Witches of New York

Books 1 - 3

Kim Richardson

Witches of New York: Books 1-3

Cover designer: Karen Dimmick/ ArcaneCovers.com

www.kimrichardsonbooks.com

The Starlight Witch

Witches of New York

Book 1

Kim Richardson

CHAPTER 1

I stood in the doorway, staring at my husband's naked body with his prominent, hard manhood. The voluptuous pretty brunette who climbed off him had guilt etching her face like she'd been caught stealing from the homeless. With her full cheeks and flawless skin, she appeared to be in her twenties, around half my age, with perky breasts and a tight body. She had no evidence of cellulite on her, either, but don't worry. It'll come.

"Leana? What? What are you doing here? You're back early," stuttered my husband. He covered his penis with the bedsheet made of Egyptian cotton, the ones I'd bought, not that it mattered. And not like I hadn't seen his tiny jolly stick for the last fifteen years. He wasn't much to look at, just a lanky body, balding head, and creeping beer gut.

Yet none of those things would've mattered if he had been kind.

We'd married young, both of us in our mid-twenties, and our marriage had never been perfect. From the beginning, I saw signs of his temper and narcissistic ways, but I chose to ignore them, thinking that's what good wives did. She soldiers on, right?

The last two years had been rocky, and this past year was a total mistake. I should have called it quits years ago, but I'd been lazy. Part of me had been afraid of finding myself single again at forty-one, after all these years of being with someone—even if that someone was all wrong for me.

But not anymore.

I'd been faithful. At the very least, Martin could have done the same until we'd both declared it officially over.

This past year, I'd had my suspicions that he was cheating: the late phone calls, leaving the room to speak on the phone with his so-called boss, and the late-night office hours, when he never came home until the early morning.

I couldn't blame only him for the marriage falling apart. First of all, he was human. I was a witch. That there should have been my red flag from the beginning. I couldn't be totally honest with him about who I was. He could never understand me or the paranormal world I worked in. Without honesty, the marriage was doomed to fail from the beginning, and that was on me.

Yet it was fun to see him squirm a little.

I crossed my arms over my chest, playing it out. "So, this is the child you've been banging?"

The brunette made a face. "I'm not a *child*. I'm twenty-three."

I raised my brows. "The response of a child."

"You're a bitch," snapped the naked brunette. "You're not even that good-looking. You're all old and saggy. You probably smell. Everyone knows old people smell."

"Shut up, Crystal," hissed my husband. His green eyes met mine, and he blew out a breath. "We haven't had sex in over a year. What did you expect? All men have needs."

I snorted. "Really? You're going to try and guilt me for your cheating?" I broke into a laugh I couldn't hold back. And once it started, I couldn't stop. All the emotions from the last year and the years before started pouring out of me until I was holding on to the doorframe for support.

"What's so funny?" growled my soon-to-be ex-husband.

I wiped my eyes. "You. This. This whole thing is like a bad joke. Or is it a *good* joke? I don't even know." I looked at the brunette, who was purposely keeping her body uncovered with a defiant look in her eye.

She might have a better, younger rack than me, but that was nothing to the wisdom built of my life experiences.

"I hope you like to clean, do laundry, and cook," I told her. "Don't expect him to lift a finger either. Oh, he might for the first few months, but then he'll stop. Then he'll get angry with you if you ask for some help. Reverse psychology at its finest. Best be prepared."

Crystal gave me an insolent smile. "I don't do housewife."

I gave a short laugh. "Good luck with that. You might want to start looking for your pacifier."

"You were always such a bitch," said my husband. He leaned back, leaving the sheet where it was and giving us a view of his man twinkie again. "You always thought you were better than me. No wonder I went looking elsewhere. And you got fat."

My smile fell as Crystal gave a fake laugh. "That's what happens when you're old," said the slut in my bed.

Forty-one wasn't old, not by any standards. In fact, I felt like I'd finally figured out who I was and what I wanted with my life. I felt comfortable in my skin for the first time, accepting all my flaws and owning them.

After many years of hard work and dedication to my craft, I was finally coming into my own as a witch, harnessing my magic and understanding it. But my magic wasn't connected to Earth's elemental magic like the White witches, nor was its power channeled by borrowing it from demons as it was with most Dark witches. No, my power lay elsewhere. Granted, it was more potent at night, which stood out among witches. But that didn't mean I couldn't draw on it now.

It would be weak. But I only needed a little.

I'd never told Martin what I was. He had no clue. I'd never had much of a reason to. Not until this very moment.

"You know, Martin," I said, smiling. "I never told you this, but I'm a witch." I tapped into my will and channeled the energy that went way beyond the boundaries of the earth. It was faint, but I felt a ribbon of power churning in my core. I held it there.

Both Martin and Crystal started to laugh as expected.

"And as humans, you can't see magic, just like you can't see the paranormal around you."

"She's fucking crazy." Martin laughed harder, and Crystal joined him.

"I'd like to give you this parting gift," I told them after their laughter had subsided.

Martin watched me with clear amusement. "What?"

I flicked a finger, and a slip of brilliant white light sprang from my hand and crossed the room to hover above his penis.

I matched his smile, pulled on my magic, and said, "This—"

My husband let out a girlish wail of pain and terror as he stared at his penis, the tip bent at a ninety-degree angle like a broken candle. *Whoops.*

Crystal flew off the bed like she thought his broken penis was contagious, her eyes wide as she backed into the wall.

As the wailing heightened in pitch, I strolled into the walk-in closet, grabbed my carry-on bag, stuffed it with as many clothes as possible, and made my way out.

"What did you do to me? You crazy bitch! You fucking whore!" howled my husband.

When I reached the bedroom's doorway, I turned around, seeing my husband red-faced with tears streaming down his cheeks. It was a good look on him.

I shot him a finger gun. "Keep it up. What? Too soon?" I couldn't help myself. He was kinda asking for it.

"You bitch," he wheezed, tears flowing freely down his face as he stared at his man-twig, which had nearly doubled in size and had taken on a purple color, kind of like an eggplant. Was that supposed to happen? Who knows.

"She broke his penis!" cried Crystal to someone on the other end of her cell phone. "She's a witch! And she broke it!"

Yeah, no one was going to believe that. The witch part, I mean.

I pulled my attention back to my husband. "Consider this a divorce."

"You're dead!" he howled as I walked out and left the apartment. Maybe I'd gone too far. Conjuring magic before humans was forbidden. But it was too late for that. Plus, I doubted anyone would believe them if they blabbed.

A strange weight lifted from my shoulders as I hit Greenwich Avenue and turned north, the cool September air soothing my hot cheeks. My stomach rumbled, reminding me I had forgotten to eat dinner. After the events of the past hour, dinner could wait, but wine couldn't. I needed a glass of wine.

I didn't feel any loss or even regret. Was that bad? Was I evil? Possibly. But he had pissed me off.

"God, why didn't I do this a long time ago?"

I paused at the street corner, waiting for the pedestrian light, and pulled the letter I'd received this morning by registered mail from my pocket. I'd read it a dozen times, but I wanted to reread it. Just to ensure I wasn't about to make a fool of myself. My eyes rolled over the letter as I read.

Dear Leana Fairchild,

I am pleased to extend an offer of employment on behalf of the Twilight Hotel. To officially acknowledge your acceptance of this offer, or if you would like more details, please present yourself to 444 5th Avenue no later than 7 p.m.

We look forward to welcoming you aboard.

Sincerely,

Basil Hickinbottom

Management

Getting job offers wasn't unusual. I was a Merlin and had been for the last ten years. The Merlin Group stood for Magical

Enforcement Response League Intelligence Network. We were the magical police, if you will, like the FBI.

I'd always told Martin that I worked the night shift at McGillis Pub, the local pub in Greenwich Village. He'd never suspected anything untoward. Of course, that was because he couldn't have cared less.

I'd heard of the Twilight Hotel. Hell, every paranormal—witch, werewolf, shifter, or fae—knew of that hotel. But getting a job offer from them was unusual. I'd never worked for them. Ever. And I didn't know anyone who had either. From what I knew, they were secretive and didn't like to hire out, which explained the mountain of curiosity I felt at getting this job offer.

I checked my phone: 6:15 p.m. "Still got time."

I stuffed the letter back in my pocket, hauled my bag up on my shoulder, and continued.

My blood pressure rose with excitement. Martin's broken-penis episode was forgotten as I only had room for one thought in my brain. Every hired witch knew the Twilight Hotel paid well. Maybe I could finally afford a car. Wouldn't that be something?

Maybe things were finally looking up for me—

My face smacked right into a wall.

A wall that smelled of musk and spices. It was a pleasant smell. I stepped back and blinked into the face of a handsome man with a square jaw and straight nose, the owner of the man chest I'd just assaulted with my face. Dark wavy hair brushed his broad shoulders, graying at the temples, which only made him more attractive. He was tall, the kind of tall that you had to let your head fall back to get a view. And it was quite the view.

He was hot. And he looked like he needed that glass of wine more than I did.

His eyes were dark and burned with a kind of intensity that had my insides churning. I kinda liked it too.

He wasn't human either. That part was clear from the rolling paranormal energy emitting from him. Big and strong like he was, no doubt this hot man-beast was a were. My money was on a werewolf.

"Watch where you're going," he growled, practically screamed, glaring at me like I was the most hated person in all of New York City.

Not so hot anymore.

I narrowed my eyes. "I would if you didn't take up so much space, *Wall*." He might have been built like a truck, which was how it had felt walking face-first into his chest, and maybe twenty years ago, I would have ducked my head and walked away. But I didn't. Life had made me hard.

And I'd broken a penis today. Go me!

The stranger glared at me, clearly not used to being challenged. Built the way he was, I was certain no one ever talked back. More than likely they cowered away. "The streets don't belong to you," he snarled.

"Don't belong to you either." If he was expecting an apology, he was going to wait a while. I was done apologizing in my life.

The hot man-beast watched me for a beat longer. "*You* crashed into *me*. You weren't paying attention to where you were going."

"Then you should have moved out of the way." I could do this all night. Well, not really. I had to go if I wanted that job. "And why didn't you? If you saw me coming, the gallant thing to do would be to step aside."

His nostrils flared with anger. "Why should I move for you?" He said it like the mere fact that he was standing there meant something to me, like he was someone I should know, someone of great importance.

As far as I knew, he was a rude, sexy man-beast. That was all.

"Clearly, you left your manners at home this morning," I told him. I refused to stare at his full, sensuous lips. Too late. I was staring. Damn. Those were some hot lips to go with the rest of his hot bod.

"You always walk around with your head in the clouds? That's how you get killed. That's how you get hit by a car."

I cocked a brow. "Problem solved. Right?" So why was he still here? Why wasn't he moving away from me?

The stranger watched me, his gaze intense. "You shouldn't be walking around here if you don't know where you're going."

I snorted. "Yeah. I don't need your permission, buddy. I'm late for an interview. Out of my way, *Wall*."

Confusion flashed in those damn fine eyes. He blinked and then walked away. My eyes, moving of their own volition, followed his fine behind until he disappeared through a multitude of humans meandering along the streets of Manhattan. Not one had any idea a werewolf walked among them—a hot, grumpy one. Yet I noticed how the humans moved away from him. They had no clue what he was, but even they could feel the ferocious, wild, and commanding energy emitting from him. He had an alpha vibe too. And I hoped never to see him again. Next time, I might not be so polite.

I let out a long sigh and started moving again, irritation fluttering through me. My body was burning up, like I'd had a sudden hot flash. Not exactly the composed, professional manner I wanted to present for the interview. I was probably red-faced. I'd look like I was nervous, which I was, but I didn't want management to know.

Damn the hot werewolf and his hot ass.

Just as I crossed East Thirty-Ninth Street, I took a few more steps and came face-to-face with 444 Fifth Avenue.

The large limestone façade had sandstone trim, and the design included deep roofs with dormers, terracotta spandrels, niches, balconies, and railings. It had a Gothic vibe, like something Dracula would have lived in, and I loved it. Above double glass doors were large, glowing white letters that read, THE TWILIGHT HOTEL. The main entrance had a double-height archway on Fifth Avenue. It was a glorious beast—all thirteen floors of it.

A soft shimmer fell over the building in a glittering spectrum of color. I recognized the glamour meant to keep any wandering humans from thinking they could get a room. To them, the building likely appeared as just a run-down, abandoned building or a building under construction—anything to make them move along and forget quickly.

My heart pounded against my chest, like a kid entering high school for the first time. I wiped my sweaty palms on my jeans before reaching for the handle.

It occurred to me then that I had no place to stay tonight or the nights after this one. Basically, I was homeless. All I had was the bag on my shoulder. I'd figure something out. I always did. Besides, things weren't so bad.

"Broke a penis today," I muttered, proud of myself. "Nothing can beat that."

Or so I thought.

With bated breath, I pulled the door open and walked in.

CHAPTER 2

The doors opened into a foyer and a spacious lobby, with high ceilings, lots of glass, gray paint, and rich red accents. A shimmer of sheer material slid over me, and I felt the familiar pulsing magic of a protection ward. Creating wards took some serious magic. Not all witches or wizards could create them, let alone such complex ones with so much power they protected an entire building.

The area was illuminated with soft light and had all the usual scents of a human hotel: air freshener and too many perfumes and colognes mixed together. Modern gray couches and chairs were placed throughout the space in designated seating areas. The only difference was the cold sharpness of paranormal energy.

The hair on the back of my neck prickled as I felt eyes on me. I looked over to find groups of people, paranormals, all watching me from their seats with curious expressions.

Adrenaline immediately spiked through my body.

A black-haired male witch was showing off his magic as his phone hovered and spun above the table while a redheaded female clapped enthusiastically. A band of older witches sat in the far corner with white and gray hair spilling out of their dark cowls, their knobby fingers wrapped around their drinks. Dark witches? Probably.

As I walked, a tall, blonde female in a leather jacket flared her nostrils as she sniffed me. Werewolf, if the scent of wet dog was any indication.

I passed a group of trolls gulping down pints. A cluster of male and female paranormals sat around a table topped with glasses filled with dark maroon liquid, which I seriously doubted was wine. Their unnatural good looks stood out among the other paranormals. Vampires. Everything was a blur of black eyes, pointed teeth, and fine clothing. Their faces were lovely yet feral. They whispered among themselves, and I didn't like how they were pointing and staring at me like they were wondering how my blood tasted.

I felt a spike in my blood pressure as I forced myself to keep my pace even, which was more of an I'll-whip-your-ass-if-you-get-too-close kind of saunter. No way in hell would I show these vampires the effect they had on me. Besides, I didn't want to cause a scene or call unwanted attention to myself in this hotel.

The Twilight Hotel catered to *all* paranormals. No matter whether a Dark witch, vampire, troll, or some renegade werewolf, the hotel would grant refuge or lodgings, whichever was essential at the moment.

Part of me felt like an imposter, like I didn't belong here, and this was a huge mistake. Maybe the hotel had gotten me confused with someone else? With my luck, anything was possible.

A pale man with black hair stood behind a counter at the end of the lobby, typing on a tablet. My gut fluttered with nerves, and I strained myself to walk with confidence as I made my way toward the gleaming granite check-in counter. I didn't know why I was so nervous. This wasn't my first gig.

I took out my letter, smoothed it on the gleaming marble counter, and then dropped my hands behind it to hide my trembling fingers. "Hi. I'm here to see Basil." I'd already forgotten his last name. I glimpsed at the letter. "Basil Hickinbottom."

The man wore a fitted, expensive, dark gray, three-piece suit. The word CONCIERGE was pinned on the front of his jacket. Up close, his pale skin was practically translucent, and I could make out blue veins on his thin hands as he typed. He was slim and about a head shorter than me, and I could sense the paranormal energies coming off him. He looked around my age, but it was hard to tell when it came to paranormals. He could be in his forties just as easily as he could be in his seventies.

The concierge kept typing on his tablet and never looked up. "You must check in all weapons and all magical objects relating to weapons," he said in a drone-like voice. The slight flick of a gray tongue told me he was a shifter, possibly a lizard.

"Sure. I'm not carrying any weapons."

The concierge gave an exasperated sigh. His light eyes finally rolled over me and landed on my bag. "Did you not hear me? Do you not speak English? Shall I spell it for you? *No* weapons are allowed. Hotel rules." He then pointed to an A-frame floor sign next to the counter that read, NO WEAPONS ALLOWED—MAGICAL OR NONMAGICAL.

I narrowed my eyes. He was an annoying little bastard, but I wouldn't let him rattle me. I wasn't about to screw this up. "I told you. I'm not carrying any weapons—magical or otherwise. You can frisk me if you like," I added with a smile and raised my arms.

The concierge wore a frown on his face, the kind that seemed permanently etched into the folds of his skin like he'd used it so often that it was his only expression. "So what's in the bag?"

"My clothes."

"Why? Are you going on a vacation?"

I wasn't about to blab my personal life to a rude stranger. "I'm here about a job. I was asked to come here by management. To see Basil. I have a letter." I smoothed out my letter again.

In a blur, the concierge snatched my letter from me faster than I thought possible. "Hmmm." His eyes moved over my letter. "So, what kind of witch are you? Are you a White or Dark witch?"

Here it comes. "Neither."

The concierge gave me a pointed look and dropped my letter. "You can't be a witch without being a White or Dark witch."

I sighed. "I can."

The concierge snorted. "Maybe you're not a witch. Maybe you're just a loser fae who'll do anything to get inside the Twilight Hotel. That's it. Isn't it? Well, I've got news for you. We don't let the trash in. Get out, or I'll have you thrown out."

And here I thought my day was looking up. "I'm not going anywhere, and I don't have to explain myself to you." I snatched my letter back.

The concierge raised his brow. "And I don't have time to listen to stupid people."

"Really?" My anger flared.

"Really," challenged the concierge.

"What's going on here?" came a voice behind me.

I spun my back against the counter to see a tiny man with a tuft of white hair and a matching white beard. Round glasses sat on his nose, magnifying his eyes abnormally to make him look like an owl. His black suit was a stark contrast to his white skin, and he looked like a miniature version of Santa Claus in a suit, with the no-nonsense stare of a man who could see through any bullshit. The tag on his jacket read MANAGEMENT.

"Basil?" I guessed. A familiar wave of energy hit me, sending a swirl of prickles along my skin. The scent of pine needles, wet earth, and leaves mixed with a wildflower meadow rose to meet me—the scent of White witches.

When he gave a slight nod, I added, "I'm Leana Fairchild. I'm here about a job." My stomach twisted again, and I struggled to keep my face from showing how nervous I was.

The hotel manager seemed to relax a little at the mention of my name. "You're the witch. The Merlin?"

"I am." I looked over my shoulder and smiled at the positively furious concierge. Then, I turned back to the manager and pulled my bag around to my front. "I have identification if you want to see."

Basil, the manager, clasped both hands in front of him. "That won't be necessary," he said. "You're hired."

My eyebrows rose. "Uh… okay, great. Thank you. Can you tell me a bit about the gig?" I'd never been hired this quickly before. It had to be a record.

Basil's eyes rounded as he looked over his shoulder, and then he leaned forward and said in a low voice, "We've had two murders at the hotel. You're here to investigate. To find those responsible."

"Okay."

"It's very bad for business, very bad. We don't want to alarm the guests." Basil looked around again, his shoulders tensing like he feared he was about to get jumped.

"Can you tell me about the murders?" When Basil's eyes bugged out more at the loudness of my voice, I lowered it and proceeded, "Who were the victims?"

"Both guests and no connection as far as we know," answered Basil. He looked up and smiled at a passing couple whose exquisite looks labeled them as vampires. "But that's what you're here for." I saw the concierge lean in to listen. "We discovered the first body three weeks ago and the second last week. Second and fourth floors. Rooms two oh two and four oh four. The bodies have been removed, but we otherwise left the rooms untouched."

"How were they killed?"

Basil turned to the concierge. "Errol. Give her the file, please."

Errol gave the witch an annoyed stare. "I'm not a servant."

"The file, now," growled Basil. "Don't push me, Errol. Not today."

At first, I wasn't sure Errol would get the requested file, but he bent behind the counter, pulled out a folder, and threw it to me.

I caught the file. "Thanks, Errol." I smiled at him as he grimaced. "I have a feeling we're going to be *great* friends."

"I'd rather slit my wrists," snapped Errol.

I laughed as I opened the file. Inside, I found copies of invoices and the victims' personal information. My fingers stopped at the two photocopied pictures—one male, one female. Both were covered in blood with severe lashes all over their bodies. A large, gruesome gap lay just below the male's ribs.

"Looks like he's missing some organs."

The female was in her twenties and in great condition. Well, before she was killed. It was hard to tell what killed them by just looking at the pictures.

Basil leaned closer. "I must insist on your full discretion," he said and then gave a tight smile at an elderly man who walked past the counter, looking as though he was trying to eavesdrop. "This whole... situation is bad for business. We can't risk the guests finding out. We might face closing the hotel if they don't feel safe here."

"Seriously?"

"No one will want to stay at the hotel if they believe they'll be murdered in their sleep."

"Good point. What about the pay?" I'd learned from experience never to agree or start a job without proof of finance or a signed agreement.

Basil pulled out an envelope from inside his jacket. "Here. This is one week's pay. After that, you'll get the same amount each week until the case is solved."

I opened the envelope and counted one thousand in cash. "Okay. If I accept the job, is there a way I can get a room?" I realized I was at a disadvantage after breaking Martin's penis. I had nowhere to live. "It might come in handy to be so close." Partly true, but I really needed a place to stay for a while.

Basil nodded. "I have a vacant apartment on our residents' floor. You can stay there for the duration of the job."

Okay. One problem solved.

I watched as Basil walked behind the counter and grabbed something from a lower shelf. Then he walked back around and handed me a key with a green tag. "You're on the thirteenth floor. Apartment thirteen twelve."

"Thanks." I pocketed my new key.

"So? Are you going to take the job?" asked Basil. I heard Errol muttering something, though I couldn't catch what he said.

I folded the file and stuffed it under my arm. "Sure. Yes. Yes, I'll take it."

"Good. That's good." Basil let out a sigh and said, "Because we just found another body."

CHAPTER 3

I stared at the body of a male lying on the floor next to the shattered pieces of a wooden coffee table. He lay in a puddle of his own blood, guts, and bits of clothing. The gray that peppered his chestnut hair at the temples told me he was in his late forties. His shirt was a little too tight around the middle, and his pants a little too short. His body was in a fetal position, and from the grimace still visible on his face, I'd say he died in excruciating pain.

I let out a breath. "Who did this to you?"

I knelt next to him. Splatters of blood stained the light gray carpet, and more blood soaked into the carpet beneath his chest. The ceiling light reflected on his rib cage, and I could see teeth marks. Sharp enough to eat through bone… someone would have to have strong jaws to snap through bones like that. They'd have to be paranormal.

Gauging by the slashing and many other deep lacerations on the body, it looked like he died in the same manner as the other victims in the hotel. Without weapons allowed in the hotel, I could only conclude that the killer used something innate to them, like their claws or their teeth. It could also be a curse. I'd heard of some pretty dark curses that could mimic a traditional knife-type weapon that could rip your body to shreds.

And I needed to be sure if I wanted to solve the case or get ahead. To do that, I'd have to pull on my own magic.

It wasn't that my magic had to be kept secret. I just didn't have the patience anymore to explain how my magic was different. My mother and grandmother warned me at a very young age to try and keep it private—not secret—to avoid the stares and the trouble that seemed to follow me because I was different. Even in the paranormal world, folks feared things they didn't understand or were foreign to them.

I looked over at the window, to the darkening deep-blue sky. I still had about two hours before sundown, so I couldn't tap into my entire well of magic, yet, only part of it.

But it might be enough for this.

I took a breath, tapped into my will, and channeled the emanations, the forces beyond the sky.

Immediately, I was hit by a cold, throbbing energy from the body, followed by a faint scent of sulfur and something else much darker and more sinister.

"You're a Dark witch or possibly a White witch," I muttered. He'd practiced magic here before he died. That was clear. But I wasn't getting any clear signs of what kind of paranormal did this. Could be a crazed werewolf or a werebear. Whichever, it was extraordinarily strong to be able do that to a body and had also bypassed the Merlins' magic. What could do that?

I spotted blisters on his side through a hole in his shirt and more on his arm. He'd put up a fight. The room was trashed and looked like a bomb had hit it. Chairs and tables were overturned, while broken glasses and ceramic plates with food still in them lay scattered on the floor. Cool air seeped through a broken window over black scorch marks marring the light gray walls, and the pile of feathers, foam, and fabric that dotted the floor had been a couch at some point.

"I'm sorry you died like this." I was sad at the death of a witch in his prime. It only fueled my desire further to solve this case.

I checked his pockets but found nothing, not even his identification. Weird. Maybe Basil took it. I'd check with him later. I needed this dead witch's name to further my investigation. Did he know the other two victims? He died on the sixth floor, where the others were killed on the second and fourth floors. What was the connection? Why was he killed? Who was he?

It was clear whoever did this had knowledge of powerful magic.

I stood and yanked out my phone to start taking pictures.

"You the new Merlin?"

The voice snapped my head around, and I found a tall, handsome male leaning against the doorframe of room 601, which I distinctly remembered closing.

A snug black T-shirt revealed tight muscles and a fit body. He wasn't as thick and muscular as the rude man-beast I'd bumped into earlier, but he had more of an athletic build, like a swimmer. His light brown hair was cut short on the sides and longer on top, fashioned in a modern style. His handsome face was wearing a smug smile, the kind that knew he was easy on the eyes and was used to the admiration of warm-blooded females. And I swore I could see a twinkle in his eye.

"I am," I answered, wondering who the hell he was. I wasn't getting "killer" vibes from him, though. More like he was out on the prowl for some casual sex, but that didn't explain why he was here.

At my answer, the handsome male strolled into the room and came right up to me, way too close, in my personal space.

I frowned. "And you are?" I'd have to knee him in the junk if he got any closer.

I was assaulted by his nearness, the smell of his aftershave, and a hint of pine needles and earth. The guy was a White witch.

Hot-guy flashed me a smile that would have had a group of single ladies throwing their underwear at him. "Nice," he said, rolling his eyes over me. "Never thought Merlins could be so pretty."

Heat rushed from my neck to my scalp. I wasn't immune to handsome faces. I just knew they were trouble that I should steer clear of. Besides, I had a job to do, and this guy was in my way.

I cleared my throat. "What are you doing here?" I didn't like that he wasn't bothered by the dead witch at our feet. Who the hell was this guy?

"You married?" he pressed. "No? Got a boyfriend? Girlfriend?"

"Leave her alone, Julian," said a second voice from the doorway.

I pulled my eyes away from the witch called Julian and spotted an older female strutting into the room. Again, uninvited. Again, not looking a bit traumatized by the dead guy at our feet.

She had a mess of red curly hair that brushed against her shoulders. Her tan, weathered face said she liked to spend time outdoors. Her blue eyes were lined with crow's-feet, and her thin lips were pressed into a tight line. She looked to be in her mid-sixties and wore a long denim skirt and garden clogs, with a long necklace and pendant over a green blouse that she'd folded back at the elbows.

She walked right up to us, stepping *on* and then over the dead witch. She blinked up at me and smiled. "I'm Elsa." She shoved Julian back forcefully away from me. I liked her immediately. "Don't mind him. He's just horny. Controlled by that thing between his legs. He's annoying but harmless." She pressed her hands on her hips as she studied me. Her cheeks lit up in a rosy hue as she flashed an infectious smile that was welcoming and felt almost like family.

Julian snorted. "Depends on what you define as harmless."

"Told you, annoying," repeated Elsa, her smile stretching.

"And she's the annoying widow who likes to keep her dead husband real close." Julian tapped his chest, eyeing the locket attached to the necklace around Elsa's neck.

On closer inspection, it wasn't a pendant but a vintage brass locket, a form of Victorian mourning jewelry. Yikes. Was that a piece of her dead husband? I knew some witches kept a lock of hair from their deceased partners. I'd just never met one in person.

Elsa rolled her eyes like this was nothing new or worthy of mention. "So, you're the new Merlin, eh?"

The same wave of energy I got from Julian hit me. She was a White witch too.

I felt myself relax a little. Clearly, these two were not here to slice my throat but more to be nosy. "Yes. I'm Leana." My gaze went from a smiling Elsa to a grinning Julian. "Why are you guys in here exactly? Did Basil send you?" Irritation flickered in my gut. Maybe the manager thought I'd need some help in the witching department.

"Basil? Goddess no," laughed Elsa. "We came to see if you needed our help."

"Right." I eyed them again. Elsa was toying with that locket around her fingers, and Julian was going through the dead witch's drawers, picking up his clothes, smelling them, and putting them back.

Part of me wanted to tell them to leave. But they were the prying types, and those types knew things. Right now, I was in the market for information.

"So?" Elsa rubbed her hands together. "What can we do to help?"

My eyes went to the dead witch. "From what I gather, Basil wants to keep this under wraps. So my question to you is, how did you know there was a dead body here?"

"Lisa told me," said Julian, walking back to join us.

At my questioning brow, Elsa added, "She's one of many hotel maids our boy here is sleeping with. Come to think of it. I think he's been with all of them."

I looked at Julian, and he flashed me a dazzling smile. "What? It's all consensual."

Oh boy. But I couldn't help the smile that tugged at my lips.

"She found him this morning," continued Elsa. "Died in a puddle of his own blood."

Something occurred to me. "You call me the *new* Merlin. Was there a Merlin for hire before me?" I thought it strange that Basil would hire a stranger when the hotel had Merlins working for them. If he wanted to keep the deaths discreet, why hire an outsider?

"Yes," said the older witch. She grabbed her locket with her hand, her face wrinkled in thought. "Eddie, something? Or was it Franky? I can't remember."

"Where is he, and why isn't he here?" I didn't like that Basil decided to keep that information from me. Maybe this other Merlin was on vacation. Either way, he should have told me.

Elsa gave a nod in the direction of the dead witch. "You're looking at him."

My mouth fell open. "You mean..."

"He's the dead guy," said Julian. "Poor bastard. I was going to help him hook up with Danielle. She's a guest on the second floor. Nice, shapely werefox."

I frowned as I looked at Eddie, Franky, whatever his name was. This explained why Basil was in a hurry to hire me. I was going to have words with that tiny witch later.

The Merlin working the case was dead. This was not good. It meant that whoever killed him was more powerful, or he'd been taken by surprise.

Damnit. I should have asked for more money.

"Looks like Eddie got too close, and he got killed for it," said Elsa, rolling her fingers over her locket.

"I think his name was Franky," echoed Julian. "Yeah. Definitely Franky."

I nodded. "That's what I think." It made sense. The witch had definitely discovered something. But what?

Julian leaned on the opposite wall and crossed his arms. "You from New York?"

I shook my head. "From a small town in New Hampshire. Moved here about fifteen years ago with my husband, which I'm hoping will be my *ex*-husband shortly."

Elsa's eyes rounded. "Sounds like a good story right there. I'm feeling some anger from your tone. Did he do something to you? What was it?"

"He cheated," I answered, finding it strange that I was so open with them about my relationship. I'd keep the gory details for later. "I just want to get a divorce and get on with my life. He's human. I don't know how long that'll take."

Elsa's face brightened. "I can help you with that. I have friends in the human legal system. If you can get me all his information, I can have your divorce final within two weeks because he cheated, and we paranormals pull strings for things like that."

I felt a pang of tension release from me. "Really? That would be great." Great? That was phenomenal.

"So, where do you live?" asked Julian, his eyes on the carry-on bag I'd placed on the floor next to the entrance. "You homeless?"

I sighed. "Here for now. The thirteenth floor until I find something, I guess."

Elsa clapped her hands enthusiastically. "We live on the thirteenth floor too. All the residents do. We're your neighbors. Isn't that wonderful? I can't wait to introduce you to the others. Jade is going to love you!"

Julian gave a one-shoulder shrug. "The hotel doesn't want us mingling with the guests. We're told not to, but we never listen to them." He flashed me a million-dollar smile. "It's how I get all my dates."

The idea of being alone with a bottle of merlot and my thoughts wasn't sounding so great at the moment.

The scuff of shoes on carpet pulled my attention to the door. A group of three men and one woman dressed in black suits, sunglasses, and equipped with medical briefcases walked into the room.

"Well, well, well. The cleanup crew is here," said Julian, eyeing the female.

Basil had mentioned that a group would come by to take the body away discreetly. Not sure how they were going to do that. First, because how do you remove a body discreetly, and second, they looked like they belonged in a remake of the *Men in Black* movies. Nothing was discreet about these people.

With my arms crossed over my chest, I watched the cleanup crew take a few pictures and categorize the crime scene before one of the males pulled out a glass vial and dumped the contents over the body. A sudden prickling of energy rippled over my skin. And then Eddie, Franky lifted from the ground in his fetal position, hovering in the air.

Magic. These guys were witches. Or at least, that one was.

Next, the female sprinkled some white powder over the dead witch, mumbling words I couldn't quite catch. Energy hissed and oozed through the air as if sheer power and magic had been extracted into an invisible haze. The white powder grew and spread over the body until it disappeared. Ha. She'd cast some invisibility spell.

Damn. I wish I could do that.

"Show offs," muttered Elsa, her face wrinkled in a scowl.

But I was seriously impressed. I was more impressed as I watched the three cleanup crew members walk out of the room, a thin, white translucent tendril tethered to the female witch's hand as I imagined her pulling the floating body behind her.

The body might be gone, but my work was just beginning.

"Who's this?" A woman stood in the doorway where the cleanup crew had just disappeared a moment ago. Her blonde hair was crimped, big, and stiff like she'd used a whole can of hair spray. Her eyes were lined with blue eyeshadow, and shiny pink lipstick coated her lips. She gave off a Cindy Lauper vibe with black fishnet tights, a white ruffled skirt, and a short denim jacket. Her arms were looped with white and black plastic bracelets. I couldn't guess her age. She appeared older than me but younger than Elsa. Clearly, she was stuck in the eighties and loved eighties' music and fashion.

"That's Leana, the new Merlin," answered Julian, giving me a proud grin.

The woman's eyes rounded. "No way."

I turned to Elsa. "And who's that?"

Elsa blinked at me. "That's Jade. The one I told you about. She's one of us."

"Us?"

"Part of the gang. The thirteenth-floor gang," answered Elsa, like it would explain everything.

"Right." I looked back at Jade, who was openly grinning and staring at me like she was fanning over one of her favorite singers from one of her eighties' rock bands.

Someone grabbed me, and I cringed as Elsa hooked her arm around mine. "Come on. Let's finish this with some food in us. And a soft spot to rest my behind while we chat. I, for one, think we need to talk."

I raised a brow. "We do?"

"Yes," said Elsa. "There's a lot you don't know about the hotel. Rumors. You're new, so it's not your fault, but you need us."

"She's right. You need us," agreed Jade from the doorway.

"*I* need *you*? How's that?"

Elsa tapped my arm. "You need what we know. Trust me. You want to know what we know."

I knew she was right. "Sure."

"Good. Let's eat." Elsa dragged me with her. "And we'll tell you everything."

I grabbed my bag and let her pull me out the door with Julian and Jade following behind us.

In the space of a few hours, I'd broken a penis, gotten hired for a new job, and found myself with a newly dead body on my hands.

It was turning into one hell of a day.

CHAPTER 4

We didn't go far. In fact, they took me to the restaurant next door to the hotel, a storefront under a gray awning. The sign right below said AFTER DARK.

The restaurant door banged behind us as we sauntered into the lobby. It housed a modern interior of dark gray seats and tables in an open-concept room with twelve-foot ceilings and exposed beams and pipes. The tall windows at the front let in the last of the evening light.

Two paranormal males and a female, dressed in suits, were standing in the lobby, their voices hushed. They glanced up as we passed them and then returned to whatever discussion they were having.

"Table for four?" said the cheerful young brunette in a white shirt and short black skirt, who greeted us at the entrance.

"Unless you want to join us?" purred Julian, and part of me wanted to slap that grin off his face.

"Yes. Four, please," I said, taking the lead.

The hostess smiled at me. She blinked, and for a split second, the pupils of her hazel eyes elongated to slits, like the eyes of a cat. She blinked again, and her human eyes were back.

"You're going to love it here," said a smiling Jade. "The food's amazing."

I glanced around, recognizing the familiar energies from all walks of paranormal life. It seemed the restaurant catered to us paranormals like the Twilight Hotel, but I hadn't gotten a glamour vibe when we'd stepped through.

We followed the pretty hostess as Julian moseyed a little too close next to her, to a table in the middle of the restaurant.

A male waiter came rushing our way, winding expertly through a sea of tables and chairs with a tray under his arm.

He rushed at Jade, expecting her to move. When she didn't, he gave her an annoyed look and growled, "Move, freak."

Jade flinched like she'd been slapped. Her face paled, her smile fading.

Anger fired up in my belly. I don't know why, but I felt a sudden overprotectiveness toward her. I wanted to grab his tray and smash it over his head. Twice. No, make that five times.

The waiter released a frustrated sigh and moved around a stunned and embarrassed Jade.

"Ignore him," I said. "People like him are not worth the time."

Jade gave me a tight smile as she dragged over a chair and sat. Pink spots colored her cheeks, and she'd lost that spark about her. I glanced at Julian and Elsa, whose faces mirrored my anger.

I pulled out my chair and let myself fall into it, realizing how exhausted I was—not physically but mentally. And sometimes that was worse.

"I need a glass of wine," I said.

"I'll have the waiter bring you a bottle of our house wine," said the hostess. "Red or white?"

"Red," interjected Elsa. She looked at me and said, "I know you prefer red."

I did. But how did she know that?

"Not that waiter," I instructed the hostess as I pointed to the asshat across the restaurant. "Someone else."

"Of course," she answered and then walked away.

I watched as Julian angled his head to get a better view of the pretty hostess walking away.

He caught me looking at him. "I'm going home with her at the end of this meal. It's a guarantee."

I tried not to smile, but my traitorous lips quirked upward. He was growing on me. "So," I said, leaning forward and glancing around at my new friends. Were they my new friends? Guess I would know soon enough. "What do I need to know about the hotel?"

Elsa interlaced her fingers on the table. "Well, for one, it's haunted."

Jade snorted but didn't say anything.

"Okay. What else?" A haunted paranormal hotel wasn't new to me. Ghosts and spirits were attracted to all things supernatural. The energies we gave off were more than the average human times a hundred. It only made sense they'd frequent these types of hotels.

Julian leaned back in his chair. "She means she thinks a ghost is doing the killing."

"A ghost?" I stared at the witch. "From what I can tell, the last victim was killed by brute force. Something powerful. Ghosts lack the physical strength. They don't have bodies. You need to have a physical body to kill someone like that." Or so I thought. But I could be wrong.

"Not necessarily," continued the older witch. "Some ghosts or poltergeists have the ability to manipulate physical objects. They can kill if they want to."

I watched the witch for a moment. "You think a ghost killed those guests and the Merlin?"

Elsa widened her eyes. "I do. I know it."

"Says the witch who still speaks to her husband like he's alive," said Julian as he crossed his arms over his chest.

Red blotches appeared on Elsa's face. "You'll never understand true love. All you do is screw and leave before your victim wakes up," she shot back.

Jade pointed her finger at Julian, and her plastic bracelets clacked around her wrist. "She's got you there, lover boy." She caught me looking at her, and she smiled. I was glad to see her smiling again.

Julian shook his head. "Love is messy. Besides, I'm not selfish. I like to share—share my body with the ladies. Why shouldn't they experience *The Julian*?"

I rolled my eyes and then looked at Elsa across from me. "Okay, let's say a ghost is killing these people. Do you have an explanation as to why?"

Elsa grabbed her cotton napkin and started folding it. "Not yet. But it explains why no one saw the killer coming or leaving the room. You can ask Basil to show you the feed from the cameras. You only see the guests coming and going into their rooms. No one else. It's a working theory."

"It's a stupid theory," Julian shot back.

Elsa clenched her jaw. "You got a better theory? Spill it."

Julian shrugged. "I think it's something to do with sex. A husband or wife caught cheating. Then they got whacked. Happens all the time."

Like breaking penises. "It does. But it doesn't explain why they killed the Merlin. And why two deaths so close together? What's the connection? What did Eddie or Franky discover? Was that the reason he was killed?"

"He found the ghost responsible," said Elsa. "And it killed him."

"What ghost?" came a deep, manly voice.

I looked up to an expression of intrigue on a handsome face that belonged to a muscled man, tall and virile, with tattoos peeking out from his sleeve down one arm. His dark eyes made me wonder what kind of lover he was in bed.

My heart slammed against my rib cage like a car hitting a cement wall.

Shit. It was the man-beast I'd crashed into earlier. He locked eyes with me, not bothering to hide the annoyance in his expression.

My eyes moved to his large hands. He held four glasses in one hand and a bottle of red wine in the other.

"You work here?" I asked.

"Sometimes," he growled. That same frown returned as he carefully placed our wineglasses, cut the foil below the lip of the bottle, and began to rotate the corkscrew. "What are you doing here?" He said it like I wasn't allowed to be here, like I should have asked his permission.

Anger rolled through me. "It's not illegal to have a meal in this city. My friends and I want to sit down and have a nice meal. You got a problem with that? Or am I not allowed to walk the streets *or* sit and eat?"

The man-beast leveled the cork out of the bottle and poured a little wine into my glass. "Taste it."

I frowned. "Giving me orders too? Wow. Full of yourself and rude. How wonderful."

Jade sucked in the breath through her teeth, and I could see Julian shifting in his seat while Elsa fondled her locket.

"You need to taste the wine," said the man-beast, his voice low and dangerous. "If you don't like it, I can get another bottle."

Heat rolled off my scalp. I knew my face was probably red. What was it about this guy that made my blood boil? "Fine." I took the glass and sipped, not bothering to swirl it around a few times or give it a sniff, like I should have. But to my surprise, the wine was delicious. A perfect balance of alcohol and sweet fruit.

"It's good." I swallowed and put my glass back down, watching as he filled it and then proceeded to fill the others' glasses.

He set the bottle on our table. "I'll have another waiter come and take your orders in a few minutes."

"Good. You do that." The last thing I wanted was my meal to be ruined by this grumpy werewolf. I'd had enough of men and their drama for one night. I wanted some time to de-stress with some wine while not having to deal with this guy.

The muscles around the man-beast's shoulders popped and jerked. It was a nice display, but I was anxious for him to leave. He watched me a second longer, too long for it to be considered polite, and then walked away.

I laughed softly and reached for my glass of wine. "Still got it. What?" I said, staring at my new friends, who were looking at me like I'd just stripped out of my clothes and decided to walk around the restaurant.

"You've got some serious lady balls," said Julian, shaking his head at me. "Either that or you're crazy."

"I've been told both," I said, still smiling. "What? Why are you all staring at me like I've lost my mind?"

"That was the owner." Jade leaned over the table, her voice low. The quirks at the edges of her lips suggested she was holding in a nervous laugh. "Valen."

My insides churned. Great. Now I'd just made an enemy at a possible regular hangout. "Is he always this pleasant?"

"Worse." Julian watched me with a curious expression. "Do you know him? I kinda got a vibe that you did."

I shook my head. "No." Not unless you counted me crashing into him earlier.

"Damn." Julian ran his fingers through his hair. "I got all kinds of sexual tension from you two."

I choked on my wine. "Stop." I swallowed. "Trust me. There's nothing there." Who was I kidding? He turned me on in a way I hadn't felt in a very long time. Hell, more like never. But I squashed those feelings. I didn't need this right now. I had a job to focus on. Not sexy man-beasts.

"It did feel like there was history between you," said Elsa, an inquiring frown on her brows.

"It did," agreed Jade, that hint of a smile still lingering over her lips.

"None whatsoever." I took another sip of wine, maybe a mouthful. "I'd remember someone like him."

"He can be a bit grumpy," said Elsa as she took a sip of her wine.

"Asshole is more the correct term," said Julian. "Just don't let him hear you say it. He's got a temper to match his large size."

I wasn't sure what to make of that. "What's his problem? Why does he have to be this way?" I'd had enough assholes in my life. I didn't have the patience to deal with one more.

Julian swirled his glass of wine. "That's just the way he is. I wouldn't get on his bad side. Those who do… seem to disappear."

I laughed. "Is he like a mob boss or something?"

He nodded. "Or something."

Awesome. Now I'd really done it. Not only did I have to figure out who was killing the guests in the hotel, but I'd have to watch my back for the man-beast.

"So, the werewolf restaurant owner hates me. Maybe we should find another place to eat next time." I took another sip of my wine and then let out an inappropriate moan.

Elsa looked over her shoulder before answering. "Not a werewolf. A vampire," she said, her eyes wide.

I swallowed hard. "Really? He doesn't look like a vampire. I thought for sure he was a shifter. Werewolf or a wereape." He definitely didn't have the unnatural good looks most vampires possessed. He had a more rugged edge. He was handsome. Just not over the top like most vampires. But if he was only *part* vampire, that might explain the harshness of his looks.

"He's not a vampire," said Jade, rolling her eyes. "Everyone knows he's a werecat. A tiger, I heard."

Julian gave a snort. "You ladies have it all wrong."

"Oh yeah?" Elsa crossed her arms over her chest. "What is he, then? If you're so smart."

"Easy." Julian popped a piece of fresh bread into his mouth. "He's a werebear. Just look at him. His size? Can't you tell?"

Elsa and Jade frowned at him, and I tried hard not to laugh.

"Whatever he is… what's his story?" I couldn't help myself. The sexy man-beast intrigued me.

"No one knows," said Elsa. "He just showed up about five years ago and bought the place. Keeps to himself. Not very talkative."

Julian tipped his head and finished his wine. "The guy's a jerk. He needs to get laid more often."

"Why do you come here if you don't like him?"

Jade shrugged and said, "The food's amazing."

And they were right.

I ordered roast duck with figs and moaned every time I brought the fork to my mouth. Elsa had a vegetable dish I couldn't remember the name of for the life of me, which looked like a big salad with nuts spread on top. Jade had fettuccini alfredo that smelled divine, and Julian had a giant steak with sweet-potato fries. When we were done, our plates gleamed like they'd just been washed.

After two bottles of wine and eating so much my belly looked like I was a few months pregnant, we paid our bills and made our way toward the main exit.

I was trying to act cool and walk a straight line while the restaurant's floor seemed to be moving. I spotted Julian speaking to that pretty brunette hostess. She grabbed his phone and typed something before handing it back, sex written all over her face. It was obvious they were going to hook up later.

I laughed as I shuffled toward the front door where Elsa and Jade were waiting for me. They could hold their wine better than me. Not fair. Maybe that came with more years of experience. I looked forward to that.

I felt better. Wine could do that to a person. After the day I'd had, I needed it. Turned out Elsa, Jade, and Julian were wonderful company—funny and kind, the way real friends should be. And informative. I hadn't felt this good in a long time. I hadn't realized how much I missed the company of others. I'd been so immersed in my work and too busy pretending my marriage was okay.

The skin on my back prickled like I'd been touched with electricity. The hairs on the back of my neck rose as I felt a pressure there, the same kind I got when someone was staring at me.

I turned around. Valen stood in the lobby staring at me, but he didn't look angry this time. His face was carefully neutral, but those dark eyes were as intense as before, perhaps more. Maybe that was the wine talking.

Too bad he was such a dick. He was nice to look at, so I kept staring, not wanting to turn away first. He was a fool if he thought he could intimidate me by staring—a handsome one but still a fool. I, too, could play the staring game. I was exceptionally good at it.

"Come on, Leana," called Elsa from the doorway. "You need to meet the others."

Valen, the man-beast, was still staring at me. Why? Who knew. Maybe he was contemplating ways to kill me.

The wine in my veins was still pumping and making me bold and foolish.

So, I gave him a smile and a finger wave before walking out of his restaurant.

CHAPTER 5

I'd never been on the thirteenth floor of any hotel or building. That was because most building designers were superstitious and avoided numbering a level as thirteen, like the plague. But this was a supernatural hotel where all things paranormal were embraced.

Still, I wasn't expecting this.

I stepped out of the elevator, stumbled, and righted myself with my carry-on bag around my shoulder, feeling much heavier than before as I gawked at my new residence.

The thirteenth floor had twelve doors, all open at the moment.

Music, TVs, and the sounds of people mingling reached me as I followed Julian and the ladies down the hallway. It opened up to us with an array of lights, music, food, and the paranormal, like stepping into a fairyland or something similar.

A few passing paranormals waved at us as they came and went from each other's apartments like it was the normal thing to do. I peeked into the first apartment to find an ample space occupied by an elderly gentleman sitting in an armchair, with a TV tray in front of him as he watched an episode of *Jeopardy*.

Across from his apartment, another room was filled with teenagers all bouncing and head bobbing to some music they were all listening to at the same time, though I couldn't hear a thing from the small white headphones pressed into their ears.

Next, was a female in her forties with too much makeup, leaning on the doorframe of her apartment while smoking a cigarette as she eyed Julian, like she wanted to strap him down to her bed and lick him all over.

"Julian, darling," she purred, her voice husky like someone who started smoking at the age of six. She took a deep drag of her cigarette. "You coming over tonight? I've got a bottle of whiskey we can share." Plumes of smoke rolled out of her mouth and nose as she traced a finger down her cleavage.

Julian rubbed the back of his neck, the top of his ears turning red. "Ha ha, Olga," he laughed awkwardly. "Maybe some other time. I'm showing the new girl around."

Interesting. It looked like Julian drew the line at smoking, crusty-looking ladies.

At that, Olga scowled at me like I'd just stolen her husband. "Who's she?"

I opened my mouth to answer, but Elsa beat me to it. "Leana. The new Merlin."

"The new Merlin?" Olga was still giving me the stink eye, but then she smiled. "You won't be here long."

"Was that a threat?" I laughed, tracing my finger down my much smaller cleavage. I couldn't help it. Damn wine. "By the way, you're smoking. You're the one who won't be here long."

Olga pinched her barely there lips together and spun around, slamming her door.

"Was it something I said?" I snorted. Crap. I had to remember to stop at two glasses of wine. Four. Well, four was going to get me into trouble.

Yet Julian had a tiny smile on his face when he looked at me. Guess we were friends now.

"Move!"

I flattened myself against the wall as twin ten-year-old girls in identical pink, sparkling princess dresses came skipping past us, the scent of animal and grass following them as energy bit my skin. They were shifters—werehorses or weredeer—and really cute.

I flinched as a dozen house cats came barreling down the hallway and vanished into an apartment on the right.

"Luke's cats," said Jade, watching me. "He picks up a stray whenever he goes out. He's got them trained to use his toilet. And he has some spell that brushes them daily, so you won't find any hair in his place."

I smiled. "Love cats." The truth was, I'd always wanted a cat or a dog. But I was never home. These furry babies needed love and attention. One day I would have a cat, catspiration. That was me.

"Elsa. I'm out of milk," commanded a tall, thin woman in her seventies wearing a long nightgown, her long, white hair flowing behind her like a cape.

"In the fridge, Barb." Elsa pointed to an apartment down the hall that could have been any door.

The tall woman walked past us and disappeared three doors down to what I could only assume was Elsa's place.

It was like the entire floor was one big family residence. It was weird—a good weird. And I loved it.

"Move!" chorused the twins as they skipped past us again. It seemed they had acquired a third wheel as I spotted a boy running clumsily after them.

"See?" Julian pointed to the boy. "That's how I started. Attaboy, Terry!" he encouraged. "Don't let them run away."

"You're the last apartment on the left," directed Jade as she strolled before us. She stood at the doorframe of what I guessed was my new home and posed with a hand gesture that would make Vanna White proud.

The number 1312 was stenciled in black just above the open door.

"After you," said Julian, bending from the waist.

I laughed and stepped into the apartment. I was half expecting it to be occupied by a horde of teenagers, but it was empty.

I walked down a small hallway into a decent-size living room and connecting dining room. The salmon-and-white wallpaper was peeling in long strips. The carpet was a dark green and felt more like sandpaper than actual carpet.

Moving on, just off the kitchen were three doors. Two were bedrooms, and one was the bathroom with light green tiles around the bath and shower combo.

It was furnished with lots of white and green-colored lamps and décor that looked like they belonged in the nineties. Not my style, but it was clean. I wouldn't have to buy anything, seeing as it was furnished. Being the last apartment meant that I didn't have neighbors on one side. And instead, I had extra windows, which meant more light.

I put my bag on the bed in the largest of the bedrooms and let out a sigh, my mind on the day I'd had, specifically on the two encounters with Valen, aka man-beast. I didn't know what it was about him, but my thoughts kept finding their way back to that burly man and that intense way he'd glared at me, like I'd stolen his spot at the gym.

I shook my head and left the room to join Elsa, Jade, and Julian in the living room.

"Laundry's in the basement," said Elsa. "The hotel only does the laundry for the guests. Not us rebels." She winked.

I came to sit next to her on the dingy yet comfortable beige couch. "Easy enough. Didn't bring much with me anyway."

"Hello! Hello!" A generous-sized woman carrying a plate of food came waltzing in. "Is this the new girl? Oh, she's pretty. Bet you can't wait to get in her pants, huh, Julian?"

Heat rushed to my face. I hated the attention and leaned back into the couch, trying to disappear.

"Her husband just cheated on her, Louise," said Julian, like that was supposed to explain it all.

The woman's eyes widened. "Well, well, well. I bet that's a

fascinating story. I bet you have tons of interesting stories to tell. Goddess knows we need some good stories up here." Her green eyes sparkled. "I hope you gave him something in return."

I grinned. "I did. I took care of his package."

"Good." Louise chuckled. "Here. I brought some of my famous tuna tartare and my cheddar dip." She settled her platter of diced tuna served on a bed of sliced avocado and mounds of tortilla chips on the glass coffee table.

"I've got wine!" I raised my head and saw a woman about my age with short black hair and dark skin walking in with a bottle of wine hung from each hand.

She was followed by a man with gray hair and a short beard. He held up a six-pack of beer. "I've got the beer," he said joyously.

More and more people followed, carrying some kind of beverage or food. I blinked, my head spinning as I realized most of the tenants from the thirteenth floor were in my new apartment. Even the twins made an appearance, skipping around the room.

The rest of the night went like that: chattering, making new friends, drinking more wine, and eating until my stomach felt like a brick wall.

Around one in the morning, Elsa shooed everyone out and said her goodbyes. I wasn't twenty anymore and didn't bounce back as quickly after a night of drinking. I needed sleep, especially after the day I'd had, if I wanted to make good on the new job.

I stumbled into bed with a stupid tipsy grin on my face, finding it exceptionally comfortable.

I went to bed and dreamed of broken penises chasing me.

And a pair of dark, smoldering eyes.

CHAPTER 6

I didn't know how long I lay in bed, refusing to open my eyes. I knew once I did, it would mean I was awake. My head throbbed like I had miniature jackhammers smashing against my skull.

I felt a sudden pressure on my chest. *Martin*.

Martin was trying to choke me again. It wasn't the first time I'd woken to him with his hands wrapped around my neck, his idea of fun sex. He'd nearly killed me the last time, and I'd had a ring of nasty bruises around my neck to prove it. Enough was enough.

"Martin, stop!" My eyes flashed open in a jerk of adrenaline, and my breath came fast.

A wooden dog's face was staring at me. And when I say staring, I mean its eyes blinked.

"Ah!" I screamed, scrambled back, slipped, and fell hard on the carpet. When my head hit the side table, all fragments of sleep fell away. My husband—soon-to-be ex-husband—wasn't here. The room was different. The smells. And then it hit me. I wasn't in my old apartment. I was in the Twilight Hotel.

The toy dog rolled to the side of the bed. Its eyes blinked again as it stared down at me. "That's going to leave a nasty bump."

Holy shit. The toy could speak!

"Definitely had way too much to drink last night," I grumbled, blinking the sleep fuzz from my eyes.

"I'll say," said the toy dog, its voice strangely human and male. Its painted eyebrows twisted in a bemused expression. "You snore like a trucker in your sleep."

Okay. Now I was freaking out.

I sat up in a flash, my heart thumping in my throat and trying to squeeze through my teeth. The toy looked like a beige beagle with dark spots covering its back. Instead of legs, it had four red wheels, a metal spring tail, droopy wooden ears, a head that rotated on a metal joint, and a moveable jaw, like a ventriloquist puppet, which I suspected enabled it to speak. To speak!

This was definitely not a dream. The toy dog was real. It was male. And it was in my room.

"Who are you, and what the hell are you doing in my room?" I clasped my arms around myself, content I had a T-shirt on and wasn't naked. That would have been much worse. Still pretty creepy to wake up to a magical toy staring me in the face.

The toy dog wagged its tail. "The name's Jimmy."

I frowned at the toy. My pounding headache etched around the backs of my eyes and made its way to my eyebrows. "What the hell do you want?"

The wooden dog blinked. "I came to see you, of course. The hotel's buzzing with news of the new Merlin. I needed to see you with my own eyes."

I didn't sense any dark, magical energies coming off the toy, but that didn't mean it wasn't sent by the ghost or whoever had murdered those people. "Do you belong to one of the kids?"

The dog's ears swung back. "I don't belong to anyone. I'm not a toy."

"You sure look like one."

Toy dog Jimmy's eyes narrowed. "I wasn't always like this. I was once a man, you know."

"That's even creepier."

Jimmy watched me a moment, and then he sprang off my bed and rolled out of my bedroom. "Get dressed. We've got work to do," he called back.

"Excuse you?" Part of me wished I was still sleeping, but I found myself getting up and locking myself in the bathroom. I didn't trust the damn toy.

After a shower, I pulled on a pair of dark jeans and a T-shirt before grabbing the bottle of Tylenol from my bag and walking into the living room. The air smelled of fresh coffee, and I found Jimmy on the counter next to the coffee maker.

"You don't have legs," I told him, wondering how the hell he got up there and then made coffee.

"How observant of you," snapped the toy dog. "Did anyone ever tell you how grumpy you are in the morning?"

"Yeah. My husband." I moved to the coffee maker and poured myself a cup. "How did you get on the counter?" And my bed, for that matter. Even more disturbing was that he'd made coffee without hands.

Jimmy swung his ears forward. "Magic."

"Funny." I downed two Tylenols with a sip of coffee. "You said you used to be a man. What's your story? Cursed?" I'd heard of people being trapped in animals before, but a toy dog was a first.

Jimmy's tail lowered. "I was thirty-seven, in my prime, when the sorceress cursed me. She loved me, see, but I didn't love her back. So, she decided if she couldn't have me..."

"No one else would." Damn. Poor bastard. "How long ago was this?"

"Nineteen fifty-four."

I choked on my coffee. "Damn. That would mean you've been inside that toy for…"

Jimmy sighed. "A very long time."

Okay. That did change things a bit. I couldn't imagine being stuck inside a toy for that many years. Here I thought I was in hell, stuck with my husband for the last few years of our marriage. This was a lot worse.

"Has no one ever tried to break the curse?"

"Many have tried, and they've all failed. It's fine. I've accepted my fate. This is who I was supposed to be."

"A toy?"

The dog frowned with his painted eyebrows, which was really trippy. "A helper. A guide. I help people."

"Hmmm." I took another gulp of coffee and finished my cup.

"Elsa asked me to help you with your investigation," said the toy dog. "She's at her sister's place in Brooklyn, weeding her garden. Her sister has a bad case of arthritis."

"I usually work alone," I told him, though a guide or guide dog sounded pretty helpful since I still was new to the hotel and didn't know where everything was. Maybe this wasn't such a bad idea.

"Not anymore. Well, at least not while you're staying at the hotel. Your business is everyone's business."

"I noticed." Last night was an awakening. I set my empty cup on the counter next to Jimmy. "Did you help the last Merlin?"

"Eddie?" said the toy dog, his metal spring tail wagging. "I did. Good lad. Decent witch."

That was good news. "Do you know what he discovered? He found something out, and it got him killed. I'm sure of it." That was the only logical explanation.

"Well," said the dog as he rolled back in what I imagined was his attempt to sit. "I remember him saying that there was no connection between the two victims, excluding him, of course. And that the killer, or killers, killed only at night and somehow were able to move through walls."

"Move through walls?"

"Like ghosts."

I raised a brow. "You've been talking to Elsa."

The dog dipped his head. "It's the only thing that makes sense. We can see the victims entering their rooms. Only them. And then the maids finding them in the morning."

It was Elsa's theory. But I didn't buy it. "I'd like to see that footage. I'll ask Basil to show me."

"Eddie has copies on his laptop," said the toy dog. "He showed me."

"You know where the laptop is now?" I didn't remember seeing a laptop in the room. If I had, I would have grabbed it.

The toy dog nodded. "Yes. I'm betting it's still there. The maids haven't touched the room yet. They're afraid the ghost will kill them if they come inside the room."

"So much for keeping this discreet." If one of the maids had found the body of poor Eddie, I was sure the entire hotel staff knew by now. It wouldn't be long before the guests knew as well. But a laptop with notes from the previous Merlin was golden. It meant I would know what Eddie knew before he was killed.

It also meant I would be a target. It wouldn't be the first time.

"You're a Dark witch. Aren't you?" asked the toy dog after a moment. "You channel your magic through demons? Not that there's anything wrong with that. But are you?"

I looked away from the toy dog. It was too early in the morning for that conversation, and the Tylenol hadn't kicked in yet. "I'm a witch. Let's just keep it at that."

The toy dog's ears swiveled forward. "Fine. Keep your secrets. It'll come out eventually."

He was right. It always did.

"So, is Martin your husband?" asked Jimmy.

"You're a nosy little creature. Aren't you?"

"That's how I know so much," answered Jimmy. "I make it my business to know what happens in this hotel."

I let out a sigh. My body tensed at the memory of Martin squeezing my throat last year, and the excitement in his eyes when I woke up to find him on top of me, me not able to breathe, which somehow turned him on. My blood pressure rose at the recollection. I felt sick, partly that I'd ever loved a monster like that. But mostly I was angry with myself that I didn't have the courage to leave all those years ago.

"He's my soon-to-be ex-husband," I found myself answering after a moment.

Jimmy rolled forward. "Ah. So, that's why Elsa asked me to drop off those files on the table for ya."

"What files?" I moved to the dining table and saw a manila envelope. A single Post-it note read *Fill out the forms and give them back to Jimmy*.

If Elsa was right, I'd be free of him in just two weeks. It seemed too good to be true. Hell, I needed a little bit of happiness in my life.

My heart leaped with the news. "Let's go, Snoopy."

"It's *Jimmy*," said the dog, though I could see the smile on his wooden face. He leaped off the counter and rolled to the front door, which—surprise, surprise—was wide open. "You coming?"

I smiled and grabbed my shoulder bag from the wall hook rack in the hallway. "Right behind you, Snoopy."

CHAPTER 7

It turned out Jimmy was right. The Merlin's room had remained intact. It wasn't even locked, to my surprise, as I pushed us through. I caught a glimpse of a maid, judging by the white-and-gray, short-sleeved uniform dress, looking over her shoulder at us. Her eyes widened in terror, and then she jerked her head back around before hauling her cleaning cart with a speed that suggested she was late for an appointment.

The guest rooms were smaller than the resident apartments. The main difference was they didn't have separate rooms, just one big space that included a bed, a small desk set before a window, a modest bathroom, and a kitchenette that hosted a small fridge and coffee maker.

The sound of wheels grinding caught my attention, and I saw Jimmy roll to a stop on the carpet next to me.

"So, where is it?"

"He hid it in the bathroom," said the toy dog as he rolled away.

"He hid it?" That wasn't good. It meant he knew someone or something was onto him.

"Yeah," called Jimmy. "In here. I can't reach it. You'll have to get it for me."

For him? I shook my head but followed him to the bathroom.

His ears swiveled forward. "Up there in the vent."

I stepped around Jimmy and then pushed up on my toes. Slipping my fingers under the metal casing, I pulled, and the frame came free. Setting it on the bathroom vanity, I stuck my hand through the vent cavity, and my fingers touched cold, hard metal. I yanked out the laptop and grinned at the toy dog.

"Not bad, Snoopy."

"You're welcome, Merlie."

I laughed. "Come on. Let's see what Eddie discovered and why he felt the need to hide his laptop."

I sat on the edge of the bed and flipped the laptop open. Jimmy leaped on the bed and rolled next to me. The computer turned on moments later.

"Shit. It's password protected." Of course, it would be.

Jimmy leaned forward and said, "*Trustnoone*. The one is the number one, and trustno is all lower case." At my questioning brow, he added, "What? I saw him type it more than once."

Seriously. This toy dog was proving to be an excellent assistant or guide. And I was glad he was here. Without Jimmy, I'd never have found the laptop. And if, by a miracle, I had, it would have taken days to find someone to crack the password. I was happy Jimmy was here.

"Looks like Eddie was an *X-Files* fan," I said, remembering the countless times I'd rewatched the entire eleven seasons. "He had good taste."

I typed in *trustno1* and pressed enter. "We're in." The desktop had about fifty folders, some labeled with dates, some just letters that didn't mean anything. "He's not that organized. Wait—here." I clicked on the folder called MERLIN. "This is only a spreadsheet of the hours he worked," I said, feeling some of my excitement fade.

Jimmy cycled forward until his front wheels bumped my thigh. "Try that one. The one that says TH. Twilight Hotel."

I scanned the screen for the folder and then clicked on it. "Here we go."

The folder opened to a list of multiple files, documents, images, and more folders. I clicked on the pictures first. The first image was of a woman lying on the floor above a green carpet. It was hard to see her face from this angle, but I could just make out the frown and the squinting of her eyes, recognizing the pain she must have felt before she died.

"That's Patricia," said Jimmy. "The first victim."

I nodded. "I recognize her from the photo Basil gave me. Looks like she died in the same way as Eddie." I flipped through the pictures until I landed on the second victim. A male.

"That's Jordan," informed the dog.

I studied the image. "The only thing that connects them all is how they were killed. Whoever did this killed them all the same way." It didn't say much, but it told me the killer was consistent.

After that, I clicked through more files and documents. "Where is it, Eddie?" I said to the screen. "What were you afraid of?" I wanted to know why Eddie felt the need to hide his computer. So far, I couldn't see anything that would give him a reason.

"Click the video file," suggested Jimmy. "It's where he downloaded the camera feed from outside the rooms."

Following the toy dog's instructions, I clicked on the folder that said VIDEO. Only two videos were inside. My pulse quickened as I clicked the first one.

The clip opened to reveal footage from a hallway of the hotel. The dim lighting and orange glow from the wall sconces were enough to make out the numbers on the doors. They all started with the number two, so I knew I was looking at the second floor. I sat there in silence with Jimmy and watched for a few seconds until, finally, a figure stepped out of the elevator. A woman dressed in dark clothing crossed the hallway and, with her key card, opened the door to room 202.

"That's Patricia," said Jimmy.

I watched as the door to her room closed and then nothing. I scrolled through the video, seeing people come and go, and finally, a brighter video as the morning sun shone through the windows.

"Here comes the maid," announced Jimmy.

Sure enough, I saw a maid push her cleaning cart to room 202, knock twice, wait, and then use her key card, unlock the door, and push in.

"Wait for it," said the toy dog.

"For what?" I asked, glancing at Jimmy.

"Look."

I stared at the screen just as the maid came crashing out of the room and ran off camera.

"See?" Jimmy shifted on the bed. "No one was in that room except for the victim and the maid. How do you explain that? Ghosts? Elsa seems to think so."

I shook my head. "I don't know. I don't think so. A vengeful ghost? Could be. But something doesn't make sense. She was killed sometime during the night. Same as Eddie and the other guy. All were killed at night and then discovered by the maids the next morning. Hmmm."

"What does *hmmm* mean?"

"It means if it was a ghost or ghosts, why doesn't Eddie mention that in any of these files? I mean, I haven't gone through all of them, but if he thought ghosts were responsible, shouldn't we have seen some evidence of that? There's nothing on ghosts in his notes."

"It doesn't mean it *wasn't* a ghost."

I shook my head. "No. But if it was a ghost, why here and why now? Why these people?"

"Good question." Jimmy rolled back. "What are you thinking? If not a ghost or some kind of evil spirit haunting, then what? Who did this? The last I knew, living paranormals can't walk through walls."

"You're right. We don't."

"Like Dark witches?" pressed Jimmy. "You're a Dark witch. Right?"

Ignoring him, I leaned forward and clicked the play button on the other video. And just like Patricia, no one entered the room after Jordan did. Just the maid who came running out the following morning.

I didn't believe a ghost did this. I didn't think Eddie thought that either. I thought something in his computer got him killed—something we hadn't seen yet.

I scrolled through the video again, all the way until Jordan walked inside his room, shut the door, and then let it play. Scrolled a bit. Let it play. And then—

"Wait a second." My heart sped up as I moved through the video frame by frame.

"What? Did you see something?" Jimmy leaped up onto my lap. "What?"

I looked down at the toy dog, thought of smacking him off my lap, but then thought better of it. "Here." I moved back, pressing a few frames with the left arrow key on the keyboard. "Here. Look." I moved from one image frame to the next. "See how the light from the moon reflects on the wall here?"

Jimmy rolled forward until the tip of his wooden nose hit the screen. "Yeah."

"Watch." I pressed on the next frame. "See. It doesn't match."

Jimmy whistled and rolled back. "Holy smokes. Someone tampered with the video feed."

"Exactly." I beamed. "This is no ghost. I'm sure of it. This is someone very much alive. I'm willing to bet Eddie figured this out too. It's what got him killed."

Jimmy stared at the screen. "Look. The time frame didn't change."

I stared at the video. The bottom of the screen read 11:31 p.m. "I know," I said, moving through the video again to where I'd spotted the glitch. The clock never lost time. "That would have been a dead giveaway. They made sure the clock stayed correct throughout the video. It was probably missing a few minutes near the end, but no one noticed."

"You're like a modern Sherlock Holmes. Does that make me Dr. Watson?"

"If this helps solve our case, you can be anyone you want, Snoopy."

Jimmy laughed, which sounded so human that it was almost like he was right here next to me in his human form.

I stared at the toy dog. "Who has access to the cameras?" I had a feeling I was onto something.

"As far as I know, Basil and the security chief," answered the toy dog.

I smiled. "That is excellent news, my friend. It narrows down our list of suspects."

"We have a list?"

"Now we do." I scratched under his chin, only realizing then that I didn't know if Jimmy felt anything. He was a wooden toy dog, not a real puppy.

Jimmy closed his eyes in delight. "Julian owes me twenty bucks. He bet that you wouldn't find anything. And you found something big."

I wasn't sure if I was more offended that they had put bets on me or that Julian didn't think I was up to the task.

I looked at my new partner, wondering where he slept, if he even slept. Did he have a room or an apartment, or did he just wander through the hotel all day and night. I wanted to ask him, but that could wait for another time.

"Let's go." I jumped up. Jimmy leaped off my lap easily onto the floor, and I grabbed the laptop, securing it under my arm. I wasn't letting go of this baby. Besides, I left my own computer back at my old place, and I wasn't going back.

This find was excellent news. I didn't take Basil as the murdering type, but if he had access to the camera feed, he was now on my list of suspects, along with whoever this security chief was.

I grabbed the door handle, yanked it open, and smacked into the chest of none other than my favorite man-beast.

CHAPTER 8

I stepped back, my face flaming from irritation and embarrassment because I'd just smeared it against some of his chest skin. "What are *you* doing here?" I really had to stop meeting this guy this way. I really had to stop thinking about him too. And dreaming about him. And why the hell did he have to smell so nice?

The man-beast wore a shirt that did nothing to constrain the muscles that pulled against it, like they were begging him to tear it off. It was buttoned low, which explained why part of my face had splattered against his man-beast chest skin. My eyes flicked at the tattoos peeking from the collar of his low V-neck shirt. He wore a pair of dark jeans that fit his slim waist and were snug against thick thighs. He looked predatory, ready to fight and kill something. Like I said, man-beast.

I quickly tore my gaze away from his distracting, extremely virile chest.

Valen, the said man-beast, looked mildly surprised at my tone. "I was asked to come here and take a look."

"By who?" I looked past him and saw two pretty women huddled together, both dressed in identical white-and-gray maid uniforms, both twenty years my junior. Now I understood. I was pretty sure he had lots of women drooling in his wake. He had that alpha thing down to a T. It was hot. Not hot enough to tempt me, though. Okay, maybe a little. Yeah, I was a total liar.

Jimmy rolled ahead and stopped at my feet. "Hey, Valen. What's up?"

"Jimmy," said Valen in the way of greeting my new friend. So, they knew each other. Interesting. I had a feeling Jimmy knew a lot more than he let on. He was proving to be a valuable ally.

"Everything smooth over at After Dark?" asked Jimmy.

The large man nodded. "It is."

"I heard there was a fight between two shifters last Friday," continued Jimmy. "I heard it got bloody. Heard one guy busted a few ribs and the other lost some teeth."

A muscle feathered along Valen's jaw as he kept his eyes on me. "I took care of it."

"Of course you did," answered the dog, rolling around Valen's ankles and stopping next to his left foot. "Your restaurant. Your fists."

Valen's dark eyes shot to the laptop tucked under my arm. He looked at me. His unwavering stare beat into me like the pounding of a drum. Tingles washed over my scalp and spread over my skin.

This man was dangerous. Not because of his size and bulging muscles. It was more in his presence, the energy he gave off. Something deadly and brutal glinted in his gaze, concealed under his rugged and handsome exterior. He was like a lion. Unpredictable and lethal, which set me on edge.

He said nothing as he brushed past me and entered the room. That damn fine cologne touched my senses, and I had no choice but to inhale some. I expected the two maids to follow, but they stayed outside in the hallway, their faces tight with fear.

I followed him. "What are you doing?"

Valen strolled into Eddie's room and went straight to the bed. He lifted the mattress with one hand, like it weighed nothing more than a bedsheet, and looked under it. Thick muscles flared along his back in quite the show. I wondered why the women weren't in here enjoying the view.

"There's nothing there, apart from bedbugs," I said, though I hadn't thought of looking under the mattress. Not very thorough in my investigation.

Valen let the mattress fall and then went through the drawers of the two night tables, clearly looking for something. "You're Leana, the new Merlin."

"That's right." I wasn't thrilled that he'd been asking about me. "And you're the grumpy, rude restaurant owner, Valen." There. I knew his name too.

Jimmy made a weird sound in his throat. "You two know each other?"

"No," Valen and I chorused with the same amount of ire. Okay, that was weird.

Those dark eyes rested on me again. His face was carefully blank of any expression. "The last Merlin died in this room."

I narrowed my eyes. "Who told you that?" My gaze went to the two maids clustered together in the hallway, both avoiding my eyes. Clearly, the two maids had blabbed. If he knew about the deaths, it wouldn't be long before the guests in the hotel knew. No way could Basil keep this quiet much longer.

Valen crossed the room and opened the cabinet of the kitchenette, the coffee maker and cups rattling above it. I was next to him in a heartbeat.

"You shouldn't be here. This is my case."

Valen shut the cabinet door and turned to me. "Your case."

"That's right," I said, my heart thrumming in my chest. Jimmy rolled past me and joined the two maids in the hallway as I turned my attention back to the large man. "I've been hired by the hotel to look into the Merlin's death." I didn't want to say too much. I didn't trust this guy. He was giving off all kinds of different vibes, and none of them were trustworthy. For one, I didn't like that he was snooping around Eddie's room like he was looking for something.

"Have you discovered anything?" asked the man-beast.

"Right. Like I'm going to tell you." The nerve of this guy.

"So you haven't discovered anything."

"I've discovered that you're very rude to strangers," I shot back, my free hand on my hip.

"I could say the same about you," said Valen, his eyes narrowing slightly.

My temper rose, and I reined it in. I did not want to start a fight, especially while on the job and with a very dangerous-looking man. "You should leave," I told him. "You're messing up my crime scene." I wasn't sure how much authority I had with the hotel. Basil and I never really discussed it. I was hoping I had carte blanche, as I usually did whenever working on a case.

His intense gaze was making me uncomfortable. I leaned my hip against the cabinet. And when I went to steady myself with my right hand, it hit one of the coffee cups.

I blinked as the cup slid off the counter.

Valen's left hand shot out so fast, I only saw a blur, and then he placed the cup back on the countertop.

I jerked, squeezing the laptop against my armpit. Okay, so this guy was fast. Vampire fast. My skin prickled and danced with fear and a little excitement. Something was seriously wrong with me. I blamed it on my soon-to-be ex-husband's years of neglect in the bedroom.

"How long have you been a Merlin?" asked Valen suddenly in the silence, leaning back and studying me. He crossed his arms, the muscles on his chest bulging, clearly wanting out of that shirt.

I didn't want to answer, but I did anyway. "Ten years. I know what I'm doing. This isn't my first murder case."

"So you've worked on a case like this before?" asked the man-beast, his voice carefully neutral.

I frowned. "I've worked on many cases. Never one like this, but every case is unique. I have to treat them as such." I wasn't liking where this conversation was going. He shouldn't be grilling me. *I* should be peppering *him* with questions.

Valen stood there, watching me. "You're different from the other Merlins."

My battle to stop flushing wasn't going well. "Really?" I snorted. "In what way? That I'm not afraid of you? All those muscles don't scare me."

I thought I saw a tiny smile form on those thick lips, but in a flash, it was gone, replaced by a tight mask of indifference. "I seriously doubt you know many Merlins." Just like there weren't many powerful witches, even fewer of them became Merlins. We were a select few.

Valen's gaze went sharp, and for the briefest of moments, a look of pure, primal hunger flashed over his face.

I stiffened, and then my traitorous body fluttered in response to whatever that was. And it wasn't fear.

"You're married to a human," stated Valen, like this was old news. His face again, carefully blank. "Interesting choice."

My lips parted in surprise. "Soon to be unmarried," I shot back, pricks of unease working through my body. I didn't particularly appreciate how he'd said "interesting choice," like I'd lowered myself by marrying Martin. Maybe I had. But I didn't like having it thrown in my face. "You've been checking up on me?" I wasn't thrilled that this stranger knew personal things about me when I knew pretty much nothing about him, apart from the fact that he was usually a prick and owned a restaurant that served fantastic food.

"It's my business to know about strangers in my city," said Valen. "We don't like strangers."

"*Your* city?" I gave him a hard stare. "Are you saying you own New York City?" Wow, this guy was infuriating. He was pushing all my buttons.

Valen flicked his gaze across the room, not really settling on anything. "No. I don't own the city. But the Twilight Hotel is in my territory. I'm responsible for the paranormals in this sector. What goes on in here is my business."

This conversation was all kinds of weird. I knew there were

paranormal bosses, alphas, and heads of clans and packs in certain large city districts like Manhattan, but I'd rarely had to deal with any of them. I also knew that paranormals tended to disappear if you pissed them off. "Listen. I don't know who you are or if any of that is true, but I know I have a job to do. You're messing with it right now. You're making it impossible for me to work." I made a mental note to investigate this man-beast, along with my case. He'd checked up on me. It was only fair that I returned the favor.

A female voice rose in pitch from the hallway. I couldn't make out what she was saying, but I was pretty sure Jimmy would give me a rundown later.

Valen's intelligent gaze regarded me for a beat. "Did you like the duck?"

My eyebrows shot up, completely taken off guard by that question. "Huh?"

"The roast duck with figs... was it to your liking?" Valen's deep voice rumbled, and I found myself entranced by it.

I blinked. "Yes. It was good. Very good." Why the hell were we talking about food?

The man-beast watched me again, almost like he was wondering if he should put a hit on me. That, or rip off my clothes. I thought he was going to say something, but he moved past me and headed right for the bathroom.

Only when I stood in the bathroom's doorway did I realize that I'd forgotten to put the metal vent back. Whoops.

Valen's eyes went to the duct cavity in the wall and then back to me, resting on the laptop again.

"Stealing hotel property?" Valen's gaze bore into mine. "That's a crime. Even here."

At that, my face was scorched like I'd doused it in molten lava. "I didn't *steal* anything. This is my laptop." I was a terrible liar. It didn't help that I stuttered and avoided his eyes. *Nice one, Leana.*

But it didn't explain why he suspected it wasn't mine. If I

didn't know any better, I'd say he knew Eddie had hidden his laptop somewhere in this room. He'd come for the computer.

I thought he was about to rip into me about the computer, but he said nothing. Without another word or glance in my direction, Valen walked out of the bathroom and into the hallway as I made my way to the door. I stood there, Jimmy at my feet, watching the man-beast and the two maids step into the elevator at the end of the hallway.

Valen looked my way. Our eyes met and held for a beat as the elevator doors slid shut.

"What can you tell me about that guy?" I asked Jimmy as I pulled the door to the room shut.

"A lot," answered the toy dog.

"Good."

We'd made good progress by finding the laptop and seeing that the video was tampered with. But I couldn't suppress the feeling that Valen somehow knew something about the murders. What was his connection?

I only knew for sure that he'd come for Eddie's laptop. I was certain of it. Did he know about the videos? Was he here to destroy the evidence?

I was going to find out.

CHAPTER 9

"Have you seen Basil?" I leaned on the front desk, careful not to hit the laptop still tucked under my arm.

"Why are you looking for him?" Errol was picking his nails with a letter opener, a bored expression on his face.

"Because I need to speak to him. Where is he?"

"Why?"

I gritted my teeth. "Hotel business."

Errol let out a dramatic sigh. "*I'm* the hotel business."

"Not this one."

"Tell me why you want to see him, and maybe I'll tell you."

Part of me wanted to jump over the desk and strangle him. "You're particularly shitty this morning."

The concierge made a face like I'd just spat on his expensive suit. "I don't like you."

"Come on, Errol, this is important," shot Jimmy from the floor. "Just tell us where he is."

"I don't respond to wooden toys. Go find a child or something. Or better yet. Go jump in a fire."

I laughed. "How the hell did you get a job in hospitality?"

Errol's pale face reddened. "Because I'm *excellent* at my job."

I pushed back from the counter. "Looks to me more like whoever hired you is a moron."

"That would make *me* the moron," said a voice.

Crap.

I turned slowly. An average-looking man with a forgettable face stood behind me. Most of his scalp showed through his thinning hair, and he'd attempted, very poorly, to comb over the strings of hair he had left. Dark circles marred his eyes, like someone who hadn't slept in years. It was hard to guess his age due to his sickly looking face. Maybe fifty? Sixty? His skin was oily, and his dark suit looked like he'd picked it from a thrift shop. In his hands hung a stained cloth and a bottle of disinfectant.

"I'm Raymond. The assistant manager of the hotel. How can I help?"

I felt a little relief wash through me. "Hi. I'm Leana."

Raymond was nodding. "Yes. I know who you are."

"Good. We're looking for Basil. Have you seen him?"

Raymond moved over to me, nudged me off the counter with a shove of the cloth in his hand, sprayed where I'd touched it, and began to scrub the surface.

I wasn't sure if I should be insulted. He was paranormal, no doubt, but all I was getting from him with the scent of vinegar and bleach. The dude was a germophobe.

"He left for some personal matter," said Raymond as he buffed the same spot continuously. "He'll be back later in the afternoon." He eyed the spot one final time and then looked at me, blinking pale eyes. "There. Must keep the hotel looking its best at all times."

Jimmy snorted, winning a glare from Raymond.

"Sure." He was a strange creature.

Raymond raised his bottle and aimed it at me like he was about to spray. "Shall I take a message? Or maybe I can help you."

"It's fine. I'll wait for him to get back." The fewer people who knew about the footage, the better.

"As you wish." Raymond cast his gaze over the lobby, his eyes settling on something, and he took off. He crossed the lobby to a group of guests lounging on the couches and sprayed his disinfectant on a coffee table to the many outbursts of annoyance from the guests.

"Come on. Let's check with security," called Jimmy from the floor.

I followed behind the toy dog as he rolled ahead. He stopped at a black metal door just off the lobby. The sign on the door said HOTEL SECURITY.

I knocked once and pushed in.

The first thing that hit me was the strong cigarette smell. The second was how tight the space was, like the size of the bathroom in my new apartment. The back wall was covered in floor-to-ceiling screens. A desk sat before the screens, topped with four laptops. The largest man I'd ever seen was squeezed into the only swivel chair. Dark hair covered most of his face, and light eyes peered from under thick brows.

"Yes?" said the man in a thick voice that matched his frame. "What do you want?"

I took a step back. My heart pounded at the threat in his voice and the way he was looking at me. He could easily snap off my head. The scent of wild animals hit me. Yup. This guy was a shifter. Werebear, judging by his size.

"Oh, hi, Jimmy," said the large man, his demeanor switching in a second to something soft and even possibly brotherly. "I didn't see you there. You here for another game of chess?"

"Hey, Bob. Not today." Jimmy rolled inside the room. "Bob's a werebear," informed the toy dog. "But don't let his size scare you. He's a big teddy bear."

"Mmm," I said, still a little taken aback by his enormous size.

"We want to ask you about the security cameras," the toy dog went on.

"Ah. You want to know about the murders?" His eyes looked me over. "You the new Merlin?"

"I am." *Please don't eat me.* "Can you show me the feed from those nights? Start with room four oh four." The clip was still fresh in my memory. I didn't take Bob for the murdering type, maybe just the killing type. But unless I could clear him, he was one of the only people I knew who had access to the cameras. And by looking at his setup, he could easily have altered the video. I wanted to see his reaction with my own eyes.

Bob moved a beefy finger over the keypad of one of the laptops. He clicked on something, and then one of the larger screens on the wall flashed. Suddenly I was staring at the same footage I saw on Eddie's laptop.

"Can you fast-forward to around 11:31 p.m.?" I instructed.

Bob did as I asked without a second thought, and then we were looking at the same spot where it jumped frames.

"Did you see that?" I squeezed around the desk and pointed to the frame. "Stop and go back a few frames."

Bob did as I asked. "What am I looking at?"

"The lighting." I pointed at the screen. "Look. It changes. Someone erased a part of your footage. The time frame was also manipulated. There's no difference in time. Just the video."

Unless Bob was an Oscar-quality actor, he was genuinely surprised and shocked at what he saw on the screen. Then… then he got mad, and that was truly scary.

He jumped up, the floor and walls shaking with his brute force. The top of his head hit the ceiling, though he barely took notice. "Who would do that?"

"That's the million-dollar question," said Jimmy. "Or is it billion-dollar question these days?"

"Bob?" I squeezed back around the desk. "If I were to take a chunk out of the video recording, how would I do that? How would I manipulate the feed?"

"Yeah," agreed Jimmy. "How would someone do that?'

Bob looked from me to the laptop. "You'd have to change the original. Go into the editing program and manually change it."

I tapped my chin with a finger. "So you'd have to be *inside* this room to do it."

The big man frowned. "Yes."

"Unless they did it remotely. Could they?" I asked. With so many hackers these days, anybody could be a potential hacker.

Bob shook his head. "Our network system is not like the human networks. You can't log in remotely, and you can't hack it from outside either. It's protected. Magically protected. Wards and such. There's only one way someone did this—inside this room."

"You've got cameras in here?" I looked around, hopeful.

"No. Sorry."

"Apart from you and Basil, does anyone else have access to this room?" I asked, following his logic. So whoever changed the feed had to get into this room and get past Bob, which was no easy feat.

Bob looked troubled as he squeezed his large behind into that chair. It was a mystery that it fit and didn't crush the chair under his weight. "Just me and Basil."

"Who works this office when you're on break or when you go home?" Jimmy asked, pulling the question right out of my mouth.

Through his thick beard, Bob's lips pursed. "No one. It's just me."

"So there's a time when no one is in here," I said out loud. Someone could have easily waited for Bob to finish his shift and made their way in to sabotage the footage. Which meant we weren't any closer to finding who that person was.

"Thanks for your time, Bob," I told the giant werebear. We weren't going to get much else.

Someone had screwed with the footage. I just didn't know who. I doubted it was Basil. He didn't look like the type who would know how to navigate and edit digital footage and then make it nearly impossible to catch, but I was still going to talk to him.

Teeth flashed, and I jerked back, only noticing that big Bob had just smiled at me. To anyone else, it could have looked like he wanted to chomp down on my head.

"Anytime," said Bob.

I started out the door. Jimmy rolled along next to me but then halted and spun around. "Did anyone else ask about the cameras?"

Bob blinked as he thought about it. "The other Merlin before you and Basil."

"Thanks."

I closed the door behind me. "Looks like Eddie knew something was up."

"Looks that way," answered the toy dog.

I looked around the lobby. It was around ten in the morning, and the hotel was buzzing with guests. One glimpse in Errol's direction, at the frown on his face while listening to a couple speaking to him at the front desk, made me smile.

We walked through the lobby. Well, I was walking, and Jimmy was rolling next to me. Not a single person looked our way. No one seemed bothered by the fact that I was waltzing around with a wooden toy dog at my feet in a fancy hotel, but this wasn't the average human hotel. This was a paranormal one.

"Do you want to put the computer in one of the hotel's safes?" inquired Jimmy as he rolled to a stop.

I stared down at my wooden friend. "The hotel has safes?"

"Yup. It's where the guests put their valuables, precious stones, jewelry, magic wands, orbs, weapons that were confiscated —that kind of thing. I'm sure it'll be safe."

I thought about it. "I think I'll keep it with me for now. I still have to go through it. There's still a lot I don't know about Eddie." I tapped the computer under my arm. "I think I'll take him to bed with me."

Jimmy laughed. "Where do you want to look next?"

"I have some errands to run. I need to stock my fridge. And I need clothes. I kinda left in a hurry from my old place. You wanna come with me? I can stuff you in my bag. No one will notice."

The dog's tail bent down almost between his back wheels. "Can't. I can't leave the hotel."

"Ever?"

"Ever."

"Have you tried?" Of course, he had, but I wanted to know.

"Many times, and it's always the same."

"What?"

"Excruciating pain," said the toy dog. "And if I stay outside longer than a few seconds, I will die."

I narrowed my eyes suddenly, a bitter taste in my mouth as anger flowed through me. The fact that the sorceress had done this to this poor man bothered me. "What was her name? The sorceress."

"Doesn't matter anymore." Jimmy rolled away. "See you later, Leana." I watched as he rolled down the lobby, no one bothering to look at him.

"Wait!" I called. "How do I get ahold of you? Do you have a room or something?"

Jimmy halted and spun around. The wooden toy dog looked sad for a moment, if that were even possible. "Just holler, and I'll find you."

I watched with a heavy heart as my new friend rolled away. Not only was he a prisoner in a toy dog's body, but he was also a prisoner in this hotel.

I felt a rush of hate for this sorceress. She might still be alive. And if she was, I would find her and have words with this bitch.

CHAPTER 10

My first stop was Macy's on West Thirty-Fourth Street. With my cash advance, I was able to buy a crapload of new underwear, bras, T-shirts, jeans, socks, bath towels, and some cotton sheets for the bed. I even bought a new leather shoulder bag for the laptop, so I could carry it properly without any nosy man-beasts asking too many questions.

Speaking of said nosy man-beast, I needed to know more about this Valen character and why he wanted the laptop in question. Was he working for someone, or was he trying to get his hands on the evidence himself?

It didn't help that I found him ridiculously attractive, with all those manly muscles and big, rough hands that I was sure would feel amazing on my skin. Yeah. I was losing it. Just a few days ago I had walked in on my husband banging some woman and had walked away, and now this handsome, dangerous dude was haunting my thoughts.

I blamed it on my hormones. Premenopause, or whatever it was, made your woman hormones go out of whack in your forties.

The truth was I didn't need a man to feel complete or comfortable in my own skin. I just needed me. I was my own hero. But that didn't mean I didn't think they were pretty to look at. I didn't trust them, especially after being with Martin, but I wasn't so naïve to think all men were bastards. I knew some were good guys, but most of the time, the good ones were already taken and settled with families.

I was lonely and had been for years. And with my luck, I would stay that way for another while. Good thing I had this new job to keep me busy.

On my way, I stopped at the small bodega on the corner of Park Avenue and East Thirty-Seventh Street and got some groceries to last me a few days until I had to go out for more. Of course, I popped into the nearest wine shop and grabbed two bottles of whatever they had on sale.

A glass of wine would be welcomed with all the research I had to do tonight, mainly with Eddie's computer. I wanted to know what he knew before he died. Maybe I'd find more than just the video feeds. Perhaps he'd discovered something else, and I needed to know.

By the time I made my way back to 444 Fifth Avenue, the clock on my phone said 6:53 p.m. No wonder I was so hungry. I didn't have breakfast, and I'd forgotten to have lunch.

I swept my gaze around the street. The hotel was nowhere in sight. Damn. I'd been so immersed in my thoughts that I'd walked right past it and didn't even notice.

"Definitely need to eat," I muttered to myself.

I turned on the spot and walked back a few steps, only to realize I *was* at the correct location. My eyes flicked to the green street sign with the words stenciled in white that read Fifth Avenue. Then my eyes settled on the restaurant After Dark. I was standing *right* in front of the restaurant. The Twilight Hotel should be there, right there, but I was staring at a dark alley. No hotel. Nothing.

"Oh shit."

Panic licked up my spine. Was this how the humans saw it?

What was going on? I knew the hotel was there, but for some reason, I couldn't *see* it anymore.

My heart rate shot through the roof. I couldn't panic right now. Humans were all around me, and the last thing I wanted was to draw unwelcome attention to myself.

I took a deep breath, gripped my shopping bags, hauled my new leather bag on my shoulder, and walked forward. I might not see it, but I'd feel it.

I walked straight with my right hand in the air. I got a few looks from some humans walking past me. They probably thought I was some crazy lady or I'd lost my sight.

But when I'd reached halfway down the alleyway, seeing the sign West Fortieth Street at the other end of the block, I started to panic. I'd crossed the entire block without feeling so much as a solid wall.

"This is bad." What the hell was happening?

With my bags gripped tightly in my hands, I turned around and doubled back, going right back the way I'd come, all the way back to the wide sidewalk on Fifth Avenue… but nothing. It was as though the hotel had never existed.

Fear pounded through me, making me irrational. Had I imagined the whole thing? Was I so messed up with my marriage that I had created this part to help me cope? Of course I had a wild imagination, but I was pretty sure I'd lived this experience. Hell, I'd slept in the damn hotel.

No, something was definitely wrong. Somehow the hotel wouldn't reveal itself to me anymore.

"Maybe I need a password. A magic word." Yeah, I wouldn't be surprised if Basil had forgotten to tell me that I needed a special password to get back into the hotel after spending more than a few hours out. It made sense.

I dropped my bags on the ground and rubbed my hands. "Open sesame," I muttered and got a few laughs from a passing group of teenagers.

"Abracadabra," I tried again, waving my fingers for good

measure, but still nothing. I didn't even feel the magical pulsing of the glamour that hid the hotel from human eyes anymore.

"The Twilight Hotel. Reveal yourself!" I said and waited. Soon my fear was replaced by irritation and a bit of my sanity. I stomped my foot on the ground. Yup, very mature. "Open up, you damn hotel, or I'm going to clog all the toilets!"

Nope. Still just an alley.

I let out a breath and rubbed my eyes with my fingers. "I can't freaking believe this."

"You lost?"

I flinched but kept my hands covering my eyes. I didn't need to see the person to know it was the man-beast from the restaurant next door.

"Go away," I said, still hiding my eyes. When I heard his chuckle, I dropped my hands, spun, and glowered at him. "What's so funny?"

Valen, being himself, stood with his arms crossed over his broad chest, amusement flashing in his dark eyes. "You can't find the hotel. Can you?"

Shit. If he knew, that meant I was right. I needed a password or something. Heat rushed to my face, a mixture of embarrassment and the fact that he was so damn fine and right next to me.

A black leather jacket hung over his broad shoulders, drawing my eyes down to his narrow waist. His dark jeans fit his long thighs perfectly, and the T-shirt did nothing to hide his muscled chest.

I puffed out some air. "Of course I can see it." I totally couldn't.

His dark eyes fastened on me. "Really? Then why aren't you going inside?"

"I thought I'd get some fresh air first."

Valen raised a brow. "You mean some exhaust fumes?"

I flashed him a smile. "Nothing like the toxic air to unclog my pores."

Valen laughed again, the sound a deep rumble that sent delicious tingles over my skin. I found myself liking how it sounded. Crap. I had to stop this. He was bad. Hot bad, but still bad. And he knew about Eddie's laptop, which put him on the list of "possible suspects."

When I realized he must have seen me lose my cool and walk up and down the alley like someone who'd lost her mind, more heat rushed up from my neck and settled around my face. And now I was sweating. Excellent.

I glanced at him again, realizing he'd been staring at me. His eyes were intense as they beheld me. I felt mesmerized by them. I couldn't help it. I felt a pull toward him, even if he was lethal.

"If you *can* see it," challenged Valen, "then go on ahead. Go in."

"Why? So you can stare at my ass? I don't think so."

Valen smiled. It transformed his face from ruggedly handsome to a whole new level of sexy.

He stared at the ground, laughing silently. "You're a witch. Right?"

"Yes. We've already been through this. I'm a Merlin. Remember?"

The corners of his eyes crinkled with laughter. "And you don't know when someone puts a spell on you?"

Oh shit. I swallowed hard. *There goes my reputation.* "You think? No. Are you serious?" What he said made much more sense now that I thought about it. Why hadn't I thought about it?

Valen nodded as he glanced in the direction of where the hotel was, though I still couldn't see it. "Someone spelled you so you can't see the hotel."

Now that I knew what had been done to me, I recognized the faint magic as it swept around me, crawling over my skin like hundreds of ants until it faded all together. I wasn't much for glamours, but I knew of them. I knew whoever had put this spell on me was an experienced magical practitioner with a high level of magic. Especially to put a spell on me without my knowledge.

I stared at him. "How would you know this?"

The big man shrugged. "The Twilight Hotel will forever ensure that all of us paranormals can find it. It's always visible to us unless a spell keeps it hidden. Like you right now. You looked like a human looking for her lost cat."

Damn. So he had been watching me.

I clenched my jaw and looked in the direction he was staring. Someone inside there had spelled me. Motherfrackers.

"So, there wasn't a password to get back in?" I felt like a fool. A big ol' fool. Maybe that person had been watching me make a fool out of myself the whole time too.

"No password," said the man-beast with laughter in his voice. "Just a spell. Or whatever magic you witches use."

"This isn't funny," I snapped.

"Yes. It's very funny."

I sighed. "And here I thought I was having a good day." I glanced at him. "Was it you?" What? I had to know.

At that, Valen chuckled, his wide chest jumping up and down. "I don't do magic. Not my thing."

I raised a brow. "All paranormals have some magic flowing in them. Whether it's the wild magic of shifters or the cold magic of demons."

Valen's face went still. "It wasn't me. If it was, why would I be here now?"

Good point. "So, what's *your* thing, then? You know about me. It's only fair I know about you."

Valen just kept staring at me with those damn dark eyes. I could still see a spark of laughter in them. The guy was having a blast at my expense. Great.

"Who would do this?" I asked after a moment, but I knew the answer as soon as the words left my mouth.

The one who'd committed the murders, that's who. They didn't want me back inside the hotel because I was onto something. I knew about the cameras. And this spell led me to believe I was about to discover more.

The fact that they did this to me only made me want to solve the case even more.

I was going to find these bastards.

We stood in an awkward silence for a while, my heart making music in my ears in the swirl of conflicting feelings while my entire body thrummed with heat that had nothing to do with my warm jacket.

Valen bent down and grabbed my bags. "Come on. I'll take you inside," he said finally, his tone caring and soft, which threw me off a little.

I didn't say anything as I followed closely behind him, not wanting to miss anything. If he should disappear, I'd find myself alone again and unable to find the hotel entrance.

I felt a little more relaxed that he didn't look or sound angry. I took that as a good sign.

I'd barely noticed the change in air pressure as the world around me changed. Suddenly I was staring at the inside of the hotel and not eyeing an alleyway.

"Is the spell gone?" asked Valen, and I turned to meet his eyes.

"Yes. You were right. Thank you," I added a little awkwardly.

He opened his mouth to say something but then stopped. Steadying himself, he tried again. "Here." He gave me my bags.

I took the bags from him, and before I could thank him again, he'd turned his back on me and made his way out the front doors.

I watched him go, more confused than ever about this guy. Why did he help me get back inside the hotel if he was truly bad? It could be to throw me off, to make me *think* he was one of the good guys when in reality, he wasn't.

I watched him through the front lobby windows until he turned left and disappeared.

CHAPTER 11

The smell of cooking had my mouth watering as I entered my apartment. The door was already open wide, which was why I'd smelled the cooking before I saw it.

The sound of voices wafted over to me, both male and female. I reached the end of the hallway and walked into the kitchen.

Elsa stood at the stove, the sleeves of her orange blouse folded at the elbow as she mixed a tall stainless-steel pot on the burner.

Julian lounged on the couch. He had one arm around a young woman with long, blonde hair, who I didn't recognize, and a beer in the other.

Jade was busy setting the table with wineglasses. She wore a black, vintage Def Leppard T-shirt with baggy jeans and had her hair in a punk-esque updo with a black bow. She saw me and raised a glass in salute. "Hey, Leana. Hope you're hungry. Elsa's making her famous chili con carne."

"Oh, hi, Leana," said Elsa as she smiled at me over the steam of her chili. "Hope you like spices. Oh. You eat meat. Right?"

I laughed. "I do." I was trying to cut back, but I didn't want to take away her thunder.

"Leana, this is Carmen," said Julian, raising his beer. I gave the pretty blonde a smile, but she seemed to be only interested in Julian.

I looked around. "You guys bought food? And wine?" I couldn't believe these witches' generosity, and I barely knew them.

"Of course we did," said Jade, flashing her big smile at me. "You're family now."

A surge of warmth wrapped around my heart and tightened my throat. My eyes burned, and I quickly looked away.

The sound of wheels whirring on the carpeted floor brought my attention behind me as Jimmy rolled into the apartment.

"How did the shopping go?" asked the toy dog, his spring metal tail wagging behind him. He might not be a real dog, but he was cute as hell.

I raised my bags. "Good. Let me drop this off." After putting the bags containing my new clothes, sheets, and towels in my bedroom, I returned to the kitchen and set the bags with the food and wine on the counter.

Elsa looked at me. Splatters of chili spotted her face and her blouse. "Dinner will be ready in about fifteen minutes. Need to let the chili cool for a bit. If it's served too hot, it'll just spoil the flavor."

I smiled at the older witch. "Thank you for doing this. You guys are amazing."

"Have some wine," said Jade as she handed me a glass of red.

"Thanks. I really needed that." I took a sip of the wine, moaned a little at the fruity taste, and started to stock my fridge with the fruits and vegetables I'd bought earlier.

Jade came to stand next to Elsa, hands on her hips. She leaned over and said, "You're putting in too much cayenne pepper."

"Don't be ridiculous. I've made my chili thousands of times. I know what I'm doing."

I joined the witches at the stove. "Can I help?" It was a strange feeling having people cooking dinner for me, let alone having my apartment filled with people.

The last time I had people over at my place, it was with my husband. He'd invited his parents for dinner about five years ago. Let's just say the evening didn't go so well. I ended up excusing myself, lying that I had to work, just to escape their condescending stares and hateful remarks that I hadn't given them any grandchildren yet.

Not for the lack of trying. But after countless tests, I was told I was barren. The initial shock of being told that I couldn't do the one thing I was supposed to be able to do as a woman sent me into a deep depression. It didn't help the marriage, either, and Martin pulled away after that. I was damaged goods in his eyes.

Needless to say, that was why I'd immersed myself with work. Those wounds healed as I accepted the cards I'd been dealt. It took years, but I was finally happy again.

Elsa pointed a finger at me. "You just relax. We'll take care of everything."

"Go sit," said Jade, pushing me out of the kitchen. "We've got this."

"Okay, okay," I laughed. They didn't have to tell me twice.

My eyes found my divorce papers tucked neatly on the counter next to the fridge, and I made a face. I did not want to ruin the night by filling those out. I'd handle them tomorrow.

I grabbed my wineglass and moved to the living room. Julian was whispering something in Carmen's ear, making her giggle. Giving Julian and his lady friend some privacy, I slumped into the chair next to the window. The sounds of the busy street slipped in from the open window, carrying a bit of cool air.

"So, how are you finding the hotel so far?" Jimmy rolled to a stop at my feet.

I set the wineglass on my lap and looked down. "I like it. It's not what I imagined. It's better. Well, apart from the three deaths."

The toy dog swiveled his ears forward. "Glad to hear it. It does grow on you after a while." His eyes flicked around the room.

I wanted to ask him how long he'd been at the hotel, but then I remembered that he'd been cursed all those years ago. I didn't want to make him any sadder than he was.

I leaned back in my chair. "What can you tell me about Valen?" I figured this line of conversation was better. Better for me, of course.

The dog's jaw flapped down. "Lots. What do you want to know?"

"Everything," I told him. "Start with his history. Who is he? Where did he come from?"

"Well, I'll tell you what I know," began the toy dog. "I know he moved here from Chicago after his wife died from ovarian cancer."

"Oh no." My heart tugged at his words, and I found myself nodding and speaking around a rather tight throat. I knew all too well what losing a loved one to that horrible disease was like. Even paranormals weren't immune to some of the human diseases, cancer being the major one.

"Bought the restaurant next door," continued Jimmy. "Fixed it up and made it more modern, or so my spies tell me."

I gave a little laugh. "You've got spies?"

"Everywhere," said the little toy dog. "I have eyes and ears outside this hotel." After a moment, he added, "I think he needed a change. A new place that didn't remind him of the past."

"Must have been horrible for him." I was sure it also contributed to his short temper and irritability. Losing a loved one changed a person.

"I'm sure. He dates, nothing long-term, and I don't remember ever seeing him with the same woman more than once. He told me he'd had enough of high-maintenance women and all the drama. Wants no commitments."

I laughed. "You asked him?"

"Yeah. I mean, we already have a man-whore in the hotel. We don't need two."

"Heard that," called Julian from the couch, though when he

caught me looking at him, he winked, seemingly delighted at the nickname.

I turned my attention back to Jimmy. "What can you tell me about his business? Not the restaurant, the other part. He told me that he's responsible for the paranormals in this district. What is that about?"

"Well," said the toy dog, his left ear swiveled back. "I'm not really sure. The guy is very secretive. But I think he meant it more like as a paranormal. It's his duty. He feels a responsibility to keep others like him safe."

"Doesn't explain why he showed up at Eddie's old room," I said. "And how he knew there was a hidden laptop."

Jimmy rolled back. "That I don't know."

"Does he have people working for him? Like the maids?" I asked, remembering the two pretty maids from this morning.

"Possibly," answered Jimmy. "Or the maids might just be some of his lady friends."

"Right." Damn. Just how many women did this guy sleep with? "So, he's like an alpha?"

"Yeah, I guess," said the dog.

I leaned forward. "What kind of shifter is he? No one seems to be able to give me a straight answer." I had thought werebear at first, but now after meeting Bob, I wasn't so sure. He didn't give off the same kind of energy that Bob did. Whatever Valen was, he was different.

"Beats me," answered the dog. "I went through all the list of shifters and weres with him once, but he never told me. Believe me, I kept asking him that the whole first year he'd moved here. Never let it slip once."

I pursed my lips in thought. "Sounds like he doesn't want anyone to know." And in my experience, if you hid something, it was because it was bad, and you didn't want others to know about it. So, the question was, what was Valen hiding? Because he certainly felt the need to hide his animal self from us.

The dog cocked his head to the side. "You're a witch. Don't you have a spell that could reveal that?"

I shook my head. "Not that kind of witch."

Jimmy's jaw fell open to ask the obvious question, but Elsa interrupted him.

"Dinner is served!" she called and clapped her hands. "Let's eat before it gets cold."

I leaped to my feet, wine in hand, and looked down at Jimmy. "You don't eat, right?"

"No," said the toy dog, not sounding a bit saddened by the fact. "But I do like to watch."

I frowned. That sounded kinda dirty.

I moved to the dining table, Jimmy in tow, and sat next to Julian and his lady friend.

The table setting wasn't fancy. In fact, there wasn't one, not really. The centerpiece was a giant pot of chili surrounded by six bottles of wine. A collection of different place mats was set in the designated spots. It was a mismatch of tall and short glasses, some plastic with faded patterns. The utensils were dull and old. The plates, well, they looked like they were from the 1970s. Not a single plate matched another. The only thing they had in common were the scratches.

And I loved it.

It was like us, a mismatch of witches, none of us the same, but we fit remarkably well together.

"Oh. We're missing a chair?" said Jade, scratching her head. "I'll go get one from my place." She disappeared while Elsa filled each bowl with a generous scoop of chili and reappeared moments later with a chair she squeezed next to Elsa's at the end.

I helped myself to some salad, a mix of yellow and red tomatoes, cucumber, and diced feta cheese, dripping with olive oil and balsamic vinaigrette.

Next, I tore into the chili. It took every bit of effort not to moan as my taste buds exploded with all the wonderful flavors. Elsa could cook up a mean chili con carne.

"Mmmm," I said to Elsa around chews. "Excellent chili. What's in the sauce?"

Elsa's smile widened to her ears as she poured herself a substantial amount of wine. "Ah. It's my secret." I couldn't help but notice that she'd wrapped her hand around her locket as she'd said it.

Jade stood up suddenly and raised her glass of red wine. "I'd like to make a toast."

Following her example, we all took our glasses and raised them.

Jade's eyes fell on me. "To Leana. Welcome to the family."

"To Leana!" chorused the voices around the table.

"To me," I said, the tips of my ears burning as I finished the toast with a large gulp of my wine through a colossal smile.

For the first time in a long while, I felt welcomed and a part of something, like a real family. I could get used to that nice, comfortable, familiar feeling.

"Help!"

And then maybe not.

I spun around in my seat to the sound of a terrified voice and recognized the elderly, tall, thin woman wearing a long nightgown.

"Barb?" Elsa shot to her feet, and so did I. So did everyone. "What's the matter?"

Barb's eyes widened in terror as she clutched the front of her nightgown. "Demon!" said the older woman. "There's a demon in the hotel!"

Guess my wine was going to have to wait.

CHAPTER 12

Everyone in the room looked at me with expectant expressions mirrored on their faces.

Right. I was the Merlin.

I stepped around my chair and came to face the older woman. "Are you sure it's a demon?" The odds that a demon was in the hotel were slim to none. I'd felt the wards the first time I'd stepped through into the lobby. They seemed carefully crafted by probably some of the most powerful witches or wizards to keep malevolent demons from entering. The hotel was a sanctuary, a safe haven where paranormals went if they had a demon on their tail.

The Veil also protected our world, like an invisible supernatural layer. But sometimes the Veil had cracks called Rifts, where demons got through.

Unless someone had *let* them in.

Barb's fear turned into anger, her wrinkled face making her look harsh. "I know a demon when I see one. I've been a witch longer than you've been alive, girlie girl."

I stared at the older witch, seeing her eyes clear, and she seemed alert. "Okay. How many demons?" I was still not 100 percent sure she'd seen a real demon, but it was clear she *believed* she had.

Barb let out a sigh. "One. Just one, I think."

I was nodding as I started for the door. "Where's the demon?"

"The ninth floor," said the older witch as I rushed out of my apartment.

I stopped at the elevator, changed my mind, instead, pushed the emergency exit doors, and hit the staircase. By the time the elevator reached the top floor, I'd already be on the ninth.

I took the stairs two at a time. The adrenaline coursing through my body helped my thighs push me forward. I wasn't twenty anymore, I wasn't as fast as I used to be. I had to rely on my profound hatred for demons to fuel my legs. I was fit, but I wasn't an athlete.

My breath came fast as I pulled open the door to the ninth floor and stepped into the hallway. I stopped to listen as I blinked into the darkness, looking for signs of the ceiling lights but saw none. The faint whisper of water running through pipes answered back. Then nothing. The dim scent of sulfur lay in the air followed by the pulsing of something cold and vile and not of this world. A demon. The old witch had been right.

I looked to the window at the end of the hallway. It was small, and I could just make out the dark, clouded sky through two tall buildings.

With my heart pounding in my ears, I stepped forward. The sound of glass crunching under my boots stopped me dead in my tracks

"Okay. Who turned off the lights?" I muttered into the darkness. I yanked out my cell phone and switched on the flashlight.

I looked to the side wall, and as my eyes adjusted to the darkness, I could make out the two adjacent light fixtures, their glass bulbs shattered.

Not knowing which hotel door the demon had slipped through, I walked to the first door on the floor and checked the knob. Locked.

The sounds of feet running and the click of a metal door opening and closing spun me around with my heart in my throat.

The emergency exit door slammed shut as Jade, Elsa, and Julian clambered into the hallway behind me.

"What are you guys doing here?" I hissed. Not that I didn't appreciate the help, but I was the Merlin here, and I didn't want my new friends to get hurt.

Elsa slipped forward. "You're going to need our help," she said, tapping her locket as though it might contain some great power.

"We might not be Merlins like you," said Jade, "but we can help."

"We can," Julian reiterated. When my flashlight rolled over him, he was wearing a long leather duster that I'd never seen on him before.

I opened my mouth to tell them to go, but looking at their defiant faces, I doubted it would make a difference.

"Just don't get killed," I said as I turned back, staring at the dark hallway. The cold pulsing in the air intensified, matching the throbbing of my heart in my chest.

"Where is it?" asked Julian. "Where's the demon?"

Screams erupted from down the hallway. "Follow the screaming," I whispered and started running.

I rounded the end of the hallway and took a right. Soft-yellow light shone from the only door that stood ajar, the faded sticker indicating 906. I rushed to the door and pushed it farther open as quietly as I could to step inside. The air was filled with the stench of blood—not exactly the best sign. The room was lit with nothing more than a table lamp that wasn't knocked down.

A body lay on the ground not ten feet from me.

Damn. I rushed to the bundle. She was lying on her side. Female—from her sheer size and the width of her shoulders under the thin, black jacket she was wearing—at least what was left of her.

My lips parted as I ran my eyes over the body. Because, yes, it was a body. No one could be alive and look like that.

The skin over her face, hands, and neck was torn, like something with long claws had attacked her, and she lay in a puddle of her blood. A large gash was torn through her abdomen. A hole meant something inside her had been taken out. Yeah. Pretty gross.

"Oh my," said Elsa, terror flashing across her face.

Jade knelt next to the body, careful not to get any blood on her. "What could do such a thing?"

"Demon," said Julian, taking the word out of my mouth.

"He's right," I said, pulling my eyes away from the dead woman and looking around the room. "So, who let it in? Did someone summon it? And where is it now?" No way could a demon slip through the wards of the hotel. No, I was willing to bet someone had let this sucker in, and I had to find it before it killed anyone else.

As if on cue, another scream erupted from somewhere on the ninth floor, raising my neck hair.

I jumped to my feet, not waiting for anyone as I hurled out of the room and dashed toward the still-screaming male voice.

A door to my left stood open, and I rushed in.

The first thing I saw was a man pressed against the wall, a hand clutched to his bleeding chest. The second was a creature that looked like an overgrown lizard.

The monstrous, mismatched nightmare of scales, fur, claws, and fangs had a collection of black eyes in the front of its flat skull. Its tail ended in a thick talon that whipped menacingly from side to side.

"That's a gutuk demon," said Elsa, joining me at the entrance. "Nasty bastards. Killing machines."

I raised my brow, impressed at her insight. "You know your demons."

"Among other things," said the witch.

The demon wailed and drove itself into the air with its powerful lizard legs, hurtling toward us with frightening speed.

I drew up my will, channeling the emanations and harnessing that celestial energy beyond the clouds. I felt a tingling as it answered.

A spool of blinding-white light curled up in my palms and wove through my fingers in a slow crawl.

And then I let it rip.

Blazing white light soared forth from my outstretched fingers, and I directed it at the demon. It hit the beast in the face, covering the gutuk's body in a sheet of white light.

A shriek of pain came from the gutuk, and then it fell to the ground in a heap of charcoaled, blackened flesh and ash.

"Holy shit," breathed Julian, his eyes wide as he stared at me. "What the hell was that?"

I looked over at Jade and Elsa, who were both staring at me with equal amounts of fascination. Well, I'd done my magic in front of them, so no point in avoiding this anymore.

I opened my mouth to answer. "My magic is different."

"No shit," said Julian.

I took a breath and said, "It's—"

A scream split the air.

Crap. "There's more than one," I said. My eyes found the still-bleeding man. "Can someone stay with him?"

"I'll look after him," said Elsa, waving us away. "You go. Hurry."

I doubled back and was out the door in a flash. Well, not really. More like half a stumble and a decent jog.

The odds of another demon inside the hotel proved my theory that someone had let them in. No way did two demons slip inside a highly warded establishment.

I made it back into the hallway.

Make that three demons.

Two vile creatures turned at the sound of my approach, just as

I caught a glimpse of a mess of black hair as a door slammed shut at the end of the hall.

I could see them, even in the dim light, and I wished I couldn't. These were different than the demon I'd just evaporated. They were naked and horribly misshapen humanoid monsters—hideous, foul, and heavily muscled.

Damn. I wasn't paid enough for this shit. I should have asked Basil for double what he gave me.

"What are they?" asked Jade.

I shrugged. "Ugly bastards." I had no idea. "Naked, ugly bastards," I corrected.

"How many more of these things are there?" Julian was next to me, his hands inside his coat pockets.

"Two," said Jade. "Can't you count?"

I shook my head at these two witches. This wasn't the time to start bickering.

One of the demons, the closest one, charged.

I rolled my shoulders, getting ready, and stepped forward to meet it.

It leaped, swinging one of its long, misshapen arms, ending in talons, at me. I tapped into my will and channeled the celestial energy. I felt a slight tug, and then with a throb, my cosmic power went out.

Uh-oh.

Instinctively, I ducked and rolled as I felt talons pull the top of my hair. I slammed into the wall, my breath escaping me.

"What the hell, Leana?" cried Julian, moving forward and catching the demon's attention.

I pulled myself up. "It happens sometimes. It's not a clear sky tonight."

"What?" yelled Julian, his focus still on the advancing demons.

The same demon that came at me rushed toward Julian. It leaped at him in a blur of grotesque limbs, bringing forth a stink of feces.

Julian pulled his hands from inside his coat, and two twin

glass vials shot from his outstretched palms. The demon took them in the chest.

After a clap like thunder, an explosion threw the demon back and up into the air. It was held there for a moment, wreathed in a ring of blue energy. It thrashed and howled, its misshapen limbs flailing and kicking.

And then the demon exploded in a mess of black blood and guts.

Dripping bits of demon rained down around us, landing with little, wet plopping sounds on the carpet, walls, and doors.

Julian caught me looking and grinned. "I'm a potion master. Poisons are my specialty."

Huh. I'd never have guessed. More like love potions were his thing.

A door to my right cracked open to reveal a startled-looking face belonging to a middle-aged man.

"Close your door and lock it," I warned him as I pushed to my feet.

The door slammed in my face as another opened down the hall from us.

"I'll go," said Jade as she ran to the young woman who was staring at the mess in the hallway, with a confused expression.

A scream sounded near us. The voice was young, possibly a teenager. The cry turned high-pitched and then became a strangled sound.

I made a wild dash toward the scream, rounded the end of the hallway, and halted.

The body of a young witch, maybe twenty, lay on the floor in the hallway, her feet hidden inside what I believed was her room. She'd tried and failed to escape.

She rested in a large puddle of her blood, forming a sticky pool around her. Her face was covered in a mask of blood and ribbons of torn flesh. Bile rose in the back of my throat.

Another gutuk hovered over her, eating strings of what looked like her intestines. It had ripped open her throat, too, and gotten her jugular. Her beautiful light eyes stared upward at nothing, glazed and dead.

My vision turned red.

The gutuk turned and looked up at me, strips of the young woman's flesh still hanging from its mouth.

Fury bloomed in my chest. Emotions were always the key to reaching more power. I drew on the celestial magic again, focused all of my will on it, and homed in on one single goal—obliterating the demon.

Putting all my rage into it, I let it go.

Two balls of pure white light hit the demon.

The blow knocked it off the woman to collide with the floor, rolling like a flaming sausage from hell. The white light filled the hallway, illuminating it like sunlight. Heat from the white energy rose, and I took a step back, watching as the demon's body snapped in half and then disintegrated into a pile of ash.

Breathing hard, I sagged with a bit of tiredness. Channeling so much power was like running a marathon, and a sudden weakness in my limbs made me sway.

The ding from the elevator sounded down the hall followed by the aggressive thumps of feet.

Errol came round the corner, his face a mask of horror and disapproval as his eyes met mine. "Who's going to pay for all of that?"

"Bill me," I said.

Julian walked forward. His eyes were on my hands, which had blazed with white light only moments ago.

"What the hell was that?" asked Julian. "What kind of witch are you?"

"That was starlight," said Elsa, coming around to join us with Jade. "Leana is a Starlight witch."

CHAPTER 13

"What the hell is a Starlight witch?" asked Julian for the third time, sitting on the couch facing me. When we'd returned to the apartment, his date was nowhere to be found, but he seemed more interested in my magic than missing out on sex.

Only Jimmy remained, wagging his tail like a real dog, thrilled to see us back. I wanted to squeeze him. He was so cute. But then I'd remembered that inside that wooden puppy was a grown man, which might have made things a bit awkward.

We'd waited for the cleanup crew to come and take the two bodies away, which was about five minutes after Errol had arrived at the scene, complaining about the mess. Guests were spying on the whole thing from the safety of their rooms. It'd be impossible to keep this attack quiet. Now Basil would have a full-on panic on his hands.

"I'm going to get sacked," Basil had said, appearing on the scene moments after Errol, his hands on his head and looking as though he was about to keel over.

"You're not going to get sacked." I patted him on the shoulder as I watched the same female witch from the cleanup crew, I'd seen yesterday, sprinkle the same white powder over the dead witch. The body had shimmered before vanishing. Not that it mattered. Nearly the entire floor was out watching these developments. "This is not your fault."

"Of course it's my fault," said the tiny witch, his voice rising in hysterics. "I'm the manager. I'm supposed to make sure guests are safe. *This* is *not* safe! This is death. Demons loose in the hotel? It's never happened in over a hundred years since the hotel's been open for business. This is a catastrophe."

I felt for the small witch. Clearly his job was essential to him, just as mine was to me. "I'm going to find who's responsible. It's why I'm here." Two people had died on my watch, and I wouldn't let it happen again.

Basil turned his face and looked up at me. His expression twisted in what looked like a mix between nausea and fear. "You'd better hurry. If you don't stop these killings soon, we'll have to send everyone away and close the hotel."

Okay. No pressure. "Everyone? Even those of us in the apartments?"

Basil nodded. "Everyone. The hotel cannot afford to lose any more people."

His statement only cemented the urge to find out where the demons were crossing over as well as those who'd either summoned them or let them in.

Now back in my apartment, with the air still smelling of chili, I'd taken a quick shower to wash away some of the demon bits that were still stuck to me and then joined my friends in the living room.

I pulled my focus away from Julian and stared at my glass of wine, the one I hadn't finished. "Well, it's—"

"Isn't it obvious?" stated Jade, sitting crossed-legged on the floor right in the middle of the living room. Her crimped hair stood on odd ends like she'd stuck her finger in an electrical socket. "Her magic lies in the stars."

Julian whistled. "That's impressive. How come I've never heard of a Starlight witch before?"

"Because they're very rare," said Jade. She leaned forward,

excitement rippling through her. "We know living beings generate magical energy; life force itself is a form of magical energy along with the human heart and emotions," continued Jade. Jimmy sat next to her on the floor. She reached out and petted his head.

"Her inner nerd witch is coming out," said Elsa with a smile. "Brace yourselves."

"Souls are also a source of magical energy," Jade continued. "There's the power of the elements. Elemental magic, like what we use, and ley line magic. Then you have magic with the help of demons by borrowing their magic."

"And magic in potions, like Julian here," said Elsa, tipping her glass of wine at him as he sat next to her on the couch.

Jade rocked forward. "There's power in words, magic words, just like there's power in sigils and seals—if you're a strong enough witch, that is. All witches are born with some level of magical powers inside them, some innate energy given to us by our demon ancestors. Still, not all witches are created equally in strength and magical abilities. Some are born with almost zero powers and are practically human." Jade wiggled her bent legs. "But starlight magic, well, it's power from the stars and constellations, *celestial* power," she added, her eyes wide.

I shrugged it off, feeling a little self-conscious that I had everyone's attention. "You make it sound wonderful. Too bad it's not a reliable source of magic like elemental magic or potions."

"What do you mean?" asked Julian. "I saw you blast that demon. We all did."

"And you also saw me not being able to do squat." I leaned back in my chair and crossed my legs at my ankles. "My magic is limited to a specific group of stars, the ones closest to us, a triple-star system called Alpha Centauri. And it's limited during the day. See, even if the sun is technically a star, it's a bully star. It blocks me from drawing my power from the other stars during the day."

"The sun cockblocks you," said Julian, his lips pursed in a smile.

"Exactly. Which is why starlight magic is best drawn at night," I continued. "Especially when the sky is clear. If it's cloudy like tonight, it's harder to draw and not very reliable."

"So what you're saying is," said Julian, leaning forward. He tipped a short glass with a clear liquid that was either vodka or rum to his mouth and took a sip. "If it's a clear night sky, you're basically unstoppable."

I laughed. "It's when my magic is strongest. Yeah. But like I said, sometimes it can be unreliable."

The sound of metal thumped on the ground as Jimmy wagged his tail. "Wow. I feel like I'm meeting a celebrity."

I burst out laughing. "Good one. Most celebrities aren't broke and homeless." Not that I was at the moment, but I had been.

The toy dog cocked his head. "You'd be surprised."

"Are you the only Starlight witch you know? What about your family?" asked Jade.

"I don't have any family," I told them, my chest squeezing. I was never comfortable with this conversation. "My mother passed away a long time ago, and I never met my father. My mother never talked about him, and she died before I had a chance to ask her. She was a White witch, like you. No siblings. No aunts and uncles. So to answer your question, I've never met another Starlight witch. I just know there are some. We're just rare, I guess."

After that, the silence was so heavy around the apartment that I could almost feel it against my skin like a mist as all of us became lost in our thoughts.

My conversation with Basil came back to me. "Does the hotel have any enemies? Like competing hotels?"

Elsa shrugged. "Not that we know of. The only other paranormal hotel near here is in Boston. The other is in Chicago. Why? What are you thinking?"

I shook my head. "Just something Basil was saying. Sabotage from other hotels, maybe? He told me that if I don't stop these killings, he will have to close the hotel and send everyone away."

"What!" Wine flew from Jade's mouth. "But… where are we supposed to go? This is our home. I've lived here for twenty-three years."

"There goes my casual sex with the ladies on the lower levels," muttered Julian.

Jimmy's head swiveled my way. "What exactly did Basil say?" I noticed the tinge of fear in his voice. If we all had to be forced out, what would happen to Jimmy?

I shifted my weight, unease gnawing in my belly. "Exactly that. He was going to lose his job and that if I don't stop these killings soon, he'd have to send everyone away and close the hotel."

"But what about Jimmy?" asked Jade, echoing my thoughts. "He can't leave."

The toy dog pivoted his ears back. "I'll be fine. I'll have the entire hotel to myself." However, his voice said the opposite.

This wasn't very good.

"Some of the tenants have never lived anywhere else," said Elsa, red spots coloring her cheeks, and I envisioned her blood pressure rising. "Closing the hotel would put us on the street. Families here have children and the elderly. We're like a big family. I've had the same neighbors for as long as I can remember, and now we'd have to be separated."

Jade was running her hands over her thighs, a pained expression on her face. She looked scared. She was more terrified at the prospect of losing her home than facing a demon.

Though Julian was trying to play it cool, his eyes were fixed on his glass. He looked tense and paler than usual.

They were terrified of losing their home, friends, and family. And I'd be damned if I was going to let that happen. I happened to like it here too. I wasn't ready to give it up.

I set my wineglass on the side table. "The hotel won't close. I won't let that happen. Look, there's still time to stop what's happening here."

"Do you have an idea of who's behind this?" asked Jade, her voice hopeful as I felt all their eyes zeroed in on me.

I sighed through my nose. "Not yet. But someone is letting in demons. You saw it yourself tonight. Only a very powerful magical practitioner could do it. Someone with the knowledge of how to bypass the wards in the hotel. Someone with enough skill to bend the Veil enough to let the demons slip in. Or they could be summoning them from inside the hotel."

Elsa shivered and rubbed her hands over her arms as though she was cold. "You think a witch inside the hotel is summoning demons?"

"I do," I said. "I think the one responsible is here, inside the hotel. You can't summon a demon from the outside and hope it'll get through. It wouldn't. Just like the demons that actually do escape the Veil can't get in with the wards in place. They're too powerful." I leaned forward. "The only way in is from the inside. And somewhere inside this hotel is a gateway for the demons to cross over—a hole, a crack, whatever you want to call it. A doorway somewhere lets them through."

"Okay," said Julian. "Say that's true. Then it means we have some crazy-ass witch or wizard letting in demons while we sleep. Nice."

"Is there a connection between the previous deaths and tonight?" asked Elsa.

I shrugged. "I'm still working on that. So far, it looks as though the killings were random, no real logic behind them," I said. "Except for Eddie. He was a target because he knew too much. He found out that someone had sabotaged the security cameras." Once the words came out, I sort of let it all out. I knew I could trust Jimmy, and my gut told me I could trust everyone in this room. "Which tells me that whoever's behind this is doing it on purpose. There's a reason they've opened the gates from hell and let the devils in."

"But why?" asked Elsa. "Why would they do this to us?"

"To close the hotel," answered Julian before I had the chance. "To get rid of us."

"But why do they want that?" asked Jade, her back stiff with tension and fear. "We haven't done anything. We just live here. We don't hurt humans or other paranormals. Our lives are very boring."

"Speak for yourself," said Julian. "I happen to lead a full and very vibrant lifestyle."

Jade made a good point. And it was the only real lead so far. Now I had to find out who would profit from the shutting down of the Twilight Hotel. But first, I had other more urgent matters to attend to.

Because the real culprit was still out there, and none of us were safe until I stopped them.

I cleared my throat and stood. "I need to go."

"What? Now?" asked Elsa. "It's nearing midnight."

"Yes. I do my best work at night. It'll be easier for me to draw on my magic. And I'll need all of it if I need to look for possible cracks in the Veil. Or traces of a summons."

Julian stood. "I'll come with you."

"Me too," said Jimmy.

"No," I told them, smiling.

Elsa pressed her hands on her hips. "You can't inspect the entire hotel on your own. It's too damn big."

"With many secret doorways," interjected the toy dog.

I stared down at him. "Secret doorways?" I wasn't sure if that was true or if Jimmy was just saying that so he could come along.

The toy dog's head bounced. "There's a lot you don't know about this place. I've been here a long time. You need me."

He made a good point. So far, he'd proven to be a perfect partner.

"Okay. Jimmy's with me," I said, and the toy dog started to spin around my ankles. "But I need the rest of you to stay here and keep an eye out. Protect the tenants on this floor should anything happen."

"You think more demons are in the hotel?" Jade's eyes were round.

"It's a possibility," I told her. "Tonight might be just the beginning. There could be more. We just don't know." I pulled out my phone and checked its battery life. I still had about forty-eight percent left. "Call me if you see anything."

"We will," answered Elsa. "Be careful."

"I will," I said, dropping my phone back into my pocket. "Same goes for all of you. No one is safe until I stop whoever's behind this."

"Let's go, Leana." Jimmy zoomed out of the living room and was already at the door by the time I stepped around the coffee table.

I walked down the hallway toward the elevator. I knew two things for sure tonight. First, I knew that more people would die if I didn't find those responsible. And the second, I was on their target list now that I had proof someone had sabotaged the cameras.

I smiled. *Come and get me.*

CHAPTER 14

"Why the basement first?" Jimmy rolled next to me, his wheels crushing the small dirt and pebbles on the cold cement floor.

"I like to work from the ground up," I told him.

The basement was huge and ran the length of the building, with many hallways and doors leading to many rooms. The ceiling was low, and the cement floor smelled of urine and cigarette ashes. I smelled the musty, moldy scent of old things long abandoned as well as a few traces of cigarette smoke and perspiration. Halogen lights hummed and buzzed overhead.

We checked the first room. Shelves and filing cabinets lined the walls. A couch and some chairs sat in a corner next to a coffee table littered with magazines and boxes. More books and boxes cramped the shelves. A room without windows was depressing. I could never work here. It was cold, and I didn't want to stay here any longer than necessary.

Jimmy rolled to a stop and looked up at me. "How do you plan on checking the entire hotel? How are we going to find this crack in the Veil?"

"I'll send out my senses," I told the toy dog.

"Like what? Witchy instincts?"

I gave a short laugh. "There's that. But I'm talking more about my magic. Here. Let me show you."

I stepped out of the room and waited for Jimmy. Then, I closed my eyes and tapped into that well of magic, to the core of power from the stars and the constellations high above me.

The air buzzed with raw energy. My hair and clothes lifted as I felt the humming of power from the stars, waiting to be unleashed.

With a burst of strength, I pulled on the stars' magical elements and combined them with my own. Energy crackled against my skin, tingling like cold pricks.

My back arched as a giant slip of that power ripped through me. I was careful not to take too much. Too much would kill me.

I opened my eyes and stared at the ball of brilliant white light that hovered over my hand.

And then I blew on my palm.

The globe rose in the air, hovering just above the ceiling, and then with a pop, it burst into thousands of tiny stars of light. Then, with a final push, the miniature stars shot forward, leaving a trail of bright light in their wake like pixie dust.

"What *is* that?" asked Jimmy, the wonder in his voice nearly a palpable thing.

"My starlights. My starlight magic," I told him. "I can manipulate the starlight into smaller versions. They're like sensors. I feel what they feel."

The toy dog blinked. "You'll be able to sense if they find any more demons."

"And if there're any cold energies here in the basement. If there's a crack in the Veil, I'll sense it. And if someone's stupid enough to make a summoning circle here, I'll sense that too."

"And if we find them? Then what?" inquired Jimmy.

"Then," I exhaled, my body shaking as I kept my focus on my starlights. "I'll kick their ass and bring them in. Let the Gray Council deal with them. My part will be done by catching them. What they do to them after that isn't my problem."

The Gray Council was the governing body created after centuries of conflict between the paranormals. It consisted of one member from each paranormal race, whose mandate was to keep the peace between the races. They were also the owners of the Twilight Hotel and similar establishments.

"I can't wait to see that," said Jimmy. "Anything?"

I sent out my senses to my starlights. "Not yet. Come on. We've got a lot of ground to cover."

"I've got all the time in the world," said the toy dog, riding ahead. "So, are you more powerful with a full moon?"

I chuckled. "Yup." A full moon wasn't only when all the crazies came out but when rituals were most potent, when magic was its most vital, and when the Veil that kept the demons from entering our world was the weakest.

But it was also when my starlight was strongest. On a full moon, well, you better watch out.

I smiled and followed behind him. I was still getting used to working with someone. Having worked alone for more than ten years without a partner, I was set in my ways. But having Jimmy with me proved to be worth it. He was like a scout, a spymaster. The toy dog knew all the "secret" doorways and rooms in this hotel that might host some vile persons wanting to harm the hotel and its tenants. Plus, he was good company, and he laughed at my jokes. What was better than that?

We walked along, every now and then, I'd pull on my starlight, see if anything vile and demon-esque came back at me, but nothing so far in the basement.

"There at that spot right there," commented the toy dog. "Was where I first saw Evonne Dubois, the famous sorceress."

"Right." No idea who he was talking about.

"She was busy… you know… with one of the locals, a much younger werewolf," continued Jimmy. "In 1962, Harry Tarrio came to stay. You know. The vampire turned actor? And then in 1983, the Ogre twins came to stay at the hotel… unfortunately, they ate one of the maids. It's hard to control your inner ogre…"

As I listened to Jimmy commenting on various other famous paranormal stars who visited the hotel through the years, I found myself thinking of a man-beast with dark, intense eyes and a smile that set my panties on fire.

Totally inappropriate at the moment, but my mind had other plans. He infuriated me, yet I felt an attraction to him. I was drawn to him, and the fact that no one seemed to know what kind of paranormal he was made him more appealing. Mysterious. Here I was on the job, hunting demons, only moments out of a bad and extremely long relationship, and my head was full of Valen. Valen. Valen. I even liked saying his name in my head.

Yup. I totally needed therapy.

After three hours of searching the hotel, even the ballroom—yes, an actual ballroom—the kitchen, and Jimmy's secret rooms, I'd discovered no traces of a crack in the Veil or a demon summoning. Whoever had done this had done an excellent job at getting rid of all the evidence. Immaculate, really. I was beginning to fear that we weren't going to find anything.

"Anything?" asked Jimmy as we walked out of the elevator and found ourselves back on the ninth floor.

Again, I sent out my starlight, and again they swooped around the hallways like hundreds of white pixies out of sight. Tiny ripples of cold energy prickled my skin as my starlight answered back. It wasn't much.

"Just the traces from the attacks. Nothing else." I was tired, exhausted, sweaty, and shaking. I was beginning to feel the effects of hours of pulling on my abilities and, by doing so, draining my magic and energy. Channeling my starlight magic like this was taking its toll. Soon I'd have nothing left to pull on. I'd have to rest and let my magic rest as well.

The thought of my bed made me walk slower. I had to drag my legs forward, feeling like they were filled with lead.

"Don't forget the envelope," blurted the toy dog.

I wiped the sweat off my brow. "The what?"

"Your divorce papers. Don't forget to fill them out and give them back to me."

"Yes. I have that to look forward to. I'll do them in the morning." If Elsa could get me a divorce in two weeks, she would be a real miracle worker.

"I'll remind you again if you forget," said Jimmy.

I laughed as we rounded the corner. "Thanks. I'll probably n—"

I halted. "Wait." The cold hit as my skin erupted in goosebumps. I felt as though I'd just stepped into a man-sized refrigerator.

The toy dog rolled to a stop. "You got something?" he whispered.

I nodded. The thing with my starlights was I felt what they felt, and right now, they felt something bad. Very bad. The energy they were giving off was cold, dark, and evil.

I pressed myself against the wall and slowly peeked around the corner. My starlights were plastered against a door, making it seem like it was made of light. Something was inside that door.

I pulled on my starlights, and then I let them go. The light on the door faded, and I could see the black number stenciled on the top, 915.

"Something's in that room. Could be a demon. Could be where all this started." I hadn't felt it before. I'd been too busy fighting off the demons to take notice. But something was there.

"Well, let's go see," began Jimmy, and then he halted as I stiffened.

The door opened.

My heart leaped in my throat at who I saw stepping out.

Valen stepped out of room 915 and shut the door behind him just as the last of my starlights vanished.

If he'd seen them or felt them, he didn't show it.

My heart suddenly pounded a lot faster than before. My abdomen contracted like my intestines were playing jump rope in my gut as my eyes rolled over him slowly. He was wearing the same clothes I'd seen him in earlier. I saw the confidence, broad shoulders, muscular arms, and that hard chest I'd been lucky enough to feel with my face. I found myself incapable of looking away.

But then his head turned our way—

I pulled back my head and hid against the wall. "Quick. Stairs," I whispered, but Jimmy was already rolling ahead of me toward the emergency exit door.

I ran as quickly and quietly as I could, which, let's face it, was little more than a lousy waddle, and my steps were loud. I wasn't a small nor a light woman in any aspect. I grabbed the door and pushed it open. Once Jimmy was inside the stairwell, I pressed it closed as softly as possible.

I kept my hand on the door. "What is he doing in that room?" I stared down at Jimmy, who moved his head as though he had shoulders and had given me a shrug.

I pressed my ear to the door, listening for any indication that Valen was headed our way. I prayed to the stars he wasn't.

A heavy tread came near, and I held my breath. But then the tread stopped, and the vibration of metal wheels and cables grinding echoed as the elevator jerked to a stop. I heard the sound of the doors opening and closing and the same twisting of metal on metal as the elevator set in motion again.

I cracked the door open. The hallway was deserted. No sign of Valen.

"Come on." Holding the door for Jimmy again, the two of us rushed back along the hallway until we faced door number 915.

"I know Valen," Jimmy was saying. "He's a good guy. I know it. He wouldn't do this."

"But you don't," I told him, going for the handle. "You told me only a few things about him and his past. But the fact is, you don't even know what kind of paranormal he is." He could be a witch or a wizard. It wouldn't be that hard for someone of high caliber to disguise their magic. A good glamour would do it, which would explain why no one could figure out his paranormal race. He was hiding it.

And here I was fantasizing about his damn fine lips and his enormous hands when he could be the guy letting the demons out.

One way to find out.

"If there's nothing in here," I began, though I seriously doubted it, "you can go on thinking he's a good guy."

I turned the handle, found it unlocked, and pushed in.

The first thing that hit me was the cold like the temperature had dropped ten degrees from just outside the door. And then there was the smell, the putrid stench of rot, carrion, and death—the scent of demons. Next, the faint scent of candles found me, along with something else. Blood.

A large blood circle sat in the middle of the floor with the head of what looked like a goat lying in its center. Runes and sigils painted in blood marked some spots around the circle's exterior. Burning candles sat on the floor, each strategically placed around the circle.

Next to the circle on the wall was a large smear of black tar, tall as a man. I knew what that was. I'd seen it before.

"That's a Rift," I said. "What's left of it. A demon portal, a doorway into the Netherworld."

Jimmy froze, his ears halfway through a swivel.

"Don't worry." I walked and stood right in front of the Rift, dragging my finger in the tar-like substance. "It's closed. Nothing can come in or out." But I knew without a doubt this was the place where the demons had escaped from. And it looked like someone had opened the Rift with a ritual—the someone being Valen.

The toy dog seemed to relax a little. He rolled toward the blood circle and whistled. "Demon balls. Would you look at that?"

I turned and looked at the circle. "I hate to say it, but your friend Valen's not looking all that innocent right now." I didn't like admitting it to myself either.

The dog twisted his head up at me. "I'll admit it is strange to find him here. I just don't understand why he'd be involved in something like that."

I exhaled. "Well, for one thing, if he did do this, and it's looking a lot like he did, he's some kind of witch."

"You think so?"

"My guess would be a wizard. A Dark wizard."

"But it doesn't explain why he would do this," said the toy dog. "Why he would have these demons kill the guests? What reason would he have?"

I thought about it. "Maybe he wants the hotel for himself. He's an entrepreneur. Maybe he's got ideas for the hotel. What better way to get it at a cheap price than when it's plagued by demons."

It made sense, but it left a bitter taste in my mouth. I'd never take the guy as a psychotic killer. But I didn't know him at all.

"Jimmy." I knelt next to the toy dog. "I need you to keep this between us for now."

"You don't want me to blab about Valen?"

I shook my head. "No. Not until I get more proof. Something's still off here. Something's bothering me. And until I can put my finger on it, I'd rather not say anything. I don't want Valen to know that I'm onto him. He's got a lot of friends here. I'm sure he'll be the first to know if we tell anyone. So don't tell the others."

"I won't," answered Jimmy. "Even Basil?"

"Even Basil. I'll tell him when I have more proof."

The fact that Valen stepped out of the room wasn't solid proof that he opened a Rift, I didn't actually *see* him performing the ritual, but it proved he was involved. How else would he have known about the room?

I pulled out my phone and started taking pictures of the blood circle, the runes and sigils, and what was left of the Rift. When I was done, I swiped the screen on my phone and then tapped it.

"Who you calling?" asked the toy dog.

"Basil. He needs to know I found the source of our problem."

Jimmy was silent after that. I knew he was struggling with the idea that Valen was responsible. I felt sorry for him, but the evidence was undeniable. We'd both seen him leaving the room.

I'd discovered where the demons had come from. Seeing as the Rift was closed, no more would be showing their faces tonight. But I knew this wasn't over.

I didn't want to admit it. Hell, I really, really didn't, but the proof was staring me in the face.

Whether I liked it or not, Valen was involved. He was implicated in opening a gateway to the Netherworld and had let the demons out.

Oh dear.

CHAPTER 15

Three weeks had passed since the night Jimmy and I had gone inside room 915 and discovered the Rift, and so far, there had been no more demon attacks.

I'd patrolled the hotel every night, searching with my starlights for any signs of demon activity, and had discovered only a few teenagers bumping uglies in one of Jimmy's secret rooms, which apparently weren't that secret, and a group of old paranormal males gambling in a smoke-infested, body-odor-laden room in the basement level of the hotel.

Every night I'd worked until dawn, knowing demons couldn't be on this side of the Veil come morning unless they wanted to suffer their true deaths. Not that I minded either.

Yet my nights had been uneventful, to say the least. I'd even dined six times at After Dark, hoping to get some information out of Valen or maybe corner one of his waitresses, but he'd been conveniently absent, and everyone refused to speak to me about him. They all got kind of the same deer-in-the-headlights expression and walked away.

But he was still my number one suspect. Hell, at this point, he was my *only* suspect.

By the time I rolled out of bed—and I actually did roll—the clock on my phone said 1:34 p.m.

The aroma of coffee pulled my legs from the bedroom to the kitchen.

"Oh good, you're up." Elsa came at me with a fresh cup of delicious-smelling coffee and a manila envelope in the other. "Here," she said, handing me both. "I've got some good news for you."

"Excellent news," said Jade, coming around the kitchen table with an Iron Maiden black T-shirt and some pink highlights in her hair. "You'll see. Open it."

"Give the poor witch a break," called Julian from the living room. His long legs were stretched over the coffee table as he lounged and watched a soccer game. "She's been working all night like me."

Elsa scoffed. "No, you haven't."

Julian flashed a grin. "I've been working all night on Janet Vickers."

I took a gulp of coffee first, hoping the caffeine would unstick the crust from my eyes. Next, I set my mug on the counter and, using both hands, tore the top of the envelope. "You did it." I looked at a grinning Elsa. "This is my divorce decree. I can't believe it. I'm divorced. I'm really divorced." I did a little dance.

"Thank the heavens," said Jade, lifting her mug in a salute.

"Now you're free to screw any hot guy you want," said Julian. "Or lady."

I blinked and stared back at the paper, my hands trembling slightly. I was both happy and a little bit sad. Not because I was officially divorced, just that it took me so long to do it. I should have done it years ago when I'd first suspected Martin of cheating on me. But at the time, I'd been afraid of being alone.

Not anymore. I was a different woman now. And I wasn't afraid of being alone. I just needed me.

I stared at Elsa. "I can't thank you enough."

Elsa's cheeks turned a little pink. "Ah"—she dismissed me

with a wave of her hand—"it's nothing. Besides, I didn't do the work, my friend. Nimir did. And it was her pleasure to help."

"Well, please thank her for me." I set the paper down, feeling a sense of lightness and freedom. It was an awesome feeling.

Jade leaned on the counter next to me. "Did you find anything last night? Any more demons or Rifts?"

Of course, I had told my friends about the blood circle and the Rifts I'd found in room 915. I just left out the part about Valen. For now.

"No." I took another sip of coffee. "Just old Craig and his buddies in the basement again. And, of course, one of them was naked."

"Nice," laughed Julian.

"I wasn't prepared to see the naked man parts of an eighty-five-year-old."

Jade widened her eyes, a twinkle of a smile happening around her mouth. "Oh dear."

Julian slapped his thigh and let out a laugh. "I'm playing tomorrow night. I'm going to break these old-timers."

My eyes found Elsa, who smiled as she rubbed the locket around her neck with both hands. My heart gave a tug. She missed her hubby dearly. Part of me wanted to know what had happened to him, but this wasn't the time to ask. If she wanted me to know, she'd tell me.

The sound of wheels turning pulled my attention to the doorway.

"So, who's ready for the ball tonight?" Jimmy came rolling my way, a grin on his face, the way only a stiff, wooden dog could.

I swallowed another mouthful of coffee. "I'm sorry. Did you say ball?" I laughed. "Good one."

Jade clapped her hands together. "The Midnight Ball! It's tradition. Every year on the last Friday in September, the Twilight Hotel throws a ball."

I blinked. "You're serious?"

Elsa moved next to me and picked up a black piece of paper

from the counter I hadn't noticed. "Here. This was on your doorstep this morning. We all got one. Everyone in the hotel is invited."

I took the invitation. Gold letters were stenciled elegantly on the black paper:

Dear Leana Fairchild. You are cordially invited to the
MIDNIGHT BALL
An evening of cocktails, music, dinner, and dancing
Hosted by the Twilight Hotel
Friday, September 30th
From Midnight to 4 a.m.
Vampire Hall
The Twilight Hotel, Manhattan, New York

I'D HEARD of the Midnight Ball over the years. Every paranormal in the city had. The rumors had it as being a lavish, magical affair you'd never forget. But you needed an invitation. And now I had one. I just wasn't sure I wanted to go. I wasn't the ball-going type, if there was such a thing. Hell, I'd never been to a ball or anything similar. The only thing that came to mind was Martin's cousin's wedding I'd attended four years ago at some snobby country club in Upstate New York. I got so bored I made friends with the wine table and couldn't remember how I got home. Not my proudest moment.

"It's the most sought-out event of the year," said Elsa as I looked up from the invitation and met her eyes. "Anyone who's anyone in our paranormal community will be there. Leaders. Heads of councils. Everyone. It's a great way to make new connections. And for you, it could mean new clients."

"And single ladies," said Julian. "I always leave with at least a dozen new lady friends."

I snorted. "I bet you do."

"And... you need to celebrate your divorce," said Jade. "This is a big deal. What better way than to dance until the wee morning hours?" She wrapped her arms around an invisible dance partner, waltzed out of the kitchen, and spun around the living room.

I stared at the invitation again. "I don't think hosting a ball right now is a good idea," I began, wondering what the hell Basil was thinking. I could only wager he was thinking if he hosted the ball, the hotel wouldn't look like it was infested with demons and hopefully would stay open.

But this was dangerous. Foolish. My investigation was still ongoing. Nothing was over yet. My inquiry into Valen hadn't been conclusive, but it didn't mean he wasn't involved. I just needed more time.

Elsa pressed a hand on her hip. "Why not? I think it'll lift everyone's morale. We need this. *I* need this."

I sighed, not wanting to burst her bubble but feeling an obligation to do so. "Because demons might still be wandering the hotel. Unless you want them to come to the ball."

Elsa narrowed her eyes at me. "There haven't been any demon or monster sightings for the past three weeks. They're gone. You found the Rift. It was closed. Right?"

"Right."

"So that settles it," continued the witch. "The person responsible is gone. They were found out and left. They know you're here. I think whatever scheme they were planning didn't work, and they've gone for good."

"Me too," said Jade, still spinning around the room with her imaginary dance partner.

I shook my head. "They're not gone," I said, thinking of Valen as I met Jimmy's worried eyes. We still hadn't told them about seeing Valen, nor would we until I had more. "I might have temporarily stopped them, but they're not gone. This isn't finished. Maybe I can get Basil to cancel—"

"No!" Julian, Elsa, and Jade shouted at me.

I raised a hand in surrender, a smile on my face. "Okay. I won't. If it means that much to you."

Julian pressed a hand over his chest. "Sex with beautiful women always means that much to me."

"Good. It's settled." Elsa gave a nod. "You'll see. You'll come, and you'll have a wonderful time. You'll dance and drink. You'll meet new people and forget about all that demon business for one night. I think you need this distraction more than us."

She wasn't wrong about that. "I can't. I'm working."

Elsa pressed her hands to her hips. "Not tonight, you're not."

"You can skip one night. Can't you? Oh, please, Leana." Jade joined me next to the counter, staring at me like she'd just lost her beloved puppy, and I was the only person in the world who could find it.

I let out a puff of air. "You're torturing me here." Then something occurred to me. "Is it a masquerade ball?" For some strange reason, that idea made me nervous.

"No," answered Jimmy. "Though some do wear the masks. Henry and Harriette Moonspirit always wear masks at the ball. It's up to you, but it's not an official masquerade ball."

"Well, okay. Not sure that makes me feel any better about it."

"You're just a bit uptight because you need to get laid properly," said Julian, standing up and coming around to join us in the kitchen. He flashed me a smile. "Don't worry, Leana. I'll hook you up."

I frowned, not sure if he meant with him or some other manslut, but he wasn't off. I hadn't been with a man in a very long time. I probably had cobwebs down there.

Maybe he was right. Maybe I was just a little uptight and needed to unwind. Maybe a ball was exactly what I needed to relax. One night off the job wouldn't be disastrous, but I was still unconvinced.

Julian put a hand on my shoulder. "Trust me. I'll get you laid by the time the ball plays its last song."

Oh boy.

"Jimmy, help me here." I looked over to the toy dog, my partner for the last three weeks. Surely he could help me out. Surely he saw the danger in hosting a freaking ball right now.

Jimmy wagged his tail. "Sorry. But I'm going too. It's really a nice ball. You're going to love it. Promise."

Jade clapped her hands together. "So, you're coming?"

I opened my mouth to answer, but Elsa cut me off. "Of course she's coming."

I rubbed my eyes. "Look, even if I wanted to come, I can't. I have nothing to wear."

Elsa pursed her lips. "That's not a good enough excuse. We'll find you something."

"But it's *tonight*. I have nothing to wear to a ball. And I'm pretty sure I can't wear jeans."

"Of course not, silly," said Jade. "You need to wear a dress. It's a *ball*."

I raised both hands. "I don't have one. I don't have anything that's ball appropriate." The only dresses I had were back in my old apartment with my ex-husband, who'd probably burned them when he got the divorce papers. The thought of his angry face made me smile.

"Fine." Elsa grabbed my arms and dragged me to the bathroom. "Go take a shower, and then we're taking you shopping."

CHAPTER 16

Vampire Hall was a vast circular room festooned with draperies of the Gray, White, and Dark councils and shields with grotesque faces, figures, and armorial emblems.

Ornate vases hung on the wall, displaying huge arrangements of red and white flowers, and similar bouquets sat in bowls around the room. Windows stretched the walls, and pretty much anything that didn't move was draped in garlands. A few small tables had been set out and were covered with bright linens. Little bits of glittering confetti sparkled on the tabletops. Ornate bows adorned the backs of chairs.

Glass lanterns sat in the middle of long tables, stacked with food and drink, adding a soft radiance to the scene's effectiveness.

It felt like I had stepped into a world made of ancient fairy tales and dreams come to life. I'd checked the ballroom every night on my rounds, and it generally looked nothing like it did tonight. It truly had a fairy-tale vibe, and I loved it.

A string quartet was set up at the far wall up on a dais. The mood in the room was lively and joyful. Couples were dressed in lavish gowns or colorful suits and tuxedos, some in the modern style, while some had more of a medieval flare with layers of skirts and lace.

Just like Jimmy had said, I'd spotted a few people with masks on. Some were dancing. Some were standing in groups near the tables at the room's edges, conversing happily with others in similar masks.

"You look beautiful," came a voice down around my feet.

I looked at Jimmy and smiled. "Who put that bow tie on you?" I asked, staring at the silver bow tie wrapped around his neck. "You look nice. Perfectly handsome."

"Thank you," said the toy dog, his tail wagging enthusiastically. "Jade put it on for me. I always wear one to the Midnight Ball. Reminds me of when I used to wear a suit, back when I was… when I was younger."

My throat tightened at the pain in his voice. "Well, you look great."

Jimmy tilted his head back. "Your dress looks… it looks like starlight. Is that why you picked it?"

"Hmm?" I looked down at myself and brushed a hand over the silver gown with a tight V-neckline bodice held with spaghetti straps and embellished with crystals. A fitted skirt with streams of satin pooled around my feet. The gown was made of material so fine and so delicate that it shimmered like liquid stars. I couldn't stop staring. I could see a subtle but unmistakable pattern of stars etched into the silk. The gown, well, it *was* divine.

Jimmy was right. The way the light was hitting it made the dress sparkle. It did look like starlight. I didn't even realize it until this moment. "I guess it does. Doesn't it?"

It had not fit perfectly at first, and since there was no time for a seamstress to work miracles, Elsa had spelled it.

"Don't worry," she'd told me earlier in the dressing room. "I've got a dressmaker spell that will fix all the gaps and make it as snug as though the gown was made just for you."

So, once the dress was on, and Elsa had cast her spell, a few seconds later, it fit me like a glove. I'd left my hair down with some last-minute big curls, a bit of lip gloss, and mascara, which had made my dark eyes pop with a thin line of kohl over my top and bottom lashes.

"Ah, there's Matias," said the toy dog. "I've got a bone to pick with him."

I laughed at his pun. "You better save me a dance."

"I will. Later." And with that, Jimmy zoomed across the ballroom, avoiding dancers with skill, like he was a race-car driver swaying through obstacles.

I looked down at my dress again. I felt pretty and feminine, something I hadn't felt in years—maybe a decade. In my line of work, dresses weren't the go-to attire for fighting and vanquishing things that went bump in the night.

A shape danced in my peripheral vision. A man stood just off the entrance, his back to the wall. A tuxedo that might have been in style in the early 1800s hung on his thin frame. Raymond, the assistant manager of the hotel. He looked as excited as me to be here, and I had a feeling he was forced to show up. Kind of like me as well.

I spotted Julian looking like a hot version of 007. A voluptuous brunette in a tight, black cocktail dress sat beside him in the seating area pushed against the far wall. She sat primly with her back straight and her breasts out. They looked like they might pop. Julian seemed oblivious to the gathering of people around him. Instead, he made a show of staring openly at her enormous cleavage.

I laughed as I walked to the table with rows of empty wineglasses. A waiter stood behind it at the ready.

"A glass of red wine, please," I told the young waiter, a vampire, if his incredible good looks were any indication. He looked like he should be on the cover of some fashion magazine and not serving wine.

He gave me a coy smile as he handed me my drink, openly staring at my breasts. They weren't much, but he could stare all he wanted.

I took a small sip of wine, not too much because, technically, I was still on the job. I turned and observed all the strangers in the ballroom, looking for one in particular. I would be a liar if I said I wasn't wondering if Valen would show up, but he wasn't here. Maybe only hotel guests and tenants were allowed.

I caught a glimpse of Basil in a heated discussion with Raymond, his tiny arms raising and falling. *Oh dear. I wonder what that's about.*

I made to move just as Elsa stepped into my line of sight. She wore a navy-blue-velvet gown that moved like liquid night as she neared. Her hair was pulled back smartly into a low bun, her locket tucked neatly between the girls.

"There you are," she said as she joined me. "We were beginning to think you'd pulled a fast one on us."

"I wouldn't spend money on this dress if I wasn't going to show," I told her with a smile. "At least for a little while." That was the plan. I was going to stay about an hour, and then I was going to sneak out, change, and go about my job.

Elsa's eyes brightened. "So? What do you think? Isn't it marvelous?"

I matched her smile. "It's beautiful. Very enchanting. Far better than I had imagined."

Elsa exhaled. "I could have told you that."

"You guys!"

I looked over Elsa's shoulders to see Jade rolling our way. Yes, I said, *rolling*. She wore a pink taffeta dress with a full skirt at the knee, off the shoulder with a sweetheart neckline. Her hair was curly, like she'd given herself an instant perm. Sizeable white plastic earrings hung from her ears. She'd completed her outfit with—no, not pretty sparkling heels to match her dress—but with roller skates.

She was one odd lady, and I loved it.

Jade dragged her left foot behind as she pulled to a stop right before us. "You'll never guess who's here!" she said, slightly out of breath.

"Who?" Elsa and I asked at the same time.

"Samuel Constantine," said Jade. She made a dreamy face.

"You're kidding?" Elsa craned her neck and looked out into the dancing crowd.

"Who's Samuel Constantine?" I asked.

Jade beamed at me. With her roller skates on, she was taller than me. "Only the most famous paranormal bachelor in all of New York City. He's a werewolf, and he's rich. Look, there. He's the one in the black tux. Isn't he dreamy?"

I looked in the direction she was pointing and saw a tall, fit man in his sixties. He was handsome in a Sean Connery way. I could see why my friends thought him attractive. But apparently, so did the four other females surrounding him at the moment.

"You've got competition," I said.

Jade flashed me a smile. "Well, I so happen to be rolling over there next, and maybe I'll just lose control and plow right through them."

"Oh!" Elsa clapped her hands together. "What a great idea. Make sure to strike them so they can't get back up."

I laughed. These two were seriously deranged.

"Hello, ladies," came a female voice, and I turned to see a tall woman with a pointed face in a black gown that looked as expensive as the diamonds she wore around her neck and in her ears. Her pale skin was pulled and stretched tightly over her features, making her appear older than she probably was. Maybe she was forty. Perhaps she was sixty. Her blonde hair was styled in glorious waves. As she approached, the scent of pine needles and wet earth emanated from her. She was a White witch and a powerful one.

"Adele," said Elsa in the way of greeting.

I noticed how fast Jade lost her smile and that spark she'd had in her eye. I'd never seen this witch before. I wasn't so sure I liked her if she could put my friends in such an uncomfortable state.

Adele looked over Elsa's dress and then Jade's, her face pinched tightly in disapproval. She held herself in the way the rich and noble do, as though the rest of us are peasants and servants at their beck and call. "You're both wearing the same dresses from last year's ball. Really? Couldn't you have worn something new? Are you struggling that much these days?" The smile in her voice made me want to grab one of Jade's roller skates to hit this woman in the head.

Elsa shut down and started to rub her locket between her fingers, her cheeks flushed. Jade was staring down at the floor, slowly swinging her body from left to right, like she wanted to bolt.

Adele flashed a fake-looking smile my way, the kind that showed too many bottom teeth and never reached her eyes. "And who might you be?" She was staring at me with open curiosity. "Are you a guest at the hotel?"

Irritation pounded through me. I didn't like this witch. In fact, I think I hated her on the spot. "Leana Fairchild," I told her, my voice strong and steady. "I'm the new Merlin the hotel hired."

"I see." Adele was still smiling, though I noticed the slight narrowing of her lips. "Your name does sound familiar. Where is your family from?"

I knew she was trying to decipher whether I was from a powerful witch family, wondering if it was a good idea for her to continue talking to me or if I was a good connection for her. I doubted it.

"Not from New York," I said, wanting her to leave so my friends could have a good time.

Adele stepped closer, right into my personal space, which I didn't appreciate. However, I stayed where I was. "You're a witch. But the energies you emit are... strange. Not White. Not Dark. What kind of magic do you practice?"

"Witch magic," I said, and Jade snorted.

"Hmmm." Adele was still watching me like I was a rare jewel. "I just might have to make some inquiries about you."

"Inquiries?" I looked at Elsa and Jade, who both seemed to pale. Why? Because she had money?

"Yes," said Adele. "I sit on the White witch council."

Ah-ha.

"I am curious to know about you, Leana Fairchild," she said, saying my name like she was committing it to memory.

I shrugged. "Inquire away." I had nothing to hide. Being a Starlight witch wasn't a crime in our world. And I didn't like this witch. I didn't care that she sat on the council and could easily take my Merlin license away. I wasn't giving her anything. I hated bullies.

"Leana," said a deep, masculine voice behind me.

I didn't have to turn around to know who that voice belonged to. My heart rate increased as I spun slowly toward it.

Hot damn.

Valen wore a black suit and tie that could scarcely hold all the muscles. The material had a shine to it and molded perfectly to his body. His dark hair was slicked back in a ponytail, accentuating his high cheekbones and smoldering dark eyes. I'd thought he was handsome in a rugged kind of way before, but seeing him dressed like this boosted his looks a hundredfold. It took me a few seconds to stop staring and to get my head back on straight.

"Valen?" A sputter of relief shot through me that my voice was steady and didn't betray my stupid hammering heart. I hadn't seen him since the night he stepped out of room 915.

The sexy man-beast held out his hand. "Would you care to dance?"

Oh shit. Oh shit. Oh shit.

I had not expected this. Hell, I didn't even expect him to be here. Why *was* he here? I'd been waiting for weeks to speak to him. He was here now.

Adele was staring at Valen like he was a man-lollipop she wanted to lick all over. But Elsa and Jade were beaming at me, clearly wanting me to dance with the mysterious restaurant owner.

What does a witch do in this situation?

She accepts, of course.

"With pleasure," I said and placed my hand in his.

CHAPTER 17

I let Valen guide me to the dance floor, his hand warm and rough, and I hated that it sent delicious little thrills through me.

When he found his spot, he turned, holding on to my hand, and put his other hand on my waist, nudging me closer. The heat from his touch soaked through my dress's fabric as I draped my left hand on his shoulder.

If you'd ask me, I couldn't have even told you what music was playing right now.

Valen led with confidence on the dance floor, and I found myself falling in rhythm with him. Obviously, this wasn't the first time he'd danced or even attended this type of ball.

Women stared shamelessly at him, and I even spotted a female licking her lips sensuously at him as we twirled past. Even some of the men stared, but Valen never took notice.

I had two left feet, but Valen didn't seem to notice that either. In fact, all he did was stare at me. The heat of his gaze was intense.

My face flushed, and I ignored the silly butterflies assaulting my stomach.

"So, where have you been?" I thought having a conversation now was better than the uncomfortable silence between us. Might as well get it over with and pull the Band-Aid off.

A smile tugged on those damn pretty lips, and the hand at my waist curled around the small of my back. "You've been looking for me?" His warm breath caressed my face, smelling of mints and something spicy I couldn't place.

I swallowed. "Yes, as a matter of fact, I was. I am. I was looking for you." Damn, I sounded like a blathering idiot. "I wanted to ask you something."

Valen was still smiling at me. "What did you want to ask me?"

I couldn't outright tell him that he was my number one suspect. It was over if I told him I saw him leave room 915. I needed more proof—a real motive as to why he was doing this. Was he working for someone else? Was he doing this alone? I had my suspicions, but I needed to make sure.

"How's the restaurant business going?" I asked instead, aware that I wasn't getting any of the witch vibes from him being so close. I could sense prickles of energy rolling off him, like most paranormals, but the specific type impossible to pinpoint. He could pass for a werewolf or any kind of shifter. But I didn't know any shifters or weres who were capable of that level of magic. And he could be a powerful witch or wizard with a glamour.

"It's going," he answered, clearly not wanting to discuss it. "You look beautiful tonight."

Ah, hell, the way he said it had my traitorous heart flapping like it had sprouted wings.

"Uh... that suit suits you well," I said, totally missing the mark. My tongue seemed glued to the floor of my mouth. It sometimes happened when I got nervous.

Valen's luscious lips spread into a smile. "Thank you."

Stupid tingles erupted over my skin, and I cleared my throat. "So, are you planning on expanding?" I tried again.

His dark eyes seemed almost black as they skimmed over my

face and landed on my lips before snapping back to my eyes again. "Is that why you were looking for me? Do you want to invest in my restaurant?"

"No. Even if I wanted to, I don't have the money for it." The only cash I had was what Basil had forwarded me. "I was just wondering if you were going to expand your business. Maybe you're looking for another building? Or maybe wanting to venture into something else?"

Valen's thumb rubbed my back, and I felt a pool of desire flutter through my core. "Why? Why so interested in my business affairs?" I heard no annoyance in his voice at my questions, just interest.

I shrugged, trying not to inhale that musky cologne or after-shave he was wearing. "Just curious. You are a curious guy. Some might even say mysterious."

Valen gave a small laugh and looked away. "Not really. If you knew me, you wouldn't say that."

I took the opportunity to look at him while he wasn't staring at me. He had a tiny scar above his right eyebrow and another on his neck.

Our fronts were almost touching now. I hadn't even noticed that he'd pulled me tighter. My body was getting confused between the cold air-conditioning and the heat pumping off his spectacular body.

I realized I was enjoying the feel of him, his hands, and his closeness. I also realized he could be the psychotic killer who let in demons that killed people. I was losing my mind.

"I heard you got a divorce," said Valen after a moment.

I stiffened. "How did you know about that?" I didn't think Elsa or my friends would have told him. Maybe the hotel staff had overheard me talking about it.

"Word travels fast in the Twilight Hotel," said Valen, his lips twitching as he tried but failed to hold back a smile. "Nothing ever stays secret here."

But you're *keeping secrets*. "I did get a divorce. Some might say it was my fault for marrying a human over our people. But I can't change that now. It does nothing to dwell on the past. Gotta move forward."

"What happened between you?"

Wasn't he a curious man-beast? "Just a falling out. Drifted apart, you know, the usual. I'm just glad it's over." I did not want to talk about my ex, or his cheating ass, with Valen. I was here to talk about him, not me. Funny how he managed to turn this interrogation around.

We danced in silence for a while after that, both stealing looks at one another when we thought the other wasn't looking. The music stopped, but Valen never let go. And then another slow tune played, and we kept on dancing.

"I wanted to talk to you as well," said Valen after a moment, his jaw clenching as his hold on me tightened.

"Really? About what?" I felt a nervous tickle at the back of my neck. Had he seen Jimmy and me? Had he felt my magic?

The man-beast sighed, and I felt myself leaning forward. "I wanted to apologize."

"Apologize for what?" Jade rolled past us and gave me a thumbs-up with her free hand, a large glass of wine in the other.

He leaned forward, his gaze was penetrating as it beheld me. "The first time we met on the street…"

"When you were incredibly rude."

Valen flashed me his perfect teeth. "Yes. I was incredibly rude. You caught me on an off day. It was… I was…"

"An ogre?"

"Angry," he answered with a laugh, and I found myself wanting to hear him laugh over and over again. "Maybe I was an ogre. I had gotten bad news. I was upset. I went out to walk it off. And then you were there, and you bumped into me."

"Which isn't a crime."

"No. It's not." Valen pulled me tighter, my heart thumping so hard I was sure he could feel it through the fabric of our clothes. He stared into my eyes. "I'm sorry I was rude to you. Can you forgive me?"

I thought about it. "No," I said playfully, catching myself as I realized I was flirting. This guy was messing with my head. I didn't know if it was my hormones or how my body reacted to him, but this was dangerous.

I had to move away. I had to go. I had to stop dancing...

But nope. I didn't.

I felt eyes on me and looked past Valen to see Adele watching us, or rather, watching me. A tall, bald man stood next to her. I didn't like the way he was staring at me like he was onto me or something.

I pulled my eyes away to find Valen still observing me. "What?"

"Who are you looking at with a frown?" he teased, that thumb rubbing of his returning on my lower back. Damn that magic thumb.

"A witch called Adele," I said, trying my best not to look over at her again. "Don't like her. Don't like the bald guy next to her either."

"Declan," answered Valen without even a glance in their direction. "They both sit on the White witch council. Both pricks. Powerful, though. I'd steer clear of them if you could."

Damn. Was I starting to like him? Why was he being nice all of a sudden?

"Too late for that." I exhaled. "I think I just made two new enemies by the way they're looking at me."

"Are you worried about your Merlin license?"

I looked at him. "You seem very aware in all things witch." *Because maybe you* are *a witch?*

"I like being informed." He watched me for a beat. "Did she threaten you?"

I shook my head. "Not in so many words. But she did say she

would *inquire* about me, whatever that means. Who my family is and how high it stands on the paranormal hierarchy."

"And where does it stand?"

I pursed my lips. "At the bottom."

Valen laughed again, and I felt mesmerized by the sound. He was very different from the first day I'd crashed into him. He was kind, attentive, and incredibly sexy. No, he'd been sexy the first time I'd slammed my face into those rock-hard pecs. I stared at his chest, wondering what it would feel like to trace my hands over them.

Valen was full-on rubbing his hand on the small of my back, which was distracting. "What else did she want to know?"

"What my magic source is," I told him, flicking my eyes again and finding Adele and her pet bald guy still staring. "It must be love 'cause they can't stop staring."

Valen gave a small laugh. "Which is what? What's your magic?"

I flicked my eyes over his face. "I'll tell you all about my magic if you tell me what you are?"

At that, Valen visibly tensed and then shut down. His smile was gone, the intensity of his gaze nonexistent. He was all taut, like the man-beast on the street. When he moved back, I felt a physical loss of heat from him, and I found myself disappointed.

Okay, so I'd found a touchy subject. But his reaction was proof I was right. He was hiding his true identity. The question was, why? Why hide it if not because you were up to something untoward?

Like opening portals and letting demons into the hotel.

Valen's attention snapped to something behind me, and more tension rippled over his broad shoulders. He stopped moving, let me go, and moved away from me. Okay. Now I was curious.

I turned and followed his gaze. And then, as if on cue, a man came barreling into the ballroom, howling. Couples shouted and jumped back to give him space. I tried to hear what he was saying, but I couldn't make it out from the screaming in between words and the loud music still coming from the band.

Then the music stopped. And I caught one word.

"Demons!" shrieked the man, blood oozed from a scratch on his neck. "Demons in the hotel!"

Well, shit.

CHAPTER 18

The ballroom, which had been a glorious, enchanted event with happy chatter and food and drinks, was now a full-on panic show.

Everywhere I looked, paranormals were making a mad dash for the exit. I spotted a male with a large gut climbing his way over two smaller paranormals on their knees on the floor. If they were too slow to react, people got punched, slapped, and kicked by the rushing horde. Shouts and screams replaced the wonderful music that had been playing just a few moments ago.

It was a freak show.

"Leana!"

Jade rolled my way, Elsa running behind her with impressive skill in her high heels, her eyes round like twin moons.

"What's going on?" Jade tried to put the brakes on, miscalculated, and came flying into my chest. Good thing I'd seen her coming and reached out to stop her.

"I don't know." I steadied her and then let go before turning to Valen. He was gone, though. I cast my gaze over the room, but it was impossible to spot him with all the paranormals scrambling to get out. He'd abandoned me. Figures.

"There goes my sex tonight," said a disappointed Julian as he joined us. "And it was hinting on a threesome too. Just my luck. That demon owes me big."

I rolled my eyes and rushed over to the bleeding man as fast as the dress would allow. He'd fallen to his knees. Some paranormals who'd stayed were watching him, but no one got close, as though his bleeding were contagious.

I knelt and heard a rip. Ooops. There went my expensive dress. "What happened?"

The man's face slid from human to something not quite human. I blinked, and it was back to his normal, petrified visage. Sweat covered his pale face, and if I didn't know any better, I would say he was about to be sick. The wound from his neck didn't look too bad. He'd need stitches, but he'd live.

"Demons," was all he said. Then his mouth continued to flap, but nothing else came out.

"Yes, you said that. But where? Is anyone else hurt?" I know he said "demons" plural and not demon singular. "How many were there?" I needed to be prepared.

The man began to shake. "I… I don't know. Three? No, six."

When it came to demons, three versus six was a colossal difference. "Three or six? Which is it?"

The man shook his head but didn't answer.

Basil bobbed into view, his face redder than I'd ever seen it. It took on a dangerous purple color at the sight of the injured man. "This is the end. I'll never recover from this," he said in a weak voice. "Everyone will remember this night as the night Basil let the demons into the Midnight Ball."

I stared at the tiny witch, seeing how much he liked to overdramatize the situation and how he made it about him.

Basil took out a handkerchief and patted his sweaty forehead. "I'll never work again," he said, his voice taking on a higher-pitched tone by several octaves. "I'll be shunned from all the important events and social parties. I'll be ridiculed."

I rose slowly and glowered at him. "Get ahold of yourself," I growled. "You're the manager here. You're making the guests freak out with your little meltdown. It's bad enough without your hysterics." So, maybe this wasn't the way to talk to your boss, but someone needed to. I'd slap him if I thought it'd help.

At first, I thought he would fire me right on the spot, but then his face brightened a bit. "Yes. Yes, you are right, Leana. I... I need to set an example. I must stay calm and collected. *I* represent the hotel."

"Is there a healer on staff here?" I asked. My eyes flicked to the nasty gash on the man's neck.

Basil nodded. "Yes. The cook. Polly. She's our healer. Best one on the East Coast."

"Good. Then you should go get her." I looked at a handful of guests loitering around the ballroom and the lobby. "You should take the guests back to their rooms."

Basil glanced around the ballroom. "Of course. I need to take care of the guests. I'm the manager, and that's my responsibility. Yes. That's what I am. The manager."

"The healer first, Basil." I watched the slight witch hurry out of the ballroom, unsure he heard me. Raymond greeted him, and the two of them ushered the last of the guests out and into the lobby.

"Here. For his neck." Elsa handed me a handkerchief she'd pulled out of her bag.

I took it and placed it on the man's bleeding wound. "Keep pressure on it," I told him and waited until he did as I instructed. His face was pale. "What floor did you see the demons on?"

The man blinked a few times. "Twelfth floor." His voice was just a whisper, and that worried me.

"What room?" I waited, but he didn't answer. Well, the twelfth floor would have to do. I stood and looked at my friends. "Can you stay with him until the healer comes?"

"We will," said Elsa, a frown on her face. "But you're not going after the demons alone. Leana?"

"Yeah, you need us," said Jade, rolling slightly to the left. Her face was flushed from all the wine she'd drunk and the excitement of what was happening. Her eyes were slightly unfocused. She was tipsy. A tipsy witch going after a demon would get herself killed.

"Thanks, guys, but you've all been drinking. You're in no shape to fight demons with me."

Jade frowned at me. "I've only had two glasses."

"Four," corrected Elsa.

A soft ticking sound spun me around. "Jimmy? What the hell happened?"

My toy dog friend shuffled his way forward on three wheels. One of his back wheels was missing.

"I was trampled on," answered Jimmy. "I'm missing a wheel. I can't find it."

"We'll look for it," said Julian, motioning Jade to follow him.

"I'll see you later," I told them, and then I was off, running as fast as I could out of the ballroom while cursing the stupid dress that wouldn't allow me to move as quickly as I would have liked.

I got to the elevator and stepped on the hem of my gown multiple times, my heart pulsating violently in my throat. "This is ridiculous."

I slammed my finger on the elevator button. I didn't have time to go to my room and change. There was just one thing to do.

Resolute, I reached down, grabbed a fistful of the skirt, found a seam right at the knee—and pulled.

The sound of fabric tearing was loud in my ears as I kept pulling until I'd freed a ring of fabric around myself. With a final tug, the material ripped off. A breeze tickled my upper thighs, and I realized I'd ripped off more fabric than I'd intended. If I were to bend down, everyone around me would see my tummy-control, grandma undies. Too late to do anything about that now. I stepped over the material and caught Errol from the front counter shaking his head in disapproval, his face pinched in disgust.

"Don't like what you see? Then don't look." The elevator was stuck on the seventh floor. "Damn it." I kicked off my heels and ran toward the stairwell door across from the elevator.

I hit the first set of stairs two at a time. Look at me go! Adrenaline fed me with superstrength and stamina. But as I got to the fifth floor, my thighs burned in protest, and I could only run up the stairs one at a time. I needed to work on my cardio.

When I reached the eleventh floor, my thighs feeling like jelly, I heard the screaming. It was coming from one floor above me.

With a cramp from hell in my side, I climbed the stairs as fast as I could. I halted at the door to the twelfth floor, my heart pounding in my ears. Would Valen be here? Is that why he left so abruptly? To erase the evidence? I hated to admit it wasn't looking good for the handsome shifter, witch, whatever he was.

I didn't want to fight him, but he wasn't giving me much choice.

I tapped into my will, reaching out to the stars and pulling on their energies, their galactical emanations. The tickling of starlight power buzzed in my core. It was ready. I was ready.

I pushed open the door and stepped into the hallway.

But Valen didn't meet me.

It was much worse.

CHAPTER 19

Bodies were strewn across the hallway like discarded old rags. The scent of blood and rot was nauseating. At first glance, I saw four bodies. No way of determining if they were alive or dead. They'd been screaming moments ago, and now they weren't. I hadn't gotten here fast enough.

A grunt pulled my attention up.

And there, standing at the end of the hallway, was a trull demon.

The trull demon was about six feet tall and nearly as wide. Its flesh was red and raw like it was turned inside out. Its features twisted grotesquely with a mouth that could fit a whole chicken. It was more apelike than humanoid, its talons skimming the floor where it stood, hunched back and waiting, next to the corpse it had been feeding on.

Trull demons weren't the sharpest tools in the Netherworld shed either. They were big and dumb. But where they lacked brains, they made up for it in strength. It only took one powerful strike to break your neck.

I wrinkled my nose at the stink of sulfur and carrion. I hated trulls. They were mean and just wanted to rip you apart for fun. But it was here now. And I knew I'd find a new Rift here somewhere that wasn't there last night. I had to close it before more of these bastards walked out.

"Eat. You," said the trull, around a mouthful of fishlike teeth, its voice croaky and wet.

"I don't think so," I told it, my eyes resting on the body it had been feasting on before I'd interrupted it.

"Witch. Eat. Good," said the trull, speaking in low, crude tones, and I brought my attention back to its putrid face. "Me. Like. Witch."

"How wonderful. You like the taste of witch." Bile rose in my throat at the idea of this thing gorging on my body.

The trull's yellow eyes rested on me. "Eat. Witch," it said again.

"I heard you the first time. But it's not going to happen. I won't let it. See, I'm going to kill you."

The trull demon stretched its face back to a vicious smile. "Hungry." The demon's throat vibrated in what I could only guess was delight. Its eyes shone with fury and a savage hunger.

Yikes. I flicked my gaze over him, but I couldn't see if there was another trull or any other kind of demon. The man had said "demons," so I was betting more were here.

"Did you bring any friends with you?"

The demon cocked its head, eyeing me like it was contemplating which part of me to feast on first.

My eyes watered at the stench of rot, like I'd rubbed them with a fresh slice of onion. "Man, you stink. Do you bathe with sewer water? Or do you use poop as your bodywash?"

The trull demon grinned at me, and then it lunged.

"Oh shit."

It pounced at me, slashing with talons and fangs so swift, it would have killed most humans. Good thing I was born a witch.

Dancing back on my toes, I pulled on my magic and flung out my hands.

Bright light emanated from my palms and fired at the trull, hitting it in the chest.

The creature wailed, thrashing as the white light grew until consuming it entirely. The light crackled, drawing a scream of rage from the trull. The next second, the trull fell to the floor in a heap of burning flesh until nothing was left of it but a pile of ash.

I exhaled a breath. "There. That wasn't so hard—"

Something hard struck me in the back just as I was assaulted by the sharp pain of teeth perforating my scalp.

Teeth perforating my scalp?

"Ah!" I let out a girly shriek as I grabbed something cold and slippery—while trying not to freak out more—on the back of my head. I ripped it off and tossed it.

Then I reached up and felt warm liquid where the thing had sunk its teeth into my head.

The thing I tossed… well, it was a thing, a demon thing. Small, the size of a house cat, but where a cat was cuddly and exotic, this creature was quite the opposite.

Its black eyes were unnaturally too large for its head, and it had a long neck and batlike ears. A short nose sat above a mouth filled with teeth. Its fur, well, it had tufts of black grime-infected hair over its dark green skin. Its feet ended in sharp yellow claws. And unlike a cat, it didn't have a tail.

A gremlin demon.

I'd never actually encountered one. I'd just seen a picture of it somewhere I couldn't remember.

My scalp throbbed where the gremlin had taken a chunk. "You bit me, you little shit."

The gremlin stood on all fours and hissed at me, not unlike a cat but deeper and creepier.

Keeping my focus on the little bastard, I called to my starlight again, aimed my hand and—

I stumbled forward as something hit me in the back again. Not something. *Some things.* And then the backs of my thighs. My waist. And, of course, my head again.

I looked down at the gremlin demons latched on to my legs, opening their mouths as they sank their teeth into my flesh.

Okay. I was going to have a girly freak now. The idea of tiny little teeth and claws all over me was horrible, I'd admit. There. I wasn't all strong all the time. Sometimes I needed a good ol' freak-out.

I screamed as I felt teeth sinking into the flesh all over my body. I blinked as a green shape threw itself at me from the ceiling and landed on my shoulder.

"Get off me!" I screamed again, grabbing the gremlin on my shoulder and throwing it as far as I could. But it didn't matter. I had another six latched on to me, their teeth and claws tearing at my skin.

Panicked, I grabbed and yanked the gremlins off me as fast as I could, not waiting for their claws to slash me or sink their teeth into my flesh. I slipped on something wet, possibly blood or something even grosser. A gremlin on the ground hissed at me, ready to leap, but I sidestepped and kicked it in the face.

The fact was, I was losing. What the hell was I supposed to do now?

Blood pounded in my ears as I spun around. Then I threw my back against the wall, hearing the crunching of bones and then feeling its teeth let go as its weight lifted from me.

I shivered. "So, so gross."

I cried out in pain at what felt like twenty needles which pierced my scalp again and sliced at my ears. My eyes watered, and I reached up and swiped with my free hand, hitting something solid—a gremlin—and some pain stopped. I rubbed the top of my head with my hand, and my fingers came back slick with blood.

"I'm not getting paid enough for this shit." I was seriously going to have a talk with Basil about a raise.

A door to my left cracked open, and a male teenager with a face full of zits stared at me, openmouthed and wide-eyed.

"Shut your door!" I howled at him and cringed as I felt more teeth sink into my thighs.

I gritted my teeth as tiny clawed hands worked their way over my face. How many were on me now? Ten? Twenty? I had no idea.

But I couldn't keep doing what I was doing. The more I yanked them off me, the more seemed to launch on me.

If I didn't do something quickly, these little bastards were going to chew me to death. Or, at the very least, blind me by poking my eyes out.

I only had one thing left to do. I'd only done it once before, but they'd left me no choice.

With my heart thrashing, I took a deep breath and called to the magical energy generated by the power of the stars. I felt a tug on my aura as it answered.

But this time, I didn't release it. I kept it with me. Inside me.

My breath came in a quick heave as a jolt of power spun, overflowing my core to my aura. Magic roared. A gasp slipped from my mouth, and energy from the stars flooded me. The rush was intoxicating, and then bright light exploded into existence.

The starlight magic raced all around and through me in an invisible kinetic force.

The bright light was all I could see as it consumed me. I was a star—a brilliant star. And like a star, I burned with energy.

The gremlins weren't thrilled.

They screeched in pain as starlight power thrummed in me. I heard a sudden collective intake of tiny breaths, and then the gremlins fell, like wasps sprayed with insecticide, and landed on the floor in soft plops.

I released the starlight with a breath, blinking in the bright light until it subsided and I could see the hallway again.

I stared, breathing heavily for a moment and trying to see if any of the gremlins stirred. But I doubted it, given the crispy piles of charred meat that was left of their bodies. The starlight had taken care of that. The gremlins would never move again.

I looked down at a substantial burned mark on the carpet at my feet. Yup. I'd done that. It was one of the reasons I didn't use the starlight that way. It tended to burn whatever was near me.

"Leana? Where are your clothes?"

And my clothes were part of the said things—one of the major reasons I didn't use starlight on myself.

I glanced up to find Elsa, Julian, Jade, and Jimmy stepping off the elevator. Elsa had Jimmy in her arms and laughter in her eyes.

Fantastic. Here I was in my birthday suit for all to see.

Julian's smile made my face burn. "Nice." He stared at me in a way that people didn't do in polite company. And then he clapped. Actually clapped.

I was in hell.

Jade clamped her hands over her mouth, but it did nothing to hide the choking sounds that bubbled in laughter.

All I could think of was thank God I'd waxed my bikini area and hadn't decided to go native like I had for the last eight months. 'Cause, *that* would have been embarrassing.

I wrapped an arm over the girls and squeezed my legs together. "Can I get some clothes, please?"

CHAPTER 20

I woke a few hours later with a migraine from hell, which happened when I used the starlight on myself, and with scratches and bite marks to about 60 percent of my body. It was not a pretty sight. My face was swollen and red from the gremlins' venomous claws and teeth—little bastards.

"Stop fidgeting. Do you want me to help or not?"

I sat on a chair in the middle of the kitchen, wearing only a bra and underwear, and stared at the generous woman with red cheeks and bright green eyes, wearing a traditional white, stained chef jacket, a little too tight around the middle. She sported blonde pigtails under a toque blanche and an infectious smile, though at the moment, she was glaring at me.

"I'm trying," I snapped. "It burns." I motioned to the large jar of a pink substance that looked like Pepto-Bismol in her left hand. She was smearing the substance on me with a basting pastry brush.

Polly, the healer, pursed her lips. "It's a healing ointment. It doesn't hurt. Stop fussing. Or do you want to look like you've fallen face-first in a wasp's nest?"

Jade snorted. "You do look like that."

I exhaled. "Fine. Okay."

"I've gotta see this." Julian came around the living room with a chicken sandwich in his hand. It didn't bother me one bit that I was half-naked in front of him. He'd already seen me rare and bare.

Polly giggled as she carefully painted my face, ears, neck, and parts of my scalp with her pink healing ointment.

"Smells like poo," I told her.

"And it works like a charm," she snapped back.

She was right. It did burn for about half a second, and then I felt a nice cooling sensation afterward. But I wasn't about to tell her.

"Okay. Stand up and spread your legs," ordered Polly, swinging the basting brush in her hands.

"What?" I cried, mortified. What the hell was this?

"Just kidding," said the healer. Jade burst out laughing, and I gave her the stink eye. "But I do need you to stand. I can see many teeth marks on the backs of your thighs. You're lucky they didn't do more damage. It's a miracle you got out of that alive. Gremlin demons are like piranhas. You fall into a group of them, and you're left with only your skeleton."

After standing for another twenty minutes while Polly finished brushing her ointment on me, she stood back and said proudly, "There. My best work yet."

"Okay." Not sure what to say. "Thanks."

Polly grinned, so genuine and glorious that I found I had to smile back. "Okay." She smacked her hands together, casting her gaze around my apartment. "Who's my next patient?"

"Me."

I turned slowly to see Jimmy jerk-rolling-limping, if that was even a thing, toward us. His tail was bent behind him, and his ears swiveled down. He looked miserable.

My heart fell to my feet at the sight of him. It was bad enough that he was stuck for all eternity in the body of a toy dog. But a broken toy dog? That stung.

"Here's the broken wheel." Elsa moved and placed a wooden

wheel on the table. Then she bent down, picked Jimmy up, and set him on the table.

Polly jammed her hands in her chef's jacket and pulled out what looked like a glue gun. How it fit in her jacket was truly a mystery, and I had a feeling her coat was spelled with deep pockets or something.

"Don't worry, Jimmy," said Polly as she bumped her stomach against the table and leaned on her elbows. "I'll have you rolling again in no time."

Jimmy stayed silent, which only made me feel worse. Who knew what was going on in his head? I prayed to the goddess that Polly could fix him.

I watched as the healer squirted a rainbow-colored substance that glittered in the light, not unlike fairy dust, onto the broken wheel. Next, she carefully placed the wheel onto the axle and squeezed some more of the rainbow-colored goo while muttering a spell under her breath. After a flash of light and a soft boom, she placed Jimmy back on the floor.

"There," she said as she straightened. "Good as new."

Jimmy rolled a few feet forward, testing his new wheel—or rather, his old wheel, which was now fixed. "Thanks, Polly," he said, his voice grateful, but I could sense some sadness there too.

"My pleasure, sweetie," said Polly as she wiped her brow with her free hand.

My throat constricted as I watched Jimmy roll away and turn right out of my open apartment door to disappear down the hallway.

Polly saw something on my face. "He'll be all right."

"Will he?" That wasn't the feeling I got. "You seem very skilled with that thing. Is there anything you can do to un-curse him?" I studied Polly as she jammed her magical glue gun back into the large pockets of her chef coat. I wondered what else was in there.

Polly beamed. "Thank you. I take that as a compliment from a Starlight witch. Yes. I know all about you." She lost some of her smile with a sigh. "Unfortunately, the curse on Jimmy can't be undone. At least, not with any tools I possess. Don't think I haven't tried over the years. I have. I've contacted my healer friends and some of the most powerful witches on the East Coast. None of us were able to remove the curse."

"Who can?" I wasn't about to let it go. Something about cursing that man into a toy dog as someone's idea of a sick joke made my blood boil.

Polly blinked and said, "The one who cursed him is the sorceress Auria. And before you ask, no one has seen or heard of her in over sixty years. I believe she's dead."

I didn't believe that for a minute. And at that moment, I promised myself I would find this sorceress and make things right again for Jimmy.

"Well, if there's nothing else, I need to get back to the kitchen," said the witch-cook.

"Thanks, Polly." Elsa grabbed her into a hug.

"Yes, thank you," I told her as she waved goodbye and made her way out.

Curious, I walked into my room and went straight to the mirror that hung on the wall, expecting to see my face with streaks of thick pink cream, but there was nothing. My skin had consumed Polly's ointment, or it became invisible after a while. Still, the scratches and bite marks on my face were much less visible and were already healing. Some I noticed were completely gone, without even a trace of a scar. Wow. Basil wasn't kidding. Polly was an amazing healer.

I grabbed a clean pair of jeans, a T-shirt, and a jacket, and stuffed my feet into a pair of short, flat boots. Then I pulled my hair into a messy bun at the top of my head before walking out of my bedroom.

"Where are you going?" Elsa had her hands on her hips. "I don't think you should go anywhere right now. You need to rest. You don't want to overexert yourself after what happened last night. You *were* attacked by demons."

"I'm perfectly fine." I grabbed my shoulder bag from the wall hook rack in the hallway and looped it around my neck. "I need to speak with Basil. I want to know what he plans on doing with the hotel." Last night, after Jade and Elsa had found me some spare clothes, I'd searched the rest of the twelfth floor and discovered another Rift. The portal seemed to be closed, but that didn't mean there weren't more doorways all over the hotel.

The guests were in danger. With the body count that kept climbing, they couldn't be in the hotel while demons were roaming at large. Not until I caught the culprit. I didn't like it, but Valen was the only suspect at this point, and he needed to be stopped.

Jade stepped into the hallway, a grilled cheese sandwich in her hand. "Hey. Apparently, most of the guests fled the hotel last night. We're the only ones left—the tenants. I heard that Mr. and Mrs. Swoop from apartment thirteen oh three left as well. It'll be a Midnight Ball we won't soon forget."

The fact that most of the guests had left was good news. But to keep everyone safe, the hotel had to evacuate everyone. Even us, the tenants.

"I'll be back later."

I left my friends in my apartment and took the elevator down to the main floor. My thighs were sore from all the climbing last night, but other than that, I felt good. Polly was indeed a miracle worker.

"You're still here?" sneered Errol as I passed the front desk. "I thought they would have fired you by now. You can't even do your job. And now, more people died. We should ask for a refund."

My anger flared, but I kept my mouth shut and headed for Basil's office just off to the right of the front desk. I didn't have the time or the energy to deal with stupid people.

"Basil..." I knocked and pushed in at the same time. "I need to talk to you." I blinked and stared at the empty desk and chair. His landline phone was off the hook, the receiver dangling off the desk like someone had dropped it and forgotten to put it back. At first glance, I thought he wasn't here, but then the soft whimper pulled my attention around.

Basil sat on the floor, his back against the wall. And in his hand was a half-empty bottle of bourbon.

"I'm finished," said the small witch, his words slurred as his bloodshot eyes rolled over me, not settling on anything. His face was red and blotchy, and he looked like hell.

I moved closer. "Have you been drinking all night?"

"I'll never be a manager again," garbled the witch. "So many dead. Dead. Dead. Dead."

I exhaled, shaking my head. "Listen, you can blame yourself all you want, but you still need to pull your head out of your ass. There're still people in the hotel. And while people are here, their lives are in danger. Basil?" I wondered if the witch could comprehend what I was saying or if I was wasting my breath.

A tear slipped from his eye. "Gone. The guests are gone."

"Not all of them. And the tenants are still here. Well, most of them."

Basil gave a fake laugh and raised his bottle. "What would you have me do? They hate me. They all hate me. I'm the laughingstock of New York. The worst manager in history at the Twilight Hotel." His wandering eyes finally settled on me. "They're closing the hotel." He hiccupped and then said, "I got the call this morning. One week. The Twilight Hotel will be no more."

I rolled my eyes. "I'd love to join you in this pity party, but I've got a job to do. And that's to ensure that the remaining guests and tenants leave the hotel—alive. It's not safe for them anymore."

Basil pinched his face together like he was struggling to make a coherent thought in his inebriated mind. "What do you want?"

"You need to evacuate everyone in the hotel. The sooner the better."

The witch blinked a few times, and I waited a few seconds' delay for the information to sink into a drunk mind. "What? You want me to force everyone out?"

"I do. It's not safe. They can find another hotel, maybe even a human hotel for now."

Basil stared at me like I'd lost my mind. "The tenants. Where will they go?"

I rubbed my eyes. "No idea. How about you and Raymond work on that? You can use Errol too. He won't have much sneering to do now that most of the guests are gone. See if you can find temporary housing for now."

Hell, that included me too. I didn't think Elsa, Jade, and Julian would be pleased about looking for a new place to live on such short notice. And that left me. But I wasn't going anywhere until I stopped this madness.

"I'll be back to check on you," I told the drunk witch. "I need to do something first."

Basil's head was stuck between a shake and a nod.

I didn't have time to deal with him now. I had something more important to handle.

I was going to confront Valen with what I knew. I was done waiting.

CHAPTER 21

My blood pressure rose as I made my way to the restaurant. I clenched and unclenched my hands, trying to rid them of the tension. This wouldn't be a pleasant encounter with the restaurant owner.

I was nervous. Part of me hated what I was about to do, but I didn't have a choice.

It didn't help that I kept playing and replaying our dancing last night, how close he held me, how he smelled, his dark, mesmerizing eyes, and how he made me feel. I wasn't going to lie. I was hot for the guy. Real hot. Something about him drew me in, and I wanted to know more about him. I wanted more.

I was mainly focused on how he tensed when I asked him about his paranormal side, his race, and how that subject made him nearly physically uncomfortable. And then the part when he'd just left when the demon attacks started.

I didn't know if it was because he wanted to hide the evidence, though that couldn't be it since I found elements of the ritual and the closed Rift in one of the guest's rooms. Maybe he wanted to be gone so no one suspected him of having a hand in all of this.

With a deep breath, I yanked open the door and marched into Valen's restaurant. Even if it was just after eleven in the morning, the lighting was dim, which kept the ambiance intimate and relaxed. A few customers sat at the tables, eating an early lunch. I glanced at a waiter balancing plates topped with food as he made his way through the maze of tables and chairs.

I walked past the hostess booth and made my way toward the back of the restaurant near the kitchen, which I suspected was where I'd find his office. My heart thumped the whole time, like I'd jogged here.

I didn't think someone like Valen would come voluntarily with me so the Gray Council officers could show up and then take him to one of their holding cells while he awaited his trial. I hated this part of the job the most and knew having a partner would have come in handy. But I'd always worked alone.

Plus, if he wasn't going to come willingly, the fact that it was daytime, my starlight magic was at its most vulnerable. If he was as powerful as I thought he was, I was going to need backup.

Damn. I should have asked my new friends for help. But then I hadn't told them everything I'd discovered about Valen. I hesitated a moment, thinking about leaving right there and then to come back when I had more help with me, but I was already here. I also wasn't sure they'd be so inclined to help me with this mess. And that's precisely what it was—a mess.

The idea that he was behind the Rifts left a bitter taste in my mouth.

I saw a short hallway with two doors on either side. This must be it.

"Can I help you?"

I turned to the sound of the voice and saw the hostess standing behind me with a concerned frown on her pretty face. I recognized her from the many times I'd come to eat here with my friends. She'd told me her name, but for the life of me, I couldn't remember.

"Yes. I'm looking for Valen."

The hostess was still eyeing me suspiciously. "He's not here." She crossed her arms over her chest.

I noticed how she didn't want to volunteer where he was. I was getting a kinda overprotective vibe from her. That or she liked him, and she thought I was competition. "Do you know when he'll be back? It's important that I speak with him."

"What about? Maybe I can help you." The hostess kept staring at me. Yeah, something was definitely going on between the two.

"It's a private matter." I saw her eyes widen at my comment. "Do you have a phone number for him?" I had to try and get him to come to me somehow.

At that, the hostess seemed to brighten a little. "Sorry. But I don't give out Valen's number to strangers."

I frowned. "I'm not a stranger. You've seen me in here multiple times. And I've spoken to him." I gave her a smile. "You could even say we're friends." Yeah, that was a long shot, and by the narrowing of her eyes, I knew she didn't buy it.

"You can come back later this afternoon and see if he's here." The hostess walked away with nothing else to say.

Maybe Elsa or Jade had his number. I'd even ask Julian for it. Yeah, I'd have to spill the beans about him, but I couldn't wait any longer. Valen was tied to the demons in the Twilight Hotel, and I was going to figure out how.

I stepped out into the sunlight on the sidewalk, maneuvered around a few humans, and headed back to the hotel. The hotel's limestone exterior blazed in the sun. I could see it now. The spell that had rendered it invisible to me only happened once. And then Valen had conveniently showed up. Was he the one behind that too? Possibly.

The thought that maybe the hostess knew where Valen was and wouldn't tell sprang into my head. Yeah, she definitely knew where the man-beast was hiding. And then I realized that maybe he was in his office. On the other hand, perhaps she just wanted me to think he was gone when he was inside the restaurant.

Yeah, she got me. Got me good. But I was onto her.

"You haven't seen the last of me," I muttered.

Making the split-second decision to go back to the restaurant, I made to turn around—

Something hit me on the back of my head. Black spots marred my vision as I fell to my knees. Agony stabbed me in the head as ice picks plunged into both temples. I cringed and doubled over. Oh God. It hurt.

Fingers grabbed the back of my neck, and I was hauled up and dragged. My vision was dancing from black to blurry to dangerously close to passing out. But I couldn't do anything. My body and limbs were hanging down like a lifeless puppet.

After a moment, I was tossed, and I landed on something hard: pavement, I was pretty sure. My head throbbed, like my skull was cracked open from the back, and warm liquid oozed down the back of my neck.

"You fuckin' bitch," said a voice I knew all too well. "Thought I wouldn't find you. Well, I did. I fuckin' did."

I turned my head slowly through the pounding behind my eyes as I strained to focus on my ex-husband, who was only a shape. "Martin?" A wave of nausea hit, and I turned my head and vomited.

The shape loomed over me. "Did you know I needed surgery after that performance? Surgery to fix my dick."

I knew one day I'd pay for my folly. I just didn't realize it would be this soon. And the bastard had cheated on me multiple times over the years. I'd call that a fair exchange.

I spat and then opened my mouth to tell him exactly that, but he kicked me in the stomach. My breath escaped me as I rolled on the hard pavement. My ribs were on fire. Yeah, he'd broken some with that kick. Tears fell down my face, and I looked up at the shape I used to be married to for all those years, not recognizing the person standing over me. I knew he'd become a bastard. Guess I just didn't know how far that bastardry stretched.

"You humiliated me," hissed Martin, though I couldn't see his face clearly, I could imagine the fury. "You're dead. I told you I'd kill you."

He leaned over, but before I could react, his fist made contact with my face. Pain exploded as my head snapped back. I tasted blood and pain. This was not going well.

"I don't care if you're a witch," Martin said over the white noise pounding in my ears. "You're fuckin' dead. And the divorce? You think I'd forget what you did to me because you paid someone to get a divorce? Never. You gonna pay for that. Pay for it good."

I rolled on my side, trying to blink away the double vision, but it didn't work. "I did what you deserved." Okay, probably not the best thing to say to someone who was trying to beat me to death, but I couldn't help it.

Martin's shape pulled his hand back, and I braced myself as he backhanded me. Stars exploded on the backs of my eyelids as darkness slammed into me. The same pain hit—only more intense. Everything kind of switched off, and darkness settled in.

I didn't know how long I was out, but when I woke from the searing pain around my neck, I couldn't breathe. I blinked into what was a blurred version of Martin's face.

Panic filled me. I hit and pulled at his hand around my neck, trying to pry his fingers apart, but it was like trying to bend steel with my hands. His grip on me was iron tight.

I was going to pass out again. I knew it would be the death of me. I needed to do something, and I needed to do it fast.

The panic was too deep. It clouded my focus. Still, I closed my eyes and drew my will, calling out to the stars. And nothing happened—just the constant throbbing in my head and ribs, along with the realization that Martin was going to kill me.

Over the pounding in my ears, I heard Martin's sharp intake of breath. His hold on me lessened, and I dropped to the pavement.

"What the fuck are you?" came Martin's terrified voice, high-pitched and filled with fear. I'd never heard him speak like that before. Not even when I broke his teeny pee-pee.

Who was he talking to? I raised my head, but all I saw were

shapes—a small shape and a massive one. Or was that a tree? I had no idea.

I heard the sudden sound of fists pounding on flesh and then Martin's shape, what I thought was Martin, flew in the air, followed by the horrifying sound of bones crunching as he hit the side of something. Maybe a building… or a car.

Was Martin dead? Who had done that?

A large shape loomed over me, but I was too hurt and nauseated to be scared. If it was going to kill me like it did Martin, well, get on with it. Maybe then the pain would stop.

Something rough slipped under me, and the next thing I knew, I was floating. Then something warm and soft was under me like a duvet made of leather. The scent of perspiration and musk blended with something else filled me. Wait a second. I'd smelled that scent before.

"You're going to be okay. I'm here now. I've got you."

I moved my face toward the sound of the voice. "Valen?"

"Yes. It's me. He can't hurt you anymore. Close your eyes. I'll take care of you."

I tried to see his face, but it was blurry and, like, four times its normal size. Boy, Martin had seriously hit me hard. And Valen's voice was different too. More profound, not like before, but booming, more guttural, and louder, like my head was next to a speaker.

"Sleep," soothed Valen.

And then the darkness took me.

CHAPTER 22

When I opened my eyes again, I had another full-blown panic episode. I was lying on a bed or a couch or something. The room was dark, except for the light of a side lamp. The curtain or blinds or whatever were drawn. It didn't smell familiar, more like spices and a bit of musk. This wasn't my apartment. Where the hell was I?

The day's events came back with a start.

Me going to look for Valen. Martin trying to kill me in an alley. And Valen again. Or who I *thought* was Valen. Martin had struck me hard, so it could have been Santa for all I knew. Possibly Batman.

What I did know for a fact was that this was not my place.

Overwhelmed by the tremors of restless fear, I tried to sit up, cried out, and lay back down. "It hurts."

"Not so fast. I think you have some broken ribs."

My heart slammed in my chest.

Valen came around holding what looked like a steaming cup of tea. He was responsible for the demons, the one I was supposed to bring in to the Gray Council.

"Valen? Where am I?" I pulled myself up slowly, this time to a sitting position. I was aware that I was covered by a lovely, soft, expensive-looking throw blanket, and my head was propped up with soft pillows. It hurt too much to try and wrap it around what I was seeing and experiencing. He was the bad guy. Right?

"My place. Just above the restaurant."

I stared at the ruggedly handsome man, beast, witch, whatever, as he handed me the steaming cup. "It was you? You saved me?" I was a little humiliated that he'd found me in such a state, but I was more shocked that he'd helped me.

"Drink," he ordered, not answering my question.

I doubted he would poison me at this point, so I took the mug. "What is it?" The smell it gave off wasn't unpleasant and could have been citrus, maybe ginger.

"Healing herbs," answered Valen. "It'll help with your concussion and your ribs. You took quite a beating."

I nodded, images of Martin's brutal attack coming back to me. If Valen hadn't intervened, I'd be dead. So why did he?

I took a sip and winced. "It smells better than it tastes." I looked at Valen, and he had a smile on his face. "What happened to Martin? Is he dead?" I hated the bastard, more now after what he did, but I wasn't sure I wanted him dead.

A muscle twitched in his jaw. "Not dead. But he won't hurt you anymore." He sat in the leather chair next to me, leaning forward until his forearms rested on his thighs. "Who is he?"

"My ex-husband," I said, remembering Martin's voice and the pain he inflicted on me. The coward had clobbered me from behind. I reached up and felt some gauze where Martin had struck the first blow.

I met Valen's gaze and held it, aware that his dark eyes were doing all kinds of things to my body.

"Why? Why did you help me?" *Because we all know you're behind the demon attacks.*

Valen looked away from me. "Because a man who beats on a woman is no man. He's a coward. He's weak. He deserved what he got."

I took another gulp and found it more bearable the more I drank. "He was mad at me because I broke his penis when I found him in bed with one of his floosies."

Valen's eyes twinkled, and a grin curled up his face. "That deserves a broken penis."

I smiled, realizing I was suddenly feeling a lot better—a bit drowsy but better. "Yeah, well. He was pissed." I exhaled, tipped the cup to my lips, and drank the rest. "I should have left him a long time ago. It just wasn't healthy for either of us."

Valen took the cup from me. "Relationships are complicated." He moved to the kitchen, which was an ultramodern white kitchen with metal accents.

I took the opportunity to look around. His apartment was maybe three times the size of mine with contemporary manly leather furniture but cozy with large Persian rugs and lots of wood. It was also immaculate, and I wondered if he spent much time here.

I didn't see any pictures of a wife or any other kinds of photos. At least not in the living room.

Valen came back and sat in the same chair. "Should I call someone? A family member? You have a nasty welt at the back of the head. You should be in bed for a day or so."

"I don't have any family," I slurred, my eyes watering at the thought. "My mother died almost sixteen years now. Never knew my father. It's just me."

"I'm sorry to hear that."

"What was in that tea you gave me?" My words were coming out garbled like I was tipsy from four tall glasses of wine.

Valen met my eyes, his dark gaze intense. "A special brew that I make for myself. It'll make you tired, but it'll help. I promise."

"Promises, promises," I said with a laugh. What the hell was wrong with me? I was getting way too comfortable with this guy.

Now that he was here, I needed some questions answered before whatever I'd swallowed wouldn't let me make coherent sentences. Might as well get it over with.

"What were you doing in room nine fifteen?" There. I'd said it. Well, I think I said it, but the tea was making me doubt if I'd just said it in my head or if actual words had come out of my mouth.

The big man watched me for a moment, his eyes widened for a second, and I knew then that he hadn't realized I was there with Jimmy. Then his eyes went distant, and I couldn't tell if he was trying to come up with a story to give me or if he didn't want to answer at all.

"Are you spying on me?" asked Valen.

Oooh. He's trying to answer my question with a question. "Yes. I'm a Merlin. It's part of my job to spy on everyone." I took a breath, doing my best to focus. "So, why were you there?"

"Someone tipped me off about a possible demon portal," said the man-beast. "I came to check if it was true."

Good answer. But I didn't believe him. "Who whipped—*tipped* you off?" Oh dear. My lips were starting to feel numb.

"A guest in the hotel. Someone I know and trust."

I searched his face. "So, you just came to wee—see? What were you going to do if you faced a demon?" I really wanted him to tell me he was a witch or a wizard.

Valen's brow cocked. "I have ways to deal with demons and other devils from the Netherworld."

I bet you do. "How exactly do you do this?"

He narrowed his eyes. "You can ask your questions, but it doesn't mean I'll answer them."

"So you just came to look and then left without letting anyone know about the Rift? That doesn't sound like someone who wants to help or cares about the guests in the hotel."

Valen stared at the floor, a smile on his lips. "You think I did this? You think I let the demons in the hotel and killed all those people?"

I tried not to let the humor in his voice bother me. No, it did bother me. "You were seen leaving room nine fifteen and didn't advise management. That's the behavior of someone who's hiding something."

Valen shrugged. "I forgot."

I burst out laughing. Totally unprofessional. "Sure you did."

The big man leaned back in his chair. "I didn't do this, Leana. You have to believe me."

I shook my head. "You're making it really hard to." Maybe he was working for someone else, and he was just the muscle.

Valen surveyed my face. "So what now? You going to arrest me?"

I felt my mouth fall open, and it kept flapping as I tried to close it. "I had thought about it."

"Is that why you came to the restaurant looking for me?" asked Valen.

I narrowed my eyes. "So, you *were* there. I knew it. The hostess. Your girlfriend lied to me." I knew she was hiding something.

Humor sparkled in his eyes. "Simone is not my girlfriend. She was just doing her job."

"What's that? Banging the boss?" Oh shit. Did I just say that? A spark of jealousy crept over me at the thought of that hostess and him going at it in his office. Clearly, I was losing my mind.

Valen laughed. "I asked her not to be disturbed. I needed some time alone."

"Why did you leave last night during the ball?" Okay, I didn't have to ask this question, but it had been burning in the back of my mind since it happened. "You give the impression that you care about the guests. We could have used someone like you to help."

"I needed to check something," said Valen, leaving it like that.

I lay there for a while, not knowing what to make of this man-beast. He was hiding something—more than just one thing. Not only was he hiding his true nature but what he was doing in room 915 and why he'd disappeared last night from the ball. His answers didn't fit. Nothing fit. I wanted to keep pestering until he cracked, but I was in no shape to do so. My head didn't throb anymore, but it was numb, and the sudden urge to giggle became overwhelming as I fought the urge to sleep.

"Is Valen short for Valentine? Like Valentine's Day?" I broke into a fit of chuckles.

Laughter crinkled around his eyes. He had such pretty eyes. "No. Just Valen."

I lifted my hand to point at him, but it kept moving around, so I dropped it back down. "Are you trying to get me drunk? You want to take advantage of me?" At this point, I was all for it. It had been way too long since I'd had some nice assault with a friendly weapon. Hell, it had been years.

Although he shook his head, his smile said otherwise. "No. I would never do that. If I wanted to sleep with you, I wouldn't do it while you were... inebriated."

My eyes rounded. "You *do* want to sleep with me!" Take me, man-beast. Take me. Take me!

Valen leaned forward until his knees were brushing up against the couch. "I think the tea is working. You'll feel a lot better in a few hours. You should get some rest."

I knew I really shouldn't sleep here, not with a possible demon summoner so close to me. He knew I was onto him now. Maybe I'd suffer the same fate as Eddie. I should be scared. I should be terrified and try to plan my escape. But whatever was in that tea made it hard to feel anything other than sleepiness mixed with some horniness.

My eyelids felt like they were made of lead, and it took an enormous amount of effort just to keep them half-open.

I squinted my eyes to try and see only one Valen because right now, there were two of him. I poked a finger in his chest. "You are a bad man. Bad. Bad. Bad."

"Sometimes," came his soft voice. "You really should get some sleep."

"Sleep, sleep, sleep." I giggled and found it hard to stop once the motor started. "I know... let's get naked!" Oh dear. There went my Merlin license. Sleeping with the enemy.

Valen laughed. "You are a strange one, Leana Fairchild."

Just as I felt the weight of sleep rushing over me, I felt a brush of a hand over my cheek, gentle and caring, and then I didn't remember anything more.

CHAPTER 23

I peeled my eyes open and blinked into the darkness. Dread fuzzed the edges of my awareness, and deep breaths helped clear my vision. As my eyes adjusted to the darkness, I recognized the plain white walls, the small room I'd grown accustomed to, and the window that overlooked a neighboring high-rise building. It wasn't much of a view. But it was mine.

I was in my bed in my apartment. But how the hell did I get here? Memories came flooding in. The last thing I remember was being in Valen's place and saying some pretty inappropriate things to him. Heat rushed to my face at the recollection of my words. His tea had something in it all right. It had made me stupid, but he'd been right. The pain in my ribs was a manageable dull ache, and the searing pain from the back of my head where Martin had struck me was a subtle throb.

Still, how the hell did I get here?

I swung my legs over the bed, relieved to find I still had on the same clothes. I spotted my phone on the side table and grabbed it. The clock flashed 9:13 p.m. So I'd slept a good part of the day. It explained why I felt so rested but not how I magically appeared in my bed.

Voices drifted from outside my bedroom door. I smiled. The gang was here. Good. I had work to do, and I needed their help.

But it also told me that Basil hadn't evacuated the tenants —yet.

I stood, feeling surprisingly better than I would have imagined. Following the smell of coffee and the murmurs of voices I suspected were trying not to wake me, I stepped into the kitchen.

Elsa looked up at me, surprise in her eyes. "Oh. Did we wake you? We were trying to keep it low. But you know how Jade gets excited easily, and her voice rises." She sat across from Jade, her fingers wrapped around a coffee mug.

Jade gave her a look. "My voice doesn't rise when I'm excited."

"See?" pointed Elsa. "It just did."

Jimmy rolled his way toward me. "How you feelin'?"

I reached up and felt the bruise at the back of my head. "Better than expected."

Jade jumped up from her chair, grabbed a clean mug, and poured fresh coffee into it. "Here. Have some caffeine. It'll give you a nice boost."

I took the mug. "Thanks." I cast my gaze over my new friends. "How did I get here?" I had no recollection of entering the hotel, let alone getting to bed. I had a feeling I knew who did, but I wanted to hear it from them.

"Valen," answered Jade, beaming. "He carried you in his arms and everything." A dreamy expression crept over her face. "Such a big, strong man with big, strong arms."

My face felt like I'd stuck it in an oven. "He brought me here? In his arms?" Damn, so everyone had seen Valen carry me back into the hotel? There went my reputation. But more so was the confusion I felt about the man-beast. Why was he being so nice? Especially after I'd accused him of letting the demons out into the hotel.

"And put you to bed," said a grinning Julian, lifting his brows suggestively and leaning back in his chair.

"Urgh." I closed my eyes and slapped my forehead. That was humiliating. A dangling, passed-out witch in the arms of her savior who was also—possibly—the bad guy.

"Don't be embarrassed," said Elsa. "Every single paranormal female in this city wishes it was her."

"And some of the married ones," laughed Jade.

I sighed. Valen was a complicated man-beast. I didn't want to like him. But he was making it extremely difficult not to.

"Who else saw this?" I had to know.

Jade shrugged like it was no big deal. "Not many. Most of the guests are gone. But Errol, Basil, and most of us on the thirteenth-floor saw."

I sighed. "Great. Wonderful."

"Don't be so down on yourself," said Elsa. "He only carried you. It's not that big of a deal."

"It is when you're a Merlin and unconscious." It made me look like I couldn't do my job. If Basil didn't fire me next, that in itself would be a miracle. Maybe he'd been too drunk to even notice.

I shifted in my seat, remembering some of the things I'd said to Valen. I'd sounded like a horny middle-aged woman. He must have loved seeing me like that.

"How long did he stay?" I asked, wondering what other humiliating aspects of my life he'd been subjected to.

"Not long," said Elsa. "We offered him coffee, and he stayed until he finished his cup."

"What did you talk about? Did you talk about me? What did he say, exactly?" I sounded more interested in what he thought of me than him being my only suspect.

Jade slapped her hands together. "I knew it! I *knew* you liked him."

My lips parted. "I don't like him." Cue in more heat crawling up my face.

"Sure you do." Jade stared at my face. "Why are you turning red, then?"

"Because I have high blood pressure," I told her. "I'm still a bit tense after what happened."

Jade's grin told me she didn't believe a word. "Uh-huh."

"We talked about what had happened to you," said Jimmy, coming to my aid. "When we saw him carrying you like that… well…"

"We all freaked," said Jade.

"We knew something terrible had happened," said Elsa. "I demanded an explanation."

Julian lost his smile, and I saw something dark cross his face. "Apparently, you were attacked by your ex-husband?" Julian's frown told me that he, too, thought men who beat women weren't men at all.

"He told you about that?" I supposed he had to tell someone. It made sense as they were the closest thing I had to a real family. And I felt a warmth in my belly at the fact that they actually cared for me. All of them worried for me, and I had to blink quickly to hide the treacherous tears that threatened to say hello.

"Of course he did." Elsa fondled the locket at her neck. "When we saw him with you in his arms, well, you can imagine the hysterics that followed."

"We made him tell us," said Jimmy, his tail wagging behind him. "Said he left the ex-husband in a bit of a pulp and rightly so." He seemed in much better spirits than when I'd last seen him, and I was glad for it.

"Yeah. He told me." I walked over to the table, grabbed a chair, and let myself fall into it. "It was all a bit blurry. See, Martin, being the asshole that he is, took me by surprise and hit me in the back of the head. I couldn't function or think after that blow. He hit me several times. I blacked out. I think he'd dragged me into an alley, but I'm not sure. And then he was choking me. He meant to kill me. All because I broke his penis." I knew it wasn't the only reason. Martin was unhinged. And it had felt like once he got the taste of beating me, he couldn't stop. He liked it. And I was sure he'd have gone through with it if Valen hadn't shown up when he did.

"You *broke* his penis?" Jade eyed me like she wasn't sure who I was. "Was it a twist?" She gestured with her hands as though she were opening a jar of jam. "Or was it a *break*, break? Like a broken toe?"

I nodded. "A break, break."

Jade's smile widened. "You're my hero."

I laughed, but it was cut short by Julian's growl. He sounded like a werewolf at the moment.

"I would have done the same as Valen," said the male witch. "Worse maybe. Guys like that don't deserve to be walking around the streets."

Jade came to stand next to me. "And Valen saved you. It's like a movie when the strong, dark, silent stranger saves the girl. You have to admit. It's romantic."

I wanted to tell her that being beaten within an inch of my death hadn't been romantic at all, but she was so happy, I decided to keep my mouth shut.

"If Valen hadn't shown up when he did," I said, "Martin would have killed me, and I couldn't do anything to stop him. My magic… well… I couldn't reach it. If he hadn't hit me so hard, I might have gotten away."

"He shouldn't have hit you at all," said Jimmy. "How did he find you?"

I shook my head. "No idea." The fact that Martin had been searching the streets of Manhattan for me gave me the creeps.

"It's my fault." Elsa's face went ashen. "This is all my fault."

I leaned forward. "What are you talking about?"

The witch clasped her locket until her fingers turned white. "I wrote the address of the hotel as your forwarding address on the divorce papers. I saw that you had left it blank. I just… I didn't think."

"Oh." Damn. So the bastard had known where to find me. And had waited for the perfect moment to strike.

"He couldn't find the hotel since he's human," Elsa prattled on. "He couldn't see it. How did he know where to find you? Unless he watched that area for days, hoping to get a glimpse. He shouldn't have been able to find you."

"But he did find me."

Elsa's eyes watered. "I'm so, so sorry, Leana. He could have killed you, which would have been my fault."

I felt my irritation leave as it was replaced with compassion. How could I be angry with a witch who'd only tried to help me get a divorce from this animal? "It's not your fault. I would have told you that Martin was incapable of doing what he did. Even I would have never guessed the asshole was psychotic."

She nodded, but her eyes kept watering until a tear escaped, and she quickly wiped it away.

At least now I didn't have to worry about how Martin found out where I lived.

"He won't be back," I told Elsa and the others, though I had difficulty believing my own words. "Not after what Valen did. I kinda wish I had seen it." Valen told me that Martin was still alive. I had the horrible feeling he'd come back one day to finish the job, but I'd be ready this time.

"Well, I think Valen likes you," said Elsa, her face stained with red blotches. "I can always tell when a man likes a woman."

Jade chuckled. "Sure you can."

Elsa glared at the other witch. "I can. It's one of my gifts. Anyone with a brain could see how much he cared. He took you to his place, patched you up, gave you some medicine, and then brought you home. That, to me, sounds like a guy who likes you. He didn't need to do all that. He could have called one of us. We would have come to fetch you. But he *wanted* to do this."

I knew what she was implying, but it didn't matter. If they knew what Jimmy and I knew, they might not be so inclined to this fantasy of theirs.

Speaking of Jimmy, the toy dog was staring at me with an expression of "Tell them or I will."

I cleared my throat. "Listen, I have to tell you something about Valen."

"You screwed him already?" Julian clapped his hands together. "I knew it. That's why you're all glowing. You got laid."

More heat rushed to my face. "No. Something you're not going to like."

"What?" said Jade and Elsa together.

"The night I found the first Rift in room nine fifteen, well, Valen was there. He'd been in the room."

Jade shrugged. "And?"

"And, it means he knew about the room. Knew what was in there. It means he could be a witch or a wizard. And that he's been opening portals from the demon realm in the hotel."

Elsa waved her hand dismissively at me. "I don't believe it. Being in a room doesn't prove anything. He could have been there to investigate, just like you."

"Yeah," said Julian. "I'm not sure I'm buying that this guy is hurting people."

"But we saw him," said Jimmy. "We saw him leave the room."

"You knew about this, and you didn't tell us?" Elsa's frown was frightening.

"I told him not to tell you," I began, not wanting Jimmy to suffer any more than he'd already suffered in the last few hours. "Not until I was sure."

"And now you're sure?" asked Jade. "Because you saw him exiting a room?"

"He also took off during the ball when we heard of the attack," I said, losing some of my earlier conviction. "I'll admit. I'm having some serious doubts." I sighed. "I don't know anymore. None of this is making any sense." And now, if I didn't think Valen was behind the Rifts, I was back at square one. I basically had nothing.

Julian shook his head. "Valen's not your guy. He keeps to himself, and yeah, we don't know much about him, but why would he do this? It doesn't make any sense. The guy keeps a nice restaurant and makes sure his customers are happy. Why would he kill the very people who eat in his restaurant?"

He made a valid point, and I shrugged. "Maybe to buy the hotel at a lower price once it's closed?" Okay, that sounded lame now. My earlier theories weren't matching up.

"If it's not Valen, and I never believed it was," Jimmy said, "then who? Who's doing this?"

"Good question." Laughter spilled from the hallway, and I looked up to see the twins running past the doorway. "How many tenants are still here?"

"Only two families have left," said Jimmy, his head angled toward the doorway. "Basil came earlier and tried to evict us. Everyone else refuses to leave."

"Like us," said Jade. "I'm not leaving."

"Me neither," said Julian.

Elsa raised her brows. "The demons will have to try and remove me and see what'll happen."

I pulled my gaze back, thinking. "So, the tenants are refusing to leave, even after being told about the demons. They're not budging." I felt proud that they weren't frightened of what could happen, but I was also afraid for them. I thought about all the guests in the hotel, from the first floor to the very top floor, and how quiet it was going to be now.

And then it hit me like a baseball to the gut. I stood up.

"What?" Elsa was on her feet, rubbing her vintage locket. "Demons?"

"I'll just have to catch them in the act." A smile curled up my lips. "We'll set a trap. I'm hoping you'll help me with this."

"Of course, we'll help," said Elsa. "But how will you set a trap? We don't know where or when another Rift will appear."

My heart thumped with excitement. "But we do." I looked at my friends. "See, I didn't realize until now. It might not be Valen, but whoever is doing this wants all of us out. It makes sense. There's a pattern. The Rifts have been climbing up this whole time. First, the victim was on the second floor, then the fourth floor, and then where Eddie was killed on the sixth floor. The ninth floor, and finally the twelfth floor, the night of the ball. They're going up. Which means..."

"Ours is the last one," said Jade, stealing the words out of my mouth, though she paled. "The demons are going to attack our floor. But there are kids here. Old people," she said and pointed to Elsa.

"Watch it," Elsa growled. "You're only a few years behind me."

I gulped some coffee, almost forgetting I was still holding the mug. "I know, and you're going to keep them away until we catch these bastards."

"They won't want to leave," said Jimmy.

"Tell them it's not permanent. At least have the children and the elderly moved somewhere else. Somewhere safe."

"My friend Janet will put them up for a few days if I ask her," said Elsa. "She's in Queens."

"Good, thank you," I said. This felt good, solid. "I don't know if they'll strike again tonight, but they'll do it soon since we're all still here." That was if my theory was correct, and they wanted the hotel empty. I still hadn't figured out why exactly they wanted that, but it didn't matter. What mattered was setting up the trap correctly.

"So," said Jimmy as he rolled around and then settled near my feet. "How do we set this trap? How are we going to do this?"

"Easy," I said, smiling. "We use us as bait."

CHAPTER 24

How do you set up a trap for someone when you don't know where they will be in a hotel with too many rooms? No idea, but I was about to find out.

Forget about trying to make the tenants leave, even the families with children and the elderly. No one was moving.

"This is my home," the witch named Barb had said, her nightgown floating around her tall, lean frame. "And I'll be damned if I let something as trivial as a demon force me to leave."

"It's for your own protection," I'd told her.

She glowered at me and said, "Make me."

Okay then.

"So, how do we do this?" Jimmy looked up at me from the ground.

I scratched the back of my head. "No idea. I was hoping to have the thirteenth floor cleared. A stakeout would have been preferable. But now… well, we'll just have to wing it." My super plan of catching these bastards in the act was slowly getting jumbled.

"Sometimes the best plans are the ones on a whim," said the toy dog.

"Maybe." I watched the twins as they pick-pocketed Julian's

wallet and proceeded to run in circles around him as the male witch tried to snatch his wallet back but missed every time. "I'm not even sure they'll attack again tonight." Maybe they wouldn't now that everyone seemed to be having a party instead of taking this seriously.

"Air Supply is the best soft rock band in the world," Jade was saying to another paranormal male as she pulled out the front of her T-shirt with an image of two men on it. "I've got three in different colors."

I cast my gaze around the hallway of the thirteenth floor, seeing it like the first time I'd stepped into the hotel. Every apartment door was open, the tenants wandering in and out of the rooms like the entire floor was one giant house, and every room was an extension of their own.

It was a disaster.

"They're not scared at all," I said, watching as Elsa and Barb laughed at something they were sharing. "They should be scared. Demons are not a laughing matter. This is serious. Some of them could get killed." It was clear they didn't think demons were going to show up. Nope. They were more interested in having a party.

My thoughts wandered over to a sexy man-beast who'd saved me from a deadly beating. I was furious at Martin for doing what he did. Furious and disgusted. Never in a million years did I think the man I was married to for fifteen years would have tried to kill me in a back alley. The fact that he'd been stalking me sent a chill through my body.

And Valen had been my knight in shining armor.

The guy was a mystery. He didn't have to save me, but he did. And if he was truly the one behind the demons, he would have let Martin finish the job. Which only reinforced my feeling that the restaurant owner wasn't the one.

My skin prickled at the memory of being held by him, how easily he had carried me, and how warm and gentle his hold was on me. I'd felt safe in his arms. It had been a lovely feeling. Too bad it hadn't lasted very long.

Yet I couldn't shrug off the sensation something was broken about Valen. He had a sadness in his eyes. His wife's death? Maybe it had something to do with the fact that he was hiding his true identity. His beast or his witch powers. Maybe I'd never know.

And maybe I should stop thinking about him and focus on the task at hand.

I let out a sigh. "I'm going to check all the rooms again."

"You want me to come?" asked Jimmy.

I shook my head. "No. You can keep watch here. Holler if you see anything."

I continued on my rounds by just checking each room, making sure no one was busy preparing a ritual for a Rift. But the more I walked around and checked the rooms, the more I realized it wouldn't happen. At least, not tonight.

I stepped into room 1307. "Hi, Felix, just me again."

Felix looked up from his chair, and his wrinkled face pulled into a smile. "Do your worst, girl," he said and turned back to whatever he was watching on the television.

I wrinkled my nose at the faint smell of cabbage and poked my head into the bedroom. Nothing. Just the same bed and furniture I'd seen when I checked it out the first time about half an hour ago. I let out a sigh. "This is pointless."

"What do you think you're doing?" shouted a voice from the hallway. "You can't do this!" Elsa. And she didn't sound happy.

I rushed out of Felix's room and came face-to-face with at least a dozen strangers dressed in gray robes—both male and female but primarily male—ushering the tenants from their rooms. Ushering was not the correct word, more like throwing them out forcefully.

I rushed forward, right into the onslaught. "What the hell is going on?"

Elsa's face was red, and I knew her blood pressure was dangerously high. "They're forcing us to leave."

"They're evicting us," said Julian, a dangerous expression on his face as he glared at one of the males in the gray robes hauling a teenager out of his room by his arm.

My insides turned. I was partly responsible for this. I'd told Basil to evacuate the hotel. Just not this way. This was wrong.

"Basil hired these mercenaries?" I'd never seen these types before, and I didn't like how rough they were being with the tenants. They were being treated like convicts.

"I had them come," said a female voice.

I flicked my eyes to a tall woman with a pointed face, her pale skin blending with the white of her robe. Her blonde hair was pulled back into a low bun, exposing her thin face severely and adding more depth to her frown. I recognized her. Adele.

"They didn't listen when hotel management asked them nicely to leave, so here I am, asking *not* so nicely," said Adele as she stepped forward, and I hated the fact that she was taller than me.

I gritted my teeth. "On what authority?"

Adele smiled coldly. "On *my* authority. The Gray Council happily lent me their officers."

"Hired thugs to move families and old people," I seethed. "Nice touch."

I caught a peek at the other witch named Declan as he manhandled Barb and pinned her against the hallway wall. My anger soared.

"You can't just do this. You have to have places for them to stay," said Elsa as she came to stand next to me. So did Jade. So did Julian. "We'll be out on the street! All of us!"

Adele flashed a smile in Elsa's direction. "But I can. That's called power, Elsa. Something you'll never have and can't possibly understand. And I have more than you can imagine. You can sleep in the gutter for all I care. You've been given fair warning."

"Less than a day to look for new lodgings isn't a fair warning,"

I told her. "You need to give them at least a week." I had no idea if that were true. I wasn't well-informed about our paranormal laws regarding the rights of tenants and landlords.

"But I don't," said Adele, giving me one of her fake smiles. "The hotel is closed as of this moment, and everyone needs to leave. Including you, Leana Fairchild, the Starlight witch. Yes. I've done some inquiries. I know everything. What did they call you back at the Merlin trials? Oh yes—Star*dud*."

Ouch.

"Couldn't even work the simplest of spells." She sidled forward. "And I know about that pathetic human you married." She laughed. "We get what we deserve. Don't we?"

"Not fair," I said, hands on my hips, smiling. "All I know about you is that you're a bitch."

Elsa's intake of breath nearly sent me into a fit of giggles. Yeah, this bitch could revoke my Merlin license, but I couldn't help myself. What she was doing was wrong. Worse was that she knew it and didn't care.

Adele's light eyes darkened. "Careful now, Stardud, or you'll be out of a Merlin license as well as out of an apartment. Don't think I won't ruin your Merlin career, because I will." She stepped closer until she was practically touching me, and the scent of something acrid like vinegar rushed up my nose. "I can make it so that you will never work again on this continent. You don't want to test me."

But I did. I really, *really* did. It wasn't the right time, though. I needed my license to finish the job. And I'd never, ever, *not* finished a job.

I felt a hand around my arm, and then I was pulled back a step into Elsa. "Don't," she whispered. "This isn't the time."

She was right, of course, but it didn't stop the fury that seemed to spill through my pores. I detested this witch as much as I despised bullies.

"You'll be able to go back to your homes once I apprehend those responsible for the demons," I told the terrified tenants who were all lined up together in the hallway with just a few bags filled with their belongings. Some faces brightened at the news I'd just relayed, and I felt a pang in my heart.

It was hard to watch the tenants being evacuated, but this was only temporary. As soon as I caught the culprit, the threat would be over, and the tenants could return to their homes.

"That won't be necessary," said Adele, staring at me like I was an annoying mosquito she was aiming to smack.

I shook my head. "This is a huge problem. Not to mention irresponsible. Someone's opening Rifts all over the hotel and letting demons out. That's got to be stopped. You can't just let it be. The demons will continue to escape into the hotel. It will never be livable again."

"It won't have to." Adele drew herself up to her full height. Yeah. The bitch was a tall one. "The hotel will be destroyed, so no more demons. Problem solved."

"Destroyed!" yelled Jade.

"But you can't," cried Elsa as she fisted her hands. "It's been around for over a hundred years."

"This is our home," said Barb, her eyes filled with tears. "It will be the death of us. Where are we to go?"

"I don't care," said Adele, the slightest satisfied smile on her lips. "I hate having to repeat myself to simpletons. The hotel is going to be destroyed tomorrow morning. If you are still inside, you will die with it. I don't care."

Every time she opened her mouth, I hated her more. The witch had no conscience. "Don't you think destroying the hotel is a bit overkill? It doesn't need to be destroyed. All you have to do is stop the one who's creating the Rifts, and you've solved the problem."

"The decision has been made." Adele's face spread into an icy grin. "The hotel will be destroyed at eight tomorrow morning. That is all."

That is not all, you tall, skinny bitch.

Then something occurred to me, and I felt all the blood leave my face.

Jimmy!

If they destroyed the hotel, Jimmy would die with it. He couldn't leave because of the curse.

I cast my gaze around the hallway and spotted the toy dog. With his ears low and his tail between his back wheels, he knew what destroying the hotel meant.

Tears burned my eyes. I would not let that happen. I would find a way to stop this.

The problem was I only had a few hours, and I had no idea how.

CHAPTER 25

With a heavy heart I watched the gray-robed officers usher out the last of the tenants. Barb actually gripped the edges of a doorframe until an officer hit her fingers, followed by the twins with their faces streaked with tears, taking turns hugging Julian.

When only the gang and me were left, Adele walked into a waiting elevator with her hired thugs. She turned to give us a last coy smile. Her features were drawn with a cold satisfaction, the kind people with power have when they ordain us little people. Her ugly face was the last thing I saw as the elevator doors slid shut.

It seemed that after she'd declared her intentions of destroying the hotel, she wasn't as adamant about getting everyone out. She didn't care if we stayed and died. She truly was an evil bitch.

But right now, I had more pressing matters.

"How do we stop her from destroying the hotel?" I asked. I sat on the floor in the hallway with my back to the wall. "We can't let that happen. There's got to be a way." I looked over to Jimmy, who'd been silent this whole time.

Elsa shook her head. "I don't think there is. I mean, we could try to contact the Gray Council. That would be the only way to stop her."

My heart leaped. "That's good. Okay. So let's do that."

"But it'll take a while," said the older witch. "It's not like you can just make an appointment. You know how hard it is just to reach them by phone? They don't take calls from just anyone. And it's past midnight. You need to go through your court."

"I don't belong to any court," I said, knowing full well that in order to belong to one of them, you needed to harness either magic, which I didn't. As a Starlight witch, I didn't fit into any of the factions. It had bothered me a great deal when I was in my twenties and left me feeling like an outsider. Now, I couldn't care less.

"But we do," answered Elsa. "And our court is the White Court, and Her Highness's ass sits on one of the seats. If she gets wind of what we're trying to do, she'll put a stop to it."

"That's a problem." I never had to contact the Gray Council directly. It had always been the Merlin Group or whoever I was working for at the time.

Jade rolled over to us. She'd put on her roller skates in solidarity with Jimmy. "I think I might know someone who knows someone on the Gray Council," she said, slightly out of breath.

"Who?" Elsa and I asked at the same time.

"Margorie Maben," she answered. "We're in the same Eighties Forever group on Facebook. She's married to Oscar Maben. He sits on the Gray Council."

I jerked. "That's great. We wouldn't have to go through the White Council. Can you call her?"

Jade screwed up her face as she yanked out her phone from her back pocket. "I don't have her phone number. We've only just chatted on social media. But I'll try to reach her there. It's late, though. I don't know if she'll answer."

"Keep trying." I watched as she began typing on her phone. This was good. If we could reach her somehow and give her our version of what was happening, we'd have a chance at stopping this ridiculous demolition. It was a small chance, but it was better than nothing.

I rolled to my knees. "Is there a spell or something that could allow Jimmy a temporary leave from the hotel? Just in case?" I stared at the toy dog, but he wouldn't look at me.

"I tried for years to find something just like that for him, a potion," said Julian, sitting on the floor across from me, his long legs nearly touching mine. "I never could find anything. The curse is too strong."

Elsa let out a sigh. "Spells are useless unless you have what was used on him. Polly tried. We all did. Without knowledge of the curse the sorceress used, we never got close."

"It's fine, Elsa," said Jimmy, finally speaking. "I know you tried. But let's face it. It's over. Maybe it's a good thing. One can only survive so long as a toy. It's time for me to go."

I frowned. "Don't talk like that. It's not over."

"But it is," said the toy dog. "You have no idea what's it been like for me. To be this… this toy. Not being able to be with a woman ever. Not being able to have a family of my own. I've suffered enough. I'm done, Leana. I'm tired."

Okay, so I had no idea what it must have been like for him all these years. And I would never know. The pain must have been unbearable, and he was a remarkable creature to have endured it for so long.

But I'd just met Jimmy. He was my friend, and I wasn't ready to let him go.

Both Elsa and Julian sounded defeated, like they'd given up on finding the counter-curse. Good thing I wasn't good at letting things go. I wasn't done yet. Not by a long shot. The best thing for Jimmy now was to stop the hotel demolition, and then I was going to find a way to remove the curse.

The ting from the elevator sounded, and then the doors slid open.

Basil stumbled out, and for a moment I wondered if he was still drunk from this morning. His eyes were wide as he took us in. "Hell's bells, what are you all still doing here? I've asked everyone to leave."

Errol walked behind him, like his taller, skinnier shadow. A happy cruelty lurked behind the calm of his features, a contemptuous grin hiding within the ordinary posture of his body. He was loving this. Why? He was out of a job if they tore down the hotel. Still, I didn't like that hidden smirk of his. Something was definitely up.

Basil stood over me. "You even asked for everyone to leave. Why are you still here? Haven't you heard what they plan on doing to the hotel?"

"I have," I said as I stood. I didn't like to have Errol looking down at me. "And yes. I did ask for you to evacuate the tenants. But not like this. Not without having accommodations for everyone. And why the gray robes? Seriously? You didn't need to do that. These people, your tenants, didn't deserve that."

Basil looked uncomfortable, and he flattened the front of his shirt. "That wasn't my decision. There was nothing I could have done to prevent it."

I could tell he wished it had gone differently, but like us, his power stopped at managing the hotel. He wasn't an owner. Adele held all the power now, granted by the Gray Council, the owners of said hotel. And an icy-cold bitch with that kind of power was a dangerous thing.

Elsa pushed herself slowly to her feet. "You could have warned us, Basil. We've lived here for years. Never caused any trouble."

Basil's face darkened a shade. "You think I don't know that. I didn't get a warning either. They just showed up."

"And you grabbed your ankles and took it like a man," said Julian, staring at Basil with a scary amount of fury. His long coat hid whatever deadly potions and poisons he had there at the ready. I was reminded not to get on his bad side.

"I had no choice," Basil cried, spit flying out of his mouth. "I have a reputation to think about. They're considering me for another management position in Florida. If I spoke out of turn, I'd be finished."

"Oh, you're finished," threatened Julian, and the hairs on the back of my neck rose at the insinuation in his words. "Those were my friends you threw out on the street. I'm not going to let that go, old man."

Basil pointed a finger at the other witch. "Is that a threat?" he shrieked, and Errol snorted behind him. "Are you threatening me?"

Julian's jaw twitched. "Yeah. You're a fucking coward." With a sweep of his coat, Julian was now standing, very tall, before Basil.

The tiny witch lifted himself onto the tips of his toes. "Take that back! I'm not a coward."

Julian had his hands inside his long coat, gesturing that he was about to toss something evil on Basil.

Basil caught on. "Don't you dare!" He flung his hand at Julian's jacket pocket. "If you poison me, you'll end up in the witch prison. And then what'll you do?"

Julian smiled coldly. "It'll be worth it."

"Stop with the pissing contest." I put myself between the two. "You're acting like idiots. Put your sausage fest back in your pants."

Basil's wide eyes met mine. "He threatened me."

I shrugged. "You sorta asked for it."

Basil's mouth fell open, his lips flapping, but nothing came out.

I turned to Julian. "Keep your temper in check. Right now, we need you calm. We must figure out a way to stop Adele from destroying the hotel and save Jimmy."

"What are you talking about?" Basil looked over at the toy dog, who was now staring at the wall, like he was hoping he could burn a hole through it with his eyes. "What's this about Jimmy?"

"Really?" I pressed my hand on my hip. "You've been the manager here for..."

"Thirty years," answered Basil proudly.

"And you didn't realize that destroying the hotel would also kill him?"

Basil blinked a few times, and his eyes went from me to the toy dog. "But I... I didn't realize..."

"Guess not."

Basil stared at the toy dog as though it was the first time he'd laid eyes on him. "Jimmy, I'm so sorry. I never imagined... I forgot," he added at the end, looking ashamed.

"It's fine," answered the toy dog, still staring at the wall.

"It's *not* fine." I glared at Basil. "You must have some connections. Who do you know on the Gray Council that could help us?"

Basil was shaking his head. "No one."

I gritted my teeth. "No one? You don't know a single soul on that council? Bull."

The hotel manager narrowed his eyes. "I don't. Okay?" And then his face changed as he'd just remembered something. "But I have a friend who might."

"Good. If you want to save Jimmy's life, you'll find that person and tell them what's happening here."

"Yes, yes, very good." Basil cast his gaze over us. "What will you do?"

I sighed. "Someone is still conjuring up Rifts. And as long as they're out there, it's my job to find them."

At that, Errol clapped his hands and hopped on the spot. He looked like a penguin at the circus.

"Okay." I turned to Errol. "What's with the creepy-ass smile? It's starting to freak me out."

Errol's eyes rounded with glee, and he actually rubbed his hands together like some mad scientist from a cartoon.

"Can I tell her?" he asked Basil. "Oh please, it'll be such fun. I want to look her in the eyes when I tell her."

Okay, now that was even creepier. "What the hell is he talking about?" I couldn't help my heart from hammering inside my chest.

Basil let out a long sigh through his nose. "I came here to tell you something."

"What?" I asked, seeing Jade looking our way with her phone still in her hand. Julian and Elsa were staring. Even Jimmy had stopped watching the wall to look over at me.

Basil pressed his lips into a thin line. "You're fired."

"You're fired!" repeated Errol like an eerie, large parrot.

I glared at him, contemplating kicking him in the throat as a parting gift.

"You can't fire her," said Elsa, coming to my defense. "We need her. If we can manage to keep the hotel from being demolished, who will you have to keep us safe?"

"She's the best defense you've got against the demons," said Julian. "It's a mistake."

A vein on Basil's forehead throbbed. "Well, if she had done her job in the first place and stopped these Rifts, we wouldn't be in this mess."

Ouch. Okay. That stung.

Jade rolled up to Basil and stared him down. "You can't blame her. This isn't her fault."

I grabbed her by the arm and pulled her back. "It's fine. People are always looking to blame someone else."

But the fact remained, what Basil said was true. If I had found those responsible, the hotel would still be open, and we'd all still have places to live.

I stood there like an idiot with shock and anger rippling through me, fighting for first place on the emotion list. I couldn't find the words.

"No hotel, no demons, no need for a Merlin." Basil pulled out an envelope. "Here is what I owe you. Thank you for your services."

The tiny witch turned on his heel and walked away but not before Errol gave me another nasty grin. He'd lost his job, too, but it seemed he was much happier that I'd lost mine.

"Don't forget Jimmy," I called out. I didn't care that I'd lost my job. We were talking about a life. "Please, Basil. Call your contact."

The small witch turned and gave me a nod. It wasn't much, but I knew he'd keep his word. At least now we had two possible ways to reach the Gray Council.

The elevator doors shut, and Basil and Errol were gone.

"I never thought I'd hate Basil so much in my lifetime," said Elsa. "He's like a different person."

"Don't blame him," I told her. "He's just following orders."

"Yeah, Adele's orders," said Jade. "Hate her and her snobby friends."

Silence soaked in, but I could almost hear my friends formulating deadly plans in their heads.

My heart beat loudly in the silence. My strong friends looked defeated and angry. Jade clutched her arms around herself, a sad look in her eyes.

This was wrong. All wrong.

"What do we do now? Where do we go?" asked Jade, her voice loud in the sudden silence.

Elsa sighed. "I'm sure my friend Janet can put us up for a few days until we find somewhere new to live." She looked at me. "That means you, too, Leana."

I gave her a smile. "Thanks. But… I don't know…"

"Why not?" asked Jade. "You don't want to stay with us?"

My insides squeezed at the hurt on her face. "Of course I do. It's just…" My eyes flicked to Jimmy. "This isn't right. I can't just leave Jimmy. Any luck with your Facebook contact?"

Jade stared at her phone. "Not yet."

"Keeping trying—"

A blazing, green-blue light exploded from somewhere outside the window. And then a sonic boom blasted around us, making me jump. The lights went out. Darkness fell, sudden and complete, and I fumbled for the wall as my heart lurched in panic.

Then an invisible force hit us, and we all went hurling violently across the hall. I slammed into the wall and slumped to the carpet. The light subsided, and I blinked rapidly, trying to rid my vision of the white spots as the lights flickered and came back on.

"What the hell was that?" asked Julian as he stood up and went to help Elsa and Jade to their feet. Jimmy seemed fine as he turned to look at me.

I pushed to my feet and stared at the ceiling. "It came from above. Outside. From the roof." I knew it in my gut.

And then I was moving.

My breath came in fast as I rushed to the emergency exit. I pushed it open, climbed a few more steps and, using my weight, shoved the roof door open with a slam of my shoulder to step onto the roof.

Part of me dreaded what I was about to discover. I didn't want it to be Valen here on the roof. So far, his actions were quite the opposite of someone who caused harm to others. But the truth was, I didn't really know him. Not really. And he could very well be the one who was behind all this. He could have played the hero card to throw me off my game.

But when I marched onto the roof, I didn't see Valen standing there. It wasn't anyone I would have guessed.

"Raymond?"

CHAPTER 26

I had a few seconds of a what-the-hell moment, but then I quickly recovered.

"You? You're behind this?"

Raymond, the assistant hotel manager, the average-looking man with the unremarkable face and just plain forgettable altogether, stood on the roof.

His strings of mousy-brown hair lifted around his head in the wind. Even in the semidarkness, I could make out the dark circles under his eyes. His face was gaunt, thinner than I remembered, but then again, I didn't really remember. He could have looked this way before, and I wouldn't have remembered. Like I said, he was forgettable.

Yet I did notice something different. His eyes were sunken but burned too brightly, like he had a fever.

The scent of rot and carrion snapped my attention to a spot in the middle of the roof.

Above a blood-drawn circle, six dead chickens lay in the middle of the roof floor. The same runes and sigils I'd seen before, painted in blood, marked some areas around the circle's exterior, next to burning candles.

A rippling wave of black waters shimmered in the air, a foot above the blood circle. The Rift was open.

It was huge, at least three times the size of the other ones I'd seen, which explained the thundering boom that shook the hotel.

I had to admit seeing him instead of Valen was a huge relief. It meant I'd been wrong about Valen, but it also meant I was losing my touch if I had totally dismissed Raymond as a suspect. He'd had access to the security cameras. He'd been in my face the whole time, yet I'd never *seen* him.

"You're a witch," I said and carefully stepped forward. "I never got that vibe from you. You hid it well. As well as your forgettable appearance." His unmemorable presence had been his weapon. And he'd milked it.

Raymond's face cracked into a smile, his eyes wide with a madman's gleam. Blood trickled from his nose, and a layer of blood covered his teeth when he spoke next. "Yes. Who would ever suspect poor, little, old, frail Raymond."

The sound of heavy breathing and the tread of many feet had me snap my head back.

Julian rushed forward, followed by Elsa and a rolling Jade.

"Holy shit," cried Julian as he joined. "That's the assistant manager. What's his name? I can never remember it."

See, totally forgettable.

"Raymond," I told him.

"Him?" said Elsa as she stood beside me on my right. "He's the one? You're kidding!"

I shrugged. "Looks can be deceiving."

"I'll say." Jade rolled to a stop next to Elsa.

"But he's the janitor?" asked Elsa, which was more of a question than a statement.

A growl emitted from Raymond at that. "*Assistant* manager," he spat at us. Yup, he had some serious insecurity issues.

I looked behind again, expecting to see Jimmy, but he wasn't there. Maybe he couldn't go on the roof, which was technically outside the hotel.

My anger twisted in my gut at the thought of all this clusterfuck because of Raymond.

The night sky was clear, and my starlight sang to me, ready and waiting. "You put a spell on me so I couldn't see the hotel?"

Raymond gave a sick, wet laugh. "I did."

I clenched my jaw, my anger redoubling. "You let the demons in and killed all those people. You had Eddie killed because he was onto you. Wasn't he? Why would you do this?" Crazy people did crazy things, but they always had a reason.

With my starlight in tow, I could sense Raymond's magic now, cold and unfamiliar. Most of it was directed at the Rift. For now. He might not look it, but he was a powerful witch. He'd fooled me, but I wasn't going to make that mistake again and underestimate him.

"Why? Why?" Raymond threw back his head and let out an unsettling and creepy laugh. He sounded pleased that he'd orchestrated it all, delighted that he'd brought the demons to the hotel and killed all those people.

The demented witch gave out a wheezing cackle. "All my life, I've been ignored and overlooked for jobs. Women don't even give me the time of day."

"Maybe if you'd clean yourself up a bit," muttered Julian. "Hair plugs can go a long way."

"Nobody ever cared about me," continued Raymond, the words rushing out of him with loads of emotion, like he'd been wanting to tell someone for years, but no one would hear him. "Every time there was a new position in the hotel, I'd be overlooked. I've worked harder, longer than anyone at this hotel. And when Jabbar, the old hotel manager, died thirty years ago, the position was open. But did they offer it to me? No. They gave it to Basil. That job should have been mine. And I had to work beneath him all these years knowing he'd stolen my position."

"Okay," I said. "You didn't get the job. I still don't get it. That was a long time ago. But what does that have to do with anything?"

Raymond's eyes narrowed on me. "Because. Because I knew they'd never offer me the job. The only way I could get rid of Basil was to get him fired. To ruin his reputation." An evil smile contorted over his face. "Only when a hotel manager is fired can the assistant manager fill that position."

"Holy shit," I breathed. "All this? All these deaths because of a goddamn position? You *killed* people because you wanted to be the hotel manager?" Clearly, he was insane.

"The guy is nuts," said Julian.

Nuts and a powerful witch. Dangerous combination.

Raymond lifted his head proudly. "I will be the hotel manager soon." He laughed, his eyes gleaming with a manic glee. "The job was promised to me. With this last demon portal, I'll be rid of you, and then Basil will be fired. And then *I* will be the Twilight Hotel manager!"

Elsa sucked in a breath through her teeth. "He doesn't know."

"What a dick," said Julian.

"They didn't tell him," added Jade.

Raymond's confidence cracked as his gaze swept around us. "Tell me what? What are you talking about?"

My skin prickled at the sudden pull of Raymond's magic, and I felt his fury rippling under the surface.

The Rift wavered, and I heard the hissing and guttural moans of creatures from the other side. A breeze brought forth an odor of blood, and a cloud of foul energies struck me in the face. Better to keep them on the other side of that portal.

I took a breath. "They're going to demolish the hotel," I said, keeping my voice calm. "They're going to destroy it tomorrow morning at eight."

Fury darkened Raymond's features. "Liar. You're all liars. You're just jealous because you want my job." He pointed at us. "You want to be the manager. But you can't. I'm the manager now. The job is mine."

"A total nutcase," I muttered. "Listen, Raymond, I have a job, and my friends here wouldn't dream about being the next manager. But I am telling you the truth."

"If it were true, why are you not leaving?" asked Raymond, the suspicion in his voice still there, though I could feel the uncertainty in his words.

"Because of Jimmy. We're trying to figure out a way to free him of this curse. You know Jimmy. Right? Of course you do. Then you know if the hotel goes down, so does he."

Jade rolled forward a bit. "It's the truth. Why don't you call Basil? He'll tell you."

Surprisingly, Raymond had a phone on him. He grabbed it, texted something, and waited. We all heard the answering ting of someone messaging him back.

He went still. As he stood there, Raymond's face seemed to take on a different cast, the shadows under his eyes growing to make him look ill.

His phone slipped from his hand and smashed against the hard surface of the roof, breaking into pieces.

"See?" I told him. "You did this all for nothing. You weren't going to get the position because there would be no position for you." Shit, I realized that was not the right thing to say to an already unstable individual. But it was too late.

Raymond's face rippled grotesquely. *"No!"* he shouted. "No. They can't do that to me. I've worked here for years. Years!"

I felt a pull from the Rift. It was connected to Raymond. All he had to do was give it a push of his magic, and it would open.

Raymond coughed and spat the blood from his mouth, but most of it remained around his lips, dribbling off his chin.

"You're sick, Raymond. Let us help you." I knew whatever dark, Black magic he'd been dabbling in took a chunk of payment from him. He'd been changed, corrupted every time he'd used it. He'd been made insane from it. I didn't know if he was already too far gone for me to help him, but I was going to try.

Raymond thrashed around on the spot, looking more and

more like a creature, a beast from the very place he'd been summoning them. "Mine. My job. Mine!"

"The guy's lost it," said Julian. "We need to act now."

I nodded. "You're right. That portal's about to burst open. Can't let that happen. You got something on you to hold him? Like an immobilizing potion?"

"Yes," answered Julian. "It'll take care of him."

"Good." I took a deep breath. "And I'll close the portal."

But it was already too late.

I felt a sudden buzz of energy, a pull of magic; a pop displaced the air.

The hair on the back of my neck rose, and I stood horrified as the Rift shimmered and cracked into existence forty feet from us. Twisting, corrupted masses of demons spilled out in search of their human feast.

The air cracked, and demons of every shape and size let out howls of fury as they surged from the portal, the light of the moon glinting on their teeth, talons, and horrible, hungry, sunken eyes. They rushed out, animal-swift, in a blur of twisted, bulging faces and limbs.

I counted thirty before I lost count.

And they all came for us.

CHAPTER 27

My first thought was, *I'm not even getting paid for this shit.* The second was that I needed to do something if I didn't want to become part of the demon buffet.

Demons spilled out of the rippling portal as though hell itself had vomited them out. At least the sudden reek of rot, bile, and sewage smelled like it.

I channeled my starlight, feeling the power in the stars as they hummed their power through me, and held it just long enough before letting it go.

A brilliant ball of light fired from my outstretched hand and crashed onto the first demon. I didn't even have a chance to see what my starlight had consumed as it illuminated and wrapped itself around the creature like white fire.

"Nice one," said Julian, vials of red liquid in his hands. "Why are there so many at once?"

"Full moon," I answered. "It's always easier for the crazies to show up and the demons to cross over when the Veil is at its thinnest."

"Good to know." Julian rolled his shoulders. "My turn."

I watched as the tall witch hit one of the demons—some lizard-like thing with a mouth of sharp teeth—with one of his vials. The creature howled in pain and shuffled forward, clumsy and slow. It shivered once and then exploded like a piñata, showering Julian in black oil and strips of its flesh.

But the witch didn't seem to care as he pitched another of his vials at another demon with brown fur and a ratlike skull.

Latin rose around me, and I turned to see Jade, spinning around some giant wormlike demon with rows of black spikes covering most of its body. She was firing orange fireballs at it.

Elsa stood with her legs apart for better balance as she fired bursts of wind at a treelike creature, sending it crashing into the massive air-conditioning unit.

A flash of sensation flickered over me as the witches drew in power—a lot of it. Shock waves of our magic shook the roof like a thunderstorm.

A laugh echoed around me. "You're too late. You're all going to die. You will never laugh at Raymond again," said the crazed witch, speaking about himself in the third person. He started to thrash around the blood circle in some creepy ceremonial dance. Yeah, the guy was seriously disturbed.

The sound of hissing reached me, and I spun with my hands at the ready.

Strings of starlight discharged from my hands and hit a demon in the chest with a burst of light, sending it sprawling to the ground sixty feet away. The demon hissed one last time before disintegrating into a clump of ash.

I'd fought my share of demons over the years but never so many at once and never on a roof of a glamorous paranormal hotel.

Too bad I'd be out of a job in the morning.

My body shook with adrenaline as more demons slipped through the portal. Three more. Six more. Ten more.

The difference between this Rift and the others Raymond had risen was that he'd been careful and closed those off after letting out a few demons. But now, it seemed the witch didn't care how many slipped out or how many people died. If the Rift wasn't closed, thousands of demons would cross over to our world before sunrise.

A collection of four demons that looked like enormous rats, the size of bears, with claws and jaws full of fishlike teeth came at me in a rush.

I called to the stars, pulled on my magic, and thrust out my starlight.

Four shoots of starlight strings volleyed, one in the direction of each demon. The starlight twisted and shifted, moving of its own volition like heat-seeking missiles searching for their aircraft targets.

They hit.

The four ratlike beasts lit up with white light. The demons staggered, cries emitting as they fell on their backs, legs flailing. The light went out, and nothing remained of the creatures but clumps of ashes that blew away in the wind.

I cringed at the scent of burnt flesh, my body pounding with starlight. I didn't have time to take a breather. The roof shook under my feet as more demons spilled out onto it.

"We have to shut down the Rift," I cried.

"I'm on it." Julian rushed over to the rippling black wave. He pulled his right hand from his coat pocket and fired a glass vial into the portal's mouth.

I couldn't see Raymond anywhere. Did the coward leave? Probably. But I'd find him. And then I'd make him pay for what he did.

Like a seasoned baseball pitcher, Julian shot vial after vial into its depths, causing the roof to shudder with each impact. I didn't know what kind of potions he was using, but whatever they were kept the demons inside. However, it wasn't closing the Rift. It was just a temporary fix. And Julian couldn't keep this up for much longer. Soon he'd run out of his vials.

We needed to close it.

Without Raymond's help, it could take hours to decipher the ritual and spells he'd used to conjure up a Rift of this magnitude.

Or you needed a crapload of power to shut it down. Enough to short circuit it in a way.

I looked to the black sky, to the shining white disk looming over all of us. I didn't draw from the full moon often. More like I tried to avoid it. Too much would kill me. The key was to balance the starlight from the moon, which was more challenging than it sounded. But I needed to try.

"I need you tonight," I whispered.

And then I was sprinting toward the portal. I saw Raymond lying on his back, moving his arms and legs like he was doing snow angels. His eyes were open, staring at the sky above.

The guy was lost, but I didn't have time to worry about him for now.

I got maybe fifteen feet before the pain hit.

I cried out as the scorching agony exploded around my left calf, dragging me down to the ground as sharp claws raked my leg. My focus shattered, and my hold on my starlight collapsed. Instincts kicked in, and I kicked out with my other leg.

My boot made contact with something solid. I heard a small yelp of pain, and then I could move my left leg again. I scrambled to my feet. The wetness that soon followed told me a demon had taken a chunk out of my calf.

Favoring my right leg, I straightened to find a wolflike demon shaking its head, red eyes watching me. It had a scorpion-like tail with a stinger at the end. Nice.

"A little help here," cried Julian as he tossed another vial into the Rift.

"I'm trying!" I shouted back and started limping forward. I pulled on my starlight once again, straining to focus. I was nearly there—

My breath escaped me as something long and hard slammed into my chest.

I grunted in pain as my back hit the hard rooftop. Hot carrion breath hit my face as its weight pinned me down. In a flash, the wolf-scorpion demon went for my neck. I raised my arm just as teeth clamped around it.

Pain racked me as the demon bit down, harder and deeper. I couldn't move. I couldn't speak. I couldn't breathe. My arm was slick with my own blood. My focus fell, and so did the hold on my magic.

Tears filled my eyes. Using my free hand, I made a fist and smashed it against its head over and over again.

But the wolf-scorpion demon wouldn't let go.

Its tail curled up behind it as it drew near until its stinger hung just above my head. Demon venom was not something you could cure. One sting of its tail, once the demon poison was in me, there was no getting it back out.

I blinked. The stinger moved closer and closer to my head.

"I'm running out!" shouted Julian over the pounding of blood in my ears. I could just make out his silhouette next to the rippling Rift. "I'm out!" He leaped back, and the hissing and grunts sounded from the portal.

Movement caught my eye as Jade limped across the roof, a roller skate on one foot but the other with just a sock. Blood was smeared on the left side of her face, and she looked tired, done in. Her elemental fire around her palms was faint, like the mild burning of a candle. She was running out of her magic.

Behind her, Elsa was pinned to the air-conditioning unit. A line of demons stood before her, pounding and throwing themselves on a thin, shimmering wall of light blue. She'd managed some sort of shield. But from the look of pure terror and the shifting in her shield, it wouldn't last.

There were too many demons. We weren't strong enough. We weren't going to make it.

Something moved in my peripheral vision. I saw the blur of a body, and then the weight of the wolf-scorpion demon on my chest vanished.

I blinked up to see Valen haul the wolf-scorpion with his bare hands, across the roof.

And then the next thing that happened, I'd never have believed if I hadn't seen it with my own eyes.

Valen, the hot restaurant owner, ripped off his clothes, which I would have really enjoyed if not for what came next.

A flash of light was followed by a tearing sound and the breaking of bones. I stared as his features shifted with a sort of rippling motion just beneath the surface of his skin, causing a widening of his head. His face twisted, enlarging and expanding unnaturally until his head was about five times its normal size.

Valen's body grew in length and width until he stood at about eighteen feet. Muscles bulged with arms and thighs as large as tree trunks. His face was different, with a stronger brow bone, resembling a Neanderthal, but it was him. It was like staring at a version of the Hulk, but much bigger and taller.

Holy shit. Valen was a *giant*.

CHAPTER 28

I'd never seen an actual giant. Giants were things of myths and legends. I barely remembered reading about them in the thousands of paranormal books I'd read over the years. No one even talked about them because we all knew they didn't exist. And I say *we,* as in the paranormal community, where shifters and vampires and fae were among our people. Giants were not supposed to be real. I mean, unicorns were rare, but I knew they were real. Some had been spotted in Ireland. But giants? Giants weren't real.

Yet I was staring at one.

"You're... you're a giant," I told him. From my vantage point, I could barely see his face.

With my heart in my throat, Valen, the giant, crushed a nearing demon with a slam of his fist. The roof shook like an earthquake.

He turned to me and said, *"I am."*

I winced at the sound of his voice. It was ten times as deep and loud with a more guttural tone to it.

I couldn't help but stare at this magnificent, yet terrifying, naked giant. The muscles on his chest flexed as he stood protectively in front of me, giving me an excellent view of his giant manhood. What? I had to look. Trust me. You would have too.

In response to a flash of fur and teeth, Valen, the giant, spun around to meet the onslaught of two demons. I heard a cry and the sound of tearing flesh. Valen, the giant, tore at the demons with voracious rapidity.

It was both exciting and terrifying to watch.

And then I realized this was what he'd been hiding. He was hiding the fact that he was a giant. But why?

A growl came from behind me. Valen stepped forward, grabbed a handful of demons, and lifted them as though they weighed nothing at all. Then he crushed their skulls together, like they were nothing more than eggshells, before tossing them.

"Leana! Help!"

I turned to the sound of Julian's terrified voice. He had a metal pole in his hand, swinging it at an oncoming demon that looked like a panther with an eagle's head. He had no magic to defend him.

I struggled to my feet. "Can you protect them? I need to get to the Rift and close it. Can you help my friends?"

Valen stared down at me with those same dark eyes. *"I can. You can close the portal?"*

"I'll do my best."

Valen turned, stepped on a demon in his way, and hurried over to Julian. I wanted to stay and watch this giant beat the crap out of the demons. It wasn't every day you witnessed a mystical creature that wasn't supposed to be real. But I had a Rift to shut down.

Picking myself up again, I limped across the roof, glad that Valen had cleared me a path. I made it to the Rift without being attacked, where Raymond was still lying with his back on the roof, staring up at the sky. He was a deranged sonofabitch.

I let out a breath and then called to my will, to my starlight. I felt the soft tug of its power as it answered, the flow of brilliant white energy churning inside my core. I held it there for just a moment. I planted my feet for better control, as I knew my injuries might make me stumble.

I stood before the demon portal. The air sizzled with cold energy as the scent of death, blood, and evil hit me in the face. It pulsed like a constant humming from a power line. The reek of sulfur and rot was overwhelming, and my ears popped with the pressure shifting. A mighty wind blew around me, lifting my hair off my shoulders and slapping it against my face. It was unnatural, acidic, and poisonous to us mortals. I recognized it. It was the Netherworld's air, coming from inside the portal.

I could see shapes through the gateway. Thousands of forms were rushing toward the opening of our world.

Shit. If they reached us, I wasn't sure even Valen could stop them.

I grabbed all the starlight magic I could to spindle it inside my core, channeling the emanations and harnessing that celestial energy beyond the clouds. I felt a tingling as it answered.

A spool of blinding white light curled up in my palms and wove through my fingers in a slow crawl.

Blazing light soared forth from my outstretched fingers, and I directed it at the Rift. It poured out of me like a never-ending shoot of white energy, illuminating the roof like it was daylight.

Screeches echoed from somewhere deep inside the portal. I couldn't see them anymore, but their voices were near. Too near. I had to hurry.

Again, way harder than it looked, and I kept my magic ready, like a loaded gun. I was ready to blast any sonofabitch who came through the portal while I tried to close it.

And then, as I held on to my starlight, I called to the moon's power.

I reached out my will to the moon, to its energy.

It answered.

Another, larger, blast of white light fired through me and hit the portal.

Pain hit my body, like my insides were liquifying. Dizzy, my balance wobbled as the magic gushed out of me like a fountain, drowning me in a flood of fatigue.

Calling up the power of the moon was not an easy feat. Like I said before, too much and it'd kill me. Fry me right there on the spot, like fried chicken.

But it was working.

The portal shifted, and it started to fold on itself.

"What are you doing!"

I turned to see Raymond on his feet next to me, staring wild-eyed at the portal as it continued to get smaller and smaller.

I didn't have the energy to waste speaking to him. One mishap and I could be finished.

"You can't do this! Stop! Stop it!" he shouted.

Yeah, I was never very good at taking orders.

The starlight kept firing out of me and into the portal. Sweat broke out along my forehead, and I started to feel the beginnings of tiredness along with a bit of nausea. But still, I held on. Only a bit more, and it would be all over.

Distant cries and howls of outrage found me. I squinted into the Rift. Countless shadows appeared in view, getting bigger and closer. I could make out wings and tails and tentacles. Their movements were frantic and desperate. The demons saw what I was doing, and now they were making a run for it.

Hands appeared out of nowhere and wrapped around my neck. I blinked into the mad face of Raymond, his eyes crazed, as he tried to crush my neck with his cold, stiff fingers.

"I'll kill you! Kill you!" he screamed, his spit flying into my eyes as he pressed harder, taking away my ability to breathe.

Again with the choking? Seriously? I wasn't afraid anymore. I was angry. Pissed. I'd had enough of men trying to choke me to death.

I couldn't let go of my starlight, and I couldn't use my hands.

So I used the only other thing I had at my disposal.

And I kneed him in the balls.

When in doubt, go for balls. And it worked like a charm.

Raymond let go and bent over, hands on his man berries. "Bitch," he wheezed.

Of course, I had to kick him again after that.

Raymond stumbled backward and fell right into the portal, vanishing.

Oops. I hadn't meant to do that, but it was too late. The witch was gone.

Adrenaline flooded me. The moon's energy seemed to shred me into thousands of pieces, held together only by my skin and my will. Searing pain exploded in my head, and blackness flooded my eyes. I couldn't see, but I still held on.

Guttural shrieks rose from the depths of the portal, but it was too late. Their cries of outrage rose, echoed, and then vanished.

With a pop of pressure, the Rift was gone.

CHAPTER 29

I let go of my starlight and the moon's energy and collapsed to the floor. Dizziness hit, and my heart was hammering, like I'd just run around the block ten times for fun. I was burned out but still proud that I'd managed to close it, something I'd never have been able to do without my friends. Without Valen.

The scent of body odor wafted up. I sniffed myself and winced. "Definitely need a shower." I stank!

Worse, I was buck naked, the cool air rolling over my lady bits. All that starlight had once again burned away my clothes. Whoops.

"You did it. You fucking did it," said Julian as he walked over to the spot where the portal had stood. "That was incredible."

"We all did." Speaking of my friends, I turned around on my butt and stared at the jumbled mess of what was left of the demons. Some were stacks of bones and heaps of meat, and some were just piles of ashes. But they were all vanquished. Not one demon remained standing.

Jade came limping our way, still missing one of her roller skates, but otherwise she seemed okay. Elsa was hobbling along behind her. She looked exhausted, but her smile was vibrant as she stared at me.

And Valen? Valen was still huge. Still naked. Still glorious.

"That was quite something," said Elsa as she neared. "It was like watching a star being born."

"Yeah. It was amazing," echoed Jade. "Wish we didn't have to fight off those demons so I could have watched. Pictures would have been nice, too, maybe a few videos."

"Here." Elsa pulled a green shawl from her bag and handed it to me.

"Thanks." I wrapped it around myself, my face burning as I felt Valen's eyes on me.

Elsa turned on the spot. "What happened to the janitor? Did the demons get him? I hope they did. Can't believe he did what he did for a promotion."

"A promotion he'd never get," interjected Jade. "Have you seen my roller skate? I swear I saw it here somewhere?"

I shook my head. "No." I gestured at the space that had held the portal. Only a few streaks of a black, tar-like substance remained. "He fell through the Rift."

"Fell or pushed?" asked Julian, a smile on his face.

"Accidental push?" I told them with a shrug. "He was trying to choke me, so I kicked him, and he fell over and through it. Oopsie."

Julian laughed. "Serves the bastard right. The world's a better and safer place without him."

Probably. But I still wished he hadn't fallen through. Prison would have been a better option. Now, who knew what had happened? All those demons on the other side probably ripped him to pieces—a bad way to go.

"Good riddance," said Jade, yanking the sleeve of her shirt with a long tear in it. "Always gave me the creeps anyway. Oh, the goddess help us." Jade's eyes widened, and I turned to see Valen coming our way in all his naked, giant splendor. Man berries and stem swinging. Yup. It was hard *not* to look.

"That's a big boy," said Julian, giving Valen's junk an approving nod. "A king of kings."

I shook my head. Men and their junk. I'd never understand.

The giant had splatters of dark blood all over him, not his blood. *"You okay?"* he asked in that deep, profound voice.

"I'll live," I told him, still trying to wrap my mind around the fact that I was staring at a giant and wasn't dreaming. Giants were real. Holy shit.

"Here. Take this." Julian tugged off of his coat and handed it to the giant. "You shouldn't be allowed to walk around exposing a thing that big."

Valen stared at him, and for a second, I thought he would refuse. But then he wrapped the coat around his man parts and tucked it in like a pair of makeshift briefs.

Julian raised his brows. "You can keep it."

I laughed. "This has been a strange night."

Elsa had her head back as she took in all of Valen. I could tell she wanted to ask him about being a giant. Hell, we all did, but we stayed silent. Call it respect. It was obvious he wasn't comfortable talking about it. But he'd revealed it to us. Without his help, we would have been toast.

"What time is it?" I asked.

Jade yanked out her phone. "Uh... two a.m."

My heart gave a jolt. We still had time to save the hotel. "Did you reach your friend?"

"Just a second." Jade frowned as she swiped a finger across the screen of her phone. "Oh. I missed a message from her." Her eyes widened as she read whatever her friend had written. And then her mouth fell open.

"What did she write?" My heart pounded, and I felt Valen's eyes on me, which were seriously more intense than before, being in his giant state.

"Oh my God," said Jade after a moment.

"What!" we all chorused together.

Jade looked at us. "She says she told my story to her husband and that he was already contacted by Basil to ask for an extension for the hotel's demolition. Listen to this! Turns out not all of those on the Gray Council were aware of this. And they weren't happy to find out so last minute."

"That bitch," I said, realizing Adele was abusing her power. She hadn't even told the rest of the council what she was up to. It was also scary to think what else she was doing without proper approval.

"They've canceled the order." Jade smiled, tears filling her eyes. "The hotel stays. It won't be destroyed."

Elsa hid her face in her hands as she sobbed openly, only to get grabbed in a hug by Jade.

My eyes burned at the sight of them crying but also because Jimmy would be okay. Basil had done well, but I wouldn't tell him that. What he should have done was double-check with the council before letting that skinny bitch Adele into the hotel and believing any word that came out of her mouth.

"Ahhhh." Julian took in a deep breath and threw his arms out in a stretch. "Nothing like a good screw to end a battle." He rubbed his hands together. "See you gals later. I've got some ladies waiting for me."

I laughed. "Can you find Jimmy and tell him?" My chest nearly exploded at the news that he'd be okay. I wanted to tell him myself, but I didn't think I could stand at the moment. My legs felt like jelly, and I was still a little bit dizzy from all that starlight and moon power.

"You bet." Julian walked away with a hop in his step.

Hot tears fell down my cheeks as I watched the tall witch exit the roof door. Valen was still watching me when I turned around, and I couldn't tell what he was feeling. And I found I couldn't look away either.

Elsa looked between us. "Come." She grabbed Jade by the hand. "We need to find Basil and tell him what happened. About Raymond. About all of it. And we need to get everyone back into their apartments." She walked away with Jade, throwing me looks over her shoulder as she let the other witch pull her.

I wiped my tears with the back of my hand, waiting for Valen to say something. When it became apparent that he wouldn't, I opened my mouth. "So, a giant? Have you been able to transform like that, for long?"

The giant bent his head to look at me. *"I was born this way."*

"Right. Of course." What a stupid question. I craned my neck. "You think you could... lower yourself? I'm getting whiplash just trying to look at you."

The roof squealed and cracked as the giant settled himself down next to me. *"Better?"*

I stared at his face. "Better." Even sitting down, he was like six feet tall. "How did you find us?"

"Jimmy told me," answered the giant, and I found myself staring at his lips while he talked. *"When I heard about what the council wanted to do with the hotel, I came to help."*

I turned my leg over, where the demon had bitten it. My calf was soaked with blood. So was my arm.

"You're hurt," said the giant, and I heard something like worry in his voice.

"It's not that bad. The wounds aren't deep. I don't need stitches." But I'd need to clean it before it got infected. "Thank you for saving me. Without your help, we would have all died, been eaten away by those demons, or been pulled back into that portal."

A noise erupted from his throat that could have been him agreeing. *"It's my job to keep everyone safe."*

"Your job?"

"I'm a watcher."

"A watcher?" I repeated like an idiot. What the hell was a watcher, and how come I'd never heard of them?

"All giants are watchers. Protectors."

It made sense, being as they were so freaking big and robust. "So how come no one has really seen or heard of you giants? As far as I can remember, giants weren't real. You were just stories parents told their children when they misbehaved."

Valen nodded and looked to the ground. *"There aren't many of us left. Over centuries ago, we were feared because of our size and strength. We were hunted. Killed. Only a few left all over the world."*

"That is sad," I told him. "Is that why you don't want people to know?"

"Partly."

"If you had told me that you were a giant, and weren't so secretive, maybe I wouldn't have thought you were behind the portals."

The giant frowned, which, let me tell you, was a scary sight. I found myself leaning back.

"Would you have believed me if I told you I was a giant?"

"By the skepticism I can hear in your voice, I'm going to go with… no?" I said. "Okay, I probably wouldn't have believed you because, well, giants aren't real." I smiled at him and felt warmth in my belly as he smiled back. "Those are some big-ass teeth."

Valen laughed, sounding like a cross between a roar from a lion and the grinding of rocks.

"I'm sorry I accused you," I said to break the sudden silence.

"I should have told you. We are on the same team."

I twisted my face. "What do you mean?"

"The hotel hired me." Valen was silent for a moment. *"I came here five years ago. To work as a watcher for the hotel and for the surrounding area."*

"Ah." Things were starting to all make sense now. "So when I saw you in room nine fifteen and then before that in Eddie's room…"

"I was asked to be there by the hotel."

"So why did they ask me to work for the Twilight Hotel when they already had you?"

"Not the same." Valen's eyes glimmered in the moonlight. They were so big and beautiful, I felt myself leaning forward. *"You are an investigator. An agent. I'm just the muscle."* He flashed me another one of those big-ass smiles. *"I'm the guy you want with you to bring in the bad guy. I protect."*

I winced on the inside. I can't believe I had ever thought he was the bad guy. *Good one, Leana.*

He'd saved me twice now. Yes, he'd been a brute when we'd first met. But all that was in the past. What did that mean now? And why was he still here with me? Why didn't he leave with the others?

"Tell me," I said, staring at all those ginormous, manly muscles and finding myself wildly attracted to a giant. Did that make me weird or just horny? "What exactly does a watcher do? I get the watching part. The… overseeing and making sure there's no evil lurking in the shadows. But do you work only when you're a giant? Or is it a constant thing? All day… all night. I mean, you do have a restaurant."

"You ask a lot of questions."

He was smiling, so I didn't think he took my pestering as a bad thing. "I've got more. How long are you staying?"

Again, the giant laughed, and my heart skipped a beat.

"I'm always a watcher," answered the giant. *"But I patrol the streets at night in my giant form."*

"Really? You must have a huge invisibility cloak." I laughed. "How can you hide"—I made a gesture with my hand over his body—"all that from human eyes. If you were a pixie, that wouldn't be a problem. But you're like a thousand times bigger than a pixie."

A smile broke over the giant's face. *"Natural glamour. Don't need cloaks."*

My lips parted. "What the hell is that?" I'd never heard of such a thing. Potions and spells that put a glamour on you or objects like the hotel, but never a natural glamour. I began to realize that I knew close to nothing about giants. And I wanted to get a crash course right about now.

"All giants are born with an inherent glamour. No human can see us. Only paranormals, shifters, vampires, witches, like you."

"That's really impressive, and I'm kinda jealous. Walking the streets at night and no one seeing you. Must be nice."

Valen grinned, and then the sounds of police sirens pulled his attention toward the skylight.

"Are you working tonight?" I asked, searching his face. The longer I stared at it, the more I liked it. Yes, it was a larger, more primal face, if I could describe it like that, but it was also soft, and his eyes were the same… but bigger.

The giant looked at me, making my stomach flutter. *"Yes. You want to come with me?"*

A burst of excitement rushed from the top of my head all the way to my toes. "Hell, yeah."

Valen leaped to his feet surprisingly fast for such a big, big man. The roof whined and trembled under his weight, and I bounced along with it.

With effort, I struggled to my feet, feeling tired but also excited. "There's a problem," I told him, my head tilted back so that I could see part of his face. "I'm a bit tired from channeling all that magic. I don't think I can keep up with you." He was probably really fast. He'd take one step, and I'd have to take ten. Yeah, I'd never catch up.

"You won't have to," answered the giant.

"Uhh?"

Before I could protest, Valen's gargantuan hand reached out and grabbed me, not hard, but gently, like he was holding on to an egg that he didn't want to accidentally crush because he could. He really could. One accidental flinch, and I was as flat as a pancake.

I leaned into his hold and then squealed like an idiot as he lifted me up and onto his shoulder. I sat very comfortably there, my legs dangling over his collarbone. The world looked different from this high. Eighteen feet high. I did not want to fall. I reached out and wrapped my hand into his long, dark locks, inhaling their woodsy scent. He did smell good.

My butt was literally on his shoulder, on his skin, and I prayed to the goddess I didn't accidentally let out a nervous fart. That would be embarrassing.

Valen walked across the hotel's roof with me rocking back and forth but finding it pleasantly comfortable. He stood at the edge of the roof.

I looked down. "Wow. That's high. How are we going down? There's no way you can fit inside the elevator." As soon as the words escaped me, I knew. "Fuck me."

"*Hang on,*" said the giant, my stomach finding its way to my throat.

And then he jumped.

CHAPTER 30

I stood on Cherry Street, staring at one of the piers of the Manhattan Bridge. The sky was a dark blue, the sun coming up in a hazy line. It was hinting at the horizon, but I still had about forty minutes left before I would run out of my starlight magic. It would have to be enough.

I'd spent nearly the rest of the night riding on Valen's shoulder as he walked through the streets of a city that never slept. It had been amazing walking among the humans but them never seeing us. Because I was riding on him, touching his skin, I'd guessed that his glamour had also hidden me from human eyes.

He was careful not to touch anyone as he walked, twisting and avoiding them as much as possible. Roofs were his thing, apparently, as he'd showed me by leaping from one to the other. It seemed he was not only gifted with strength but with the power of leaping great distances. I was jealous about that too.

I didn't realize I'd fallen asleep on his shoulder. And when I'd woken up, I was back in his apartment, and he was back in his normal size and fully clothed, unfortunately.

"How long was I out?" I'd asked him, sitting up from his couch.

"About an hour. How you feeling?" He handed me another tea.

I took it and stared at it. "Is this…"

Valen laughed. "It won't make you sleep. This is just regular tea."

I stretched and yawned. "Like a new me. I feel great, actually." It made me wonder if giants had healing abilities or something because I shouldn't feel this rejuvenated. I took a sip of the tea and placed the mug on the side table.

The couch bounced as Valen sat next to me, his thigh brushing against mine. It felt nice, and I didn't move.

I stared at his face. "You must be tired?"

"Not at all," he said, staring at me with such intensity that I felt about to spontaneously combust. "I'm used to it." His eyes moved to my lips, which sent a spike of desire to my core.

"I'm sure you are." He was close. So very close.

"You're very beautiful," he purred, and I think I actually moaned.

"I saw you naked," I said. Why the hell did I say that?

Desire flashed in his dark eyes. And without so much as a warning, he tilted his head and kissed one corner of my mouth. Then the other side, pulling gently on my lips.

I stiffened in surprise. His lips moved against mine, warm and soft, my heart pounding as I kissed him back. When he slipped his tongue in between my lips, my pulse jumped, and heat bloomed over my skin, alluring, spinning a thrill through me from my lips all the way to my toes.

I'd forgotten how good it felt to be kissed like that, with passion and desire, the kind of kissing that set your lady drawers on fire, like this one.

He slid a hand around my back, the other at the back of my neck, edging me closer. I felt myself move my arms around his waist and his back. My breath came fast as he darted his tongue deep into me. He tasted faintly of coffee, and his kisses made me ache for more.

I let out a little moan and wound my fingers at the nape of his neck, pulling him closer.

He made a surprised sound, and his kiss turned more aggressive. His hands tightened around me. I felt his desire and his need in them. It sent a surge of heat through me, my lady bits pounding. A part of me wanted to rip off his clothes, to feel his hard body against my skin.

Damn, he was a good kisser. Did all giants kiss like that?

My breath left me in a moan as I eased against him, one hand wrapped around his neck and the other in his soft, silky hair. I felt his muscles tighten, and it was all I could do to keep from ripping off his clothes.

His hands moved under my shirt, and the roughness of his callouses sent my skin tingling. Sensing my desire, his touch became aggressive, and hot ribbons of pleasure spiraled through my core.

And then he pulled away.

"I'm sorry. I can't," he said, his voice low and full of emotions. His breath came out in a slow exhalation. Not only did he pull away but he walked away, too, like, to the kitchen.

It was hard not to feel hurt or hit with a giant ball of rejection. We were on our way for some bedroom rodeo. I'd felt his hard desire for me, but something held him back. Or someone…

I sat on the couch in silence for as long as I could before it became awkward. "How much did we patrol? How far did we go?" I asked, breaking the uncomfortable silence and looking up at the man who wouldn't meet my eyes.

Valen surprised me when he returned and took the chair next to me. He remained a good distance away from me but close enough I didn't feel rejected again. Yeah, still a little. "All the way to Harlem and then back down to Chinatown and then here."

I raised a brow. "That was a lot of ground you covered. You must know the city pretty well." A thought occurred to me. Being a watcher, Valen had patrolled the streets of Manhattan for years. He knew where all the dark, vile critters lived, renegade demons, outcast werewolves, and vampires. Among others…

"I do," answered the giant, his dark eyes holding me for a moment.

I swallowed. "Do you know of a sorceress named Auria? She'd be old. Past her one-hundredth birthday."

Valen's brows met in the middle as he thought of it. "Not the name. But I do know of an old sorceress who lives under the Manhattan Bridge. She's been there for many years, apparently. Why?"

My heart slammed in my chest as I stood. "I need to go." I really did need to put some distance between the hot giant and my thumping lady regions. I had to do something else, keep my mind from feeling that rejection again. Because it hurt. I wasn't going to lie.

Valen stood up slowly. "Now?"

"Yes. Before sunrise. I still have time."

I wasn't surprised when he didn't offer to come with me. It was obvious Valen had some inner demons to take care of, and I was just making it worse. Yeah, that didn't make me feel a lot better either.

I'd left his apartment with my heart a little sore. But nothing that couldn't be mended. I didn't want another man in my life. Or so I thought until I'd met Valen. But I wouldn't let myself get too attached to someone who wasn't ready, or someone who couldn't let go of the past.

And now here I was. A half hour later and staring at the stone pier.

Part of me had wanted to stay with the giant. I felt a definite pull between us. But I had something more important I needed to do.

Feeling rejuvenated because of Valen's giant magic—though he hadn't confirmed it—I stepped toward the stone pier and looked for the door. At first, I couldn't see a door or doorway.

After going around the pier, it was obvious it wouldn't be easy to find.

"There has to be a door. Right?"

Being a powerful sorceress, Auria would have the door glamoured and hidden by a spell. Good thing my starlights could find it.

Looking over my shoulder to make sure no curious humans were around, I pulled on my starlight magic, held it, and then lifted my hand and sent it out.

Hundreds of brilliant white miniature globes shot out of my hand and hit the stone pier, draping it in a curtain of white light. The starlights moved around the stone wall, and I followed them. Then they came together on a spot on the stone. Their inner lights shone brighter. The starlights shimmered and then dissolved to reveal a door carved into the stone.

I smiled and, putting my shoulder into it, pushed it open and stepped through.

CHAPTER 31

I found myself in some sort of hallway with a low ceiling that stank of old rugs, mildew, cat pee, and other fouler things I tried not to think about. Nasty. I wrinkled my nose at the scent of incense and candles as I stepped over the dirt-packed ground chamber that ended in shadow. It was dimly lit by glowing flames from a few wall torches.

It was cold, about ten degrees colder than outside, and I wrapped my arms around myself.

Just as I took three more steps, a sudden, cold tingle of magic energy rippled over my skin, making it riddled in goose bumps. Hard to tell if it was Dark or White magic. But an evil energy definitely pulsed around me, slow and thick like the beating heart of a giant beast.

The sorceress's magic. With something extra in it.

"You put a curse at the entrance," I muttered, feeling the cold thrumming and familiar pulse of a curse.

"Ooh. It's a bad one. Kill-me-on-the-spot kind of baddie." But I'd been prepared for it.

With a burst of strength, I pulled on my starlight. Energy crackled against my skin—the energies from the stars tingling over me.

I gave a burst of my starlight, lighting up the hallway with white light and eating away at the darkness. The pressure in the air drifted and disappeared. With a crack, the cold pricks in the air vanished as though they'd never been there.

The curse was broken.

If she didn't know someone had come through her door before, she would now.

I kept going, following the stench and feel of her cold magic. Cobwebs stretched out along the stone walls. The floor sloped slightly up, where a mound on the cave floor gave rise to a larger space.

The room sported a small kitchen area, where a collection of cauldrons were pushed to the sides, a cot that I guessed was her bed, tall bookcases crammed with books, and a long table covered with melted-down candles, books, and bowls. Shelves and racks lined parts of walls, packed with an assortment of jars with unidentifiable objects, all covered in a thin layer of dust. Candles, animal bones, crystal balls, pendulums, chalk, scrying mirrors, cauldrons, and books were crammed in every corner.

I saw no bathroom, which possibly explained the smell.

And there, staring at me from her chair next to what could only be described as a magical fire with green-blue flames, was a woman with more wrinkles and folds around her face than a Shar-Pei dog.

Even bent with age, she had a powerful quality to her. Wisps of white hair fell loosely around her face, her arms and legs hung weakly, and she was painfully thin.

She looked like she had celebrated her two hundredth birthday recently. But her eyes shone with sharp intelligence.

Auria. The sorceress.

Laughter echoed around the room. The old woman lifted her chin haughtily and pointed a gnarled finger at me. "You are a fool. Only fools venture into my home." Her voice was scratchy, old, and withered, just like her.

"Possibly." I was a fool, but I wasn't stupid. I knew she was powerful. But I wasn't leaving until I got what I came for.

I walked in closer, my skin tingling with the pressure of her magic. I was on her home turf, where her magic was strongest. But I had my magic with me too. The old sorceress didn't scare me.

She watched me, sizing me up. "You broke my curse. You a Dark witch?"

"No." I stood as close as I allowed myself. The old woman gave off a horrible stench of an unwashed body.

Auria made a disapproving sound in her throat. "Who are you? What do you want?"

I clasped my hands behind my back. "My friend wants his life back, and you're gonna give it."

The old sorceress narrowed her eyes at me. "Who's your friend?"

"Jimmy." I knew with the slight arch of her brow and the way her lips pressed tightly, she realized who I was talking about. It also confirmed that she was indeed Auria, the sorceress.

"Why should I care what your friend wants?" said the old woman, a smile in her voice.

"Because you cursed him into a toy dog. I think you made your point. Jimmy suffered enough. It's time you break your curse and let him go."

The sorceress's jaw moved like she was gnawing on food. "Never."

Irritation flared as I took a step closer. "You will. Don't make me hurt an old lady because I will. He's my friend. He's a good person. He doesn't deserve this."

The old sorceress laughed a wet laugh. "He's a fool."

"Why? Because he didn't return your love? It happens. Grow up and move on."

Auria leaned forward in her chair. "You're an insolent creature."

"And you're a bitch. I don't care how old you are. You will tell me how to remove the curse. And I'm not leaving until you do. But I'm hoping it's soon, 'cause... you really stink."

The sorceress snorted. "You think you scare me? You're just a witchling. Your White or Dark magic can't do nothing to me."

"How do I remove the curse?" I asked. "The sooner you tell me, the sooner I can leave you to get back to whatever you were doing." I did not want to know.

"I will never tell you or anyone," said the sorceress. "He deserves what he got. Men are nothing but tools for reproduction. They're weaker than us. And I don't care."

I shrugged. "Sure, some are scumbags like my ex-husband. But not all men are bastards. Just like not all women are bitches."

Auria glowered, which was a scary sight, and she nearly lost her eyes in the folds of her wrinkles. "I don't like you."

"I don't like you either."

She waved a crooked hand at me. The other hand I noticed was over a book on her lap tucked neatly in the creases of her robe. "Leave, or I'll do to you worse than what I did to your friend."

"I told you. I'm not leaving until you tell me how to remove the curse from Jimmy." The old sorceress didn't look like much. She seemed like a gust of wind would blow her to ashes. But we all knew in our paranormal world her frailty might just be a cover. I wasn't going to let her play me.

"Others have tried and failed to get their hands on the curse," she said, her voice proud, and it made me feel sick. "Our curses are an extension of our power, of who we are. We don't give out our secrets. Otherwise, we wouldn't be powerful. We wouldn't be feared. Like you... like *your* secret."

I frowned, not liking that she was trying to guess what kind of magic I wielded.

My blood pressure rose. I knew I didn't have much time left. I had to finish this.

"Give it," I told her and took another regrettable, holding-my-breath step closer to her.

She watched me silently, her eyes gleaming with the promise of pain and death. Her face pulled in a grimace. "Fuck you."

Yikes, that was all kinds of weird coming from an old lady's lips.

I was so shocked by that, I missed that flick of her hand and the word, "Atucei!"

A gust of energy rippled out of her like a wave of death.

My arms snapped to my sides as red misty tendrils wrapped around me like a rope. Searing, white-hot pain exploded around my body as though teeth sank into my flesh and back out again. Yikes. That hurt like a bitch.

"Okay," I wheezed and then laughed. "You got me."

In a blur, I was yanked across the room, the wall acting as my savior when I hit it instead of crashing through the window. I slipped to the floor like a rag doll.

"I'm going to enjoy killing you," said the sorceress, and I lifted my head to see that she was still sitting in that damn chair.

Yup, she was powerful. They were right about that. But so was I.

With my heart hammering, I took a deep breath and tapped into my core, my will, and reached out to the magical energy generated by the power of the stars.

Bright light exploded into existence as my magic mixed with my hatred roared in. It overflowed my will and poured into my body. In a rush, the starlight magic raced all around and through me, like a pounding high-voltage conductor until it consumed me.

Starlight magic blasted out of me, breaking through her spell like breaking through chains.

The blast hit the old woman, and she was thrown out of her chair, landing somewhere behind it.

No. I was not sorry.

I stood, dusted myself off, and walked over, looking for what I had the feeling contained my answers.

A book lay a foot away from the sorceress—the same book

she'd been protecting on her lap the whole time I was there. I bent down and grabbed the book.

"That's mine!" She crawled on her hands, pulling herself forward. "Give it. Give it back!"

With my phone's flashlight on, I balanced the book with my right hand and hip and flipped it open. The thin book didn't have a lot of pages in it, which was good. I cringed at the many brown smears and stains on practically every page.

"You take the meaning of dirty witch to a whole other level," I told her.

"No one can break my curses," she spat. "No one. I'm the only one who can."

"But I just did," I said, flipping through the pages.

She looked up at me and started screaming as loudly as a banshee.

It didn't matter. I found what I was looking for. There, on the top of a page, written in scribbly letters, was *Maledicere Alicui Rei*.

My Latin was rusty, to say the least, but I knew *maledicere* meant curse, and the little dog that was drawn next to it gave it away.

My pulse quickened. This was it. I knew it in my gut.

I snapped the book shut. "Nice doing business with you." I stepped over the witch, wanting to put as much distance between me and her horrible body odor as soon as possible.

"What are you?" asked the old sorceress.

I turned and tucked the book under my arm. "A Starlight witch."

And with that, I left a wide-eyed, stinking sorceress on her dirt floor and walked away.

CHAPTER 32

"You think it's going to work?" Jimmy stared at me from my kitchen floor, inside the chalk circle I'd just drawn around him.

"I do." I placed Auria's book back on the table. I was about 90 percent sure, but I wasn't about to tell him that. By the time I'd returned to the Twilight Hotel, the sun was up and bathing the sky in pinks, oranges, and blues.

Echoes of rich voices reached me, and I turned to see Barb, a hand on her hip in a scolding, grandmotherly manner while she pointed at the twins in the hallway. Word of Raymond's defeat and the hotel's reinstatement spread quickly, or Elsa and Jade had been busy waking up the tenants from wherever they had taken up temporary lodgings while I was out and had come back to their homes.

The thirteenth floor was just as vibrant and noisy as it had been the first time I'd set foot on it.

"I can't believe you found her." Jade was on her knees on the floor, carefully lighting each candle that encircled Jimmy, with a whisper of words. It was truly impressive, something, unfortunately, I would never be able to do, being a Starlight witch.

"We looked everywhere for that horrible sorceress," said Elsa, fiddling with her locket in one hand as she flipped through Auria's book with the other. "We even paid a private werefox investigator. Cost us a fortune, and he never found her."

"How *did* you find her?" Julian stood with his back to the wall, looking refreshed and smelling like soap and aftershave. Next to him on the counter was a bundle of clothes I'd asked him to bring for Jimmy. I had no idea if he'd come back fully clothed or as naked as a newborn.

"Valen helped me," I said. Then, knowing they'd all seen his giant shape, I continued. "He patrols the city at night. Sees a lot of what we don't see. Hears rumors. Anyway, he knew of an old sorceress who lived under the Manhattan Bridge. It was her." The memory of that passionate kiss we'd shared was still very hot in my mind, and my body tingled at its recollection. It had been a kiss of *giant* proportions.

Jade leaned back on her heels. "I wish I could have seen the old hag's face when you took her book."

Elsa picked up Auria's spell book. "I would have enjoyed kicking her in the ass," she said, surprising me.

I laughed. "I doubt she'll be bothering anyone anytime soon." The sorceress was powerful, but she looked in poor health. She'd probably not left that place she called home in many years, from the smell of it. And if she ever did crawl out of her nest, I'd be ready for her.

"Are we doing this?" Jimmy's eyes flicked from me to the others, his tail swishing behind him in a nervous whip.

"We are." I shifted my weight and looked to the witches in my kitchen for help. My starlight would be of no aid at the moment, and curses and counter-curses weren't exactly my forte. I was going to need their help to make this work.

Elsa came to stand next to me, Auria's curse book in her hands. "I've studied her curse. Sorcerers' and sorceresses' magic is different from ours. The words they use. The way they draw their power. But nothing here is too complicated. We have her exact words, enough to produce a counter-curse. Enough to unmake what she did to Jimmy."

I smiled down at the nervous toy dog. "See? We've got you."

Elsa glanced at us. Her eyes sparked with something hard and determined. "Auria's a powerful sorceress, more powerful than any of us when she made that curse. We'll need to join hands and combine our magic if we want to match it."

I took a breath, excitement rising through me. "Let's do this."

We all took our places in a circle around Jimmy. Then I took Elsa's hand and Julian's as he took Jade's, and she closed the circle with Elsa's. We were all connected physically.

My hand shook with sweat and nerves, and I hoped Elsa and Julian were too focused on the counter-curse to notice. I took a calming breath as a tiny thrill of excitement rushed in, knowing we were about to pool our magic together. I'd never done this before, shared magic with other witches. I had always been a lone gunman—gunwoman. I wasn't sure what to expect. I felt vulnerable. Open. But I'd put aside my fear and insecurities to save a friend.

"Okay," I said, feeling the warmth in my friends' hands. "I'm guessing we have to say the counter-curse together?" I remembered the conversation I'd had earlier with Elsa when she was studying the curse and preparing the counter-curse.

"Yes," answered Elsa. "Do we all remember the words? We've been over it for the last half hour."

I nodded as Julian and Jade both said, "Yes."

Elsa let out a breath. "Together now."

"We call upon the forces of the Dark Mother," we chanted in unison as I reached to the powers of the stars. "Let flesh be flesh and bone be bone; return what was taken, and remade whole. Make right again that we must; reverse the curse that made this mutt. Undo the magic acted here; reverse the spell, so all is clear."

I drew what energy I could from the stars in the middle of the morning, which wasn't much.

But then my pulse quickened at the sudden surge of magic,

my friends' magic, sending my skin rippling with goose bumps as magical energy poured into me through our hands.

My hair lifted in a sudden wind, carrying the scent of wildflowers, earth, and pine needles—the scent of White magic. The air hummed with power, and I stared, startled as a visible shimmer of blue, orange, and yellow rushed through me and the others.

With a flash of blinding light, I closed my eyes.

When I opened them, instead of a wooden toy dog, stood a man in the chalk circle. An ethereal shimmer rippled over him like a mist, and then it was gone. He had fair skin and hair, graying at the temples. He was about an inch shorter than me. And yup. He was naked.

"Oh my God! It worked!" cried Jade as she let go of the others and began clapping. "It really worked!"

Jimmy's blue eyes, his *real* eyes, stared at me in wonder. "You did it. I can't believe you did it."

I smiled, happy that his voice was the same as it had been when he'd been a wooden toy. "*We* did it. All of us." Which was true. I'd felt the magic of the other witches pour through and around me. Without them, it wouldn't have worked.

Jimmy raised his hands in front of his face, wiggling his fingers like he was trying them out for the first time. That's probably how it felt after being in a wooden body without fingers for so long.

"Here. Cover your junk before the ladies throw themselves all over you." Julian handed Jimmy a bundle of clothes, and we all turned around as he pulled on a pair of jeans and a shirt.

"You can turn around now," said Jimmy.

I spun around, smiling. "You look good, Snoopy."

Jimmy laughed. "Thanks, Merlie."

"You're going to need to hem those jeans," I told him. His feet were entirely hidden by the jeans' bottom hem. The shirt was also too big. He looked like a kid trying on his dad's clothes. He was so cute.

"It's fine." Jimmy folded back the sleeves of his shirt. "I don't care that the clothes don't fit. It's me. I'm me again." When he met my eyes, his were brimming with tears. "Thank you," he said, freely crying now. "This would never have happened if you hadn't accepted the job at the hotel. You gave me back my life."

"Ah, hell," I said, my eyes and throat burning. "Now you're going to make me cry." Shit. Now I was crying too. Big, thick tears poured out of my eyes, like the emotions of the past weeks just starting to make their appearance.

"I'm already crying," said Elsa as she grabbed Jimmy into a hug, which had his head smacking into her armpit.

"Me too," said Jade as she squeezed herself into their hug. After another squeeze, Jade released her hold and stepped back. "Who wants coffee?"

"Me," I said, suddenly realizing how tired I was.

"I'll have one too," said Jimmy, his eyes round with excitement. "I haven't had a coffee in… more than sixty-eight years."

Damn. The poor man hadn't had food or anything to drink all this time. Damn that Auria. I was pretty sure I hated her even more now.

We all watched in silence as Jimmy accepted a steaming cup of hot coffee and took a sip. When he started to cry, hell, we all started to cry again. Damn, what a day.

"I wish Cedric were here to see Jimmy," said Elsa, rubbing her locket.

"How long were you married?" I asked her, guessing she was talking about her dead husband.

Elsa blinked some tears from her eyes. "Thirty-seven years. He loved Jimmy. He would have been so happy to see him like this. The two were very close."

"What happened to him?"

"He died in his sleep. Healers say it was a heart attack."

I felt a heavy pang in my chest. "I'm sorry, Elsa."

Elsa sniffed as she leaned over and popped open the vintage

locket. "He's always with me." And there, resting inside the locket, was a lock of brown hair.

"He had good hair," I told her, my chest squeezing at her smile.

"He did." Elsa snapped the locket shut and kept her hand on it, visibly shaking from a rush of emotions. She cleared her throat. "You hungry, Jimmy?" she called out. "I'll make you anything you want. Just say it."

Jimmy grinned. "Bacon and eggs would be great."

Elsa flashed him a smile. "Consider it done."

A few minutes later, rumors of Jimmy's miraculous transformation spread throughout the thirteenth floor, and soon my apartment was filled with every single tenant on that floor.

"It's nice to meet you man to man," said an older paranormal man whose name I couldn't remember.

"You're just as cute as you were when you were that dog," said Barb.

"You're short," chorused the twins.

My heart swelled with emotion again. Just seeing Jimmy's happy human face made everything okay.

And then my heart started to speed up, not because of Jimmy, but because of the big, husky man who just sauntered in.

Valen walked into my apartment, all smiles, as he shook Jimmy's hand and, with the other, gave him a manly pat on the shoulder.

I traced my eyes slowly over the giant—yes, the giant. It was still mind-blowing. I took him in. All in. My eyes grazed over him very, very slowly. I saw the confidence, the strength in those broad shoulders and muscular arms, and that hard chest I'd been lucky enough to feel with my face.

"OH GOOD. YOU'RE STILL HERE."

I turned around to see Basil standing behind me. "Yeah. I haven't packed yet." I was so tired. I was hoping they'd let me sleep off some of the exhaustion. But it didn't look like it. "I'll be gone in an hour. If that's why you're here."

Basil shook his head, and I noticed the bags under his eyes. He hadn't slept yet either. "It's been a rough night." He blinked at me. "I'm told you were the one who found Raymond and defeated him."

"I found him on the roof. But we all defeated him. Well... his demons."

"But you closed the Rift."

I nodded. "I did."

"So Elsa told me," said the hotel manager. "Never imagined Raymond would do this. I thought he liked his job. I thought he liked me."

"Pretty sure he hated you."

"I know that now." The short witch exhaled. "What a disaster."

"At least you were able to stop Adele and her plans to destroy the hotel."

Basil frowned and stroked his beard with his fingers. "Yes. I'm glad *that* is over. Glad I still have a job."

I pursed my lips. "Good for you, I guess." What the hell did he want? A pat on the back?

Basil cleared his throat. "I'm sorry I fired you. It was a bit hasty. I wasn't myself."

"We were all under a lot of pressure," I told him.

The hotel manager sighed. "Well, if you'll reconsider working for us, the hotel would like to extend a permanent position."

My pulse raced. "Really?"

The witch smiled at me. This time it was a true, genuine grin. "We owe you a lot. The owners feel that having you here full-time would put their minds at ease. They want a Merlin assigned to the hotel permanently."

"And Valen?" I asked. "I know the hotel hired him. I don't want to take his job."

Basil waved a hand at me. "No, no, no. Your jobs might be

interlinked, but we need you both. You each have different responsibilities. So, what do you say?"

"Yes. I'll take it. Thanks." I shook his hand when he offered it.

Basil gave me a nod and walked away. I watched him make his way around the paranormals to Jimmy.

I stood for a moment, emotions high, as I felt a sense of pride and joy mixing with a sense of relief. Faces blurred as I cast my gaze around them, their voices distant, like hearing them from a radio far away.

I got my job back.

I felt eyes on me and darted my gaze back to where Jimmy was. Valen was watching me from across the apartment and gave me one of his drool-worthy smiles.

My heart sped up as I found myself incapable of looking away. I smiled back as a fluster rushed through me at the memory of our kiss, practically hitting me in the face. Those dark eyes had held both a promise and a desire.

Valen, the rude guy I'd bumped into on the street, turned out not so bad after all. He was a rare race of paranormal—a giant, watcher, and protector, and he'd done just that. He'd saved my ass twice.

We held each other's gaze for a moment, my body prickling and reacting to the heat between us.

Damn. Damn. Damn.

I didn't want to be in a relationship with anyone at the moment, not after the years I'd spent in a bad marriage. I wanted time alone. To be myself. Time for me. I didn't want to get involved with someone who clearly had some serious baggage.

But then… then there was Valen.

Yup, I was definitely in trouble.

KIM RICHARDSON

CHAPTER 1

I hadn't seen or heard from Valen since we'd removed the curse from Jimmy and put him back in his human body. That was five days ago. Maybe the giant was avoiding me. Perhaps he regretted the kiss he'd planted on me. Just thinking about the kiss sent a flash of heat through my nether regions. But it didn't stop me from doing a little research on my own.

I spent days browsing every Google link, trying to decipher myth from reality, because sometimes fairy tales hid a bit of truth. I didn't want to overlook anything. We'd all heard the stories and seen the movies about vampires and werewolves, and they were as real as you and me. So why not giants?

Still, I couldn't find much on giants. I'd discovered from human mythology that giants were described as stupid and violent monsters, sometimes said to eat humans. That totally wasn't like Valen at all.

Yes, he was violent. I'd seen it with my own eyes. But that was because he had protected me and the others from demons who wanted to eat our faces. He'd described himself to me as a protector, a watcher. So the stuff on the internet was a bust, despite my best efforts.

I'd even searched the Merlins' mainframe database and was

seriously disappointed when I found nothing. Only when I'd called the Gray Council and spoken to one of their secretaries to ask for permission to look at their archives here in New York City did I find anything of real value.

"Can you point me in the direction of giants? I'd like to see everything you've got on them," I'd told a frowning old man, who'd gone bald many years ago, as he sat at the archives' front desk.

"*Giants?*" he'd repeated, like I was a simpleton.

"That's what I said. *Giants,*" I repeated, louder than was necessary.

"Why? Giants have been extinct for hundreds of years. I'm afraid someone is leading you on a ghost hunt."

He was wrong, but at least he knew they were real. "So, where to?"

Even though the old bookkeeper thought I was mental, in the end, he took me to a restricted section and handed me a single, thin tome.

"Here," he said. "It's the only material we have on giants. Written by Theodore Paine himself, head of the White witch court at the time."

I'd never heard of Theodore Paine, but the tome dated back three hundred years. It seemed to be a journal of sorts, depicting his own experience with a giant called Otar.

From his entries, I'd learned both parents didn't need to be giants in order to produce a giant offspring. Interesting. Female giants were often barren, most suffering stillbirths and miscarriages if they did become pregnant. I'd learned these facts because, apparently, the Gray Council had taken to trying and breeding an army of giants to protect them. However, according to the entries, that hadn't gone all that well, and many babies had died.

And like us, giants had demon blood. They were descendants of a demon called Gigas, described as big as a house, though the giants were considerably smaller.

Unmatched in their strength, giants also possessed healing abilities. I believed that after the direct contact with Valen's skin while riding on his shoulder had healed my wounds. This just validated that.

I couldn't find anything about a giant's glamour or other abilities, but I'd experienced them as well, so there was that.

After my discovery in the archives, I decided to take a more hands-on approach to my research.

I decided to stalk Valen.

Yup. I was a total stalker. For the last three nights in a row, I'd waited on the roof of the Twilight Hotel around midnight. All three nights, I'd caught glimpses of Valen taking his clothes off in the alley between his restaurant and the hotel. Then, with a flash of light, he transformed into his magnificent giant self—all naked, all glorious, and all very *big*.

I wanted to see what he did without having me tag along, like that night when I sat on his shoulder. At first, it was easy enough to follow him. I blended in with the Manhattan crowds, the human population oblivious that they had a giant strolling among them, and protecting them, as I followed him through the streets.

But when Valen leaped and soared to the rooftop of some building, I couldn't follow. If I could fly, I would have, but I didn't have a flying broom or magical levitation spells. I wasn't that kind of witch. Some magical aspects were just out of reach for a Starlight witch.

My body fluttered with warmth at the memory of the kiss we'd shared a few days ago. It had only been a kiss, but you'd think by how my body was reacting, we'd done the assault-with-a-friendly-weapon more than once.

"Earth to Leana?"

"Hmmm?" I turned and found Jade standing next to me in the hotel lobby, her blonde hair done up like a beehive. Pink, plastic earrings hung from her ears, grazing her denim jacket. She didn't have her roller blades on today. Instead, she'd opted for a pair of black-and-white Converse sneakers.

Right above her, secured over the lobby's front entrance, a sign read CASINO WEEK AT THE TWILIGHT HOTEL.

After the dealings with the Rifts and the demons, guests avoided the Twilight Hotel like the plague. Word had spread of the deaths, and although we'd handled the issue, the hotel was only filled to a quarter capacity, if I were being generous. It felt like less than that.

Basil had the idea of hosting a casino event to get more guests to stay at the hotel and, in turn, keep his job. The lobby and conference rooms were transformed into game rooms with blackjack, baccarat, roulette, poker tables, and way more slot machines than were necessary.

I spotted Errol in an expensive blue three-piece suit, his pale skin practically translucent. He was adjusting an A-frame floor sign next to the front counter that read CASINO CHIP EXCHANGE—NO REFUNDS! He caught me staring and sent a disdainful look in my direction. With his sharp features and jerky movements, he really did look like a lizard, now that I knew his shifter animal.

Today was the first day of Casino Week, and so far, only three guests were sitting at a blackjack table in the lobby. Two females were nestled next to Julian, who caught me looking and flashed me a you-know-I'm-getting-laid-tonight kind of grin. The other was an elderly witch male, who kept hitting his cane at one of the slot machines. Guess he couldn't magic his winnings.

Errol dragged another A-frame floor sign across the lobby and settled it at the entrance. This one read NO MAGIC USE ALLOWED ON THE GAMES. CHEATERS WILL BE CURSED AND REMOVED.

In fact, a group of very powerful witches and wizards had come this morning to put special wards and spells to keep magical practitioners from cheating. They could try, but they'd end up with a nasty case of hives or warts—their call.

Sounded acceptable to me, if only we had more guests.

"You're totally gone," said Jade, pulling my attention back to her and seeing her smile. "I'd love to know what you're thinking about. Is it dirty? I bet it's dirty. It is. Isn't it?"

Yup. Yup. Yup. "No. Just… thinking about boring stuff."

Jade snorted. "Sure. I bet you're thinking about a certain *giant*," she added with a whisper.

Damn her perception. "He might have circled around my thoughts."

The five of us, including Jimmy, had sworn not to tell anyone about Valen being a giant. The guy hadn't shared his true nature with anyone apart from the hotel owners and Basil, and he had only revealed himself to us to save our asses. We decided to respect that and keep his secret to ourselves.

"Where is he, by the way?"

"Who?"

Jade rolled her eyes. "Valen. You know, the not-so-grumpy-anymore-since-he's-met-you restaurant owner?"

I shrugged. "No idea. I haven't seen him in a while." Total lie. I'd seen him last night.

The way Jade was staring at me told me she didn't buy a single word coming out of my mouth. "Well, I think you've changed him."

My pulse gave a tug. "How so?"

Jade attempted to brush a strand of hair, but when she touched the side of her hair, the entire section moved like a single entity, like it was superglued. "He's not so grumpy anymore. Haven't you noticed? He's not smiling or doing anything that crazy, but he's… nicer. A lot nicer. And I think that's because of you."

I made a face. "No, it isn't. I barely know the guy. Why would I have any effect on him?" But her words had my pulse racing, and heat pooled around my middle.

"Because you do," said Jade. "He's different now. You've had a real effect on him. I can tell."

"What can you tell?" asked a female voice.

We spun to see Elsa joining us. Her mess of curly red hair

brushed against her deep-orange blouse. As she walked forward, green garden clogs peeked from under a long, navy skirt.

"That Valen is into Leana," answered Jade with a grin.

"I could have told you that," replied the older witch, smiling, her blue eyes lined with crow's feet. "He lusts over her."

Heat rushed to my face. "I don't think so. Besides, I don't think he's over his wife's death. Not that he should be. I mean, if I loved someone deeply, and they were taken away from me too soon by a horrible disease, I probably wouldn't be over them either." No. It just made me like him even more.

Elsa smacked my arm harder than necessary. "Don't talk like that. No one deserves to be alone. I'm sure his wife wouldn't want him to be lonely. You can love again, you know. Have more than one love in your life."

"Says the witch who keeps the locks of her dead husband close to her neck," said Jade, eyeing the vintage locket hanging from Elsa's neck.

Elsa stiffened and grabbed her pendant. "That's different. I choose to be alone. Cedric was my one and only true love, and I know in my heart I will never love again. And I'm okay with that. I have no regrets. I'm perfectly content. I feel lucky to have had a great love. Not everyone can say that. And I don't need another."

"You're really lucky," I told her, meaning every word.

Elsa wrapped her hands around her locket. "I know. I'm one of the lucky ones."

I didn't need a great love, or a man, to feel happy, but having experienced a great love the way Elsa had did sound amazing. Not everyone was so lucky, though. I'd married a man who'd tried to kill me in a back alley just because I'd broken his penis. That was my luck.

I hadn't seen or heard from Martin since, and I was hoping he'd gotten the message from Valen—the I'll-pound-your-head-in-if-you-come-near-her-again message.

I'd seen something dark in Martin's eyes that day—blurry, but

I'd seen it. Maybe it was more of a feeling, an instinct, that told me he wouldn't let it go.

A tiny man with a tuft of white hair and a matching white beard stepped into my line of sight. His dark suit fit him perfectly, and his typical pale skin was blotched in red.

Basil, the hotel manager, marched over, his eyes wide under his glasses. "What are you doing? You're supposed to be greeting the guests, not chitchatting with your friends."

He pushed his round glasses up his nose, his fingers trembling lightly. The scent of pine needles and earth hit me, along with a familiar prick of energy.

His magic was in full mode, like it was leaking out of him. That happened when witches were upset or in a battle. The guy was stressed.

"You told me to be in the lobby at one p.m., and here I am," I told the small witch. "I'd greet the guests if there *were* actual guests. What else do you want?"

"The hotel is paying you," said Basil, eyeing the main entrance door behind me. "You are an employee, and your job requirement is to welcome the guests—oh! Here they come now!"

I turned to see a middle-aged couple, dressed in expensive-looking clothes and wearing identical looks of disdain, walk through the front doors, their eyes traveling over the game tables.

Basil grabbed me by the arm with strength that surprised me, given his size, and hauled me with him.

"Hello, hello! Welcome, welcome!" said Basil, his voice high as he addressed the new guests. "Welcome to Casino Week, where games are your heart's desire. We have everything you could wish for. We have themed game rooms, dice, blackjack, roulette tables, and slot machines."

The couple stared at Basil like they thought he was insane. He did sound a little mad, if not a whole lot desperate.

When their eyes flicked over the lobby with concerned brows, Basil blurted, "This is Leana, the hotel's Merlin." He pushed me forward as I gave them an awkward smile. "She singled-handily defeated the demon that had taken residence in the hotel."

I noticed how he said "demon," like there had only been the one.

"She's the Starlight witch everyone's talking about. Say hello, Leana."

"Hello, Leana," I said, feeling like a pet Labrador retriever.

The couple seemed to visibly relax at this bit of news, though I wasn't sure I appreciated him parading me around in hopes of having the guests unwind and stay. Especially the part where he disclosed my magical attributes. Not good.

"Let me get you settled in." Basil ushered the new couple to the front desk to an awaiting, disgusted Errol.

"Do you feel dirty?" asked Jade as she joined me.

"No, why?"

"To be used like that?" she added with a smirk. "He's whoring you around to the guests. You do know that. Right?"

"Leave her alone," said Elsa as she stood with her hands on her hips, watching Basil with a frown. Guess she didn't like it either.

"Oh, there's Jimmy." Jade gestured to the conference room, now a game room, where Jimmy came strolling out. A dark suit wrapped his lean frame. His light hair was shorter than it had been, telling me he'd gotten a haircut. He smiled at the guests, his back straight, as he walked with a nice confident gait.

"He seems to be enjoying his new post," I said. "Assistant manager suits him. He knows the hotel better than Basil, so he's perfect for the job." The post had opened after the late assistant manager, Raymond, had been killed… or rather fell into a Rift and then was most probably killed by the hundreds of demons waiting on the other side. Jimmy hadn't wasted a single second and had asked for the job, which Basil had happily given him.

After the curse was removed, Jimmy took one of the vacant apartments previously belonging to one of the families, who did not return to the thirteenth floor after the demon attacks. With his own place and a new job, our Jimmy looked complete.

"He looks very happy," said Elsa. "But I do miss the toy dog. He was so cute."

I laughed. "He was, but don't tell him that."

"He looks great. Doesn't he?" said Jade with a strange, dreamy expression on her face, like she was staring at Jon Bon Jovi.

"He does." I nodded. "And it looks like he's coming our way."

Jimmy's face beamed as he took us all in. "Ladies," he said, and Jade's face flamed a bright red.

It looked like Jade was developing a crush. I bit the inside of my cheek to keep from laughing. "Assistant manager," I teased, bowing my head.

Jimmy laughed as he tapped his flashing name tag. "Has a good ring to it."

"It does. It's the perfect job for you." Basil couldn't have found a more eager and perfect assistant. "You looking for someone?"

Jimmy nodded. "Yeah. You, actually. This just came in." He handed me a small white envelope.

I took it. "Who's it from?"

"The Gray Council," he answered as my eyes found the inscription on the front.

The Gray Council? I'd never received a letter from them before. Why would they send me a letter when they could reach me by phone? I wasn't sure how I felt about that.

Elsa crossed her arms over her chest. "I'll never understand why they can't contact people through email like everyone else. They're still in the Stone Age. I wonder what they want?"

"Maybe you're going to get a promotion!" said Jade, excitement in her voice. "Or maybe that's a big bonus check. You can finally get that car you wanted."

I shook my head. "No. The hotel pays me. Not the council." I tore open the envelope, hating my shaking hands, and took a breath as I read the letter.

• • •

Dear Leana Fairchild,

This letter confirms that we will be investigating a matter that concerns you. A complaint has been made about your conduct. We can change or add to these concerns in light of our investigation. We take all complaints seriously and will investigate thoroughly and fairly. After the investigation, a decision will be made as to whether further action (including disciplinary action) is needed.

You must cooperate with our investigations and answer any queries. We will set up a time to meet with you and give you a full opportunity to provide your account of events.

Yours sincerely,
Clive Vespertine
Gray Council

"What's it say?" asked Jade. "You look pale, like you're about to throw up."

I stuffed the letter back inside the envelope. "There's going to be an investigation. Someone has launched a complaint about me. And I bet I know who."

"Who?" Jimmy was watching me with a frown.

"The only person I pissed off lately whose ass sits on the White witch council," I told them, my heart pounding as anger swept through me.

"Adele?" Elsa's face twisted in horror. "You think so? You think she would do that?"

I nodded. "I do. This is her. For the Gray Council to open an investigation for someone means that someone must have some power and leverage. Merlins are always bad-mouthing each other, comes with the job, but we don't seek to ruin others. And we keep our problems within the Merlin group. We don't go crying to the Gray Council. Ever."

I knew Adele didn't like me and was pissed that, with the help of my friends, we'd managed to save the hotel and expose her psychotic plans. This was her payback.

"Okay, so what?" asked Jimmy. "You didn't do anything wrong. We can attest to that to the investigator. We know what happened."

"It's easy to twist the truth," I told them. "She could have told them I put everyone's lives in danger when I refused to help her force people out of the hotel when I knew there were demons. She could make it seem like I was responsible for some of the deaths. Like maybe I should have come forward sooner. She can make it look horrible."

Elsa was shaking her head. "So, what does that mean?"

I let out a breath. "It means, if I'm found guilty of whatever trumped-up charges, or if they think I've done something wrong, then… then… I'll lose my license and my job. I'll lose everything."

CHAPTER 2

After spending the rest of the day forcing myself to smile as I welcomed guests, which was just another handful, I was back inside my apartment. My anger was making me on edge, and I wanted to punch something, preferably Adele's face. Still, the way Errol kept throwing me snotty glances and correcting me as I explained the game table settings, I'd settle for his ugly face.

I was irritable, and Basil finally told me to leave around 7:00 p.m. "Go have a rest. You look like you need a break. But I expect you back here tonight. Tonight, more guests will come. You'll see. It'll be just like the old days. We'll have to turn away guests!"

He was so happy at the thought I didn't have the heart to tell him I doubted it. Casino Week was a great idea. I just didn't think the paranormal community would easily forget what had happened here. A lot of ugly rumors were circulating, one in particular that demons were still in the hotel, and management had lied to keep their jobs and the hotel open. And well, it seemed it was keeping guests away.

I paced my apartment, clenching and unclenching my fingers as a deep dread filled my gut. If I lost my Merlin's license, I'd lose my position here. I liked it here. I liked the people. They felt like family, and I didn't want to lose them.

If Adele wanted me sacked, she was pulling all her cards to make it happen. Sure, she could have my Merlin's license, but that didn't mean I couldn't find work as a witch for hire. I could be a private paranormal investigator, a rogue agent, or just a plain witch for hire.

There were other ways to make a living. She wouldn't get rid of me that easily, and I wasn't going to sit back and let her ruin my reputation either.

The letter hadn't said when they would send an investigator, just that there would be one. That being said, I was pretty sure they would send someone local—someone who'd done this before with loads of experience.

Valen knew a lot of people in the paranormal community. I was willing to bet he knew who they would send as an investigator.

I yanked out my phone and decided to text him at the phone number Basil had given me. Yeah, okay, I'd told him it was for work stuff, so he had grudgingly given it to me.

Me: *Hi it's Leana. Do you know any investigators who work for the Gray Council?*

I stared at the text, feeling both nervous and stupid. Then I changed my mind and erased it. It would be better if we spoke. I could show him the letter. Plus, then he wouldn't know I'd gotten his phone number.

Using that as an excuse—because we all know I'd use any excuse to talk to the giant again and see how he'd react to seeing me—I grabbed a jacket, looped my shoulder bag over my neck, and left my apartment. After a short elevator ride, I found myself back in the lobby, which was practically deserted.

"Leana! Want to join us?" Julian sat at the same blackjack table he'd been at since this afternoon. The only difference was he was surrounded by four females, all trying to get his special attention. Everyone was different, in terms of age and weight. The only thing they had in common was how they were all glaring at me. Clearly, they didn't want any more competition.

I laughed. "Maybe later, *darling.*" I winked at the females. Their collective anger made me all giddy inside.

I spotted Elsa and Jade bickering at one of the slot machines. I hoped they didn't spend too much money on these things.

I thought about going over there but then changed my mind and made for the front doors.

"Leana! Where are you going?" shouted Basil, marching toward me, as red-faced as this morning. If he didn't calm down, he was going to give himself a heart attack. "You need to be here!"

"I need to step out for a bit. Be right back. Promise." I pushed the doors open and hit the sidewalk. The doors closing behind me cut off whatever Basil was shouting after me.

I had no idea why he was yelling. The guy had told me to take a break. This was me taking a break.

I walked over to the building next door, Valen's restaurant, my heart thrashing the whole time, like I'd jogged here. I was nervous. Why was I nervous?

The AFTER DARK sign was illuminated in soft red lights as I walked under it. The restaurant door banged behind me as I went in. The familiar smells of cooked food were welcoming. My friends and I had eaten here twice since the whole demon episode with Raymond, but Valen wasn't around either time. Or at least, that's what the hostess had told us. Whether that was true or not, I didn't know. But she was annoyingly loyal to the giant. He could have been in his office.

The interior housed modern dark-gray seats and tables in an open-concept room, with twelve-foot ceilings and exposed beams and pipes. Floor-to-ceiling windows at the front let in the last of the evening light.

The lighting was dim. Most of the tables were occupied by paranormals enjoying their dinner. None of them glanced up as I strolled through. They were all preoccupied with their meals, and I didn't blame them. The food here was incredible.

"Eating alone?"

I looked up to the sound of the voice and saw the same irritating hostess standing behind her podium. She had long, flowing brown hair, a perfectly tight body under her white blouse, and I was guessing a black skirt behind the counter. She was pretty, cold-pretty, if that was even a thing. But if you looked closely enough, her skin had a subtle rippled effect, and I swear for a second, I saw gills. Maybe she was a mermaid.

Valen had told me her name, and of course, I'd forgotten it the moment it left his lips.

"No. I'm actually looking for Valen."

If she told me he wasn't here, again, I would deep-fry her and serve her bits to the guests at the hotel.

Her face went from blank to her lips curling at the corners. "He's busy at the moment," she said, tapping her long fingers with blue fingernails on the counter.

Okay, cue in the anger now. "It's important."

The hostess gave me a mocking smile. "Of course, it is. It's always important with you. Isn't it? Always more important than anyone else."

"That's because it is." That's it. I was going to smack that grin off her face.

The hostess laughed, actually laughed. "He's over there." She pointed to the left, to a spot across the restaurant.

I cast my gaze to where she gestured, and my heart sank, heat rushing to my face like I'd poured hot coffee over it.

Valen *was* here. I hadn't spotted him when I came in. Trouble was, he wasn't alone.

A beautiful blonde sat across from him with her hand over his. The way they were both leaning across the table to get closer to each other told me this was a very intimate encounter. They were so close they could probably kiss at that distance.

Worse was that he was… smiling. Valen was *smiling*—a pretty rare emotion for him. I could count how many times I'd seen him smile. Okay, maybe not. But it was few and far between.

I'd never seen this woman before. Maybe she was his girlfriend? Was he dating her? Was she the reason he'd pulled back from our kiss? Well, if he had a girlfriend, he had no business kissing me at all. Jimmy had said that Valen had *many* girlfriends. He was a fool if he thought I was okay being in his harem.

The hostess leaned over the counter, her expression giddy at what she saw on my face. "Told you he was busy. But by all means… go see him. I'm sure he won't mind you *disturbing* him right now."

I stiffened, and a flame of anger hardened my insides. Without another word, I turned on the spot and headed back out of the restaurant. The laughter from the hostess only added more heat to my face, like I had a mega sunburn.

I knew I was acting like an immature fool. He wasn't mine, and we were by no means a couple. He could date or sleep with whoever he wanted. And now I'd basically told the world how I felt about him with my reaction. *Nice one, Leana.*

That hostess would have a real laugh at my expense. She already had.

I was humiliated, and I felt let down. I'd been an idiot to think Valen and I had shared something special. Apparently, it was all in my head.

With my heart pounding, I pulled open the door and marched out. I hit the street, turned right at the first block, and kept going, my legs pumping with a charge of adrenaline. My pace was fast, and I kept it without slowing down. Cars and cabs honked as I crossed the street, but I barely noticed.

While I walked, I kept replaying that kiss over and over again. I wasn't perfect, and sometimes I wasn't as strong as I thought, my emotions taking over my mind. I hated when that happened. It meant I couldn't think straight. That my feelings got in the way of making decisions.

I needed to be rational. I needed to think with my head and not my heart. Because this was how people got hurt. I knew if I wanted to keep my job and live in the Twilight Hotel, I needed to push away these feelings and learn to live with the giant since he was so near and had such a close connection with the hotel.

And I knew I could never share a kiss with Valen ever again.

I let out a long breath as I reeled in all those conflicting emotions. It wasn't the end of the world. So, the guy had many women in his life. I wasn't about to let it break me down into a thousand sad pieces. It would take a hell of a lot more to break me. All this meant was Valen and I weren't meant to be. It was that simple.

And with that thought in my head, I walked straighter, feeling better that I had chatted with myself. Of course, chatting with oneself happened a lot over forty.

The moon was a solid, glowing white disk in the inky sky. The lengthening shadows began to trigger streetlights as the town's skyline cast deep, cold shadows over me. Even surrounded by tall buildings, I still felt it was darker than it should be.

I slowed to a stop, realizing I had walked off, not caring where I was going. And looking around now, I was somewhere behind the hotel on one of the small side streets, more like an alley. Still, it shouldn't be this dark.

Dark windows stared back at me from the neighboring buildings. The streets were quieter than usual for a Friday night as darkness rushed in, filling the spaces not lit by the streetlights.

That's right. It was Friday night. I should have been having fun, not walking off my emotions.

"I should be playing at the game tables with the girls," I muttered.

I spun around and smiled at the thought of enjoying a nice glass of wine and laughing at Elsa as she lost more money at the slot machine.

Small pools of water from last night's rain cast silvery hues from the moonlight. I walked faster, wrinkling my nose at the sudden stench of garbage. I'd been so focused before that I hadn't even noticed it, which seemed nearly impossible given how potent it was. The stench was a mix of dirty feet, smoke, and rot, like the bins hadn't been picked up in weeks.

Holding my breath, I kept going. My eyes flicked to the large metal garbage bin next to one of the buildings.

And then I halted.

There, sticking out from a pile of black garbage bags, at the base of the bin, was a leg.

No, *two* legs.

"What the hell?"

I stepped forward, still holding my breath, and clasped my hand over my mouth.

There wasn't just one pair of legs. There were three. Three bodies, judging by the degree of decomposition. I yanked out my phone and switched on the flashlight.

I could make out the first body as a male. The others were piled under him, and I wasn't about to touch them without gloves —no need to be putting my DNA on that.

Judging by the waxy, gray color of his skin, the blue on the tips of his fingers, and the pale lips, the body was still in the "fresh stage" and hadn't begun the second stage of decomposition, which put his death around the six-to-twelve-hour mark, if I had to guess.

But the fact that I'd just discovered three dead bodies wasn't the reason I nearly dropped my phone or felt the sudden spike of dread in my gut.

It was the long canines peering from the lips of the dead male.

"Holy shit. You're paranormals."

CHAPTER 3

"What do you think happened to them?" Jade had a cloth over her mouth as she leaned over the three cadavers. "God, they stink." She pulled out a small perfume sample mini bottle and sprayed the air above the dead in great big arcs. She was contaminating the scene, but I didn't see the point in stopping her. It was too late now.

I shook my head, a dark feeling creeping into my gut. "No idea. And why are they here? Like someone just dumped them next to a human garbage bin."

"Because whoever dumped them was hoping for the human police to find them," answered Elsa, her fingers fumbling with her locket, something I now realized she did when she was nervous and stressed.

Julian was leaning over the bodies, next to Jade, with his mouth open. I knew he was breathing through it to avoid the stench, but that seemed worse to me. "This poor bastard's a vampire. Are they all paranormals? I can't see the faces of the two others. They could have thrown the vamp in with a couple of dead humans and hoped no one would notice his fangs. It's possible they didn't know he was a vamp."

I was surprised he'd ditched his lady friends to come and help when I called Jade. It meant a lot.

"Let's find out." I looked at Elsa. "Did you bring me some gloves like I asked?"

"Here." Elsa drew yellow kitchen gloves from her soft cloth bag. At my reaction, she said, "I'm not a healer. I don't have latex gloves at my disposal. It's all I could find on such short notice."

"It's fine. Thank you." I pulled on the kitchen gloves, grabbed the dead vamp's leg, and began dragging him off the others. "Damn. He's a heavy sonofabitch." I'd barely pulled him halfway when I felt resistance, like he was tangled with the others.

"Let me help." Julian joined me, grabbing the other leg with a pair of blue latex gloves, which appeared out of nowhere. He easily hauled the dead vamp to a spot on the pavement.

Seeing as he was a lot stronger than me, I let Julian pull the other two bodies next to the bin until he'd lined them up, side by side, on the pavement. The streetlight illuminated enough of their faces to see that one of the dead was female. The other two were males.

"Are they all vampires, you think?" asked Jade, the cloth still over her mouth.

I'd gotten used to the smell now. What did that say about me? "Let's see." I knelt next to the female and gently lifted her top lip. "She's got sharp canines. Yeah. Wait a second. Something's here." I grabbed my phone from my pocket and flashed the flashlight over the dead female. "Look. She's got a hairy neck."

"That's something I never want to hear again," said Julian, looking mortified.

I rolled my eyes. "Well, she does." I grabbed the female's hand. "It's more like fur. She's got furry hands too. And I'm pretty sure she's got some seriously woolly toes."

"Urgh." Julian shook his body like he'd just felt some cold shiver running over him.

"She's not a vampire." Elsa's clogs appeared at my side as she leaned over me. "She's a werewolf or some kind of shifter.

Vampires don't like hair on their bodies." She caught my eye and added, "So, I've been told."

"What about the other guy?" asked Jade. "Is he a werewolf too?"

I crabbed-walked over to the next one and checked his teeth. "Canines. No signs of fur on him. Vampire." I leaned back on my heels. "So, one werewolf and two vampires. Killed and then tossed here like garbage? That doesn't make a lot of sense."

I was glad the alley was nearly completely covered in darkness. I wouldn't want some wandering human to happen upon us because that would be bad. We didn't need the human police involved here. This was clearly a paranormal issue.

Elsa took a breath and let it out. "It means whoever did this didn't give two hoots about these people." I had to agree with her on that.

"What do you think killed them?" asked Jade.

I let out a sigh. "I can't see any blood. Let's see if I can find signs of a struggle or something." I moved to the closest dead vampire and checked his neck and arms. When I lifted his shirt to check for wounds, I saw a smooth chest—a decomposing one, mind you, but so far, no cuts, bruises, nothing that would give us an idea of how he died.

"Maybe she was boning both dudes, and they got in a fight," said Julian. "Jealousy is an ugly thing. Plays with the mind."

"Okay. Say that's true. So one of the vampires kills the other vampire for stealing his girl, and then kills the girl and offs himself? That doesn't sound like a vampire. And there'd be blood. Lots and lots of blood."

"She's right," agreed Elsa. "Vampires are brutal. When they fight, it's usually to the very violent end. I'm not seeing any signs of violence here."

Jade lifted the cloth from her face. "What about poison? That could be it if there's no sign of violence. I bet they were poisoned."

I looked at Julian. "You're the poison expert. What do you think?"

Julian knelt next to me and shone his phone's flashlight over the corpse's lips. Then he carefully opened their eyes one by one. When he was done, he stood up. "It's not poison."

"How can you tell?" I asked.

He pointed with his free hand. "See their lips? If it was poison, they'd have sores around the mouth. And their pupils are normal. They would be enlarged and red. They're not. And there's usually a lingering smell when poisoned."

I frowned. "You mean this isn't smelly enough for you?"

The male witch shook his head. "No, what I mean is that each poison gives off a certain smell. If they were poisoned, I'd be able to smell it and tell you which poison was used."

"I'm not sure how I feel about that," I told him with a smile. Yet, part of me was impressed. I knew next to nothing about poisons. Julian clearly was a master of his craft.

Elsa wrapped her arms around herself. "How dreadful. Their families must be worried sick."

Something occurred to me. "They've been dead for a while... how come we didn't hear of anyone missing?" The paranormal community was small and tight. We took care of our own. If some were missing, we should have heard something. Even Valen. He would have known and would have been looking for them.

"I'll check their IDs." I checked the vampire closest to me first, feeling bad that I had to go through his pockets, but I didn't have a choice. "Nothing. No wallet." Weird. Then I checked the last two. Again, nothing. "Okay, this is even weirder. No wallets on any of them. How are we supposed to identify them without their wallets?" And then it hit me. "Because we're not supposed to."

"I don't like the sound of that," said Elsa. "Sounds premeditated."

"Yeah, it does," I said. "Whoever did this, I'm willing to bet they're hoping they'd be found by the human police and marked off as John and Jane Does. Problem solved." Pretty psychotic.

"Maybe they were robbed?" Jade's worried face was cast in shadow. "It's New York City. A lot of people get mugged here. Maybe they were killed and robbed by humans."

"But that's just it," I told her. "They weren't. There're no wounds on the bodies. Humans couldn't have done this. Not to mention that paranormals can easily get rid of a few human muggers. We'd be staring at dead humans, if that were the case. Not dead vampires and a shifter."

The longer I thought about why or who had killed these paranormals, the worse I felt. The fact that we had found no evidence of how they died left a dark feeling wrapped around my chest.

"I don't think they were killed here," I said, knowing it was true. "It would explain the lack of evidence and blood and why they were dumped. They were killed somewhere else."

"So, who did this, then? And why?" Elsa's eyes were round, the whites showing from her eyes in the dark.

"Good question." I looked over my friends' worried faces, sharing their sentiments exactly. "My guess is paranormals. Not humans. But as to why? That's the million-dollar question."

"How did you find them?" Julian was staring at me, and from this angle, shadows covered half his face. "I mean, this is, like, nowhere near the hotel. What were you doing out here?"

My face flushed at the memory of seeing Valen smiling at the pretty blonde, and I was glad for the cloak of darkness. That way, they wouldn't see the redness on my face. I pushed back to my feet, my thighs burning in protest. I needed to do more yoga and stretches. "I went for a walk." I wasn't about to tell my friends about my humiliating episode at Valen's restaurant. Sometimes it was better to keep the humiliation to oneself.

"Here?" Jade turned around on the spot, a frightened expression on her face. "In this creepy alley? With mountains of garbage? At night with places for rapists and muggers to hide?"

My lips parted at the seriousness on her face. "I just went for a walk. Wasn't really paying attention to where I was going." No, because my head was full of Valen.

"Well..." Elsa sighed. "It's good you found them. At least one of us did. Maybe with the help of the courts, we can identify these poor people. They deserve better."

"I agree." I felt sick to my stomach at how callous the scene was. "Let me call Basil. We need the cleanup crew here. He can contact the paranormal courts. See if anyone's gone missing."

Elsa shook her head. "But this is far from the hotel's borders. You sure this isn't maybe Valen's territory?"

"Yeah, call Valen," agreed Julian. "He's the right giant for this job. He might know something."

More heat rushed to my face. "He's busy," I said, my voice rougher than I would have liked. "I went to see him before." I swallowed. "He's not available. So… Basil, it is."

Guilt fluttered through me at lying to my friends, but I just couldn't handle Valen right now. I needed some more time to process what I'd seen. Like a few days. More like a few months.

I pressed Basil's number. After four rings, it went straight to voicemail. "Basil, it's Leana. We found bodies in an alley. Call me back." I ended the call and texted him a 9-1-1. Hopefully, the witch would get the message.

"I doubt he's going to answer," said Jade. "He's really busy with his"—she made finger quotes—"Casino Week."

I shrugged. "He barely has any guests."

"Don't tell him that," laughed Julian.

"Why don't you want to call Valen?" Elsa pressed her hands to her hips, the light of the moon highlighting her red hair. "Did something happen?"

I belted out a fake laugh that came off way too strong. "I didn't say I didn't *want* to call him. I said he was busy."

Elsa pressed her lips into a thin line, searching my face. "I don't believe you."

I cocked a brow. "What makes you say that?" I was a terrible liar.

"Yeah, you're acting weird," said Jade, narrowing her eyes. "Oh, my God! You slept with him!"

"What? No." If I could have melted into the pavement, I would have.

"Yes! You slept with him, and he's not calling you back!" Jade continued and clapped her hands, like she'd just won big at one of the slot machines. "That's why you went to see him just now. You wanted to confront him."

I shook my head. "I wanted to ask him about the letter I got from the Gray Council. I didn't sleep with him." Who was I kidding? I did want to sleep with him. *Had* wanted. Not anymore.

Jade made a face, clearly sticking to her story. "Yeah, right."

A snort came from Julian, and when I looked at Elsa, she had an I-don't-believe-you smirk on her lips.

"I'll prove it," I told them, feeling nervous all of a sudden as I swiped the screen on my phone. His name was on my list of contacts. Weird. I'd put him as my number one contact and never even remembered doing it. "I'll call him right now."

I didn't want to, but it wasn't like she was giving me a choice. Besides, maybe it was better that Valen got involved. Perhaps he could shed some light on these bodies too. The giant was still a mystery. Who knew what other abilities he had? Maybe he'd know how these paranormals were killed. From the looks of it, the werewolf and two vampires had been in their prime—strong, capable, and healthy.

A werewolf and two vampires, I repeated in my head.

A werewolf and two vampires!

"Hang on." I stuffed my phone back in my pocket, my heart hammering hard.

"Told you," said a smiling Jade. "Sex, sex, sex."

Ignoring her, I stepped forward and leaned over the bodies. "Something's off about them."

"What do you mean?" Elsa joined me. "Like what? Other than they're dead, and we can't seem to figure out how they got that way."

I shook my head. "Not that." I knelt again, knowing in my gut that I was onto something. "They're not giving off any energies."

"What? Are you sure?" Elsa threw her palms over the bodies like she was searching for heat waves. I felt a tug of her magic, like a change in air pressure, and then it was gone. She lowered her hands. "I'm not getting anything either. But maybe that's just because they're dead."

"No, Leana's right." Julian stared at the body with a confused frown. "We should be able to sense something. Even dead paranormals still have an energy pulse. It'd be faint, but I'd sense it. And I'm not sensing anything."

"Me neither," said Jade after a moment of silence.

I rubbed my eyes. "Could be… could be a curse or something to hide their true nature," I said, thinking of Valen. "Let me see if I can dig deeper. See if anyone put a glamour on them."

I took a deep breath and called to that well of magic, the foundation of power from the stars high above me. My hair and clothes lifted as I felt the thrumming of power from the stars. The air hissed with energy, crackling against my skin and tingling like cold pricks.

I yanked on the stars' magical elements and merged them with my own. A sphere of brilliant white hovered over my hand like a miniature star.

Then I blew on my palm.

The globe climbed in the air, and then with a pop, it burst into thousands of tiny stars of light. The miniature stars fired forward, leaving a trail of bright light in their wake like pixie dust, before settling over the three bodies.

I was as connected to my starlight as they were to me. I felt what they felt. And at the moment, all I felt was a whole lot of nothing.

No cold pulses of vampire energy, no prickly tingles from the power of werewolves.

Nothing.

I gave a final tug on my starlight and let them go. Then, with a soft plop, they vanished.

"Nothing," I said. "No glamour and no paranormal vibes."

Jade began to rub her arms. "I don't like this. Nope. Not at all. What do you think it means?"

"I don't know what these are," I said. "But they're not paranormals. It's almost as though… it's almost as though they're human?" I knew that couldn't be, but it still needed to be said.

Julian made a sound in his throat. "But that's impossible. Clearly, they're not. I mean, look at them. Even the biggest idiot can see that they're not human."

"I know, but that's the feeling I got." Staring at the bodies, and seeing with my eyes that they were indeed paranormal, but they didn't *feel* it, was starting to freak me out. "They're paranormals, but they're not paranormals. This is crazy."

"But…" Elsa shared a look with Jade. "If they're not paranormals, what are they?"

"Good question." That was an excellent question. Because if they weren't, I had no idea what they were.

And they were dead.

CHAPTER 4

Basil's cleanup crew—a group of two men and one child—showed up about ten minutes after he'd called me back. Well, the young one looked about fourteen, and in my book, that was a child.

They were dressed in black suits without the sunglasses this time but equipped with medical briefcases. We all stood in silence and watched as the cleanup crew took a few pictures and cataloged the crime scene. But when the kid took out a vial from his briefcase, I couldn't hold it anymore.

"You're a kid?" I said to the youngest of the cleanup crew gang.

The kid, boy, teen, glared at me with brown eyes and a fatty face filled with zits. "I'm not a kid."

I raised a brow. "You've got a kid's voice. Do your parents know what you're doing?"

The teen straightened. "I graduated years before everyone else. I'm one of the best. Better than you old geezers. And now, you're in my way."

I raised my hands in surrender and stepped back. "Go for it."

"Boy genius who likes to pick up dead bodies as his career of choice," said Julian. "Think about that."

Yup, that was creepy. The teen dumped the contents of the vial over the bodies. A sudden prickling of energy rippled over my skin, and then the three corpses rose from the ground, hovering in the air. After the same kid sprinkled some white powder, the bodies disappeared, just as I'd seen happen before, and the cleanup crew left. Three white, misty tethers followed the teen boy, like the bodies were floating behind him.

It took all but about ten minutes, and then it seemed as though the bodies had never been there. But not before I'd taken as many pictures as I could. My memory wasn't as sharp as it had been in my twenties, so every bit of saved information would help.

After leaving Elsa, Jade, and Julian in the lobby at the game tables, I went back to my apartment to start up a file on the two dead vampires and the werewolf. I had kept Eddie, the last Merlin's, laptop and used my dining table as my designated workplace. Call it morbid, but why waste a good computer when I was in the market for one? Besides, we were both Merlins, so that kind of made it mine in a way. Not really, but that's what I told myself.

Eddie, being the highly organized and thorough Merlin he was, had blank files already prepared as templates. So, with a glass of red wine, I began to fill them out with as much detail as possible while they were still fresh in my mind.

I logged on to the Merlin central mainframe, wondering if I'd even be allowed since I was under investigation. But as soon as I typed in my login and password, I was in.

I searched the database for any missing persons and found nothing recent. A witch by the name of Karrin Weber had been missing since 1993, but she was never found, and the case was still open. Other than that, I found nothing. It was possible these paranormals hadn't been missing long enough to alert their loved ones of their disappearance. I'd keep an eye on that.

Next, I searched the database's list of all known paranormals, creatures and all, for a clue as to why I wasn't sensing their energies. But after an hour of exploring all the files, I came up with nothing. According to the database, all paranormals gave off a thrum of energy.

Except for the ones I'd found.

The sound of the floorboards creaking under the carpet pulled me around.

Valen crossed the short hallway in my apartment and came forward.

My heart did a funny bungee jump at the sight of him. The dim light in my apartment only accentuated his rugged good looks—his square jaw, straight nose, and dark, wavy hair brushing his broad shoulders that I wanted to run my hands through.

He wore a brown leather jacket over a black shirt and a pair of dark jeans that fit his slim waist and were snug against his muscular thighs. My eyes rolled over his ridiculously powerful and broad chest, and I wondered what it would feel like to have his hot skin under my palms.

Heat blossomed over me, and I hated that my body reacted this way at seeing him. My hormones were out of control. Maybe I needed meds?

We stared at each other for a moment. My insides felt like they were being rearranged in my belly and swirling up into my throat with an added uncomfortable silence accented by the ticking of the refrigerator.

"Don't you knock?" My voice came out rough. Apparently, I was not over seeing him with that pretty blonde. I really shouldn't be. We weren't a couple or really anything apart from being friends.

Valen's eyes narrowed at my tone. "The door was open."

I pulled my eyes away from him and stared at my screen. "Still, should have knocked. I'm kinda in the middle of something."

"The something being the bodies you found?" He came up right behind me, looking down at my laptop. "You kept Eddie's laptop."

"I did. I didn't think it was right to toss it. It's practically new." I let my head fall back to see his face. "Can I help you with something?" I hated how impersonal my voice was. It was betraying me, betraying what I was feeling for him. I didn't know why I was feeling like this. I was acting like a jealous twenty-year-old girlfriend, which I wasn't. I was a grown-ass woman, and I needed to start acting like it.

Valen leaned back and crossed his arms over his ample chest. "You found bodies in an alley behind the hotel, and I had to hear it from Basil. Why didn't you tell me?"

"I forgot." Which was partly true. The whole thing about the paranormals not giving off energy had kind of thrown me.

"You should have told me," said the giant, his tone a little harder now.

Should've. Could've. Didn't. "I told you, I forgot. Things got a bit strange."

"Strange, how?" His eyes flicked to my computer screen and then back at me. "What did you find?"

Valen had been hired by the Twilight Hotel and was responsible for ensuring the safety of its paranormals and the paranormals in Manhattan. We were both employed by the hotel, and we shared the responsibility. I had a duty to tell him, just like he would if he'd discovered the bodies. He needed to know.

I moved my hands over the keyboard and pulled up the images I'd taken of the dead. "What you see are two dead vamps and a dead werewolf female."

Valen's eyes were fixed on the screen. "Okay."

"No cause of death that we could see. And they didn't give off any energies. No paranormal vibes. It was almost like they were human. But obviously, they're not human. See my dilemma?"

I searched his face for traces of recognition. Possibly he'd seen something like this before, but nothing was there. "Have you seen this before?" I figured I'd give it a shot.

Valen flicked his eyes over to me. "Never. First I've ever heard of something like this. Where are the bodies now?"

"At some paranormal morgue," I answered. "I told Basil to inform them that I wanted autopsies performed on them. I want a cause of death. See if maybe the way they were killed could explain the no-vibes thing. And it wasn't a glamour. I checked. No IDs on them either. I checked my Merlin database for missing persons and got nothing." I let out a sigh. "We have no idea who these people are."

Valen was silent for a moment, giving me a chance to look over his face. His features rippled like he was struggling with something internal, like he wanted to tell me something but couldn't.

"I could have helped you," he said finally, a softness to his voice. "You didn't have to do it alone."

I looked away from his luscious lips, which were seriously distracting me. "I wasn't alone. My friends were with me. Besides, I'm used to working alone. I get my best work done when I'm alone."

Valen let out a breath through his nose, his jaw clenching. "You're angry with me? Why?"

Because you kissed me, and now you're with someone else? "I'm not. Just tired." I gave him a quick smile. I was a horrible liar. But I seriously needed to get my head straight.

Valen's gaze intensified, like he could read my thoughts and knew I was lying. Could giants read minds? God, I hoped not. 'Cause *that* would be embarrassing.

"You came by the restaurant," said Valen. "You didn't stay. Were you looking for me?"

My heart jumped as a new wave of heat rushed from my neck up to my face. Ah, crap. I couldn't lie myself out of this one. "I was. But your hostess—whatever her name is…"

"Simone."

"Told me that you were busy," I continued, watching his reaction, which was nothing apart from staring at me. "So I left."

Valen's face was carefully blank. "What did you need?"

I noticed how he didn't specify what he was busy with, like

that pretty blonde. "I'm being investigated by the Gray Council. Someone… someone of high ranking made a complaint."

"And you think it's Adele," said the giant, pulling the words out of my mouth.

I nodded. "It's the only explanation. I did ruin her plans and expose her."

"It wasn't just you." Valen's eyes traced my face and settled on my lips, sending a jolt of electricity rippling through me.

I cleared my throat. "Maybe not. But she's focused her hatred on me. I think it has to do with me being different, being a Starlight witch. Listen, I came to ask you if you knew of any investigators. I thought if you knew any, it might give me a better chance at being prepared."

Valen ran his fingers through his hair. "The only one I know is Drax. And he's retired now. Moved to Florida."

I let out a breath of air, disappointment running through me. "Okay. Well. Thanks, I guess." I'd just have to wait and see who they were going to send and hope Adele's influence wouldn't be a factor.

An awkward silence followed for a while, my heart making music in my ears in the swirl of conflicting feelings while my entire body thrummed with heat that had nothing to do with my warm apartment.

Part of me wanted to ask about the blonde, but I knew it wasn't my business. Plus, the moment those words left my lips, he'd know I liked him. Liked him a lot.

It didn't help that the giant had saved my ass twice. He was gallant, strong, and sexy as hell… but he wasn't mine. And I didn't share my men.

Valen stepped forward until his knees brushed up against my thigh. "Something else is wrong. What is it?"

I looked away from the giant. How could I tell him without betraying myself? Because I thought I felt something between us, something real. But I wasn't going to be that woman. I was too old for this.

And that's when Jade came in.

The witch hurried through my apartment, took one look between Valen and me, and halted, hands in the air. "Sorry, am I interrupting something?"

"No," Valen and I said at the same time.

"Oookaay," said Jade. "Well, Basil sent me to fetch you. Says he needs you in the lobby, pronto."

"Great. Sounds like fun." Without looking at Valen, I grabbed my bag and jacket and headed out of my apartment behind Jade. I needed to put some space between Valen and me, which would be nearly impossible since he lived next door, at least until I got over these feelings.

But something made me turn around just before exiting the door. I looked over.

Valen stood there next to the table, staring at the floor. His features were tight and guarded, but I could tell he was worried about what I'd just told him. I was concerned too.

Because I had a horrible feeling this was just the beginning.

CHAPTER 5

The lobby didn't look at all like it did an hour ago when I strolled through and hit the elevators. Instead of being sparsely inhabited by guests, it was packed.

Paranormals stood in little knots, talking while drinking from their glasses. Some even sat in comfortable chairs as soft music played with a steady rhythm. But most sat behind the game tables or clustered around the slot machines. The smell of cigarettes reached me, and somewhere in the middle of all that, I felt a quiet, quivering pulse of energies—paranormal vibes.

I recognized a few faces. Barb, the elderly witch, sat at a poker table. She wore sunglasses to help hide her eyes as she held her cards, and she looked like a pro. This was not her first time gambling. I didn't recognize the others sitting at her table.

I saw Luke, our thirteenth-floor cat-man with a big, fluffy orange tabby cat sitting on his lap as he pulled the lever from one of the slot machines. Olga, the chain-smoking witch, who had the hots for Julian, sat at a roulette table. She had a cigarette in one hand while she held a short glass with what could be water in the other. I doubted it was water. Her purple eyeshadow was a bad call. But I wasn't going to tell her.

Hands waved in the air, and I saw Basil gesturing me over

next to a tall male and a female shorter than him. Possibly a hobbit.

"She's the Merlin. That's right. Leana Fairchild. The Starlight witch who..."

I ducked behind a large, beefy man with hairy hands. I was tired of being Basil's star of the moment and found myself face-to-face with the front counter.

Movement caught my eye, and for a fraction of a second, I saw a fly sitting on the countertop. Then, with a blur, Errol's hand came out of nowhere. I blinked. The fly had disappeared, and a flick of Errol's gray tongue told me where it had gone.

"Did you just eat a bug?" I stared at him, wide-eyed. Now that was gross, even for him. Or was it?

The concierge glowered at me. "Are you mad?" he spat at me. "You're being especially stupid today. You should stop taking those meds. Now, go away. You're disturbing me."

I smiled at him. "You did, you nasty little creature. You ate that fly. I saw you." What? I had to have a little bit of fun.

Errol's pale face darkened, and he splayed his fingers on the counter. "I don't know why you're still here. The hotel made a mistake hiring you back. I would have thrown you out on your ass. You don't belong here."

I leaned over the counter, right in his face, and waved my finger at him. "Don't change the subject. You ate that fly. You know it. I know it. What else do you eat? Cockroaches? I bet you *love* those. All those juicy cockroach guts. Like gravy."

"Cockroaches? Ew." Jade appeared at my side and leaned on the counter. "I thought the hotel took care of that last year. Without Luke's cats, it would have been an infestation." Her eyes widened. "They were everywhere."

I grinned at Errol. "I'm sure Errol took care of that. Didn't you, Errol?"

Errol's face was practically purple with anger. "I can assure you, there are no cockroaches in the hotel."

"Of course not. You took care of them." I couldn't stop smiling. He was so easy.

I pulled Jade away with me before the concierge's head exploded.

"You like to torture him. Don't you?" asked Jade, yanking up her sleeves. The plastic bracelets tinkled around her wrist.

"A girl's gotta have fun sometimes." I looked around the lobby. It was full of people I'd never seen before. Some were my age, but most of them were older, hovering at Elsa's age and older. They talked and laughed and drank. All seemed pleasantly cheery to be here. "The hotel's pretty full tonight. It's nice." More than nice. It was great. It meant I could easily hide from Basil.

Jade's gaze shifted from side to side. "It is. Looks like most people like to gamble at night."

"Possibly. I don't gamble, so I wouldn't know." I worked hard for my money. The idea of throwing it away on a "possible" win sounded foreign to me. I wasn't rich, and every dime counted. Trust me. I counted them.

Jade gave a laugh. "Look. There's Elsa."

I followed her pointing and saw a frustrated red-haired sixty-five-year-old woman with a drink in one hand as she kicked a slot machine and was apparently cursing at it.

"Let's go help her before she breaks her foot." Jade hooked her arm in mine, and together we joined a crimson-faced Elsa.

The older witch's eyes rounded as she saw us. "That damn machine took my money!" she howled. "Give it back!"

I pressed my lips together. "That's what they do. People rarely win."

Elsa made a fist with her free hand and raised it. "It took all of it. All of it. And it won't give it back. I've tried a reverse number spell, a magical jackpot sigil, and a pandora lottery curse. Nothing worked."

Jade shared a look with me. "That's because the machines are warded against cheaters."

Elsa sucked in a breath, looking scandalized. "Are you calling me a cheater?"

Jade shrugged. "Well, you lost, and now you're trying to spell the machine to give you back your cash. I'd say that's kinda cheating."

Elsa clamped her mouth shut. Then she took a swig of her amber-colored drink, finished it, and said, "You're right. I'm an asshole."

I spurted out a laugh. "Never imagined that word coming out of your mouth. I like it."

Elsa wiped a strand of hair from her sweaty brow. "Have you discovered anything about the bodies?"

"Yeah. Do you know who they are?" pressed Jade.

"Ah," I said as a waiter walked forward and lowered his tray of wineglasses for us. Jade and I each snatched up a glass of red. "I couldn't find any files on any missing persons," I told them. "Now, I'm waiting to hear from the autopsy. Hopefully, that'll shed some light as to what killed them."

"True." Jade took a mouthful of her wine and winced. "Not as good as Valen's house wine."

She was right about that. The wine tasted very strongly of alcohol and had a vinegar taint.

"Basil doesn't seem too concerned about it," added Elsa with a frown. "He seems more concerned about the turnout of his Casino Week than those poor dead souls."

I cast my gaze over the crowd and found Basil chatting with an important-looking man in a dark suit. When I turned around, Elsa was mumbling another spell at the slot machine under her breath, thinking we didn't see her.

Jade caught me looking and twirled a finger near her temple.

I snorted and looked away before Elsa saw me looking. Poor her. She probably lost a lot of money.

My heart leaped when I saw a pair of dark eyes watching me across the lobby.

Valen stood with a predatory grace that commanded attention.

Those surrounding him gave him a wide berth, a king among his peers. Even in his more diminutive human form, he was huge, at least a head taller than anyone. He was all confident and destructive with his arms crossed over his ample chest, making his broad shoulders stand out, and his pecs bulge—a virile man-beast.

Even from a distance, I could see an intensity in his gaze as he watched me and the hair on the back of my neck prickled. The feeling was intoxicating.

Finally, he pulled his gaze away as Jimmy joined him, and the two men started a conversation.

"Did you and Valen have a fight?" asked Jade, which made Elsa stop cursing the slot machine and turn to face me.

"What? No. What made you think that?"

"So why the cold shoulder?" pressed the eighties-loving witch. "You practically wanted an excuse to ditch him to come with me. What's up?"

I contemplated telling them about the kiss I'd shared with Valen but decided against it. The fewer people who knew about it, the better. "I was an idiot," I told her. "I thought… I thought there was something between us. But I was wrong. There's nothing," I said, thinking of the blonde I'd seen with him. "We're just friends."

Jade cocked her head to the side. "What makes you say that?"

"I saw him with someone today." I thought I might as well tell them. They'd find out eventually. "A very pretty blonde. They were holding hands, sort of, and sharing an intimate moment. There was definitely something between them."

"You saw him with another woman. So what?" Jade pressed her free hand on her hip. "Valen knows a lot of women."

I shook my head. "I know what I saw, and what I saw was a man and a woman really into each other. There's nothing between Valen and me." At least, not on his part. "Why are you looking at me like that? It's fine. We didn't even go on a date. I imagined something between us… and now I realize I was wrong. That's it."

"Pfff." Elsa downed the last of her drink and slammed it on the top of the slot machine, her cheeks redder than usual. "Nonsense. We all see the way you two look at each other. Like you want to rip each other's clothes off. Something is definitely there. Don't you try to deny it."

"She's right, you know." Jade took a sip of her wine. "I remember how close he held you when you were dancing at the ball. Just look at the way he's watching you now… like he wants to take you to bed and give you *multiple* orgasms."

My face flamed as Elsa fist-pumped the air and started to sing, "Ah, ha, ha, ha, orgasms, orgasms," to the Bee Gee's "Stayin' Alive" chorus. Clearly, the witch had too much to drink, but she was a fun drunk.

Nearby guests stopped chatting and turned our way, wanting some of the "orgasms" action. They stared at Elsa, who was still chanting and shaking the slot machine with both hands like she'd lost her mind. Maybe they thought orgasms were the secret word to win at the slot machines. I laughed harder.

Jade exhaled long and low. "I wish someone would watch me like that."

I leaned over and noticed Jade staring at Jimmy instead of Valen. Looked like she was still crushing hard on the guy.

Elsa exhaled. "He is a complicated beast. Very handsome beast. But complicated."

"Yeah." I had to agree with that. "Complicated beast."

A sudden cheer filled the air, and I spotted Julian jumping up from his seat and looking rather pleased with himself. "Winner, winner, chicken dinner!" he shouted.

"Julian's having fun." I turned my attention back to Valen, because why the hell not, and saw a woman next to him. Not a woman. A witch. A tall, skinny-ass witch who had my blood boil in not a good way.

"What the *hell* is she doing here?" I growled.

Adele appeared in the lobby wearing a tailored navy pantsuit, a pressed white blouse over her thin frame, and a radiant smile.

Her long, blonde hair flowed in loose waves down her back. Her glowing smile reminded me of a ventriloquist puppet's smile—fake and orchestrated. Eyes bright, she glanced around the room, and when they settled on me, she smiled without showing teeth.

I met Valen's eyes across the room and saw concern cross his features. And then Adele turned her body so her back was to me. I guessed this was an attempt to hide Valen from me, but the guy was huge. She was just a thin pole obstacle standing before him, allowing me to still see him perfectly… along with the frown on his face as he spoke to the witch.

Both Elsa's and Jade's postures stiffened, and Elsa seemed to sober up a bit at the sight of the other witch.

I put my glass of wine on top of one of the slot machines. "I think I'm going to have words with her."

Elsa's hand shot out and grabbed my arm. "No." She gripped me. "Don't. Nothing good will come of it."

I tried to yank my arm free, but Elsa had it in a death grip. "I want to know why she filed a complaint. No. I want to confirm it's her." I knew it was her, but I wanted to hear it from her own thin lips.

"We know it's her," said Elsa, fear making her voice high. "Leave it alone. If you go there, you'll just make things worse. Trust me."

I shook my head, my eyes returning to Adele's skinny back. "How can they be worse than they already are?"

"She can make it worse," agreed Jade, her face pale. "You don't know her like we do."

I narrowed my eyes. "Are you speaking from experience?" I cast my gaze over my friends. "What did she do to you?"

Jade looked at Elsa, and then finally the older witch spoke: "My husband lost his post because of her."

"What?" A flame of anger ignited in my gut.

"Of course, it was a lie," said Elsa, tears brimming her eyes. "My Cedric would never steal anything. She'd just said that to get rid of him. See, he worked as a bookkeeper at the White witch court office here in New York City. He was the only one who stood up against her. She bullied everyone around, but not my Cedric." She wiped her tears with her hands and then smiled down at her locket.

I gritted my teeth at the sudden crazy need to run over there and yank Adele's hair. Then, slowly, I turned my attention back on that horrid witch, imagining her head exploding instead. "Now, I really want to talk to her."

A man came rushing across the lobby and met with Valen. He leaned forward and exchanged a few words. Then I watched as the giant pulled out his phone and put it to his ear.

"What's this?" asked Elsa, leaning forward too much and nearly falling over. She righted herself.

"Not sure." I stared as Valen's face went through a few shades of emotions—shock, anger, and a sense of obligation. His features hardened again, and then he met my eyes.

"Looks like we're about to find out," said Jade. "He's coming over."

I caught sight of Adele's indignant face as Valen left her to come to me. It was a small victory, but I'd take it.

The big, muscular giant came right up to me. "Something's happening in Brooklyn. A group of vampires is attacking humans."

"What?" we all said together.

"Just got confirmation," said the giant. "The head vampire has a team there, but they need help. It's getting out of control. Three deaths already."

Shit. That was bad. "I'll go."

"I'm coming too," said Elsa, hanging on to the edge of a side table so she didn't tip over.

"I think it's better that you stay," I told her, staring at her empty glass.

"I'll stay with her," said Jade, though I had a feeling she wanted to be where Jimmy was.

"Fine." Elsa pressed her hands to her hips. "Then I'll have

words with Adele." Before any of us could stop her, Elsa marched across the lobby like she was going off to war, toward Adele.

"Oh, no." Jade looked at me. "I think I better stop her," she said and took off, running behind Elsa.

"Where in Brooklyn?" I asked the giant.

His dark eyes met mine as he said, "Marine Park, near the nature trail. Come. I'll drive."

CHAPTER 6

It was the most uncomfortable twenty-minute drive of my forty-one years. Not because of the car, though. The black Range Rover Sport SUV was extremely comfortable—luxurious, spacious, sexy, and very manly, just like Valen.

I sat in the front passenger seat, and though the seat was practically molded to my butt, my insides were on a roller-coaster ride. Valen hadn't said a word since we left the hotel. I kind of just followed him to the parking lot behind his restaurant and got in his gleaming SUV.

The last time we'd been this close and alone was the night in his apartment when *he'd* kissed me. And let me say it again—*he* leaned in and kissed me. Yeah, I thought about it, but he was the instigator. And after he'd pulled away from the kiss, he'd also pulled away from me entirely.

But I had a job to do. I knew this would eventually happen where Valen and I would have to work a case together. I had to reel in my emotions, and hormones—let's be honest—and put the safety of our people and the humans first. I had to stop with the naked images of that splendid giant, preferably with me naked too. No wonder I was so horny. I hadn't had sex in over a year, and that had been with Martin, the one-minute man. More like a twenty-second man. Let's be honest here.

As we sat there in silence, my insides kept rearranging themselves in my belly, going from a tango to a somersault, accented by the whoosh of igniting gas, and the come-and-go flashes from the streetlights and cars flashed in my eyes.

Yet I felt his eyes on me. Valen kept throwing covert glances, thinking I couldn't see him. I could see him all right. I just didn't want to look at him right now.

But this was ridiculous. "What can you tell me about the attacks?" I said after I couldn't bear the silence between us anymore.

Valen stopped his SUV at a red light. "Just that a group of vampires is out of control and killing humans. The head vampires are trying to get things under control, but looks like they need our help."

"Have there been other vampire attacks in the city lately?" I asked as the SUV started forward again, pressing me back against my seat.

Vampire attacks were rare, just like werewolf attacks were uncommon, but they did happen occasionally. Usually, the paranormals in question were either sick or had some mental issues, not unlike humans when they had a psychotic break. But it was usually contained to just one vamp or shifter, not a whole gang.

"Three in the last five years since I've been here," answered Valen, handling the steering wheel with one burly hand. "Each time, the heads had the issue under control before it got out of hand or the human police got involved."

I rolled my eyes over his face, watching as the streetlights and shadows raced across his features. "You think these attacks and the dead paranormals are connected?" I didn't believe in coincidences. What were the odds of finding dead paranormals who were stripped of their essences, and now an unusual vampire attack?

Valen's hand gripped the wheel harder. "I don't know. Guess we'll find out when we get there."

"Why do you think they're acting like this? Group psychosis?"

Yeah, that sounded pretty lame, but I couldn't come up with a reason why a bunch of vampires decided to chew on some humans.

A muscle feathered along Valen's jaw. "Could be a sickness? Something contagious to vampires only?"

"Hmmm. It's odd behavior." I stared in front of me, watching the car lights passing us.

I felt Valen's eyes on me again as he said, "I know you've been following me."

Kill. Me. Now.

I cleared my throat. "What?" When in doubt, play dumb.

"For the last three nights in a row, you've been following me," continued the giant. "You think I didn't know?" His lips curled into a smile.

Irritation and embarrassment sizzled inside me. "If you knew, why didn't you say something?"

I felt like an idiot. I thought I'd been clever in my stealth, like Catwoman or something. Guess I wasn't as clever as I thought. The idea that he knew I was following him this whole time was mortifying. I was a big ol' fool.

"And stop you from feeling that you had the upper hand?" teased Valen. "I didn't want to ruin your thunder."

My face flamed. "Well, it is now."

"So, did you find what you were looking for?" asked Valen, humor in his voice.

Shit. Did he think I wanted to see him naked? I played off a shrug. "I'm a curious beast. I'd never met a giant before. I wanted to experience it without you knowing I was watching. It was for work." Partly true. The other part was because he intrigued me.

"Right." Valen turned to look at me, and laughter danced in those damn fine eyes of his.

I raised my hands. "Okay, you found me out. I'm a stalker."

Valen burst out laughing. "At least you're a beautiful one."

Heat rushed over my body, sending little tingles all over my skin. Okay, now I was baffled. Valen wasn't a player. I didn't get that vibe from him. But I knew he dated many women simultaneously—casual dating, if you will. I wasn't that kind of woman.

"If you must know, I won't be stalking you anymore. I got all the information I needed. Thank you very much."

"If you say so," said the giant after a moment, his voice hinting that he didn't believe a word I said. He turned his attention back to the road, a thoughtful expression smoothing his handsome features, his posture confident and strong.

We hit Marine Park after that and continued on until we neared the nature trails. Shadows of tall grasses and shrubbery lined the area. At 10:00 p.m., it was hard to see through the darkness that had settled. The only illumination was the moon and a few streetlights near the parking lot.

Valen pulled up next to another dark SUV and killed the engine. I slipped out of the SUV and looked around.

Oak and ash trees as tall as three-story buildings loomed over us, and acres of marshes spread out all around. Leaves rustled, and a wind blew through the trees—brisk, calm, and unnatural. The smell of moist earth and damp leaves rose with the wind, and for a moment, it almost felt like we were walking through a natural forest. But the thickening scent of blood gave it away. Something was definitely wrong with this nature trail.

I spotted another car parked behind us with the front passenger door open. A man hung from his seat, his legs inside the vehicle while his upper body lay on the ground. I hurried over and slowed my steps as I saw the mess of what was left of his neck. It was like a lion had taken a chunk out of his jugular. Blood was everywhere. The man's lifeless eyes were open, staring at nothing.

I felt Valen come up to me. "I didn't know a human body could bleed this much," I told him. "Don't vampires just drain their victims of blood? I mean, call it a cliché, but why waste fresh blood like this? And look at his freaking neck? Looks like he was mauled to death."

Valen was shaking his head. "I've never seen this before. This looks more like something a werewolf would do or another shifter of some kind. Even then, they'd have to be mad to go this far."

"But your guy said vampires. Right?"

Valen's body hardened in unease. "He did."

I felt bad for the human man. He looked young, not more than thirty, with his whole life ahead of him. "Bad way to go." But we couldn't do anything for him now.

High-pitched screams reverberated somewhere in the marshes. A man's voice let out a ringing, defiant shout.

I looked at Valen. "Let's go."

"Stay sharp," he warned, his stance predatory, emanating a threat. "These are not your regular vamps. Crazed vampires are ruthless. And this feels more like wild animals. There's no thought in the killings. They're just hunting for sport."

I let out a nervous breath. "Got it."

Valen's face was a display of determined rage, sharp like a dagger. "If they come at you, don't think. Just do. Thinking will get you killed."

"Got that too." This wasn't my first rodeo with a mad vampire, but the fact that Valen was clearly edgy about it was making me more nervous. If these attacks were putting a giant on edge, what the hell did that mean?

Without another word, Valen took the lead and ran toward the constant screaming, with me galloping behind him on a sandy path, okay more of a light jog. My legs were already cramping, and the wine I'd had earlier was threatening to come back up.

I didn't know what we'd find once we got there, but I was glad for the clear sky. I tapped into my will and channeled the celestial energy. With my heart hammering, I took a deep breath, tapped into my core, and reached out to the magical energy generated by the power of the stars.

I was ready.

Tall grasses and phragmites as tall as me flanked either side of the path. Valen wasn't much ahead of me. I could tell he wasn't running as fast as he could, more like he was making sure I could keep up. See, things like that only made me like him more. Yup, I was in a mess, but I couldn't think of that right now. This was too important to let my feelings get in the way.

I wondered if he'd change or if he could fight off vamps in his human form. I knew he wanted to keep being a giant secret, or rather private, but I couldn't help but wonder if others knew, apart from me, my new friends, and a handful of others. Did the head of the vampires know? Was that why they called him and asked for his help? I figured I was about to find out.

The giant stopped up ahead and leaned over something in the path.

Breathing hard, I rushed over to him. Lying on the path was another body, female this time. Bile rose in my throat at what I saw. Not only was her throat a stringy mess, but her clothes were shredded, leaving what remained of her chest and stomach exposed. Her jacket, shirt, and jeans had been torn to bloody ribbons along her forearms and legs. I felt ill and angry at the horrific scene.

"This is sick," I said, shaking with adrenaline and anger, knowing we were about to face some seriously messed-up monsters, not vampires. No, these were more like what demons would do to us.

Valen's face was set in anger. "Come." That was all he said as he hurried off again.

I followed the giant, adrenaline pumping through me to help me push with my legs and keep up with him. I didn't have to go much farther.

The moon reflected on a pond, its silvery water rippling in a slight breeze. And there, just on the other side of the pond, were not a handful of vampires, but about a hundred.

"Oh, shit."

CHAPTER 7

The scene was like something out of a horror movie, where a horde of zombies was suddenly upon the frightened humans, who didn't know how to fight or do pretty much anything else but die.

The air shook with the bloodcurdling chorus of battle cries and the shouts of the dying. Bodies—human and nonhuman—lay scattered across the marshes, too many to count and too dark to make out an accurate number.

The vampires were bent from the waist with their taloned hands grazing the ground in an apelike stance. They had a distinctive animal-like gait to them, almost as though they'd lost their humanity and were just animals. Creatures.

I caught sight of a male paranormal with supernatural speed fighting off one of the crazed vampires. He moved with precision, light on his feet. His attack was skilled and organized with deadly grace. This wasn't the movement of a deranged vampire. This was one of the sane ones, for lack of a better word. In a blur, he lashed out with his talons and severed the head of the other vampire.

Now that I knew what to look for to determine the not-crazy ones, I could see about a dozen "normal" vampires battling the other vampires. They were strong and agile with incredible speed, but so were the others. And the so-called crazed vamps fought without any thought process, wild and uncontrolled. They only wanted to kill. To annihilate. The other vampires wouldn't last. They didn't have the numbers.

That's where we came in.

Vamp heads turned at our approach. That drew screams and growls of rage from the mass of vampires. Rows upon rows of sharp white teeth shone in the moonlight. Damn. That was a lot of sharp teeth.

"Stay close," said Valen as he exhaled. The tightness in his voice pulled my eyes back to him. Tension flashed across his features.

"What are you going to do?" A knot formed in my gut at the torment in his eyes.

The muscles along his back tensed. Valen's face was troubled. His features kept flicking from frustration, rage, and uncertainty. He splayed his hands. I could easily see he was struggling with the notion of whether he should Hulk out or not. His secret wouldn't be so secret anymore after this.

"You don't have to change," I said, recognizing the turmoil. "I can take them." I'd never fought so many at the same time, though, so I would have to pull some serious magic out of my ass. I had a sizeable ass, so it might just work.

Valen clenched his jaw, his eyes on the battle. "I don't have a choice. They're going to die if I don't."

"You always have a choice. I can slow them down and wait for reinforcements."

Valen looked at me, a softness in his eyes that had my throat close. "It's too late. You can't take them all. Look at them. See how they move? You fight off one, and then five more will tear you apart. I can't let that happen. This needs to stop."

With a pull of his muscled arm, Valen ripped off his clothes. In a sudden flash of white light, instead of his normal six-foot-four frame stood his eighteen-foot one. Muscles bulged on arms and thighs as large as tree trunks. His face was different, with a stronger brow bone, more ferocious and harsh, but it was him. Valen was his giant self.

I felt a tautness throughout my chest. Valen was exposing himself to save lives, and it was tough not to like him more after that.

With a powerful thrust of his back legs, the giant shot forward and rushed to meet the onslaught of vampires. I heard a cry and the sound of tearing flesh. The giant tore at the vampires with barbarous rapidity, his mighty body a force to be reckoned with and scary as hell.

I'd forgotten to ask him if I should shoot to kill or if we were just going to subdue them until we figured out what the hell was happening.

But then I got my answer.

A vampire threw itself at Valen's thigh, its fangs sinking into the giant's flesh as it began to munch on his skin.

Valen reached down, grabbed the vampire by the neck, and lifted him as though he weighed nothing. The vampire looked like a child in the hands of the massive giant. Using both hands, Valen split the vampire in half and tossed it.

Okay, that was kind of gross. But now I had my answer. Definitely shoot to kill, but I'd try to knock them out first.

A flash of dark clothes caught my attention to my right, and I twisted around. A group of three vampires rushed me like a great, black wave of death. It was impossible to distinguish the males from the females with all the blood splattered over their faces and their clothes.

They were fast—damn fast—and a hell of a lot faster than me.

"Stop!" I cried out in desperation. I didn't want to kill them. "Stop right there! Don't come any closer!"

Even as they rushed me, I could see the vacant look in their eyes, nothing but a hunger to kill. Whoever they'd been before was gone.

I yanked on my starlight, feeling the power in the stars' answer as it thrummed through me—and let it go.

Twin balls of brilliant white light fired from my outstretched hands and crashed into the first two vampires.

The starlight exploded around the vampires, lighting them up in flames of white light. The vamps thrashed, howling in pain as the starlight burned through them. I gagged at the smell of burning, rotting flesh. The air stank of burnt hair and charred fat. These weren't demons I was roasting with my starlight. These were vampires. With a sizzling pop, the vampires crashed to the ground, lifeless. They didn't explode into ash like demons did. Demons didn't belong in this realm, but vampires did.

Two down. One to go.

Not sure how I felt about that, I had a moment of regret, feeling the ramifications of what I'd done. I'd killed those two vampires. I mean, vamps weren't my favorite of the paranormal races. Their good looks kind of pissed me off, and they were arrogant as hell. But I'd been sworn to protect them and all the paranormals. However, when the third vampire came at me, its eyes gleaming with manic hunger, those emotions kind of went away.

The vampire moved with unmatched supernatural speed, much faster than the other two.

Terror-fueled adrenaline rushed through me and kicked me into high gear. I willed my starlight to me and hurled a shoot of brilliant light at the vampire.

And missed.

Oh shit.

The vampire slammed into me with the force of a moving van. Pain reverberated all the way up my back as I hit the ground with the vamp on top of me.

I smiled at the male vampire, seeing it up close and personal now. "You know, you're moving way too fast for me. I'm not that kind of girl."

I waited for a glimpse of a human-vampire emotion, but all I got was an openmouthed growl, putrid breath, and some thick, stinking drool hitting my face.

"Thanks for that."

The vampire lowered his head as his black eyes found my neck, and he licked its lips.

That was my cue to get the hell out of there.

It was male. And what do males have that we don't? This—

I lifted my knee and smacked it in the vampire-nads.

The vampire's black eyes widened in pain as he rolled over, screeching in agony.

I pushed to my feet. "Be a good vamp and stay down."

Obviously, he didn't listen.

The vamp leaped to his feet, hissed at me—actually hissed like a mad cat—and sprang.

I gathered my starlight, joined my wrists together, and let it rip.

A thick shoot of brilliant white energy lashed out and hit the vamp. The vampire staggered, crying out in sudden agony, his body tightening helplessly as his muscles convulsed just as they would if electrocuted.

The vamp fell to the ground, thrashing his limbs and writhing, but it didn't last long. He flailed around for a moment and then stopped.

I let out a breath. "God, I hate this. See what you made me do? I killed you."

I stepped back and cast my gaze around the ongoing battle, looking for Valen, who wasn't hard to spot.

He swung his great big fists at the crazed vamps with a terrible ferocity. They launched themselves at him like a swarm of wasps, their faces deranged, but Valen brought down his enormous fists. Bones crunched. Heads looked like smashed cherry pies. It was disgusting, but I found I couldn't look away. I was seriously demented. But I was confident that Valen, in his human form, wouldn't have stood a chance at this horde of deranged vampires.

I couldn't distinguish the regular vamps from the deranged ones anymore. All I saw was a blur of teeth, talons, and death.

The sound of something heavy approaching pulled me around. Four more vampires stepped in my line of sight.

The odds weren't exactly in my favor, but I almost always beat the odds.

I was ticked. Pissed that they wanted to kill me, yes, but angrier that I had to kill them too. Clearly, something was wrong with them. I didn't want to kill any of them, but if they came at me, I'd have to defend myself.

Yup. They were coming for me.

The first vamp, a bald one—let's call him Baldy—came at me swinging with a kind of vampire speed that was truly impressive. His swings were fueled with fits of deranged anger instead of any sort of skill or precision. It was the only thing that gave me the advantage. If these were normal vamps, I'm not sure I'd have made it out alive. I still wasn't sure.

Baldy came with a burst of speed, but I slipped aside. His strike went wide before he realized his mistake. I twisted around, pulled on my starlight, and gave a clap of my hands.

Thousands of brilliant mini globe-like stars fired from my hands and surrounded the vamp like frenzied wasps out for revenge.

The starlights danced around the vamp as he howled and flailed his arms in an attempt to stop them from attaching to him. The starlights kept attacking until the vampire was covered in them, wrapped around him like a glowing mummy. He reeled and then keeled over.

My temples throbbed at the giant migraine that had made its appearance. Channeling all that magic so quickly was getting to me, and my body shook with tiredness—payment for the service of conducting all that starlight power.

But there was no rest for the wicked.

Just as the vampire-mummy fell, the three others came at me.

"Seriously?"

Again, I yanked on the powers that came from the emanations. I aimed and sent it free.

A shoot of white energy slammed into the three rushing vamps. It hit the closest one with the tremendous power intended. With a startled cry, the vamp flew back into a pair of his buddies. All three of them went down in a tumble of teeth and taloned limbs.

I heard a snarl to my right.

Willing my starlight magic back to the surface, I spun, and a ball of white light fired out of my hand. It slammed into the oncoming vamp straight in the chest. The vampire shrank back, howling, his body consumed in white flames. It lasted three seconds before the vampire collapsed to the ground.

The smell alone was enough to make me want to vomit. "Damn it. See? See what you made me do again?"

I whirled around at the sound of nearing claws and growls.

Four more vampires lunged at me.

This was becoming ridiculous.

I let out a growl of my own as I swatted the four of them with a blast of my starlight. I winced as waves of pain washed through me, the starlight magic settling and taking payment once again.

Dizzy, I took a breath and steadied myself, wrinkling my nose at the stench of burnt skin and hair. Sweat ran down the sides of my temples and my back. I was tiring. I couldn't keep this up. There were too many. Just too many.

My pulse raced as I spotted Valen. He was covered in vampires. Yup, that's what I said. Maybe thirty were attached to the giant, their fangs and talons biting, cutting. He pulled them off like they were annoying rats, crushing their skulls.

But just as soon as he yanked one off, ten more came.

"Stop this!" I shouted, panting as my magic coursed through my body. "I don't want to hurt you. Listen to me, you idiots. Just stop!"

Another two came—two females, from what I could tell. The two leaped together, flinging themselves at me with their talons extended and jaws open, like I was their midnight buffet.

No rest, then.

I planted my feet as I dove deep into my will and channeled the power from the stars.

And then the two female vamps fell facedown into the dirt.

I stared at my hands. "Weird. I hadn't even fired yet."

I looked over the marshes. Then, like a domino effect, the vampires, one by one, started to collapse. They weren't just collapsing but hitting the ground in convulsions until every last deranged vampire was down. Their limbs jerked and flailed for a moment, like dehydrated fish washed up on the shore. And then they were still.

With my boot, I kicked the nearest one to me. It didn't move. Its black eyes were open but without movement. No breathing. The vampires were dead.

My eyes found six vampires standing amid the sea of dead bodies. Nothing seemed unhinged about them, but they were bent with exhaustion. These were the "normal" vamps. Judging by their lack in numbers, they'd lost a few.

The ground shook, and I saw Valen, the giant, step in next to me. He was bleeding from hundreds of minor cuts and bite marks. Yikes. But the big giant didn't seem to be bothered by it at all.

"What did you do?" came his loud voice.

I'd heard it before, but it was still a little bit shocking and nerve-racking to hear it so close.

I shrugged. "Nothing. I didn't do this. They just… died. All of them. Almost like… it's almost like their time was up. Like they were running on fumes and then poof. They expired."

I scanned the scene, and even if these vampires had tried to kill us, seeing so many of them dead was still disturbing. "What could do such a thing?"

"I don't know. Never seen this before."

"There's no way this many vampires suddenly went crazy," I said, my head throbbing. "Someone did this. Someone did this to them. It's the only thing that makes sense." But why? I had no freaking clue. I had to find out, though, because I had the eerie feeling this wasn't over.

A thought flicked to the forefront of my mind. "Wait a second." I knelt next to the nearest body. The cold, familiar feeling of dread settled in me, and my gut clenched. "I'm not getting any vamp vibes. Nothing."

A growl rumbled deep in the giant's throat. *"I don't like this."*

I crabbed-walked over to the next body, a young male in his twenties. "Nothing here either." Then moved on to another female. "Yeah. I got nothing." I kept going until I'd checked another twenty bodies. I looked up at Valen and shook my head.

Holy shit. Just like the bodies I'd found next to the dumpster, these vampires had no vamp vibes. No paranormal energies were emitting from them. There was no way they weren't vampires by the way they moved and attacked. Hell, they would have kicked my ass if they hadn't just stopped and died.

But why *did* they die?

"They're connected," said the giant, reading my thoughts. *"These vampires. The bodies you found."*

I nodded and slowly straightened, my thighs protesting. It'd be worse tomorrow. "They are. Maybe the bodies near the dumpster had run out of time too."

That was so bizarre on many levels, but I couldn't decipher the cause of death, just like these vampires. They just upped and died.

The only thing that could help now was what the autopsy would reveal. "We need to take at least one body to the morgue and have it checked against the other bodies. See if they can tell us how they died."

"We'll need to take the bodies away before daylight. Before humans start coming through here for their morning jogs."

"We wouldn't want that."

Valen's features were twisted in agony. I could tell the whole thing saddened him. It did me too. *"I'll make a call. Phone's in the Range Rover."*

I nodded. "Right."

Valen watched me for a beat. *"This is bad, Leana."*

I exhaled. "You don't have to tell me." I looked over at the remaining vampires, seeing the distress on their faces and their postures. "I don't know what's going on, but we need to figure it out before it happens again."

Because we all knew in my life, things could *always* get worse.

CHAPTER 8

I looped my hands around the coffee mug and suddenly wished I had some Baileys in it instead of just coffee. I was tired, and at my age, lack of sleep not only made my body ache but made me grumpy.

I'd barely slept the night before with the images of all those dead vampires haunting me. I'd waited with Valen for the vampires' cleanup crew to show up and take the bodies away. It had taken ten nondescript vans, with about ten bodies in each of them, to haul out the dead vampires. All that took a mere twenty minutes. The vampires were highly organized.

According to Valen, one body was to be taken to the paranormal morgue in the city. If the other bodies couldn't be identified, they would be cremated and buried in the vampire cemetery in Queens. Yes, it exists.

After he'd returned to his smaller human size, and grabbed a change of clothes from a duffel bag in the back of his SUV, Valen took me back to the hotel. Neither of us spoke a single word during the ride back. We were both exhausted and possibly a little shocked by the events we had witnessed. No matter how you played it, a hundred dead vampires who had just upped and died was pretty traumatic. Unheard of, actually. And it left us both confused, and let's be honest, a little freaked. Well, I was.

Was this some kind of disease that only affected the paranormals? Was this a vicious attack on us? Three dead the night before and now a hundred? Something was definitely happening in our city, and I was going to find out what.

I wasn't even bothered that the giant hadn't said a word to me as I rolled out of his SUV and shuffled inside the hotel. I was just too damn tired to have a conversation. I just wanted my bed. So I was grateful he drove me back, and I left it at that.

I'd turned as the Range Rover pulled away from the curb and caught a glimpse of the giant. The emotions that darkened Valen's face told me he wasn't ready to talk, either, and I wouldn't push it.

"Tough night?"

I looked at Elsa across from me, her red, frizzy hair higher and fluffier than usual, like she'd fought with her brush this morning. "You can say that."

I took the opportunity to look around, my nose filling with the smells of cooking and spices. We sat around a circular table in the hotel's dining room. A large orange banner above the doorway read CASINO BUFFET.

The soft clink of glasses and the loud racket of conversation wafted around. I'd never seen the hotel's dining room this packed, ever. It seemed Basil was doing something right. Just the smell of the delicious, mouthwatering food would have anyone walk in from the street.

"Are you going to tell us what happened after you left with Valen?" inquired Jade, sitting to my right. She popped a piece of cubed cantaloupe in her mouth. "We're feeling a little left out over here." Her blonde hair was pulled into high pigtails, and she'd rolled the sleeves of her acid-washed denim jacket over her Kate Bush T-shirt.

Elsa put her fork down, where she'd been busy tearing into her spicy Portuguese chicken. "Spill it. Don't leave anything out."

"Don't forget the part where you and Valen rip off your clothes." Jade raised her brows suggestively. "That's the part I want to hear about."

Valen had ripped off his clothes, but it wasn't like that. Just as I opened my mouth to answer, Julian appeared, carrying two plates piled with food. He pulled out a chair with his foot, set the plates down, and sat.

"What'd I miss?" he asked.

I stared at the dark, bruised mark on his neck, just above his collarbone. "Is that a hickey?"

Julian winked. "You bet, darling. I've got more. Wanna see?"

I snorted into my coffee. "No, thanks."

"Don't change the subject," ordered Elsa, giving me her stink eye. "You look like you haven't slept a wink. I can tell. Something happened. Something that kept you up all night."

"Sex kept me up all night." Julian smiled as he ripped into his thick steak with a knife and fork, looking famished, like whatever—whoever—he'd been doing all night had left him ravenous.

I exhaled and leaned forward. Then, keeping my voice low, I told them all about the deranged vampires, how they all suddenly died, and how they didn't have any vamp vibes. I watched their eyes widening when I was done.

Elsa paled and leaned back in her chair. "Goddess, help us. How horrible."

"Tell me about it. It was much worse in person." I sighed and stared at my grilled cheese sandwich, unable to bring myself to eat. The scent of burnt flesh and blood was just still too fresh in my mind and my nose. The only thing I could keep down was coffee.

Jade was shaking her head. "But how can that be? I don't understand how they all died like that. And so many of them." Her eyes were round with fear. "Is it contagious?"

I shrugged. "I don't know. I don't think so. If it was, I'd be sick or something," I said, remembering my encounters with the crazed vampires. I'd been drooled on and had contact with a lot of them. If it were contagious, I'd have gotten it.

"But I'm hoping the autopsy results will tell us something about what happened to them. They're going to compare the first victims with one of the vampires... see what comes up." I'd been to New York City's paranormal morgue a few times. Maybe I should have gone straight there. Perhaps I would have gotten results if I did.

Julian pointed his fork at me. "But you think it's the same? What killed these vampires and the bodies near the dumpster?"

I took a sip of my coffee. "That's what it feels like. I didn't see how the others died. But my gut is telling me they're related. Valen thinks so too."

Jade's face brightened at the mention of Valen. "Did you ask him about the *other* woman?"

I choked on my coffee. I cleared my throat and said, "Um. No. Wasn't really the time to talk about that. Besides, it's none of my business." It really wasn't. Valen could sleep with as many women as he wanted. He was a grown-ass man with no attachments.

My face flamed at the recollection that the giant knew I'd been following him at night. Clearly, I needed to improve my stealth skills.

"Lovers' quarrel?" said Julian as he shoved a potato in his mouth. "You need me to take care of this *other* woman? It's not a problem."

"Uhh..." I shifted in my seat, not sure what he meant by that. Did he mean he'd poison her? I did not want that to happen. I had some insecurities. I wasn't perfect. But I wasn't a murderer.

The handsome witch winked at me. "I can easily steer her my way. And after spending some time with The Julian, trust me, she won't want anything else. She'll be begging me for more."

I really shouldn't have laughed, but I couldn't help it. "You're crazy, you know that?" But the thing is, he was dead serious.

Would I be a bad witch if I was tempted by his offer? Yes. Yes, I would.

Julian waved his fork at me again. "Think about it. I'm always here for you." It would have been touching if I didn't suspect this to be something he rather enjoyed, stealing females from other males, like sport.

A generous woman, who was wider than she was tall, walked to our table. Red splatters that looked suspiciously like blood stained her white chef's coat. It almost looked like she'd just killed a chicken or something. Guests whispered as she walked by, eyeing her with disparaging expressions, but she never took notice.

"Hello, my dear witches," said Polly. She tipped her white hat, and I could see her hair pulled back into a French braid. The same Polly had healed my wounds from my gremlin demon attack and was apparently as good a cook as she was a healer. She bumped her large stomach against our table, a tray of food resting in her left hand and a spoon in the other. "Can I offer you some jambalaya? Or some chicken gumbo? Fresh off the stove."

"Yes, please," said Jade, making room on her plate with her fork.

Polly's smile widened as she plopped two generous helpings of her Cajun dishes on Jade's plate. Her eyes flicked around our table to finally rest on me. "You want some?" Her words came out more like an order than a question.

I shook my head. "I'm not really hungry. But thanks. It does smell delicious."

"It is," moaned Jade as she swallowed. She had some sauce smeared on the side of her mouth. When she took another mouthful, another blot of sauce sullied the opposite side of her face. At least she was consistent.

The chef narrowed her eyes at me. I could see the thoughts moving at the speed of light behind her eyes. Polly pointed her spoon at me, sending chunks of her jambalaya and chicken gumbo splattering on our tablecloth. "Stay out of trouble."

I grinned. "I can't promise anything."

Polly flashed me one of her infectious smiles and pulled away. And with that, the chef moved to the following table of waiting guests just as Jimmy headed our way.

"Basil's looking for you," he said as he joined our table, the distinctive scent of dog rolling off him. I never noticed before. Looked like the longer he was in his human shape, the stronger his paranormal side intensified. Jimmy might be a werewolf. He was some kind of dog. It might explain why the curse took on the shape of a dog. I was going to ask him later.

"Tell him he can find me here," I told Jimmy. I pulled my eyes from his and saw Jade's flushed face as she stared at her plate and did her best to try and shrink down in her seat. Yeah, she had it bad.

Jimmy gave a short laugh. "I will." His eyes moved around our table and settled on Jade. "Oh. You've got something here," he said as he pulled out a handkerchief and carefully dabbed Jade's face with it.

Her arms clamped to her sides as though she'd just been hexed with a solidifying spell. I didn't think she was breathing. And her eyes were wider than I'd ever seen them.

"There. Good as new," said the assistant manager, smiling at what could only be described as a petrified Jade.

Julian snorted at his plate and shook his head.

I looked up at Jimmy, wondering if he was oblivious to Jade's crush or if he knew. But it didn't look like he did.

"Enjoy your meals," he said, and then he was off, probably to find Basil.

"He's gone. You can breathe now," said Elsa, laughter in her voice.

Jade blinked. "I've never been so humiliated in my life. I think I wet myself."

"Stop. That was nothing. Just a bit of sauce," I told her, seeing redness creeping up her face and neck.

Jade shook her head. "I'll never leave my room ever again."

"Don't be ridiculous," snapped Elsa as she wiped her mouth with her napkin. "He was just being nice. Nothing to be embarrassed about. So what if your face was covered in sauce like a five-year-old."

"I want to die," muttered Jade, and we all started laughing. At first, I thought she'd be furious at us for our shared lack of support, but then she began to laugh too. "I can't believe I just sat there like an idiot as he wiped my face," she said, laughing. "What must he think of me?"

"That you're a wonderful person with a great sense of humor," I told her. When her eyes brimmed at the compliment, I felt a tug around my heart. Jade definitely deserved a good man. And Jimmy, well, you couldn't find any better, in my opinion.

"Leana!"

The sound of my name spun me around in my chair to see Basil marching toward our table.

"Oh dear, he's got his business face on," muttered Elsa. "Wonder what he wants."

"We're about to find out," I said as Basil grabbed an empty chair from the neighboring table.

"I need to speak to you." Basil pulled his chair next to mine and sat. He had a folder in his hand.

"What about?"

"Here." He handed me the folder. "These are the autopsy reports." At that, my friends all leaned in closer.

My pulse spiked as I grabbed the folder and flipped it open. "And?" I asked, my eyes tracking the file.

"Inconclusive," answered the male witch.

"Inconclusive?" I repeated and then glanced back down and read that exact word at the end of the report—in bold letters, mind you.

"What is it, Leana?" asked Elsa, worry filling her tone.

I looked up and glanced at my friends around the table. "They can't find a cause of death. Not on the ones we found next to the dumpster. Not on the vampires. They don't know how they died."

"But that doesn't make sense?" said Julian. "They died of something."

"Shhh!" hissed Basil, looking over his shoulder. "Keep your voices down," he said as he turned back around.

I stared at the file. I'd hoped to get something back from the autopsy. But now, it was worse than before. It meant that whatever killed these paranormals was untraceable. Undetectable. And that was a hell of a lot worse.

Dread filled my gut like it was loaded with cement. I had no leads, no cause of death, and no explanation as to how they died.

But someone did this.

That I was sure of. Someone killed all these paranormals, and I had to find them before they did it again. Because I knew they would.

Basil leaned over. "Listen. I don't know what's going on, but you need to put a stop to it."

I frowned at him. "I'm trying."

"Try harder," ordered the small witch. "See this?" He gestured around the hotel. "It's never been this busy in twenty years. The hotel needs this. *I* need this. And I want to keep it that way."

"Of course."

He pointed a finger at me, which I didn't exactly appreciate. "Figure it out. I don't want anything to interfere with my Casino Week."

"I get it."

"Do what the hotel pays you for, and fix this." Basil got up, not bothering to put his chair back, and pulled his face into a fake smile as he moseyed over to another table and started a conversation with the guests.

"Sometimes I want to punch him in the face," I said through gritted teeth.

Elsa smiled at me. "We all do."

I understood that Basil was worried about his job. His Casino Week was turning out to be a great idea. I didn't want these mysterious deaths to interfere with that either.

My stomach gave a sudden squeeze, not because of Elsa's comment but because of a certain tall, big, and muscled man-beast who had just walked into the dining room.

My eyes were immediately drawn to him, to his black shirt carved around his thick muscles, broad shoulders, and thin waist. His dark hair was pulled back into a low ponytail, which only emphasized his rugged good looks. It was hard *not* to look. The guy was huge. He commanded respect in a way that only the strongest alphas did.

But then, everyone else was eyeing him. More than usual, that is.

I turned in my seat as the murmurs of voices rose in the dining room. Straining my ears to catch every nuance, I stiffened at the nervous pitch, the rise and fall of their voices mixing with their restless energy.

"...that's him," said a male paranormal from a table to our left.

"...apparently he's a *giant*," said a female paranormal from another table.

"...his name is Valen," stated another voice from behind me somewhere.

"...giant..." came another voice, until the word "giant" echoed all around us, replacing the happy chatter from moments ago with more of an excited, urgent hush, like they were all looking at a freaking unicorn.

"Looks like his secret is out," whispered Elsa, concern etched all over her face. "Everyone knows."

A muscle pulled along Julian's jaw. "The guy looks like he's in hell."

He wasn't off. Valen halted in the dining room, his eyes scanning the space and the people sitting there, pointing at him like he was an animal at the zoo.

I knew this was the result of Valen showing his true self to help the vampires. And now, to thank him, they'd revealed his secret.

Damn it.

Valen's face was tight, and I could see emotions and thoughts flashing behind his eyes. Our eyes met and locked for a beat. I opened my mouth to tell him to come over, but my jaw just hung there, the words evaporating in my throat.

And then he spun around and exited the dining room.

"That's not good," said Jade. "Poor Valen. He didn't look good."

"He didn't." I was torn. Should I go to him? Speak to him? Emotions pulled me every which way until I felt like my limbs were stretching paper-thin. Part of me wanted to go to make sure he was okay. But then the other part felt he'd rather be on his own. He was a solitary creature.

Guess which part won?

The one where I stood up and walked out.

CHAPTER 9

Was I an idiot to go to a man who was most likely seeing other women? Possibly. Yes, I had feelings for him that I had to reel in, but Valen had proven to be a friend to me and had saved my ass more than once. He'd been kind to me, apart from when we'd first met. He'd been a total jerk then, but he'd apologized since. That said a lot. And right now, my friendly giant looked like he needed a friend to talk to.

I knew Valen had been careful to keep his giant nature a well-kept secret. Only a handful of people knew, including me. Probably because the man wanted to avoid all the attention. Not to mention, few giants were probably left in the world. Let's face it. He was a freaking unicorn in the room—a sexy one too.

By the looks of things, the guests in the hotel knew about him, which meant they'd told their friends and their families. Damn. That meant soon, every paranormal in the city would know what Valen was. He'd had to know that one day his secret would be out. He couldn't keep it for long, not with the work he was doing for the hotel.

When I exited the hotel and hit the sidewalk, the giant was nowhere in sight. So, I made for the only place he could be.

With the autopsy folder in one hand, I yanked open the door

to his restaurant, After Dark, and strolled in. I cast my gaze over the tables and booths and, not seeing him, went straight to his office.

I went to the first door and pulled.

"Hey! You can't go in there!" cried a voice behind me.

I knew it was the hostess what's-her-name, so I didn't bother turning around. The room turned out to be his office. I'd been right about that. A large wood desk occupied most of the space, the top scattered with papers and a mug. Bookcases flanked each side of the room, but Valen wasn't there.

"I'll have you thrown out!" shouted the hostess, her face flushed with anger, rippling with what looked like fish scales. Yeah, definitely mermaid or some finfolk. She looked like she was about to beast out into whatever fish she was, but I didn't care.

I pushed her out of the way and moved to the only other door, which turned out to be a storage room.

"Valen will know about this," she threatened and yanked out her cell phone.

"Good. You be a good girl and tell him."

I heard her sharp intake of breath, but I wasn't here to fight her. I was already near the front doors when I heard her voice shouting something.

I was back outside, standing in front of the restaurant as my eyes went to the second floor. The building had only two floors, and the entire top floor was Valen's apartment.

Heart pumping, I moved to the right of the building where the side entrance to his apartment was. I yanked open the door, hit the stairs, and when I made it to the landing, I knocked three times.

I moved back, a little out of breath from climbing those stairs so quickly. My heart thrashed in my chest, and I was a little dizzy from not eating. I had a moment of panic then. *What the hell am I doing here?*

I should go. I shouldn't be here. What would he think when he saw me? He'd be irritated because he didn't want to be disturbed, that's what. This was a mistake. I was an idiot.

I whirled around and made to leave just as I heard the door swing open.

"Leana? What are you doing here?" Surprise flashed across Valen's face as I turned back around. His eyes went to the folder that was still clutched in my hand and back at my face.

"Uhh..." Damn it. My mouth wasn't catching up with my thoughts. "I wanted to make sure you were okay." There. At least that came out right.

His dark eyes rolled over my face. "Come." He stepped aside and held the door for me.

Did I go inside? Hell yes.

I stepped in, and the familiar scents of leather and spices filled my nose. I'd only been inside twice, but it looked exactly the same.

"Can I get you a glass of wine?" Valen walked past me to his kitchen and started opening cabinet doors.

I hauled off my boots and followed him. "I really shouldn't. I haven't eaten anything since last night. Can't seem to hold anything down. Just coffee, so far."

"Last night was bad." Valen watched me for a beat longer, but I couldn't tell what he was thinking. "Sit." He gestured at the kitchen island. "I'll make you something that'll help with your stomach."

"I won't say no to that," I said, smiling. He smiled back, and my insides gave a jolt. I pulled my eyes away before my face gave away my feelings. I grabbed one of the stainless-steel stools, which were more comfortable than they looked, let the folder drop next to me on the counter, and sat.

I watched as Valen went to work, staring at his broad shoulders, the way his back muscles danced and pulled as he set pots and pans on his stove. He grabbed some veggies from his fridge that was the size of two of mine and started chopping them on a cutting board. Then he expertly poured the mix into a pot and added seasoning. It was quite the show, and I had front-row seats.

He was so different from the first day I'd assaulted his chest with my face. Then he'd been a man-beast jerk. Now, he was sweet and caring, which didn't help my conflicting emotions.

The last time I was here, he'd kissed me. And it was a hell of a kiss, the kind that made you want to rip off your clothes and shout, "Hallelujah!" The type of kiss that whispered we were about to get our freak on. Which, let's be honest, I would have allowed to happen.

But Valen had pulled away, and I'd seen a sadness in his eyes that had sobered me right up. I'd first thought he wasn't ready to be with anyone. But then Jimmy had told me Valen had many girlfriends, and I'd seen him just yesterday with one of them. So that couldn't be the reason.

It hurt. I wasn't going to lie to myself. Maybe Valen had realized he didn't like me in that way after the kiss. And that was perfectly fine. These things happened. I couldn't be angry at him for it.

I just had to get used to it.

"So," I began, wanting to say what I came here to say. The sooner I did, the sooner I could leave. "The guests were pretty excited to see you. They know. Won't be long before the entire city knows."

My eyes trailed down his back to his very fine behind. His ass looked spectacular in those jeans. "I'm sorry you had to reveal yourself last night." Reluctantly, I yanked my eyes back up to his shoulders. "But if you didn't… I don't think we would have made it."

Without him, those vampires would have reached Manhattan in no time and killed maybe hundreds of innocent humans.

"I knew it would happen one day," said the giant as he added butter to a frying pan. The scent made my stomach grumble.

I rested my elbows on the counter. "So, you're not upset?"

He shook his head, his attention never leaving his cooking. "I was hoping to stretch it out a bit longer. But after last night, I knew it was over."

I wouldn't say I liked his choice of words there. "So, what does that mean, exactly? Do you still work for the hotel?" God forbid if it meant he'd lose his job. I'd gotten used to the idea of a giant living next door. It made me feel safer knowing he was there, patrolling the streets at night, even when I was stalking him. I might not be his girlfriend, but I didn't want to lose him either.

Valen turned around. A smile touched the corners of his mouth. "Is that why you came? You thought I'd be fired?" His eyes pinned me. They were mesmerizing as they beheld me. It was all I could do not to pull away. Did giants have hypnotizing abilities?

I shrugged, my insides churning, and not because of what I'd seen last night. "I don't know. Basil is a bit of an ass. He doesn't want anything to disrupt his *Casino Week*."

"He puts on a big front, but he's a real softy, that Basil," said the giant as he turned back around. He dumped the contents of the frying pan into the boiling pot. The smell of butter and spices and God knew what else was making me salivate.

"Are those the autopsy reports?" he asked as he whisked the contents into the pot.

I sighed as I grabbed the folder and flipped it open. "Yes. And it's inconclusive. They can't find a cause of death on any of the bodies, which makes absolutely no sense. But there you have it."

At that, the muscles along Valen's back tensed. Obviously, we both knew this was the worst possible outcome.

Without a cause of death, we didn't have much to go on. Basically, we had a whole lot of nothing.

I folded the file shut. "Jade thought it could be a virus or something, which could have accounted for so many of those vampires last night, but the autopsy would have said as much. And we're both fine. So it can't be that. Damn it. I have no freaking clue what did that to all those paranormals." I rested my head on my hands, recalling the scene from last night and trying to pinpoint something. The only thing that stood out was how wild, unfocused, and out of their minds the vampires were.

And they all just died like a mass suicide.

"Here."

I looked up as Valen set a bowl of steaming something with floating vegetables, chicken, and what looked like rice in front of me. Next, he placed a spoon fit for a giant, which made me laugh, and a white napkin.

I stared up at him. "You made me chicken soup?" My throat contracted. Apart from my mother, no one had ever made me soup or anything. Not even Martin. All he ever made for me was a whole lot of nothin'. Damnit. Why was Valen being so damn nice?

He leaned over the counter until his face was practically over my bowl. "It's my own recipe. It'll help to settle your stomach. You need to eat something."

I narrowed my eyes. "This won't make me drunk. Will it?" I still remembered his special brew of tea, which made me feel like I was drunk.

The giant chuckled. "No. This will make you feel better. Trust me."

I shrugged. "Well, if you say it like that." I stared at the spoon, not sure it would fit inside my mouth. I lifted the massive spoon. "Ready for your spanking?" I laughed and then caught myself. Why did I just say that?

Valen flashed me his perfect teeth. "I'm ready if you are."

Kill. Me. Now.

I lowered my head toward my soup, barely feeling the steam on my hot cheeks. Hell, I probably had some steam of my own shooting out of my ears. I dipped the mega spoon in the bowl, scooped up some of the soup, put the spoon to my lips, and sipped.

"Mmmm, good," I said as I swallowed. "Spicy good. Don't think I've ever had chicken soup that tasted so good."

Valen beamed. He crossed his arms over his chest and leaned

his back on the counter next to his stove, eyeing me. "Glad you like it. It was my wife's favorite."

I froze, spoon halfway in my mouth. "Uh… huh…"

Valen never stopped smiling. I couldn't detect any sadness in his eyes, just warmth. "She was a lot like you, headstrong, fierce, impulsive."

I swallowed. "Was she a giant like you?"

Valen shook his head, losing some of his smile. "A werewolf. We used to shift together at night. She'd lose me the first five minutes. She was too fast for me, and she thought that was hilarious."

My heart clenched at the thought of his wife dying of cancer. "I'm sorry for what happened to her."

"I am too." Valen looked away for a brief moment, but then his eyes were back on mine, bright and softened ever so slightly. I saw something I couldn't put my finger on. "You should start feeling better soon."

He wasn't kidding. As soon as I gulped down another three huge spoonfuls of soup, my stomach wasn't queasy, and the night's aches and pains—both physical and mental—were gone. I felt good. Great.

I eyed the giant in his kitchen. He looked good, edible. "You like taking care of people."

He looked at the floor. "I do. It's in my nature. It's something all giants share."

I waved my spoon at him. "All those muscles have to be put to good use."

Valen laughed, and it sent delicious tingles over me.

"You're not having some?" I asked, shoving another spoon topped with shredded carrots, celery, and some other vegetable I didn't recognize. I didn't care that he heard me slurping and moaning. Once I started with the soup, I couldn't stop. I was ravenous.

"I've eaten."

When I looked up, Valen was still staring at me with a strange smile. "Don't tell Polly." I waved my spoon at him. "She'll freak if she knows you can make a mean chicken soup. Probably'll have you sign an NDA."

Valen laughed, and my heart melted a little. Shit. I had to get out of here. I was not falling for this guy. Nope. No. No siree, Bob.

I grabbed my bowl with both hands, tipped it to my lips, and drank the rest. Every last drop. Why waste a good thing? Am I right?

I set my bowl down and wiped my mouth with my napkin. "Wow. That was good. Thank you so much." I slipped off the stool and grabbed the folder.

"You're leaving?" Valen uncrossed his arms.

"Yeah. Oh. You need help with the dishes?" The man had made me chicken soup from scratch. The least I could do was clean up.

The giant watched me for a long beat, and I thought he would take me up on that offer. But instead, he said, "Have dinner with me tonight."

Uh-oh.

The folder slipped from my hand. Blood rushed to my face as I bent and picked up the file, only to find Valen two inches from me when I straightened.

I raised a brow. "How'd you do that?" The proximity to his hard, muscular chest was making me a little drunk, like he'd given me his special tea again. We were almost touching.

"Have dinner with me," he repeated.

I was hot, flushed, with my body tingly all over. I swallowed hard. "Huh?" Okay, this was not the plan. The plan was to go see the giant, make sure he was okay, and then skedaddle. See? Good plan.

He looked down at me with those dark eyes I could get lost in. "Dinner tonight. I'll have something special prepared for you downstairs."

My heart pounded in my ears. "At your restaurant? You want

me… to have dinner with *you*?" I sounded like an idiot. But I wanted to make sure he knew what he was saying.

Valen inched closer, his eyes dipping to my lips and then up to my eyes again. "Yes. I'd like to have dinner with you, unless you have other plans."

Images of the pretty blonde flashed in my mind's eye. The way he'd smiled at her, the way they were touching, their closeness… definitely something between them.

What I should have done was tell him no. I licked my lips, preparing to turn him down gently.

"Okay. Sure. What time?" Seemed my mouth had other plans.

"Seven o'clock," said the giant, his eyes gleaming as they narrowed in on my lips. A cocky smile spread over his own, like hot males got when they knew they had you.

Damn you, hormones.

I spun around before they got me into trouble. I pulled on my boots and headed out.

Only when I was out and had reached the sidewalk did I remember to breathe.

Holy hell. What have I done?

CHAPTER 10

"Not that. You'll look like a slut," said Elsa, grabbing my low-cut black blouse from me and tossing it on my bed. "It screams desperate. You don't want to give him that impression."

"She's right," said Jade, going through my closet. "You don't want to give him the *wrong* impression. You want to be sexy, not slutty. There's a difference."

"I get it," I said as I moved over to my bed and sat. "But I don't have much. I don't have a 'dating' wardrobe. I have a work wardrobe—a killing-baddies wardrobe. I never thought I'd be dating right now after what happened with Martin." The cheating and, of course, the trying-to-kill-me part. That would turn off any woman from dating.

"Things change," said Elsa. "When you know it's right, it's right. Time won't make a difference when the right man comes along. Why do you have so many T-shirts?" She held a cluster of white and gray T-shirts.

I shrugged. "Because I love cotton? I told you I don't have anything worthy of a date." I knew Valen would be wearing something expensive and exquisite on his muscular frame. I hadn't really gone shopping for going-out clothes. The only thing

I'd bought recently was that silver gown for the Midnight Ball, and I ended up ripping it so I could maneuver in it. The dress was ruined, and I'd tossed it.

"You know," said Jade, as she poked her head out of my closet, "I have a really nice blue taffeta dress I think would look amazing on you. It makes a swooshing sound when you move!"

I kept my face as blank as possible, not wanting to hurt her feelings because the idea of me in a blue taffeta dress was more horrifying than going on a date with Valen.

"Thanks, but I'd rather wear pants or jeans. I'll be more comfortable. More relaxed. Pants are good. Especially if I have to work after."

Elsa huffed in disapproval. "You need to learn to have fun. Forget about work for just one night and enjoy yourself. Life is short, and the older you get, the faster it goes. Trust me. Do you know how many women wish to be in your shoes, right now?"

"In your pants," laughed Jade.

Elsa nodded. "That too. Do you?" When I didn't answer, she added, "All the single paranormal ladies, that's how many. Valen is the most wanted bachelor in our community. Some women have had the pleasure of being with him, but none of them could tie him down. A wild beast that no one can tame. But something tells me he's serious about you. You'll be the one to tame him."

I shifted my weight on my bed, my white bathrobe pooling around me. "I don't want to tame anyone." Okay, maybe that was a lie. I had the visual of me with a whip and a naked Valen tied to a bed. "I told you about that hot blonde. What makes this any different? I don't have the will or the energy to be Valen's girl of the week. I'm too old for that crap."

"I don't think that's it at all," said Elsa. "Give him some credit."

"How do you know?"

Elsa gave me a knowing smile. "I just know." She twisted around and started shuffling through my clothes on hangers. "Just like I knew Cedric was meant for me. Sure, Katie and

Samantha were all over him, but he was mine. And it's the same with you. Valen is your guy… or should I say your *giant,*" she added, laughing at her own joke.

Jade pulled her pigtails tighter as she stared at herself in the full-length mirror on the wall. "You practically told everyone how you felt about him, earlier. The entire hotel is talking about it."

I leaned forward. "I'm sorry? What?" I felt a burst of heat rolling up my body in waves.

Jade spun around to face me. "The way you ran after him. Everyone saw."

Another rush of heat settled around my face. "They saw a friend who was concerned," I said, though, by her smile, I knew she didn't believe me. "I saw his reaction when everyone in the dining room was talking about him—pointing and whispering like he was some rare animal at the zoo. I would hate that too. I wanted to make sure he was okay."

Yes, I cared for him more than I should, but I had honestly gone to make sure he was okay. The guests' reaction to him had angered me. And then, well, things just got more complicated after that.

"And that won you a date," called Elsa from inside my closet. I couldn't see her face, but I could hear the smile in her voice.

Something occurred to me. "What do you think will happen now that everyone knows about him?"

"What do you mean?" asked Jade.

I shrugged. "I don't know… maybe he won't stay. Maybe he'll start getting better job offers than working for the hotel. Giants are rare, assumed nonexistent. I'm pretty sure lots of people in power want a piece of him now."

Jade pinched her lips together, shaking her head. "He'll never leave. No. I don't believe it."

Elsa poked her head out of my closet. She didn't say anything, but from the frown on her face, I knew some of what I'd just said rang true. I mean, who wouldn't want a giant on their team or as a soldier somewhere? Not only was he the most wanted bachelor, but he was also the most wanted paranormal.

I watched as Elsa whirled around and continued going through the clothes that hung in my closet, with purpose. "Should I ask him about the blonde?"

"No," chorused Elsa and Jade, making me jerk.

"But—"

"Are you crazy? Do you want to ruin things before they even start?" Elsa stuck her head out from my closet again. One of my hangers was sticking out of her hair, but I wasn't about to interrupt her. "Not on the first date. Look, even if he was dating her, that's his business. That was before you agreed to go on a date with him. So why torture him about that? Trust me. Don't go there. Just see where things lead. After tonight, I'm sure that's the last you'll ever see of that mystery blonde."

I wasn't sure about that. Something in the way they were looking at each other. Call it my witchy instincts, but I had a feeling I'd see her again.

"And he cooked for you," said Jade, beaming. She let out a sigh. "I've never had a man cook for me. That says a lot."

"Jade's right," agreed Elsa. "You said he made a special soup from scratch just for you."

"From *scratch*," repeated Jade, her eyes wide like that was the key ingredient here.

"Men just don't whip up food for women they don't care about," said Elsa, and she tapped her nose with her finger like that was supposed to mean something to me.

"Right." Maybe they were right, but Valen's predisposition was that he took care of others. I had a feeling if Jade or Elsa had been sitting at his kitchen island earlier, he would have made that soup for them too. Yeah, he was that kind of man.

Jade pulled a pair of yellow earphones from her vintage yellow Sony Walkman that hung from her jeans' waistband. She positioned the earphones over her head, pressed down the play button on her Walkman, and bobbed her head at whatever music she was listening to. She caught me smiling at her through the reflection of the mirror.

"Best of Journey!" she yelled, oblivious to how loud her voice was.

I laughed, hearing Elsa's muffled chuckle from the closet. "You think Jimmy knows how she feels?" I asked Elsa. I chose this moment to ask the question I'd been meaning to ask, knowing Jade couldn't hear me.

"I'm not sure." Elsa's face was set in a frown as she stared down at my leather knee-high boots. "Seeing him as a man takes some getting used to. We were all so used to him as a toy dog. It's different now. But if he doesn't know, he's an idiot. Everyone with a brain can see the woman is in love with him."

I snorted and looked at Jade, who was now twirling on the spot, her lips moving to whatever song was playing in her ears. I loved her free spirit and her happy attitude. I needed some of that in my life.

I sighed and rubbed my sweaty palms on my thighs. "I haven't been on a date in over fifteen years. I'll probably end up just talking about work or the weather. Something un-date like."

My heart kept skipping whenever I thought of Valen and me sitting across from each other at his restaurant, the lights dim and romantic. I didn't like that he was making me nervous. Why the hell did I put myself in this position?

I grabbed my phone. The screen said 6:47. "I've got about thirteen minutes to get ready." I'd already done my makeup, which consisted a bit of black liner over my upper and lower lids along with a bit of lip gloss. I didn't need blush. My face was red enough without adding more. My hair was down in soft waves around my shoulders.

"Plenty of time," said Elsa, pulling out a pair of dark jeans. She observed them and then folded them over her left arm and kept going through my closet.

Jade pulled out her yellow earphones and looped them around

her neck. "Don't forget to wear sexy undies," she said, her eyebrows high.

I shook my head. "Yeah. I don't think so. Just dinner. That's it."

Jade's eyes rounded. "Sure. Whatever you say."

Part of me felt like I should just call him and cancel. Valen was a work colleague, and you should never mix relationships with work. Someone always got hurt, and the work relationship suffered. I didn't want to risk my job. I loved where I lived, and my new friends were like family. I didn't want to lose them either.

"Maybe I should just cancel," I said. My friends were more important to me than any man—even sexy man-beasts—and the idea of losing them scared me.

"Don't be a coward. You're going," ordered Elsa.

Jade snorted but sobered up at what she saw on my face. She came to join me on the side of the bed, and I could hear the faint music from her earphones around her neck. "Why are you so worried? Valen's a great guy."

"I'm sure he is. But if… whatever this is, doesn't work out… I don't want things to be awkward. We have to work together. And he lives next door."

Jade patted my hand. "Valen is a gentleman. I'm sure he can handle whatever happens." Her face went serious. "Any news on those dead vampires?"

"Nothing I haven't told you. Don't worry. Whatever killed them isn't contagious." I could tell she was still thinking about it.

"And you still don't know who they are?" Jade's blue eyes were filled with sorrow. "I can't imagine dying without anyone knowing who you were."

"It's rough. Hopefully, with more investigation, we'll find out who they are. Doesn't seem right to bury them in unmarked graves." I thought of all those vampires. "I was really hoping the autopsy would have revealed something. Now, we're still in the dark."

Jade fumbled with her fingers on her lap. "You think there'll be more. Don't you?"

I looked at her. "If I said no, I'd be lying. This is someone's twisted idea. Their sick joke. Why they're doing it? I don't know. These victims were robbed of their inherent paranormal energies."

"Do you think that's what killed them?"

"It makes sense. But why didn't the autopsy say so? And why did they die all at once?" The memory of all those vampires suddenly keeling over was still fresh in my mind, and it would probably haunt me for a good while.

Jade shifted on my bed. "You know, they could be from out of town. You said there were no missing persons in our community. What if they're not from here?"

I nodded. "Yeah. I hadn't thought of that. I'll check with the other Merlin groups. I have pictures of the three I found behind the dumpster. I'll start with that."

Jade and I were silent after that. The only sounds came from my closet, as hangers were being dragged along the metal pole.

Finally, Elsa came out of my closet looking flushed. The same pair of dark jeans hung from her left arm. "You've got nothing in here. How's that possible?"

"I told you. I've got nothing to wear. I should just go naked," I added with a laugh.

Elsa didn't laugh. The witch's face was pinched as she moved over to my bed and dropped the jeans on my lap. "Do you have a black cami?"

I nodded. "Yes."

"Okay then." Elsa sighed. "Bring out the slut blouse."

CHAPTER 11

My phone read 7:06 by the time I pulled open the restaurant doors and walked in. So I was a little late. Six minutes wouldn't kill the guy. I was late because I had to wait for Elsa to bring me a black leather clutch since my shoulder bag was a "horrible idea," according to her.

So with her clutch, a nice pair of black kitten heels borrowed from Jade—oddly, we wore the same size of shoes even though I was significantly taller—and the slut blouse that was not so slutty with a nice cami covering the girls, I thought I looked pretty good. Causal chic or whatever it was called. My dress code was I usually went with whatever was clean.

The restaurant door clicked behind me, and I strolled into the lobby. The same hostess, the one who *loved* me, had her face set into a glare as I walked past her, searching for Valen. The restaurant was packed. I couldn't see an empty seat in the whole place. I also couldn't see Valen. Shit. Did he leave because I was a few minutes late?

"The restaurant is full," said the hostess whose name I still couldn't remember, not that I cared to. She smiled at me, her eyes rolling over me slowly like she wasn't sure if she liked what I was wearing. "You can try maybe one of the human restaurants and see if they'll let you in."

"Good one," I said, suddenly feeling awkward holding a clutch and secretly wishing I had my shoulder bag with me.

"Leana."

I spun at the sound of my name to find Valen walking over.

Va-va-voom!

The light reflected off his sun-kissed skin, and his tall frame was covered in an expensive-looking, dark-gray shirt and snug black pants, showing off his fantastic physique. His dark locks were pulled into a low ponytail. In the dim light, his rugged beauty was startling, like an ageless elven king—graceful, menacing, and ruthless.

Why he wanted to date me was a mystery. I was seriously rethinking my ordinary jeans. Maybe I should have taken Jade up on her taffeta dress? Yeah, maybe not. The key point here was comfort, and I was comfortable in my jeans, albeit not as fancy.

"You look beautiful," he purred. Or did I purr? Hard to tell.

My guts were doing a jig. "Thank you." I tried to pry my lips open to tell him how amazing he looked, but they seemed to be superglued together.

"This way." The giant gestured and took my hand, gently leading me into the sea of tables. My skin tingled at his rough, calloused hand. His grip, though gentle, was just hard enough.

I looked over my shoulder and gave that uptight hostess, with a stick up her ass, my best smile. I really shouldn't have, but it was so damn fun. And totally worth it by the look of pure hatred with a smidgen of jealousy I recognized flashing behind those eyes.

I let Valen pull me with him as he led me across the restaurant to the front end, where the tall windows lined the entire front of the restaurant. A table with an arrangement of every color rose you could think of sat empty. I glanced around. The other tables didn't have flowers, just this one.

It was also, I noticed, pushed farther back from the other tables to give it more privacy.

Valen let me go and pulled out a chair for me. Yeah, ladies. He was *that* kind of man.

Smiling like a fool, I sat down and enjoyed the feeling of the giant pushing in my chair for me.

My eyes stared at his fine ass as he made his way around the table and sat in the chair directly in front of me. My eyes drifted down to his chest, where his muscles were screaming to be let out of the confining fabric, and I was willing to oblige them. Was this the hormones talking? I was acting like a schoolgirl with a crush, not a mature woman.

His dark eyes sparkled. "You should let your hair down more often. You look gorgeous."

My instant flush-o-meter soared to my face. Rolls of heat spiraled over me like a hot flash. "Enough with the compliments," I teased, though I didn't want him to stop. "But you do clean up real nice." There. I said it.

Valen's handsome face creased into a smile. "I try."

Cue in another hot flash. Hell, at this rate, I would melt before the food arrived.

Just then a male waiter with a shaved head bumped his thigh against our table. In his hands was a bottle of red wine. "Is this the wine you requested, boss?"

"Boss?" I snorted and then immediately regretted it. But Valen's smile only blossomed over his entire face. It was really hard not to like this guy.

"It is," Valen answered. The waiter poured some into his wineglass, waiting patiently for him to taste it.

After Valen gave the waiter a nod, he poured some into my glass and then proceeded to fill Valen's. I could feel the giant's eyes on me, but I pretended not to notice as I reached out, grabbed my wineglass, and took a sip.

Something was incredibly intimate about us having dinner together and him being so close.

"I'll be back with the entrées," said the waiter before he took off, winding his way through the tables and chairs.

"Cheers, Leana," said the giant, his voice low and sultry. He lifted his glass and held it over to me.

Shit. I'd already taken a sip. Nice one. My heart raced. I was nervous and felt like every nerve ending in my body pulsed into a burn. I wasn't exactly sure why I was nervous, though.

"Cheers," I said and gently tapped my glass to his. I took another sip, letting the fruity flavors sink into my taste buds. "Very good wine. Probably costs more than I make in a month."

A tiny smile crept along his full lips. "Not that much."

I frowned. "You know how much I make in a month?" I wasn't sure how I felt about that.

Valen set his wineglass down. "Basil mentioned it to me when he was having a bit of a meltdown. Does that bother you?"

I thought about it. "No. But now you need to tell me how much profit a year this place makes," I smiled, teasing. "You know. So that we're even."

Valen matched my smile. A shiver of delight went through me. He licked his lips, sending a wave of heat right to my core and pulling my stomach into knots of nerves.

"I think we'll be even when I see you naked," said the giant.

Holy shit.

A rush of heat flared from my middle to my face at the intensity of his eyes. He wasn't joking, either, and it sent butterflies in a boxing match in my belly.

Yes, I'd seen him naked many times when he changed into his giant form. And yes, I looked, a lot. I couldn't help it. Any warm-blooded female would.

"Well," I said, my heart thumping in my chest. "Let's see how this evening goes first." I could play this game too. It wasn't like I was *planning* on having sex with the giant later, but I was totally thinking about it. "You could think about having some custom shorts or something to wear… you know… when you change."

Valen's eyes crinkled in amusement. "Being naked doesn't bother me."

"I've noticed."

"It's just skin."

"Lots and lots of skin."

"When I'm out patrolling the streets at night, humans can't see me." He shrugged and leaned back. "It's like I'm not even there."

"But there's still a huge, naked man walking around," I said. "Admit it. You're a nudist."

Valen laughed hard this time, and I got a glimpse of that part of him that wasn't so serious, grumpy, or sad. It was wonderful to watch.

I took another sip of wine, enjoying my little victory. I was making this hot guy laugh. Nothing was better than that.

I turned my head and found the hostess watching us, especially me. Her face was a mask of hatred. Okay, that was definitely better.

"If it'll make you feel better, I can have some clothes made for me," said Valen.

I stared at the giant, wondering why he cared so much about how I felt. This date, or whatever it was, had all the elements of something more serious in the long run. But I was confused, mainly about the blonde I'd seen with him.

He wasn't giving off player vibes. His focus was solely on me. His eyes never wandered. I quickly glanced around and saw at least five women openly staring at him with lust in their eyes. They most probably knew what he was and were wondering what it must be like to get into bed with a giant.

Valen was a natural protector, a mighty powerful one, especially for those he cared for. It was an extremely attractive quality. What woman didn't desire a robust and protective type? It was a total turn-on, and I could understand the desire in those women's eyes.

The truth was, Valen could have any of these women if he

wanted to. But either he didn't notice, or he didn't care. I'll admit. That felt nice, more than nice.

But I couldn't ignore the fact that I barely knew this man. I had to be careful and had to protect my heart. And although I really, really, really wanted to ask about the blonde, I forced myself not to.

"I'll leave that to you," I said instead.

Valen pulled his handsome face into a grin. "Tell me about yourself. What was your life like before you moved to New York City."

I took a larger-than-necessary gulp of wine and swallowed. "My mother and I lived in my grandmother's house. And after my grandma died, it was just Mom and me for a long time." I sighed. The memory of my mother's passing was still an ache inside. "Then my mother got sick. After she died, I was a mess for about a year. I lost twenty-five pounds. I wasn't eating and drank too much. Lost my hair. I couldn't live in that house anymore. So I sold it and then I met Martin. I was still a mess. But back then, he was kinder. And I needed that. The rest, well, the rest, you know. The bastard tried to kill me."

Valen cocked a brow. "Because you broke his penis."

I laughed into my wineglass. "Good times."

A deep chuckle rumbled through Valen. "That's what I like about you," said the giant, making my pulse race. "You're real. You're not afraid of anything or anyone. You don't take bullshit. You're exactly what I see across from me."

"A middle-aged, divorced witch?"

"A badass witch," answered Valen. "The fact that you're beautiful is just icing on the cake."

Yup. I was purring now. "If you think flirting with me will get me in bed with you, you're dead wrong." Yes. It was working!

A slip of teeth showed through Valen's lips. "I'm just saying how it is. I like a headstrong woman who knows what she wants. It's sexy as hell." He stared at me. "If it'll get you in my bed, I'm all for it."

Ask him about the blonde! Ask him about the blonde! "Let's see how this date—dinner goes first. We might hate each other after."

Valen gave me a look that said that would never happen. "That won't happen."

"You never know. After a few more dates and sleepovers, when we let our true selves out, we might end up despising each other."

Valen leaned forward and surprised me when he took my hand. "You've seen me at my worst. The very first time I laid eyes on you, I was a bastard. Yet. Here you are."

"Here I am." I was very aware of his touch, his rough, calloused thumb rubbing my hand, and it sent a spike of desire through me.

Valen's smile was sly, and it went right to my gut and tightened. "You could have said no to tonight."

"I could have," I answered, my voice tight with desire. He kept rubbing my hand, and I could barely think. It didn't help that I hadn't been with a man in a very long time. My hormones were in overdrive.

A smile hovered over his features, and his gaze became more intent. A thick stubble peppered his face, black and sexy. My gaze slid down to his broad chest, muscles bulging from his fitted gray shirt.

I could have pulled my hand away, but I didn't. I let him caress it as I stared into those deep, dark eyes of his, trying to peel away some of the complex layers and get a peek of the softer, more vulnerable man.

But I also let him because it felt freaking amazing.

"Here we are." The same bald waiter arrived with plates topped with a variety of foods, and I pulled my hand away from Valen's, my heart hammering at what had just transpired between us. He was watching me with a look that made my breath catch in my throat.

The sexy-as-sin giant. The big, strong type who'd save you

from killer ex-husbands and demons. It hit me like a warm wave, ready to sweep me away. Damn.

I flicked my eyes back to the waiter as he settled the two plates, gave a nod to his boss, and then was gone again.

Food. Good. This would be a welcomed distraction to the hot, very hot attraction we'd had going just a few moments ago.

"What's all this?" I asked, knowing Valen had said he'd have something prepared for us, for me.

He pointed to the plates. "Melted calumet cheese, caramel with an emulsion of dried tomatoes and pecans. I hope you like it."

I leaned forward and took a sniff. "If it tastes as good as it smells, I might have to lick my plate."

His laugh echoed around us. "I'd like to see that."

I grabbed my fork and pointed it at him. "You just might."

At first, I tried not to moan whenever my fork reached my mouth, mainly because people were watching. But after the second mouthful, I let it all out.

"Oh, my God, this is good," I moaned, enjoying the blasts of caramel and cheese in my mouth. "You should package it up and sell it."

Valen flashed me his teeth as he took a sip of wine. "Glad you like it."

"Like it? If I could make love to it, I would."

In my twenties, with all those insecurities that came when you were younger, I would have been embarrassed to eat in front of him, concerned about how I chewed and whether I'd get some food stuck between my teeth. At forty-one, I couldn't care less. I wouldn't let a meal this good go to waste. I'd eat it. I'd eat it all.

We spent the rest of the evening laughing, talking, and enjoying each other's company. I felt at ease and comfortable, something I had never felt before with a man, not even Martin. Especially Martin. I felt myself relax, knowing I could tell him anything and he wouldn't judge me. I made sure not to talk about the blonde, though the thought did creep up on me more than once.

Before I knew it, he was walking me back to the hotel. He held the door open for me, and I walked in, seeing the hotel buzzing with guests enjoying Casino Week.

My skin tingled at his closeness, my mind fluttering with ways of how or if I should ask him back to my place. I'd have to figure out how to lock the door. Shit. What if the gang was there? No way could I have some private time alone with the giant.

"Good night, Leana," said Valen, and I turned as he took my hand. "I had a lovely time."

I smiled. "Me too." My insides fluttered in disappointment.

Valen dipped his head and kissed me. The slip of his tongue over my bottom lip sent bolts of ripples across my skin until heat pooled into my middle. He pulled back, his eyes tracing my lips. He looked at me and smiled, a glimmer of desire in his eyes, and then he walked away.

The kiss had been quick, but it screamed with need and desire, making my knees almost buckle.

I let out a breath and made my way toward the elevator across the lobby. I'd need a cold shower after that.

"You've got a message," called a voice. I turned to see Errol behind the front desk, his face pinched in a mask of derision while holding out a small message card.

I walked over to the front desk. "I've never gotten a message before."

"I don't care." Errol dropped the message on the counter and moved away.

"Who's it from?"

The concierge sighed and turned around. "I don't know. It was a phone message. No name. Just wanted to leave a message. He sounded nervous. Now, go away."

"Always a pleasure, you lizard *bastard*," I mumbled the last bit.

My insides twisted. What if this was a message from the Gray

Council's investigator? Curious, I took the message card and inspected it:

Go to 501 West 16th Street.
Look inside the warehouse, and you will find what you're looking for.

OKAY. Definitely not from the Gray Council.

Now, I was *really* curious.

CHAPTER 12

I sat in the front passenger seat of Valen's Range Rover Sport, the message card in my hands as I stared at the darkened street before us.

"How much farther?" came Julian's voice from the back seat.

I leaned over and stared at the SUV's built-in GPS screen. "Says about six minutes, and we'll be there."

The sound of leather pulling reached me. "I wonder who left that message," pondered Jade. "It almost sounded like a riddle. Or it could be a song? What do you think it means?"

"We'll know when we get there," came Elsa's voice right behind me.

My gut told me it had to do with the dead paranormals. It was the only crazy thing that was happening right now. I was looking for answers, and whoever had left that message card knew it. I just hoped I was right.

After receiving the message, I went up to my apartment, grabbed my shoulder bag and jacket, pulled on some flat boots, and searched for the gang. I'd found Elsa and Jade at the slot machines and Julian in the elevator with a gorgeous redhead, on my way down. After I'd filled them in, I called Valen.

"Miss me already," the giant had said on the first ring.

"You wish," I laughed. "Listen. I got this message just now." Once I'd read the message to him and expressed how I felt that it was somehow connected to the paranormal deaths, the giant had said, "Stay there. I'm coming to get you. We'll go together."

Tonight was a clear night, and although I could handle myself, having the giant with me was a bonus. Not to mention the three other witches. We'd face whatever this was together.

"You think it has something to do with the dumpster deaths and the other vampires?" came Julian's voice.

"Really?" expressed Jade, the surprise high in her tone. "How?"

I turned in my seat to face them better. "I do. Just a feeling. But don't you think it's weird that after I found those dead paranormals, and then the vampires last night, I get this message? I don't believe in coincidences. I think they're connected."

"It could also be a trap," said Valen. "If they've been watching you for a while, they'd know you'd come to investigate. It's how you operate."

I frowned. "Watching me?" I didn't like the sound of that. Following a giant patrolling the streets at night was one thing, but having some creepy stalker spying on me gave me the willies.

Elsa reached out and wrapped her hands around my car seat's headrest. "You think someone wants to hurt Leana?"

"Who wants to hurt Leana?" asked Jade. Her voice hitched, sounding paranoid.

Valen's jaw clenched. "I don't know, but receiving a message like that can't be good news. They didn't leave a name. They gave an address and said to go there. Sounds like a trap."

Nerves pulled my insides tight. I hadn't thought of that. "Well, we'll soon find out." I'd had my share of enemies over the years. I'd put a lot of paranormal "baddies" in jail, but they were still in prison, as far as I knew.

Elsa leaned back into her seat, her hands wrapped around her locket. "I'm glad you told us. I would have been very upset if you'd gone in alone."

I grinned. "I know. It's why I told you." My heart warmed at the feeling that I had these witches looking out for me. Only a few weeks ago, the idea of working with others would have had me walking away from jobs. Now, it felt strangely comforting that they were with me. And that went for Valen too.

"Did Errol say where it came from?" asked Jade. "Maybe he knows who sent it."

I shook my head. "I asked him. He said it came in by phone, and the person wouldn't leave their name. They just wanted to leave a message. He said the voice sounded nervous, and it was male."

Jade pursed her lips, toying with the white plastic bracelets over her wrist. "Hmmm. That is weird. But I'm surprised you got all that from Errol. He's a jerk. Never wants to help with anything if it's not in his job description."

"I had to threaten him to get that much." I smiled, remembering how round his eyes got when I told him I would dump a truckload of cockroaches in the lobby if he didn't give me more information. The actual cockroaches didn't scare him but knowing he wouldn't be able to control himself and would feast on the insects in front of everyone. We all had our demons.

"So," began Elsa, a smile to her tone, "how did the date go?"

Oh. Hell. No.

"We all know you two went on a date," continued the witch. "The entire hotel knows. And we"—she pointed to herself and then to Julian and Jade—"would like to know how it went. So?"

I clamped my mouth shut, and when I cast my gaze over a smiling Valen, a flush crawled up my face. "It went well," I said after a moment. Looked like I was going to have to do the talking.

Julian snorted. "It went *well*? Doing your taxes goes *well*, not a date. Either you knew it sucked after ten seconds and left early, or you stayed for dessert. Looks like you both stayed for dessert," he added with a sneer.

"We're going to find out later, might as well tell us," pressed Jade.

Valen was still smiling as I answered. "It was very nice. The food was perfect. The wine was excellent and the company too." I stared at Valen. "Care to add anything?"

The giant shook his head. "No. You're doing fine."

Elsa, Jade, and Julian all started laughing.

I glowered at them. "Let's talk about something else." I didn't want to talk about my date with Valen, not when I hadn't even had time to think about it myself.

I stared at the GPS. "Should be right there on your left."

The address 501 West 16th Street came into view. It was a giant wall of aluminum boxes—a warehouse. Rust stained the front and sides of the building, making it look like the metal was diseased. There were no windows as far as I could tell.

Valen pulled into the driveway, parked, and we all got out.

Julian walked over and faced the building. "Looks deserted. No lights on from inside."

"It's almost eleven at night," said Elsa, like that explained everything.

Valen walked to the back of his Range Rover and popped the trunk. He yanked out a flashlight from a black duffel bag, tested it, and handed it to me. "Here."

I took the flashlight. "Thanks. What about you? Do giants have night vision?" Vampires did, and so did most of the shifters and weres, so why not giants?

Shadows hid most of his face, though I could see a smirk. "We have better eyesight than most, but not like vampires or other shifters who can see well in the dark." He lifted another flashlight from his bag. "Better come prepared." He handed it over to Elsa, who waved a dismissive hand at him.

"Don't need it." Rummaging through her own bag, she pulled out a small globe the size of an apple—a witch light. I'd seen other witches use them before, though I'd never used one myself. I'd always wished I could do some elemental magic to have a witch light of my own.

Elsa held out her hand and whispered, "Da mihi lux." *Give me light.*

The sphere pulsated against the palm of her hand, and then a light shone through it as though she were holding an LED bulb. The globe soared into the air above her, illuminating the area in a soft yellow glow.

"Show-off," muttered Jade, though she had a huge smile on her face.

I checked the address one last time. "Well, this *is* the place," I said and stuffed the message card into my jeans pocket. "Let's see if the doors are locked."

"If they are, I have a potion for that." Julian strolled next to me, his long duster coat billowing around him as he moved. His hands rested in his jacket pockets, which contained potions and poisons.

"Could be warded and cursed," I said, remembering the sorceress Auria's secret entrance below the bridge. She'd been furious that I had broken through her curse, but even more so that I took her precious book of curses. It made me smile.

Together, we headed for double metal doors, what I assumed was the front entrance. One of the doors was propped open a crack as a silent invitation or a trap, like Valen suggested.

"It's open," I told them, turning around and seeing the worry etched on all their faces.

"I don't like this." Jade shifted on the spot, traces of anxiety on her face and fear in her eyes. "Who would leave it open like that?"

Good question. "I don't know. But it doesn't feel right." I reached out to my starlight. Energy hissed against my skin as the stars' power tingled over me. Hundreds of brilliant white, miniature globes flew out of my hand and hit the double metal doors, wrapping them in a curtain of white light. I waited as the starlights moved around the doors, expecting to feel the familiar cold pricks of a curse, but I felt nothing.

I let my arms fall. The starlights shimmered and then dissolved. "I'm not getting any ward vibes. No curses either."

"I'm not sensing the energies of wards here," commented Elsa as she held out her hands over the doors, like she was warming herself over a campfire.

I sighed. "Well. Looks like someone left it open for us."

Valen's frown and the narrowing of his eyes were truly scary. He clearly still thought this was a trap, and he probably wasn't wrong. But we'd come all this way. I wanted to know why someone wanted me to come here to see something. I wanted to know what that was.

"Let's go." I pushed on one of the heavy metal doors, and it swung easily to the side with a loud screech. "Let's see what this is all about. Shall we?" I said and walked in.

Valen was at my side in a beat. "Careful. Like I said, we don't know if this is a trap."

I nodded and flicked my flashlight forward, but I didn't need to. Elsa's witch light flew in and hovered above us, casting a soft glow and giving us a great deal of illumination. I still kept the flashlight on anyway, though, for the dark corners.

Still, I wasn't an idiot. Part of me agreed with Valen that this whole thing could well be a trap. I didn't want my friends or Valen hurt. We didn't know what we were up against, and sometimes that was worse.

The warehouse's interior was just as gloomy and stale as the exterior, reeking of disinfectant, like you'd smell at a hospital, with an underlying hint of something acrid like vinegar or blood. With the witch light dancing above us, I could make out racks that reached the ceiling stacked with boxes and what looked like wood crates, with plywood sides warped by moisture and wear.

"Smells disgusting," said Jade as she covered her nose. "Like a morgue that forgot to turn on the refrigeration switch."

She wasn't wrong. Something smelled ripe in this place.

My eyes flicked over to Valen. His features were set hard, and I could tell by the muscles popping along his shoulders and neck that he was just about to beast-out into his giant alter ego, or whatever it was called.

"Demons?" suggested Elsa.

I pulled on my starlight again, enough to send out my senses. A familiar energy prickled along my skin, the combination of cold-and-warm hum of magic. Magic was here—lots of it.

But something else, something more substantial that I couldn't decipher, was also lingering. It had the typical pulses of magic but was different, like the magical properties had been altered.

"I'm not getting any demon vibes," I said as I walked forward. "But something's here. Something with powerful magic."

"Yeah." Julian nodded. "I feel it too."

"Me too," answered Jade, and Elsa gave a nod.

We continued forward in silence, our boots clattering on the cement floor. I had no idea what to expect or what we would find, apart from mountains of crates. But someone had sent me here for a reason. Could be a trap. Could be anything, really.

We kept moving. My heart was a drum, pounding to a wild rhythm I couldn't stop. Valen stood next to me, a silent, powerful presence.

I couldn't see very well into the rest of the building because of the racks of giant crates, but whispers of energy rolled from the shadows around me. An entrance to another room came into view, and we made for it.

Just as we crept into the large workroom, the energy hit me with a full-on blast.

It was roughly the size of the Twilight Hotel lobby, teeming with computers, filing cabinets, and metal tables topped with microscopes and glass vials. I felt like I'd just stepped into a B-rated science fiction movie where mad scientists were manufacturing human and alien babies. The space looked and felt evil, wrong, and unnatural, as though whatever was happening here shouldn't be happening at all.

I halted as my eyes settled on rows of giant aquarium-like tanks. However, the tanks weren't what had me freezing in place but the people floating inside them. Tubes and wires wound from areas hooked to their naked bodies and connected to machines next to the tanks.

"What in the name of the goddess is this?" cursed Julian.

I rushed forward to the closest tank, feeling the constant thrum of magic and seeing a male floating inside. His eyes were closed. "The tanks are spelled." I stared at the tube of dark red liquid being pumped into him like a dialysis machine, but those machines didn't have magic coursing through them. These did.

"They're alive," came Valen's voice next to one of the machines. "They all have constant heartbeats."

"I don't get it. Is this a clinic?" Jade looked around. "Are they being treated for something? And why here?"

"Good question. They're being kept alive for a reason." I went to grab a file I saw resting on one of the machines when a whimper caught my attention.

I turned to my left, and my breath exploded out of me.

There, in a metal cage, was a person. No, not just one, but three terrified-looking people.

They sat, hunched in a cage fit for a large dog, their wrists and feet bound with rope. A piece of duct tape was strewn across their mouths, wet with tears. One of them, a female, met my eyes, and my chest clenched at the fear I saw.

I rushed over to the cage. "What the hell is going on here?" Anger soared as I looked for the door to the cage and found a lock. "Motherfu—"

"I got it." Julian hauled me back as he poured yellow liquid over the lock. It sizzled as the potion ate away at the metal like acid. The smell of copper filled my nose. The rattling of metal echoed around us as Julian pulled the door open.

"Thanks." I reached in and, with Julian's help, hauled out the female first, followed by the two males. As soon as we cut away their bonds and removed the duct tape, I knew something was off.

"Oh, shit," I said, staring at their scared faces. "They're human."

"What?" Valen stood next to me, his eyes inspecting the three *very* human captives. The female shrank away from Valen, and so did one of the men. I didn't blame them. The guy was still large and imposing, even in his smaller human shape.

Elsa pulled what looked like candy from her bag and offered it to them. "Here. Take this. It'll make you feel better."

The three humans huddled together and cringed from Elsa, like she was about to poison them.

She turned to look at me. "This is very odd. What were they doing in those cages?"

These were all excellent questions that needed answering. "Who did this to you?" I asked them in my most gentle voice, though a bit hurried. "Who brought you here?" I waited for a moment or two, searching their frightened faces, but I didn't think they were going to answer me.

Jade wrapped her arms around herself, staring at the tanks. "What's going on here? What the hell is this place?"

My eyes flashed to the tanks, and then I was moving. Yanking up my jacket's sleeve, I shoved my hand into the tank with a suspended female, trying not to think of what was in the water, and touched her arm. Then I moved to the front of the tank and carefully pulled back her top lip to reveal sharp canines.

I yanked it back, a cold sort of panic rushing through me.

Valen was right there, looking down at me, his eyes narrowing dangerously. "What is it? What did you find?"

I waited to have all my friends listening before I said, "She's human. I'm willing to bet every single person in those tanks is human."

Jade was shaking her head. "But I don't understand. I can sense magic here. We all can."

I shared a look with Valen. "I think... no... I *know* what's happening here. It's all starting to make sense."

"Please tell us before I have a heart attack," said Elsa, glancing over at the huddled humans with pity in her eyes.

Bile rose in my throat at what I was about to say. "These humans are being transformed into paranormals."

My friends all just stared at me like I was nuts.

"Look around you," I continued. "I'm willing to bet that blood in there," I said, pointing to the contraption that reminded me of a dialysis machine, "is paranormal blood. They're making paranormals out of humans."

"It's not that simple." Julian examined the machine I'd pointed to. "You can't just pump in some of our blood, and then you become a paranormal. It's not how it works."

"I have to agree with Julian," said Elsa. "I've never heard of humans being turned this way. Well, not if you count them being bitten by a rogue vampire or werewolf. Even then, it doesn't always take. It usually ends up with the human dying."

"I know," I answered. "But maybe all you need is a powerful spell and magic to complete the transformation. I feel it. You all can feel it. There's a spell here attached to this equipment, or maybe it's in the blood." Yeah, definitely in the blood.

Elsa's face was wrinkled in pity and disgust. "Goddess, help us all, if that's true."

I looked at Valen. He was quiet, his features carefully guarded. But I could tell by the stiffness of his posture he was upset. We all were.

"It gets worse," I said, my eyes tracing over the three terrified humans who looked like they were about to bolt any minute. I wouldn't blame them. They'd been privy to our conversation this whole time, which wasn't allowed. I'd worry about that later.

Jade rubbed her hands over her arms. "What'd you mean?"

My heart pounded as I was filled with dread and horror. "It means all those vampires we fought and those people I found near the dumpster… were human. That's why I never felt any paranormal vibes," I said as the realization hit me. "Because they were never paranormals to begin with. They were humans." I looked at my friends' shocked faces and said, "Humans that came from this place."

CHAPTER 13

Including the three terrified humans we'd freed, another fifteen were floating in the tanks being carefully carried out by the Gray Council's healers and placed on mats. I watched as the tenth human male was lifted out of his tank, the tubes and wires still attached to him. The healers, all dressed in white lab coats, proceeded to pull the wires and tubes from him.

Another group of officers dressed in gray uniforms—the Gray Council's tactical security, the equivalent of their police squad—watched from the doorway. I didn't care for them. They were arrogant and considered themselves above any laws but their own, so I stayed the hell away from them.

The warehouse lights were on now. No point in trying to be inconspicuous anymore, so I had a good view of the interior and the horror that inhabited inside.

I flicked my eyes back to the man on the mat. His skin had a grayish tint to it and was wrinkled, like that of a newborn. The hum of magic pulsed in the air as the healers mumbled some spells. The man's eyes flicked open for a second, and then they fluttered back closed. He looked like he was sleeping.

The healers were eerily silent as they worked like a group of monks after taking a vow of silence.

The sound of wheels pulled my head around to see another healer pushing a gurney toward the human man. Together, the two healers lifted the man and placed him on the gurney. Then he was hauled away out the door to a waiting van.

"Where are you taking them?" I asked the closest healer, a female about my age.

"Where they tell us to take them," she answered, her eyes flicking over to the gray officers. And then, before I could ask her more questions, she moved to the next waiting tank.

"The three humans are asleep now." Elsa and Jade came to join me.

I let out a breath. "Good. That's good. What about what they saw and heard? It's enough to traumatize them for life."

"The healers performed a very powerful memory charm on them," answered the older witch. "They won't remember a thing. Thank the goddess."

"Better that way." Jade let out a long sigh. "Some humans can go mad after witnessing something like this. It's too much too soon for them, especially since they've never had any dealings with the paranormal world, and they think we don't exist. Better to keep it that way."

"I agree." I looked over to see Valen and Julian both listening to a healer who was pointing to those weird dialysis machines. Valen's big, muscular arms were crossed over his chest, and he had that look in his eye that said I'm not sure if I like you or not.

Jade rubbed her eyes. "Well, I'm glad it's over."

I looked at Jade. "I don't think it's over. Yeah, we discovered their lab, but how do we know there's just one?"

Elsa's face paled. "You don't think there's more. Do you?"

I nodded. "I do. This was all carefully thought out and planned. It took time and effort. Probably months and years to come up with a spell to make the transition from human to paranormal work. There's no way this is over."

"But why? Why do this?" Jade's face was wrinkled in sorrow as another human was hauled out on a gurney.

I cast my gaze around the lab to the tanks and the equipment. "Looks like they're trying to make an army of some kind." As the words left my lips, they rang true.

"An army?" gasped Elsa, her voice loud enough to have Valen's head snapping in our direction.

I met the giant's eyes for a moment before pulling my attention back to Elsa. "That's what it feels like to me. Why wait years for a paranormal army when you can create one from humans?"

Jade made a disgusted sound in her throat. "Some people are just crazy."

"They are. But their army is faulty. It doesn't last. Whatever morphing is happening doesn't stay. It's not permanent. The vampires we fought last night all died when their time ran out. That's why I think this isn't over. We'll see a lot more of this before it's over because they're still perfecting the transformation. They'll keep doing it until their newly created paranormals stay alive."

This was Dr. Frankenstein stuff. But Jade was right. The person or persons who were doing this were clearly insane—psychopaths with no empathy or regard for human life.

"Why an army?" Elsa watched me for a moment.

I shrugged. "Armies are built to fight. Fight what? I don't know yet. But I'm going to find out."

Another gurney rolled our way with a female human resting on it. Dark blue veins were peeking through dangerously pale skin. She looked in worse condition than the others.

"Wait," I said and rushed over. "Will she live?"

The healer, a black male, looked at me. "I doubt it."

My mouth fell open. A heavy lump of dread formed in my chest. "No. Really? There's nothing you can do to help her?"

The healer shook his head, pursing his lips. "She's too far gone in the transformation. There's nothing we can do."

"Can't you reverse what was done to them?" My throat was tight with emotions, and I didn't care to hide it.

"We can't," answered the healer. "There's no turning back from this."

"But..." I looked at the remaining tanks with a floating human. "That means all those humans you guys pulled out are going to die?"

The healer looked at me, and I could tell he was trying to be kind. "Yes. We'll keep them as comfortable as we can. But they *will* die. All of them. Only those who haven't been subjected to the blood mixture will live."

"The three in the cages," said Elsa, standing next to me. "Oh, dear. How horrible."

My hands fell to my sides, and my eyes burned with both sorrow and anger as I watched the healer haul away the woman.

"What's going on?"

I turned my head to find Valen walking over. "The healers say that none of the humans will survive." My anger soared, forming into something as hot, brutal, and destructive as I felt inside.

"I'm not surprised," answered the giant. "Our blood is poisonous to humans. And with the amount they were given, you can't flush it out with liquids or with more human blood."

I clenched my fingers into fists. "It shouldn't have happened in the first place. This is someone's sick, twisted idea of creating paranormals."

I felt a hand on my arm. "But you saved three." Elsa's face was filled with compassion. "Think of those lives. They would have died if we hadn't come here."

She was right, but I still felt like I'd failed these people. "Who left me that message? Who left the door unlocked?"

"Someone with conflicting emotions," said Jade, casting her gaze around. "Probably worked here."

I stared at Jade. "You're right. Someone who participated in this nightmare... suddenly got their conscience back." And they'd reached out anonymously. But still, without them, we'd never have discovered this lab and saved those three human lives.

"There must be records of those people working here. Something." I looked over the machines at some metal tables piled with papers and files. "Let's see if we can find anything. Clues. All we need is a name. One name, and we'd have a lead."

We all started to go through discarded papers and files, Valen included. But after about fifteen minutes, all I'd found were just notes and data about the human patients. There were no bills, no receipts of any kind. It seemed those responsible had been very careful to keep their identities hidden.

"Nothing is here," I said as I shut a filing cabinet.

Jade held a tiny slip of paper. "I've got a McDonald's receipt. Two Big Mac combo meals. No credit card number. They paid cash."

"How will we find who's responsible without a name or something?" asked Elsa.

"Maybe whoever sent me that message will send me another one?" Yeah, I didn't think so, but if one person had a conscience, I was hoping others would too.

I turned and watched as the three surviving humans were hauled away on gurneys. Their terrified reaction to us was justified. They'd been kidnapped and forced to watch as other humans were subjected to this maniac transformation, knowing it would soon be done to them. If I'd been in that cage, I would probably have shit myself.

The only comfort I got from this cold, stale, nightmarish place was that they wouldn't remember a thing.

"Where are you taking those?" Julian's loud voice twisted me around.

The magical dialysis machines—not sure what else to call them—were being pushed and hauled out by the healers. He met my eyes across the room and lifted his arms over his head like he was making an offering to the goddess.

"What the hell?"

I rushed to meet them. "What's going on here?" I asked, putting myself in front of one of the machines, blocking their way. I was suddenly not thrilled about the healers taking the so-called magical dialysis machines. What if they could study them and reproduce the spells? Nope. Not going to happen.

Looks passed between the healers until one of them, a young male, answered. "We're following orders."

"Whose orders?" Valen was suddenly next to me, his hands on his hips. And from the deep frown on his face and the expectant glare in his eye, he was envisioning an answer.

Fear flashed in the same healer's eyes as he peered at Valen through his eyelashes, no doubt the result of knowing who and what he was. "The Gray Council gave specific instructions to bring the devices back," he answered, speaking fast, like the faster he answered, the quicker he'd be away from Valen.

I frowned. "The Gray Council?" I looked over their heads and saw another group of healers shoving all the files in those ready-made cardboard boxes with handles. "And the files? All the data? That too?"

"Yes," answered the same healer. His gaze flicked to the gray officers still standing around the doorway. "We were ordered to bring everything back."

"Back? Back where?" I asked, my pulse suddenly racing.

The healer swallowed, his body tense, and I could tell he was wondering if we were about to kick his ass. Sweat beaded his forehead, and a large vein throbbed on the side of his temple. "Headquarters."

"To be destroyed. Right? Not to study?" I waited for an answer, but the healers weren't talking.

When no one answered after a few moments, Valen stepped forward. "Answer her. Now. Or I will *make* you." The muscles on his neck and shoulders bulged in a show of strength and dominance. Not sure how he did that, but it worked.

The healer looked like he might have crapped his pants before he answered. "I… I don't know. They didn't tell us," he said, his voice quivering. "But we were told to be careful with the equipment and not to leave anything behind. Absolutely everything was to be brought back." The whites of his eyes shone as they darted from me to Valen.

I looked at the giant, seeing the same distrustful expression that I was feeling. But it's not like we could stop them.

Reluctantly, I dragged my body away, stepped aside, and let them pass. "Fine. Go on."

I crossed my arms over my chest as I watched the last of the gurneys with humans being hauled out of the warehouse a little faster than before, thanks to Valen.

Elsa stood next to me. "You've got that frown again. What's going on? What is it?"

I clenched my jaw. "I don't have a good feeling about this. Them taking all this back. It doesn't feel right." No. It felt like the Gray Council was about to set up a lab of their own.

"What do you mean?" asked Jade. "Can't be worse than all this."

I met Jade's face. "The Gray Council should have asked to have the machines destroyed."

"Yeah. They should have torched the place with everything inside," said Julian, his hands in his coat pockets. I met his eyes, and I knew he'd come to the same conclusion I had.

"But they've been given specific instructions to bring everything back," I said.

"And?" Jade shrugged. She was shaking her head, anxiety written all over her face and in her eyes. "It's better that way. Right?"

I shook my head. "These machines, with the blood mixture and the magic still in them, is not better. It means they can study the magic and the procedure. It means they can replicate it."

I let this information sink in a little while, watching the silent, collective horror spreading across their expressions.

Elsa was the first to break the silence. "You don't think... No... I don't believe the Gray Council would do that."

"I do," said Julian, his face tight. "They would."

"I do too." I stared at the now-empty warehouse. The last

evidence was carefully packed in boxes as the remaining healers walked in a line out the door, the gray officers following them out. Nothing was left of the lab we'd come across. "If they ever need to build an army for whatever reason… to fight demons or whatever… now they have the tools to do it. The procedure still needs work, but I came face-to-face with the result. It worked. What happened here, to these humans, is way too valuable to destroy."

"Maybe you're wrong," said Elsa, but the tone in her voice suggested otherwise, like she didn't believe it herself.

"Maybe," I answered. But my gut was pulling me in the opposite direction. Nope. The Gray Council was keeping all of it for a reason.

Elsa sighed. "Well, it's late. I think we should all get some sleep and speak about it in the morning."

"It's already the morning," said Julian. "Like three-ish."

"Then, the afternoon," she snapped. "I don't know about you, but my old bones need rest, especially after a night like this. We'll reconvene tomorrow afternoon. I'm sure things will be clearer after we all get some sleep."

She wasn't wrong. We were all high on emotions and adrenaline. It had been a strange night. I'd gone on a date with Valen and even contemplated asking him back to my place. And now this. I needed to sleep for a few days just to get rid of this eerie dread that had stuck to me like a cold sweat since we arrived.

Because I was pretty sure things would get worse before they got better.

They always did.

CHAPTER 14

"What are you doing still in bed!" shouted a familiar voice. "Get up. Up! Up! Up!"

Even though my eyes were closed, I knew it was Elsa, and she sounded annoyingly chirpy and giddy.

"Go away. I'm still sleeping." I lifted my comforter over my head, trying to shut out her voice. My head pounded with a migraine, feeling like I had a massive hangover but without the fun of the actual drinking part.

I barely slept a wink. How could I when we still had a demented mad scientist or *scientists* on the loose in the city somewhere? I kept waking up in a sweat, my heart pounding in my chest as I kept replaying the scene over and over again. My stomach quailed at the thought of all those humans floating in those tanks back at the warehouse, the way the humans cringed from us in that cage, like we were monsters about to devour them. The notion of what these humans had endured had my guts rolling and my eyes burning every time. It had seemed their lives meant nothing. They were just vessels, their bodies used for a single purpose. To kill? That was still unclear.

I think I started to doze off just as Elsa barged into my room.

I felt a tug, and fresh air assaulted my face as my comforter disappeared. "Up," ordered Elsa. "You're not sleeping. You're having a conversation with me. That's not sleeping." She let out a sigh. "You're exactly like my son, Dylan. I could never get that one out of bed. Slept the day away."

I blinked the crust from my eyes. "You have a son? You never said?"

Elsa smiled proudly. "Yes. He lives in Scotland with his wife. Very much like his dad." She lost her smile. "Don't change the subject. Up you go. Come on. It's nearly six o'clock."

"What?" I reached out, fumbling with my side table, and grabbed my phone. "Damn. It felt more like noonish." Crap, I really had slept the day away. Well, not exactly slept. I only dozed off here and there. Not exactly a good sleep.

Concern flashed across her face. "I know. I don't think any of us slept much. All those poor souls. Dreadful what's happened to them."

I sat up, feeling a little dizzy. My eyes rolled over Elsa, noticing her wild, red hair was carefully pulled back with a barrette, though some loose strands framed her face. Red leather boots peeped from under her flowing, striped-green-and-orange skirt.

"You look nice. Why all dressed up?"

Before she could answer, Jade came gliding into my room on roller skates. She wore pink tights under a black sweaterdress with a white belt wrapped around her waist. Long faux-pearl necklaces looped around her neck and dangled past her stomach. Her hair was scrunched up into a high ponytail like she'd done it without a mirror.

"Oh, my God, she's still in bed?" laughed Jade as she did a pirouette, settled, and braced herself on my dresser. "We're going to be late."

I sat straighter. "Late for what?"

"Hurry up and shower." Elsa pulled me to my feet. My long T-shirt was the only thing I had on me. "The hotel's throwing a special dinner. Casino dinner for the guests and tenants."

"That means us," said Jade, pointing at herself as though I hadn't gotten that part.

"Drinks start at six," said Elsa, looking at my closet like a ghoul was hiding in there about to jump out. "Find whatever you have that's appropriate, and we'll meet you downstairs."

"Okay, okay." I waved at them. "Going to shower now."

Jade laughed and rolled out of my room. "Hurry up, old lady," she called over her head at Elsa.

"Call me that one more time, and you're going to lose a wheel," threatened Elsa.

With my phone in my hand, I rushed over to the bathroom and turned on the hot water in the shower. It took a while for the water to get hot, so I took the opportunity to scroll through my phone and see if Valen had written to me or called. Nope. Nothing.

Last night had been a weird night. First dinner with the giant and then off to the warehouse. Still, I thought he would have reached out.

I stared at his name on the screen, my finger hovering above it as I contemplated calling him. No. I was not going to be *that* woman. If he wanted to call me, he knew where to reach me.

After showering in record time, I pulled on a pair of black pants and a black sweater. I brushed my hair up in a messy pony-tail, dabbed on a bit of black eyeliner and clear lip gloss, slipped on my ankle boots, grabbed my bag, and headed toward the elevator.

My stomach growled as I hit the lobby button. Dinner sounded really good at the moment. Food to heal the soul seemed about right. Hopefully, they'd have cheesecake for dessert. That would flush away all sorrows.

I hit the lobby, maneuvered around the gaming tables and slot machines, and made my way toward my favorite concierge in the history of concierges.

Errol looked up as I approached, and his face twisted in what I could only describe as a constipated look.

"What do you want?" he snapped, his upper lip twitching in a snarl, and I got a slip of his gray-forked tongue. I noticed he did that when he was upset or nervous.

I leaned over the counter and got as close as possible to him. "Any more messages for me?" It was a long shot that the person would send me another, but it was the only lead I had. Their conscience led them to me once. Maybe it would do it again.

"No." He smiled, seeing my disappointment.

"You sure?"

"Positive."

I tapped the counter with my finger. "You're not holding out on me. Are you? Because that would be bad. Bad for you."

Errol gave me an annoyed stare. "I would rather slit my own throat. Now… go away."

I raised a brow. "Ooookay. Good talk."

I pushed off the counter and made my way to the dining room that only yesterday had been set up as a lunch buffet.

The tables were placed the same, but they had a more elegant feel with white tablecloths and short candles as centerpieces. White gleaming plates rested neatly over the tables, flanked by shining cutlery and expensive-looking white napkins with gold etching.

I let my gaze travel over the room, looking for that particular wall of a man with dark, fine eyes and never-ending muscles. But I didn't see the giant anywhere. Maybe he didn't want to experience the same thing he did yesterday when everyone ogled him like he'd just arrived from Mars.

I yanked out my phone and stared at the screen. No new calls. No messages. I struggled for a moment, my fingers itching to text him but figuring the man probably needed space, so I shoved my phone back in my bag.

"Pretty, isn't it?" Elsa joined me, a wineglass in her hand, and by the pink on her cheeks, I knew this wasn't her first.

"It is." I spotted Basil across from us, waving his hands at an annoyed Polly, who was holding on to a meat mallet like she was about to use it on the small witch. "That doesn't look good. Doesn't he know never to insult the chef? Insult the chef, and you'll have spit or worse in your food."

Elsa chuckled. "Basil is a fool. The tables are already designated with tiny name cards on each plate. That's our table." She pointed across the room to where Julian was standing. He picked up a small, white, rectangular folded piece of paper and stared at it.

Jade was already sitting at the table, her head down and her chin rubbing her chest. She looked like she wanted to slide down her chair and hide under the table.

"What's the matter with Jade? She looks sick." Her usual pink complexion had that unearthly pallor of those near death.

Elsa snorted. "She asked Jimmy out."

"Noooo." I pulled my eyes back on Jade. "Attagirl." She might look like she was about to puke, but I was proud of her.

"Come. Let's sit. Everyone's starting to take their seats." Elsa pulled me with her as the dining room suddenly filled with guests and tenants, the sound of conversation and happy babble loud.

I saw Barb, the elderly witch, standing before a table. She grabbed the name cards, pulled them to her face, and smelled each of them. Okay. Not going there.

Elsa let me go, and I bumped my hip against the chair next to Jade. "I heard what you did," I said, wrapping my hands around the chair's backrest and doing my best not to laugh.

"I think I'm gonna be sick," muttered Jade, her face tight.

Julian pulled out his chair across from Jade and sat. "It took balls to do what you did. Not a lot of women ask men out. I wish they did it more. It's such a turn-on. And it would take some of the pressure off. You know what I mean?"

I laughed. "Not really." I turned back to Jade. "When did this happen?" It couldn't have been that long ago. I'd just seen her a few minutes before in my apartment.

"Like, five minutes ago," said Jade. "Right here. In front of everyone. I want to die."

"No, you don't. It'll be all right."

Jade slid farther down her chair, her eyes brimming brightly like she was about to cry. "No, it won't. I can't believe I did what I did. I'm such an idiot. Big, stupid idiot."

I felt for the witch. I'd seen the powerful crush she had on Jimmy. I swept my gaze over the room and spotted him looking sharp in a blue suit, talking to Basil. I waited to see if he would make eye contact, but he didn't. Some guys were total dicks when dealing with things from the heart, but not our Jimmy. He was a good, kind man who'd been stuck in a damn toy dog for longer than I had been alive. If anyone was sensitive to the feelings of others, it was our Jimmy.

I turned my attention back to Jade. "What did he say?" The worst that could happen to my friend was if Jimmy said no. There was a fifty-fifty chance that he would. But from her reaction, I was guessing he turned her down. Gently, I was sure, but still a blow to one's ego.

Jade's face took on a paler shade, if that were even possible. "Nothing."

I frowned and leaned closer. "Nothing? What do you mean, nothing?"

"Nothing," she repeated, staring at a spot on the table. "Who does that? It means he's not interested. It means he was so *disgusted* by my asking that he didn't even have the words to turn me down."

"Oh, dear." Elsa let herself fall into an empty chair. "Here we go."

I shook my head. "Wait a second. He didn't say anything? He just stood there and said nothing? What did his face look like?" That was strange, even for Jimmy.

"Like he was in hell," muttered Jade, making Julian laugh.

A tug pulled on my heart at the pain in her voice. "Okay, so you asked a guy out, and he didn't answer. It's not the end of the world. There are worse things in life." But right now, I could tell there weren't. Not for her.

Jade only shook her head. "I knew it was a mistake. My inner Jade told me not to do it."

"Your *inner* Jade?" Okay, I had to laugh this time. So did Julian. So did Elsa. Yeah, we were terrible friends.

"But did I listen?" continued Jade as though I'd never spoken. "Noooo. And look what happened. He'll probably never speak to me again. He'll avoid me like I'm diseased. I've seen it happen before."

"Jimmy's not like that," I told her. "He's one of the good ones." I knew she knew this, too, part of why she had such a crush on him. "Listen. He was cursed as a toy dog for a really long time. Maybe he's just not ready."

"Doubt that," said Julian. "If it were me, I'd be getting laid with as many lovely ladies as I could after being a toy."

I glared at Julian. "Not helping."

Julian shrugged. "Just saying how it is."

The truth was the only person who knew what it was like to be cursed into a toy and then turned back into themselves was Jimmy. Maybe he wanted time alone, and maybe Jade just wasn't his type.

Jade pulled at the strands of hair around her face. "It's humiliating. And now I have to look for a new place to live."

"Don't be ridiculous," snapped Elsa. "It's not like you were dating for a while and you caught him cheating."

I nodded. "Good point."

"Pull yourself together, and let's enjoy the evening," said Elsa, winning a glare from Jade. "It'll all get sorted out. Things have a way of doing that when you least expect it."

Jade pulled the elastic band from her hair and, with her fingers, combed the strands forward around her face, like she was using her hair as a shield to hide behind.

I grabbed the last empty chair, but I scanned the table before I pulled it out. "Where's my name? I'm not seeing it anywhere. And there are only three table settings."

Elsa put her wineglass down and grabbed the three name

cards, rereading them as though the others were illiterate. "Your name's not here."

"I know." I felt a flash of irritation that they'd forgotten to print out my name. But it was nothing compared to how Jade felt.

"Who cares? Sit. We'll get Polly to get another place setting," offered Julian.

"That won't be necessary." Basil stood next to our table, scrubbing his glasses with a corner of his navy jacket.

"Why's that?" I asked him, inspecting his face for a clue as to what he was hinting at but finding nothing.

Basil put his glasses on, straightened, and puffed out his chest like a proud peacock. "Because you're sitting at the *important* table with me."

I clamped my jaw tightly and tried hard not to laugh. "I am?" Maybe hotel employees sat together. Okay. I could do that. It wouldn't be as fun as enjoying a good meal with my friends, but I knew by taking on the job full time, I'd have to make some sacrifices in the name of the Twilight Hotel. Sitting and having dinner with Basil was apparently one of them.

"That's right," answered Basil. "By special request."

I frowned. "Special request?" Not sure I liked the sound of that.

Basil's face stretched into a smile that was far too wide to be considered normal as he looked across the room. "Yes. Adele asked for you to be seated next to her at her table."

Hell no.

A flame of anger ignited in my chest as I followed his gaze. There, sitting at a table toward the far end of the room, was none other than that skinny witch bitch who had nearly destroyed the hotel and cost Jimmy his life.

The one who sat on the White witch council. The one I'd bet my life made that complaint about me.

Adele.

CHAPTER 15

"Hurry up. We don't want to make Adele wait." Basil grabbed me by the arm and hauled me beside him with surprising strength for such a tiny witch.

I glanced over my shoulder at my friends, seeing their faces cast in worry. They looked petrified, like I was being dragged to the center of the village to be hanged. Even Jade looked like she'd forgotten her troubles for a second and was staring at me wide-eyed and fearful.

"Here we are," said Basil as we arrived at the said important table.

A quick glance around the "important table," and I spotted a large centerpiece of a mix of glass candles and white flowers. The white tablecloth was made of some expensive silk material with golden symbols etched into the fabric, unlike the ordinary white cotton cloth that covered all the other dining room tables.

Adele looked up from her seat where she was currently the only one sitting at the "important table." She wore a white tweed-knit belted jacket over her thin shoulders, a piece of clothing that screamed haute couture and probably cost more than what I made in a month. Diamonds fell from around her ears and neck, taking up more space than they should. Her blonde hair was styled in a chignon on top of her head, adding a catlike resemblance to her already sharp features. Her light eyes tracked me slowly, and I couldn't help but feel goose bumps rise over my skin.

I yanked my arm free. "I didn't need an escort." I glared at the male witch, my fingers twitching as a part of me wanted to wring his little neck.

"Yes, well..." Basil cleared his throat and bowed slightly from the waist. "I must see to the kitchen. Don't worry, Adele. I will make sure your lamb is cooked just right."

Adele gave Basil a patronizing smile. "Thank you."

Still, Basil seemed pleased and rushed away, heading for the double doors to the right, which I knew was the hotel's main kitchen, Polly's domain. I wasn't sure she'd take kindly to being told by Basil how to do her job. The thought made me smile on the inside.

I could feel the older witch's eyes on me, but I refused to look at her. I spotted my name on the name card placed above the table setting, next to hers.

I stood there contemplating whether I should just leave. I didn't want to be here. Sitting next to a hateful witch whose ass happened to sit on the White witch council wasn't exactly my idea of a nice dinner. This witch had cost Elsa's husband his job, had made a complaint about me to the Gray Council, and had nearly killed Jimmy. I would never forget that.

If I left, Adele would probably make my life a hell of a lot worse after everyone saw I'd slighted her in public. Yeah, she'd hate that. I didn't care. She could hate me all she wanted. At least we'd have that in common. But I did care about my job here at the hotel, and I wasn't ready to let that go. Not yet.

Gritting my teeth, I yanked out the chair and sat. I had a good view of my friends' table. They were all huddled together, talking and throwing concerned looks my way. If I didn't know any better, it looked like they were planning my rescue. Loved these guys.

"Hello, Leana," said Adele, her voice dripping with the kind of fakeness that made my skin crawl. "You know, it's very rude to ignore your guests."

"Guests?" I said, though still not looking at her. "I don't get it. You don't like me. I don't like you. So why did you want me to sit here? To torture me? Want to pretend for the world that we're besties?"

The witch gave a phony laugh. "Why are you so hostile, Stardud? Is it a crime now to want to get to know you better? I just want to share a pleasant meal in your company."

I cringed and swung my eyes to her. "Cut the crap. Why am I here? Payback? Is that it? Your revenge?"

Adele's pale face pulled into a pointed smile. She was even uglier up close. "Trust me. If I wanted revenge for that little stunt you pulled with the Gray Council, this wouldn't be it. You have it all wrong, Stardud."

I narrowed my eyes at the warning in her tone. "You nearly killed my friend Jimmy. I'm very glad my so-called stunt saved his life and ruined your plans. I'd do it again in a heartbeat."

Adele's pale eyes tracked the room and fell on Jimmy. "I heard you removed his curse. How did you achieve that?"

"Wouldn't you like to know?" Ah-ha. So, this was more of an interrogation dinner. She wanted to know how I'd managed to remove Jimmy's curse. She could ask all she wanted. I wasn't about to tell her.

Adele picked up her glass of white wine and took a sip. "The hotel's hired you full time. I find that interesting since you were an epic failure. But that's what you are. Isn't it, Stardud? A failure sort of witch. But *is* it witch? Not exactly sure you fit the bill, as they say. Your magical abilities are somewhat wanting."

If she thought she was going to upset me by dragging out my unusual and, yes, sometimes lacking, magical skill, she was sadly mistaken.

"Well, they did," I answered, keeping my voice from showing any emotion. "Must have done something right. But I'm very surprised your ass still sits on the White witch council. Especially after going behind the Gray Council and trying to have the hotel, *their* hotel, destroyed. How is that?"

Her face was screwed up with irritation, and her eyes almost seemed to glow in frustration. But then it was gone in a blink, replaced by her usual arrogant, contemptible visage. "Careful, Stardud. This ass can take everything away from you. This place. This job. Your friends. I can take it all."

I didn't like the way she said that. My voice twisted with bitter anger when I looked at her. "Is that a threat? Are you threatening my friends? Threaten me all you like, but leave my friends out of it."

Again, she plastered that fake smile on her face, the one that never reached her eyes. "You're *sooo* sensitive. I would never hurt your friends. What kind of witch do you think I am? But you should know something. In this line of work, you need to have thicker skin, Stardud. Or you'll never make it."

I frowned. "You're not as good a liar as you think. Need to work on that." I pulled my eyes away from her face before I lost control and punched her. Or made her eat her stupid diamonds.

"Has anyone ever told you what an insolent and vile witch you are?"

"So I'm a witch again now?" I shrugged. "If you're feeling agitated and frustrated, my work is done." If she thought I'd just sit here and be polite, she didn't know me as well as she thought she did.

"I guess that's what happens when you grow up with the wrong witch family," she added conversationally.

"What the hell do you want?" I was going to punch her before dinner was served.

"For starters, a pleasant conversation would be nice."

She was so full of crap, I was starting to smell it on her. "Sure. Whatever."

"Good. I heard it was quite the show on the hotel's roof," said Adele. "You defeated many demons. Closed a large Rift as well, if I'm not mistaken."

I nodded. "That's right." She'd let on that my magic was worthless, that I was a dud, practically human, yet here she was, intrigued by it. She was so easy to read.

From the corner of my eye, I saw her watching me. It was creepy. "And you did that on your own?"

Ah. Now I knew where this was going. "No," I said, looking at her. "I had help. My friends helped me."

A strange smile pulled at her lips. "I hear you and Valen are getting close. You were on a date last night. Is it serious?"

My anger resurfaced. "You spying on me?"

Adele gave a laugh. "If you wanted it to be secret, you shouldn't have dinner in a restaurant filled with people."

A waiter came then and held a bottle of white wine in one hand and a bottle of red in the other. He looked at me and said, "Can I offer you some wine?"

I nodded and pushed my empty wineglass forward. "Red, please."

When he was done, I grabbed my glass and took a sip, thinking about why Adele was so interested in my love life. Maybe not even my love life but Valen. I'd seen how she looked at him like he was sex on a stick. Obviously, she had the hots for him. She was jealous that I'd been on a date with him. Now she wanted to know if it was serious or not.

"You want my advice?" asked Adele after a moment.

I laughed. "No."

"He's not the settling-down type. He's been with many, *many* women over the last few years. But to my knowledge, he's never found any of them worthy enough to be serious with. To settle down with. Not one. And there've been many."

"Yes, you said that already." I took another gulp of wine. "Are you hoping he's going to ask you out? Is that it?"

"You like him. Don't you?" continued the witch in that same condescending tone she'd used on Elsa. "You think you have what it takes to tame him. You think you can tie him down?"

"He's not a wild dog. He's a man," I said, irritation flowing in my tone.

"A giant," corrected the witch.

I narrowed my eyes at her. "What's your point?"

Adele leaned back in her chair, balancing her wineglass in her hand. "A giant and a Stardud. Interesting pair. One would never imagine that sort of *union*."

Damn. She could really piss me off. I could feel my blood pressure skyrocketing until it pounded behind my eyeballs in anger—beautiful, hot anger. I was furious, really.

Movement caught my eye, and I saw Elsa standing up from her chair, looking like she was about to come over here. Probably to rescue me.

Our eyes met, and I shook my head. I waited until she sat down and smoothed out my emotions. I didn't want Adele to know this line of conversation had such an effect on me.

Instead, my heart warmed at how a small group of people had become part of my family. And as family, they cared and were worried about me. Even though Adele terrified Elsa, she was willing to come over and help. That was true friendship.

"Call it whatever you want," I told the other witch. "It was a date. Just a date."

"That's not what I heard."

I whipped my head around. "What have you *heard*?"

At that, Adele smiled evilly, and it took an enormous amount of self-control not to grab that diamond necklace and shove it down her throat. "That the giant is falling for you. That he can't keep his eyes off you when you're in a room." She paused like she was hinting that the big news was coming. "That he saved you from a brutal beating from your ex."

My lips parted, and my heart slammed into my chest. "Who told you that?" How the hell did she know about that? As far as I knew, only Valen, Martin, and I knew. Okay, maybe I'd told my friends too. And maybe word had gotten out. Damn. This was not the kind of news I wanted Adele to be privy to.

I kept my face from betraying the emotions fluttering through me like I had butterflies instead of blood flowing through my veins. "That was a personal situation, which is none of your business."

Adele threw back her head and laughed. "Oh, Stardud. Don't you know? Everything that happens here is my business." She leaned forward and placed her glass on the table. "But I can't say I'm surprised. Human males are often filled with uncontrollable emotions. They're weak. Under my council, witches are forbidden to marry out of their race. I would have never allowed it if you were in New York then."

I snorted. "Wow. That itty bit of power really got to your head."

Adele's eyes gleamed. "Power is power. Nothing else matters."

"Hmmm. I'm guessing you're rooting for a spot on the Gray Council. Is that it? You really think they'll give you a chair? The crazy witch who wanted to destroy their hotel?"

"I'll let you in on a secret since… well… since you're so interested and all," said Adele, as though speaking to a five-year-old child. "The thing with the Gray Council… they don't care about you. Witches, vampires, and werewolves all are disposable. One dies and is easily replaced. But the Gray Council, well, it will always stand, and it will always come first."

I shook my head, wishing I was sitting with my friends instead of this crazy bitch. "Quit the Yoda talk. Say what you mean."

A hint of devilry lay in her voice as she said, "Not yet. Soon. Soon you will understand."

I rolled my eyes. "This is going to be a long night."

Just when I thought about excusing myself to the bathroom with a case of intestinal failure, Jimmy showed up at our table.

"Hey, Jimmy." I perked up at the sight of him. "Please tell me you're sitting at this table."

"Uh…" Jimmy's eyes flicked over to Adele and then back to

me. “Yes. But that’s not why I’m here. Someone’s at the front desk asking for you.”

Saved by the bell, or rather, the assistant manager. I sat straighter. “Who?” Thinking this must be one of Julian’s schemes to get me away from Adele, I flicked my gaze to my friends’ table, and my heart sank. They were all still sitting there. Staring over here, but still all present. Jade was staring at Jimmy like she was about to hurl.

“I don’t know,” answered the assistant manager. “Never seen him before. I told him you were at a dinner party, but he won’t leave a message. He’s really adamant about speaking to you in person. He’s a bit of a twitchy fella.”

I beamed at Adele. “Duty calls.” I took the last swig of my drink and left, not bothering to say anything else to that icy bitch. The more distance between us, the better.

“You’re pretty cool around her,” I muttered once we were out of earshot.

Jimmy stopped when we reached the end of the dining room. “I don’t let her get to me. You should do the same.”

“Touché.” I looked him over. “You gonna tell me what happened with Jade?”

Jimmy’s face twitched, and then he grimaced. “I… I gotta go.”

My mouth was still open as I watched the assistant manager hurrying away from me, like he was late for a meeting.

“What is up with those two?” Shaking my head, I made my way back to the lobby to the front desk. My best pal, Errol, was there. And for the first time, he was looking at someone else the same way he looked at me—like they were walking poop.

The someone was a middle-aged man with reddish-blond hair. He was heavyset, short, with a white shirt halfway tucked into the belt of dark pants that were too long for him. He looked like a mess, which explained why Errol was glaring at him.

The stranger’s eyes widened when he saw me approaching. “Leana? Leana Fairchild? The Merlin?” he said in an accent I couldn’t place.

"Yes." I came to stand next to him. "Do I know you?" He had a forgettable face, kind of like Raymond.

He grabbed my arm and pulled me with him.

"Hey!" I yanked out of his grip, pulling on my magic as I felt a burst of nervous energy coming from him. Okay. He was a witch too.

"Grab me like that again, and you'll be kissing the floor," I growled.

He let go, pulled out a handkerchief, and started to dab the sweat from his face and forehead. "Apologies. I just"—he looked over his shoulder, his eyes darting nervously around and not settling on anything—"I don't want to be overheard."

I crossed my arms over my chest. "What's this about? Who are you?"

The man leaned forward and muttered, "My name is Bellamy Boudreaux. I'm the one who left you the message about the warehouse."

Okay, then.

CHAPTER 16

I took Bellamy back through the hotel lobby to one of the slot-machine areas that was now vacant and away from Errol's eavesdropping.

Once I was sure we were alone, I turned to the witch. "You're a witch?" I had to be sure.

"Yes." Bellamy nodded. "I'm the chief—*was* the chief—witch scientist on the HTO project." At my bewildered expression, he added, "Human Transference Origins."

"Wait—there're witch scientists?" Of course, there would be. I don't know why I said that.

Bellamy nodded. He looked over his shoulder. "Yes, well, as you have probably guessed by now, after seeing the warehouse, I was charged with altering humans' genetic material. To transform them into us. Into paranormals."

"I noticed. It worked."

The witch shook his head, his body twitching like he had a spasm. "No, not always. What you saw was a small percentage of humans that survived the actual transference."

Dread clenched my chest as the images of those floating people came back, slamming into me like a physical blow. I cocked my head to the side. "So you're saying a lot more humans have died for this?"

I thought it strange that I hadn't found any mention of masses of humans disappearing in the human news. I made it a habit of checking social media for anything suspicious.

"Unfortunately"—Bellamy pulled out his handkerchief to dab his sweaty forehead and face and then shoved it back into his pocket—"mostly prostitutes and the homeless."

I didn't like the casual way he'd said that, like they didn't matter somehow, as though that made them lesser humans. "Still people. Still humans. Still illegal to harm them." Every paranormal child knew that harming a human was forbidden. We were all raised to know our laws inside and out.

"They didn't all take to the paranormal transference," said the witch, and he blew out a heavy breath like that had been highly tedious for him.

"You said that." I was starting to dislike this witch scientist, possibly more than Adele at the moment.

Bellamy seemed to cower at my heavy glare. "No. What I mean is we were able, more or less, to administer modified werewolf blood into a human host. Vampire blood worked, too, but we were not able to manipulate the blood of a witch. I still don't know why, but the witch gene could not be transferred."

"Good." The idea of a bunch of crazy, brand-new witches loose in the city was not a good thing. It was horrible enough we had a bad case of crazed vampires. But witches? Witches could do magic. And I didn't want to think of the horrors they would have bestowed on the human population.

The witch scientist sighed. "Even then, it was not enough. It was never enough."

I stared at him for a second. It seemed like whoever he was working for had high expectations. "But your science project has flaws," I told him, seeing him narrow his eyes at me. "I fought a horde of newly created vampires and then they all just died. Like they had an expiration date. Care to explain?"

"Another unfortunate consequence of the transference," said Bellamy, shifting his weight. "We tried to have them last longer. At first, it was only a few seconds. Then a few minutes. Hours. But we couldn't get them to last more than six hours."

A cold sliver of dread slid through me at the thought of all those test subjects. Human test subjects.

But in an instant, my anger took over my dread. I didn't like this guy. Yes, he'd given us the location of the warehouse, but he'd still participated. He made this happen. You'd have to be pretty demented to work on something like this and call it science. It wasn't even fringe science. It was barbaric.

I swallowed, feeling the tension rise in me. "Why did you do it? *How* could you do it?"

Bellamy clenched his jaw and swallowed. It looked painful. "Money. Power. Prestige. I thought I'd be published in our science journals. But I quickly realized that would never be the case." He hesitated. "There's no excuse. I just... couldn't do it anymore. Couldn't. All those humans. Terrible. I had to tell someone. Now, I'm on the run."

I stared at him, still wondering if I should punch him. "Telling me was the only good thing you did about this whole situation."

Bellamy's pale eyes rounded, and he reached out and grabbed my arm. "You have to protect me! They're going to kill me!"

I peeled his hands from my arm. I did not want this guy touching me. Ever. "Take it easy. You're safe here."

"No. No. No. They have spies everywhere." His head spun around as he surveyed the lobby, like he thought we were being watched. "They're after me. They know what I did. I'm a dead witch if you don't protect me!"

"Who? Who's after you? Who's behind all of this?" I had my suspicions, but I wanted to hear it from him.

Bellamy's bottom lip trembled. "Never got a name. But they just sent instructions to be followed by their mediators. They have lots of money and power. I think... I think it has to be someone on the Gray Council."

I let out a breath through my nose. "My thoughts exactly."

Bellamy paled at the mention of the council. "It's why I couldn't go to them. What if I was right, and then they'd just kill me to silence me." His wide eyes flicked behind me. "They have eyes and ears everywhere. Everywhere!"

Right. He was a bit of a drama queen, but I knew he was scared. He had intel, the only intel about this whole nasty operation. He was my key witness. My only witness. I had to keep him safe.

"You're a Merlin," said the witch scientist. "You're sworn to protect the vulnerable. Those who need help. That's me."

Not exactly. But I wasn't about to explain my role as a Merlin.

"I'll protect you," I told him and saw tension leaving his posture. "First, I need to find a safe place for you, like a safe house. Somewhere they won't think of to look for you."

"Here?" Bellamy looked around, not at all that comfortable with the idea of staying in a hotel owned by those he was allegedly running from.

"No. I don't think here is a good idea." I stared at him, wondering if I should find him a hoodie or a hat to hide his face, but I decided we didn't have time for that. "Come with me."

I grabbed Bellamy, and together we exited the hotel. I looked over my shoulder when we got to the front entrance to see if anyone was following us, but no one was there.

"Where are we going?" asked the witch scientist, who was now sweating profusely in the cool September weather.

"A friend's place," I answered.

I yanked out my phone and called Valen. After the fourth ring, it went to voicemail. I hung up. It wasn't ideal, but Bellamy would be a lot safer in Valen's apartment than he would in the hotel. And I didn't think the giant would refuse to let him stay, either, as a protector and all.

Besides, Valen needed to know what was happening.

Exhaust fumes and the stench of garbage displaced the night air as I hauled Bellamy with me to the building next door. The gathering dark rushed in to fill the spaces where the streetlights couldn't reach.

When we arrived at the storefront, I looked up and found Valen's apartment windows black as night. I didn't think he was there.

"Are you taking me out to eat?" asked Bellamy, squinting his eyes at the glass like he was trying to get a better view of the restaurant inside. "I am kinda hungry."

I rolled my eyes. "Come on." Grabbing Bellamy by the arm, I hauled him through the restaurant doors and came face-to-face with none other than Valen.

And the mystery blonde.

"Oh," I said, jumping back and pulling Bellamy with me.

"Leana?" Surprise flashed across Valen's face. "What are you doing here?"

I narrowed my eyes at his reaction. I'd expected a "What's the matter" or a "Are you okay." Instead, I got a "What are you doing here?" Yeah, something was definitely up with him and the blonde.

Speaking of said blonde, I took my time to really look at her. She was about my height, but with a more voluptuous body and curves in all the right places. Her lean figure was perfectly enclosed in a snug black pantsuit under a black cashmere coat. She wore her hair in a slicked-back, low ponytail, which only accentuated her pretty features. She was classy and put together, the total opposite of me. If I were to guess, I'd say she was a paranormal lawyer.

Annoyingly, she was even more beautiful than I remembered, with large blue-green eyes and full lips, reminding me of a young Christie Brinkley. Seeing her up close was playing with my insecurities, but I could also see her horizontal pupils. She was a shifter.

But I couldn't let my imagination get in the way. I came here for a reason. I waited for Valen to introduce us, but he just stood there, looking slightly awkward and, did I dare say... guilty?

Bellamy leaned forward. "What are we doing here? Are we eating or not? I'd go for a large steak with fries. Smells decent in here. But you can never tell what's really going on in the kitchens. You know what I mean? You can never be too careful when picking out a restaurant."

Valen watched me and then moved his gaze over to Bellamy, sizing him up. A slow frown creased his brow.

I ignored Bellamy and spoke to Valen. "Are you going to introduce us?" I should have gone straight to the issue at hand, but I couldn't help myself. I'd wanted to know who she was for days. Now, she was right here in front of me.

At that, the mystery blonde raised her perfectly manicured brows, and a coy smile reached her lips. She thought I was hilarious. Great.

I heard a snort and looked past Valen to see my favorite hostess smiling at me, the kind of winning smile like she knew I'd been played. Either that or she knew something I didn't.

Two people thought I was hilarious. Fantastic.

Valen's eyes darted between Bellamy and me. He gestured toward the blonde. "This is Thana. A friend."

I looked over at the woman called "Thana. A friend," expecting to see her hand out for a shake, but she just stood there with that amused look in her eyes.

Okay, either she didn't want to shake my hand because she thought I was beneath her, or maybe she didn't want to shake it because I was the competition?

My gaze fell back to the giant, expecting him to say something else, but he just stood there, looking more uncomfortable than anything.

A painful silence settled in, and my anger welled.

"That's it?" I looked at him. "That's all I get?" Okay, so maybe I wasn't exactly entitled to know all about his personal life and whether he was dating other women, because it certainly looked like it. It's not like we'd made what we were—what were we, exactly?—exclusive.

But it still pissed me off.

"Let's go." I grabbed Bellamy and hauled him out of the restaurant with more force than necessary.

Valen didn't call out my name. He didn't come after me either.

Nope. He let me leave.

It hurt. I'm not going to lie. It hurt a lot. But that was my own damn fault.

I should have never let myself fall for a man I barely knew. That was all on me.

CHAPTER 17

"You think I'll be safe here?" asked Bellamy, staring at all the open doors on the thirteenth floor, like he thought a monster was going to sprout out and grab him.

I snickered. "Don't worry. Everyone's downstairs at the special dinner. No one's here but us."

"But is it safe?" pressed the witch scientist, the whites of his eyes showing.

I had no clue. "It's the safest place we've got for now."

Valen's place would have been ideal, but it looked like he was going to use his space for some sexy time with the blonde later.

I cringed on the inside, trying not to think about it, but it pounded against my skull like a migraine. I wasn't perfect. I still had those insecurities that crept up from time to time, and having lived with a cheating husband didn't help them from springing up again. It just brought them all back with force.

My eyes burned. No. I would not cry. Not for any man. Not anymore.

It was my own damn fault I'd let a stranger into my heart. And now I had to pull up my big-girl panties and get to work. I had a job to do, something more important than my personal life. Besides, I would get over it. I always did.

"Why are all the doors open?" asked the witch, walking a little faster whenever we got to a doorway and then slower when we hit the hallway wall. "Is that normal? It's like everyone left in a hurry. Maybe there's a fire?"

"No fire. Trust me. This is how it is here. This entire floor is kinda like one big apartment," I said, feeling a warmth creeping in and filling that little part of my heart that was aching. "I was a little taken aback at first too. But I love it now. Everyone's amazing. We all look out for each other. Like a family."

"Hmm." Bellamy's face was screwed up in irritation, his shoulders going stiff. Clearly, he didn't think this was a good idea. I didn't care. I didn't really care about his feelings. The witch had been involved in torturing humans and had subjected them to horrible experiments. He could be *bothered* all he wanted.

"Right here," I said when we'd reached the end of the hallway and my apartment. I gestured to Bellamy to follow me inside.

I took five steps and then halted. "What are you guys doing here?"

Elsa, Jade, and Julian looked up from the living room as we entered.

"Waiting for you," said Elsa, her eyes on Bellamy with a questioning frown.

Jade stood up and rolled over to me in her skates. "Who's your friend? And why is he sweating like he's in a sauna?"

Bellamy let out a squeal like a frightened mouse, doubled back, and started for the doorway.

Good thing I caught him.

I grabbed a fistful of his shirt, spun him around, and dragged him forward, helping with a little shove. "This here is Bellamy. He's a witch scientist with the ho project."

Julian grinned as he leaned forward. "The ho project? Count me in."

"HTO project," corrected Bellamy, enunciating every letter.

I cocked a brow. "Whatever. He's one of the witches who performed those experiments on the humans."

At that, I watched as my friends' faces darkened with a mistrustful cast. Yeah, they liked him as much as I did.

"He's the one who left me the message about the warehouse."

Bellamy looked at me, horror written all over his face. "What are you doing?" he hissed. "I came to you for protection! And now you're telling them everything about me. Might as well kill me now."

I rolled my eyes and heard a chuckle from Julian. "Bellamy has a flair for drama."

Bellamy scowled at me. "This was *not* the plan."

"These are my friends," I told the witch scientist, scowling right back at him. "I trust them with my life. So, you can trust them with yours. Okay?"

Bellamy didn't answer, but he really didn't have a choice. If he wanted my protection, well, it came with my friends.

I looked back at my friends. "What about dinner? It can't be over so soon?"

"We left before dinner was served," said Elsa as she stood from the couch. She saw my disappointed look and added, "It just didn't feel right. We saw how uncomfortable you were sitting with… her. I didn't think it fair that we would have a good time while you looked…"

"Like your guts were being pulled out of your mouth," said Jade, smiling. Her face stretched into a bigger smile as she caught Bellamy looking at her, but the witch scientist pulled his face into a glower and quickly looked away as though someone like Jade shouldn't be ogling him. What a tool.

"It got better when you left," informed Julian, piquing my curiosity.

"What do you mean?"

"Adele was furious you just left her like that," he said, and I saw Bellamy stiffen at the mention of that witch's name. Guess he didn't like her either. "She started to scream at Basil to go get you back. Poor bastard. He tried, but you weren't in the hotel."

Ah, hell. I didn't want Basil to get mixed up in my mess. "So, what happened?"

"He found someone else for her to torture." Julian shared a look with the others.

"Who?" I didn't like the sound of that.

"Jimmy," he answered, and I felt a wash of anger flow over me. "Don't worry. Jimmy can handle himself. He was all smiles when he sat down too. Probably gonna try to get some info out of that cold bitch. He was still with her and Basil when we left." Julian stretched and crossed his ankles on my coffee table. "I can't wait to hear all about it."

"Me too," said Jade, and she rolled off to the kitchen to pour herself a glass of water.

Bellamy leaned forward and whispered in my ear, "Isn't she a little old for roller skates?" His voice was filled with mockery. "She looks ridiculous. And look at her hair?"

"No, she's not," I snapped. I leaned forward until I got right in his face. "Another comment like that about my friends, and I'll personally send you to the Gray Council wrapped up in a bow. You got that?" I wasn't kidding either.

Bellamy's face went from shock to irritation, but he was smart and kept his mouth shut after that.

Seems my little encounter with Valen still had me on edge.

"Why are you so tense?" Elsa's eyes inspected my face. "You look flushed. Did something else happen?"

I shook my head while grabbing Bellamy and pushing him into the armchairs. I wasn't about to relay what had happened with Valen. It wasn't the time. And I didn't want to bring up all those feelings.

"More humans died than we first thought," I told them instead and began to communicate everything Bellamy had told me about their experiments.

"I think I need to sit down." Elsa's face was pale as she fell back onto the couch.

Julian pressed his feet on the floor and leaned forward, resting his elbows on his knees with his attention on Bellamy. "And you don't know who's behind this?"

Bellamy swallowed hard. "I believe it's someone on the Gray Council. But I don't have any proof. We never met them. They paid really well and just gave out orders through other people."

"And you kept killing humans because it paid well?" came Jade's voice as she rolled back into the living room.

The witch scientist's face flushed red, and he wiped it with his handkerchief again. "We believed it was for the greater good. For our people."

"Who's we?" I crossed my arms over my chest, staring down at him.

"The other witch scientists," he said. "That's what we were told. We believed them."

"Through these mediators?" I pressed.

Bellamy nodded. "Yes. Through phone calls and emails. It was something they kept repeating." He hesitated like he was trying to recollect a memory. *"The time of the paranormals has come. We must rise and protect our people.* It was repeated constantly. Texts. Emails. It just became normal."

"When did this all start?" Elsa's voice was filled with anger. "When did you..." She gestured with her hands.

"About a year ago," answered Bellamy. "At first, it was just to get the lab going. People don't realize how much work it takes just for pre-op. And then we got our first human subject."

I cringed at how excited he sounded at the prospect of using a human for his experiment. "So, what you're saying," I began, "is basically you've killed what... hundreds? Maybe thousands of innocent humans?"

Bellamy's mouth dropped, his eyes darting around the room but not settling on any of us. I could tell he was quickly trying to find a way to defend his actions. "We thought—"

"It was for the greater good of our people." I felt bile rise in the back of my throat. I really hated what he'd done. I despised him for it. But so far, he was our only proof that the Gray Council, or someone in it, was responsible for killing those humans. It could never happen again. I had to stop it. And for that, I needed more.

"I'm going to need names."

Bellamy shook his head. "I told you. I don't know who they are."

"Names of the other witch scientists you worked with," I told him, seeing his eyes rounding. "And a copy of all those emails and texts. You still have them. Right?"

"Yes," answered the witch scientist, dribbles of sweat running down his temples. "What will happen to them? To me?"

"Well, first, we need to keep you safe and alive," I said with a sigh. "You did come forward. I'm sure that will swing in your favor when your case goes to trial. You'll probably get off with maybe six months to a year in prison."

"Prison! I can't go to prison," cried Bellamy. "I have an IQ of two hundred and five!"

Julian snorted. "Anyone else feel really stupid at the moment?"

Elsa pressed her hands to her hips and glared at Bellamy. "Well, you should have thought about that before you started torturing humans if you're so smart."

Jade rolled over to him. "That doesn't sound smart."

Bellamy stared up at Jade like she was an annoying child. "I told a Merlin. I stopped. I gave you the message. That has to mean something. I cannot go to jail."

"That's not up to me to decide," I told the witch scientist. "Once we have all the evidence and a solid case against the Gray Council member or members responsible, you'll know. I wouldn't be surprised if your colleagues get life in prison."

Bellamy's complexion went a tad green at that point. "That *cannot* happen to me. I still have plans, projects that need pursuing."

I didn't think Bellamy should be anywhere near another lab in his lifetime. Not after what he'd done. He was dangerous. What he did was unethical. Yeah, okay, so he had a teeny conscience, which was the only thing that would save him right now.

"There's more," said Bellamy into the sudden silence.

My pulse was fast and still rising, and I felt my anxiety pulling me stiff. "What?"

The witch scientist wiped his forehead and face again with his damp, sweat-covered handkerchief. So gross. "If I tell you, do you promise to keep me out of jail?"

I clenched my jaw. The nerve of that little bastard. And then I realized this was his plan all along—string us along, and when he knew it was the best time, play his only card. His "get out of jail free" card.

When my gaze traveled over the others, they were all looking at me. Waiting. Fear echoed in their faces. Fear of something worse. It rattled them.

I stepped closer until my thigh bumped against Bellamy's chair. "What is it?"

"Promise," he said, pointing a trembling finger at me. "Promise me, or I won't tell you."

"We could just beat it out of him," suggested Julian, staring at Bellamy like he wanted to test one of his newest potions on the witch. "He kinda deserves a beating. And worse."

I couldn't agree with him more, but seeing his resolute face, I had a feeling he wanted to tell me. And I knew how to do it without a well-deserved beating.

"Fine." I kept my face from showing any emotion. "I promise to keep you from jail. Tell me." Total lie. And for once, I felt like I'd pulled it off, but only Bellamy's reaction would tell.

The witch scientist relaxed and leaned back into his chair. He believed me. "Thank you." He let out a breath, met my eyes, and said, "There's another lab in the city."

Ah, hell.

CHAPTER 18

The cab ride to Upper Manhattan was silent and uncomfortable. First, well, because we had a human driver, and second, we were all dreading what we were going to find. Would it be worse? A more extensive lab with more humans being experimented on?

I'd really hoped the lab we'd discovered yesterday had been the only one. I'd never imagined we'd find more of these human workshops around the city. Bellamy knew of one more, but what if there were more than he knew? The thought sent pricks of fear through me.

I'd left the witch scientist back at my apartment. No way was I going to risk his life. He was too important—a bastard, yes, but a bastard I still needed.

"You stay here and lock the door behind us," I told him about five minutes after he'd given us the news of another lab. "Don't let anyone you don't know in. Got it?"

Bellamy gave a nod. "I'm hungry. Do you have any gluten-free food in that contraption you call a fridge? Something of quality?"

I'd slammed the door in his face. I was protecting him. I didn't have to like him or be nice to him.

The silence was suddenly interrupted by the loud ringing of my phone. Damn. I'd forgotten to put it on vibrate.

The cab driver looked at me. "You gonna answer that?" He was a middle-aged white male with a scruffy beard and a receding hairline. At first, he'd refused to take us all in his cab since there were four of us and the back of his sedan only fit three. Although Julian offered, I was not going to sit on his lap. The cabbie finally agreed after I'd pulled out a hundred-dollar bill.

I gave the cab driver a look, pulled out my phone, and switched it to vibrate mode.

"Who was that?" asked Jade from the back seat.

I turned my head and stared out the front, blinking at all the oncoming car lights. "Nothing important."

I heard the pulling of leather and then Elsa's voice. "The same *nothing important* as the restaurant owner next door?"

"Possibly." I was going to tell them about my abrupt visit with Valen earlier. They were going to find out anyway, just not right now in a dingy cab with a human stranger sitting so close and staring at me more than was considered comfortable.

After another ten minutes, the cab pulled inside a long driveway and stopped his car. "That'll be a hundred and thirty-two bucks," said the driver, a grin on his face.

Julian whistled. "Expensive ride."

I paid the cab driver. "Maybe. Still cheaper than owning a car." With the gas prices up and all the insurance and maintenance of a car, I didn't think I was going to buy my own anytime soon. "Can you wait for us?" I didn't feel like waving down another cabbie who might not want all of us in the cab.

The driver flashed me a toothy grin with more spaces than teeth. "It'll cost ya."

"Fine."

Still smiling, the driver pressed on his meter box and turned it on. "What are you guys, anyway? You're not cops. You ghost hunters or something?"

I winked at him. "Or something."

The driver gave me a look like he thought I was full of crap and started to scroll through his phone.

I got out and shut the door just as the others climbed out. I glanced around to see we stood on a tight street stacked with warehouses and apartment buildings that looked like they'd survived a world war. Across from us an empty lot was blocked off with a sagging chain-link fence, and tall grass grew through the fissures in the pavement.

Before us loomed a lengthy gray building with a flat metal roof and no windows. It looked more like a container than a building, like the mother of all containers.

"Looks like someone left the door open *again*," said Julian as he moved closer to the container-like warehouse and headed for the large metal door.

"Just as charming as the one we found last night," muttered Jade, rolling beside me. She was still in her roller skates.

I frowned, unease rippling through me. "Stay close and be alert. We don't know what other *things* they're creating in here."

"I don't like the sound of that," said Elsa, hanging on to her bag.

Julian was the first at the entrance, a vial clasped in his hand as he pulled open the door with the other. After a loud screech, we all stepped into line behind him—you guessed it, in complete darkness.

"Hang on," said Elsa as she whispered an incantation and drew a glowing, silver witch light from her hand before tossing it in the air. The globe rose above our heads, illuminating the space in a nice soft yellow glow.

We stood in a sort of entrance, if you wanted to call two metal walls with an opening an entry.

Jade reached out and steadied herself on the side of the metal wall. "What do we do if we meet any of these witch scientists?"

"Probably have to fight them." I hadn't thought about that. I was hoping they wouldn't be quick on the magical draw. We could also face some opposition with those mediators Bellamy talked about.

As a precaution, I tapped into my will and called my power to the stars, my starlight magic. A cool tingle of magic washed over me, and I held it. If these intermediaries came at us, I'd be ready for them.

I didn't sense any other magic, either, but I didn't think it odd. The other human subjects hadn't emitted any paranormal vibes either.

"I need something that'll connect this lab to the Gray Council," I said, keeping my voice low in case we weren't alone. "The entire warehouse is a big evidence pile. This time we'll be taking some of the evidence back."

I wouldn't be putting out a call to the Gray Council until I knew who among them was in on it. And if they were all corrupt, I would talk to the head of each paranormal council and show them the evidence. It might even cause an overthrow of our government. The thought had my guts in a twist, but what choice did I have? None.

"If only one of those transformed humans had stayed alive," said Jade, pulling that thought right out of my head. "We could have nailed them with that. That's all the proof you'll ever need."

"Or those we found in that cage, if they hadn't wiped their memories," commented Elsa, her face pinched in thought.

With my temper rising like a fever at the idea of finding more transformed humans, we walked past the entrance and stepped into a much larger space—the only space since there were no signs of doors, hallways, or other compartments in the massive container.

As soon as the reek of disinfectant and bleach reached me, I knew something was wrong.

I swept my gaze around the area. I saw no signs of wood crates that had littered the other warehouse, and the racks that reached the ceiling were empty. I saw no tanks with floating humans in them and no cages with terrified humans. Not one of those magical dialysis machines. Not even a single file remained. Nothing. It was as though the lab had never been operational. Either that, or it had been wiped clean.

"That son of a bitch lied to us," cursed Julian, pacing until he reached the middle of the warehouse, his voice echoing off the walls of the space. "He's dead. He's fucking dead."

I felt the air move next to me as Jade rolled ahead. The screech of her wheels reverberated over the concrete floor. "Why would he lie? What purpose would it serve?" she called as she took on speed, clearly enjoying the empty space.

"To throw us off, maybe?" Elsa had a frown on her face as she placed her hands on her hips, looking very much like a mom about to scold one of her kids.

I looked around. "Throw us off from what?" I didn't think Bellamy had lied. He wanted to stay out of prison too much.

My phone vibrated in my bag, but I ignored it.

"You know you can share with us," called Jade from the other side of the warehouse. "We won't judge."

How did she hear my phone? "I know. Just don't want to think about that right now." I crossed to the other side of the container warehouse and then turned around and did the same, walking the length of the structure and hoping to find something, anything. But there was nothing.

I began agreeing with Julian about Bellamy lying to us until something caught my attention. It was small, a miracle I even saw it in the dim light.

A drop of blood.

I grabbed my phone and switched on the flashlight mode, carefully shining it on the spot. "Definitely blood."

"What? You got something?" Elsa joined me, Julian following closely behind, her witch light hovering and bathing us in enough light for me to see.

"Not just a drop. A *trail* of blood," I said, seeing it clearly with the witch light. A long splatter of blood led to the door we came from.

"What?" Jade came speeding toward us, tried to stop, missed, and just kept rolling by.

Not wanting to take any chances, I tapped into my starlight. A ball of white light, the size of an apple, hovered over my palm, and I blew out a breath, causing the ball to burst into a hundred smaller globes. They flew over the trail of blood and fell on it like an illuminated walkway.

As soon as the starlight hit the blood, I felt it—the pricks of paranormal energy and something else I couldn't decode.

"He didn't lie." I watched as my starlight vanished. "That's paranormal blood. Shifter blood. And it's been tampered with." I knew in my gut this was the same type of blood that had been pumping into those humans at the other lab.

Jade came rolling back and this time managed to slow to a stop. "Did I hear you say you found shifter blood?"

"I did." I pointed to the trail of blood. "Bellamy told the truth. This was the same kind of lab he worked in. My guess was they knew about the raid on the other one and packed everything up."

Elsa sighed. "There goes our evidence."

"Not necessarily," I said, looking at my friends. "We still have a witch scientist."

And now, more than ever, I knew I needed to keep him safe.

CHAPTER 19

Of course, when I got back to my place, Bellamy was gone.

My eyes went from my open apartment door, the door I distinctively remember Bellamy locking behind us, to the living room area just off the hallway. I strode through, dread clenching my chest as I already knew I wouldn't find him even before I checked the other rooms.

The witch scientist was gone.

A series of curses flew out of my mouth as I rubbed my temples and my eyes. The night was proving to be one of the worst in my career—first with the empty warehouse and now with the only witness disappearing.

"He split," said Julian, stating the obvious. He started to laugh. "That little shit just took off. He's dead. He's so dead."

"He left?" Elsa sounded incredulous. "Why? Doesn't he know you're the only one he can trust? Who will protect him? What an odd thing to do."

I shook my head, frustration filling me. "I don't know. Maybe he got spooked. He didn't want to stay here. He didn't trust the hotel. But I never imagined he'd leave." He'd come to me to protect him, so why did he just leave?

"Maybe he just got bored and decided to gamble some of his

blood money downstairs." Jade walked into the kitchen barefoot. Her roller skates hung down from her neck, tied with their laces. She grabbed a glass and filled it with water.

"Yeah. That's it," said Julian, his hands on his hips as he gave the room a final glance. "Let me go check." Before I could stop him, Julian strolled out of the apartment and disappeared.

"More like there are a few ladies he wants to go see," laughed Elsa. She sounded tired as she leaned on one of the dining chairs.

I let out a sigh. "I should have left someone with him. Damnit. I shouldn't have left him alone. Now the only person who can expose those on the Gray Council is missing." I was angry with myself. If I could kick my own ass, I would. This mistake would cost me. It was a rookie mistake, and I wasn't a rookie.

I'd screwed up because I wasn't focused. My head had been filled with Valen and that blonde. I'd been hurt and angry at the giant but mostly at myself for letting my heart fall for this man. I'd tried to clear my head of him and focus, but I'd failed. And that had cost me my only witness.

Crap. This was bad. I rubbed my eyes, looking over the room for clues, anything that would give me an indication as to where Bellamy had gone.

My pulse raced as something else occurred to me. In a burst of speed, I rushed around the living room, checking the side tables, sofas, and chairs, trying to look at everything all at once.

"What are you looking for?" Jade put her empty glass of water in the sink.

"I'm not sure." I spun on the spot, not seeing anything out of place. "I was wondering if maybe Bellamy was taken."

Elsa sucked in a breath. "You think?"

"Possibly. I'm not seeing any signs of a struggle, but that doesn't mean they didn't put a gun to his head." More like a magical gun or something to threaten him with. The more I thought about it, the more it started to make sense. Someone had come here and had taken Bellamy. But who? And where did they take him?

"But how did they know he was even here?" asked Jade, coming around the kitchen to where I stood in the living room.

Elsa let herself fall into the chair with a flop. "They must have recognized him with Leana. They must have seen him downstairs. The hotel is filled with guests and strangers. I'm willing to bet they saw Leana with him."

"And they put two and two together. They knew I'd put him in my apartment, and then they just had to wait for us to leave and…"

"They took him," added Jade. She looked at me, determination on her face. "Then let's go find him and bring him back."

I gave her a weak smile. "I wouldn't even know where to look first. I'd say to check his house or apartment, but I'm sure those who are after him have already been there. And he'd come here, knowing his home was compromised." I flicked my gaze between the two of them, seeing dark circles under their eyes. They were drained. "Besides, you guys look exhausted. I'm not going to make you run around the city looking for a scared witch scientist, when we don't even know where to look."

"I'm not that tired," said Jade, though her droopy eyelids said otherwise.

"I still have about three hours of investigation left in me," said Elsa. "If I don't have to run, I'll be fine."

I smiled at her. "There'll be no running tonight." I moved to the coffee machine, flicked it on, and went to fill it with water. I wasn't tired at all. Quite the opposite. I'd slept half the day, so I was still running on adrenaline and energy. "This is my fault. My mess." I had to find him. And I wouldn't rest until I did.

"Fine," said Jade, moving next to Elsa by the table. She wrapped her hands around her roller skates that hung from her neck. "We'll go. But only if you tell us what happened between you and Valen."

I cringed as I turned around and rested my back on the counter. "Do I have to?"

"Yes," they chorused.

"When I first found Bellamy, I took him to Valen's restaurant. I figured it was a better place to hide him than the hotel."

"Makes sense," said Elsa. "No one would have thought to look there."

"That was what I was thinking," I continued, seeing their focus on me, their eyes gleaming with interest.

"You didn't find Valen?" asked Jade. "Is that why you brought Bellamy back here?"

I turned and poured myself a fresh cup of coffee. "Oh, I found him, all right. I found him with that pretty blonde."

"You caught them having sex!" Jade smacked her roller skates together, looking positively thrilled.

I sighed. "No. They were leaving the restaurant when we got there."

"And you think he's dating you both? Is that it? Is that why you're angry with him?" Elsa watched me, her lips pressed in a tight line.

I took a sip of coffee. "I know what you're getting at. I have no right to be upset. We've only been on one date." The fact that he hadn't reached out after that date did sting. "But I reacted. I didn't use my head."

A slow smile worked Jade's lips. "What did you do?"

"I didn't do anything. Bellamy was with me. I left and brought Bellamy here."

"Leana," began Elsa. "It doesn't mean he doesn't care for you. I mean, you don't know who that blonde woman is."

I thought about when I asked him to introduce us, the way Valen didn't want to elaborate on who she was. It only cemented my belief that he was in a relationship with her.

"It doesn't matter. That's it. That's all that happened. And you know the rest." I was done talking about it. I needed to find Bellamy, and I wouldn't let my emotions get in the way of work. I wouldn't make that mistake again. "Off to bed, you guys," I said as I ushered them out of my apartment.

When we reached the doorway, Jade turned. "What are you going to do?"

"I'm going to start downstairs and ask around to see if anyone saw anything. If he was taken by force, someone must have seen something." I wasn't sure I'd be so lucky, but I had to start somewhere. I had to do something. I couldn't just sit here and wait for Bellamy to show up, because I doubted he would.

"You come and get us if you find anything," ordered Elsa, her back hunched with tiredness.

"Sure," I lied. My friends had done enough tonight. I was going to drag Bellamy by the ears on my own when I found him. *If* I found him. "Who knows, maybe Julian has something."

We said our good nights, and I headed to the elevator. When the doors slid open to reveal a lobby, loud with the murmurs of people, the clanking of chips, and the binging of slot machines, I made my way to the front desk.

"You still here?" I leaned over the counter, knowing it would anger Errol that I was contaminating his space with my dirty witch DNA.

The concierge lifted his lips into a snarl. "The night shift is late. Happens all the time. What do you want?"

"Any messages for me?"

"No."

"You sure?"

"Do I have three eyes?"

I grinned. "Maybe? It's hard to tell sometimes under that frown."

Errol grimaced. "Go away."

"Did you see a short, heavyset male, kinda disheveled looking with a white shirt, by any chance?"

Errol gave me a mock laugh. "Lots of dirty-looking guests fit that description."

I raised a brow. "He might have been with someone else. Being dragged by force? Anyone like that?" I knew Errol watched the lobby. He might be a lizard shifter, but he had the keen eyes of a hawk.

"No," he said. "You stink." He moved away from me to the other side of the front desk, where a female guest in a short red cocktail dress was waiting.

I gave my armpits twin covert sniffs. They weren't shower-fresh but nowhere near as bad as Errol led me to believe, especially after the night I was having.

Disappointed, I pushed off the counter and went in search of Julian. He was pretty easy to spot. You just had to look for the handsome, tall male surrounded by three females.

Julian sat at a blackjack table with a brunette on his lap. A redheaded female stood behind him, rubbing his shoulders, and another darker female whispered things in his ear that kept him grinning like a fool.

Yeah, he didn't look like he was trying hard to find Bellamy. Still, it wasn't his fault we'd lost him. That was on me.

"Julian," I called as I squeezed in. The three females all glared at me. "Got anything on Bellamy?" I asked, ignoring them.

"Oh, hey, Leana," said the witch. "Blow on this for luck, darling," he said to the brunette on his lap as he held his fist with dice toward her. She gave him a lustful smile and blew on his dice. Satisfied, Julian tossed the dice, and from the winning cheers all around, I was guessing it had worked. I didn't really care for those games.

"Julian?" I pressed again.

"Oh." The witch turned to me. "No. Sorry. He's not here."

I wanted to press him with more questions, but the way the three females were staring at me meant it wouldn't be long before their nails came out.

Shaking my head, I left Julian and his harem to search for Jimmy. Maybe he'd know or had seen something. What I did not expect was to see Errol coming my way.

"Here. This came for you." Errol all but threw a message card at me.

I caught it before it hit the floor. "Thanks, gecko."

"You're welcome, *witch*." We all know that's not the word he used.

I laughed because why not. Plus, I was beginning to feel a little bit tired now that the initial rush of losing Bellamy had passed. I flipped the message card over.

Sorry I had to go. Meet me at 599 East 120th Street. Come alone. I don't trust your friends. You are the only one I trust.
—Bellamy.

A WASH of relief fell over me. Okay, so he hadn't been kidnapped. The witch scientist had snuck out on his own because he distrusted the hotel and its owners. Now that I knew where he was, I could still build my case. All was not lost.

I frowned at the slight on my friends. But I got it. He was scared. It had taken what courage he had to find me and trust me, as he said. I would have to respect that. Besides, my friends were either preoccupied or already sleeping.

First, I was going to find him, and then I'd figure out where to put him. Even if it meant I had to go back to Valen's, seeing as it was still the perfect spot to stash a critical witness.

And this time, I wouldn't let Bellamy out of my sight.

CHAPTER 20

By the time the cabbie dropped me off at 599 East 120th Street, it was one in the morning. I looked at the massive gray-brick building standing before me with tall chimneys jutting from the top, like a crown of a giant beast. Lines of blackened windows stared back at me, and darkness stretched in the arches and doorways. No lights shone from the inside to give any hint of where Bellamy could be. Not even the soft glow of a candle.

"Why did you come here, Bellamy?" I whispered to myself. "Should've stayed in my apartment."

The fact was, the building gave me the creeps. It was huge. Thousands of square feet. Six stories high and the size of a large hospital. Bellamy could be anywhere. It would take me hours to scout the entire building.

I sighed. "Couldn't you at least have given me a clue?"

My phone vibrated and made me jump. I pulled it out of my bag, saw Valen's name flashing on the screen, and hung up. The giant was persistent. Maybe his guilt was talking. Either way, I was going to speak to him. But now wasn't the time.

Part of me wondered if I should call Elsa and Jade to see if they were up to searching a creepy building with me. But just the memory of how tired they'd been when I left had me stuffing my phone back in my bag and abandoning that notion with it. Bellamy might not even be here.

No. I was doing this alone.

I crossed the street toward the colossal and grotesque building. The windows from the front entrance shone in the half-light from the distant streetlamps. Graffiti plagued the exterior walls like mismatched murals, but the bright colors did nothing to improve the decrepit structure.

A door lay open, dark and frightening like the mouth of the beast. Yet, even in the semidarkness, I could still make out worn, red letters just above the frame that read ENTRANCE.

I sighed and adjusted the strap of my bag higher on my shoulder. The tightness in my gut reappeared tenfold at the massive, eerie building. If Bellamy was in there, I was going to find him.

I pulled out my phone again, realizing I should have kept it in my hand, given the darkness reflecting inside the building. With a swipe of my finger, I turned on the flashlight mode. A shoot of bright white light bathed fifteen feet beyond in its luminance. Good enough.

I halted just before stepping inside and looked to the sky. It had clouded over, and dark gray-black clouds raced across the night sky. It would be harder to tap into my starlight magic, but I might not have the need to. I might just knock Bellamy over the head and drag his ass back with me.

I stepped through the doorway. A tingling presence of magic and something much stronger hit me like I'd walked face-first into a wall of mist. I took a deep breath and let it out, exhaling anxiety with it before I kept going. I met darkness and shadows and nothing else. Even though my senses weren't as acute as a White or Dark witch was to paranormal energies and the vibrations of magic, I still felt a cold transition of energy as soon as I'd stepped through the entrance. The shift in the air had nothing to do with the wind that moved through the open door behind me.

Magic was here. And a crapload of it.

My pulse raced as I moved inside, holding my cell phone

before me like a weapon. After a moment, my eyes adjusted to the darkness until I could make out shapes and familiar-looking objects. *Very* familiar-looking objects.

"Oh… shit."

Similar to the first lab I'd seen with my friends, the space was filled with rows of tanks, crates, and machinery, all hooked up to humans submerged in huge liquid tanks. I could hear the clicks and taps of the machines over the blood pounding in my ears.

This was the same setup but on a much larger scale. The ceiling was probably thirty feet high or more, and the edge disappeared into shadows. Here, there weren't just a dozen or so tanks paired with a single floating human inside, but hundreds of tanks.

An uneasy feeling settled in my core. This was the mother ship of labs. The other two were just the offspring. This was massive.

"Bellamy?" I called out, my voice echoing around me. I waited about a minute or so, listening, but I didn't hear anything apart from the constant beeping of the machines and my own damn heart. Maybe this was Bellamy's way of telling me there was another lab. Perhaps even where everything originated? Yeah, that had to be it.

I rushed over to the first human-tank setup, snatched up all the files that would fit in my bag, and stuffed them inside. I needed proof. *Proof!* I grabbed my phone, switched off the flashlight mode, and started to take pictures of the tank, the miserable suspended human inside, and everything around it, like a paparazzi on a coffee high. Once I had about thirty pictures or so, I sent copies to myself by email. Just in case.

That's when I heard the footsteps.

Instinctively, I dropped my phone, yanked on my starlight, and spun around with twin balls of star power hovering in my palms.

"Bellamy?" I lowered my hands, my starlight vanishing, but not before I got a clear view of his face. He looked… he looked *off*. The witch scientist shifted his weight like he had ants in his pants or he had a prostate problem.

"Shit." I bent down and picked up my phone. Even in the dim light, I could see a long crack all the way across the screen. Relief washed over me as glowing icons stared back over the multitouch display. It wasn't dead. I stood and switched on the flashlight mode once again. With a flick of my wrist, I shined it in Bellamy's face, and I watched him squint his eyes.

"I told you to stay put." I glowered at him. "It's not safe for you. Especially not here. Please tell me why you thought coming here was a good idea?" When he didn't answer, I kept going. "You could have just told me about this place instead of me chasing you around the city. It would have been a lot easier and cheaper. I'm spending way too much on cab rides." I swept my gaze around the space. "It's huge. It's where it all began. Right? Where it all started?"

Bellamy's hands twitched nervously as he yanked out his dirt-smeared handkerchief and dabbed his face. "Yes. That's right."

I frowned and moved closer to him. "You look nervous. More than usual. Why did you bring me here?" Something was definitely up with him.

Bellamy's face was sweating, and his hair was damp like he'd gone for a dip in a pool before meeting me. "I'm sorry. I had no choice."

My gut tightened at the fear and guilt in his voice. "What are you talking about? What the hell is going on?" I stepped closer. "Start talking. Why did you bring me here?" I looked around again at the gargantuan lab. "I thought you were running away from places like this. That you'd be too afraid to set foot in here again." It didn't make sense that he'd want to meet here.

"I'm… so sorry." Bellamy spun around and ran.

"Wait!" I hurried after him. Adrenaline spiked through my thighs, helping me put on a burst of speed. The witch was in worse physical shape than I was, and I caught up to him in no time. I was going to tackle him like a linebacker.

But then something stepped from the shadows and blocked my way.

I skidded to a stop. Bellamy's shape veered left behind a wall or a tall cabinet, and he was gone.

The said something that had blocked my way wasn't just a something—but *some things*.

Miraculously, I still had my phone in my hand, and I flicked it up.

A group of paranormals teemed before me. And guessing from the smells of wet dog, old blood, and what I thought was feces, I knew I was looking at newly formed vampires, werewolves, and shifters. Some were naked, and some were partially clothed. One male had only a pair of boxers on him. Their hair was damp, and their skin shone with moisture.

Tension tightened my muscles. "Fantastic. Fresh out of the tanks. Am I right?"

I gritted my teeth, anger welling inside my core. Bellamy had set me up! The witch bastard brought me here, hoping these newly created paranormals would kill me. And all after I tried to keep his sweaty ass safe.

Note to self, never trust a profusely sweating individual.

Well, he was wrong about one thing. I wasn't planning on dying tonight.

I dropped my phone in my bag, freeing my hands. "Let me pass," I ordered, pulling on my starlight again and hoping they still had some humanity left in there somewhere. Perhaps their transformation had been successful this time, and they weren't deranged like the previous vampires I'd encountered with Valen.

A dark male flashed me his teeth and did a swipe of his sharp black talons at me in a show of violence and strength.

I guess not. "I don't want to hurt you, but if you come after me… you'll give me no choice." I knew these were humans, tampered with paranormal blood, no less, but still human at the source. I didn't want to kill them, but I wouldn't let them eat me either.

But all notions of guilt evaporated as the first swarm of human subjects threw themselves at me.

"I'll get you, Bellamy!" I shouted as I threw out my hand.

A brilliant ball of starlight hit two paranormals. They lit up like twin white Christmas trees, twitched, and then they collapsed ungracefully to the floor.

"I'll find you, and then you'll get it, Bellamy!" I cried out. "You're gonna get it!" I didn't know what I'd do to him when I found him again—because I would. I just knew it would involve me smiling and him crying.

Movement caught my attention to my right. My body flooded with the tingling starlight energy that gushed from my core and raced along my hands.

A female vampire rushed toward me, fangs and talons out like she was ready to make me her late supper. Or was it early breakfast?

A burst of white light fired forth from my outstretched fingers, and I directed it at the vampire. It hit her in the chest, covering her body in a sheet of white light.

A shriek of pain came from the vampire, her long limbs flailing like she was attempting a backstroke. And then she fell to the ground in a heap of charcoaled, blackened flesh.

I didn't have time to feel guilty about killing her as another paranormal came at me from behind.

I spun around, my hands ready. A male of considerable size advanced with more muscles than he seemed to know what to do with and crushing fists. He growled, spit dripping from his mouth. My eyes burned at the stench of vomit and something else I didn't want to think about.

"You are mine," he roared, in a voice that was two voices, like the part of blood from whatever paranormal that was used to create this thing had formed its own voice along with the human's. Damn.

"So, you can speak?" I said, surprised.

It appeared as though the newly transformed humans were capable of thought. How much of it was still to be determined. But they weren't mindless zombies.

The male paranormal threw his head back in a deeply amused laugh. "I can do more than just speak." And then he rushed me.

A sledgehammer of flesh and bone barreled my way. He scared the crap out of me. Just as well, fear added fuel to my magic.

Gripping my will, I blasted him with shoots of my starlight. It hit the male human subject on the shoulder, causing him to stagger back. And before I could conjure up my starlight again, his mouth was wrapped around my arm.

I cried out, and tears filled my eyes. His jaw tore into my flesh with his needlelike teeth. I swore as white-hot pain ripped through me, and I felt hot wetness trickling down my arm.

I kicked out with my leg, and my boot vibrated as I made contact with his knee. He stumbled back, but in a flash, he went for me again.

Fear and anger rising, I thrust out my hand and hit him with a single thin burst of starlight, coming at him horizontally like a glowing white blade.

The blade of starlight sliced through him like he was made of butter. I saw a surprised look on his face as he glanced down at himself. And then his upper body slid off his waist and landed in a clump next to his severed lower body.

"I told you to stay back. Damn it," I told him, though I knew he was dead.

I looked up to find a row of paranormals smiling evilly at me, their eyes traveling over my body like they were wondering what part to rip off first or what I tasted like.

Crap. I was seriously regretting not picking up the phone, when Valen called. I could have used the giant's help right about now.

I thought about dialing his number, but that thought died as a shadow sprang at me from the left.

Before I could stop it, we hit the wall together with frightening force. The impact of pain took the breath from my lungs, and I felt my hold on my starlight slip. A shower of wood fragments, and what might have been wires, blasted into the air, falling over my hair as dust blew into my eyes. I was pinned to the wall and couldn't move.

The male vampire shrieked with laughter, and his warm breath assaulted my face as he spoke. "I will tear the skin off your bones slowly until you beg for mercy… and then I'll suck out your blood like water through a straw."

I coughed, blinking the tears away. "That's really gross." I yanked on my starlight, reaching out to the magic of the stars, and let it rip.

A burst of light emanated from me and blasted the vampire, sending him end over end across the lab. A sudden crashing sound seemed like maybe one of the tanks had busted, but I couldn't see that far out in the dark.

I pushed myself forward, staggering as I felt the effects of drawing on my starlight. My body weakened as the magic took its compensation.

Growls echoed, pulling me around. A group of human subjects fell on their hands and knees. Their bones cracked and popped, their arms and legs lengthening. Their faces warped and stretched until their jaws elongated into a hideous blend of human and wolf.

A fluff of silky, thick gray-and-black fur appeared over their skin as their yellow eyes tracked me. Nothing human was left in them, just animal. Their lips curled in a threat with steady growls in a promise of death.

I felt a rush of panicked anger. "Super." I exhaled. "I'm getting too old for this shit. Should have stayed in my apartment. That's what I should've done."

I barely had time to register how quickly my plan had gone down the crapper as the wolves came at me.

I flung myself under one of the tanks, twisting while ducking and rolling until I barely missed a swipe of razor-sharp claws from the black wolf.

But then something grabbed my foot, and I was dragged back out.

Rolling, teeth and claws slashed at me, shredding and tearing at my clothes and skin. It hurt like a sonofabitch, but I was up in a heartbeat. Good ol' adrenaline could do that.

A fist came out of nowhere and down onto my face. Blackness plagued my vision as I stumbled, and my cheekbone screamed in pain. I felt the warm trickle of blood from my nose as I blinked the wetness from my eyes while the shadow of vamps loomed over me. Even with the starlight energy that flowed in me, I was no match for a vampire's supernatural speed. They were still way faster than me and stronger, able to dodge my attacks with fluid ease.

My face throbbed, and I felt it swelling up like a balloon. No need for fillers. A male vamp lunged at me, teeth bared and unnaturally white. I leaped back, but not fast enough, as his fist connected with the side of my head.

I stumbled, bending forward and nauseated as the walls of my skull drummed. I was barely aware of my legs that were miraculously still supporting me. A hand shot out, and the same vamp grabbed me, throwing me to the ground.

I was *so* going to kill Bellamy.

"Playtime is over," said a voice that sounded vaguely familiar.

With my head throbbing, I struggled to sit up, but something grabbed my arms.

"Hold her down," ordered a female voice.

Flashes of white lab coats assaulted me, and the next thing I knew, I was pinned to the cold cement floor, unable to move.

Fear cascaded down me in waves, ice-cold and chronic. I tried hard not to think about the throbbing in my head or the fact that these human subjects were listening to someone.

The sting of a needle prick pinched the side of my neck.

Immediately, I felt a rush of something warm, the feeling of fatigue rushing through my veins. And for some strange reason, I couldn't make my legs or arms move.

Uh-oh.

Straining, I tried to will my legs, arms, even a finger to move, but it was as though I'd been hit with a freezing spell. My body wasn't responding.

Shit. This was really bad.

That fear boosted me with the last burst of adrenaline, keeping me awake. I couldn't move, and that alone terrified me.

The lights flickered on, and I blinked into the light, letting my eyesight adjust to the sudden brightness as the entire warehouse lab was suddenly bathing in bright light.

A shape drew my eye. And then the figure stepped forward into my line of sight.

"Stardud," said Adele, a smile in her voice. "How nice of you to come."

CHAPTER 21

Adele? My mind seemed to be suffering from the effects of whatever they'd given me, because that person looked exactly like Adele. Unless she had an evil twin? Yeah, didn't think so.

Nope, it was her. I'd recognize that demented twinkle in her eye and her false smile anywhere.

"You?" I said, my lips strangely tingly and numb, like when the dentist injects your gums with Novocain. Tendrils of tension squeezed my chest, and all my warning flags went up.

Adele looked down at me. Her white council robe hung on her tall, lean frame, and gold etching weaved around the sleeves and collar in sigils and runes. It was an exquisite robe. Too bad it draped the shoulders of such a cow. "Yes. It's me. Who else?"

"You drugged me." I stared at the syringe she still held in her lengthy, spindly fingers. "What did you give me? What is this?" I tried to move, but it was no use. It was as though my limbs were made of cement, and they were part of the floor.

In a flash of white, I could just make out three people dressed in white lab coats standing above me. Not just people but witch scientists like Bellamy.

"A powerful muscle relaxant," answered Adele, her voice silky and venomous like a snake's. "A neuromuscular-blocking drug, like human doctors give patients to keep them still before operating on them."

Operating on them? I tried to frown, but it seemed my facial muscles were all out of whack too. I might have been smiling. I might have been glowering. "But your bony ass sits on the White witch council. How could you do this?" Yeah, she was just the sort of narcissistic psycho to come up with something so twisted.

"Poor little Stardud, caught in a web." Adele stepped calmly toward me.

The other remaining paranormals stood watching, their faces peering down at me with excitement flashing in their eyes as they anticipated what Adele was about to do. Whatever it was, I was betting it wasn't good.

Straining, I tried to focus on my starlight as I called to it, but it was like something was blocking me. Some kind of invisible wall or obstacle kept me from reaching out to the stars. It felt similar to when the sun cockblocked me, as Julian had said, like it was high noon even though it was, like, one in the morning.

"You can't call on your starlight magic," commented Adele, apparently having seen me struggling with something internally. She glanced at the syringe in her hand. "I made sure to add a magic-barrier component in that shot I gave you. Bellamy prepared it for me. Your magic can't save you now, Stardud."

Damn that Bellamy. I'd never heard of a magical blocker used through a syringe. From what I knew, you could potentially block another witch or any magical practitioner from using their magic with a spell or a hex. I'd even heard of magical handcuffs that could break the magical link. Adele had figured out a new way to jam my starlight frequency.

I tried to grimace, but I'm sure I looked more constipated than anything. "My friends will come looking for me. They know where I am." Total lie. I should have at least texted Jade or Elsa, telling them where I'd gone. The fact was, no one knew where I was except for Errol, who took the message down from

Bellamy. I was as good as dead if I expected Errol to come to my rescue.

"It's over," stated Adele. "You think too highly of yourself and your abilities. I noticed that flaw the first time we met. So arrogant. So self-absorbed. You will always be a nothing, a dud. The fact is, you were never going to win this. For the strong to survive... we must rid ourselves of the weak."

"Blah, blah, blah," I muttered. "You really like listening to yourself talk." But that was good in a way. I wanted to know the full extent of this plan of hers. Because when I could move again, I was going to come after her hard. For that, I needed her to keep talking.

Because I would move again, just as soon as this drug wore off, and then her ass was mine. I just didn't know when that was going to happen.

Adele snapped her fingers. "Put her in a chair," she ordered. Those three white-coat idiots picked me up, dragged me, and then dropped me in an office chair none too gently.

My head lolled to the side. Thank God the chair had a high enough headrest to keep my head from snapping off of my neck. I knew technically that wouldn't happen, but that's how it felt. The only good thing about my new chair was that now I had a good view of my surroundings.

I felt a string of drool starting to trickle down the corner of my mouth. Damn. I was drooling. I tried to suck it back in, but that didn't work. I could feel it but could do nothing about it. I was a paralyzed, drooling Starlight witch. Fantastic. The next thought in my head was thank the goddess Valen wasn't here to see this.

I heard the scrape of a shoe on the floor and flicked my eyes to see Bellamy crouching behind one of the human tanks.

"You're dead," I threatened. "You came to me for help, and you do this? I'm coming for you next. Just as soon as I can move, you lying sonofabitch!"

At that, Bellamy's face went from pale to paler. But as he continued to watch me, I could see the realization on his face, the way his posture seemed to relax a bit. He knew I wasn't going to get up anytime soon. Once he found some courage, he came around from his hiding place and stepped forward.

"I'm sorry. But she gave me no choice," said the witch scientist. "It was either my life or yours. And I'll always choose me. You're a Merlin. There're lots of those. But you can't replace me on a whim. I have an IQ of—"

"Shut up, you sweaty little prick," I howled. "When this is over, I'm going to kick your ass. And then I'm gonna do it again because it's fun. You can count on it. I'm a woman of my word."

Bellamy clamped his mouth shut, his eyes darting over to Adele. It was almost as though he wasn't sure who was scarier, me or the skinny witch. Yeah, he was right to be scared.

But Bellamy, the traitor, was the least of my worries.

I turned my gaze to Adele, trying to think of a plan to get myself out of this mess. "This is the revenge you were talking about. Right?" I was glad my voice came out level and strong, even though my stomach was in chaos. "You want to kill me because I stopped you from destroying the hotel? That's a bit extreme, even for you. Don't you think?"

The corners of Adele's mouth twisted at my defiance. She shook her head, looking at me like I was her human subordinate who'd picked out the wrong robe. "The hotel needed to be replaced with something better. Bigger. Bigger is always better." Her thin lips stretched into a terrifying smile. "I will make that happen. One day soon. But I can't be distracted from my work." She moved to one of the desks and dropped the syringe.

I tried to lift a brow, but I might have flapped my upper lip instead. "What's that? Queen bitch? I think you've already achieved that goal." Okay, so this was probably not the best way to talk to my captor who had the means to rip me to shreds. But I hated this witch. And sometimes my mouth got ahead of my brain.

Adele turned and looked at me. "Haven't you been paying attention, Stardud? Look around you. What do you see?"

"If I could move my head, I could help you with that." I blinked. "What I see is your science experiment gone wrong."

The witch walked over to my chair and stared at me. "I thought you were smarter than this, smarter than those fools of witches you call your friends. But your name says it all. Doesn't it, Stardud? You're just an idiot with a pretty face."

At that, Bellamy snorted. He caught me staring, and whatever expression he saw on my face was enough to make him look away.

I flicked my eyes back on the witch. "Very mature." Still, it was clear she wanted me to see something or just validate what she'd done here.

The constant beeping of the machines pulled my eyes toward the tanks and the tubes filled with paranormal blood pumping into the human subjects.

"How did you get all the blood? Volunteers?" The amount of blood pumping through those magical dialysis machines was probably equivalent to ten liters or more. More than half of the average for a human body.

At that, Adele's eyes sparkled. So I was getting somewhere. "For the creation of the races, it required great amounts of blood from specific paranormals. So I took it."

"Meaning what? You killed them?" She was crazy. Not only did she kill humans, but I had no doubt she'd killed some paranormals as well to get what she wanted.

"Not always," answered Adele, coming closer still. She was so close, I could smell the bursts of her rosy perfume and something else like old onions. "Some gave blood in exchange for money. But sometimes, they didn't survive the retraction. Sometimes their bodies couldn't handle it. And well, maybe we took too much. Guess we'll never know."

"I said we were taking too much," expressed Bellamy, the faint tightening of his jaw the only sign of his resentment. "You didn't listen."

Adele gave him an irritated glance before returning her eyes to me again. "They were a means to an end."

"A very excruciating end, no doubt."

The twinge of indignation on Adele's pallid face almost made me smile. Hell. It felt good to piss her off. I should do it more often.

"You still haven't said why you're doing this," I tried again. And seeing that satisfied gleam in her eyes, I knew she was about to tell me. It looked like Adele wanted to brag about her achievements before she got to the punchline.

A slow, deeply satisfied smile came over the witch. "It's time for the paranormals to rise. Time for us to take back what was ours in the first place."

"What's that?"

She raised her arms. "This world."

Uh-oh.

Adele sneered, her features pulling back and making her look feline. "Humans are weak, greedy, and stupid. Too long have we lived in the shadows of the weaker species. Not anymore."

"If I could throw up, I would."

"See," continued Adele. "We will remove the human race, but we'll keep just enough to sustain our thirst. They will continue to provide us with their blood, you see. We'll contain them. They'll be right where we need them."

"Like a prison?"

"Like a prison," she repeated joyfully. "My dear Stardud." Adele looked down at me. "I'll let you in on a little secret since… well… you're going to die."

I wasn't surprised to hear her say it. "And what's that?"

Adele surveyed my face, like she was making sure she had my complete attention for the full effect of what she was about to say. "There's no room for humans in *my* new world," said Adele, speaking clearly and emphasizing the word *my*. Her eyes traveled to the tanks and back to me.

"*Your* new world?" Yeah, she was most definitely nuts. I felt dizzy. This was too much information. "Holy shit. You're trying to breed out humans. Only you can't wait that long, so you're manufacturing paranormals?" It sounded even more insane as the words left my mouth.

"Vampires, werewolves, every kind of shifter," said the skinny witch. "Some species are more difficult to recreate, but soon we will achieve the impossible. Right, Bellamy?"

Bellamy looked up from a file he was staring at. "Yes. Yes, that's right. Witches are posing a small problem but nothing that we can't adjust for."

"Excellent." Adele's face twisted in a wicked smile.

Heat rushed to my face. I tried to move again, but it was no use. My body was just as useless as Bellamy's trust. "But your experiments are flawed," I spat. "They don't last. All of these… these *things* have an expiration date. It's not going to work."

"Long enough to achieve what I need," said Adele. She glanced at me, her smile widening at what she saw on my face. "The complete and utter destruction of the human world. My *experiments,* as you so delicately put it, are the key. No longer will we be kept in our cages. No longer will we live in secret. Paranormals will walk the earth. This is the end of the human world as you know it. It's a shame you won't be around to see it. Billions of humans will be replaced and will eventually die. No skin off my teeth."

Yikes. A mix of anger and fear rushed through my core. "You're insane."

At that, the witch's cool demeanor seemed to crack on the surface. "And just like everyone here, *you* have a part to play in my new world, Stardud," she added, her eyes gleaming.

My blood went cold as I suddenly understood what I was doing here, paralyzed in the chair, why Bellamy made me come here. He didn't mean to kill me—well, not at first.

"No. You can't take my blood. You can't make other Starlight witches. It doesn't work like that." I gritted my teeth, praying to the goddess to give me the use of my magic again, but as I tried to reach out to the power in the stars, I felt the same blockage as before. I looked at Bellamy. "You can't create witches. Tell her, Bellamy. Tell her!"

Oh, shit. I shouldn't have come here.

Bellamy looked at the other witch scientists, like he was hoping they were going to back him up. But they glanced away and turned their backs on him, looking just as terrified of Adele as he was.

Sweat trickled down Bellamy's temples. "Witch transference is a problem..." His eyes went to Adele. "But nothing we can't overcome. I assure you," he added quickly.

Damn. They were going to take my blood and probably kill me in the process. I couldn't do anything about it.

Worse, no one knew where I was. I felt foolish and terribly alone at the moment. Tears brimmed my eyes.

"Are you crying?" laughed Adele. "I thought you were made of stronger stuff, Stardud. Crying's for losers."

Tears from anger, desperation, and regret fell. I didn't care that they all saw. What did it matter anyway? They were going to use me like a lab rat.

Adele tsked and leaned over me. I heard some rustling, and then she hauled my bag from my head and pulled it to her.

"What are you doing?" I asked as she rummaged through it.

Adele reached in and pulled out my phone. "Like I said. You give yourself way too much credit, Stardud. In a few minutes, you'll be dead," she cooed. "Your life will have never mattered. Soon, no one will even remember Leana Fairchild, the Starlight witch. You're nothing, and you'll die nothing."

My expression warped as I searched for an answer that wasn't coming. Panic redoubled, clouding my mind and my focus. I didn't want to die like this, paralyzed and unable to defend myself.

"It's not going to work," I hissed. "My blood can't help you."

Adele gave a mock laugh. "Oh, Stardud. This isn't about you. It was never about you. You're not that special."

"What?"

"What is the rarest, most special of all of us?"

Oh, fuck…

Adele held my phone in her hand. "I told you. It was never about you. It was always about the giant. To make more giants, well, I need a giant." She smiled wickedly and said, "I need Valen."

CHAPTER 22

I was a fool. The biggest fool in the universe of universes of fools.

The blood left my face. I'd been wrong. I knew where this was going. It all made sense now. Why I was coaxed here and carefully kept alive. Adele was going to use me to lure Valen somehow.

I stared at my phone in her hand. "It's not going to work."

"Yes. Yes, it will."

"It won't."

Adele looked up and said, "He'll come. He'll come for you. I've seen the way the giant looks at you. The way a man desires a woman. You're all he thinks about. He's in love with you, I think."

My face flamed at her comment. "He's not. I know that for a fact. He's seeing other women. Just tonight, he was with someone else. You've got it all wrong." But did she?

Adele's fingers moved over the screen as she typed. "I don't think so. I've been watching you two for quite some time. It was nauseating, but the work had to be done. He's that handsome, strong, overprotective type of male who will come if he thinks his woman's in trouble."

"I'm not his woman." Though, I liked the sound of it.

She pocketed my phone inside the folds of her white robe. "He cares about you deeply, though I have no idea why. Still, he'll come. I'm always right."

"What do you want from him?" I knew what she wanted, but I wanted to hear her say it.

"With a giant army at my disposal," she said, straightening, "the humans will never be able to resist. There'll be nothing left of the humans after my giants take care of them."

"You're one twisted bitch," I snarled. "You won't get away with this. The Gray Council will stop you." I wasn't entirely sure, not anymore. Even if Adele had orchestrated this lab, I had a feeling she had some admirers within the Gray Council. "And I'm pretty sure you'll get some resistance from the paranormal courts. They won't let you destroy all the humans. Because... well... because that's crazy."

Adele tidied the front of her robe. "You're right. Resistance is inevitable. And they'll be taken care of just like the human resistance. With my giant army."

Dread was a sudden finality. I felt useless and ashamed. No way could I get out of my chair. My body wasn't my own anymore, but I still had the use of my mouth.

"Bellamy, listen to me," I said, talking fast. "Do you hear what's she's saying?" The witch scientist angled his body toward me from one of the workstations, but he wouldn't make eye contact. "Don't you know this is genocide? You can't do it. If you let her, you're part of it. You're just as guilty as her. Even if you manage to get her plans up and running, we will stop you. You hear me! And when we do, you won't make prison. You'll be killed." His shoulders tensed, so I knew I was reaching him. "You can stop her. Just don't do it. Say you won't."

Bellamy finally lifted his eyes to mine. "You don't understand. I have no choice."

I growled as I tried to move, more angry tears leaking from the corners of my eyes. "If I could move, I would kick you in the ass! You *do* have a choice, Bellamy. Don't. That's your choice. Don't do it."

The witch scientist looked away and turned his attention back to whatever he was doing. When he shifted his weight, I got a glimpse of three syringes with fluffy red ends placed carefully in a line next to a dart gun. Not syringes, more like darts filled with whatever they'd used on me. "Are those for Valen?" I practically spat. Yes, I was certain there was moisture there. "You sonofabitch, Bellamy. You're just as nasty as her."

Adele laughed like I was some comic show put on just for her, but the witch scientist hunched his back—whether from guilt, tiredness, or fear, I didn't know. I didn't care. He'd prepared to do the same thing to Valen that he'd done to me. He was just as culpable as Adele in my book. He deserved a good ol' ass whooping.

Anger burned through my misery and my feelings of betrayal. I went somewhere far, far away from myself. Silent tears slid down my face and neck, puddling around my clavicles. Yup, some snot was mixed in there as well, and I could do nothing about that.

My own fury and fear evaporated at the thought of Valen, replaced with an overwhelming need to protect him. So what if he dated other women? Valen wasn't a bad guy. I wouldn't let her hurt him.

"Why don't you take my blood instead? Am I not good enough for your science experiment? I'm right here. Aren't I? Ready for the plucking?"

Adele threw back her head and laughed. "Why would I want more Starduds? You're the weakest sort of witch... you can't call on the power of the goddess or the elements, and even demons won't give you the time of day. I don't think it's accurate to even call you a witch. You're more human than anything else." She let out a breath. "I want a giant, and a giant I will have."

"He's not an object. He's a person."

Adele raised her brows. "He's whatever I want him to be. He's what I want and need at the moment."

My eyes burned as more tears fell down my cheeks. "You're a sick bitch. You know that?"

"I've been called worse."

"He won't come," I said. "He's busy." It was true. He was with that hot blonde.

The sounds of voices drifted over to me above the loud humming of my heart in my ears.

My pulse quickened, and I deeply regretted my decision to meet with Bellamy.

Adele's eyes rounded with excitement. "He's already here."

I darted my eyes over and saw some white coats rushing over to the table with the tranquilizing darts. One of them grabbed the gun, and then they all disappeared off to the sides, out of my line of sight. The paranormals were next as they all scattered like frightened rats behind crates and disappeared.

"No!" I clamped down on my jaw as I struggled with all my might and my strength. I might have farted, but it was hopeless. I couldn't move.

Adele snapped her fingers, and to my horror, Bellamy advanced with a roll of duct tape.

"Don't you dare," I growled. "Don't! Valen!" I shouted, looking over Bellamy's shoulders. "Don't come here! It's a—"

Bellamy slapped a piece of duct tape on my mouth. "I'm sorry." He leaned forward like he wanted to say more, his lips flapping, and then he just said three words in a whisper, "It won't last."

"Mrrghh!" I cried, my words muffled.

Bellamy pulled away from me, and he moved off somewhere behind my chair.

When I searched for Adele, I couldn't see her anywhere. Everyone was gone. It was just me, the chair, and… Valen.

Valen strode into the warehouse with a fluid, predatory grace, but his movements had a hurried edge as though he were uncomfortable or anxious. Though his rugged face was warped in worry, he was just as handsome and mesmerizing as ever. A black leather jacket covered his wide shoulders over a snug T-shirt and jeans. Even in the distance of the room, I could see a darkness in his gaze and tension over his face. Such concern lingered there.

Our eyes met, and my heart lurched.

Valen's eyes widened for just a second as he took in the chair, the duct tape over my mouth, my inability to move, and my tear-stricken face.

Raw emotions crossed his features—fear, guilt, and then a deep fury.

"Mmhhh!" More tears leaked out of my eyes as I tried to tell him no with just a stare, but Valen was already closing the distance between us at a sprint.

The tears kept falling, and Valen's speed increased. This was wrong. All wrong.

From the corner of my blurred vision, I saw dark forms fall from the ceiling, and then a blur of shapes surrounded Valen. Their black eyes flashed with a dark hunger, talons thrashing. Vampires.

Valen halted.

The sound of growls pulled my eyes to the left. More shapes came into view with fur and bodies that were too big to be considered normal wolves, their ears pinned and lips curled to show teeth the size of short blades with paws the size of my head.

In a blur of limbs, Valen ripped off his clothes. Next came a flash of light followed by a tearing sound and the breaking of bones. His face and body twisted, enlarging and expanding until he stood at his eighteen-foot giant form.

And then they rushed him.

Hot anger welled over my skin, though I could do nothing but watch.

Vampires and werewolves attacked Valen from each side. The giant moved fluidly and with the skilled grace of a killer. He swatted them with his great arms, sending two vampires crashing into one of the water tanks.

Valen ducked, spun, and came up with a great swipe of his

fists, crushing the skulls of about three werewolves at once. They let out choked screams of pain and shock as blood fountained from their bloody stumps.

If I didn't know he was here to help me, I would have been scared shitless.

A thud of metal hit bone, and I saw one of the vampires holding a sword. Valen grabbed the sword, snapped it in half, and then did the same to the vampire.

Damn. That was pretty nasty. But I couldn't look away.

More vampires fell from the ceiling like big, ugly spiders and clung to the giant, sinking their teeth and talons into his flesh.

I heard a cry and the sound of tearing flesh as Valen peeled the vampires from his person, two by two, before smacking their heads together. I heard a sickening sound like the crumpling of bones, and he tossed them.

He crushed their bodies with voracious rapidity, his massive body unstoppable.

A flash of brown fur appeared in my line of sight. With a torrent of paranormal speed, a werewolf sank its teeth into Valen's thigh.

The giant cried out, more in anger than in pain, and with a swipe of his great fist, he pummeled the werewolf's head. The beast slid off the giant's leg and crumpled to the floor.

Another group of werewolves threw themselves at Valen in a flash of fur and teeth. A black werewolf opened its maw as it roared, its yellow eyes glowing while it snapped its huge teeth. It came up behind him. Valen spun and brought down his foot over its head, killing it instantly.

Strangled cries and yelps rang out all around me, followed by the horrid sound of flesh being torn and the fast, thrashing sound of fists pounding on soft flesh. Again. And again. And again.

Then a sudden silence hit me. Blinking through tears, I looked around.

Valen stood in a sea of broken, crushed, lifeless paranormals. Everywhere I looked, bodies of vampires and werewolves lay crumpled and very dead. I pushed aside the guilt that threatened to rise as I knew these were human subjects, well, most of them. But I couldn't know for sure. Some real paranormals could have sided with Adele.

My eyes found Valen again. He met my gaze, and a strange, warm thrill vibrated in my belly.

Glee and hope filled me. Valen had beaten them all, and no one was left. Not alive.

He turned his head to me, and I tried to smile, but the tape was too damn tight.

"*Leana,*" said Valen, and my heart cried a little at the worry in his voice. Worry for me.

I heard a sudden loud pop, like the sound of a firework.

A small object flew past me and hit Valen in the chest. The fluff of red feathers stood out against Valen's skin.

Shit. The darts!

My eyes rounded in fear. "Mmgghmm!" I felt the blood leave my body and heard the intake of breaths from behind me. A wisp of panic unfolded like a leaf inside my chest.

Valen reached up and pulled out the dart, staring at it a moment before he crushed it in his hand.

The giant's face rippled in anger. And then he was moving toward me again.

Another pop. And I blinked to see another dart speared in Valen's neck.

The giant pulled that one out, too, and tossed it. He faltered for a moment, and I hissed through my teeth.

He took another step toward me just as a third dart sank into his right bicep.

"*Mmhhmm!*" I cried through my bound mouth.

Valen yanked out the third dart. He teetered and then he fell to his knees, the dart still in his hand. I watched in horror as the dart slid out of his palm.

And then the warehouse walls and floor shook as the giant hit the floor and collapsed on his side.

CHAPTER 23

"Finally." Adele came out from somewhere behind me. Her white robes billowed around her as she crossed over to where Valen lay. His head was turned in the opposite direction, so I couldn't see his face.

Adele stood over the giant for a moment, and then she pulled back her leg and kicked him with her boot.

"Grrrrrh!" I shouted.

She glanced over her shoulder at me and smiled. "He's ready."

I heard the muffled sounds of voices followed by the sound of many feet crossing the warehouse floor as the white coats came into view.

I narrowed my eyes at them. *Cheaters*. If they had fought Valen with the other paranormals, they'd be broken and crushed, lying on the floor with the rest of them.

"Don't worry," said Adele as she met my eyes. "He won't feel a thing," she added with a satisfied smile.

I watched in horror, unable to move or work my magic, as the six white coats dragged a thick chain that looked like the anchor chain from a large boat, from somewhere off to my right. They wrapped the chain around Valen's arms, and then with a sudden click, a machine turned on. Suddenly Valen's large, heavy body was being hauled across the floor.

They dragged him to a lab station and laid him on his back. Then quickly began to stick needles all over his body until he had tubes connected to his neck, wrists, arms, legs, and chest.

The sound of wheels drew my attention to two white coats pushing a cart. Tall glass jars clinked together as they parked the cart next to one of those magical dialysis machines.

"Where's Bellamy?" Adele tossed her head around, her eyes darting across the warehouse.

"He left," said one of the white coats, a male with a short, brown beard. "Couldn't handle it." The others all laughed at that.

"He's a rat," said the only female white coat. "We should have killed him."

"That's not up to you," snapped Adele, and the female white coat's face flushed red. "*I* make the decisions. Bellamy served his purpose." Her eyes moved to Valen on the floor, and then they flicked up to me. "Without his traitorous ways, I wouldn't have my giant." Adele moved to stand next to Valen's head. From my vantage point, I could see only part of his face. He was staring up at the ceiling.

Terror pulled my throat tight. "Hhhhmmm."

"What about her?" The bearded white coat pointed at me. "She knows too much."

"We could perform a memory charm," said another white coat, the oldest one of the group, with his short white hair and a face draped in wrinkles.

The female white coat shook her head. "They never last. She might not remember a year from now. Or maybe in two years, it'd all come back to her. It's too risky. We should kill her."

What was up with that one and the killing? My heart jumped to my throat, and I could feel the beginnings of a panic attack.

"More Starlight witches could come in handy," said the bearded white coat. "We should bleed her. Save her blood for when we're ready for a witch transference."

"Have you not heard a word I said?" Adele leaned her tall frame over the smaller witch scientist. "I make the decisions. Besides"—she looked at me, a curious frown on her face—"Darius wants her alive."

Darius? Who the hell was Darius? Was he the one on the Gray Council calling the shots? I bet he was.

"But..." Adele smiled coolly at me. "He never said we couldn't play with her first."

The white coats all laughed at that, sounding like a pack of wild hyenas, and I saw a flicker of fury cross over Valen's face.

"We're ready," declared one of the white-coat males standing next to that dialysis machine, his hand next to a large, red button.

Adele let out a sigh of satisfaction. "Let us begin."

The white-coat male pressed the button, and the rumble of a motor came to life, beeps and clicks ringing throughout the warehouse.

I felt sick to my stomach as shoots of Valen's blood rushed through long tubes and disappeared inside the dialysis machine. Then drops of red liquid began to fill the glass jars.

"Quickly," ordered Adele, snapping her fingers. "Bring in the human."

Bring in the human? Was she going to create another giant now?

Yup. I blinked at another group of white coats hauling a heavy, water-filled tank on wheels with a floating, unconscious female inside.

Shit. They were going to try and create a giant with this human female.

I looked over at Adele, trying to tell her with my eyes that she was a demented bitch, but she was just staring at Valen like he was a prized diamond. She was pacing. Her excitement for torturing and killing people was sick.

Bile rose in my throat, and I pressed it down. If I threw up now, with my throat partially paralyzed, I might choke to death.

I pulled my eyes back to Valen, and my breath caught. His skin was pale, sweaty, and almost had a greenish tint. His face was a mask of distress. He looked sick, like he had a fever.

I tried to thrash, giving it my all, but all I did was let out more gas. *"Mmmm!"*

Adele looked at me and flashed me a smile. "You're thinking that we're just wasting her life like the others. That her weak human body can't withstand the transformation." Her smile grew. "We've added a special mix this time. A key element to preserve all magical properties of giants. As though she were born a giantess. If she lives through the mutation, there's a good chance she'll survive. She'll never be human again. She'll be a giantess."

I frowned, or at least I tried to, a feeling of dread filling up to my eyeballs.

"Count yourself lucky. Not many have witnessed the birth of giants."

The birth of giants? She was a freaking lunatic.

The female white coat grabbed tubes attached to the human female and connected them to the same machine that Valen was connected to. They were bleeding him and trying to create a giant at the same time. They were going to kill him.

My eyes rolled over Valen again, seeing his face and body weaken.

The sound of chanting broke over the beeping of machines. The white coats and the witch scientists were working their magic. The chanting took on the edge of fierce, vindictive satisfaction and continued to rise in pitch until it sounded almost like shouting.

The scent of white magic twined around me like a vine. A cold, icy feeling hit me that wasn't from the September wind. My skin pricked at the shift in the air like tiny electrical currents. I swore as I felt the sting of them mixed with the scent of candy and rotten eggs.

The human in the tank jerked, her limbs flailing as Valen's blood was pumped into her. She looked like she couldn't breathe, like she was being held underwater by force. She turned her face, and we locked eyes for a moment. Through the glass, I saw the fear and despair in them. I wanted to help her, to do something. I got a flash of her frightened human face, and then her eyes went dull, her head hanging. Was she dead?

I'd never witnessed something so terrible, so inhumane and vile in my entire life. I could never unsee it. It was imprinted inside my eyelids forever.

"With my army of giants, I will be invincible!" cried Adele, her face set in a manic smile. "I won't need Darius or any of them. I will crush all who oppose me. I will have my new world. And I will be queen!"

Total psycho.

The witch scientists kept chanting. A blue-white light flashed so brightly, I had to close my eyes for a moment if I didn't want my eyeballs to burn.

Next, came a sizzling sound and then a pop, like a campfire, followed by the overwhelming scent of wet earth mixed with sulfur. The light diminished, and I stared at the human female floating in the tank. She was the same size as before. Nothing had changed as far as I could tell.

Adele snapped her fingers impatiently. "Drain it. Come on. Come on."

Obeying their mistress, one of the white coats pulled on what I could only call a black tub plug, and the water released into a thick, black pipe that stretched all the way to the side of the warehouse.

"Take her out," ordered Adele as soon as the tank was empty of water.

The white coats yanked the naked human female out and placed her on the cold cement floor, wet and most probably dead. Somewhere deep inside of me, I hoped she was.

The anger on Adele's face made me smile. Well, I tried to. Oooooh. She was mad.

The witch stood over the human. "Get up. Up! Get up and change, or I will burn you alive!"

The female human's eyes snapped open. Holy shit, she was alive!

"Get up, you filth." Adele moved and kicked her in the stomach hard.

The human yelped in pain and rolled to her side.

"Rise!" Adele called out, her arms stretched wide. Yeah, total Dr. Frankenstein wannabe.

I took the opportunity to glance at Valen, and fear choked me. His skin was wet and almost transparent. Blue veins shone through that looked as thin and delicate as tissue paper. I could almost see the blood being sucked out of him.

They were killing him. He wasn't going to survive this.

And it was all my fault.

Dread twisted my guts, and more tears spilled down my face as I stared at the man, the giant, who I obviously cared for more than I wanted to admit to myself.

"Up! Get up! You stupid human whore!" Adele kicked the human female again and again. Even her white coats had the smart idea of moving back and giving her space.

The human female let out a scream, and then she started to convulse. At first, I thought this was the end. But then I felt a hum of magic in the air and saw a flash of light.

The human woman went down on all fours, howling as her face and body rippled and stretched to unnatural proportions.

"Yes! *Yes!*" shrieked Adele.

The female subject's face swelled, and so did her limbs until her body was triple her normal size. The floor trembled as she pushed to her new, giant thighs and then feet. She had a prominent brow ridge and a protruding upper jaw, giving her more of an ogre-like look, just like Valen. She wasn't as big as Valen in his giant form, but she was close. Maybe fourteen feet tall. She was frighteningly big and strong.

Adele had done it. The bitch had made a giant.

When I looked back at Valen, his eyes were closed. And his

body had returned to its human size. He looked... he looked dead.

My despair worsened. My gut twisted as I let the panic in until it felt like the world dropped out from under me, and I was falling through the chair.

And then something strange happened.

I felt a tingle. A prick. First along my toes and then up toward my knees, sneaking over my skin, like I had thousands of creepy insects crawling inside and out of my body. Totally disgusting. But the tingling continued throughout me until it reached all the way up to my scalp.

The tingle lasted a few seconds, and then I felt a release, like a sudden unbridling of a tight rope that had bound my limbs.

I was free. I could move again.

Bellamy's words made sense now. *It won't last*. He'd meant the paralyzing drug. He'd tampered with it. He'd only given me part of that drug. Enough to fool Adele. Enough to set me free.

I reached out to the stars, to the powerful emanations. The Starlight answered as it hummed through me, waiting to be unleashed.

I ripped off the duct tape and leaped off my chair. "Get away from him!"

And then I let my magic fly.

CHAPTER 24

The anger, the fear, the desperation—all of it consumed me as I hurled my starlight at the machine that was pumping Valen's blood.

A white coat jumped in my line of fire. Too bad.

I blew the fucker into pieces just as I shattered that damn machine in a blast of my starlight.

The metal contraption flew back, end over end, and crashed against a far wall. All the wires and tubes that were connected to Valen were yanked and torn away from him. He still wasn't moving, nor had he opened his eyes. Red rage filled me as I turned slowly and faced my enemies.

"Get her," I heard one of the white coats say and saw the only female, with another syringe in her hand.

"Not this time, bitch." I flung out my hand and fired a brilliant white blade of starlight.

It hit the female just below her jaw. Her eyes went wide. She didn't have time to cry out as her head slipped from her body, and she crumpled to the ground, taking her syringe with her.

The white coats were witches. And they brought their magic down on me.

But I had magic too.

Like a storm of wild magic, the white coats exploded into motion.

"For the new world!" one of the males cried as he vaulted forward with purple flames spewing from his hands.

Anger. Fear. Pain. The tidal surges of my emotions fueled my magic. I would use it.

I planted my feet, pulled on my starlight, and clapped my hands once.

A white, glowing disk sprang in front of me like armor. Purple light flooded around me as the witch's magic hit my shield and then bounced off.

I stood my ground, my starlight pumping through and around me as it bathed me in its brilliance.

The same witch hit me again with a volley of purple flames. The flames angled off my shield, redirecting the magic, and a burst of his own magic slammed into the oncoming witch.

I lowered the shield and looked up in time to see the witch I'd struck flying back. His body sizzled in purple flames. That could have been me.

I saw Adele's shocked expression at my starlight shield. She didn't know I could do that.

Surprise, bitch!

The mumblings of a curse spun me around to face another witch.

He moved awkwardly, stiff like he wasn't entirely sure what he was doing, or maybe he'd never dueled one on one before with another witch.

I smiled. "You ready? I'm ready. Bring it."

He snickered at what he saw on my face, probably a combination of anger and fatigue.

"You're dead," he snarled. Green magic coiled around his arms, and it reminded me of Jade's plastic bracelets. Love her.

"Iqtz M'atx!" he cried, flinging his palms at me.

Green fire rings burst from his outstretched hands, and my face flamed from the heat of his magic.

I flung out my hand as a sheet of starlight knocked his magic rings away, a foot away from my face.

I didn't want to hurt or kill anyone, except for Adele—and maybe Bellamy—but this was self-defense. Kill or be killed. And the witch was trying to fry me.

The witch's lips moved in a dark chant or a hex, I had no idea, but I was way ahead of him.

With my starlight still pounding inside me, I arched my body back and hurled my shield with both hands. It fired straight and true, spinning like a disk and catching the witch on his right side.

He let out a cry of rage, and then I heard nothing but the sound of flames burning his robe and flesh.

I barely had time to catch my breath as two more white coats leaped my way.

"Damn. How many of you are there?" I asked, spotting another two waiting in the shadows, like a wrestling tag team anticipating their turn to pound my head in.

The nearest white coat's eyes met mine, and he smiled lazily as if pleased that we were about to duel. "We're going to bleed you, and then we're going to take you apart… little piece by little piece."

I pursed my lips. "Let me think about it… screw you."

The same white coat's eyes gleamed with orange magic. And then he flicked his wrist, and a flaming orange whip materialized.

Nice trick.

I jumped aside, the end of the whip grazing my hip. I hissed at the pain. But his strike went wide before he realized his mistake. I spun around and fired a ball of starlight at him. It caught him in the chest and sent him stumbling away just as a larger white coat took his place.

He struck more proficiently than his colleague, fireballs whistling as they soared in the air, aimed at my face. I had a split second to whirl before they struck.

I jumped back, his balls going wide—yeah, I know how that sounded. "You guys lack in your defensive magic. You should stick to what you know. Being dicks." It was obvious these witches, these white coats, weren't trained in this type of magic. They were all over the place, uncalculated, their strikes untrained.

But I was.

The beefy white coat snarled at me, sweating profusely, and he reminded me of Bellamy. "I'm better than you. You're not even a real witch."

"Gotta stop listening to your mistress." Speaking of mistresses, I stole a look to my right and saw that Adele was still standing by the new giantess. The look of pure joy on her face was enough to nearly make me hurl.

"You're going down for a very long nap... the forever kind," said the same white coat, pulling my attention back around. His hands were dripping with orange flames. "I see it now. Your fear. You know you're going to die, and you can't do anything to stop it. Your miserable friends aren't here to help you. You're all alone." His lips curled up almost in a smile, his eyes widened in victory. "And you're going to die alone."

"I'm not dying tonight, buddy." My fear of dying wasn't what spiked the sweet adrenaline in me and through my limbs. It was the horror and the pain of what these assholes did to the innocent. But mostly to Valen.

My pain was lost in my fury. I pulled on my starlight and pushed out. A shoot of white light fired out of my hand—

"Ignitu det!" shouted the white coat, waving his hands, and a sheet of semitransparent orange haze rose before him. My starlight hit the protection shield like it had hit a solid concrete wall and fell away.

The white coat's grin widened at the shock he saw on my face. "See? You're not the only one who can work shield magic."

I shrugged. "And you just said I wasn't a real witch? Which is it?"

He widened his legs, his stance firm with his hands moving confidently. "You're not," he panted, as though that bit of magic took some enormous effort and energy from him. I didn't see him pulling another shield. He was done.

He smiled at me again and opened his mouth to throw another insult.

But I didn't have time for this shit.

I flicked my wrist at him. In a blur of white, a starlight arrow speared his chest.

He stumbled, blood bubbling out of his mouth as he fell to his knees.

I felt a shift in the air behind me, and I whirled to see five white coats approaching, their magic dripping from their hands. From what I could tell, these were the last five.

And I'd had enough.

Straining, I took a deep breath and reached into that spring of magic, to the core of power from the stars. Clamping my jaw, I pulled on my starlight, letting it rip through me until five balls of blazing white light hovered over my hand.

And then I flung them.

Five shoots of starlight magic soared straight and hit the white coats. Cries erupted with the scent of burning flesh. I blinked at the sudden white light as their bodies were engulfed in the starlight, like they were lit by a million LED lights.

I staggered, feeling a sudden wave of dizziness. The more I pulled on my starlight, the more my body felt like it had been beaten with a two-by-four wood plank.

And then, the last white coats went down in wailing screams of fire and ash.

I bent at the waist, sweat pouring down my back and between my breasts. My lungs felt raw, like I'd just finished a five-K run. I was drained. I needed rest. But first, I needed to take care of Valen.

"Kill her!"

I turned to the sound of the voice and saw Adele pointing at me and motioning to the giantess, her arms beating the air like she was trying to fly.

Crap. I'd forgotten about her. I was exhausted. I'd never fought a giant, or rather a *giantess,* before, and I doubted I'd survive if I did. From what I'd observed with Valen, not much could harm them. I wasn't even sure my magic would serve me against a giant.

Adele's face was red and blotchy as she pointed at me, a slight tremor to her hand. "Kill her! I command you. What are you waiting for? I told you to kill her. Kill her now, you idiot. You will do as I command. I am your god! Obey me!"

Yeah, like I said, total nutjob.

Fear spiked in my chest as I surveyed the giantess's massive hands that could easily bludgeon me to a pulp. Those were some seriously big fists.

"Kill her, you stupid giant!" shouted Adele. "Kill her now, or I will end your miserable life." She stood there, hands on her hips with that same self-satisfied expression, as though she ruled the world and was above all of us peasants. She felt she could do as she pleased with us, which included killing us.

The giantess looked at me from across the warehouse, and I felt my bowels go watery. Her expression was cast in a frown, and I wasn't sure if she was angry or if this was her thinking face.

But what happened next, I did not expect.

The giantess's face rippled with anger as she turned back and looked down upon Adele.

"*No,*" she said, her voice loud and deep like Valen's but with a more feminine edge to it, if that were even possible.

"No?" Adele's rage was palpable. "What do you mean, no? I'm your creator! I'm your god, and you will—"

The giantess's hand shot out and wrapped around Adele's neck, pulling her effortlessly off her feet and into the air.

"Oh, shit," I said, unable to look away.

"Let me go!" shrieked Adele as she hit the giantess's hand with her fists. Her lips moved in a chant or a spell, and I saw sparks of orange, green, and red magic slamming into the giantess. But the massive woman didn't even flinch.

The giantess's eyes were filled with anger, but I could see the anguish, the sorrow, and the hatred there. She hated what Adele had done to her.

The giantess's lips curled into a snarl, and the hand around Adele's throat tightened. The witch's eyes bulged, the whites showing.

I heard a snap like the breaking of a twig, and Adele's head was bent at an unnatural angle. It happened so fast, a part of me thought I'd imagined it.

But then the giantess tossed Adele's body to the floor. Her limbs splayed out. Her head turned my way. I could see her lifeless eyes.

Adele was dead.

CHAPTER 25

I had a somewhat freak-out moment as I stood there staring at the dead witch and the giantess who'd killed her. Who knew what the giantess was thinking right now? She could turn her anger on me and break my neck too.

I could make a run for it, but I wouldn't leave Valen.

I wasn't sure how long I stood there, staring at the massive human woman who looked… lost? But then the giantess looked my way, and all I saw was sorrow and pain. I might have been scared, but I felt her anguish too.

The giantess then lowered herself to the floor and sat, dropping her head to her knees as she sobbed. Damn.

I swallowed, looked over to where Valen still lay, and made a run for it.

I slid to my knees, my thighs bumping into him as I scrambled on the floor and pulled myself next to him. I grabbed his arm and winced at how cold his skin felt. It was like ice.

"Valen?" I shook his arm, big, hot tears spilling down my face. When I didn't get a response, I wrapped my fingers around his wrist. A sigh escaped from me as I felt a pulse. It was weak, but he was alive. He needed help.

The sound of great, slobbering sobs twisted me around. I

looked at Adele's dead body and then at the giantess who was still weeping. Her shoulders shook as another cry released from her.

"This is a strange night."

I pushed to my feet, and I was off again. I knelt next to Adele's body, lifting her heavy robe as I searched for my phone and doing my best *not* to look at her bruised neck. Too late. I looked. Damn. It was even worse up close. Deep-purple marks wrapped around the dead witch's throat. A piece of her cervical spine perforated her skin where her head was bent at an unnatural angle. Yikes. I yanked my focus back to search for my phone. I slipped my hand inside Adele's robe and felt something solid and flat. I yanked out my phone and rushed back to Valen's side. I stole a look over my shoulder. The giantess hadn't even looked up.

Valen needed help. He'd lost so much blood. I didn't know if he'd survive.

Fingers shaking, I quickly texted my friends a 9-1-1 to send help and Basil to contact the Gray Council. I knew a so-called Darius was corrupted, but I was hoping the others on the council weren't. They were going to find out about this sooner or later.

My phone beeped.

Elsa: *On our way. Gray Council too.*

I let out a staggered breath.

"Leana?"

I jerked as I stared at Valen's dark eyes staring up at me.

"Oh, my God, Valen!" I reached down and pulled him over my lap, cradling his head. My vision blurred by the sudden tears. I didn't care that he saw me bawling my eyes out and would know how much I cared. I was over that. This wasn't about me, and he needed help. I cringed as I stared at his face. Blue veins shone through his skin, and his eyes were sunken. He looked weak.

"What can I do? I don't know what to do. Do you need my blood? I know you're not a vampire. I have to do something. I—"

"Not your blood," said Valen, his voice depleted, and it brought a sob over me.

I looked around the room to where the remains of the machine I'd destroyed lay scattered across the floor, not realizing at the time that I'd also destroyed his blood. He could probably use that blood right about now. I'd ruined the only blood that could save him.

What have I done?

Fear rushed through me, stealing my breath at the memory of losing my mother. Tears welled in my eyes, and my throat throbbed. I couldn't lose Valen. Not when this was my fault.

"Why did you come, you fool," I told him, more tears spilling down my face. "You should have stayed at the restaurant."

"You texted… said you were in… trouble… needed me," he said, his voice harsh and weak.

"That wasn't me. It was Adele." I knew she was dead, but I still hated her for what she'd done.

"I figured." A feeble smile pulled his lips, and I felt a stab in my heart.

I wiped my nose on my sleeve. "I'm so sorry. This is all my fault. I shouldn't have come alone. But I wanted to get Bellamy back. That's the guy I was with when I went to your restaurant." My jealous reactions from before felt so foolish. And I regretted them. "You should have stayed on your date with that pretty blonde. Think about it. You missed out on some sex." I flashed him a smile. "Instead, you came here and got… well… this."

Valen blinked slowly. "Wasn't a date. I hired her."

I cocked a brow. "Okay, so she's an escort. I guess you didn't get your money's worth. Sorry about that."

Valen opened his mouth to speak but instead broke into an agonizing, wet cough, sounding like someone who'd smoked three packs a day all their life. Every breath looked painful, like his lungs weren't working properly.

I rubbed his arms with my hands, trying to get him warmer and his blood flowing. "Don't talk. Keep your strength."

"She's not," Valen cleared his throat. Then he closed his eyes, his face twisted in pain. He opened his eyes again and wheezed, "Not an escort. A private investigator."

I did not expect that. "You're dating a private investigator?"

His face shifted into an expression of effort. When he spoke, his jaws stayed locked together, but I could understand the words. "No. I hired her to look for others like me. Giants. She's been looking for six years."

Now I really felt like a fool. Six years was a long time to get to know someone. It explained what I saw on their faces, a friendship. Not lovers.

So Valen had wanted to find more of his kind. I could understand that, being the only Starlight witch I knew. I knew others like me were out there. I just didn't know where they were at the moment. But it wasn't the same. I was still a witch, and plenty of witches lived in our communities. Not giants.

A weak smile curled his lips. "She found some."

My mouth flapped open, and I let his words sink in. "Giants? She found other giants? Where? Who?" My body warmed at the spark in his eyes.

"Two. Brother and sister. In Germany."

I squeezed his arms tighter, not feeling any warmth in them. Was his skin getting colder? "I'm really happy for you," I said, trying to keep my voice from showing the fear that was redoubling. "If you want… I can be your travel guide to Germany. Though I've never been, I've always wanted to go and see the Neuschwanstein Castle. Pretend it was mine and all." It was true, but I couldn't afford to go anywhere, especially Europe.

Valen let out a breath. "No need. They're coming here."

"That's great." I waited for him to say more, but he didn't. "Then we'll just have to throw a party in their honor when they get here. Oh, wait. Maybe they're secretive like you, right? They won't want us to know."

"They are," said Valen. His voice was so low, I had to lower my head near his lips to hear him properly. His eyes flicked over to the giantess. "Is she… is she all right?"

I followed his gaze. The giantess was still quietly sobbing, her shoulders shaking and her head still hidden between her knees. My eyes watered at seeing her like this.

"No, she's not," I told him. "They took her. Imprisoned her. And transformed her into a different being, a creature she never thought was real. She'll never be all right." Ever. If she'd been a paranormal, it might not have been as traumatizing, though still disturbing to be morphed into another creature. But she was human. Only yesterday, she didn't believe in vampires and ghouls and fairies. And tonight, she was a giant. The woman would probably go insane if she lived long enough. And *if* she lived, she'd need serious therapy. But after seeing what happened to Adele's science projects, it didn't look like she had a bright future.

"Adele is—*was*—a crazy bitch," I said to Valen, seeing he'd gone silent again, his eyes closed. "She wanted to create a new world without humans, where she wanted to be queen or a god. A goddess? Anyway, the point is, she wasn't alone in her insanity. She was taking orders from someone called Darius. Do you know anyone by that name who sits on the Gray Council? Valen?" I had to keep him awake. I knew if he fell asleep, he might never wake again. "Valen?" I shook him, and his eyes popped open.

"Hmmm?" He blinked at me, his eyes unfocused, like he wasn't sure who I was.

"Do you know someone called Darius? I think he sits on the Gray Council."

Valen's dark eyes searched my face. "No. I don't think so."

Shit. I could barely hear him. His eyelids started to shut. "Got to keep awake, Valen. You hear me. Don't you fall asleep on me."

"So… tired…"

"I know." I rubbed his arms again, I had to keep doing something, or I'd lose it. "But you have to keep fighting. You hear me? Valen? Valen!"

Valen's eyes shut. I shook him and then again harder, but he didn't open his eyes. He looked like he'd gone into a coma.

Panicked, I put my ear to his mouth. I heard a soft breath. He was still breathing but barely.

Okay, now I truly did have a freak-out moment. My insides twisted. Raw terror radiated through my guts. I felt sick. My breath caught, and I blinked a few times to keep the room from spinning.

Valen was dying.

By the time the team got here, it would be too late.

CHAPTER 26

I needed to do something. *Think, Leana!*

And then I remembered something. Giants had healing properties that were different than anything I'd ever seen. Maybe… maybe it was worth a shot.

Carefully, I lay Valen's head back on the floor and pushed myself up. With my heart lurching in double time, I ran over to the other giant. A cold sweat trickled down my back as I flung a long strand out of my eyes.

"Excuse me," I said, standing about five feet from her, my pulse hammering. My eyes darted over her hands the size of car wheels. I'd just seen what she could do with those giant hands. I wanted to keep my neck from being crushed.

I took another breath and repeated, "Excuse me—"

The giantess snapped her head up.

"Ah!" I jerked and fell back on my ass hard. I might have broken my coccyx. Her glare was enough to make me pee my pants, but for some strange reason, I kept my bladder in check. Looks like those kegel exercises weren't so useless after all.

Still on my ass and cowering, I raised my hands. "Please don't kill me. I'm not here to hurt you," I said quickly. "You've got a serious glower, you know? Like big. Um. Listen. My friend is dying. Can you help him?"

The giantess looked over to Valen, but I couldn't read what crossed her face. She was still glowering.

I decided to try another approach. "My name is Leana. What's your name?"

At that, the giantess's features seemed to soften a little. "*Catelyn*."

I winced at the ferocity of her voice. "Nice to meet you, Catelyn." I waited and then said, "My friend's name is Valen. That evil bitch that did this to you, well, she hurt him too. He's dying. And I think you can help him."

Catelyn stared down at her hands like she couldn't believe they belonged to her. "*I don't want to be like this. I want to be me*." Her eyes met mine. "*Can you change me back?*"

Oh, shit. "I'm not sure. But I promise you I will do whatever it takes to change you back. Back to you. To the human Catelyn." I wasn't sure if she could change back into her human part. I'd seen Valen do it, so maybe she could. Perhaps she just needed coaching on how to do that.

Catelyn shook her head, tears trickling down her face. I looked over to Valen. His eyes were still closed, but somehow he looked worse, like thin or thinning.

"Please." I pushed to my feet and faced her. "You saw me tied up in that chair. I know you know I had nothing to do with this. I tried to stop it. I don't want any more people to die. And right now, you're the only person who might be able to save him. Please, Catelyn. Will you help my friend?" Okay, now I was really crying. My voice cracked with emotions.

Catelyn brought her tear-filled eyes to me and said, "*Okay*."

I wiped my tears and rushed over to Valen, trying not to despair at how frail he looked.

"*What do I do*?" asked Catelyn as she pushed to her feet and went to stand over Valen.

"I think you need to touch him," I said, hoping I was right. "If you could lay your hands on him for a bit, I think it'll work." Goddess, let me be right.

Catelyn did as I asked and knelt down next to Valen, who looked tiny in comparison to her massive frame. She placed her hands gently over his chest, her eyes roving over him. I saw confusion there, but I also saw a spark of worry in her eyes for Valen.

After about a minute of Catelyn's hands touching Valen, I was expecting to see something. Maybe sparks. Him opening his eyes. But after two minutes of nothing, I realized I'd been wrong. Catelyn couldn't save him. No one could.

My eyes burned, and I shook my head, dread forming a hard knot in my stomach. "It's not w—"

Valen's skin began to glow, softly at first and then with more intensity.

"Look! It's working! Catelyn, you did it!"

Catelyn flinched, as whatever she was doing surprised her too. The giantess had a determined look on her face now as she kept her hands on Valen's chest. She wanted to help him. Save him. Even after what had been done to her, she still wanted to help. Wow. She was my hero.

Soon, Valen's skin went from a dangerous, deadly pastiness to his natural golden, healthy color. The veins that webbed over his face disappeared, leaving his skin smooth.

I searched his face. "Valen?"

Valen's eyes snapped open. "I'm all right." He looked at Catelyn and smiled. "Thank you."

The giantess blushed and pulled her hands away, realizing she was touching a seriously handsome and seriously naked man.

I pressed my hand on her shoulder. "Thank you. You saved his life."

Catelyn looked at me, her eyes sad. Her lips parted, but she nodded instead, seemingly unable to formulate words.

I felt a little tear in my heart. "Valen," I said, looking at him. "This is Catelyn. She was made from you. Damn, that sounds so strange. Um, listen. Does that mean she can transform back into her smaller version? Like you do?" I knew if she went back to her original body, her human size, it might not be so daunting. Scary still but manageable.

Valen propped himself on his elbows with a small moan on the exhale. "Catelyn. All you need to do is calm yourself. Take deep breaths. Think about yourself before the change. Keep that image, and let the change undo itself. Try it now. You can do it."

I didn't know if I could have been calm after such an ordeal. It would take some serious self-control.

"I'll try," said the giantess, and I was genuinely impressed by this woman's inner strength. I thought I was badass, but she was badasser.

I watched as she closed her eyes, seemingly in a meditative state. And then, just as I'd seen Valen change multiple times, with a flash of light, Catelyn's body shrank on itself, smaller and smaller until she was about my height and size.

She did it.

"You can open your eyes now," I told her.

Catelyn's eyes flashed open. They were red from all the crying, her face blotchy. She looked to be about my age, maybe a few years older. She raised her hands slowly up to her face, turning them over as she inspected them. She looked down at herself and then at me. Her mouth started working soundlessly, and her eyes overflowed with tears. It took her several seconds to let out a little choking sound, followed by the words, "I'm me. I can't believe it."

"A very naked you." I laughed and hurried over to one of the dead witch scientists. I yanked off a white coat and gave it to Catelyn so she could cover herself.

"Thanks," she said, wrapping her arms around herself, her eyes wide and anxious.

"I know you must have loads of questions," I began.

"I do," she said. "All this… all this is real. It's a lot to process."

"It is, Catelyn. I think it's best that you stay with us for a while. My friends and I stay at this really nice hotel. You'll be safe there. And you'll have friendly people to talk to. To coach you and explain what's happening. Do you have a family?"

She nodded. "I do."

"Okay, then call them." I handed her my phone. "Tell them you're okay and that you're staying with some friends for a while."

"Will I ever see them again?" Catelyn's bottom lip trembled, catching my heart.

"You'll be able to go see them… once you get your big-girl-self under control." I didn't know what else to call it.

Catelyn's eyes brightened. She took the phone and walked away for some privacy.

A labored breath spun me around. Valen was lying on his back again. He turned his head and looked at me. "I think she's going to be okay."

I nodded. "Yeah. I think so too." Strangely enough, it rang true. I knelt next to him. "She's going to need your help to explain all the"—I waved my hands around his body—"giant stuff."

"She has it."

"Are you cold?" I asked, rolling my eyes over him, our eyes locked.

"No." Valen's face transformed into one of his sexy smiles. He looked just as handsome as ever, naked, no less, his thick, dark hair brushed just above his eyes. But he did look fine.

And the man was still naked. I liked him naked. He rocked, naked. Still, I needed to find something to cover him up before the others got here.

"Just a sec."

I pushed myself to my feet with a tiny moan, my thighs and knees protesting. Still, I moved across the room without falling over. I was tired and still bleeding from some of the wounds bestowed on me by those vampires. I'd have to see Polly later so she could fix me up. But Valen came first.

Finding what I needed, I yanked another lab coat from a dead witch scientist, a little too roughly as his head kept smacking the hard cement floor, but the guy was dead.

"Here you go." I knelt down next to Valen again, and placed the coat over him. Obviously, it was too small, but it did cover the larger-than-average important bits.

His lips curved toward his eyes. "Kiss me."

"What?" My core pooled with warmth, and I whipped my head around to see whether Catelyn had heard, but she was busy talking to someone on my phone.

"Come here and kiss me."

I turned my head back around. He looked at me expectantly, cocky as hell, like he knew he had me—had me good. Was it wrong that I was turned on?

My heart thumping like an idiot, I leaned over, stared at his dark eyes for a moment, and then lowered my lips to his.

I was expecting a soft kiss. Nope. That's not what I got.

Valen's hands wrapped around my back and my neck, pulling me down farther, closer, as he crushed his lips on mine.

His kiss was different this time. Cautious. But it had an intensity. Emotions poured into it. My breath came fast as he slipped his tongue into my mouth, and a thrust of desire went right to my core. The heat of his mouth, his tongue, was an exquisite kind of torture.

A tiny gasp escaped me, and he moaned. His rough, calloused hands slipped under my shirt and moved around my back, down to my waist.

I never wanted to stop kissing Valen. It felt too damn good, intoxicating, like a sugar buzz after eating four scoops of rocky-road ice cream. But this wasn't the place for such a sensual kiss.

I pulled away, breathless. Waves of desire pulsed through me as I leaned back on my knees. "A guy who was close to death shouldn't be able to kiss like that."

"I can't help myself," he breathed huskily. He winked and added, "Especially with you. I just want to keep kissing you."

Okay, that did all kinds of great things to my ego. And the way he was staring at me did all kinds of things to my lady bits.

The sound of running feet had me twisting around.

Jimmy came jogging toward us, his lean legs propelling him with speed and his face set in concern.

"Jimmy?" I said, surprised. Behind him came Julian, Elsa, and Jade. The thirteenth-floor gang was here.

Jimmy skidded to a stop. He looked over us and then to the dead white coats sprawled between some of the dead paranormals. "Shit. What the hell happened?"

"Long story."

"Is that Adele?" Elsa was staring down at the dead witch. She wasn't smiling, but she didn't look bothered either. She looked... curious.

"It is," I answered.

"What happened to her neck?" asked Jade as she joined her. "I can see her trachea." She had a pen in her hand, and she poked the witch on the floor like she wasn't sure she was dead and thought she might spring back to life. Not with a neck like that.

My eyes flicked to Catelyn, who was off the phone and staring at my friends like she wasn't sure whether to change into her big-girl form and break their necks too.

"These are the friends I was telling you about," I told Catelyn. I waited for her to make eye contact. "You can trust them."

She gave me a nod, but she still was watching them with uncertainty and fear. It was going to take some work.

"Where's Bellamy?" Julian was staring at one of the tanks with a human floating inside. I saw anger creep over his face as his jaw set, and the veins at his temples stood out.

I shrugged. "He took off just when things got interesting." The bastard had slipped away, but I would find him. He carried the knowledge and the expertise to do this again. He was dangerous, and he would have to deal with the consequences of his actions. He might have tricked Adele and the others by only subjecting me to a part of that paralyzing mixture. But he had betrayed me and lured me here under false pretenses that had nearly killed Valen. Yeah, he needed to be dealt with.

"I bet he did." Julian's eyes locked on Catelyn. He flashed her a smile, but she didn't smile back.

"The Gray Council should be here soon," said Jimmy as he swept his gaze around the room. "This place is creepy."

"Tell me about it," I answered.

"Who is she?" Jimmy was looking at Catelyn, wondering if she was one of the good guys or in alliance with Adele.

"That's Catelyn. She's—*was*—just an ordinary human."

"She's one of the human subjects." Jimmy looked back at me. "A were or a vamp?"

I shook my head. "A giantess."

Jimmy's mouth flapped open as the rest of the gang all looked between Catelyn and me.

"Long story," I told them, smiling at their collectively shocked faces. "I've got lots of them. Catelyn is staying with us for a while. We need to look after her."

"Of course she is," said Elsa, giving Catelyn one of her motherly smiles. "We're going to look after you, Catelyn. Don't you worry. You'll fit right in with the rest of us crazies."

And when Catelyn gave her a weak smile back, I knew she'd be okay.

I let out a breath, tension still ringing through me. Tonight could have turned out to be one of the worst nights of my life, but it didn't.

I was alive. Valen was alive. And the threat, well, Adele was dead. I wasn't a fool. I knew this wasn't over. I still needed to find this Darius, but I'd take this as a win for tonight.

"You ready to go? Valen?"

When I looked back down, Valen's eyes were closed. A light snore emitted from him, and he had the tiniest of smiles on his face.

CHAPTER 27

I stood in the lobby of the Twilight Hotel, a glass of red wine in my hand as I cast my gaze around. The air smelled like grilling meat and buzzed with happy chatters. The clanking of chips echoed from the multitude of game tables splayed around the lobby and neighboring rooms. I peeked through the door to the dining room and saw long tables stacked with food and every alcoholic beverage you could think of. Polly stood behind the table with the meats, a pair of metal tongs in her hand, and her white toque over her head as she served happy, hungry-looking guests.

I'd never seen the hotel so cramped before with so many guests. Basil's idea to hold a Casino Week had helped revive the hotel. No one spoke of demons and devils in the rooms. Everywhere I looked, I saw happy, smiling faces peering back.

It was the final night, and it looked like he'd gone all out.

"Not a bad turnout." Jimmy came to join me, looking dashing in a dark-gray, three-piece suit, his hair styled in the 1950s side part. He looked like a classic mobster from that era.

"Not bad at all. It's good for the hotel. For us. We won't lose our homes after all." Even though we'd stopped Adele from destroying the hotel, part of me feared that the lack of guests would eventually ruin the hotel's reputation, and we'd all have to look for someplace else to live. Now it looked like we'd be okay for many years to come.

"It'll die down after this," said Jimmy, nodding at a couple of vampires passing by us. "But it'll be better than it was. I gave Basil some ideas for the next theme."

I cocked a brow. "The next theme?"

"Yeah, we're thinking of keeping this as a regular monthly to bimonthly occurrence to keep the guests happy and attract new guests."

"I like it. A different theme every couple of months?" I was curious. "What's your planned next theme?"

"Rock and roll," said a smiling assistant manager. "It'll be awesome. You'll see."

I smiled. "I have no doubt." I studied him for a moment, getting the pricks and tingles of his supernatural shape. "You know, you never did tell me what type of shifter you are."

Jimmy chuckled and adjusted the sleeves of his jacket. "True." He turned around, and when he blinked, his eyes flashed a golden color. He blinked again, and his eyes were back to their normal blue color. "Werefox."

"Is that why Auria's curse turned you into a toy dog? Foxes are canines."

Jimmy let out a long breath. "No idea. Maybe. Or this was just her sick, twisted way of making me suffer. Make me feel useless. Like a fool."

"Never useless. Definitely not a fool either." I stared at his cute face. His sneaking around the hotel, knowing all the nooks and crannies, definitely attributed to his werefox ways. He was sly as a fox. "So, how old are you anyway?"

"What?" Jimmy laughed. "Ninety-eight."

"Well, shit. You're pretty hot for a grandpa."

I broke into a laugh I couldn't hold back, and then Jimmy joined me. Once we started, it was like a switch had turned on. We couldn't stop the fit of giggles until tears streamed down our faces.

"Hey, guys. What's so funny?"

I wiped my eyes and looked over Jimmy's shoulder to find Jade coming to join us. Her blonde hair was dyed pink. She wore a vintage black hat, a floral pink-and-red scarf, a long, black retro blazer, and a floral vest over a white blouse. She finished the look with pink bracelets and brooches.

Looked like she was going for a *Pretty in Pink* movie vibe. I loved it.

"That Jimmy looks younger than us, but the fact is, he's an old geezer."

Jade looked between us. She opened her mouth to say something, seemed to think better of it, and turned her head around. "Basil did good. Didn't he?"

"We noticed," I said. "Is Elsa with you?"

Jade gestured over to the slot machine area. "She's with Catelyn. She's doing really well for a human. I mean, she's only had a few freak-out cries. Two last night and one this morning. That's pretty incredible for a human."

I looked over at the human, now turned giantess. Catelyn's face was tight. She looked like she was the new kid in school—part terrified, part excited—as she was listening attentively to whatever Elsa was telling her. The witch looked positively enthralled that someone was digging her wisdom.

Both women had glasses of wine in their hands, though Catelyn's was empty. I felt for her, and I was glad Elsa had given her the spare room in her apartment for the time being. Elsa was just the sort of soft-tempered, tolerant, and caring, motherly figure Catelyn needed right now. Plus, we needed to keep an eye on her. We weren't sure if she would go insane like the other human subjects I'd encountered. Or worse, die suddenly. So far, she wasn't showing any signs of mania. And she was still alive. Thank the goddess. Maybe giant blood was different. Maybe Adele had figured out the missing link to the transference like she'd said. Maybe, just maybe, Catelyn would survive this.

"You ready?" Jimmy held out his hand to Jade.

My lips parted in surprise as I looked over at Jade, whose face turned a beet color. "You two…"

Jimmy smiled proudly as he took Jade's hand and placed it in the crook of his arm. "Date night."

"Date night," I repeated. My heart swelled as I watched Jimmy and Jade walking away. The two were absolutely perfect for each other. I laughed as Jade looked over her shoulder and gave me a thumbs-up.

I was in such a good mood after that, I had to keep up the good vibes. So, when my eyes found Errol eyeing me with a look of disdain from across the lobby, I knew I had to go say hi.

I leaned over the gleaming stone counter. "Any messages for me?" I had put out the word that I was looking for Bellamy, but so far, nothing had turned up. Earlier this morning, I'd taken a cab out to his fancy apartment on 499 East 34th Street, with a view of the East River, to find it ransacked with no witch scientists. When I checked his bank account, with the help of Jimmy's hacker skills, it had been emptied the day before. Looked like Bellamy was on the run.

Errol looked like he wanted to spit in my face. He reached down, pulled out a message card, and threw it at me.

If I hadn't expected it, it would have hit me in the face. But I knew the little lizard bastard well enough to anticipate what he was about to do. He was conveniently predictable.

I caught the card. "Careful, Errol. Stuff like this will land you in trouble. Buckets-full-of-cockroaches trouble."

Errol glowered at me. "I hate you."

"Right back at you, lizard."

I glanced down at the card.

Stop looking for me. You'll never find me. I'm sorry for what I did to you, but I had no other choice. —Bellamy

"YEAH. I'm not going to stop." I stuffed the message card in my jeans pocket, catching a view of Julian playing cards with our thirteenth-floor twin ten-year-old girls in identical periwinkle-blue, sparkling princess dresses. Tilly and Tracy were the twins' names, though I couldn't tell them apart for the life of me. Julian kept throwing glances at the pretty woman standing over the girls, their mother, Cassandra, I think her name was. But she was completely unmoved by his attention. More like she was ignoring him. That was interesting. Looked like Julian had his lover-boy work cut out for him.

I sighed and gulped the last of my wine. No way would I stop looking for Bellamy. He had to pay for what he did, and I *would* find him. I wouldn't rest until I did.

The Gray Council's officers showed up a few minutes after my friends returned to the warehouse. Again, they packed everything up and hauled it away, not even leaving a single piece of paper. Nothing. But I'd taken enough pictures and stolen some files to keep me busy. I was still building a case against this Darius character.

If Adele was following his orders, he was perhaps even more deranged and dangerous than she had been. I had to find him. The Gray Council was corrupted, and I had to weed out the mess. I'd start with Darius.

"You look nice tonight."

My heart sputtered at the sound of that rough, deep voice. I twisted around to find Valen standing there, all manly, all sexy as hell, all man-beast-like. A brown leather jacket hung over his thick shoulders under a tight, black top and tucked into a pair of snug jeans. A waft of musky cologne and spices filled my nose, sending my skin into tiny ripples. Just his smell turned me on. Yeah, my hormones were still out of whack.

Damn, he looked good. Yet, even if he smelled good enough to eat, he still had shadows under his eyes. He wasn't fully recovered.

"You look pretty good yourself for a man who nearly died a few hours ago. Shouldn't you be resting?"

His dark eyes gleamed intensely. "No." His eyes traveled to Catelyn. "How's she doing?"

I let out a breath. "Better than expected. Really good, actually. She's still in good health too. She knows to tell us if she feels off… more off than when she turns into a giant."

"I talked to Polly, and between us, we'll start Catelyn on a weekly specialized tonic. Like an energy drink. To keep her as healthy as possible."

"That's a great idea."

Valen shrugged. "Who knows. She might outlive us all."

I nodded, knowing giants had inherent healing abilities. Maybe that was the secret ingredient to allow the humans to change into paranormals and stay that way forever without having to worry about their time running out.

My eyes drifted over his broad shoulders and down his chest. Valen caught me staring and gave me a smug smile, the kind that sent my nether regions pounding. His dark eyes pinned me, and I saw a glimmer of desire in them.

He took my hand, and the next thing I knew, the giant was pulling me just off the front desk and into Basil's office.

Valen closed the door behind him. His larger-than-life body pushed me up against the wall.

My pulse throbbed in my throat. "What are you doing? This is Basil's office."

Holy shit. He wanted to take me right here! Not that I was complaining, but I'd always imagined having sex with Valen back at his place, on his comfortable, very private bed. But I could do spontaneity. Spontaneity was my middle name.

His hard body pressed against mine. "You're so fucking sexy tonight. You drive me crazy."

I swallowed hard. "I try."

Valen growled and planted his lips over mine. His tongue darted into my mouth, and I felt my knees go weak. My pulse skittered to high gear as his hands slipped under my shirt and grabbed my breasts. Taking his lead, I slid my hands under his shirt, feeling the warm, hard muscles of his back, which were a stark contrast to his cold skin last night.

His fingers expertly found the back closure and unhooked it, letting the girls fall free. I moaned as he cupped them, my skin erupting in goose bumps at the rough callouses of his hands.

I dragged my nails into his back. He moaned again, or maybe that was me?

I pulled my mouth away. "Are we doing this now? Here?"

Valen's eyes snapped to mine. "We can stop if you want. Is that what you want?"

"Hell no." My lady bits were pounding.

Valen laughed and then dipped his head. His mouth found my neck and sent little kisses, his tongue teasing.

I shivered as my hands found his belt, and I yanked it hard, undoing the top button of his pants. The button fell. I might have yanked a little too hard. Blame it on the raging hormones.

Valen laughed again, and the next thing I knew, he'd scooped me up in his strong arms and hauled me over to Basil's desk. Papers, memorabilia, and mugs all went flying as the giant lowered me onto it.

"Basil's going to kill us," I mumbled through kisses.

"He can try," said the giant, his hands on my breasts again. He pushed himself right between my legs, and I felt how hard he was for me. Yup. We were going to do it in Basil's office!

I was dizzy with lust and emotions. And the fact I hadn't had sex in a long while was making me crazy.

I pulled my mouth away for a second. "It's been a long time

for me," I said, knowing he was most probably a destroyer of vaginas from what I'd heard.

"Good," said the giant, going for my belt.

"Could be cobwebs down there," I said.

Valen let out another laugh. But when he looked at me, all I saw in his eyes was desire and a vulnerability that squeezed my heart.

I felt slightly embarrassed at my lower-than-average skill in the bedroom. Martin was more of a wham-bam-thank-you-minute-man kind of lover. Hell, you can't call that a lover. More of a one-way, selfish shag.

"What in the name of the goddess is going on here?"

I looked up from behind Valen's shoulder and saw Basil standing in the doorway. He pushed his glasses up his nose as if that would somehow help him interpret the scene in his office.

Oops. I bit down on my tongue so I wouldn't burst out laughing. Poor Basil. He did look like he was in hell.

But a dark chuckle rolled out of Valen as he slowly slid away from me. "Did you need your desk?"

Basil's face flushed, his eyes moving everywhere but at my disheveled shirt and bra. My eyes found Valen, and I snorted.

"Someone's here to see you," said Basil, staring at the ceiling. He held an ashtray in his other hand. That was odd. The last I knew, the tiny witch didn't smoke.

"Me?" asked Valen.

"No, Leana," said the hotel manager. "I'll wait outside." And with that, Basil tripped on his own chair, caught himself before he fell, and hurried out of his office.

"I'll join you. Need a minute," said Valen as he adjusted the tented region of his pants.

"Wonder who it is." I hooked my bra and pulled my hair back into a messy ponytail. I felt a little irritated that Basil had interrupted what could have been the best sex of my life, but in a way, I think it was for the best. Best to have that experience elsewhere and in private.

I turned at the door. "See you later."

Valen grinned, desire still in his eyes. "Count on it."

Woo-hoo. It was on later!

I was smiling—feeling like I was in a dream with things finally looking up in the relationship area—as I left Basil's office, closed the door, and joined him near the front desk. At first, I thought Bellamy might have been surrendering himself, as any weasel should. But it wasn't him. And it wasn't anyone I recognized.

Three men stood with Basil. Two wore heavy gray robes and frowns that would scare off little children. The third one sported a black suit made of the finest silk. Their eyes all tracked me as I approached.

I didn't remember meeting these guys before. Maybe they were going to hire me for a job. My heart was still pounding in my chest from Valen's kisses and his touch.

"You looking for me?" I planted myself before them, crossing my arms over my chest. I got a mix of pine cones, sulfur, and vinegar, the scent of both White and Dark witches. Okay, now I was really curious. Why would a Dark witch seek out my services?

The suit-wearing witch frowned at my forwardness, his light eyes assessing me as he took a drag of his cigarette. Basil held out an ashtray, trying to catch the ashes as they fell but missing. That explained the ashtray.

Suit-guy's eyes were too bright, too clever for my liking as they traveled over me, lingering on my neck, where I probably had one hell of a hickey, and I resisted the urge to put my hand there.

Speaking of said hickey, the sound of a door closing twisted my head around, and I saw Valen heading our way, no tented pants. He caught my eye and winked, sending a spike of desire to my core.

I bit down on my smile and turned my attention back to the three male witches.

"Leana Fairchild?" asked the one in the dark suit. The soft yellow light from the hotel lobby gleamed on his dark, slick hair.

"Yes."

"I'm Clive Vespertine, the investigator from the Gray Council," said the witch. His voice grew airy, almost sarcastic, and it triggered something in me.

"Okay. Good to know." Crap. I'd totally forgotten about the investigation with all that had happened. "How can I help you, gentlemen?" I wasn't sure I liked how they were looking at me, like I'd done something wrong.

Clive took a step forward and smiled. "You're under arrest for the murder of Adele Vandenberg."

Well, shit, that was unexpected.

Witches of New York

Book 3

Kim Richardson

CHAPTER 1

I always wanted to see the inside of the Gray Council headquarters building in New York City. I just never imagined I'd be a prisoner when I did.

It happened so fast, I barely had time to react. Clive Vespertine, the investigator, and his goons handcuffed me in front of everyone in the lobby. One minute, I was about to have some incredible sex—probably the best sex of my life with Valen, in Basil's office, no less—and the next, I was being hauled away, humiliated, and treated like a convict.

As soon as the cool metal hit the skin of my wrists, I knew something was different about these cuffs. A cool energy climbed over my wrists and seeped into my skin. And I felt light-headed for a moment, like I stood up too quickly.

My frustration spilled out again. Straining, I pulled against my restraints, the metal cutting into that delicate flesh around my wrists, but I was only a Starlight witch. I didn't possess a giant's strength. I couldn't break through metal, but I might be able to melt it.

When I reached out to my starlight, I knew.

Similar to what Bellamy had injected me with, I couldn't tap into my magic. Something was obstructing my starlight. The handcuffs. They were anti-magical handcuffs made to block a witch's magic.

Shit.

I looked over at Valen. His face was dark with anger, his eyes burning with cold fury. He kept clenching and unclenching his fists, like he wasn't sure who to pound on first. I could tell he wanted to morph into his giant form and beat these creeps into a pulp. I would have welcomed that. But then, that would only make me look guiltier. Not to mention what it would do to his reputation and his career. He'd never work for the hotel again after that.

Our eyes met, and I gave him a silent shake of my head, hoping he'd get the message. He nodded. It was good enough.

I glared at Clive. "You're making a mistake. I didn't kill Adele." My shoulders ached from being pulled back and twisted at an odd angle. I yanked at the restraints again, even though I knew it was hopeless. Call it an instinctive reaction. I loathed being trapped.

Clive took a drag of his cigarette. His eyes flicked around the lobby, like he was admiring the décor and didn't really care that he was causing a scene or perhaps ruining my reputation for the rest of my life. "We'll let the courts decide. But there's a mountain of evidence against you. You have no case. You can kiss your freedom goodbye."

Blood pounded in my ears. "What?"

Clive blew out a shoot of smoke. "And we have an eyewitness. Saw it all happen."

My lips parted. "That doesn't make any sense." I didn't remember seeing anyone leave the lab. But then again, I was busy fighting, or being tied up, or trying to save Valen's life. It was possible a few of Adele's cronies had left.

Reluctantly, I cast my gaze around, seeing that most of the guests had stopped playing at the gaming tables and were more interested in what was happening to me.

Basil cleared his throat. He was jumping and chasing Clive's cigarette ashes with the ashtray in his hand. "I must agree with Leana. This is a mistake. A mistaken identity. She's no murderer. She's a Merlin. Tell them, Leana."

I doubted that would help. "I'm a Merlin?"

Clive's mouth twisted in a smile that was part amusement and part arrogant. "We know who she is. She can be a Merlin or a fairy queen. I don't give a shit. You killed a member of the White witch court, and you're going to have to pay for what you did." He gave a flick of his head, and the witch who had handcuffed me yanked on my wrists and hauled me forward none too gently.

The next thing I knew, Valen was in front of the witch. He put a finger on the guy's chest, looking like he wanted to rip it open with his bare hands if he dared to take another step forward. "You take your hands off her."

The witch smiled, showing a slip of teeth. "Or what, big guy? You gonna make me?" He laughed. "Go ahead. I would love to take a giant down. I'll add that to my bucket list."

Valen glowered. "You're no match for me."

"Wanna see if that's true?" Purple flames hovered above the witch's palms. A sort of zealous glee glimmered in his dark eyes. He wanted to fight Valen.

The muscles on Valen's neck and shoulders popped. "You're not taking her."

The witch sneered, loving what this was doing to Valen. "We are. And there's nothing you can do to stop us." He raised his hands, the purple flames curling around his wrists and spilling over his arm.

Valen moved closer until he was about an inch from the witch, towering over him easily. "I won't let you." The giant's face was scary, with an uncontrollable fury rippling over him. It was practically a living thing. But I could see some desperation in his eyes, and fear. Fear for me. Fear for whatever they were going to do to me.

I dreaded it too. "Valen. Don't. He's not worth it. He's just trying to get you angry enough so you'll fight him and end up just like me. I can't have that. I need your help."

At that, the giant's eyes fell over me, and I could see his expression soften. Agony crossed his face, and I tried to ignore what it was doing to my heart. He moved back, not a lot, just a step, but his body was still turned toward the witch with the purple magic, as though he were telling him one wrong move, and he'd crush his skull.

I would have been totally turned on if I wasn't angry and scared. Of all the things that could have gone wrong tonight, I would have never imagined I'd be arrested for Adele's murder. It almost seemed like a dream. Too horrible to be true. I felt like I was in denial, just like after my mother passed away. She looked so peaceful in the bed, like she was sleeping. She couldn't be dead. She was still warm.

I blinked, my eyes burning. I would not cry. I would not give Clive and his pets the benefits of seeing me crumble like a sad female. I was strong. Stronger than they knew. I'd get through this. I was innocent of this crime, though part of me wished I had killed Adele myself. I wasn't so naïve to think it would be easy. Just that I'd figure out a way. I always did.

"What is going on here? Why is Leana in handcuffs? Who are you?"

Elsa pushed past a few guests who had formed a circle around us. Her face was red with what I could only guess was the result of the amount of wine she'd been drinking. Catelyn came up behind her, like a child hiding behind her mother's skirt. Her eyes were round with fear, and her mouth fell open when she saw the handcuffs on my wrists.

"Gray Council investigators. They're arresting her for Adele's murder." Basil threw himself forward and caught some of Clive's ashes again. Clive flicked the butt of his cigarette onto the floor, causing Basil to let out a whimper as he dashed forward like a soccer goalie and, miracle of miracles, caught the damn butt in the ashtray.

Elsa made a low sound in her throat. "She didn't kill Adele, you fool. You have it all wrong."

Clive reached inside his jacket and pulled out a small metal box before flipping it open and plucking out a cigarette. He put it to his lips. I saw a small puff of fire as the cigarette lit on its own. Not on its own but with magic. I might have been impressed if I didn't already hate the guy.

Clive took a long drag of his cigarette and blew the smoke out from his nose. "If she didn't kill her, who did?"

Elsa stiffened, and my eyes trailed to Catelyn, who looked like she was about to throw up any second. Yeah, Catelyn had killed Adele with a simple flick of her hand, breaking her neck and killing the witch instantly. And in the process, she saved my life. Adele wanted her to kill me. She'd ordered her to do it. But the giantess had turned on Adele instead. I didn't blame her. I probably would have done the same.

Catelyn's eyes teared up. She looked trapped, like a wild animal in a cage, gnawing at the metal bars.

My heart grew heavy at the sight of her. She thought we were going to tell them. Catelyn had been through enough. I didn't think she could handle the Gray Council prison. She wouldn't make it. And I wasn't about to turn her in either.

Clive chuckled at our collective silence. "Lying won't save you either." His eyes met mine. "I don't care that you're a Starlight witch with a giant as your lover. Adele was my friend." The way he said it, with that bit of emotion he let slip, I knew they'd been more than friends. Lovers.

Shit. He thought I'd killed his girlfriend, and now he would get his revenge. This was bad. Very bad.

Catelyn seemed to relax a little, but she hid behind Elsa, like the older woman was her shield.

Clive swept his gaze around the lobby. "Nice hotel." He looked at me. "You like luxury, just like most women." He smiled, looking mildly entertained. He blew out a row of smoke from each nostril. "Better take a good look. 'Cause where you're going, the only luxury you'll have is when they let you have a bathroom break once a day." His lips quirked with what looked like a laugh.

The bastard thought this was funny?

"Take her. Let's go."

Without another word, Clive moved away and headed toward the front hotel doors.

I winced as Dumbass One (I needed to give them names) grabbed me from behind and pushed me forward.

The last thing I remembered was looking over my shoulder at my friends. Basil was on his knees, trying to pick up some ashes he'd missed from the floor. Red blotched Elsa's face and neck, her blood pressure rising. And Valen... Valen's eyes connected with mine. He looked torn as his face took on a world of pain that made my throat burn.

"Leana..." He couldn't finish whatever he was going to say. His anguish knocked the breath out of me.

My eyes burned, and I could feel the tears forming as my vision blurred. I spun my head back around. My legs were heavier than usual as Dumbass One pushed hard against my back. But I'd cried enough in my life. Tears wouldn't help me now. They would only make Clive feel like he'd won.

I heard a growl and turned in time to see Valen punch a massive hole in the hotel's wall. He placed both hands on the wall and hung his head. That's the last I saw of him as they dragged me away.

That was three days ago. And I was still here, sitting on the floor of my ten-by-ten cell with no windows to keep me company or tell me what time of day or night it was. Only the occasional cockroach visited me.

"You're lucky Errol isn't here," I told it as it scampered through the small opening under the metal door.

I'll admit, it hurt that my friends hadn't come to see me. Not even once. Not even Valen. It's possible the Gray Council forbade visitors. Maybe they were hoping to let me rot in here alone for a few days until I confessed my crimes.

Okay, I'll confess to my crimes. There were many, just not the one they'd put me in here for.

As soon as they removed the cuffs and shoved me into my new, tiny home, I felt it—the waves of the magical barrier. Just like the handcuffs, the walls of this place kept me from doing any magic. It didn't surprise me. All kinds of wizards, warlocks, and witches had likely come through these cells. If they could use their magic, they'd have no problem escaping.

Without the use of my magic, I was basically useless.

I'd been to the Gray Council's archives once to gather all the information I could on giants, but this wasn't the same place. The archive building was more of a library, with the smell of books and knowledge. This place smelled of fear, desperation, and the forgotten.

Being alone meant all I had was time to think about who would want me here in the first place. With Adele dead, the only name that came to mind was Darius.

I still needed to figure out who this Darius was. All I knew was that he sat on the Gray Council, and Adele had been taking orders from him. Possibly this guy had figured out I planned to put a stop to whatever crazy new-world project he and Adele had orchestrated, where only the paranormal would exist. It sounded fine until she said they'd kill all the humans to achieve this. He didn't want me to stop his plans, so he'd devised an excuse to lock me up.

He'd also told Adele to keep me alive. That was interesting. But why? Why not just kill me? Why put me here? To make me suffer? It didn't make sense.

I was as stubborn as hell and hadn't cried once. I wouldn't put it past them to have some magical, invisible cameras in my cell, which was why I kept flipping off every corner of the room and telling the walls to fuck off.

Clive was doing this on purpose. He wanted me to break, but I wouldn't. It was going to take a lot more to break me. I wasn't afraid of solitude either. I liked my alone time. Always had.

Growing up without siblings, cousins, or even a father, you sort of figure out things on your own. You make your own fun. You adjust until it becomes your routine. Even married to Martin, I felt alone. So, being in a small cell was nothing.

I wouldn't say I liked bathroom breaks once a day. At my age, my bladder wasn't as strong as it used to be, and I needed to pee every couple of hours. Now I was seriously working hard on my kegel exercises so I wouldn't leave little puddles on the floor. If they had left me a bucket, I would have used it. But I had nothing.

There was no bed, blankets, or chair to sit on—just these cold, hard stone floors and walls.

I hadn't seen Clive either. The last time I'd seen his chain-smoking face was when he smiled at me and shut the metal door of the cell in my face. I thought I'd see the bastard again, but he never showed.

My ears pricked up at the sound of keys rattling. My bathroom break? It seemed a bit early, but then again, I had no idea what time it was. They took my phone and my bag. I had nothing.

But I welcomed my bathroom breaks. Not only could I empty my poor old bladder, but I also got the chance to look around and figure out the layout of whatever basement dungeon they'd stuck me in.

All I saw when my jailor—let's call him Ben—took me for my daily bathroom trip were just rows of more cells identical to mine. The doors were all closed. But I could hear the constant moaning of lost souls. It made me wonder how long they'd been here and if they would ever get out.

I'd never even had a good look at the Gray Council's first floor. They just hauled me downstairs to my waiting cell. The space had been too dark to really make out any other doorways or possible escape routes.

I pushed to my feet, my lower back and knees protesting from being in the same position for so long. The cold floor was not helping. A short walk to the bathroom would do me some good and get the blood flowing to my limbs.

The door finally swung open, giving me a good look at my jailor.

"You're not Ben."

Nope. I'd never seen this man before. Unlike Ben, who wore a heavy, brown robe that looked like it had belonged to some monk in the 1970s, with dirt on the hem and holes—you get the picture—this guy was more refined.

He was a tad shorter than Ben, and where Ben was rough around the edges with his looks, this man oozed sophistication and intellect. He held himself like a cross between a college professor and a politician. His expensive light-gray, three-piece suit fit him perfectly. No doubt it was tailored to him. The only odd thing about him was his long silver hair tied back in a low ponytail.

"You a Targaryen?" I laughed and regretted it as I felt a tiny release in my bladder. Whoops.

The silver-haired man stepped inside my cell, giving me a good view of his eyes. They were gray. Cold energies wafted through with the scent of sulfur. The Targaryen wannabe was a Dark witch.

He smiled, but I saw no warmth in it. "My name is Darius."

CHAPTER 2

Darius. So, this is you.

I'd wanted to meet the person who gave Adele her orders. I just hadn't expected to have the pleasure so soon. Still, I would take that as a win.

"So, you're the Darius Adele told me about." I stared at his face. It held the same assured smile of a crooked politician lying through his teeth and believing his constituents were oblivious. "Can't say I'm sorry for your loss. She deserved what she got and worse after what she did."

Darius shrugged like she had meant nothing to him. "Adele had her issues."

"Mental issues."

Darius laughed. "I'm glad to finally meet you. Shame it's under these unfortunate circumstances."

"Can't say the same about you." I'd never met a member of the Gray Council before. I'd expected to see a weathered, old, wrinkled person in a gray robe. Not some silver-haired guy who didn't look much older than me. Maybe fifty. Maybe even forty-five. It was hard to tell. His skin was... delicate, like he never went out into the sun. Not the same kind of smooth that vampires sported. This was different. Fake.

Darius clasped his hands together. "Understandable. I'd be pretty upset, too, if I were in your shoes." His voice was the same as his appearance: cultured, smooth, politician-like. I hated it.

I crossed my arms over my chest. "Am I ever going to get out of here? I do have a life and a job." I wasn't so sure about the job part. The guests at the hotel had seen the whole thing. If Basil believed somehow my arrest would bring shame to the hotel and keep guests from booking, I was confident he'd fire me.

Darius watched me. "You'll have to go through the process that every paranormal does when they come here. You'll have your day in court to plead your case." He let out a long, exaggerated breath as though what he was about to say was final. "But in your case… I'm afraid it doesn't look good."

"Which means what exactly?"

"Means that you *will* be found guilty of murdering Adele. You'll be sent to Grimway Citadel, the witch prison in New York, where you'll spend the rest of your life. Unless, of course, you do what most of those sent there do and take your own life. The more cowardly way out."

I shook my head, feeling the anger rushing back hard. "I didn't murder that skinny witch. Though I sometimes wish I did. Hell, lots of times. I'm just glad she's not around to hurt anyone else."

Darius raised a brow. "You're just a hired witch, whereas Adele was a respected member of the White witch court. See where I'm going with that?"

"Right. Because I'm a nobody, I'm automatically labeled as guilty?"

Darius smiled. "Precisely."

Despair hit, and I pushed it away, not wanting to give this creep anything. "What about a lawyer or something?" I wasn't schooled on the whole paranormal judicial system, but I knew we had lawyers. Just like in the human courts. "Don't I get a chance to defend myself? And where are my friends? I know they tried to see me. You stopped them from coming. Didn't you?"

"Yes." Darius gave me a lazy smile. "Visitors are not permitted. Not for murderers."

I swallowed hard, my throat constricting. "When's this court date?"

Darius glanced at his watch. It was a Rolex or one of those really expensive ones. "In a few minutes."

"What!" Holy hell. "But I'm not prepared. This isn't right. You know this isn't right." Obviously, this guy didn't care. So, why was he here? Was he here to gloat?

"There's a witness who saw everything. It doesn't look good for you."

"I heard. A *paid* witness." They would have said a giantess killed Adele if there was an actual witness. Not me. Her messed-up neck was proof. Clearly, this was sabotage, a way to get rid of me.

Darius stepped into my cell and started to pace. Whenever he came close, I quickly moved out of the way. No way did I want this creep to brush up against me.

The Dark witch halted and spread his hands. "I could make this all go away."

I stared at him hard, not trusting the words that were coming out of his mouth. He was all smiles, but somehow his voice rang false.

"I'm not sleeping with you," I told him and took a step back. I was desperate, yes, but not *that* desperate. Besides, his silver hair was freaking me out a little.

Darius smiled. "You are lovely, like a rare flower. But you're not my type."

"What's that? The ones with meat on their bones." Thank the gods.

The Dark witch's eyes narrowed, and I saw the first flicker of annoyance. "I'm not here to sleep with you. If I wanted that, I would have taken you to my manor directly. Then I would have forced myself on you. Over and over again. As much as I wanted. I take what I want. I don't want you in that way."

Bile rose in the back of my throat. "So what, then? How can you make this go away?" I would never trust anything that came out of this witch's piehole. But that didn't mean I didn't want to hear what he had to say.

Darius brushed a long strand of his silver hair over his shoulder. "I seek something of great value."

"What's that?" I had a strange feeling he wanted me for a job. Something he didn't want the rest of the Gray Council members to know about.

"A jewel."

"A jewel. Like a diamond?"

The cunning smile on Darius's face only ticked me off more. "It's called the Jewel of the Sun." His eerie gray eyes rested on me. "And I need you to find it and bring it to me."

I thought about it for a moment, Adele's words coming back. She said Darius didn't want me dead, and now it all made sense. He needed me to look for this jewel for him.

"And why can't you find this jewel on your own? You look like someone of means. I'm pretty sure you can find anything you want. Why me?"

Darius watched me, and I couldn't tell what expressions crossed his features. "I've been following your progress for a while. You're resourceful. Clever. And you always get the job done. You're what I need."

I didn't believe him for a second. I couldn't help but notice how he avoided the question. "So it's dangerous. Am I right? That's why you're sending me?" It wasn't the first time I'd faced danger. "I'm going to need more to go on. Like, what kind of jewel is this? What does it look like?" The guy was scum. Any so-called jewel was something he would use for his own gain. And it wasn't for the good of humanity or our people.

"What does it do?"

Darius smiled, and I saw a slip of his perfectly straight teeth. "It holds great power. What else?"

Of course it does. The last thing I wanted was to give this guy a device of great power. But I was kind of stuck. "And if I refuse?"

Darius's smile faded. "Then you will be condemned to spend the rest of your life in prison."

"Even if I'm innocent. Nice system." I pressed my hands over my forehead. I was trapped. He knew it. I knew it. And I had a feeling this was all his doing. He'd done this on purpose. Orchestrated this sham of a murder charge to force me to do his bidding because he knew I would have never accepted otherwise.

A mix of resolve and irritation shone on his face. "What will it be?" The tone of his voice suggested he knew he had me trapped, and I would accept. Bastard.

"Fine." I sighed. "I'll do it. Do you have any clues as to where it is?" If this jewel was somewhere in Europe, it might be fun to sightsee and visit another country. More like a vacation. I was due for a break.

He was silent for a long while, watching me. Then he pulled a manila envelope from inside his jacket. "This is what I've gathered over the years."

I took the envelope and pulled out what looked like photocopies of files.

"I've found three possible locations for the jewel," said Darius, his hands clasped in front of him once again. "All in New York City. One possible location is the Sisters of Compassion convent. Trinity Church in Manhattan is another. And the last is in Hell's Kitchen Psychiatric Ward. All the information is in that file you're holding."

I was a little disappointed that I wouldn't have to take a plane, but it meant I'd be with my friends while I worked. And Valen. "How will I find it? What does it look like?"

Darius cocked a brow. "With your unique starlight skills, you shouldn't have a problem. The Jewel of the Sun will show itself to you and only you."

I frowned. I wasn't sure what he meant by that. "How much are you going to pay me?" I knew I was pushing it, but I wanted to be paid if this was a job. And if he was seeking my help, he was desperate. Everyone knew the desperate paid.

"Giving you your life back isn't enough?"

"I need to eat and pay rent."

I didn't like the way Darius's eyes were wide with wonder and admiration. Instead of answering my question, he walked to the doorway and picked up something from the floor. My bag. Guess I wasn't going to get paid.

Darius handed me my bag. I checked inside. My phone was there. But the battery was dead. No surprise. I'd been here for at least three days without a charger.

"How will I contact you when I find your jewel?" I knew this guy didn't want the Gray Council knowing what I was doing. He wanted this off the books. He was also a cheap bastard.

Darius stared at the file I was holding. "I'll know when you've secured the jewel. I'll come find you."

Interesting. "Is there a time frame I should know about? This doesn't sound like an easy job. It's going to take some time."

He shook his head. "A few days should be plenty of time. And, Leana, I will be watching. Don't even think about keeping it for yourself."

"I wouldn't dream of it."

"Because without me, you'll have no life. Find the jewel, and you can return to your mundane existence."

I hated how he'd said that. But I'd rather return to my mundane life than to spend another minute with this creep.

"One more thing." Darius stared at me. "Your friends can't be involved."

"Why the hell not?" It would go a lot faster if they were with me.

"It's simple." His gray eyes rolled over my face, slowly down my body, and back up again. "I need a Starlight witch. You're the only one who can find the jewel. They'd only be interfering."

I seriously doubted that. "Well, you're the boss. Right?" Just saying that had my stomach churning. If I had actual food in there, I might have puked.

A small, devious smile showed on his face. "I will see you very soon, Leana Fairchild."

"Let's hope not."

"I'll get you a cab." With a last smile, Darius walked out of my cell, leaving the door open. I stood there for about a minute. Knowing that, either way, I was trapped. He'd conned me into working for him—for free, I might add. I knew this jewel was bad news. He wanted me to retrieve it for him. Why? Because he couldn't find it? Was he too busy? A lot of this didn't make any sense. The guy probably had loads of witches and wizards on his payroll. Why me?

And then I lifted my bag on my shoulder and left the cell that had been my temporary home for three days.

CHAPTER 3

My legs felt like wooden boards as I made my way across the hallway of the thirteenth floor. On the ride home, I'd asked the cab driver for the time while he drove me to the hotel.

"Seven-ten p.m.," he'd said as he'd taken the next right.

After Darius had left, I had climbed the staircase, reached a heavy, black metal door and pushed it open, only to realize he was nowhere to be found on the main floor of the Gray Council building. Only Ben, my jailor, was there. He led me out and had the cab waiting for me when I exited the building.

I smelled like sweat and whatever muck I'd accumulated on my jeans from sitting and sleeping on the cold stone floor. I needed a shower first, and then I needed some food.

A few tenants eyed me as I walked past their apartments, but I was too tired to say anything to them, so I avoided eye contact and kept walking.

Finally, when I made it to my apartment, the familiar sounds of voices reached me. Elsa, Julian, and Jade were gathered around the dining table with papers scattered all over the top. I'd made it to the living area before they saw me.

"Leana!" Elsa was the first one to see me. She clapped her hands together and ran to me, her eyes wide.

Then Julian and Jade spun around and rushed to greet me.

When I noticed Elsa going in for a hug, I lifted my hand in warning. "Don't. I smell like I've been living on the street for a month."

Big tears rolled down her face, and she wiped them away. "What happened? How are you here? Did they drop the charges against you?"

"We tried to see you." Jade's face flushed, and I could tell she was holding back tears.

"They wouldn't let us in." Julian's brow lowered, and he clenched his teeth, his jaw muscles standing out sharply. "We even hired three lawyers, and they wouldn't let them see you either." He ran his fingers through his light-brown hair, cut short on the sides and longer on top.

My heart felt heavy, and it was nearly impossible to keep the tremor from my voice. "Damn. I'm sorry. That must have cost a fortune. I'll pay you back. I swear it." I didn't know how I would, seeing that I had most definitely lost my job. Or close to it.

Elsa waved a hand in my direction. "Never mind that. Come and sit. You look exhausted. And thin."

"Did they starve you? Oh my God, they did!" Jade's blonde hair had blue highlights that reflected in the light. Her Best of Journey T-shirt had an extensive wine stain on the front.

I shrugged. "They gave me water and this disgusting stew, which was basically questionable things floating in lukewarm water. I didn't eat it."

"Come." Elsa grabbed me by the hand and sat me at the dining table. "I'll make you something before you collapse."

I stared at all the papers and what looked like a building's blueprint. "What's all this?"

That drew a small, sly smile out of Julian. "We were going to break you out of jail."

"What?" My chest warmed at the thought. "You guys are crazy. But I like it." The fact that they were going to risk their own butts for me said a lot. My eyes burned, and it was a miracle I didn't start to sob right there and then. Guess staying in that cell for three days affected me more than I wanted to admit.

"Jimmy was going to help too," said Jade, a proud smile on her face. Looked like things were going well in that department. I was happy for her.

"We were going to blow a hole with one of my potions." Julian pointed to a spot on what I imagined were the blueprints of the Gray Council building that meant nothing to me. "It was the closest to the basement entry. Best spot to hit without hurting any paranormals in the cells."

It probably would have worked, but then what? Live life on the run? Nope. I'm glad they didn't have to do it.

Julian grabbed the chair next to me, pulled it out, and let himself fall. "They let you out?" By the question still lingering in his voice, I knew he wanted to know what happened.

"In a way," I said as Jade bumped her hip against the table, her arms crossed over her chest. "I met Darius. The guy Adele was working for."

"Darius?" Elsa whirled around with a frying pan in one hand and a carton of eggs in the other. I saw her face make the connection. "He did this to you. Didn't he? That bastard." She swung the frying pan like she wished she could use it on his head. I did too.

I nodded, feeling tired and wanting to take that shower. "He did." I gave them a brief account of what had happened to me during my stay in the cell and what Darius had proposed.

"So, of course, I said yes."

"Any of us would have done the same." Julian leaned back in his chair, and a flicker of anger crossed his features. "So he did all this: starved you, kept you away from your friends in a stinking cell, just so that you'd agree to find this jewel?"

"That's what I'm thinking. He's a bit twisted." And let's not forget creepy.

Jade's face was screwed up. "And you're really going to go through with it? I mean, look what he did to you."

"I know what you think," I said, watching Elsa crack two eggs and let them slip into the now-hot frying pan. "Why would I give this guy something that will most probably hurt or kill people?"

Jade shrugged. "Yeah. That."

"She didn't have a choice, Jade," called Elsa from the stove. "It was either that, or they would process her, and she'd end up in prison. Forever."

I felt a chill roll up my spine at the thought of being in an identical cell for the rest of my witch life. I liked my solitude, but at some point, I would need some companionship. And the gang had become more than friends to me. They were family. I needed them in my life. And Valen. Let's not forget the uber-hot giant.

"I know *that*," said Jade. "I don't know. It just doesn't seem right to help this Darius. Not when we know he's responsible for changing humans into paranormals."

"I get it." She had me there. I didn't want to help him. But he hadn't given me a choice. I wanted to get out of that cell more than anything. He knew it, which was why he kept me there without even a damn blanket, for three days. It was enough to imagine life like that for a very long time—a life I didn't want.

Also, out of that cell, I could continue my investigation on Darius. Now that I knew more about him, what he looked like, and what he wanted, I was closer. If I could get my hands on the proof I needed, I could bring it to the Gray Council, and inadvertently, it would be enough for them to wave away the charges they had on me. Get rid of Darius while working for Darius. It sounded insane. But that was *the* plan. Well, it was the *only* plan I had at the moment.

I yanked out the envelope from my bag and placed it on the table. "If I find it, I'm not about to hand it over to him either. I want to know more about it. What it does."

"And if it does what we think it does?" pressed Jade. "Kills more innocent people?"

"Then I'll figure out a way to keep it from him until I have a solid case," I told her. "I'm hoping the Gray Council is not all corrupted. Hopefully, some members still have a conscience and don't like Darius. That's what I'm betting on. So, if I get the proof I need, I'll present it to them. But I'll have to find a member I can trust to do that." And I didn't know a single soul on that council.

"We can help you with that," said Julian. "We can test them. See who the liars are on that board."

"How're you going to do that?"

"Feed them lies. See who takes the bait."

I smiled. "I like how your mind works."

Julian smiled, stretched, and leaned back. "Me too."

I laughed as I looked around at my friends, feeling something was missing. "Where's Catelyn?" My gut clenched at the thought that maybe something had happened. Like her time had run out.

Elsa came over with a plate of steaming eggs and veggies. "She's studying. I gave her a few books to look over. You know, to get to know about our world and who we are. She's an outstanding student."

I felt myself relax at her words. I stared at my plate. "Wow. Real food."

Elsa flashed a smile and pointed to my plate. "And it tastes real too. Eat. Or I'll spoon-feed you."

"Yes, ma'am." I filled my fork with some yummy veggie omelet and shoved it in my mouth. No point in trying to be proper. I was starving. Funny how something as simple as an omelet tasted amazing when you hadn't eaten anything real in three full days. It was like tasting food for the first time in my life. My taste buds were prickling and tingling with flavors. They were doing a line dance in my mouth.

I moaned. "Wow. This is *soooo* good." Once I had a taste, I couldn't stop. No one said a word as I finished my plate. I stared at it, disappointed that it had taken me a whole two minutes to finish.

Elsa handed me a tall glass of water. Then she grabbed my plate. "I'll make you some more." She twirled away, seemingly pleased that she would make me seconds. At this point, I thought I'd likely go for a third or even a fourth serving.

I gulped some water and moaned too. "Who knew that clean water could taste this amazing."

Jade laughed. "Poor you. Sounds like you had a horrible time."

"Could have been worse." I thought about what Darius had said about forcing himself on me. Over and over again. My gut tightened. *That* would have been way worse.

My silence after that seemed to draw Jade's features in worry. "Well, you're home now. Valen is going to be thrilled!"

"He's been out of his mind with worry," said Elsa as she whisked some eggs and veggies in a ceramic bowl. "I thought he was going to give himself a heart attack. I don't think he's slept since you were taken."

Valen. The look of pain on his face tore the edges around my heart. "Can I borrow someone's phone? Mine is dead." I pulled out my cell phone and stared at the black screen.

"Take mine." Julian handed me his phone. He took mine and moved to the kitchen counter where my charger was to plug it in. I didn't even have to ask or tell him where it was. That's how close we all were. He walked back. "He was going to break through the Gray Council building with his bare hands. Told me so. If I didn't have the potions to make a big enough hole. Part of me wanted to tell him I'd run out of potions just to see him in action."

"I'm glad none of you had to do that. Trust me. You don't want this guy Darius on your bad side." I dialed Valen's number that I'd committed to memory, but it went to voicemail after the fourth ring. I hung up and texted him instead.

Me: *It's Leana. I'm out. I'm back at my place with the gang. My phone is dead so I'm using Julian's. I'm okay.*

I wanted to write more, but it would be easier face-to-face. So I gave Julian back his phone. "Thanks."

"No problem." Julian picked up the envelope, dumped the contents, and spread them out on the table. "Where are we going to look first?"

I smiled. I loved that he said "we," like this was going to be *our* task and not mine alone. "Maybe the church? I need to look over this again. Not tonight. My brain is mush. But after I sleep a few hours, I'll study them. I'll get back to you on that." Darius had warned me to do this alone. Too bad I wasn't very good at following instructions.

"Do you trust him?" Jade watched me, her features tight.

"Hell no. But what choice did I have?" I also agreed because I wanted to know about this jewel.

"Jade's right." Elsa returned and filled my plate with another, more significant veggie omelet. "What if you do all the work, get him that jewel, and then he throws you back in jail?"

I nodded. "He could. That's what he's thinking, I'm sure. But let him think that. It's not like I'm going to let him do that to me." Again.

"What are you thinking?" asked Jade, her eyes curious.

"That I need more time." I sighed and tore into my second omelet. "I need more time to figure out my next move," I said, with my mouth full. "Turns out Darius just gave me that time."

"I need to tell Jimmy." Jade pulled out her cell from her back pocket and began moving her fingers over the screen.

"Is Basil still here? I should speak to him. Let him know I'm back and hopefully still have a job." I knew I had to speak to him. The troubled look on his face when Clive and his goons handcuffed me was like I'd caused a scene on purpose just to make the hotel look bad. It was always about him, with Basil. Still, I needed my job.

"Don't worry about Basil," said Elsa, like I was overreacting. "He can wait. You can speak with him after you've rested. You just relax and eat. You need to gather your strength. After this, you can take a nice long shower and go straight to bed." She said it like it was an order. "I'll stay here and make sure no one bothers you. You want more?"

I eyed my empty plate, not even remembering eating all the omelet. "No. I'm good, thanks. Full."

"Well then, let's get you clean 'cause you stink." Elsa tapped her nose and made her way to my bathroom.

"See you when you wake up," said Jade. "Come on, Julian. Let's let her get some sleep."

I waved them goodbye and followed Elsa into my bathroom.

The older witch took a good long look at me, the kind of look someone gives you when they know you're holding back.

"A good shower will wash away all the aches and pains and… all the rest." I knew what she meant. The horrors. The might-have-beens. That maybe I had slept on decade-old fecal matter.

"A shower sounds amazing," I said, not realizing at the time just how amazing it would be.

Elsa was nodding. "I'll make you a nice herbal tea to help you sleep." She stared at me for a moment and then set her hands on my shoulders. "I'm glad you're back." Her words were clipped. Her blue eyes were bright, and they welled with tears.

My bottom lip trembled, but I managed a "me too." My throat tightened. I didn't think I could have uttered another word.

I was thankful when she left and closed the door behind her.

I wiped the one tear that had escaped my right eye, glanced at myself in the mirror, and winced. Damn. My face was hollowed around my cheekbones. Dark circles were painted under my eyes like I hadn't slept for days, which I hadn't. I looked sick. My hair stood out on odd ends, not like I had a brush with me, and my three-day-old eyeliner and mascara were smeared under my eyes from my oily skin. I looked like hell. Guess three days of fasting would do that to a person's face. I was glad Valen hadn't seen me like this.

Slowly, I pulled off my clothes: jeans, shirt, bra, and undies. I gathered them and stuffed them in the small garbage bin I had in the bathroom. I was never going to wear them again. It would only remind me of my time in that cell. I didn't need reminders. A good laundry detergent would get the smell out, but it couldn't wash away the memories.

I stepped into the hot shower, and a huge sigh escaped me as the water fell over my face. As soon as the water splashed over my face and body, I couldn't hold it together anymore. Like the water was the last thing that undid me.

At first, it was a small cry, like when you're watching a sad movie, the part where the child is ripped away from the mother's arms—or when the dog dies. Why do they always kill the dog?

Then, well, the emotions hit like a tidal wave of grief.

I let out a strangled cry, sank to the floor, and put my head between my knees as the waves of raw emotions overcame me. Water splashed over my head into my mouth as I continued to sob, each one shaking me between bouts of tears and chokes. It hadn't hit me until now. I hadn't even realized I'd been holding in so much—the thought of losing what I had, my friends, my new family, Valen. The idea of never seeing Valen again was almost unbearable.

But it wasn't just him. It was the life I'd made for myself.

I hadn't wanted to admit my fear and that sometimes it's okay to cry. Sometimes it's okay not to be strong all the time.

I knew Elsa could hear me bawling my eyes out, but I suspected that's what she wanted me to do, what she had planned. Cry it all out.

And I did.

CHAPTER 4

I woke in a startled panic. At first, I thought I was back in my cell with only cold stone walls as my constant companions.

But as my eyes adjusted and sleep left me, I recognized the surrounding walls of my bedroom. I was back in my apartment and in my own bed.

But something had woken me—the smell.

The scent of cooking, specifically butter, wafted into my bedroom from the space between the floor and the door. I also noticed a lingering sweet smell, like maybe French toast or pancakes. French toast sounded divine. My mouth started to salivate.

I grinned. Elsa was making me breakfast. I grabbed my phone. The screen read 11:14 a.m. Definitely not breakfast, then. The last thing I remembered was hitting my pillow last night and finding it the most comfortable bed I'd ever slept in. Then nothing.

Still smiling, I swung my legs off my bed, dressed in a clean pair of jeans and a T-shirt, and sneaked into the bathroom. After I brushed my teeth and relieved myself, I sauntered down the hallway and into the kitchen.

Only Elsa wasn't standing at the stove.

"Valen?"

The giant turned around. The sunlight through the window hit his face at all the right angles, making it seem as though he were glowing. I always thought he was handsome, but somehow, seeing him now after being apart and thinking I might never see him again made him all the more beautiful. He wore a black T-shirt that barely contained all those thick muscles, and a pair of black jeans.

He smiled, and my heart did three somersaults and a dive. "You're up. Did I wake you?"

I closed the distance between us. "The smell of whatever you're cooking did. What is that? Smells fantastic."

"French toast."

I moaned. "I *love* French toast." I glanced at a plate next to the stove with a pile of French toast already prepared.

Valen caught me staring. "I was going to make these, and then you could heat them later when you woke up." His eyes slowly dragged over my body without revealing a single thought. But then his gaze narrowed, and his mouth drew tight like he wanted to say more.

"I'm up now, and I'm starving."

"Good." Valen was holding a spatula in his hand, but he hadn't looked away from me yet. "How are you feeling?"

I loved that he was so concerned about me. He was smiling again, but part of it seemed forced, as though he was still upset about my arrest. He couldn't quite let it go just yet.

"Better than I felt four days ago." Which was the absolute truth.

Valen stared at the ground for a moment, his jaw clenched. It was impossible to read all the emotions that ran across his face, so many of them. But the winner was anger. Yup. He was still livid.

The giant flipped over the French toast in the frying pan. I could tell he didn't want to bring it up, for my sake. I didn't want to bring it up either. It wasn't a very good story.

I watched as he grabbed a plate, piled it with two French toast slices, and set it on the kitchen island. "Eat these while they're still warm. I'll get the syrup."

"And the butter." I grabbed a stool and sat, inhaling that sweet smell of cinnamon. "I feel spoiled. First Elsa, last night, and now you. I could get used to this life."

Valen placed the butter next to me and handed me a fork and knife. "I'll make you breakfast every day of your life if you want."

My face felt on fire at his comment. *Was that some sort of proposal?* I didn't know how to respond to that, so I just kept staring at him like an idiot. Breakfast with Valen, every day of my life, sounded like a dream. It didn't sound real.

Next, the giant moved forward and placed a mug of steaming coffee on the table for me, never making eye contact with me. I wasn't sure if this was his way of torturing me, seeing how I was going to react to that comment.

But then his gaze met mine. When he smiled, I felt it inside my stomach, and it stayed there. But there it was again, that not-quite smile that didn't reach his eyes. It was as though he was relieved I was back, but he was battling his anger. And it was winning.

I tore into my French toast, feeling the need to say something. "I'm okay. You don't have to be upset. It's over. I'm back. Things will be back to what they were." I sure hoped they would. But I had a few things to take care of before I could really believe that.

Valen's smile disappeared, and he crossed his arms over his chest. "Elsa said they let you go on the condition that you find the Jewel of the Sun."

I swallowed the piece of French toast and had to try not to roll my eyes in the back of my head. "You know about that?"

Valen gestured to the dining table, still covered in papers and blueprints. "I spent the morning looking over the files Darius gave you." At my questioning brow, he added, "I came over last night as soon as I got your message, but you were asleep. I wanted to wake you up, but Elsa would have killed me."

I laughed and pointed my fork at him. "She would have."

"We talked for a bit. She told me what had happened to you."

The giant's features tightened, and he uncrossed his arms as he grabbed the counter's edge. He hung his head, staring at the floor. "I should have come and gotten you. I should have never let you spend a single minute in that place."

"It's fine. I'm out now. It wasn't that bad." Yeah, it was.

Valen's dark eyes met mine, and something dangerous flashed across them. "Only after they bribed you. The guy orchestrated this whole thing so he could force you to do this job for him."

"I know."

Valen looked at me, and then he glanced away, seemingly uncomfortable with what he wanted to ask me next. "Did they… did they…"

"Force themselves on me?" I knew that's what he wanted to know. Seeing him now, like a beast on the verge of a killing spree, I wasn't sure he could handle that if they had. "No. No one touched me in that way." Thank the goddess for that.

The giant was nodding, but my answer didn't do much to the fearsome frown on his face. "I should have stopped them." Valen was shaking his head. "In the lobby. I shouldn't have let them take you. But I thought if I did something… it would have been worse for you. I just never imagined they wouldn't let anyone see you."

My insides tightened at the emotion in his voice. "What happened to me isn't your fault. None of it is."

When his eyes met mine, they were filled with sorrow. "I should have done more."

"And then what? End up in a cell next to mine? Well, I guess that wouldn't be so bad, then." I smiled and could see a hint of a smile in those damn fine eyes. "Listen. I agree that Darius coordinated my arrest to force me to do this job for him. And I doubt anything you or anyone could have done would have stopped him."

"For the jewel." Valen was quiet for a moment. And then he spun around like he'd just remembered the stove and the French toast that was close to burning.

I watched as he turned the knobs off. "Do you know anything about this jewel? Ever heard about it before?"

Valen wiped his hands on a dish towel. "No. From what Elsa told me, it might hold magic?"

I pushed my now-empty plate forward so I could lean my elbows on the island. "Obviously, Darius wants it for that reason. I don't think him getting his hands on it is a good thing."

"You're not going to look for it?" Valen sounded genuinely surprised.

"Oh, I am. I'm just not sure I'm going to hand it over to him when I find it." I knew Darius had spies everywhere. He'd know if I just pretended to look for the jewel but didn't really, just to get out of the cell. He wasn't so easily fooled. And he'd be watching me.

A smile spread over the giant's face, the kind that had me falling for him the first time I saw it. His shoulders seemed to relax a bit. He didn't look like he wanted to make holes in the walls anymore.

"You're still marked as a criminal." Valen watched me. His smile was replaced with a narrowing of his brows.

"How do you know that?"

"I have a friend on the Gray Council here in New York City. I asked her to look into your file. There's no indication that Darius granted you a compassionate release or some kind of probation. Or even a dismissal."

A slip of anger and fear settled in my gut. "Well, can't say I'm surprised."

"It means they can arrest you again whenever they want."

"Excellent." The French toast didn't feel so amazing in my stomach anymore. The thought that Darius and his cronies could take me away again just because he didn't like how I laughed or smiled had my blood pressure rising. He could very well put me back into that cell, and I couldn't do anything about it. But he wouldn't. Not until I found the jewel. I still had time.

"I'm having some of my contacts look into this so-called eyewitness," said Valen.

I looked up at him surprised. "You are?"

"I know it's bullshit. All of it. And to clear your name, we need to prove it. Prove that this witness is lying."

"But won't that get Catelyn into trouble? The last thing I want is for her to end up in one of the paranormal prisons." I took a sip of coffee, letting the warmth fill the coldness I suddenly felt inside.

"Not after what Adele did to her," said the giant. "She wants to come forward."

My lips parted, and I blinked. "Excuse me?"

"The Gray Council can't charge her with anything. She's a human who was changed into a giantess against her will by an illegal procedure. She's willing to confess what she did to Adele."

"But the Gray Council is corrupt. Darius can't be the only one."

"Maybe," said the giant. "But we can go public. Let all the communities know what's happened. Jimmy is already setting up a website."

I felt an incredible sense of gratitude that Catelyn wanted to help me, but that didn't mean I was okay with it. "How do you know this? Did Catelyn speak to you?"

Valen flicked a strand of hair from his eyes. "She did. We've been spending a lot of time together. I've been helping her manage better control of her inner giant, which has been helping me not kill anyone while I waited to hear from you."

I sighed and rubbed my eyes. "This is such a mess, but I'm going to fix it. If your guys can find this witness, and if I can figure out what this jewel is, and why Darius is so adamant about having it, I think we might be able to get rid of him. For good." I knew I'd never be safe as long as Darius was a member of the Gray Council.

We stared at each other for a long while until Valen broke the silence.

"I can't lose you, Leana," he said, his voice sincere and full of emotions. "You're the best thing that's happened to me in a very long time."

I smiled at him. "Don't you forget it," I teased, but his words clung to me, sending my heart into bouts of flips and backflips.

The next thing I knew, Valen was beside me, his big hands gently cuddling my cheek as he stared deeply into my eyes. "I won't," he whispered, sending tiny thrills over my skin.

He leaned forward and pressed his lips against mine, and the first thought in my head was that I hoped I didn't have chunks of French toast stuck in my teeth. His tongue slid against my lips, and I opened them, welcoming it.

I moaned into his mouth as our tongues interlaced. He deepened the kiss, and I could feel all the words he couldn't communicate before, within the kiss. Then he spun me around so our fronts were facing. He dragged his hands down to my hips and then along my thighs. Next, he moved his hands and grabbed my knees, spreading my legs. He pushed himself against me, and a surge of heat rushed inside my body.

I slipped my hands over his back, letting the hot skin soak into my fingers. I whispered against his mouth, "I missed you."

Valen let out a growl and kissed me hard—the kind of kiss only confident bad boys were capable of that had your eyes rolling in the back of your head and begging for it never to stop.

"I want you," he said around his kissing. "Right now." His mouth was ferocious and needy. He pulled off my T-shirt in an interlude of moans and kisses.

I'd never been wanted in such a fierce, passionate way, as though I was irresistible. And it was doing some pretty crazy things to my nether regions, not to mention my ego.

I was sitting on the stool with Valen between my legs, in only a bra and jeans. If any of the gang came in now, that would be embarrassing.

But all those thoughts evaporated from my mind as he

grabbed my hips and lifted me. I wrapped my legs around his waist as he carried me to my bedroom, our lips still connected.

"Lock the door," I breathed around his mouth.

The giant did as I asked, shut the door, and locked it with me still hanging around his hips. Next, he laid me gently on the bed, fumbling clumsily with the top buttons of my jeans before managing to undo them. I felt a pull, and then my jeans were yanked off my body before Valen tossed them to the floor.

I grinned. "Now, that's what I call experience." I reached behind me and unfastened my bra, setting the girls free. Before I could stop him, Valen slipped his fingers over my panties and pulled them off as well.

Okay, so I'm completely naked now, and the giant is fully dressed.

Valen's eyes traveled very slowly over me like he was committing every inch of me to memory—all my flaws and imperfections—yet somehow desire soared in his eyes.

"You're beautiful." The giant ripped off his shirt and jeans, and the next thing I knew, he was standing there in all his naked glory.

And let me tell you, it was glorious.

It wasn't like I hadn't seen him naked multiple times. It was just that for the first time I saw him naked with a hard-on just for me.

His manhood? Well, he *was* a giant, and I'd never seen the likes.

My eyes studied his manhood, and I had a momentary fear of, *that thing won't fit in me.*

I spun around, trying to hide my goofy grin, and reached for a condom in my night table drawer. I bought them last week, thinking I might get some time alone with Valen.

Valen took the condom, and when it was in place, he didn't hesitate. He gave me a long, meaningful kiss as he lowered himself on top of me.

"Leana," he growled my name as he dropped his mouth over my neck, kissing and licking. His kisses were like a kind of torture, increasing in pressure and making me dizzy.

I moaned and arched against him. The nerves I used to feel about my lack of bedroom skills were gone because I knew Valen would take care of that. I knew he'd attend to my needs.

His rough hand slid down my waist to my thigh, and I gasped as his magical fingers found my sweet spot. Martin could never find that spot, even if it came with instructions.

Valen growled in my mouth while his magical fingers did their thing, sending me over the edge. My body rippled with trembles as I moaned, possibly shouted. At one point, I was fairly sure I was seeing double. I had no idea sex could feel this good, this amazing, and this addicting.

Boy, had I ever been missing out.

As his expert hands and mouth did their thing, I dug my fingers into his back. Wrapping my legs around his waist, I pulled him against me, never wanting to let him go.

We moved together in a tangle of moans, kisses, and emotion. Pools of desire ignited in my core, seeing this beautiful man on top of me and seeing his own passion and need for me.

And as Valen pushed into me, I let him take all of me.

CHAPTER 5

I stood in the elevator, grinning like a fool. It was hard not to, especially after experiencing mind-blowing sex with the giant a few hours ago.

Did I mention it was mind-blowing? With earth-shattering orgasms? Yes, *orgasms*. More than one. Woo-hoo!

It was nearly impossible to concentrate after that. But the nagging thought that if I landed in prison, I'd never experience that again sobered me right up.

If I didn't find the jewel to save my ass from prison, I'd do it for Valen's orgasms.

I shook my head, trying to clear the aftermath of those intense, carnal feelings.

"Where you going?" Valen had asked a few minutes ago. He was lying on my bed, on his back, with his arm folded under his head. He'd looked positively edible. "I'm not finished with you. Come back here." He growled delectably, sending my heart into a gallop.

"Hang on, you dirty giant. I need to speak to Basil," I told him and grabbed my bathrobe. "He has to know I'm back. See what I missed since I was... gone." I remembered the hotel manager's face all too well, how he was more concerned about what my arrest was doing to the hotel's reputation than me. I needed to speak to him before he did something stupid. "I won't be able to relax until I speak to him." I knew if I went back to bed with Valen, I wouldn't get back out until tomorrow or next week. His touches and kisses were intoxicating.

"Hurry up." The giant watched me with a deep desire in his eyes, which told me he wasn't finished with me. Not by a long shot. I was a lucky woman.

After a quick shower and another round of deep kissing with Valen, I reluctantly pulled away and made my way to the elevators.

Following a short ride, the elevator doors swung open, and I headed toward the front desk. Seeing Errol's frown at my appearance made my heart swell. It felt like home.

I leaned on the counter, grinning. "Hey, Errol. Miss me?"

The concierge's lips pulled up into a snarl. "I thought you were dead."

"Not yet."

"Then there's still hope." Errol swiped his long, spindly fingers on his tablet.

I was so happy to be back. His negative attitude didn't even bother me. On the contrary, it just made me smile more. "Any messages for me?" I doubted Bellamy would send me another message, but you never knew. I was feeling exceptionally good at the moment. Maybe my luck had turned.

"No. No one cares about you. You're not that important," said Errol. He lifted his eyes and observed me a moment. "Why are you so disgustingly happy? It's not like you. You're more of the angry, frowning type."

Angry, frowning type? Was I really like that before? "Well, if you must know. I just had incredible sex."

"No!" Errol dropped his tablet and covered his ears, his pale face taking on a dark shade of red. "Go away. I won't listen to you and your whoring ways."

I laughed. Boy, was he ever in a mood. I loved it. I leaned

forward until my upper body nearly crossed the counter. "It's just sex, Errol. It's not a bad thing. It's a really, really good thing."

The concierge moved away from me, like I was contagious with Ebola, and stood on the opposite side of the desk, putting as much distance between us as he could.

"Is Basil in his office?" I asked as I leaned back and straightened. "Errol? Hello?"

But the lizard shifter continued to ignore me, hands on his ears, as he turned his back to me.

I rolled my eyes, pushed off the counter, and headed toward Basil's office. A smile tugged my lips at the thought that we'd almost had sex on the hotel manager's desk right before Clive and his cronies took me away.

The thought of Clive and that cell stained my happy mood. No way was I going back there. If it meant I had to find this jewel and give it to Darius, I would. Maybe I'd just steal it back. Yeah. Good plan.

I faced Basil's office door, knocked twice, and pushed in. "Oh. Sorry. You're busy."

My eyes settled on the man sitting across from Basil. He turned in his seat so I got a good look at him. His scalp shone through his thinning blond hair that was cut way too short, in my opinion. He was a slow blinker, and I noticed one green eye and a blue one. A long scar jagged from his right brow and down to his jaw. He wasn't young, possibly early fifties. I saw no warmth in his eyes, more like a cold sort of calculating look, like he was sizing me up. He seemed like someone with some life experience under his belt, battle experience if I were to guess, by the scar on his face.

A strong pulse of cold magic hit me, followed by the scent of sulfur and vinegar, the power of a Dark witch. The stranger was a Dark witch. Was he one of Darius's guys?

"Leana?" Basil's face dropped, and then his lips flapped nervously like he didn't know what to say to me.

Weird. I gave him a quick smile. "I'll come back later." I made to move back out.

"What are you doing here?" stuttered Basil. "They released you?"

I stopped and took a step inside the office. My face flamed. I wasn't about to talk about what had happened to me in front of a stranger. I'd been humiliated enough. "Yes. Last night. Listen, we'll talk later. No big deal."

"Why did they release you? Did they drop the charges?" Basil was staring at me with wide eyes, slightly shaking his head like he was in denial. He was acting weird. It was almost as though he never expected to see me ever again.

"Yes, they dropped the charges," I lied. Valen had all but confirmed that the charges were still there, and if Darius wanted, he could throw me back into jail whenever he wanted. I was basically tethered to him until I gave him the jewel he was looking for, so now I was trapped. But I wasn't about to tell Basil or the stranger. I was back. That's all he needed to know at the moment.

"Oh, well, this is awkward," said Basil, looking from me to the stranger. The said stranger had a tiny smile spread over his lips as though he was enjoying whatever *this* was. I wasn't sure I liked him.

I frowned, looking back at Basil. His fingers twitched over his desk, like he didn't know what to do with them, and his face was redder than usual. "How's that?" Now I was getting really worried. "What's going on, Basil?"

Basil shrugged and gave a nervous laugh. "I didn't think you were coming back. I thought you were gone for good. Sent to that witch prison up in New York state. You know, the one where no one ever leaves except in a bag or an urn."

"I wasn't there." My stomach tightened. A slip of unease found its way around my shoulders.

"They never let anyone out," continued Basil as though I hadn't spoken. He looked over to the stranger and gave him a look as though this was common knowledge and waiting for him to agree. "Especially with a murder charge. I hear they have an eyewitness who says you killed Adele."

Here we go. "There's no such witness," I said, though I wasn't sure. All I knew for sure was that their so-called witness was lying. "I didn't kill Adele." No. Catelyn had killed her, and that wasn't something I was willing to share.

Basil narrowed his eyes like he didn't believe me. "We never thought we'd see you again. You were charged with murdering a member of the White witch court." He pushed up his glasses with a trembling finger. "So, I did what I had to for the hotel's sake. You have to understand. We never thought we'd see you again."

"You already said that." My gaze flicked from Basil to the stranger, who was watching the scene with mild interest. Yeah. Didn't like this guy. "Who is this?" I didn't care that my voice sounded rough or rude. Something was up, and that something had to do with this stranger.

Basil shook his head. "I only did what was best for the hotel. Anyone in my position would have done the same. I had no other choice."

"Who is he, Basil?" Now I was ticked. I could see Basil was fishing for answers to appease his conscience. He looked guilty. But culpable of what? And why did I have the feeling it had something to do with me?

The hotel manager swallowed hard, like his throat was dry, and it was painful for him to do so. "This is Oric."

The stranger finally stood and turned to face me. He was maybe an inch taller than me, but not by much. He wore dark clothes under a long black leather jacket that looked as old as he was. He wore gloves, too, which I thought was weird. It wasn't cold enough, yet, for gloves. He still had that amused look, like this was entertaining to him. Like *I* was the entertainment.

"Oric. This is Leana Fairchild. The one I told you about."

Why was Basil talking about me to this stranger? I waited for this Oric to offer to shake my hand. He didn't. Neither did I.

"You going to tell me what's going on, Basil?" My nerves were shot. I felt a spike of adrenaline washing through me. Something wasn't right here.

Basil cleared his throat. "Oric is the new Merlin for the hotel."

What the hell?

I felt the blood leave my face. I blinked as I tried to wrap my brain around the words that had just left his mouth.

"I'm sorry, Leana," said Basil, though he didn't sound sorry at all, more like guilty he'd been caught at something he wanted to do. "But I thought you were gone for good. I'm only looking after the hotel's needs. And after what happened in the past, I can't be too careful. The hotel will always need a Merlin. So, you can understand why I did what I did. Nothing personal. It's just business."

The walls in the office seemed suddenly close, and I couldn't find enough air to breathe. I felt like I was back in that dark, dingy cell with nothing but the cold walls to keep me company. Alone and forgotten.

"You replaced me?" This was the last thing I expected to hear. Yes, I might have imagined Basil giving me the boot, but I always thought he'd save my spot. That I'd have my job back with some minor groveling and maybe even a pay cut. I never imagined he'd replaced me.

Basil shrugged and gave a nervous chuckle. "I needed another Merlin. Oric here comes highly recommended."

"You can rest assured, the hotel will be well looked after," said Oric, his voice deep and scratchy like his exterior.

My heart was pounding hard against my ribs as I tried to make sense of everything. I didn't have another paying job. I needed money. Money to eat. Money to pay rent. "But I was under contract." I wasn't well-read in all of our laws, but the one thing I did know and had educated myself with were my contracts and my rights as a Merlin. I knew for a fact that the hotel couldn't hire another Merlin until my contract was up.

"Null in the event of an incarceration," said Basil. "It's all legal. Checked with the lawyers. You are no longer employed by the hotel."

"I have some friends who might be interested in hiring you," said Oric, though his voice didn't sound sincere. More like he was just throwing it out there so I wouldn't freak out. I didn't know what it was about the witch, but he felt foul to me. I didn't like him. But it was most probably a reaction to him taking my place as a Merlin. Yeah, that was it. He could have been the nicest guy in the world, and I'd still hate his guts.

Basil pointed at Oric, his eyes wide. "See? That's good. You have another job waiting for you. Isn't that something?"

"I have a job here," I said, not wanting to let it go. It didn't help that I felt humiliated by this whole thing. The unfairness of it all had my stomach coiling. This was Darius's doing. The silver-haired bastard had thrown me in jail on trumped-up charges, and now I'd lost my job because of it—a secure job that I was really proud of and loved.

I was ticked and a little hurt at how quickly Basil had found another Merlin to replace me. Bellamy had once said there were lots of Merlins. I just never imagined I'd be swapped so quickly.

I remembered how nervous I'd been the first time I came to the hotel, thinking it was too good to be true to be hired by the Twilight Hotel. After what I'd survived, I felt like a fool.

"I'm sorry you're angry, Leana," said Basil, not looking sorry at all but more embarrassed by the situation. "I'm only thinking of the hotel. You must understand. If you were me, you would have done the same. I have an obligation to the guests and to the tenants."

I gritted my teeth. "After everything I've done for the hotel, I thought you could have waited a little longer before replacing me. How long *did* you wait before replacing me?"

Basil spread his hands. "I don't think that matters. Let's not get into that right now."

"Matters to me. How long did you wait?"

The hotel manager shifted in his seat, his eyes focused on a spot on his desk. "I don't know. The next day, perhaps? I'm not exactly sure of the date."

"Damn, Basil. You couldn't even wait a few days." Okay, that stung more than I would have thought. I thought management cared a little more about me. But it looked like I was just a number.

I tried to see it through Basil's eyes. As the hotel manager, he did have a duty to ensure the safety of the guests and tenants. I got why he had to look for another Merlin. Just not why he had to do it so soon. I deserved at least a month. Apparently not.

Basil cleared his throat again, and when I flicked my eyes over him, he looked even more uncomfortable. He tapped his desk with his fingers and said, "I'm going to need the key to your apartment."

Okay, now I was pissed. "Excuse me?" My face felt like it was on fire. I'd gone through three days of hell, and now this? No. I wasn't going to give up my place.

"The apartment belongs to the hotel Merlin. Well, since you're no longer that, the place goes to the new Merlin. To Oric. Key, please."

"You gave my apartment away?" I was dizzy. Dread hit, real and hard and undulating. Not only had I lost my job, but I'd just lost my home. I'd lose my friends too. My independence. It was the first place that had felt like home since I left Martin. No, since I left my grandmother's house fifteen years ago. I could feel the pricks of tears behind my eyes. I wasn't about to break down and cry. From the stiffness in Basil's shoulders, he was expecting it. Me crying. That's what these men expected me to do. I wouldn't. I was stronger than that.

But if it could save my apartment, I'd seriously consider putting on the waterworks. I'd throw in a few wails, just to see them squirm.

I stiffened, feeling a panic attack on the way. I felt trapped. Part of me wanted to just run out of this office and go back into Valen's arms.

Valen. If he knew about this, he'd probably force Basil to give me back my job. But maybe it was too late for that too.

"The owners feel that a Merlin should live at the hotel," said Basil. "After our history with the… *demons*," he added in a whisper, as though saying that word would somehow make them appear, "they would feel much better if a Merlin was staying here full time. So I need your keys."

I stood there staring at his hand. Part of me wanted to go over and smack it. Heat rushed to my face. I'd be out of a place if I gave him my key. I'd be on the streets.

"It's fine. She can keep her apartment. I have a place here in the city." Oric looked at me and smiled, but it was one of those fake smiles I'd seen so many times on Adele.

If he wanted a thank-you, he wasn't going to get it.

I let out a labored breath, feeling like my body was not my own. Feeling like this was a bad dream and I was going to wake up now. But I wasn't so lucky.

"Are you sure?" Basil was eyeing Oric. "You'd be in your rights to take it. It's the last apartment on the thirteenth floor. Great windows. Lots of sunlight."

Anger flared in me. I was so angry at Basil. It was all I could do not to rush over there and strangle the little witch. Didn't he see what this was doing to me? What this place meant to me? Apparently not.

"She can keep it," said Oric with that same amused and entertained tone, like I was being an emotional female. I could feel his eyes on me, but I wouldn't look at him. My eyes were on Basil, feeling my respect for the hotel manager evaporate as quickly as he'd replaced me.

"Well, if you change your mind," said Basil. He looked at me and said, "Would you mind closing the door on your way out?" He smiled at me like he hadn't just stabbed me in the heart repeatedly, as though he'd just done me a favor.

I didn't remember leaving Basil's office or how I ended up walking on 42nd Steet. My legs were numb. I was numb. It was like I was having an out-of-body experience and just floating into the abyss.

I got to keep my apartment. But I felt I couldn't hang on to it for much longer. It's like Basil said. That apartment was for the hotel Merlin.

Which I wasn't anymore.

But I was going to get it back. How? I had no idea.

CHAPTER 6

"I can't believe he fired you." With her mouth hanging open, Jade's chin was practically touching her chest. Her shocked expression combined with her blonde, crimped hair looked like she'd just been electrocuted.

"He didn't fire her. He let her go," corrected Elsa, sitting on my couch. "Not the same thing. Still unbelievably stupid. I could just kill that Basil. I should spell him into a rat. Would serve him right."

Julian opened my fridge, grabbed a beer, twisted off the top, and entered the living room. "Can't believe he did that." He took a long sip of his beer. "We had no idea, Leana. No idea he would do something like that."

"If we had, we would have stopped him," agreed Jade. Her arms crossed over her Bananarama T-shirt.

I'd walked back to the hotel about an hour after Basil had given me the news, half expecting it not to reveal itself to me, like that time Raymond had spelled me, but it did. I managed to find my way back to my apartment—while it still *was* my apartment. Valen was gone. Just as well. I didn't think I was prepared to see his reaction. Knowing him, he'd be livid. He already felt guilty about me cooped up in that cell for three days. I didn't want to think about what he might do to Basil when he heard I'd gotten sacked or, rather, replaced.

Elsa pulled on the locket around her neck. "We were so preoccupied with finding ways to get you out of that god-awful place, we never imagined Basil was looking for another Merlin. I thought he was pleading your case with the Gray Council. We all did."

"That's what he told us," said Jade, her eyes narrowed. "He told us not to worry and that he was going to make some phone calls. And that everything would be fine." Her lips thinned. "He lied to us. He lied to us good. I bet he did that so that we wouldn't interfere. Because he knew we would have, if we'd known."

"That little shit. He's on my list, right next to Bellamy," said Julian, and I had no idea what kind of list he was referring to. "Just took the number-one spot."

But that reminded me I still needed to find that witch scientist. Yet it seemed my plans were constantly changing and rearranging. I might have to put off finding Bellamy for now while I looked for this jewel for Darius.

I rubbed the tension behind my neck. "I think Basil's just following orders from the owners. I think they told him to find another Merlin." I didn't know why I was defending him. I wasn't a hundred percent sure about that. I had a feeling Basil was doing this more for the sake of the hotel, his reputation, and the hotel's reputation by removing the Merlin with a murder charge hanging over her and replacing her with a "cleaner" one. Yeah. Basil wanted me far away from the hotel.

Elsa let out a sigh and folded her hands in her lap. "He didn't even wait. He went looking for another Merlin the minute they took you away. I can't believe it."

"Definitely my number-one spot," growled Julian, taking another swig of his beer, his fingers tapping the bottle.

She wasn't wrong about that. I was pretty sure that's what Basil had done. No way he would have found another Merlin that quickly otherwise.

"I should have known he'd pull something like that." A mix of emotions flashed over Elsa's face. "He never thinks about anyone else but himself and his job. The hotel is his life. He won't stand for anything that would get in the way or taint the hotel's reputation. Or his. Why didn't I see it?"

I let out a breath. "It's not your fault. It's just… a giant misunderstanding." I tried to make myself believe that, just to feel a little better. It wasn't working.

"A giant clusterfuck." Julian fell onto the couch, next to Jade.

"Why don't you sit, Leana. You're making me nervous," said Elsa, waving her arms at me. She looked like she was about to have a heart attack.

I shook my head. "Can't. I don't know. I can't sit down. I'm too wired. Too angry." Too freaking devastated. I had a feeling if I tried to sit, I'd just jump back up.

Elsa stared at the floor momentarily and then looked up at me from her chair. "I'll talk to my friend Madeline. She's a paranormal lawyer. Yes, that's what I'll do. I'm sure she can figure out how to get your job back. You're not in jail anymore, so they can't replace you with this Uric."

"Oric," I corrected.

"That's what Basil said," continued the older witch, tapping her finger on her thigh as I could see her mind working behind her eyes. "The only reason you were ousted from your contract was your incarceration. So, that won't stick any longer." Elsa had a determined look on her face, making the wrinkles around her eyes and mouth more pronounced. "We'll get you your job back. Don't you worry. By this time next week, it'll be like nothing ever happened. You just wait."

I forced a smile. "That would be amazing." That would be a freaking miracle. I wasn't naïve enough to think getting my job back would be that simple. Not when Oric was already here. I had the feeling he wouldn't part with his new job that easily. He'd fight for it. Just like I was going to do.

"What's he like, this Oric?" Elsa waited for me to answer, but then before I could open my mouth, she added, "You think he can handle himself? Do the job?"

"I think so. He's not a rookie, unfortunately." I thought about the scar across his face. It was too jagged to be from a sharp blade like a dagger. It looked more like the result of being slashed by a claw. The witch held himself with the kind of confidence that only someone with loads of experience and knowledge in his craft did. "He looks capable enough. Came *highly* recommended, according to Basil."

"Urgh." Jade looked like she was about to be sick. She pulled on her Bananarama T-shirt, warping the singers' faces. "I really hate Basil right now. That's it. He's not getting his Christmas present this year."

I felt a warmth in my middle at her comment. At least my friends were on my side and saw the absurdity of the thing. Thank the goddess for friends like them.

"And you're sure he's a Dark witch?" asked Elsa, her head cocked slightly, like she was working out something in her head.

I nodded. "Positive." Dark or White, it didn't really matter. And I was curious as to why that seemed to be a detail of interest to Elsa.

"I'm going to ask Jimmy about this Oric witch," said Jade after a moment of silence. "Jimmy will know. Trust me. I'll get all the dirt on him. And then we'll get him fired." She punched her fist into her palm.

I laughed. "That sounds too good to be true." Yet I had this weird feeling about Oric. Call it a woman's intuition or my witchy instincts, but he rubbed me the wrong way. I would have still felt the same if he hadn't taken my spot.

I was glad to see that Jade and Jimmy's relationship seemed to be going well. I was saddened that I'd missed the first few days, the "honeymoon" stage because of my imprisonment. I would have loved to see the spark in their eyes. And this was all because of Darius.

"I got it." Julian straightened. "I know how to get him fired."

Jade's eyes rounded with delight and interest. "How? Tell me."

The male witch stretched his face into a sly grin. "I'm going to make his life hell."

I stared at him curiously. "How're you going to do that?"

"Easy." Julian looked at me, his grin spreading across his face, making him look years younger and boyish. "Basil only cares about his reputation and the hotel's. So, all we gotta do is make it look like Oric can't cut it." His smile grew. "I'm going to sabotage the hotel."

My lips parted, but I couldn't help my smile. "You wouldn't?"

"I would, darling. For you, I'll do anything," said Julian, making my gut pool with warmth.

Jade smacked her thigh. "I want in. I've got ideas. And Jimmy'll help too. He knows the hotel better than all of us put together."

"I can think of a few spells that will surely leave the hotel guests looking a little disheveled," said Elsa, a cunning smile on her face. "I have a few ghost spells, and I know of a witch who can sell me a demon-hologram spell that moves and looks just as real as you and me. That'll take care of a few guests."

"It'll get the guests talking," said Julian, his shoulders straightening proudly with his scheme. "They'll be scared shitless. They won't want to come back."

"Oric won't know what hit him." Jade rubbed her hands together, a smile on her face. "He'll look incompetent. Useless. Basil won't have a choice but to fire him and hire you back."

I laughed, feeling a huge weight lifting off my shoulders, like I had just shed a heavy metal blanket. Just seeing my friends' faces transforming from a palpable worry to a collective, devious cheerfulness had me wondering if this could really happen. If anyone could scare away the guests, and make Oric's life hell, it was my thirteenth-floor gang.

"Won't that force the hotel's closure?" I asked, wondering now if this wasn't as great an idea as I first thought.

"Don't worry," answered Julian. "Nothing that drastic. We won't kill anyone, if that's what you're worried about."

"Now I'm worried," I said with a laugh.

"We just need to scare the guests. We won't hurt them… much. Witches' honor." Julian held up two fingers and placed them on his heart.

I laughed hard. "Is that even a thing?"

"No. But I thought you'd like it," said Julian.

"It's perfect." Jade rocked her body on the couch. "It'll work. I can feel it."

I nodded. "It does feel like it could work. If you terrorize Oric enough, he might just leave on his own." Wouldn't that be something?

"At least you got to keep the apartment," said Julian. "One less thing to worry about. Don't think I'd want another dude on my watch. No. Definitely not."

"On your *watch*?" I stared at the handsome witch, biting my tongue so I wouldn't laugh. He looked serious.

Julian took another sip of his beer. "Yeah. The females on this floor are my watch."

I shook my head and rolled my eyes. "Well, you're wrong about one thing. I don't think I'll be able to keep the apartment."

Elsa leaned forward in her chair, her expression tainted with sudden worry. "What do you mean? I thought you said that this guy didn't want the apartment?"

I sighed. "It's just a feeling. But I'm pretty sure Basil won't let me stay. The owners want a Merlin here full time. It's just a matter of time before they kick my ass to the curb. Besides, I think this Oric was just pretending to be nice. Give it a few weeks. He'll probably take the apartment." Which meant I'd have to look for another place to live. I should start now before I ended up on the street. I doubted that would happen. I was sure Jade or even Jimmy would let me crash at their place. And there was Valen too. He'd never let me be out in the streets.

Jade shook her head, a frown on her face. "We won't let him.

He has no business coming in here and stealing this apartment. This is *your* place. *Our* place."

"Does Valen know?" asked Julian. He leaned forward and put his empty beer bottle on the coffee table.

"Not yet." I rubbed my temples, feeling a headache on its way. "I'll call him when I've had time to think about it."

Julian whistled and leaned back into the couch. "He's gonna be pissed. You know that. Heads-crushing pissed. There'll be blood."

"I know." So much was happening all at once. It was a miracle I was still standing. But that was the adrenaline. Eventually, I was going to go down. It wouldn't be pretty.

If I didn't, I'd probably fall into a horrible self-pity party of "why me?" and "why is this always happening to me?" I needed to keep busy. This wasn't the time to have a meltdown. I had things to do.

I needed to clear my name without implicating Catelyn. The only way I saw that happening was to reveal Darius's treachery. Reveal his plans, that he was responsible for all those human deaths, and that Adele was working under his orders.

Once he was removed, the charges wouldn't stick. Or at least, I hoped they didn't. But I had to keep my ass from jail. And the only way to do that was to look for the jewel and make sure Darius knew I was looking. Or saw me looking because I knew he'd have someone tail me. I was positive.

"We got you, Leana," said Jade, seemingly having seen the distress on my face. "You just think about that jewel. Leave Oric to us. Trust me. You're going to get your job back."

"And a pay raise, by the time we're done," added Julian. He winked at me. "We got you covered, Leana." He got up. "I need another beer. Nothing like beer to get the creative juices flowing."

Emotions ran through me. Excitement. Fear. Exhilaration. Fury. With my friends' help, it might actually work. This was my chance.

Just one thing was missing. Valen. I yanked out my phone. I

needed to talk to Valen. I moved my fingers over the screen as I texted him.

Me: *U busy? I need to talk to you about something.*

I waited a few seconds before seeing the dots on my phone move back and forth.

Valen: *On my way to the airport to pick up Frederick and Hanna. I'll be back in a few hours. You okay?*

Crap. I'd forgotten about that. I knew he'd made plans with the other giants. But seeing as I had been in jail for the past three days, I'd totally forgotten about it.

Me: *I'm fine. I'll talk to you when you get back.*

Valen: *Okay.*

"Is Valen on his way?" Elsa watched me, her eyes curious.

I shook my head and slipped my phone back into my pocket. "He's actually on his way to pick up the brother and sister giants at the airport. I think they'll be staying with him for a while." If I'd been kicked out, I could have never stayed at Valen's, not while his guests were there. Another great reason why my friends' plan was essential.

"Oh, right, that's true. That's today," said Jade. "How great is that for him? He must be *soooo* nervous. To finally meet others like him."

"Yeah. I'm sure he is. I'm really happy for him. Better that he doesn't know about this until he gets back. I don't want anything to ruin that get-together." Valen had been searching for six years in hopes of finding other giants like him. No way was I going to spoil that. Besides, it looked like we had things covered between the four of us. For now.

"Can I borrow this?" Julian held one of my notepads in one hand while holding a fresh bottle of beer in the other.

"Sure," I told him.

"It's time to do some brainstorming, ladies." Julian took his seat next to Jade. "You think Jimmy could get us blueprints of the hotel?"

Jade leaned forward, grinning. "You bet."

Elsa stood up. "Move. I want to see. You're going to need my input."

Julian and Jade scooted over to give Elsa room on the couch.

I stood there smiling as the three witches began to formulate their plans to add hexes, curses, spells, potions, and poisons all over the hotel, all teeny-weeny spells, of course, nothing that would harm any of the guests. Or so I hoped.

"Leana, come sit." Elsa patted a very tight spot next to her. "Four minds are better than three."

"I think I'll go for a walk, if you don't mind." They all looked at me with that same worry as when I first told them about being sacked. "Just need to clear my head. You guys keep working. I can't wait to hear all about it when I get back."

Elsa waved a finger at me. "Don't stay out too long. I'm worried about you."

"Don't be. I'm fine. See you later."

It wasn't a lie. I really did need to clear my head, but to do that I needed to be alone. I needed time to decompress. To think about my next move.

Because my life had just become a great deal more complicated.

CHAPTER 7

I didn't know how long I'd walked around the city until I sat my butt on a chair at an internet cybercafé, the name of which I'd forgotten, the moment I walked in. While I drank coffee and munched on a few biscotti biscuits, I decided to Google the so-called Jewel of the Sun. When all that turned up were anime terms and some gross, human-sized doll, I logged on to the Merlin mainframe. At first, my heart thrashed in my chest. Having forgotten for a minute that I'd been thrown in some Gray Council cell, they might have revoked my Merlin privileges. But after I entered my login and password, I was in.

I must have stayed logged on for at least an hour and found absolutely nothing on that jewel. So, I tried other combinations: sun jewel, sun diamond, sun gem, even with a misspelled *jewl* of the sun. Nothing.

If this Jewel of the Sun existed, it should have come up in the database. But it didn't. Darius didn't give me much to go on, which was suspicious. And without a clear idea of what that jewel was and what it looked like, I was starting to wonder if it even existed and that Darius had sent me off on a wild-goose chase for his screwed-up purpose.

But I'd seen that look in his eye, the one Adele got when she spoke of power—a combination of a manic desire with some addiction to the idea of more power. The jewel was real. If it wasn't in the databases, it might be because it was rare, and only a few had heard of its power. Something new.

I had basically nothing to go on except what Darius had told me back in my cell, which wasn't much. Strangely, I was curious about this jewel. And the lack of information just made me want to find it even more.

Darius had said that my starlight magic would help find this jewel. My power manifested mostly at night, which explained why I stood at the front gates of Trinity Church on Broadway at eleven o'clock at night.

I'd texted Elsa, Jade, and Julian to stay put tonight and told them where I was, in case something happened to me, like that time I'd gone alone to the warehouse looking for Bellamy, which turned out to be a trap. I'd decided, then, to have at least one person know where I was when out on a job.

A part of me also wanted to go alone to test the field, in a way. I'd call them if I ran into any trouble. I still didn't know *how* to find the jewel. Darius had said that with my starlight abilities, I could find it. I was going to test his theory.

The cool winds picked up, rustling the leaves of a massive oak tree that rose to the church's right. It was the end of September, and soon all the leaves would turn and fall, leaving the city bare with room for snow.

The church was massive. It had that Gothic Revival style I liked with a dark brownstone exterior, flanked by pointed Gothic arches—the same motif framing the stained-glass windows. It stood in the middle of the block, like a great ship, its towers rising far above the trees.

A quick Google search told me that the church was constructed in 1698 and destroyed in the Great Fire of New York in 1776. Then built again in 1790.

The entrance nameplate on a stone pillar read TRINITY CHURCH. A thick, six-foot iron fence ran the length of the block and surrounded the entire church, like they were trying to keep humans from going in.

I exhaled. "Where the hell do I begin?"

I made my way up the stone steps to the great arch entrance. The double doors were closed. Locked, no doubt. Visiting hours were over long ago.

I looked over my shoulder. A few humans treaded down Broadway. Some cars and cabs rushed by. I stood without moving for a minute to see if anyone would look at the strange woman standing on the church's steps.

After a few more minutes, it was clear no one even glanced in my direction.

Taking that as a good sign, I pulled on my well of magic to the power from the stars and the constellations. The air hummed and pulsed with raw energy as I pulled on the stars' magical components. Power crackled against my skin, and then a ball of brilliant white light hovered over my palm. I wasn't worried about using my magic in front of humans. They couldn't see my starlight. My magic was invisible to them.

With my starlight in my hand, I pressed it over the lock on the door.

The globe burst into thousands of tiny, glowing spheres of light. My starlights spread over and around the lock. I didn't have to utter a single word. My starlights and I were connected. All I had to do was think it, and they knew what to do.

I heard a click followed by the sound of metal being dragged.

With a final glance over my shoulder, and seeing no one, I grabbed the door and pulled. It came free with a slight grinding noise. I opened it a crack, enough for me to slip through.

I'd expected alarms, but to my surprise, I heard none.

I shut the door behind me with a thud and let go of my starlight. I stood in a short entrance dimly lit with yellow light in sconces that lined the walls, illuminating everything in its creepy hues. All was quiet. The air reeked of incense, candles, wood, and musty carpets.

As soon as I entered the church, its beauty transfixed me. The altar took my breath away. I swept my gaze around. I wanted to capture it all—from the fine details on the cross, and the careful choice of color on the mosaic artwork of the windows, to the arched ceiling and the stained-glass, sculpted bronze doors and marble reredos.

I moved past the entrance, with wood paneling and antique rugs, and stepped into the central area of the church. Rows of pews flanked either side of a long stretch that ended in a large altar, all under the watchful gaze of the arched ceiling and stained-glass windows.

I realized that a precious jewel of any size could be carefully tucked inside here, and no one would know.

I didn't understand why Darius didn't look for this jewel himself. It's not like he couldn't walk into a church like the rest of us witches. He'd basically ruined my life for this jewel, or what I'd recently made into a life.

"Okay then," I breathed. "If you're here, Jewel of the Sun, I'll find you."

He'd said that my starlight magic would find it. So I gave it a shot.

I willed my starlight magic again, feeling the humming of power from the stars waiting to be unleashed. As another ball of white light hovered over my hand, I blew on my palm.

The globe rose in the air and burst into thousands of miniature stars of light. They soared forward, like glowing dust particles. The starlights wrapped around the church, the walls, the ceilings, columns, and pews until every inch of it was illuminated in dazzling white light. Once I knew I had every inch covered, I sent out my senses to my starlights to see if I'd get a feeling of some kind of energy back. Something that would point me in the direction of this jewel.

But after a few seconds, I knew nothing was here. If the jewel reacted to my magic, to my starlights, then I—we—would have felt something.

"It's not here," I said, letting go of my magic. "Okay. Well, two more places to go."

The sound of a shoe scraping on the floor reached me.

I stiffened. All the hair on my body rose at the same time. I spun around, thinking it was a priest or whoever was here after visiting hours. I was not expecting someone who needed a good ol' ass whooping.

"Bellamy?"

CHAPTER 8

The witch scientist crouched behind one of the pews at the far end, closest to the exit. He stood slowly and raised a hand. "Hi, Leana."

"Hi? That's all you've got to say?" I glowered, taking him all in. He looked exactly like the last time I'd seen him—a short, heavyset, middle-aged man with reddish-blond hair, pants that were too long, and a white shirt halfway tucked into the belt, with guilt written all over his sweaty face.

I never expected to see the witch scientist in the city. If he was as clever as he claimed to be, he should have left the country days ago. He was the last person I'd expected to see now in this church, late at night.

Bellamy swallowed, his entire body twitching nervously. "Well... I did want to talk—"

"How did you know I'd be here?" And then it hit me. "Have you been following me? You have. Haven't you? You little creep."

"Ummm." The witch scientist looked over his shoulder like he was expecting someone to walk into the church.

My temper soared as all the emotions came crashing down on me like a tsunami. "Do you know what I've been going through? Do you know what your little disappearing stunt did to us? To

Valen? Do you know that he almost died!" Okay, now I was shouting. If there were apartments on the ground floor of the church, someone was going to call the police.

"I didn't have a choice. I-I'm sorry," stuttered Bellamy. "The process of the transference still needs work. It's not an exact science… yet. I was only doing what I was paid to do. My job. Just like you."

"Don't you *ever* compare me to you," I seethed, my starlight magic vibrating through me, though I didn't even remember calling out to it. "I save people. I don't subject them to experiments that kill them."

Bellamy shrugged. "I came forward. Didn't I? I gave you that location of the warehouse."

"You stupid sonofabitch," I raged. Seeing him jerk across the church from me did make me feel a tad better. "You betrayed me when I was trying to help you. And you nearly had my friend and me killed. All for what? For your chance at money and glory? To be published in some stupid scientific magazine!"

"I tried to help. *I* saved you," said the witch scientist, looking at me like that little part was going to save *him* from me kicking his ass.

I gave a fake laugh. "You didn't save me. You left. You left me like the coward you are."

Bellamy raised a finger at me and shook it. "No. That's not what happened. I only gave you enough of the magical muscle relaxant to make it *look* like you'd be paralyzed for hours. But you weren't. You got free. That was because of me."

"How would you know? You disappeared. You didn't stick around for the best parts."

Bellamy gave a nervous laugh. "I don't know how to fight. I'm not a battle witch. I'm a witch scientist. That's where my magic lies. In science."

I pressed my hands on my hips, pondering whether I should give him a tiny ass whooping. He deserved it. "Were you there when Adele died? Did you see that? Or were you already gone?"

Bellamy shook his head. He pressed his hands on the pew in front of him, grabbing it tightly like it was the only thing keeping him from falling. "I didn't see it. I heard about it." He looked at me, a curious expression on his face. "They're saying you killed her?"

"It wasn't me. I wish it had been me, but it wasn't. I didn't kill Adele." No way would I tell this creep about Catelyn. I had a feeling if he knew the transference of giants worked, and she was still alive with all the magical properties Valen had, chances were he'd use that again.

"I wouldn't blame you if you did," said Bellamy, and I knew he was trying to win some points with me. "She wasn't very well-liked among us. We were all rather terrified of her. You know, Rick Tanaka, he's one of the first witch scientists on the project. He argued with her a lot, and then… then he never came back."

"I don't care about you or your crazy scientist friends." I clenched my jaw. "They locked me up. Did you know that? Threw me in some dingy cell for days, with no bed, toilet, or food." You couldn't call that stew, food.

"Fasting is supposed to be good for you. I think more people should try it."

I let out a breath, reeling in my anger. "That's what your future looks like. But I'm sure where they'll put you will be far, far worse."

Bellamy's eyes widened, and I saw a flash of fear cross his face, not for me, of course, but for him. He no doubt feared that could happen to him. "I'm sorry you had to go through that." He shook his head, his features set in what I could only guess looked like forced innocence. "That's not my fault. You can't blame me for that." He wiped his forehead with his hand. "But they let you out. Why is that?"

Nope. Not going there. Bellamy was as trustworthy as a cheesecloth condom.

I took a few steps forward and saw him flinch. I halted and crossed my arms over my chest. "Why are you here? And why the hell are you following me?" I could just grab his ass and haul him back to the hotel or, better yet, drag him over to the Gray Council. But I needed Bellamy. He was still my only witness to this giant mess. He was my best bet to put Darius away.

Bellamy wiped his forehead with the back of his sleeve. Gross. "I was wrong. I thought I could handle it on my own but..." He looked over his shoulder again. "Being on the run is not what it's all hyped up to be. It's much harder than I first thought."

"Not all glamourous like you'd hoped?"

His expression was almost sick with fear. "I'm not programmed to be on the run. I'm supposed to be in a lab, working. That's what I'm supposed to do."

No way Bellamy should be near a lab ever again. "Did you run out of money so soon?"

"I'm being followed."

I narrowed my eyes. "You're being *followed*?" It would explain why he looked like he was about to jump out of his skin. Whoever they were, they had him spooked.

"At first, I thought it was you," he said. "But then I heard that you were in jail, so I knew it couldn't be you. And then last night..."

Okay, now I was curious. "What about last night?"

The witch scientist leaned forward until his stomach touched the back of the pew he was holding on to. "I saw them. I saw who was following me."

I shrugged. "Who are they? The Gray Council officers?" Maybe they wanted to find Bellamy and throw his ass in jail where he belonged. Maybe I should just get out of their way and let them. That would be one less thing for me to think about. I had enough issues of my own.

Bellamy's eyes widened, and he shook his head, looking frightened, like he was already locked up in one of those prison cells he feared. "Not the Gray Council. Or at least, I don't think so. They weren't officers. I believe these are the same people who hired me."

I could see the witch was visibly shaking with fear, and I couldn't care less. "The mediators? The ones who paid you to kill all those humans?"

Bellamy winced at my comment. "That's what I think. They want me dead. I thought they'd want to keep me around. You know. To do more experiments. To push our findings and the Human Transference Origins project even further. To achieve something greater."

"You mean killing hundreds, perhaps thousands of innocent humans wasn't enough to satisfy your twisted concepts?" The idea of Bellamy subjecting more humans to their barbaric testing nearly had me call up my starlight and flog the witch scientist. But we were in a church. I respected the church. Not him.

Could Darius be after Bellamy? Adele had been working for him. Maybe the silver-haired witch wanted to clean up any traces linking him to the HTO project now that it had been exposed. Bellamy was definitely one of those links.

But then again, it could also be mercenaries paid by the Gray Council who had nothing to do with the HTO project but just wanted Bellamy killed for what he did.

"I was wrong," he said again, though somehow I didn't believe him. His voice held no traces of regret, just fear. Fear for his own ass. "I know that now. I've had lots of time to think about my actions. I should have never agreed to work on the HTO project."

I shrugged. "Why don't I believe you?"

His eyes rounded. "It's the truth. I'm sorry for what happened. You have to believe me."

"Maybe you're just sorry that it ended, and now someone wants you dead."

The witch scientist clamped his mouth shut. His eyes rolled around the church like he was trying to think up a lie to feed me.

I was running out of patience. "I'm working here. And you're bothering me. What the hell do you want, Bellamy?"

His eyes met mine across the rows of pews. "I need protection."

Of course he did. "Forget it."

"Please!" Bellamy moved from behind the pew and dropped to his knees, his hands together as though he were praying. I wasn't sure if that was sacrilege or something, coming from a paranormal witch scientist who'd sacrificed humans for a chance at climbing the science ladder.

"Please!" he cried. "You have to protect me. They'll kill me if you don't. I beg you. I'll do anything you want. Please!"

His theatrics didn't move me. All of it was fake. Except for the part where he feared for his life. That part was real. "Hmmm. I'm guessing you tried to run, or you thought you could outsmart them, but you were wrong. Am I right? And now you have no choice but to come crawling back to me? I feel so lucky." More like I wanted to puke.

"Yes. It's true. It's all true." He lifted his head, and hope filled his eyes. "You'll help me?"

I pursed my lips. "I'm not sure yet. I need time to think about it." Bellamy was probably one of the only witch scientists involved in the HTO project who was still alive. He was the last piece of evidence of those horrors. They, whoever *they* were, might want him dead, but I needed him alive.

"Please!" Bellamy pushed to his feet clumsily, rushed over to me until he faced me, and threw himself at my feet. "I'll do anything. I swear. I'll even stay with you at the hotel. I won't run away again. I swear it." He reached to grab my boots, and I stepped away from him. I did not want him touching my boots.

Though he probably deserved to squirm a little more, I couldn't stand it any longer. "Fine."

Bellamy looked up at me. "Fine? Yes? You'll protect me?"

"I said fine, so yes. Now get up before I change my mind."

With some strenuous effort, the witch scientist rolled to the side and then managed to push himself back on his feet. I had to look away so he wouldn't see my smile.

"Excellent. Just excellent." Bellamy brushed his shirt and pants. Visible tension left his posture. "I knew you'd make the smart choice. I can always tell."

I rolled my eyes. "Let's go, Bellamy." I walked down the aisle and returned to the church's entrance.

"Why are you here anyway? In this church?" asked Bellamy as I reached the doors. "You a religious person? I would have never thought that you, a witch, would follow human religions."

"I'm working. I go where my job takes me. My beliefs don't matter." When I grabbed the door handle, I turned and said, "Hang on. Let me see if it's clear of humans before we step out." Not that I was sure Bellamy had done that before he entered, but the bastard had been tailing me, and I had never known. Maybe he had some hidden talents.

I waited for a human man to walk past and then grabbed Bellamy by the shirt and hauled his ass out. I closed the door and hurried down the steps.

"I'm hungry. Haven't had a decent meal in days," Bellamy whined. "You think that restaurant next to the hotel is open?"

I started walking down Broadway. "Fasting is supposed to be good for you, remember?" Reciting what he'd told me. "No. It's late. I'll find you something to eat at the hotel."

Bellamy twisted his face like the idea of the hotel food repulsed him. "I saw what you had in your fridge. Nothing. You —" He froze, eyes wide, staring at something across the street from us.

I followed his gaze. It wasn't difficult to see what had him frozen solid like a witch popsicle.

A man stood at the edge of the sidewalk across from us. He wore a dark cloak over dark clothes. His cowl rested around his shoulders. He stood with a posture that was nothing but relaxed nonviolence until he struck out, and then you died. He was a good-looking man with slender, stark cheekbones, and his demeanor was more like a businessman than that of a street thug.

He looked to be in his sixties. I didn't recognize him. His eyes were gauging. And right now, they were fixed on us.

The way he was staring was intense, almost like he was… could I say curious? My lips parted as the hair on my neck prickled, and a shudder rose through me.

"Is this the guy you were talking about?" If he wanted Bellamy, he would have to go through me first. I wasn't about to lose him again. Once was enough, thank you. I didn't know if he was a witch, a werewolf, or a vampire. He was too far away to get a good read on his energy. Yet this guy felt different in the way he was watching us both. I couldn't say what exactly, but it was just a feeling. I didn't get any violent vibes from his stance or his features. It was more of an open curiosity, like he was studying us. His eyes seemed to be more focused on me than on Bellamy. Now, that was strange.

But I still pulled on my starlight, just in case. Not that fighting another paranormal in the middle of Broadway was a good idea, but I'd do it anyway to save the witch scientist.

"His staring is starting to creep me out. Do you recognize him? Bellamy?"

But when I turned around, Bellamy was gone.

I cursed. "Bellamy?" I hissed. Cursed some more. I jogged a few paces forward, searching for the witch scientist, but all I saw were the annoyed faces of a few human passersby. Bellamy was nowhere to be found.

Double damn. Now that was twice I'd lost him.

My anger flared to life, furious at myself. I was enraged at the stranger. I should have tied Bellamy with a rope and fastened it around my waist.

And then, when I looked back at the stranger, because I wanted some words with the guy who had scared away my only witness, he was gone too.

Well, damn. Looked like my night kept getting better and better.

CHAPTER 9

I hurried back to the hotel on foot. It wasn't too far, and I couldn't afford to spend any more money on cabs now that I was out of a job. Especially since this covert job I was working on didn't pay. Well, it only kept me out of jail, in a way.

The exercise would do me some good, especially after spending three days in a small cell. It also gave me time to think about what the hell had just happened.

Damnit. I'd lost Bellamy again. It seemed the witch scientist had developed the skill of stealth while he was on the run. I tried looking for him for another half hour, doubling back, even trying the church again. But he wasn't there.

I was still thinking about that stranger and the intense way he'd been looking at me. Yes. He was looking at *me*. The more I thought about it, and the more I replayed the scene in my head, the more I realized who he'd been staring at. Not Bellamy. Sure, he glanced at him, but the stranger focused solely on me. But why? Who was he?

The first thought that popped into my head was perhaps he was one of Darius's guys following me, ensuring I followed his instructions. It would make sense. But not the way he was staring.

He'd looked at me in a curious sort of way and something else. Something I couldn't put my finger on.

Once I reached the Twilight Hotel, my eyes moved to the restaurant. My heart was doing all kinds of Olympic standard jumps and twirls. All the lights were off, even in the apartment above.

My chest squeezed at the thought of the giant, along with some hot flashes of what he could do with those magical hands and magical tongue. We'd spent an incredible morning together, one that I wanted to reproduce and soon. But it wasn't only that the sex had been mind-blowing—because it had—but I'd felt a deeper connection with Valen since the night Adele nearly killed him. It was as though I had dropped that wall I built around myself over the years, much thanks to Martin, which wouldn't let anyone near my heart.

Somehow Valen had chipped away at it until pieces of my wall fell, and then it collapsed entirely.

The man, giant, checked all my boxes. He was strong, independent, confident, and intelligent, but he also had a sensitive side. His fierce sense of protection was a total turn-on. I wouldn't lie. I missed him, I realized. And found the feeling comfortable to actually miss someone. I wanted to see him, but I knew he was busy with his new giant friends. I didn't want to interrupt that.

I pulled out my phone and checked the text message he'd sent me twenty minutes ago.

Valen: *Miss you*

Me: *Prove it*

Valen: *You just wait. I'll prove it to you… more than once*

Me: *Does it involve spanking?*

Valen: *Spanking and kissing*

Me: *Yay*

Grinning like an idiot, I stuffed my phone back in my pocket. I blew out a breath, walked into the hotel, and halted.

When Julian had said he was going to "take care of it," I'd never imagined it'd be so soon. And this messy.

Shouts rang out as soon as I stepped into the lobby. Just like during Casino Week, the lobby was packed with guests. Although this time, they weren't smiling happily and enjoying the gaming tables. Nope. They were furious.

Hands tossed in the air with angry gestures as curses flew in time with tempers. Chaos erupted. The lobby was filled with screams and shouts. And I saw why.

A couple, vampires from what I could see of their good looks, though it was hard to tell because they were dripping in red… paint? Hard to tell. I was seriously hoping it was paint and not blood. Head to toe, both the female and male vampires were doused in red liquid. And judging by the distribution, they got the full impact of it from the front.

Another female, barefoot, with a white bathrobe wrapped around herself, was screaming, red-faced, though she didn't have paint on her or whatever that red, sticky substance was. No, she was bald—completely bald—no eyebrows, from what I could tell. The top of her bald head shone with some moisture, and faint steam rose slowly, like she'd just been inside a hot tub or cauldron.

I cast my gaze around and spotted a young adult male who had his mouth sewn shut. No, not sewn. It didn't exist. Holy crap. He had no more mouth. He was mouthless.

Along the far wall, next to the front counter, a group of guests sat on the floor. Polly was there, busy rolling gauze over an older female's leg. The other four were waiting for Polly, blood seeping from their many wounds. If I didn't know any better, it looked like some gremlin demons had attacked them.

Everywhere I looked, the guests were marked with something, except for a handful who watched from a safe distance, like me. I saw Basil and Oric among the guests. Basil's face was twisted in what I could only guess was absolute mortification. Oric had an annoyed expression, like he couldn't wait to escape all the commotion. I thought it suited him.

I sneaked around a young couple, ducked behind a really tall male in jogging pants, and inched a little closer to get a better perception of what was happening.

Jimmy stood on the outskirts, a strange sort of designed innocent look on his face. I knew him well enough now. That look also said he was guilty. Not that he'd done this, but more like he knew it would happen and let it happen.

The largest male I'd ever seen, with a mass of dark hair covering most of his face, stood next to Jimmy. His arms were crossed over his chest, and his light eyes peered from under thick brows as they tracked the lobby: Bob, the hotel's security chief and werebear. And like Jimmy, Bob didn't look at all surprised either. I knew Jimmy and Bob were close. Seemed like Bob was on our side.

"I'm bald!" shouted the bald female, pointing a long finger in Basil's face, who looked positively dumbfounded and, may I dare say, speechless? "I took a shower, and I came out bald! Is this the hotel's idea of a cruel joke? You'll be hearing from the Werewolf court!"

Oh dear. That was not the right thing to say to poor little Basil. So, why was I smiling?

"I-I'm so sorry, Mrs. Wiggins. I don't understand what happened." Basil looked over a few guests and then returned his attention to her. "I don't see anyone else bald. Perhaps this was a momentary glitch in the water system. But please, rest assured. The hotel will give you a full refund."

She flailed her hands and pointed at her head. "I don't care about your stupid refund. I want my hair back." She yanked open her bathrobe for all to see. Yup. She had no hair around her lady V, not that having a lot of hair in that area was a problem, but I did understand that some of us preferred a little vagitation.

"This… this paint won't come off!" hissed the vampire male who'd been doused in red.

Basil looked over at him, and I noticed how he was keeping a reasonable distance from him, like he was afraid to get some of that red paint on him. "You'll get a refund too. You'll *all* get *refunds*," he added to the others around him.

My ears whistled as more cries and shouts erupted. Clearly, the guests didn't care about refunds.

I jumped out of the way as an older male brushed past me, his suitcase dragging behind him as he hurried out of the hotel. Behind him came a row of frightened-looking guests trailing their luggage as they made a mad dash toward the exit.

I heard more shouting and then caught Basil's voice.

"How could you let this happen!" Basil pointed his finger up at Oric. "You came highly recommended!"

I smiled—music to my ears.

I whipped my head around before Basil caught me smiling and, consequently, ruined Julian's carefully thought-out plan. I made a sprint for the front counter.

"Messages for me?" I stood with my back to Basil and Oric and my smile facing the concierge.

Errol let out a long sigh. "Why are you still here? Didn't they replace you with that ogre? Go away." He waved his hands at me like he was shooing a dog away. "Why is it when the night shift is late, you come along?"

I leaned on the counter. "Did I just detect some love coming from you?"

"It seems you have misplaced your straight jacket again," snapped the concierge.

"No, I sense that. You like me better than Oric. Oh my God, Errol. You know what that means?"

"If I say yes, will you go away?"

"Deep inside that lizard heart, we're *besties*."

Errol's mouth flapped open. "I would rather jump off the roof of this hotel to my death."

I flashed him my teeth. "I'll let you in on a secret. I don't like him either."

Errol let out an exasperated howl. "What do you want?"

"Messages?" I repeated. Bellamy had asked me for protection, and after some squalling, I agreed. Okay, so he got spooked by the stranger, but he still knew I was his safest bet. Maybe he'd show up again. Or perhaps he'd do the right thing and send me a message, telling me where he was, so I could go get him.

"No messages." Errol moved away before I could ask him anything else.

I spun around and leaned my back against the counter. My eyes went to Basil. His face was pallid, and he was sweating, reminding me of Bellamy.

And his anger? Well, it was directed at none other than my new favorite Merlin, Oric.

Movement caught my eye, and I spotted Julian, Elsa, Jade, and Catelyn all making a beeline for the hotel's exit. Jade stopped and waved at me from the entrance.

Shit. I couldn't wave back. If Basil saw them, he'd figure out it was them.

I started forward just as Jimmy looked my way. I motioned toward the hotel's front doors. He looked over and then said something to Bob.

The massive werebear walked away from Jimmy and positioned himself right in Basil's line of sight, hiding my friends from the hotel manager with his massive body.

I mouthed a thanks to Bob, who nodded, his eyes crinkling in a smile.

"Leana." Basil was staring at me, and I could see a frown forming on his brow. "Why are you smiling?"

"Gotta pee." It was the first thing that came to mind. I turned and rushed to the elevators, knowing Basil wouldn't follow.

Damn. Me and my stupid face. I did not have a poker face to save my life. Still, if this worked, and somehow my friends got Oric sacked, it was all worth it.

I stepped off the elevator when I reached the thirteenth floor and walked along the hallway. At nearly midnight, you'd think most of the tenants would be sleeping. You'd be wrong.

Every apartment door was open, the tenants wandering in and

out of the rooms like the entire floor was one giant house, and every room was an extension of their own. It was one of my favorite things about the hotel. Everyone treated their space like it belonged to everyone.

My stomach coiled at the idea of losing this. The hotel's owners wanted the Merlin to live with the tenants. They had every right to ask this. But I wasn't ready to let it go. Not when it felt so right. Not when it felt like home.

Olga glared at me as I walked past her apartment. A cigarette hung from her bottom lip.

"Tell Elsa she's out of sugar," said the senior witch Barb as she stepped out of Elsa's apartment with a bag of sugar in her hands.

"Will do," I told her and laughed. Like I said, a big ol' family.

As I reached my place, I slowed. The door was closed. The only time I'd closed this door was to keep Bellamy safe inside.

My pulse increased. "Thank the goddess. He thought to come here."

I pulled open my door and went in search of the witch scientist. "Bellamy? It's me. I'm back."

When I got to the living room, Bellamy wasn't waiting for me.

It was the stranger from the street.

CHAPTER 10

Okay, now, *this* was really unexpected. Unexpected, yes, but I was always a prepared witch.

Instincts flaring, I yanked on my starlight in a burst of fear and self-preservation, gathering a huge, brilliant globe of my magic. I didn't care if he worked for Darius. Okay, maybe a little. I was still going to blow him to chunks if he tried anything.

"You don't need to do that. I'm not here to harm you." The stranger's voice was strangely calm, though not as deep as I imagined it would be, and flowed in a way like someone who'd been practicing the English language for centuries.

"Says the guy who sneaked into my apartment." Yeah, I wasn't buying the crap he was selling. "How did you get in?" I was surprised no one stopped him from coming inside my place. Then again, I doubted the tenants even noticed him.

Now that he was close enough, I took a moment to look him over. His hair, which I guessed had been dark at one time, was primarily gray and hit just under his jaw. He had a short beard that matched his gray hair and green eyes under thick, black brows.

I couldn't see any weapons on him, but he was wearing a heavy black cloak. Plenty of places to hide weapons.

"Who the hell are you?" I stared at him. I wasn't getting any paranormal vibes. No vampires, weres, fae, nothing. Not even witch.

His face went through a myriad of emotions too quickly to pinpoint one. When he looked at me again, it was carefully blank. "I'm not here to hurt you, Leana. I would never harm you."

I wasn't surprised he knew my name. He had been following me. He probably knew a lot more about me than I wanted him to. "Tell me who you are, and what you want, and then I'll make that decision." I heard a beep from my phone and knew it was Valen, well, most probably him. I wondered what he'd do to this guy if he came here and found us like this. He'd be mad as hell. That's what he'd be. And then he might swing a few fists.

"My name is Matiel."

"Never heard of you." I stood with my hand outstretched, waiting for him to make a move, but he was just standing there with his hands in his pockets, looking nonchalant, unaggressive. His body language didn't say he was about to attack me. More like he was happy to see me. But why? He wasn't afraid of me that I could tell. Even with my glowing ball of starlight pointed at him, he didn't flinch or show that it bothered him.

His eyes tracked over my face slowly, which made me uncomfortable. "I knew your mother. I knew Catrina."

I felt a slip on my magic. I wasn't expecting that. I blinked a few times, reeling in my focus and starlight. "Nice try." It was. I'd give him that, but I wasn't an amateur. He'd have to do better than that.

His eyes lit up, and a faint smile spread over his lips. "You look just like her. Same eyes, hair, same build. I bet you laugh like her too. I always loved her laugh."

What the hell was this? "Cut the crap. What do you want, and why are you in my apartment? My patience is running thin. I've been having a bad week. Out with it." Three full days in a cell would do that to a person.

A sigh escaped him. "I've wanted to meet you for so long. This is not how I imagined our first meeting would go. Though I know now it's silly. I always thought you would be smiling. Happy to see me. But I know that will never happen. It's been too long."

I narrowed my eyes, not liking how he'd managed to turn this into some sort of twisted intimate conversation. What kind of psycho was he? "Too bad for you. I'm not playing with… whatever you're trying to do here."

His smile faded. "I can understand your mistrust. You don't know me. And that's my fault. You have every right to think of me as a threat."

My pulse thrummed in time with my starlight. "You got that right. Did Darius send you? Is that it? Want to make sure I'm not veering from the path. I'm not. So you go and tell him that. I'm working. No need to send you." If he'd sent this one, I was willing to bet Darius had more of his spies all over the city, watching me. That silver-haired bastard was cramping my style.

The stranger named Matiel shook his head. "No one sent me. I don't know anyone by that name. I came here for you, Leana."

Even if he was one of Darius's goons, I didn't expect him to admit it. But having him come to my apartment, well, that was stepping over all kinds of boundary lines. "Whatever you say. You don't feel like a witch or any paranormal I know. What are you?" I didn't know what he was, which made me nervous because it gave him the upper hand. He could be a witch or wizard using a glamour to hide behind. He could also be one of Darius's experiments, which would explain the non-paranormal energies.

Matiel pulled his hands from his pockets.

"Watch it," I threatened, my starlight hovering over my palm, ready to launch at the guy. "One wrong move."

"Just want to remove my hands from my pockets." Matiel waited. "May I remove my hands?"

I nodded, so he slowly raised his hands and twisted them around to show me he didn't have anything in them. "I'm not here to harm you. You have to believe me."

"I don't. You're a stranger who's been following me around for

God knows how long, and you just appear in my apartment and want me to trust you? I don't think so." I shifted my weight and adjusted my stance. "Tell me who you are, and what you want, or get the hell out of my apartment. I won't ask again."

The stranger watched me, his expression slightly worried as my eyes narrowed. He crossed his arms over his chest. "I'm not anything you call paranormal. Well, not in the way you think. You can put away your starlight. It has no effect on me."

"Good one." Just to prove a point, I yanked on my starlight, and a second dazzling white sphere appeared on my other hand. I was not messing around. If he knew who I was, and I was certain he did, he also knew I took threats very seriously. His being in my apartment uninvited was a major threat.

A brow lifted from the stranger as he looked at my hands glowing with starlight magic. "I'm not here to hurt you."

"You said that. And somehow, I just don't believe you."

The stranger flicked his eyes to the floor, seemingly thinking about the best lie or way to answer my question. "I'm not from this world."

I stiffened. Oh shit. He's a demon. "You're a demon." I yanked hard on my starlight, keeping it real close. "How the hell did you get past the wards? Did someone summon you here?" I seriously hoped this was not one of Julian's plans gone terribly wrong. Still, he didn't look like any demon I'd ever faced. He didn't smell or feel like a demon either. That worried me. Maybe I didn't have what it took to take him down, which was why he was so calm. He knew I couldn't beat him.

Okay, cue in a little panic.

And then it hit me. Darius was a Dark witch. And what do Dark witches have that other witches don't? The ability to borrow magic from demons as well as the knowledge and know-how to summon demons and control them. If he was a demon, I was pretty sure Darius had sent him.

Matiel's eyes widened suddenly, and then his expression became hard, dark. "I'm not a demon."

"You sure about that?"

Matiel's face shifted in irritation. "Demons are notoriously self-centered. Their giant egos were one of the reasons why they fell from Horizon. Demons are evil by definition."

I gave a one-shoulder shrug. "That description matches a lot of people I know." It really did.

A light sparked in the stranger's eyes. He was silent a moment. "I am no demon, Leana. I promise you."

"Then *what* are you?" Not that I believed him. My starlight tingled through my body, feeling my mistrust of this stranger. We were both tired of this and wanted him to leave or I'd fry his ass. What I wanted was some sexy time with my giant. That's what I wanted.

"It'll be easier if I show you." He looked at me, and suddenly his eyes sparked with an inner white light. A wind rose in the apartment, lifting my hair and my clothes, just as the air hummed with energy that felt strangely familiar, almost like my starlight or close to it. And then his skin started to glow, like he had millions of tiny lights inside his body. His entire body began to shine with an internal light and expanded until he became frayed at the edges. Still, the light grew and grew. I averted my eyes at the sudden shining blur that was too bright to look at.

Energy pulsed in the room, over the walls and in the air, and brushed against me. The power was both unfamiliar and familiar at the same time. Really confusing, but I did know that it didn't feel menacing.

It was like I was staring at Gandalf the Gray becoming Gandalf the White. I didn't know how else to explain it. It was both terrifying and oddly interesting. I think I might have peed a little bit.

When the light subsided, Matiel's body flickered, and then his inner light faded until he was just like he was a moment ago, normal and not lit up.

"I'm an angel."

"No shit." He could be lying, but somehow, I knew he was

telling the truth. I'd never met or seen an angel before, so I hadn't known what to expect. But I'd heard the rumors of their inner light. I also knew that not all angels *were* angels in the way of their morals, and they could kill you just as easily as a demon.

"Okay, Matiel, the angel," I said, still hanging on to my starlight. I still didn't trust him. "What the hell do you want from me?"

Matiel looked pained, and then for the first time since his arrival, he looked tired. Could angels be tired? "I know this is probably not what you want to hear. And I'll understand if you're angry. But you need to know. Know who you are and where your magic comes from."

I snorted. "Comes from my mother. She was a witch. A White witch, not a starlight witch. If that's where you're going with this." Where the hell was he going with this?

Matiel's eyes fixed on mine, and then he said, "But your magic also comes from your father."

Oh, hell no. "What are you implying?" I knew what he was implying. If he was going to say those words, I might have to fire my starlight at him. Would it hurt an angel? Hard to tell. He did say my magic wouldn't affect him. But I was going to try.

Matiel stared at me. "I'm your father."

I shook my head. "Oh, no you don't. Get out. Get the hell out." A strange fear started to climb up my back at his words because a part of me knew it was true. I felt it. I couldn't explain it. I just felt the familiarity that you only feel around family. But how could that be? I'd never met him before. Never seen a picture. I knew nothing about him.

Yet… he felt like family.

What if he *was* my father? My mother never talked about him. I'd always thought he was just a deadbeat dad. I had thought about who my birth father was, over the years, more when I was younger. Barely ever now. He could be the one. And he could be lying too.

"I'm your father, Leana. It's the truth. Deep down, you know it's true. I can feel it in you. You know I speak the truth."

I shook my head, not knowing whether angels could read minds. "I don't." But I kinda did.

"Have you ever wondered where you got your starlight magic? It's celestial magic, cosmic energy. Magic from the stars, given by the angels. That's... your starlight."

Was it, though? Really? Was starlight, in a way, magic from the angels?

This couldn't be happening. I was suffering from some midlife crisis. But what he was saying made sense. The stars. My starlight. It always felt cosmic. The energy I drew upon was never from this planet but from the stars. I felt a connection to him. Was that part of my starlight connection?

My heart was pounding in my chest, and I could feel my blood pressure rising. "If that's true, where have you been for the last forty-one years? My mother could have used some help."

"Respecting your mother's wishes," he answered and straightened. "We were very happy at one time, but then we drifted apart. No one's fault. It just happened. When your mother got pregnant with you, she told me, and asked that I stay away. She knew you'd be different. She wanted to give you a normal life. She wanted to raise you with her mother and keep you away from my side of the family, in a matter of speaking."

"Really? Why is that?" I couldn't believe I was buying all of this.

Matiel exhaled. "To protect you. It was always to protect you. Keep you safe. If the angel legion knew I had an offspring, you'd be hunted and killed."

I raised my brows. "If that's true, why tell me now? Won't this legion try to kill me now?" Great. I had enough problems in my life right now with the Darius thing. The last thing I needed was the legion of angels on my ass.

"No. You've proven to be guided by the light and not the darkness. And you're not powerful enough to draw their attention."

"Geez, thanks, *Dad*," I said, but the angel smiled. Damn. "Okay, so you're saying you're my father. Maybe I believe you… maybe I don't." I let go of my starlight. "You say you were respecting my mother's wishes to stay away. That's honorable. And if that's true, thank you. But I have to ask. Why now? Why did you show up here? You do know she died more than fifteen years ago."

Sadness flashed across his face. "I know. I know about her cancer. And before you ask... no, I couldn't have done anything to save her. I was there during her last moments, though you couldn't see me. I was there at the funeral."

I rubbed my eyes. "I'm going to need a drink after this. This is… this is a lot to take in. Especially at this time at night." I imagined my friends' faces when I broke the news. I'd need to sit down after that.

I was part witch and part angel. I'd need two full bottles of wine. One for each part.

"I understand," said Matiel, his voice filled with compassion, and I almost started to feel comfortable around him. Almost. "I can't imagine what it must be like for you. To meet me like this. Uninvited in the middle of the night. And I'm sorry to spring this all on you in such a short time."

"Why did you? Is something going on?" I watched him for a moment, trying to see any family resemblance, but I didn't see it. But I felt it. I figured I took after my mother's looks and my father's power. *My father's power*. That sounded so foreign to me. He might be my father, but he was still a stranger.

Matiel glanced behind me. "You can come out now," he called suddenly.

"Who're you talking to?" I turned around at the sound of footsteps.

A girl, maybe ten or eleven, stepped out of my bedroom. She had light-brown hair, kept in a ponytail, a backpack over a denim jacket, jeans, and sneakers. She kept her head down, and her fingers moved on her tablet's screen as she walked past me and made her way to the living room where Matiel stood. She joined him, turned around, so she was facing me, met my eyes, and quickly glanced back down at her tablet, continuing whatever game she was playing. She didn't look like she wanted to be here. I didn't blame her.

"Okay, why do you have a kid with you? And why were you hiding her in my room?" And why did he bring her here?

Matiel held her by the shoulders and said, "This is Shay. She's your sister. And she needs your help."

Well, crap.

CHAPTER 11

My apartment floor sort of wavered at that point.

I shook my head, hoping it would clear my hearing because those words that came flying out of that angel's mouth couldn't be true. "I'm sorry. My what?"

"Your sister," repeated my so-called angel father. "A different mother, of course."

"Of course." Was he serious? I stared at the kid, but she wouldn't make eye contact. She was most probably terrified or just wanted to get the hell away from here.

Matiel dipped his head. "Shay. Say hi to your sister."

The girl kept typing on her tablet, but she did emit some type of grunt.

The angel locked eyes with me and shrugged. "Kids."

I felt like I'd just hit a wall at fifty miles an hour. "This is crazy. You're crazy." I couldn't possibly have a sister. A kid sister. This angel said he's my father, and right now I was leaning toward a big yes. I could actually feel it now, the blood connection or whatever you wanted to call it. If she was his daughter, I guessed she was my sister or half sister. "Do you make it a habit of impregnating mortal women?"

Matiel's eyes narrowed. "Even angels get lonely."

"I can see that. Couldn't keep it in your pants." Yes, that was a bit rude, but I was angry. Ticked that this angel was my father who decided to show up after forty-one years only to tell me that I had a sibling. I watched his reaction, expecting him to be furious, but he just looked sad and maybe a little defeated. What was that about?

I tried to get a better look at her face, but she never looked up. "Is she a Starlight witch like me?" At that, the girl stopped moving her fingers over her tablet, and I could tell she was waiting for our angel papa to answer.

Matiel didn't respond right away, as though he was formulating what he was about to tell me, being extra cautious and choosing his words carefully. But then he said, "Yes. She is a Starlight witch. But her powers are somewhat... *different* than yours. Same but different."

"Not complicated at all." At that, the girl looked up, and my breath caught. Her eyes, which were green, were red and puffy like she'd been crying... a lot. I didn't know what she saw on my face, but she quickly averted her eyes and busied herself with her tablet again.

"I need to sit down." I was impressed that I hadn't fallen over yet. I moved to the living room and let myself fall into one of the armchairs. Following my example, Matiel sat on the couch, pulling his daughter with him.

It was hard not to stare at the girl. I'd never had a sibling, cousins, nothing like that. It had always been just me, my mother, and my grandmother. That had been my family. And now I had the thirteenth-floor gang as my adoptive family.

I pulled my gaze away from the girl and stared at Matiel. The angel looked more nervous than ever. "Why did you really come here? You said something about her needing my help. Help with what?"

Shay spared me a glance before going back to her tablet.

Matiel nodded and dragged his hands over his thighs, like he was trying to let go of some of his tension. "I told you it's forbidden for angels to have relations with witches or any other mortal."

"Yet you keep doing it."

The angel pressed his lips into a tight line, not impressed with me. Too bad. I wasn't impressed with him either. "And I told you about your mother's wishes to stay away because she knew more contact with me would be suspicious within the legion of angels. Just like you, if they knew of her existence, they would hunt her because of what she is. There are those who want to hurt Shay."

Now we were getting somewhere. I spoke to Matiel, but my eyes were on the girl. "Who? The angel legion?" I'd never imagined a group of angels hunting some little girl. But then again, I didn't know how angels operated. Celestial politics weren't my thing. Even human politics. Paranormal politics were enough. Thank you very much.

"Among others." Matiel met my eyes, and I saw a sort of pleading in them. "She needs your protection."

"From the angel legion?"

"That's why she needs to stay with you."

"Excuse me?" I felt like I'd just been kicked in the gut. "Stay with me? For how long?" Okay, this was not ideal. I could do a few days, but that was it. If he thought I'd be his new babysitter, he had another think coming.

Matiel had gone stiff. "Until she turns eighteen."

Holy shit. "You can't be serious." This had to be some joke. "I don't know anything about kids."

"I'm not a kid," snapped the girl. She stared at me with venom in her eyes.

Ah, hell. Now I'd done it. "See, I'm no good with *young women* her age. She already hates me." It explained why she had a backpack with her. He was planning on leaving her here with me. "Seems to me like you're trying to sneak away from your responsibilities. That's what it looks like." With me, and now with her.

"Leana, listen to me," said Matiel. "You're her guardian. You're her only living family."

"What about her mom?" Judging by her red eyes, I had a feeling I already knew the answer.

Matiel glanced at the floor. "She's no longer with us."

Damn. Damn. Damn. "What about you? You're her father. She should be with her father. Not a sister she never knew existed. I'm a stranger to her." And she to me. God, this was awful. I felt for her. Whenever my eyes settled on the girl, my heart clenched like a fist was crushing it. I knew all too well what it was like to lose a mother. But I'd been an adult when she'd passed. Shay was just a girl. A girl who'd just lost her mother, and her father was now trying to pawn her off on a stranger. Damn. Now I was ticked.

"I would if I could," said Matiel. "I'm an angel, Leana. I can't stay in this realm for very long. Only a few hours at a time before I must return to Horizon. So you see, there's no way I can care for her. I need your help. She needs your help."

I stared at Shay, and I saw her blinking fast. Damnit.

"You're the only person in this world who can keep her safe," Matiel was saying. "The only person I trust."

I looked at him. "You don't even know me."

"You're my daughter. And I knew your mother inside out. And you're just like her. Loyal. Good. Selfless and brave."

My throat tightened, and it was my turn to blink rapidly.

"She has no one else," said Matiel. "You're the only person she's got. Will you help us?"

The guilt hit. Obviously, if he knew my mother as well as he said, and if I was truly just like her, he knew what I was going to say the moment he showed up in my apartment with Shay.

"Yes." The word left my mouth before I'd even formulated it in my head. "Of course she can." Holy crap.

Matiel let out a long exhale and stood. "Thank you, Leana. I'll be back as soon as I can."

Shay jumped to her feet. "Don't go. Please. Don't leave me."

Matiel grabbed his daughter's face and kissed the top of her head. "You know I can't stay. I promise I'll be back soon."

"No." Shay hit his chest with her fist. "You can't leave me here. Take me with you."

Matiel's eyes filled with tears. "You know that's not possible."

"Don't leave me! I don't want to be here!" Shay punched her father again. And again, until her fists mixed with bouts of sobbing.

My eyes burned, and I turned my head away from them for a moment, wanting to give them some privacy. I felt sorry for the girl.

"You'll be safe here. I promise. Your sister will look after you. I'll be back as soon as I can. Then you can tell me all about it."

"I hate it here!" she wailed.

"Love you."

With a sudden citrus smell, my apartment burst with light, just like when Matiel had revealed his angel form to me. I blinked and stared at the bright light. And then the light was gone.

So was Matiel.

It was just Shay and me.

Damn. What the hell was I supposed to do now?

My pulse rose. I was nervous, but that was nothing compared to what this kid must be feeling right now.

I cleared my throat. "You hungry? I'm not a great cook, but I can find something for you to eat."

Shay wiped at her eyes and sat back on the couch, her tablet in her hand. She wouldn't look at me.

"Not hungry. That's okay. Let me get you a glass of water." I stood up, more for me. I had to do something to cure this awkwardness. I walked over to the kitchen, filled a glass of water, and returned to the living room.

I set the glass on the coffee table. "Have some water. You look like you could use some." The poor kid looked dehydrated.

"So," I began and sat next to her on the couch. "How old are you?"

"Eleven and a half," she answered, surprising me. I saw a

resemblance to Matiel in her eyes. And she had the same long, goofy legs I had at her age.

"Do you go to school here in New York City?" We had several paranormal schools around the country, although I had never attended one. My mother and grandmother had homeschooled me in all things magic and supernatural. Though I'd always felt like I would have liked to participate in the paranormal schools to see what it was like.

"Homeschool." A big, fat tear fell across her cheek, and she quickly wiped it with her hand.

"Your mom?"

Shay nodded but kept silent, her fingers moving along her screen. The beeps and tings from her game seemed loud in the silence now that it was just the two of us.

It was obvious she and her mom were close. Her mother was also her teacher, which meant that Shay had been accustomed to a schedule and a normal life, and now everything she knew and loved had been taken away. And she was dumped on my doorstep, so to speak.

"Are you tired?"

Shay nodded, and another great big tear rolled down her cheek.

"Okay. I'll make up the couch for you. I don't have another bed. I use the spare bedroom as an office. Tomorrow I'll look into getting a bed for you, and we'll set it up in the spare room. That'll be your room."

I got up and went in search of some extra blankets and pillows. I didn't have much, but thank God, I had some spare, clean sheets.

I walked back into the living room, and Shay stood from the couch and moved to stand next to the armchair. "The bathroom's just down the hall," I told her as I laid a sheet over the couch, trying to make eye contact, but she wouldn't look at me. I'd only met her a few minutes ago, and the girl hated my guts.

I might have been a tad insensitive at first. I was shocked by the whole thing. Kids didn't forget or forgive easily. I didn't know how this was going to work or how Matiel thought leaving her with me was a good idea.

Shay grabbed her backpack, disappeared into the bathroom, and slammed the door shut.

"Well, at least her actions speak louder than words."

My fingers shook as I pulled a comforter over the makeshift bed. I hadn't realized how stressed and shocked I was too. And I could feel the onset of a migraine approaching.

I went back into the kitchen, grabbed a box of chocolate chip cookies, and placed an entire row on a plate. I took the dish with me, grabbed one for myself, and set it next to the glass of water. I finished my cookie, waiting for Shay to come out.

When she finally did, I stood and moved over to the wall. "Well. I guess that's it. I'm off to bed too. We'll talk more in the morning." I watched as Shay dropped her bag and pulled off her jacket. "Good night." I waited to see if she'd answer. Nope.

I shut off the living room lights, walked over to the apartment door, made sure it was closed, and then went to my room and shut the door.

I sat on my bed and quickly grabbed my phone. Voices traveled in this place, and the last thing I wanted was to make Shay more uncomfortable than she already was, so instead of phoning Valen, I decided to text him. I couldn't type everything. It would be too long. So I gave him the short version.

Me: *Guess what. My father showed up. He's an angel. I also have a stepsister. He can't take care of her so he left her with me. She's eleven. And she hates my guts.*

I waited with my heart thumping loud in my ears. I knew what I'd just typed would fundamentally change our relationship in a big way. When we'd met, I didn't have a ward. I wasn't anyone's guardian. And I certainly didn't have an eleven-year-old sister. It was just me. Me and my baggage, but me, nonetheless. Now, I was responsible for a person, a little person who'd lost everything. It was a lot to take in. Valen and I were just starting our relationship. We hadn't even discussed kids. I couldn't have them. And when I realized I couldn't, I just stopped thinking of a life with kids. I didn't know where he stood with that. We were both in our forties. It was a lot to think about.

If he didn't want to be with me anymore, I'd have to respect that. I wouldn't force it on him. I wouldn't do to him what my angel father did to Shay and me. But I really hoped he'd stay. God, I hoped he stayed.

When I saw the three dots on the screen, my heart skipped a beat. I stared at the three dots for what felt like hours. What was he writing? Why was it taking so long?

Valen: *Wow. A sister? I think she'll be good for you.*

I frowned at the screen. What the hell did that mean?

Me: *You think?*

Valen: *Yes. I can't wait to meet her.*

Me: *I'm freaking out over here.*

Valen: *Bring her to the restaurant with you tomorrow for lunch. 1 p.m. I want you to meet Hanna and Frederick before they leave tomorrow night.*

Oh, right. I'd forgotten about the giants. Now that was a lunch I was looking forward to. I wanted to see if they were like Valen or completely different.

Me: *Okay. See you tomorrow.*

I placed my phone on my night table, plugged in the power cord, stripped, and climbed into bed.

I lay in bed for hours after that, thinking. How could things have the nerve to look so normal when my entire life had just imploded? I realized, then, that my life would never be the same again. Ever.

And I wasn't sure how to take that.

CHAPTER 12

I woke to a pounding headache. I'd barely slept and kept waking up with my heart trying to bust through my ribs because an eleven-year-old girl was sleeping on my couch, and I was supposed to take care of her.

But I'd forgotten to mention one vital thing to Matiel last night.

Darius.

Darius could snap his fingers and haul my ass to prison. He could lock me up forever if he wanted. And then what would become of Shay? See. I wasn't fit to take care of anyone. I could barely control my own life. How could I possibly take care of her?

Matiel said he'd come back. I'd just have to tell him then. He had to know if I suddenly disappeared. Then he'd have to look for someone else to take care of Shay.

Damn. When did my life get so complicated?

I tossed the sheets off me and hauled myself out of bed. My phone said it was eight in the morning. Not too late, but not that early. I didn't know Shay's schedule. Another thing to add to my list of things to do. I had to know what she did every day and try to stick to it. It might make her feel better if she had some normalcy in her life. I doubted it.

I hurried to the bathroom. Then, after I'd relieved myself, I brushed my teeth and walked into the living room.

Shay sat on the couch, playing with her tablet. The sheets were folded neatly and piled on the sofa beside the pillows. She had her denim jacket on and her backpack as though she was ready to leave or be dropped at the next person's door.

My heart shattered at what I saw. I was mad at myself for being selfish when this kid was going through something far worse than me. She was my *sister*. My only family too. My eyes burned, and I rushed to the kitchen, not trusting my voice at this moment.

I flicked the coffee machine on, swallowed hard, and pushed off the counter.

"You like eggs? I'm not really good at cooking. I have cereal too."

Shay just shrugged.

I sighed. This was going to be more complicated than I thought. Not knowing what else to do, I decided to make eggs and prepare a bowl of cereal for her too.

I reached into the cabinet and grabbed a bowl, the cereal box I got on sale, and milk, before setting it all on the dining table. Then I turned on the stove, waited a minute or so, cracked two eggs, and dropped them in a frying pan.

I opened the fridge and thanked my friends silently for supplying me with orange juice and fruit. I grabbed some grapes and the orange juice and set them on the kitchen table.

"Come eat," I told Shay. I expected her to give me a hard time, but she stood up, pulled out a chair, and sat. Then she grabbed the cereal box and began to fill up her bowl.

Okay. That wasn't so bad. I placed a clean glass next to her and filled it with orange juice. "I don't know if you like orange juice."

Shay nodded as she shoved a spoon of cereal into her mouth. She had dark circles under her red, puffy eyes. Her hair was sticking out of her ponytail. She needed a good brushing.

"Oh, hello."

Elsa strolled into the apartment, wearing a long denim skirt and a smile.

I hadn't even heard the door open.

"Who's your friend?" asked the older witch. Her hip bumped against mine as she joined me next to the dining table, her curly red hair bouncing on her shoulders.

Shay stopped eating. Her green eyes were wide as she looked at Elsa. She looked like she was about to run.

"Uh…" Okay, might as well just come out and say it. "This is Shay. She's my sister."

Elsa just blinked. I didn't think I'd ever seen her speechless before.

"Shay, this is my friend Elsa. You can trust her," I said, feeling the tension rolling over the young girl. She looked terrified.

Elsa seemed to notice that too. "Of course, you can trust me, sweetheart," she said, her voice soft and motherly. Damn, I wish I could do that. "I'm a trustworthy witch. The most dependable witch on the thirteenth floor," she added with a smile and tapped the side of her nose with her finger. She looked between the both of us. "Sisters, eh? You don't have the same eyes, but you have the same nose and jaw."

Shay and I both looked at each other.

"She's a witch too. I can tell," continued Elsa. "I'm getting some strong readings from her. Well, how about that?" Elsa clapped her hands. "I think it's just fantastic. Marvelous."

"What's marvelous?" Jade came strolling into the apartment. Her blonde hair was up in pigtails. She wore a pair of high-waist, acid-wash jeans and a baggy, oversized pink blouse with shoulder pads that made her look like she could play a linebacker in football, all held in place with a wide white belt.

"That's Jade, my other friend you can trust," I quickly told Shay, whose eyes had expanded a bit at the sight of Jade.

Jade beamed and placed her hands on her hips. "Totally."

"That's Shay," said Elsa, beaming. "Leana's sister."

Jade's jaw dropped. "No way. Why didn't you tell us you had

a sister? I *love* sisters." Jade pulled out a chair and sat. She grabbed the spare bowl I'd placed for me and started to dump cereal into it.

I shrugged. "I didn't know."

Jade and Elsa both stared at me. "Long story," I said, seeing Shay staring at her bowl. Color spotted her cheeks.

"What in the name of the goddess is that?" Elsa rushed over to the stove and grabbed the frying pan.

Damn. I forgot about the eggs. "Eggs?"

Elsa looked over her shoulder at me. "Who burns eggs?"

I shrugged. "That would be me." I glanced at Shay, and she had the tiniest smile on her face. But then I blinked, and it was gone.

Elsa mumbled something under her breath, chucked my burnt eggs, and placed the pan back on the stove. "I think pancakes are in order." She looked at Shay. "You like pancakes, dear?"

Shay looked up and nodded. I noticed Jade staring at her with a slight frown, and then her eyes went sad. It wasn't hard to see that the kid was in pain.

Damn it. I wish I was better at this stuff, but I thanked the goddess for Elsa and Jade.

Soon the kitchen smelled of delicious, sweet pancake mix and butter. Pancakes sounded divine. I was ravenous.

"Guess who I had sex with last night?" Julian came waltzing into the apartment like he was the goddess's gift to all women.

"*Julian*." I glared at him, wide-eyed, motioning with a jerk of my head to the kid sitting at the table.

"Oh shit. There's a kid here," he said. "Sorry."

"Her name's Shay," said Jade. "She's Leana's sister."

"Sister?" Julian looked at Shay, who had turned a darker shade of red, her head practically in her cereal bowl.

"She didn't know she had a sister," Jade told him.

"What?" Julian turned to look at me.

"Tell you later," I said quickly. "How about you keep that sex talk to yourself for a while."

Julian made a tying motion at his mouth with his fingers. "Done."

Jade leaned forward and said to Shay, "You can trust him too. And there's Jimmy, my friend. You can trust Jimmy. He's the best."

I smiled at the way she said that all lovey-dovey and sappy. I was truly happy that things were going so well between them.

"Move over," ordered Elsa as she placed a plate of hot pancakes, dripping with real maple syrup, on the table for Shay. "Here you go, sweetheart," she said, leaning back. "And there's lots more."

"Good. 'Cause I'm starving." Julian sat across from Shay. "Worked out quite a bit last night, if you know what I'm saying."

Jade smacked Julian with her spoon. "Shhh."

"Ow," he laughed. "Okay, sorry."

But Shay had that tiny smile reappear, and she was a lot less red-faced. I watched as she pushed away her cereal bowl and opted for the golden pancakes. Good choice.

I grabbed the empty chair next to Shay and sat just as Elsa reappeared with a plate and pancakes for me. "Thanks."

"You're welcome." Elsa beamed, looking pleased to be doing something in the kitchen. She liked feeding people and taking care of them, just like Valen.

"Where's Catelyn?" I cut a piece of my pancake with my fork and stuffed it in my mouth.

"She's still sleeping." The older witch gestured with a spatula. "She had a rough night last night. Poor dear. It was her niece's birthday."

"Right." Catelyn had to get ahold of her new giantess abilities. She had to be able to control them on a whim before she could go see her family again. She was practicing daily, and I knew Valen was helping her. But it would take time.

"She'll be fine." Elsa returned to the stove and started to whisk up some more pancake mix in a ceramic bowl I'd never seen before. I swear she brought over some of her own dishes.

We settled into a silence broken only by the brewing of the coffee machine and Elsa whisking her pancake mix. We were all lost in our thoughts, but mostly I knew my friends wanted to ask Shay questions. They knew to give the girl a break, though.

"So," I said, breaking the silence, "your master plan to get rid of Oric seems to have gone off pretty well."

Julian gave me a sly smile. "I told you we'd take care of it."

Jade let out a chuckle. "Did you see my permanent paint spell? They never saw that coming."

I laughed. "I did. And that poor bald woman? What was that?"

"That was one of mine," said Julian proudly. "Added some of my *hair removal* potions to the main water valve on that floor. She's not the only one who turned out bald, let me tell you."

"Probably the only one who wasn't embarrassed about it," said Elsa.

"She was pissed," I said, remembering how angry she was at Basil. "You think it's going to work?"

"It's already working," said Jade. "Jimmy told me that half of the guests checked out last night… after our… you know…"

Shay listened attentively to our conversation, seemingly happy not to be the center of attention.

"Oric was investigating the 'unusual phenomenon' all last night." Elsa snorted. "He has no idea what hit him."

"That'll teach him for stealing my friend's job," said Jade, and I could see more interest flicking in Shay's expression. She was getting loads of information right now.

Julian waved his fork at me. "We're just getting started."

I laughed. "Just don't get caught is all I ask."

"We won't."

I felt some tension release from my middle. Maybe this was going to work after all. "Valen invited Shay and me to lunch at his restaurant today," I said, breaking the silence. Shay's eyebrows twitched, but she didn't look at me as she continued to work on her pancakes. I met Jade's smiling face and added, "He's my…

friend," I said, not knowing what I was supposed to call him. We'd never made it official.

"He's also a giant," blurted Jade, making Elsa spin around so fast that clumps of the mix splattered over the floor. Julian choked on his mouthful of pancake.

My eyes flicked to Shay as I watched her raise her head from her plate. She looked from me to Jade and then back at me, the suspicion obvious in the frown on her brow. I could tell she didn't believe that. I mean, only a few weeks ago, I would have had the same reaction as her about giants. Because we all knew giants weren't real… until now.

I swallowed and said, "That's right. Valen *is* a giant. I didn't believe it either. Not until I saw him change with my own eyes." I had a feeling Shay was well-informed about our world, perhaps more than your average eleven-year-old, seeing as she had an angel as a father and a witch as a mother.

Shay frowned at me, and I knew from how she was flicking her eyes from me to the others that she thought we were messing with her. But I could also see a part where she was curious.

"I used to think the guy was an asshole, but he's a good guy," said Julian.

I cast him a frown, but he didn't notice as he just kept eating.

"Anyway, I thought you should know before you meet him," I told her. She was still watching me under her frown, her green eyes hard.

"Here you go." Elsa came around the table and added another golden pancake to Shay's plate. Then she moved over to Julian's and piled another two for him.

"Jade? You want some? I can make some more," called Elsa as she moved back to the stove.

Jade shook her head. "No. I'm stuffed. I want to watch what I'm eating." We all know what she meant by that. She wanted to look good for Jimmy.

Speaking of Jimmy. "Hey, you think Jimmy is busy today?"

Jade shook her head. "I don't think so. Why?"

"I need another bed and maybe a dresser for Shay's room." I could see Shay cutting into her hot pancake, from the corner of my eye. "Maybe he'd know if the hotel still has the old one that used to be in my spare bedroom."

"I can ask him," said Jade.

"No, it's fine. I'll do it," I told her. Shay was my responsibility now. I should be in charge of getting her new room ready for her.

"Let Jade do that," said Elsa. "And I'll help too." She put the hot pan into the sink and let the water run for a few seconds before turning it off. "You should take your sister shopping and get her some new clothes." She gave me a knowing glance, the one that said I should take another good look at Shay.

So, I did.

When I looked at her, her clothes seemed like they'd seen better days. In fact, if I didn't know any better, it looked as though she'd been wearing the same clothes for a while. Like a street kid or someone who'd been homeless for a few weeks. Shit. How long had she been without her mother? Why hadn't I seen that?

The only thing she carried with her was that backpack, and I doubted there was more than one change of clothes in there, maybe not even.

"Would you like that, Shay?" I watched her face. I couldn't tell what she was thinking. She gave me a one-shoulder shrug without looking at me. I took that as a yes.

"Then it's settled," said Elsa. "You take Shay shopping, and we'll take care of her room."

At that, Shay spied Elsa through her eyelashes, and I swear I could see a tiny smile somewhere hidden around that sad girl's face.

It was a start.

CHAPTER 13

By the time Shay and I returned to the hotel from our shopping, it was a little past noon. I didn't know much about shopping for a young girl, so I took her to Macy's. I figured they had everything there.

Shay didn't talk much the entire time. I got lots of head shakes, nods, and the occasional, "Okay." I knew she was uncomfortable. I was too. And I didn't push it. I'd let her come around when she was ready. She'd been through enough these past few days if her red puffy eyes and disheveled clothes were any indications.

I let her go and take what she wanted to the dressing room while I waited. After two hours of shopping, we got four new pairs of jeans, five long-sleeved T-shirts, underwear, socks, a pair of Converse sneakers, another denim jacket, and a collection of T-shirts with some manga characters on them that I was not familiar with. When I took some training bras to the dressing room for her, she shook her head, looking mortified, like I'd just signed her death warrant. Okay, maybe that was too early. My bad. As I said, I didn't know anything about kids.

It wasn't much, and I knew I'd have to get her more clothes eventually, but I tried not to have a panic attack when the lady at the cash register rang up my bill. Damn. At that moment, I knew I had to keep a paying job just to afford the basic needs of this girl. I needed to get my job back at the hotel—more than ever.

Bags in our hands, we walked into the apartment to the sound of voices. I followed the voices to the spare room and halted. The desk I had been using was replaced by a single-sized bed, adorned with a beautiful light-blue-and-white-striped comforter and four fluffy pillows. One small night table rested next to the bed, and a lovely oak dresser was pushed up against the opposite wall. A plush Oriental blue-and-red rug sat above the nasty green industrial apartment carpet. The carpet was still gross, but there was nothing to do about that.

Elsa smiled at us as she finished fluffing the last pillow. "What do you think, Shay? You like it?"

I glanced down at Shay. Her face was crimson. She nodded.

"Jimmy put your desk in the living room, just below the window," said Jade. "It's the only place it would fit."

"It's fine. Thanks." I'd have to thank Jimmy later. "Thanks, you guys. Really. This is great."

"You're very welcome." Elsa gave Shay a huge smile, which the girl tried to return but looked more like a terrified grin.

When the witches were gone, I left Shay alone in her room, letting her settle in while I took a shower and then went down to the basement to wash her new clothes. After Shay had taken a shower and dressed in a clean, new outfit, we left the hotel and went to the restaurant next door.

Once inside, I noticed Shay had brought her tablet and her dingy backpack. I wasn't about to tell her she couldn't bring them. My shoulder bag was my comfort item, so I understood where she was coming from. She wanted to have something familiar with her.

"What's this?"

I turned to see my favorite hostess staring at Shay like she was dog poop she'd just stepped in with her new Prada shoes.

Shay lowered her head and stared at her feet.

My temper flared. I really hated that one. "Where's Valen?" I glanced over the restaurant, looking for that handsome giant.

"No idea," answered the hostess, whose name I didn't care to remember. She was such a liar. The woman tracked Valen like a tick on a dog. I had the feeling she was in love with him.

I spotted him far back at the same table he'd used for our date. "Come, Shay."

The hostess mumbled something as I led Shay to the back left side of the restaurant, near the windows.

"You're alone? Where are the other…" I left the question in the air, not wanting to say *giant* in the restaurant in case they were here somewhere and didn't want anyone to know their true nature.

Valen stood, and a drift of some musky cologne rolled to me. "They left early this morning. I tried to have them stay longer, but they wanted to leave. It's okay. It was really nice to meet them."

Our eyes locked as heat poured down my back and settled in my middle at the intensity of his gaze. I couldn't help but think about his rough hands over my skin and his kisses that sent me into a wild frenzy. I wanted some more of that. Lots more.

He pulled his gaze away from me and settled on Shay. "I'm Valen." He stuck out his hand, and I was amazed when she shook it. "It's nice to meet you, Shay."

Shay gave a little smile, hurried over, pulled out a chair next to the window, and sat, her head down as her fingers swiped across the tablet.

I looked up at Valen, who was beaming. I thought he liked the idea of me having a little sister, and that did all kinds of things to my belly. I thought about kissing him. Should I kiss him? How did we act in public?

I was a little disappointed as he pulled out the chair next to Shay for me without a kiss, but still gallant. Maybe he didn't want to embarrass Shay. Because we all knew if he planted that mouth on mine, it wouldn't be a peck.

As Valen took his seat across from me, a waiter came and

handed us three menus before pouring some water for us. It was the same bald waiter who had served us during our date night.

"Wine, boss?" asked the waiter.

"Yes." He looked at Shay. "What would you like to drink?"

Shay carefully pulled her eyes from her tablet. "Orange juice," she answered, and I felt a little more relaxed that she was talking.

The waiter angled his head. "Be right back."

I let out a sigh. A glass of wine would be welcome right now. But I'd keep it to one glass. I had to work later. I still had to find Bellamy and hit the second possible location for the jewel. But I had to find him first. If he was telling the truth about Darius's guys wanting him dead, I needed to find him before they did.

"Are you really a giant?"

Both Valen and I stared at Shay.

Shit. I hadn't asked him if it was okay to reveal his secret to my newly discovered sister. And I hadn't expected Shay to come out and say it like that. I hadn't expected her to be so direct.

I waited, my pulse pounding, as I stared at Valen to see any indication that he was upset. But the giant smiled, a genuine, want-to-kiss-those-lips-now kind of smile.

"I am." He leaned forward. "Does that scare you?"

"Nope."

"Have you ever met a giant before?"

"Nope."

"Do you want to ask me a question?"

Shay pressed her lips together and stared at her tablet for a second before looking up. "How do I know you're not lying?" The skepticism in her voice was palpable.

"He's not," I told her, enjoying our conversation. "I've seen him change. Many times. He *is* a giant." Shay didn't look convinced.

Picking up on that, Valen folded back his shirt sleeve to his elbow. "Let me show you."

With a small flash of light, like someone had turned on a lamp at our table, Valen's hand and arm started to ripple and grow until they were three times their normal size.

"Holy crap," I whispered, looking over my shoulder to see if anyone else had seen Valen's arm grow in size, but it looked like the customers were too busy eating their meals. The food was excellent here. I stared at Valen. "I didn't know you could do that." I'll admit that was pretty amazing to watch. It appeared the giant still had many tricks yet to be discovered.

Valen brushed it off like it was nothing. Then, with another small flash of light, his arm was back to its standard size.

Shay's mouth hung open, her green eyes bright, not with fear but with interest.

"How big do you get?" she asked, and I held back a laugh.

Valen smiled proudly as he pulled down his sleeve. "Eighteen feet. Which is not, I hear, the biggest of our race. My friend Frederick reaches twenty-one feet. Kinda made me feel small when he told me."

I watched as Shay's eyes widened a little, and I could tell she was trying to imagine how big eighteen feet actually was.

"Whoa." Shay wrinkled her forehead in a cute way. "What about the girls? How big do they get? Are there girl giants?"

"Yes," answered Valen, and I could tell he was really enjoying talking to Shay. He hadn't stopped smiling since we arrived. "They're smaller. Fifteen, sixteen feet. There aren't many of us left."

"Why not?"

This was more than she'd spoken since I met her.

"Well, the short version is we were hunted at one point in time. Because of our size, some people feared us. Fast-forward to now, and we're just a few left."

"That sucks," said Shay. She was quiet for a second, and then she said, "I wish I was a giant."

I laughed, trying to imagine a larger version of this tiny kid. "Why's that?"

Shay stared at the table. "I could have stopped them from killing my mom."

I felt a pang in my heart as I searched the girl's face. Her mother had been killed? I ran over what my angel father had told me. If they were looking for Shay, her mother might have died defending her daughter. And maybe Shay had gotten away. Away long enough to possibly live on the streets for a week or so until her father found her.

My eyes burned, and I blinked fast. Crap. This was bad. Had she seen her mother die? She'd never get over that.

"If I was a giant, no one could hurt me," continued Shay.

She'd said it so indifferently like she knew her life was in danger, and whoever was hunting her wouldn't stop. I also felt an overwhelming feeling of protection for Shay. I barely knew her, but she had a way of growing on me in her sad, quiet, little-kid way. And I'd be damned if I let anyone hurt her.

Valen's expression went serious. I'd told him a little bit about my father and why he'd left her, but there was still a lot he didn't know that *I* didn't know about Shay.

I leaned over. "Who wants to hurt you, Shay? The angels?" The idea that anyone, angel or not, wanted to hurt this little girl had me seeing red. She was innocent. If they wanted to hurt someone, they should go after our father. He knew what he was doing when he bedded two mortal witch women. Shay was just a kid.

Shay just kept staring at her tablet, her eyes shining with unshed tears, but she'd gone all stiff and quiet again.

I didn't know what to do. I felt like an idiot. Should I hug her? I got the impression she wouldn't like that. We might be sisters, but we were still strangers. I kept throwing nervous glances at Valen, who looked just as uneasy as I did. Especially him, seeing as it was in his DNA to protect.

The waiter arrived at that moment. He gave Shay a tall glass of orange juice and had Valen taste the wine.

"I'll give you some time to look over our lunch menus," he

said, noticing our sudden discomfort, and then he disappeared again.

I took a sip of wine, but Shay hadn't touched her orange juice. "Do you want something else?"

Shay shook her head and remained quiet.

Valen watched Shay tentatively. "You know, your sister is a badass witch. I saw her take down an army of demons once."

At that, my sister looked up and stared at me curiously.

"I wouldn't say an *army*, but there were a few," I said, trying to shrug it off.

"If you're like her," Valen said, "you're a badass witch too. Which means you're strong and capable. You don't need to be a giant to be strong. You have other ways to do that. All you need is inner strength, and I can tell you have it."

Shay gave him a smile that warmed my heart like a cup of hot chocolate. Damnit. I had to blink fast again. Crying now would probably freak out Shay. When he said things like that, it was really hard not to fall for the guy. And I was falling for him fast.

I looked at Shay. "Did your mom teach you starlight magic?" I wasn't sure if bringing up her mother was a good idea, but the words were already out of my mouth.

My sister shook her head. I waited to see if she'd shut down again because I'd mentioned her mom, but she was looking at me expectantly, like she was waiting for me to say something.

"I was about your age when my mother and grandmother taught me," I said, seeing her interest that I was saying what she'd wanted to hear. "Like you, I had the magic inside me, but I didn't know how to control it. I almost burned down the house once. On Christmas Eve. I didn't know what I was doing." Shay just stared. "They taught me. How to call on it, how to spindle it, control it. And how not to use too much. Too much can kill you. Anyway, if you want, we can start lessons. I'm probably a terrible teacher, just so you know."

Shay shrugged, but her expression was still open and curious.

I took that as a yes. She took a sip of her orange juice, seemingly a little less gloomy.

She'd have to learn, and it was good that she was open to it. Like Valen said, there are other ways to be strong, not just with muscle. There was magic. And we Starlight witches had the power of the stars. Go us!

Shay would have to learn how to protect herself, just like I did. Because one day, I might not be there, and she'd have to defend herself. And if she was hunted, as my father said, she'd have to start now. A little starlight could go a long way, even at her age.

And I was curious as to what stars answered to her. She must be really powerful if the angels were after her. Apparently, I was a dud in the angel legion's eyes. Fine by me. But I had Shay to worry about now.

"You guys want to catch a movie later?" Valen set his wineglass on the table. "My treat."

Shay's eyes just grew wide as all her focus was on Valen. Then she turned around and stared at me, waiting for me to answer, waiting for my *permission*. It was strange to be responsible for another person when I'd been alone practically my entire adult life. Martin didn't count.

I should be looking for Bellamy after lunch, but one look at Shay's face, and all thoughts of that sweaty witch scientist vanished. It was like staring at a kid in a pet shop with big, hopeful eyes that she could take home that golden retriever puppy.

"Sounds like fun." I hadn't been to the movies in ages. I wouldn't even mind some of that oily popcorn that gave me heartburn every time I ate it, if meant Shay could escape her life for a few hours. My smile widened at Shay's smile—a big one, this time. I could see teeth. She had cute teeth.

She leaned back in her chair, smiling. "I still want to be a giant."

Both Valen and I started laughing.

CHAPTER 14

A cold wind blew as I headed to 326 West Fifty-Sixth Street, toward Bellamy's location, or so I hoped. Valen had put the word out to his contacts, and one of them had spotted the witch scientist or someone who fit his description.

I had to check out the lead. If it turned out to be good, I'd have my chance to bring Bellamy back with me. I didn't want to lose him. Not when I knew he had Darius's crew after him. I had to find him before they did because if I didn't, Bellamy would be dead, and I'd be out a witness.

After a wonderful two hours at the movies, I'd taken Shay back to the hotel so she could unwind and have some time to herself. Basil was in the lobby with Oric, throwing his hands around in another fit. I grinned. Julian's plan in the making again. But then Basil's attention snapped to mine and then to Shay. His eyes narrowed. I hid her the best I could with my body and ushered her inside the elevator.

I hadn't asked Basil if I was allowed to have another person living with me. I knew families lived on the thirteenth floor, but my arrangement was as a Merlin—singular. I was pretty sure there were papers to fill out and procedures to follow. But I didn't want to give him any excuses to kick me out of the apartment.

Once I cleared my name, I'd have a chat with the hotel manager, and hopefully, he'd agree.

We'd arrived to find Elsa, Jade, and Julian in the apartment. Elsa and Jade were busy in the kitchen with what I suspected was lasagna while Julian was hunkered over what appeared to be a blueprint of the hotel.

I'd gotten a call from Valen a few minutes later, telling me about the tip on Bellamy's location.

"He's hiding at three twenty-six West Fifty-Sixth Street," Valen had said. "In a motel. Room number fourteen. The curtains are drawn, so they can't confirm he's still in there."

"I'll check it out tonight. Thanks. Talk to you later," I told him and hung up. "Three twenty-six West Fifty-Sixth Street, room number fourteen," I repeated and quickly wrote the address down on a piece of paper before I forgot, and stuffed it in my pocket.

So, after a nice full meal of a home-cooked lasagna, I'd asked my friends if they wouldn't mind staying and looking after Shay, playing with her tablet, next to Julian in the living room.

"Of course, go," said Elsa, ushering me out. "She'll be fine with us. Don't worry."

"Go get Bellamy," said Jade. "Bring his dumb ass back."

I wouldn't have left Shay if I didn't have faith in my friends. I knew she'd be safe. Knew they'd protect her should anything happen or if an angel showed up. They'd face three very capable witches if they were stupid enough to pop in.

The streets were quieter than usual for a Friday night, and my boots clicked against the sidewalk as I walked down West Fifty-Sixth. Finally, the address 326 came into view.

A decrepit building, with its exterior walls painted in graffiti, was conveniently placed only a block away from a strip joint and a few pubs. My gaze lingered on the red flashing sign that read Hell's Kitchen Motel. Yikes. This place was the pits. Bellamy must be really desperate if he was staying in a place like that. Remembering how snotty he'd been just inside the Twilight Hotel, he was probably freaking out with all the bedbugs and other stains I didn't want to think about.

I crept alongside the building, which was suitably constructed practically on the sidewalk. The number fourteen, stenciled in black, hung above the door. A single window, with its curtains drawn, edged the door. I could see the flickering of light, like the illumination of a television. Whoever was in there was watching TV.

Gently, I tried the door handle. It was locked. I knew Bellamy was inside, and if I used my starlight to break down the door, I'd startle the witch scientist enough that he might not want to come with me. I could force him, but that would only make things worse for me. I needed the idiot for my case against Darius. I had to have Bellamy on my side. So, I needed to make this *his* decision. Well, make him *think* it was.

With bated breath, I knocked twice. "Bellamy," I said, my voice low but loud enough for him to hear me. "It's Leana."

The television light went out.

I waited a moment. "I'm alone. Let me in."

Silence. The only sound came from the street behind me, the cars rushing by and the distant honking in the blocks beyond.

"Bellamy," I hissed. "You asked for my help. Well, here I am. Now, open the damn door. Bellamy, open the door," I repeated.

I heard a heavy thump, like someone had jumped off a bed followed by the tread of feet approaching, and then, "How do I know it's really you?" came Bellamy's voice from beyond the door.

I rolled my eyes. "You can see me if you look out your window." God, this guy was insufferable.

The curtains pulled over a crack, and then were closed again.

"Bellamy?" I tried again.

"You might not be who you say you are," came Bellamy's muffled voice through the door. "You might be wearing a glamour to trick me. How do I really know you are you?"

My temper rushed through me. I didn't have the time or the

patience for this crap. "Bellamy, I swear, if you don't open this door, I'm going to knock it down."

Just when I was about to continue my endless pounding and shouting, I heard the twisted, slow scraping of the deadbolt, and the door swung open.

Bellamy stood on the threshold, his hair disheveled and pointing to the right. His eyes were red, looking half-crazed, half-drained, and he wore the same stained white shirt and pants that were too long for him.

"Only the real you would be this rude," he said as he stepped aside to let me in.

"Thanks." I had a few words reserved for him, but I bit my tongue, moved in, and closed the door behind me. As I stood in the narrow room, I ran my gaze over the typical motel room—one double bed, a striped-brown-and-tan duvet, with matching pillows and drapes. Tucked away toward the back was a single door, which I guessed was the bathroom. Take-out boxes littered a small table. It smelled of old cigarettes, musk, and God knew what else.

"Looks like you downsized from your old place," I said, glancing around, careful not to touch anything. I did not want to bring any *microorganisms* home with me.

Bellamy stood by the bed. "How did you find me?" His eyes narrowed as though he was upset, not surprised, that I found him.

"It wasn't hard. You were spotted. I came to check and see if it was really you."

"I didn't think anyone would look to find me here, of all places." The witch scientist sat on the edge of the bed. "This place is a lab experiment on its own."

I cringed, looking at the duvet cover and seeing the visible brown smears. I could just imagine all the *invisible* stains on there. "I have to agree with you on that." I pressed my hands on my hips to give the impression of importance and keep them from accidentally touching something. "Why didn't you come to the hotel? You would have been safe there."

Bellamy reached behind him and scratched his back. "I thought about it. But I had the feeling the hotel was compromised. They might know of our… understanding. I couldn't take the chance of showing up and being killed. I'm hunted, you know. The most wanted witch scientist in the city."

Oh boy. "The hotel is safe. Trust me. No one's been by looking for you there either. Besides, you'd have a floor packed with witches and paranormals to protect you."

Bellamy was shaking his head, his lips pressed into a tight line as he thought about it. "No. I think I'll stay here. I was fine until you showed up."

I narrowed my eyes, not appreciating his tone. "You can't stay here."

Bellamy looked up at me. "Why not? I have food and entertainment. No. I think I'll stay here for a while. Then, I've decided to move to Canada. They can't find me there."

"Sure they can."

Bellamy made a face. "Then I'll move to Australia."

I exhaled. "They'll find you there too. Don't you get it? Darius has a very long reach. A different continent means nothing to him. He'll find you, no matter what."

"You don't know that for sure."

I swore I was going to haul his ass with me by force. "Listen, if it was easy for me to find you, that means the ones looking for you are going to find you here too. It means they're probably on their way now. Do you want me to tell you what I *think* they'll do to you before they kill you? Think torture. Think slow death. They'll want you to reveal everything to them before they kill you. Trust me on that."

The witch scientist shifted on the bed, his face pale. "You think they'll torture me?" His voice had gone up an octave.

"Yes. They'll hurt you for a good long while. These are not good people, Bellamy. You don't want them to find you. You can't protect yourself. That's what you said to me in the church. You need me. So, I'm here to protect you."

"But I have to stay at the hotel?"

"Yes." I thought about it. "But if you really hate the idea of the Twilight Hotel, you could also stay with my friend Valen. You know, the giant that you almost killed? He owns the After Dark restaurant. I'll have to ask him first, but I don't think it should be a problem."

Bellamy's eyes were round as he jumped to his feet. "No." He shook his head. "Absolutely not. He'll want to kill me after what I did. He'll crush my cranium with his giant hands."

Here we go again. "He won't. He knows how important you are. Unlike you, he doesn't harm and kill people. He protects them."

A flash of anger crawled over the witch scientist's face. "That was done for the good of our people. In times of war, we must make difficult choices."

"The only war was in Adele's head," I told him, my voice rough, and I had to strain to keep my temper from going over the edge. I felt my starlight tingling, the sudden energy pressure in the room. Bellamy did this to me with his disconnect of feeling for the humans he killed by subjecting them to the HTO project. It still didn't seem to sink in that he'd taken lives. I didn't know if I could live with him to keep him safe. I might kill him myself.

He must have felt my starlight magic because he froze. The only thing that moved were his eyes that kept tracking my hands, as though he was worried I might toss a few starlights at him.

I tried again. "If you don't want to stay at the hotel, staying with Valen is another option. I won't force you." I didn't want him to bolt again. I had to make him trust me.

"And you trust him?"

"With my life. He'll protect you. I promise."

"Okay."

"Good." I looked around his room, eyeing a large carry-on bag. "Pack your things. We should go now."

Within five minutes, Bellamy had packed all his things. I

didn't offer to help. As I said, I didn't want to touch anything in here. We made our way out of the motel room.

Just as I closed the door, a shape jumped and ducked behind a parked car.

Bellamy leaped behind me, using my body as a shield. Yeah, such a strong man. "Who's that? They're here! They found me!"

"Shhh!" I pressed a hand on his shoulder and pushed him back. "That's not them." No. The shape was small and somewhat familiar.

My blood pounded in my ears as I moved over to the car, Bellamy following closely behind me like a shadow, and leaned over.

All the blood left my face. "Shay? What the hell are you doing here?"

My heart just about exploded as Shay stood from her hiding place. She was wearing her backpack over her new denim jacket. She shrugged and said, "I followed you."

"I can see that." I stared at her, taking a moment to look her over. Her green eyes were bright, eager… and happy to be with me? Was I reading her right?

"Who is that?" Bellamy stood on my side. "A street kid?"

"My sister."

"Your sister is a street kid?" The witch scientist looked over Shay like she might be something worthy of his next experiment.

"But…" I shook my head. "Did Elsa and the others let you leave?" I seriously doubted that. Maybe they'd left to do some of their "plan" to get rid of Oric and had left Shay alone? I had a hard time believing Elsa would leave my sister alone in a new place without an adult. She was a mother. Unless something had happened. Basil. Basil had found Shay out and had evicted us?

"I sneaked out when they thought I was sleeping," she answered like it was no big deal.

Damn. Elsa would have a heart attack if she realized Shay was missing. Why did I feel this wasn't the first time Shay had snuck out from somewhere? The way she'd said it told me she did this a lot.

"It's no big deal," said Shay, thinking I was somehow more worried about my friends' reactions to her missing than her being here.

This was not good at all. "You shouldn't have followed me. It's dangerous. What were you thinking!" I immediately regretted the pitch and anger of my voice when Shay cringed away from me. Shit. I wasn't good at this parenting, big-sister stuff, or whatever this was. I was going to mess it all up.

Bellamy let out a whimper. "This is hopeless. I'm going to be killed."

"Shay." I moved to be in front of her and lowered myself to her eye level. Then, keeping my anger and fear from my voice, I said, "Why did you follow me?"

Shay shrugged. "I thought I could help you find him."

Bellamy joined us. "Does she mean me? You have kids helping you? Are you crazy! I'm dead. I'm so dead. I should just stay here. Yes. That's what I'll do. I'm going back."

I snapped my fingers at Bellamy, and he froze. He probably thought I'd spelled him with my starlight magic. Good. Let him think that.

"I wanted to be useful." Shay's eyes glimmered, and I knew she was holding back tears.

Ah hell. I did not want to make my little sister cry. "Listen. I'm sorry I was mad. It's just I didn't expect to see you here. You surprised me. That's all. And it's dangerous out here. Really dangerous. If something had happened to you, I could never forgive myself. I promised your father that I'd keep you safe. You running around the city alone wasn't what he intended."

"Nothing happened. I'm fine." Shay's face was pleading, and I had the feeling she also came because she didn't want to feel abandoned.

I let out a long exhale. "Nothing happened now. But it could have."

"I can take care of myself." She set her face in determination, but I also saw a little anxiousness there.

"I know you can." I couldn't stay mad at Shay. She had such a sad, cute face, and I knew her whole world had shattered after her mother's death. She wanted to feel like she belonged somewhere again. I got that.

My throat was tight as I said, "Okay, then. You're pretty good at sneaking up on people. I'll give you that." By the way Shay smiled, I realized it was the wrong thing to say. "Let's go back to the hotel. But first, I'll text Elsa and tell her where you are before she has a heart attack." I looked at Shay and spied a tiny smile on her face as I yanked out my phone and began to text Elsa. When I was done, I stuffed my phone back in my pocket.

I noticed she seemed more comfortable around me now. She was more talkative and didn't hide her face under her hair as much. And she had decided to follow me in the hopes of helping find Bellamy. That had to mean she liked me somewhat. Or maybe she was just bored.

"It's too late," said Bellamy suddenly.

I glanced at him. "Too late for what?"

"They found me." The witch scientist pointed with a shaking finger at something down the street from us.

Suddenly, the hairs on the back of my neck rose at the fear in his voice, and I had the nasty feeling of being watched. I felt cold, like I'd just stepped inside a fridge as I whipped my head around.

From the darkness came a low laugh. My skin erupted in goose pimples, and three figures stepped forward from the shadows of the building. Dark witches, by the smell of sulfur and vinegar that wafted from them. And they were poised to attack.

Oh, swell.

CHAPTER 15

I thought tonight would have been an easy bag and tag—or rather bag and *drag*—and I'd be back at the hotel with a glass of wine, celebrating with my friends just how clever I was to find Bellamy, though I had help from Valen. We'd discuss how much closer I was to proving my innocence to the Gray Council.

I was wrong. I'd been wrong a lot lately.

"Get behind me." I hauled Shay behind me just as I pulled on my starlight. My body hummed with the power of the stars. "Tomorrow night, I'm going to teach you how to use your magic," I told her, never taking my eyes off the three witches. I knew Shay would most probably sneak out again. She wouldn't be facing witches, though. She'd be facing angels, and she needed to be ready.

Black hoods hid most of the witches' faces, but I could see that two were light-skinned, and the other was dark. Dressed all in black, they looked like spills of ink against the darkening sky. They didn't move, instead just stood there with cocky expressions, in their stupid-ass, black robes.

"That's it. I'm dead. I'm dead," squealed Bellamy, hopping from foot to foot like he needed to pee. What a tool.

"Shut up, Bellamy." A flicker of annoyance rose in me, but I quickly quashed it.

"Why did I listen to you? I'm the smart one. Not a *Merlin*." Bellamy looked over his shoulder, his wide eyes on the motel as he turned his body toward it.

Crap. "You go in there, and you're basically asking to be killed. It's a death trap. There's nowhere to run in there."

The witch scientist looked me over, thinking it through. "I don't want to die."

I stared at the witches across from us. "No one is dying tonight." Well, at least not us. "But I'm going to need your help," I told him.

He looked at me like I'd just ruined one of his experiments. "Me? What can I do? I told you I don't know how to fight." Now he really looked like he was about to bolt.

I was going to ask him to watch over Shay, but seeing him now and knowing what I already knew about him, he'd ditch her to save his own ass. Couldn't have that.

"If you won't fight them, get behind me." I had to protect him as well, just as I had to protect Shay. Damn. I should call Valen, but by the time he'd get here, it would be too late.

I'd have to fight them off. I'd been faced with worse odds before and survived. But I didn't have two people to guard at the same time.

I stole a look over my shoulder. Shay's face was pale, and her eyes had that deer-in-the-headlights look. She was terrified. Damn. Damn. Damn.

Speaking of said witches, they were still standing there, although I could see their lips moving.

"Why are they not moving?" asked Bellamy, pulling the words out of my head.

A spark of cold energy rolled our way. "They're getting ready to use their magic."

As if on cue, one of the Dark witches, the only one with ebony skin, fell to his knees and drew a circle and other symbols that were too far away for me to decipher.

"What's he doing?" questioned Bellamy, fear high in his tone.

"My guess?" I watched as the same witch stood with his arms up. "He's summoning a demon."

I heard Shay's sharp intake of breath, followed by Bellamy's squeal, and I had the crazy idea of tossing them in the motel, but I knew if I did that, I'd risk losing them both.

Instead, I pulled on my starlight, letting its energy thrum through me until it felt all-consuming. I rolled my shoulders, my hands splayed out at my sides near my waist. My fingers twitched, making me look like a cowboy ready to draw. Or was it a cowgirl?

Echoes of rich voices reached us, and the distant sound of a mocking laugh carried on the wind, along with the aroma of rotten meat, feet, and the worst dog breath ever with an underlying hint of rotten eggs.

I felt a sudden pop of displaced air, and a creature, like I'd never seen before, was in the middle of the chalk-drawn circle. It had the hairless, muscular body of a human but with a squid-like head, tentacles with suction cups on the ends, and a mouth filled with sharklike teeth. Its shoulders were hunched and powerful, and abnormally long arms grazed the ground with clawed hands.

"It's an ugly bastard," I said out loud.

It was a lesser demon. They didn't have much more intelligence than your average dog, driven by the hunger for blood and mortal life. Still, it would kill you if you didn't know what you were doing.

The few humans who walked the streets or passed us by in the cars couldn't see the demon. They'd just notice a drop in temperature and maybe even a feeling of emptiness and sorrow. Just as well. No one wanted to see a demon, especially not a lesser one like this.

"Leana."

I turned to the sound of Shay's voice. I didn't think I'd ever heard her say my name yet. The depth of the emotion in her tone had my gut twisting in a knot.

"Don't worry. I've got this," I said. My heart seemed to clench at the concern flashing behind her eyes. "I've fought demons before. I'll be fine. I can handle it."

Bellamy looked up at me, his eyes narrowed. "What are you going to do?"

His pointing out that he wasn't going to do squat wasn't lost on me. "Fight. And then save your ass." I took a breath, enjoying the excitement and adrenaline pumping through my body and making me quiver.

Just as I turned my attention back on the demon, it came at us.

We didn't have time to run for cover. We didn't have time to do anything but fight and pray for our souls that my starlight magic would survive this attack from one of hell's children. The sky was cloudy. And we all knew what happened to my magic when the night sky wasn't clear.

"Stay behind the car." I pushed Shay and Bellamy back and planted my feet. "If anything wrong should happen..."

"What do you mean by *wrong*?" asked the witch scientist.

"If things don't go as planned."

"Still not following."

"If the demon kills me, I need you to take Shay back to the Twilight Hotel. Can you do that?"

Bellamy looked at Shay as though she'd grown a third eye. "If I must."

"You *must*." Damn, I hated that witch sometimes. A part of me wanted to leave Bellamy with the demon and take Shay to the hotel with me.

"I'm not leaving you," said Shay, her tone full of determination.

"If I'm dead, you'll have to. You go to the hotel and find Elsa." I knew in my heart that should anything happen to me, my friends would look after Shay like she was their own. It was the only consolation I had at the moment. I couldn't rely on

Bellamy. I could trust him as far as I could throw him—maybe an inch.

With my heart hammering, I took a deep breath, tapped into my core, and reached out to the magical energy generated by the power of the stars.

Bright light exploded into existence as my magic mixed with my fear for Shay and my hatred for demons. And let's not forget my hatred for Darius. He was the cause of all of this, and he had to be stopped.

But one thing at a time.

My starlight flooded my will and poured into my body. In a blast, the starlight magic raced all around and through me like a pounding high-voltage conductor until it consumed me.

The squid demon—I didn't know what else to call it—rushed me with its long limbs. Its tentacles lashed out, stretching until they were so close I could smell the scent of sewer.

Starlight magic blasted out of me. The burst hit the squid demon, and it was thrown back, landing somewhere behind another parked car.

I straightened but stayed alert. I wasn't fool enough to think that was the end of the demon.

Tentacles appeared from behind the car, and then the demon leaped over it like it was nothing. It landed about twenty feet from me and wailed as it shot at me again, yellow spit dripping from its mouth. My eyes burned at the stench of rot and sulfur.

Yup. I was right. It couldn't be that easy.

Focusing, I pulled on my starlight, letting the power of the stars rush me. A dazzling ball of light appeared on my palm. I flicked my wrist sideways, and a blade of light, like a glowing sword, flew from my outstretched hand.

The starlight blade sliced through the creature, right below what I thought was its rib cage. The demon never stopped advancing until its upper body slipped off its lower body and fell into the street, twitching. I shot it again just for good measure. Its severed body went up in tall, white flames, leaving only a pile of ash when the fire went out.

I pulled my head around and caught sight of a group of humans walking by, snapping pictures of me while giving me looks that suggested I belonged in the psych ward. Of course, it would appear that I was fighting an imaginary foe since humans couldn't see the paranormal.

I waved at them, smiled for a pic, and watched them scurry off, scared the crazy lady might turn on them.

I took a moment to glance over at Shay. She was staring at me wide-eyed. I saw some fear there, but I could see admiration, envy, and excitement—the possibility that one day, she could do this with her own magic.

When I cast my gaze back at the three Dark witches, a different one was on his knees this time, drawing out symbols around his summoning circle.

We heard a clap like thunder, and another demon stood in that circle—a much bigger one this time.

The impossible creature of nightmares had thick leather hide, fur, claws, and fangs. A cluster of red eyes was set dead center in the front of its flat skull. It looked like a cross between a giant rat, an alligator, and a scorpion. Its tail ended in a thick talon that whipped threateningly from side to side.

"There's another one," Bellamy cried.

"I know that. I can see it."

My heart thrashed against my chest as demonic energies flooded around us. The Dark witch called out something in a language I couldn't catch. But I did get his meaning.

The demon turned its ugly head, all eyes on me. And then it spun around and leaped my way faster than I thought possible.

Shit. I yanked on my starlight, waiting for the feel of power rushing through my body, but felt nothing.

I stared at the sky. A massive dark-gray cloud covered it.

Double shit.

I glanced back down. With a blur, something hard that smelled strongly of feces crashed into me.

The demon collided with me, and I screamed. No, that was Bellamy.

We hit the ground together. The creature snarled and snapped. I gasped as its weight crushed my lungs, my breath escaping me. I kicked out with my legs, my boots connecting with its gut, and the demon went sprawling backward. I jumped to my feet just as it barreled at me again in a flash of claws and teeth.

These were the times I wished my starlight magic wasn't so limited or that I could somehow call upon elemental magic, anything as a backup. But that's not what life gave me.

I ducked, spun around, and managed to escape its tail as it swung it at me like a giant hammer.

"You don't play fair. Do you?" I hissed, glancing up at the sky and hoping to see a twinkle of stars in the night sky. Nope. Just a big ugly sheet of dark clouds.

The demon stilled and lifted its head in the air as though it were smelling something. Then it slowly turned in the direction of the parked car Shay was hiding behind. Its eyes gleamed with hunger as it focused on her.

And then it charged.

"No! Here! Here!" Panic spiked through my veins as I met Shay's terrified eyes. No way she could fight off a demon of that size. She was just a kid.

"Get away from her!" My legs were moving before I even knew what I was doing. I might not have my starlight magic, but I still had my body weight and a few lessons of one-on-one combat.

I hit the demon in the side with a football-style tackle, and we both hit the ground. Heart pounding, I knew I had to fight it with my physical body, which wasn't really trained for that kind of thing. But the thought that this demon could hurt, possibly kill my little sister, the only family I had, sent me into a frenzied rage.

I pushed off enough to get a view and a good inhale of its putrid stench, and then I jabbed my fingers into its eyes as hard as

I could. I winced as it was even more disgusting than I had imagined, but it was the only move I had.

Its warm blood splattered my face and hand as I stumbled away. I pushed to my feet and heard an angry, clicking growl as the demon staggered to its feet, clawing at its eyes. Did I blind it? No idea, but I was pretty sure it couldn't see clearly anymore. And I had drawn it away from Shay.

But I didn't account for its sense of smell.

Before I could move, the demon threw itself in my direction. A clawed hand hit me in the face, and my nose and left cheek exploded in pain. Stars swarmed in my eyes for a second as warm wetness trickled from my nose.

Okay, ouch.

"Behind you!" shouted Bellamy.

I spun a little too fast and wavered on the spot.

Sharp, wet teeth reached over me, snapping viciously at my face. I kicked and made contact with one of its legs as it stumbled back. I drove my fists up, not sure what I was going to do with them, but I figured that's what I was supposed to do.

Teeth sank into the flesh of my extended left arm. I cried out as fire burned my skin where the demon's fangs had punctured it. I made a fist with my other hand and punched it in the head, but it didn't let go. I punched it again, and again, and again, but still the beast didn't let loose.

I heard a scream. Shay.

A sliver of fear ran up my spine, but I also felt anger and an overwhelming sense of protection. Or maybe my fierce maternal instinct was kicking into high gear. Call it what you will, but all that mattered was keeping Shay safe.

With my free arm, I reached out and stabbed—with my fingers again—into its multiple eyes in quick succession. The creature let go. It hissed at me and faltered back.

A spark of light flickered from above. I glanced up, seeing the large chunk of a clear sky, and jumped into action.

I pulled on my starlight as much as I could and let it rip.

A shoot of white light fired at the demon and hit it in the chest.

The creature burst into flames. It made a horrible scream as it thrashed around the street, its mouth open wide and teeth snapping as flames consumed it. Its howl made my skin crawl. Hunched over, it staggered toward me, still on fire, and I backed up.

The demon burst into a cloud of gray ash. I didn't even wait for the demon ash to settle as I stepped through the falling dust.

"There's another one!" howled Bellamy. He was great at pointing things out, just not great at actually helping.

My eyes moved to where Bellamy was pointing. Sure enough, another demon came barreling my way, some hairless bear with spikes along its back, but I'd had enough.

Without hesitating, I reached inside to my starlight, unleashing my will as I thrust my hands at the bear demon. The white globe exploded into the creature, lighting it up like a flailing Christmas tree. The creature staggered and collapsed, bursting on impact into a cloud of ash. I gagged at the smell of burning, rotting flesh.

"Come on, you bastards. Come on!"

Panting, I held on to my starlight, letting it hum through me. I looked around, ready to blow me some more demons into ashes, but no more demons were ready to eat me.

And when I searched the spot where I'd last seen the Dark witches, they were gone too.

CHAPTER 16

I sat at my dining table, my hands clasped around a cup of coffee. It was my fourth cup since this morning. It was half past one in the afternoon, and the caffeine still didn't seem to want to kick in. Maybe it already had, and I was just too wired from last night to feel it.

"Oh, my." Elsa dropped her head to inspect me better. "You look dreadful."

"I feel worse." The draining of the starlight power the morning after was there, as it always was, like a bad hangover. But it was more than that. I wasn't used to the emotional drainage, the overwhelming feeling of possibly losing Shay. I wasn't used to that. That fear, that panic. Would she have made it back to the hotel if something had happened to me? Would Bellamy have bolted? Probably. And she would have been on her own.

Elsa took a sip of her coffee, set the mug down, and looked at me again. "Did you recognize the witches who set those demons on you? Can't believe they'd do such a thing to another witch. But there you have it. Our world has gone mad."

I shook my head. "No. I also asked Bellamy before I sent him off to Valen's, but he didn't recognize them." After the demons had been vanquished, and the Dark witches were gone, I'd dragged Bellamy back with Shay and me to the hotel. Once he started whining at the possibility that those who wanted him dead, mainly Darius, were friends of the Twilight Hotel, I hauled him next door to Valen's.

When Valen opened his door, I'd given him my best smile. "I'll owe you big, but could you look after this one for a while? He doesn't want to stay at the hotel."

Valen had crossed his arms over his ample chest, glaring at Bellamy. "I remember you. You came by the restaurant. You're Bellamy, the witch scientist."

Bellamy had smiled proudly, thinking that his reputation preceded him. "That's right. And you are?"

"Your new babysitter." I hauled him inside and pushed him into a chair. "Valen here knows exactly who you are and what you did. So I'd keep quiet if I were you." I looked over at the giant, who was smiling at Shay and saying something to her that made her grin. "Keep your eyes on him. He likes to disappear."

"I was running for my life. There's a difference," said the witch scientist, admiring Valen's apartment. "How much does a place like this cost? What's the square footage?"

I looked at Valen's face, seeing the flicker of irritation there. "Okay. I'll owe you really, really big."

At that, the giant's face spread into a smile. "How big, exactly?"

I could tell by the desire in his eyes just how big I'd owe him for this. I didn't mind one bit. "We'll talk about that later, but can he stay with you?"

Valen nodded. "Sure. I'll keep an eye on him. Don't worry."

Bellamy seemed to shrink in his chair at that.

I let out a breath. "Great. Thanks. Come on, Shay. I think we need to revive Elsa."

I was grateful Valen had agreed to have Bellamy stay with him. Now that Shay was staying with me, I didn't exactly have room for the witch scientist. The couch would have been his new bed if Valen had refused. It would have been crowded, but we'd have managed if it meant a chance at clearing my name.

"And you believe they were working for this Darius character?" asked Elsa.

I took a gulp of coffee, waited for the caffeine to hit, got nothing, and said, "Yeah. They want Bellamy dead. If I hadn't found him when I did, they would have killed him."

Elsa made a sound of agreement in her throat. "And then you would have lost your key witness."

I downed the last of my coffee. "I have to teach Shay how to use her powers. I keep thinking that if something had gone wrong, she would have been left alone with Bellamy, which means alone. Those Dark witches would have killed her. It was close." Tension ran through my body at the memory of Shay's frightened face. "She needs to learn how to fight. How to protect herself."

"I think that's wise," said Elsa. "She's at a good age too. Not too old to be already set in her ways and not too young to lack control. When will you start?" Elsa looked over my face, curious.

"Right away. We start tonight. It'll be a clear sky. I checked."

"Good." Elsa tapped her fingers on her mug. "It'll be good for you and for Shay."

"What do you mean?"

"Time for the two of you to bond. What better way than with your similar magic."

I hadn't thought of that. My eyes flicked to Shay's room. Her door was closed, and I knew she was in there playing her games on her tablet. The idea that she had somewhat settled into her new life had a bit of the stress loosening from around my shoulders.

"Shay seems to love her new room. You guys were amazing, decorating it."

"Thank you." Elsa clutched at her vintage locket around her neck. "I nearly had a heart attack after I got your text last night.

When I went to check her room and saw that she wasn't there... goddess, help me. I nearly died."

I smiled. "I figured."

"Dylan used to sneak out of the house, too, when he was fifteen," said Elsa, smiling at the distant memory. "But he was all long and gangly, always made so much noise trying to climb out the window. I heard him every time. I let him, of course, because I knew. But her? I never heard a peep. Sneaky little bugger."

I laughed. "Very sneaky."

"I can't believe she followed you. What was she thinking?"

A tiny stab went through my gut. "She wanted to help me find Bellamy."

"Well, her heart's in the right place, but you'll need to work on her thinking. She's too young to be roaming around in the city at night. Especially if angels are hunting her." Elsa stood and set her empty coffee mug into the sink. "At least you have Bellamy now. Valen will keep an eye on him; you just watch."

That made me laugh. "I know."

"What about that second location for the jewel?"

"I'll go after my training session with Shay." I had a feeling not only would this training help her life if an angel happened upon her, but it would also build her self-confidence, which I could see she lacked. And through no fault of her own. Having suffered what she'd suffered and being thrown into a new environment would do that to a young girl. It was inevitable.

"You think you can keep an eye on her again? Tonight?" She'd promised she wouldn't sneak out again, but I had a feeling she would do it the first chance she got. She still didn't understand how dangerous it was for her. It was up to me to keep her safe.

Elsa placed her palms on the counter, a determined look in her eye. "I'll watch her like a hawk this time. She fooled me once, and that was the one and last time."

I laughed. "I believe you. Where are Jade and Julian? I haven't seen them since last night."

Elsa washed her hands in the kitchen sink and dried them on a dish towel. When she looked up at me, she had a cunning grin on her lips. "Well, they've been—"

"Leana! Oh, good. There you are."

Basil came marching into my apartment, his face blotchy and twisted in unease. A butterfly net hung in his hand. "You need to come downstairs with me right now."

I raised a brow. "I do?" My eyes went straight to Shay's door. Damn. I hadn't discussed my new roommate with Basil yet. But Jimmy knew, so hopefully Basil wouldn't kick us out for now.

Basil stood with one hand on his hip while the other pointed at the interior of my apartment, looking around. Then his eyes settled on me. "You're still staying in this lovely apartment, when *technically* it belongs to Oric, the new Merlin. So you've got no choice but to help."

I glanced at Elsa, who looked just as annoyed at his choice of words as I was. "Help you with what, exactly? And why are you holding a net?"

"Come. Come. Quickly," called Basil over his shoulder as he marched right back out of my apartment.

I stood up. "Elsa. Can you…" My eyes went to Shay's room.

"I'll watch her," answered the older witch. "You go see what he wants."

"Thanks." I ran after the little witch and met him in the waiting elevator. "What do you need from me?" I asked him as the elevator started its descent.

"The hotel's reputation is at risk." Basil threw his hands in the air, a bit overdramatically, which reminded me of Bellamy. "After all my hard work at mending the hotel's status in the community, it's once again in danger. It's a catastrophe! I thought you had taken care of our"—he lowered his voice—"demon problem."

"I did. There're no demons in the hotel." Unless Julian and Jade had summoned a demon, which I doubted they would or could in the middle of the day. I didn't see how a demon could be in the hotel. Especially with the strong wards. There were no Rifts. I was certain of that.

"You're wrong. Something is driving the guests away. Something evil is still here. It's everywhere. On every floor. It feels like a direct attack on me."

"Why can't Oric take care of whatever this is? Isn't he your new Merlin?"

Basil shook his head. His lips pressed tightly together, seeming almost white.

"Basil?"

I heard the screams before the doors of the elevator swished open. The lobby was a war zone.

Hundreds of tiny humans the size of apples flapped multicolored wings that looked like they belonged on butterflies as they darted through the lobby, leaving trails of glimmering dust in their wake as though it were raining glitter.

"You got pixies?" I said as I stepped out of the elevator.

Pixies dived and flew around the lobby like a mob of giant, angry wasps. The hum of wings reached me, and I ducked as a throng of pixies flew at me, their tiny, clawed hands going for my eyes.

Technically, these miniature paranormals weren't dangerous unless you pissed them off by hurting one of their own or stealing from them, which was what it looked like.

A group of pixies had a male shifter pinned against the far wall next to one of the lobby sofas. His eyes widened as he swatted at them, but the pixies were too fast and zoomed in, scratching his face, his arms, and anywhere his skin was visible.

"Get away! Get away!" Errol ducked behind the front counter, his arms flailing above his head, trying to swat the two pixies diving at his head, with tiny blades in their hands.

A couple was hiding behind one of the lobby's chairs to my right, their faces cut and bleeding from multiple wounds.

I spotted Oric. He stood with his feet planted in a defensive stance as he thrust balls of purple energy at the pixies but kept missing. And he kept making holes in the hotel walls. Oh dear.

When I spied Julian leaning against the far wall with his arms crossed over his chest, and a satisfied look on his face, I knew this was another one of his master plans to get rid of Oric. I couldn't see Jade anywhere, but I had a feeling she wasn't very far.

"Here." Basil thrust the butterfly net at me. "You take care of this."

I frowned at him, giving me an order like I still worked for him. Of course, I could have told him no, but I had Shay to think about. "Okay, on one condition."

Basil looked at me like I'd spoken to him in a foreign language. "What? What do you want? Money?" He thrust the net at me again, but I wouldn't take it.

Pixies charged, exploding in clouds of orange, blue, red, and pink sparkles as they dived around the lobby, their eyes wide with manic glee. They were enjoying themselves.

A male guest howled as he swung what looked like one of the hotel's towels at a pixie, missed, and nearly tripped over his own legs. The pixie—I couldn't tell male from female at the speed they were zipping around—rose and shot toward the guest in a cloud of red sparkles and glinting knives.

Basil's eyes rounded. "Don't just stand there! *Do* something!" he wailed and swatted at a pixie. "They're attacking the guests. They're ruining my reputation!"

"I have a sister," I began, enjoying the show of the pixie war.

"Who cares!" Basil thrust the net once again at me.

"I want her to stay with me in my spare room. I want her to live with me, and I want you to agree. Deal?"

"Yes. Yes. Here. Take it." Basil shoved the net at me, and this time I took it. Though I doubted it would help.

"Great. Thanks." I moved away from Basil and made my way to the middle of the lobby. I wasn't sure what I could do to stop the pixie madness, but I was hoping I was right about this. I looked over at Julian, and he gave a single nod of his head.

Okay. I was going with my gut now. I ducked as a pixie dive-bombed my head. I straightened and then raised my hands, mumbling gibberish under my breath. Basil knew I was a

Starlight witch, but he didn't know that my magic was limited during the day. Not many people knew this, so I was going to use his ignorance.

I cast my gaze around while I was still mumbling and waving my hands for show, and I saw Julian talking to a male pixie dressed in green clothes, on his shoulder. The pixie took off and made a few spins around the lobby, his fist in the air, like he was giving some sort of signal. And then, one by one, the pixies gathered in a flock and flew out the lobby's front doors, which Jade so happened to be holding open at the moment.

She grinned at me when I met her eyes. I had to bite the inside of my cheek to keep from laughing. This was too good. At this rate, Oric would be fired at the end of the week. Or so I hoped.

"Thank the goddess." Basil came strolling through the lobby and went straight to Oric. "Thank you, Oric. You did well."

"Thank you, Oric?" I hissed loudly enough to have him and Basil look my way. Oric looked angrily at me, and if I didn't know any better, I would say he knew he'd just been played.

Basil had the nerve to look a little embarrassed, and then he dismissed me as he raised his hands and addressed the remaining guests.

"It's over. The pixies are gone. Just one of those mishaps." He laughed like it was no big deal. "Free lunch will be served in the dining room for all the guests."

"The little shit," I said. Part of me wanted to go over to Julian and have him call back his pixies.

"A big shit," said Jade as she joined me. "Don't worry. There's plenty more where that came from."

But I was worried. I'd just told Basil about my sister. And if he was this loyal, I feared it wouldn't be good for me. Or Shay.

But that's not what had my intake of breath and the sudden prickling of ice roll up my back.

It was the silver-haired witch who just stepped into the hotel.

Darius was in the lobby.

Oh, crap.

CHAPTER 17

The Dark witch sauntered into the hotel like he owned it. Maybe he did. He carried himself with a sort of sophisticated intellect. His expression was carefully blank, which I knew was as dark and empty as a crooked politician's heart.

He wore a similar three-piece suit of dark-gray cloth that fit him in all the right places, like he had a tailor on call. His long, silver hair gleamed under the lobby lights. Okay, so he had good hair. He was still an asshole.

"Who's that?" whispered Jade, staring wide-eyed at the Gray Council member.

"That's Darius," I mumbled. A crazy part of me wanted to reach out and pull his silver ponytail. I noticed Julian push off the wall and slowly come to join Jade and me.

"That's Darius," Jade whispered to Julian.

Julian nodded. "That's what I thought. What the hell is he doing here?"

Good question. He definitely wasn't here to stay in one of the guest rooms. No. He was here for me.

Two brutish-looking males walked behind him—one I recognized as my jailor, Ben, but the other I'd never seen before. Darius flicked his gray eyes lazily over to me. I didn't know what I saw on his face. Anger? Contempt? Happiness? Who knew? I just didn't like it.

"Darius. What a surprise," said Basil, his voice high and sounding like a frightened mouse. He shuffled forward and met the Gray Council member, looking like his legs were made of metal rods, his skin pale and pasty, like he was about to throw up. He seemed to know exactly who Darius was. "Is this a yearly checkup?" He laughed nervously, sounding like he had the hiccups. "You'll find that the hotel is in tip-top shape. The guests are loving their stay at the Twilight Hotel."

I snorted. Some of the guests were still cowering behind the lobby furniture. But Darius didn't seem to care.

"I'm not here on hotel business," said the Gray Council member. "I'm here to speak to Leana."

At that, I saw Basil visibly relax. Hell, he looked absolutely elated at the prospect that they were here for me and not for him. It was hard *not* to hate him at this moment.

"Yes, of course. There she is." Basil pointed in my direction. And when he found me watching him, his eyes rounded, and he flapped his hands like a seal performing at a SeaWorld, gesturing for me to join them.

Julian leaned in. "You want me to call my pixie pals back? Just say the word."

I shook my head. "No. It's fine. But if something should happen to me..."

"What do you mean?" Fear flashed across Jade's face.

"Promise you'll look after Shay. She has nobody else."

"That's not going to happen," said Julian, shaking his head. "But yes. You know we'll look after her. She'll always have us."

It was the only thing, the only comfort, that allowed my legs to move forward. My pulse throbbed as I joined Darius and Basil.

"Ah. Here she is," said Basil. He grinned at me like we were old pals and clasped his shaking hands together.

"Hello, again, Leana." Darius's features pulled into a smile, but his voice held no warmth. It was all business.

I looked at Ben and then glanced at the other one with the mustache, who I was going to call… Mustache. Why not? And then I flicked my gaze back to the Gray Council member.

"Darius. What are you doing here?" My heart pounded as my stress levels hit a high. I knew why he was here. It was one of two things. The first was to know about my progress on the Jewel of the Sun. The other was that he'd already found it and was here to take me back to jail. Forever.

Darius dipped his head. "Can we talk somewhere in private?"

"Absolutely." Basil grabbed my arm. "Leana. You can use my office. You know the way."

Know the way? I practically had sex on your desk.

"Excellent," said Darius. Again, he had a smile, but his voice was cold. I could detect a little urgency in it, too, like he was only here on hasty business—his and my business.

Without a word, I turned on my heel and marched toward Basil's office. I pushed in, looking at the desk. My face flushed as I remembered the *bodily* event that had almost happened. I moved to the left side of the office, all the way to the wall, putting as much distance as I could between Darius and me.

The silver-haired Dark witch stepped in and closed the door just before I caught a glimpse of Ben and Mustache flanking both sides of the door like bouncers, probably to keep anyone from disturbing us.

I crossed my arms over my chest to give the impression that I wasn't afraid of him, instead of what he could do to me. Because we both knew he could do plenty. He could change my life on a whim. I hated that my hands were shaking, so I stuffed them under my armpits.

"You here to throw my ass back in jail?" I'd only just gotten Bellamy back. I hadn't had a chance to finish the case I was working on, the case on Darius that I was preparing to send to all members of the Gray Council, with copies to every head of the paranormals in the city.

A cold, collected smile spread over Darius's lips. He moved

over and inspected Basil's desk. He dragged a finger along the top and then brushed what I could only assume was dust from his fingers.

"Not yet." The silver-haired witch turned and met my eyes. "Though I am disappointed in your progress."

My guts tightened. "I've checked the church. It's not there, by the way." I wasn't sure if he already knew that or not. "I'm going to the convent tonight. Maybe I'll find it. It's not like I haven't been looking. I have. And you haven't exactly given me much to go on. I don't even know what the damn jewel looks like. It would help if I knew what the hell I was looking for."

Anger sparked in the Dark witch's eyes. "You should have found it by now. The fact that you haven't suggests that you're not taking this seriously. It tells me that you think this is a joke. Trust me, Leana. I don't play games."

Maybe not this kind. "I believe you. And I'm not playing games either. I've only got one speed," I told him, my head dizzy with how fast my heart thrashed. "There've been some complications. Nothing I can't handle. I'm working on it."

"With the witch scientist, I presume?" Darius's face was tight with repressed anger. Waves of his magic pulsed around the room. He was pissed. I had messed up his plans of killing Bellamy. Oopsie.

"Maybe." No need to lie. But he didn't need to know the reason why I saved Bellamy either.

Darius observed me, and I couldn't help but feel a shiver roll up my spine at the intensity of his gaze. "I'm curious. Why are you so interested in him? I would have thought you'd want him… *taken care of* after what he and Adele had put you through."

I liked how he pretended like he wasn't the one giving orders to Adele on her HTO project. Guess that's how he was going to play it.

Because I need him to put your bony ass in jail. "He kind of grows on you after a while. Like a fungus."

Darius made a sound of disappointment in his throat. "He's

weak. The weak have no place among the strong. They only drag the rest of us down."

"Well, he asked for help. I'm a Merlin. It's what I do. Help those in need." Not exactly, but I was just blabbing over here.

"My understanding is that Merlins are more like investigators. They seek out the truth, pursue dangerous criminals and monsters. Right? When did Merlins become sad little nannies?"

I shrugged. "Sometimes a job grows and becomes something else. Like taking care of the hotel. It's not just one task. It's a multitude of tasks, but they all relate to the hotel's well-being."

Darius gave a soft laugh. "You don't work for the hotel anymore. You only work for me."

"Right," I said as I tried to calm my rising panic. "I am." I didn't have to ask how he knew this. The witch was resourceful.

"You're too slow. You need to work faster." The threat in his voice made my insides tighten. Darius walked around the desk, stared at the chair like he was thinking of sitting down, but then moved away as he thought better of it. He stood behind it instead, his hands on the backrest. "Is it your age? Are you finding yourself tired? Too old to do this job? You're at that breaking point when things start to sag, when your eyesight starts to go, when your beauty starts to fade."

I narrowed my eyes at the humor in his tone. "I'm not old. I feel fine. Better than I have in years." Ain't that the truth. Goodbye, Martin. And hello, Valen! "If you think I'm so old and useless, why did you bother to send me on this job? Why not send Ben and Mustache?" Darius frowned, and I continued. "Because you need me. You need me to find this jewel, because if I had to guess, you've tried before and you've failed. And I'll throw in another guess: I'm your last resort. You've got no one else."

Darius clapped his hands. "Very good, Leana. I knew I chose well when I selected you for the job."

I shook my head. "Whatever." The witch was creepy, and Basil's office suddenly didn't have the same exciting feelings as it once did. It felt like a prison. Like my dingy cell. And I couldn't wait to get out.

The Dark witch's gaze traveled over me, and I didn't like how *slow* it was before he reached my eyes again. It made me remember the conversation we had the first time we met in my cell, when he told me if he wanted to have sex with me, it would be by force.

"I'll give you two more days to find the jewel," said Darius. "And if you don't, well, you know what will happen to you."

"Trust me, I know."

Shit. I didn't like the position he was putting me in. But it made me realize that, for whatever reason, he needed me to find the jewel. It seemed he was on a time crunch.

That information would help me. I just didn't know how yet.

I didn't have to tell him that I never wanted to see the inside of my cell ever again because it was obvious he already knew.

"I'm going to find it. I swear it. But two days is a bit tight," I said, thankful my voice was steady. "I need more time."

"Two days," repeated Darius. "If you can't retrieve the jewel in two days, I'll have no further use of you."

A heavy weight pressed into my chest, and I swallowed. Two days wasn't much. But I had to do it. Otherwise, I'd be thrown back into that cell a second time, and Shay would be on her own. Well, not anymore. She'd have the thirteenth-floor gang. Yet I had the nasty feeling Darius wouldn't live up to his end of the bargain. Nope. I'd be next if he was hunting Bellamy to get rid of all the evidence. I was sure of it. I'd never see the inside of that cell because he'd kill me.

"I'll need your guys to back off from Bellamy," I said. "I can't be thinking about him when I need to be looking for your jewel."

"Done." Darius smiled. He didn't even try to pretend he wasn't hunting the witch scientist.

He seemed to be in a lighter mood. I was going to use that. "Can you tell me what it does? If I knew that, it would help. I'd know what to look for."

"I've already told you," said the Dark witch, an edge to his tone. "You're all it takes to find the Jewel of the Sun. Nothing else. And you will find it. Don't make me start killing off your friends, because I will. If it'll mean you'll work faster."

When I glared at him, his gray eyes were as ruthless as the churning of a winter storm.

Bastard. "I'll find it." Even if I did, and I would, I knew Darius would never let me live after that. Not after seeing him like this. Not after what he was doing to Bellamy. I needed a better plan.

"Very good. I have faith in your abilities." Darius moved away from the chair and went around the desk. He adjusted the cuffs from his sleeves. "Remember, Leana. Two days."

I clenched my jaw, trying to quell the rising dread in my belly. "I heard you the first time."

When Darius reached the door, he turned back around and said, "Ticktock." And then he closed the office door behind him.

CHAPTER 18

"Again."

I stood on the roof of the Twilight Hotel under a clear night sky. Julian, Jade, and Elsa sat in folding chairs, watching, waiting for an eleven-year-old to come into her power. But so far, Shay hadn't shown us a drop of magic. And we'd been at it for about half an hour.

Shay shrugged. "I'm not sure what I'm supposed to do."

"Okay." I planted my feet next to her. "Maybe I'm going too fast."

"You are," agreed Elsa. She aimed a finger at me. "Baby steps, Leana."

I made a face at the older witch and turned my attention back to Shay. "See, with starlight magic like ours, it doesn't come from this place, this earth, so we have to reach out and grab it. From way up there." I pointed to the sky, like she didn't already know that. "Somewhere, a constellation of stars will answer to you and only you. That's *your* source of power."

Shay's green eyes were dark under the night sky. "Do you have more than one star?"

I smiled at her curious mind. "I do. Three stars. A triple-star system called Alpha Centauri."

Shay blinked up into the sky. "Do you think those will be my stars too?"

I shrugged. "No. But you'll feel it when you're ready. The stars will tell you."

"How?"

"They'll show themselves to you, in a way, I guess." Not sure those were the right words. God, I was bad at this.

"How?"

I exhaled. "It's hard to explain. But you'll feel a connection to those stars. A sort of tug in your belly. Like a bond. A really strong bond. Once you know which stars are your stars, where your starlight magic comes from, you can easily draw on your powers."

"Okay." Shay didn't look convinced, or maybe this was too much information for her so soon.

"One thing you have to remember that's really important," I said, trying to read her face to see if all this information was sinking in or going over her head.

Shay pursed her lips. "Like what?"

"Well, you have to remember that our magic is different from other witches." At her frown, I added, "Not that it's bad or anything. Just different."

"Nothing wrong with different," Elsa called out. "It just means you're special."

"Yeah," snorted Jade, tapping her rows of multicolored plastic bracelets around her wrists. "We're all *very* special."

A spark lit in Shay's eyes at Elsa's comment. Good. I needed her to feel special. It would help draw her power. Give her a slip of that confidence she lacked. Conviction was a big part of drawing magic from whatever source.

"Our magic is different," I continued. "We can't call upon the magic of the elements. We can't summon fire or wind like Elsa and Jade. We can't summon demons either—not that you should. See where I'm going with this?"

Shay gave a one-shoulder shrug.

"Yeah, all those things sound cool, but our magic is pretty cool too. It's unique. Rare. And sometimes things that are rare have their own set of challenges."

"Tell me about it." Julian took a sip of his beer. "She doesn't even know I exist."

I shook my head, knowing he was referencing the twins' mother, Cassandra. Not going there.

I clenched my jaw and tried again. "The thing is, our magic is restricted during the day. Our magic is strongest at night when the stars shine. See, even if the sun is technically a star, it's a bully star."

"I hate bullies." Shay stared at me, a tiny frown on her cute face.

"Me too. And this big boy blocks us from drawing our power from the stars during the day. You can still feel the stars' power during the day, but drawing on their energies will be hard. Most of the time, it doesn't work. And sometimes, when it's cloudy at night, our magic can be… flawed. It doesn't always work." Wow. That sounded lame.

Shay's face went from curious to dejected in a flash. "So, our magic sucks."

Jade choked on her wine. Yes, she and Elsa were sharing a bottle.

It did suck sometimes when you needed your magic to save your ass, but you couldn't reach it. I wasn't about to tell her that, though. She had to believe in her magic first, and then I'd let the ball drop.

"Our magic doesn't suck. Let me show you."

I took a breath, stared up into the night sky, peppered with dazzling stars, and reached out to my three stars, calling to their magical energy. I felt a tug on my aura as it answered.

Power pounded through me. I raised my palm, and a dazzling sphere of light, like a snow globe, floated above my hand.

Shay leaned in closer, her face illuminated by my starlight. "Cool."

I smiled. "Watch this." And then I blew on my palm.

The globe rose in the air, hanging just above our heads, and then with a pop, it burst into thousands of tiny stars of light. I moved my hand to the right. The miniature stars moved along with me, traces of glowing particles in their wake. Then I slid my hand to the left, and again the tiny stars followed.

"Those are my starlights," I told her. "They're like an extension of me, in a way. I feel what they feel," I said, realizing that probably didn't make any sense to her. "I can reach out with my senses to them, and they can tell me if danger is lurking."

"They report back to you?" Shay was staring at the starlights like she wanted to go grab them.

"Exactly." I looked over at my friends, sitting in their chairs, their eyes tracking my starlights as though they were all mesmerized by them. Guess you didn't see that kind of magic often.

"They're like your friends." The emotion in Shay's voice was like a physical pang in my chest. She was still staring at my starlights with longing, like if she had some of her own, she wouldn't feel so alone.

"Yes, you're right," said Elsa, and sadness flashed in her eyes when I looked over at her. Jade's eyes were bright as well, and Julian stared at the ground, looking uncomfortable.

"Shay. Didn't your mother tell you all of this?"

"No," said the young girl, her gaze on the starlights. "We never talked about it."

"Why? Why didn't she prepare you?" A witch with a child had the responsibility to teach and inform their child with their own magic. Letting witchlings fend for themselves was dangerous. Reckless. And I couldn't understand why her mother never taught her anything.

"She was afraid," answered Shay after a moment. "She thought if she did, they would find us. That I would trigger something." Her face grew dark. "What did it even matter? They found us anyway."

Ah, crap. This was not the way to go. I needed her to be

excited and focused. Not sad or depressed or guilty about what happened to her mother. Because I knew part of her blamed herself for her mother's death.

"Shay..." I let out a breath. "What happened—no!" I tried to pull her hand away, but it was too late.

Shay reached out and grabbed one of my starlights.

I heard screaming, Elsa's voice, or maybe Julian's. Very high-pitched.

Panic fired inside me as I caught Shay's hands with my own.

But then the strangest thing happened.

Shay wasn't harmed, and she hadn't let go of that single tiny starlight either. She had a strange smile on her face as she cupped the starlight in her hands. It lingered there, glowing like a tame pixie.

What in the goddess?

"Has this happened before?" Elsa was next to me. "Can others touch your magic?"

I shook my head and let go of Shay. "No. No one but me. This is… new." No one had ever touched my starlight before. Well, not unless you counted all the demons and the baddies I'd killed with it. But this was different. The starlight wasn't hurting Shay. It didn't burn her. It… *liked* her?

"It's because you're sisters," said Julian, beaming at Shay, who looked like a totally different girl holding on to that one starlight than she had been at the beginning of this training session. "Your starlights recognize family."

"Maybe." That rang true, in a way. I didn't know how else to explain it. I had no idea what was happening. Shay should have been scared, but she wasn't.

My other starlights were still hovering in the air to the side, like they weren't sure what was happening either.

Shay spread her hands wide. Instead of the starlight returning to the others, it drifted above her hands the same way it did when I controlled it. But I wasn't controlling it. She was.

My sister looked at me with the biggest smile I'd seen on her face yet. "Look."

I smiled back. "I know." Goddess, that kid was cute. And her smile just about melted my heart.

"Okay, wow," said Jade, standing close to Shay but not close enough to have the starlight touch her. "Makes me want to be able to play with starlight too. I envy you guys."

Shay's smile turned into something that resembled a mix of curiosity and determination. And before I could stop her—before I knew what she was about to do, because we were still getting to know each other—she stepped into my flock of starlights.

I sucked in a breath, not knowing what to expect. I was about to end my connection to my starlights at the first sign that Shay was in pain, in danger.

Shay stood still as my starlights rushed around her like a kaleidoscope of butterflies, bouncy and excited like they were greeting an old friend or family.

I reached out to my starlights, sending out my senses. I was hit back with a hefty dose of emotions, affection, and love.

Holy shit. My starlights… *loved* her.

Shay giggled as the starlights revolved around her body, lifting her hair and clothes as they zoomed in and around the young witch. She lifted her arms, and the starlights followed, circling her arms and looping like great big, brilliant bracelets. When she moved, the starlights moved with her.

Julian whistled. "Fuck me."

Jade's eyes rounded like tiny moons. "Fuck me sideways."

"Will you look at that?" Elsa had her hands clasped around her locket, a smile on her face. She might have had tears. "Have you seen anything like this? It's magical."

It was magical. Starlight magical. If I'd had any doubts before that she was a starlight witch like me, they were gone. No way could another witch do what she was doing, playing with my starlight, if she wasn't a starlight witch. And my sister.

Shay let out another laugh as she spun on the spot, the

starlights following her every move like they were an extension of her.

I didn't know what it meant that my starlights behaved the way that they did. Maybe this was normal. Maybe all starlight witches could manipulate other starlight magic? I'd never met another witch like me, so I basically had no idea. And I didn't remember my mother ever mentioning this to me either.

I'd learned something new tonight. I'd learned that Shay could manipulate *my* starlights. Ain't that something? So, it meant she could manipulate her own.

"Okay, Shay, I'm going to let go of my starlights," I said, stepping forward.

Shay dropped her arms, and a small flash of sadness crossed her face. "No," she said. "No, please. Not yet."

I hated the disappointment I saw on her face. But it needed to be done. "You need to be able to call on your *own* starlights. I can't always be there to protect you."

"She does have a point," said Elsa, and she looked at Shay. "A witch must own her magic."

"Hear, hear." Jade raised her glass of wine. "Truer words have never been spoken—ow!" Elsa elbowed Jade, which only made the witch laugh. "You made me spill my wine."

I blinked at the light of the starlights that were still coiling around Shay. "You have your own starlights," I told her. "Don't you want to meet them?"

At that, the girl smiled and gave a nod. "Okay." She seemed even more excited at the idea of her very own starlights, like she'd just gotten a dozen puppies.

"Okay." I pulled on my starlights, and then I let them go. They blinked one last time, and then they were gone. "Your turn. All you need to do is reach out and try to find your stars. Let your senses guide you. Your inner witch. The stars will answer."

Shay let out a breath, and I could tell she was wired with excitement as she clenched her tiny hands into fists. They were shaking when she looked up to the stars, her green eyes wide.

"I don't feel anything," she said after a few moments.

"Maybe if you close your eyes, it might help you to focus," I offered. "That's how I did it the first time." I will always remember that moment when my stars answered back. It was a strange feeling. It was also the moment I knew I'd never be alone. Not with my starlights.

"Think happy thoughts," suggested Julian, and I glared at him. "Sorry." He laughed. "Just trying to help."

"I know. But that's not how it works."

"Leave them alone, Julian." Elsa pulled on his arm and dragged him back to his chair. Jade followed them. I was beginning to regret my decision to let them stay during Shay's training. Tomorrow it would be just the two of us. They were way too much of a distraction. A happy one, but still a distraction.

"It's not working." The defeat was heavy in Shay's voice.

"You can do this," I encouraged. "The stars will answer. You'll see. Keep trying."

But after another hour of the same, nothing was happening. Worry found its way into my gut. Why weren't the stars answering her?

"How long did it take you?" Shay looked at me. I could see the distress all over her face, the frustration.

"An hour, maybe? Maybe more?" It had taken me about ten minutes, but I couldn't say that to her. Not with that look of despair on her face. She seemed crushed.

Shay stopped talking after that. *Good one, Leana.* She just shook her head and shrugged now. The others all fell into an uncomfortable silence. None of us wanted to say anything that would only make Shay feel worse.

"I think it's enough for tonight." I touched her shoulder. "You did good. You did amazing."

Shay wouldn't even look at me. She just gave me her signature shrug.

"Your starlight magic will come," I told her, hating the worry in my tone as the others picked up their folding chairs. "We'll practice again tomorrow night. And the night after that. We'll practice every single night until it appears to you."

As we left the rooftop, I couldn't help but worry and wonder what was happening with Shay. I was about her age when my magic surfaced. She should be able to tap into her starlight. It shouldn't be this hard.

It didn't make sense when she was clearly a starlight witch and could even manipulate *my* starlight. Could it be that Shay didn't have magic? Or magic of her own? Was she only some kind of conduit of magic?

If that were true, why did my father give me the impression that Shay's magic was all-powerful? If not, then why were the angels after her?

CHAPTER 19

"Don't worry. We'll take care of her," said Elsa as I'd grabbed my bag and swung it over my shoulder back at the Twilight Hotel.

"I hate to leave her like this, but I don't have a choice." No. Darius made sure of that. I should have been staying with her all night, watching some action movies or whatever she wanted to boost her spirits with after she failed to summon her starlight magic. After a night like that to an eleven-year-old, I shouldn't be leaving her again with my friends.

I looked over toward the living room. Shay sat next to Julian, sharing a popcorn bowl as they watched some action movie on Netflix.

Worse, I'd made a mistake. I'd told Basil I had a sister. If word got out and reached Darius that I had a sister, he could use her against me. Crap. I should have kept my big mouth shut.

"I'll see you later, Shay," I called. I waited for her to turn around, but she didn't.

Julian glanced over her head at me and gave me a sympathetic look and a shrug. Looked like Shay was mad at me. I'd be mad at me, too, if I were her. Part of me wanted to explain to her why I had to leave again, but it was complicated. And she didn't need more worry added to her eleven-year-old brain. There was still a chance I'd end up back in jail. I didn't want her to think about that right now. I just wanted her to concentrate on her magic. Eventually, it would show. It would just take some more time. Maybe Shay was just too emotionally compromised after what she'd suffered with the loss of her mother, what she'd seen. Maybe she just needed time. Or this is what I told myself to feel a little bit better.

The night was not starting on a high note.

"Go. She'll be fine." Jade gave me a warm smile, seeing something on my face. "Go do what you gotta do. We'll watch over her, and I promise she won't escape. Not this time." She leaned forward and whispered, "Elsa is going to put a locking spell on the door as soon as you leave. She'll never get out."

Elsa raised her brows and squared her shoulders proudly. I had the feeling this wasn't her first time doing it. "She's not going anywhere. That's a promise."

I wasn't sure how I felt about that, but at least I knew she'd be safe with them.

What I needed was a conversation with Matiel. Did angels have cell phones? I doubted it. If so, I was pretty sure he would have given me his number before he just vanished. He'd said he'd be back. When? In a few days? Weeks? He'd just dropped her off and left. Is that what angels did? Come to our world for short visits, and when things got rough, they scrambled away?

I didn't know Matiel's story, and I wanted to find out more. More about him. Him *and* my mother. What the hell was that like? But especially more about Shay and those who had killed her mother. I had the impression her mom had died protecting her child. Would Shay's life always be in danger? The angel needed to answer these questions. I knew witches could summon demons. Otherworldly creatures. Following that logic, then, weren't angels otherworldly creatures too? Maybe I could find myself a witch who could call Matiel's ass back here, so he could answer some questions.

But first, I needed to follow the plan. And the plan was to find the jewel, have Darius thrown off the Gray Council, and get my life back. Good plan.

After I'd left a miserable Shay back at the apartment, I went in search of the Jewel of the Sun. My first stop was the Sisters of Compassion convent. It was closed to visitors at around 9:05 p.m., so obviously using my starlights, I snuck in through a back door that led to the kitchens. I'd triggered no alarms here either. Well, none, as far as I could hear.

Yet, after spending a good fifty minutes in the convent, searching every floor, every nook and cranny, the dungeons—technically a basement, but I couldn't even call it that because it was so awful—even the bathrooms, which were in need of serious makeovers, the jewel wasn't here.

That's why I found myself a half hour later, climbing up the steps to Hell's Kitchen psychiatric ward. By the time I'd made it to the front doors, it was half-past ten. Surprisingly, the doors weren't locked. Guess they figured no one was stupid enough to waltz right in at night, like yours truly.

This was the last location Darius had given me. The jewel had to be inside this place. It had to be. And I was going to find it.

I still wasn't sure what I was going to do with it when I found the damn jewel. If I gave it back right away, Darius would end me. Then Shay would be alone. Not *alone* alone, but without her big sister.

But if I kept the jewel, Darius would most probably try to kill me, then, too. So I was in a jam. Give it to him? Not give it to him? Both ended with my life gone. Those weren't good odds. I needed to find the jewel and then find someone I could trust on the Gray Council to plead my case. With Bellamy now on Valen's watch, I had everything I needed. I just had to have a person on my side. That said individual being one who sat on the Gray Council. Didn't Valen say he knew someone? I'd have to ask him later.

Once I had the stone in my possession, I was going to start to plan Darius's takedown. And I had less than two days to do that.

Scratch that. I had less than a day and a half. I had to move this along before whatever crazy plan Darius had going for him.

Easier said than done. But I always got the bad guy. Always.

I made my way through the lobby to a long hallway that branched off in many directions with more corridors and doors. My boots clanked on the polished, hard floors, a sea of rooms on either side.

I'd never been inside a psych ward, and it clearly had a hospital vibe: white walls, the smell of disinfectant and ammonia, the constant whisper of beeps from machines, and the whines of patients. Fluorescent lights flickered weakly while long shadows stretched out from doors and hallways.

I peered through the first door. A man lay in a single bed with white sheets covering his fragile frame. His scalp showed through strings of white hair. He looked like a corpse whose skin was paper-thin, cracked, and peeling. His eyes were closed, and for a second, I thought he was dead, but then his chest rose and fell.

I kept going. I needed a spot hidden from human eyes, somewhere out of sight, where I could call on my starlight without being interrupted. An orderly passed me, dressed in his white uniform. He was talking on the phone and didn't even glance my way as I walked the corridor. Weird. At this hour, he should have looked my way to make sure I wasn't one of the patients roaming around. Maybe the dude just didn't care.

A nurses' station sat across from me as I approached. It stood empty. Guess the graveyard shift hadn't arrived yet.

I took that as a good sign, meaning I could work without the humans bothering me. They'd probably think I was one of the patients.

Speaking of patients, I peeked through another open door and froze.

An Asian man, maybe in his sixties, was jumping up and down on his bed, naked. And he had a friend. An older Caucasian woman. Yeah, she was naked too. Bits flying and slapping. You get the picture. The man saw me and kept bouncing as he waved. "Hi."

I waved back. "Hi." It was going to be one of those nights.

Smiling, I kept going until I reached the end of the first floor, found a quiet spot next to a nurse's cart, and pulled on my starlight—

My phone beeped.

I let go of my magic and yanked out my phone, my hands trembling with the sudden spike of adrenaline. "If this is Elsa telling me that Shay snuck out again, I'm going to need a room here. 'Cause I'm about to go crazy."

I sighed through my nose as I saw Valen's name next to his text message.

Valen: *Where are you?*

Me: *On the job. Is this about Shay? Is she okay?*

My eyes warmed as my emotions ran from one extreme to the other. My thoughts went to Shay and how defeated she'd looked earlier. What if she ran away? Had I pushed too hard? It wasn't like me to second-guess myself. But I'd never had to be responsible for a little person before. This was new to me too. And it terrified me. I wasn't ashamed to admit it. It terrified the crap out of me.

Valen: *She's fine. Don't worry. Any luck with the jewel?*

Me: *Not yet*

Valen: *U need help?*

I smiled at my phone.

Me: *No. I've got this*

Valen: *Will you be out all night?*

Me: *No. Maybe another hour. Why?*

I still had the two upper floors and the basement to check. And I wasn't leaving without that damn jewel. No matter how hot my giant was. Yes, I said *my* giant. He was mine.

Valen: *I have a surprise for you when you get back*

My stomach did a pirouette and then a backward dive.

Me: *Does it involve nakedness?*

Valen: *Maybe. Meet me at the hotel.*

Memories of our sexy time came rushing back, and warmth pooled down in my middle. The thought of his rough hands touching all my sensitive spots and kisses that were both tender and full of fire had desire hissing over my skin and straight to all the parts of my body that remembered his touch all too well. A foolish part of me wanted to bolt out of this place just to feel him.

Me: *What about Bellamy?*

If he disappeared again, the next time I saw the witch scientist, I'd kill him myself.

Valen: *He's at my place. Don't worry. He won't leave. He's… happy there*

Me: *Bellamy happy? That I gotta see. Okay. I'll see you at the hotel*

I stuffed my phone back in my pocket, wondering what Valen had planned for me and why he wanted to meet me at the hotel. I tried, really, really hard to wipe all the naked images of Valen—he did rock the whole naked thing—out of my head so I could focus on my task.

I was suddenly hit with a wave of fatigue, and I hadn't even done anything. Well, not really. I realized that emotional issues drained your body, perhaps even more than physical issues.

Gathering my will once again, I reached out to the power of the stars and felt a yank as it answered. Once I made sure no one was walking along the hallway, I sent out my starlights. Thousands of tiny, brilliant balls of light zoomed from my outstretched hand, lighting up the hallway for a second, like it was daylight, before rushing down the hallway and then breaking apart as one part went left, and the other made a right.

I sent out my senses to my starlights, hoping to sense something, anything of power. But I felt nothing. No magic. No paranormal energies. At least, not on the first floor.

"Well, that's not good."

I let go of my starlight and went in search of the stairs. When I found them, I made it to the second floor, and again, I sent out my starlights, searching for whatever I might recognize as the jewel. Something my starlights were supposed to identify.

And again, I felt nothing.

It was the same for the third floor. By that time, I started to feel the beginnings of a panic attack.

A cold sweat trickled down my back as I headed down the stairwell. When I finally reached the basement level, I was drenched in sweat, like I'd just stepped out of a sauna—with all my clothes on.

The basement was huge and ran the length of the building, with many doors leading to many rooms. It was almost identical to the other three levels I'd been to—boring white walls with matching boring white tiles: cold, unnaturally clean, all lit with fluorescent lights.

It was colder, like maintenance had forgotten to turn on the heat. The air had the harsh scent of cleaning products, which overlapped the sweetish odor of decay, like a few dead rats stuck in the vents or behind the walls.

Trying to quash my feeling of dread, I looked into the first room. It was large and stuffed with metal tables, topped with various medical devices covered in dust and what looked like a few restraint chairs. The hairs on the back of my neck immediately rose.

It looked like it hadn't been used since the 1960s. It resembled a place where they performed electric shock therapy and other questionable treatments, all in the name of science and mental health.

"This is the part in the movie where the woman gets her neck slashed by the crazy doctor." What the hell was this place? In a basement like this, whatever happened here had to be something shady, no doubt.

I stepped out and sighed. "Well. This is as good a spot as any."

Gathering my emotions, I used them to tap into my magic. Again, I sent my starlights out, venturing into the depths of this cringeworthy basement.

My pulsed pounded, and I took a careful step forward, sending out my witch senses to my starlights.

And after only a few minutes, I knew nothing was here but the memories of human wails and tortures and experiments.

I shook my head. "No. This can't be. It *has* to be here. It has to."

Again, I sent another volley of my starlights, casting them out to search every inch of this eerie basement. And again, I got no sense of pulses of energies, or the hum of something magical, or even just paranormal. The only pulses that reached me were the thrums of the halogen lights above my head.

Shit. I stood there like an idiot with my mouth hanging open, feeling the panic taking over. Hard this time. Buckets of it until I felt like a rope tightened my insides, cutting through my intestines.

I let my starlights go and looked around. An awful feeling of dread settled in me, and my gut clenched.

"This is the right place," I told myself, feeling some doubt creeping in. Had I gotten it wrong? No. This was the place. I was sure of it. Hell's Kitchen had no other psych wards, and I'd searched every inch of this building.

The jewel was not here.

Unless it had been at some point, and it had since been removed? Was this some ploy to make me out to be a fool? Had Darius lied to me this whole time? Why? How would that benefit him? He made sure I was arrested, only to blackmail me into doing his bidding. I didn't take him for a man, witch, who liked to play games. At least, not when it involved something he wanted.

So what the hell did this mean? It meant I was in bigger trouble than I was when I first set out on this job. Without this jewel, I couldn't use it as proof against Darius. But I had Bellamy for that. So, it might be enough.

Still, even if I wasn't planning on giving the jewel to Darius, it would have given me an edge over him. Or even something to bargain with, like getting my life back.

He would eventually figure out that I didn't have it. He'd given me two days to find the damn thing. Day one was almost over. I had to figure out something fast.

Because if I didn't, it was back to my old cell. But we all knew Darius would kill me if I was no longer of any use to him.

Yeah, good times.

CHAPTER 20

I pulled open the hotel's front door and marched in, my emotions raw and paper thin. I'd failed to retrieve the jewel. This was an epic failure.

I was wired, angry, scared, and a hell of a lot of other emotions, all fighting and trying to make their way to the number-one spot.

Faces passed me in blurs of beiges, grays, and tans. I could tell the lobby was scarcely occupied, maybe only a handful of guests, but I didn't look up or around as I made my way toward the elevator, my legs feeling like they were filled with cement.

Just as I pressed the up button, something hit me in the back of the head. I turned around and spotted a message card floating to the gleaming floor, next to my boots.

"This came for you hours ago." Errol stood about ten feet from me.

I didn't know if it was because I'd failed to find the jewel, that I couldn't get Shay to summon her power, or the fact that Darius would most probably kill me—possibly all of the above—but I lost it.

A slow burn of fury took root. All the emotions from the days before came rushing back into me.

That line that held all of my emotions together so that I could function? Well, it snapped.

"I'm not your secretary," said Errol. "You don't even work here any—"

A ball of dazzling white light hit the lizard shifter in the gut. The force threw him thirty feet back, and lucky for him, he crashed into one of the sofas and not the hard hotel wall.

Holy crap. I'd just roasted me a lizard.

Was he dead? Shouts and screams echoed around the white noise that pounded in my head. I hit him hard, but not enough to roast him. Or maybe I had?

I stood there for maybe another moment, and then I saw Errol clambering to his feet. He was smoking, not in the smoking-hot kind of way, but literally smoking. The top part of his three-piece suit was still sizzling. Only the arm sleeves remained. His pale white skin was blistered. That was going to hurt. But he was alive.

I stared at his face. His eyes were wide, and a ribbon of fear slid behind them before he mastered it. His gray-forked tongue kept flicking out of his mouth. He was scared. So, he should be.

But damn. Any small hope of getting my job back was gone. I'd really done it now. I'd lost my temper and nearly killed the concierge.

I bent down, picked up the message card, and stepped into the waiting elevator, not caring about the guests staring at me or those who were yelling. Yeah, there was some yelling.

My face flamed from anger and guilt. Errol wasn't my favorite person. Yes, sometimes he deserved an ass whooping, but I'd never imagined I'd actually do it.

Shit. Shit. Shit.

The doors closed, and I stared at the message card just as I leaned over to press the number thirteen.

Meet me in room no. 1213

—Valen

. . .

"ROOM 1213?" What was Valen doing in a room in the hotel? I thought he'd meant my apartment?

I sighed and pressed the number twelve on the control panel, with a shaking finger. The elevator jerked as it climbed, my blood pressure rising with each floor.

"What did I do? *What* did I *do*!"

I let my head fall against the elevator wall, the anger and the fury still hammering through me, with just a small dose of guilt.

The elevator doors slid open, and I walked to the door with the number 1213 stenciled in black. I didn't even realize how I got there, my emotions still rocking my foggy brain.

I took a calming breath and knocked. I wasn't about to barge in there, just in case it wasn't Valen, though I was pretty sure it was. Why else would he text me and then send me this message?

The door swung open, and there was Valen, all sexy as hell dressed in a black dress shirt and pants. I breathed deeply, taking in his scent: a mix of musk, aftershave, and soap. Yum. He smelled good enough to eat.

He took one look at me and said, "What happened?" His eyes narrowed over my face.

The worry lines that formed over his brow added flutters to my belly. The fact that he cared spoke volumes. I was a lucky woman.

"I need a drink." I walked past him, realizing after the fact that this might be construed as rude, but I was already halfway through the room. It had the same layout as the other hotel guest rooms I'd visited under very different circumstances. But this room was a bit larger, and it had a small kitchenette. A round dining table sat next to a window with a centerpiece of flowers nestled between two lit candles. Two place settings rested on the table next to a bottle of red wine. A table for two.

I spun around, only now noticing the pots and pans on the counter next to the stove and the smell of something spicy and delicious. Nothing was more of a turn-on in my book than a man cooking dinner.

"You cooked for me?" The giant not only had cooked me what was most probably something amazing, but he'd arranged to have a "date night" in a room in the hotel so we could have some privacy. Privacy for some serious horizontal mambo. Boy, oh boy, did I need some of that.

"I did." Valen was still watching me with concern in his dark eyes. "Are you going to tell me what happened? Or should I spank it out of you?"

My lips parted. "Sounds like fun."

Valen's gaze was intoxicating. "With me, it will be."

Tingles erupted over my skin. I wanted nothing more at this moment than to jump on this hot giant. But I smelled terrible, and he smelled amazing. I was not letting him touch me when I knew I had butt-crack sweat. Yup. I did.

"I just need to wash up."

Valen smiled. "Take your time. Clean towels are in the bathroom." He walked to the table and began to turn the handle on the corkscrew from the wine bottle.

A shower sounded amazing. Trying to hold on to that feeling of joy, I stepped into the bathroom, peeled off my clothes, and stepped into a hot shower. I won't lie and say that I wasn't in there longer than necessary, but I found it hard to leave the wonderful sensations of hot water pouring over my head. Plus, I didn't want to face what I'd done. But I had to.

Still, I finally stepped out and dried myself off. I cringed, staring at my dirty, sweaty clothes and wishing I had brought a change of clothes, but I had no idea Valen had planned this surprise dinner. I spotted one of the hotel bathrobes and pulled it over me. It was a far cry from a date-like outfit, but it was clean and way better than my dirty clothes. Plus, I was naked underneath. Pretty sure that would make up for the dreary bathrobe. Win-win!

I came out of the bathroom, my body clean and fresh, but a

feeling of turmoil still clung to me. The shower hadn't been able to remove that stain.

Valen looked up at me as I entered the cozy dining area. "Better?"

"Cleaner. Not necessarily better."

"Here." The giant handed me a glass of red wine. "Now. You better tell me what the hell happened. Why are you all tense and anxious? What happened tonight? Did you find the jewel?"

I took a large sip of the wine, letting the fruity taste linger in my mouth before I swallowed. "I didn't find it. I searched both locations… and nothing. It wasn't there."

"So, we'll look again." Valen held the bottle of wine in his hand. "We'll do the three locations again. We'll take the time we need to find it. We'll find it."

I shook my head, feeling a tightening in my chest. "That's just it. I don't have much time left. I didn't tell you, but Darius paid me a visit today here at the hotel. He gave me two days to find the jewel. And if I don't find it in time… well, I'm sure you can figure out the rest."

The bottle of wine exploded. Wine and shards of glass crashed to the floor.

"Shit." Valen stared at the mess on the carpet. "Don't move. I'll pick this up."

I watched as the giant hurried over to the kitchenette, grabbed a dish towel and a small garbage bin, and hurried back.

"We'll go back first thing tomorrow," said the giant as he carefully picked up the broken shards of glass and dropped them in the garbage bin. Those big hands were meticulous at times. Trust me, I knew.

"We could, but it wouldn't make a difference. I searched those places. Every inch of them. And nothing was there. If there was anything of paranormal nature with magical properties, I would have found it. Trust me. My starlights would have found it."

Valen looked up at me from the floor. "Why only two days? Why the rush?"

"Yeah, I thought about that," I answered, watching the giant press the towel into the carpet to soak up the wine. "I'm not sure, but whatever the reason, why he wants this jewel, it's because of something happening soon." I had no idea what, but I would find out. I had to. If I could figure out why he needed the jewel, I might be able to stop whatever he was planning.

I grabbed one of the chairs at the small table and let myself fall into it. "I really thought I'd find it. This jewel. Without it, it's going to be harder to build my case against Darius."

"We still have Bellamy. I think the witch scientist is a much stronger witness than the jewel. He can testify to what he did. What they paid him to do."

"Yeah, but I don't have the proof that connects Darius to Adele's HTO project. Bellamy never got names, just orders from the middlemen. Some emails and texts, probably all from fake accounts. I heard Adele speak of Darius. I knew she was taking orders from him. But that's just my word against his. I wanted something solid."

"Bellamy can provide that," repeated the giant. "Once you file your case, there'll be an investigation into Darius. Things always manage to surface. He'll get caught. And you'll be free of him."

"You're not worried that Bellamy might slip out?" I said, staring at his wide back and relishing the way his muscles flexed and rolled. "He's a sneaky sonofabitch."

Valen gave a laugh. "No."

I frowned at the confidence in his tone. He sounded way too certain. "What'd you tell him?" Something mischievous flickered in his eyes. Yeah, I had a feeling Valen had done something to make the witch scientist stay put.

The giant flashed me a smile. "That I would crush his skull if I found out he left. He knows I'd find him."

I tried to laugh, but it came out like a weird gargling sound in my throat. "He probably deserves that." But I needed Bellamy, even though I despised him and what he did.

"Sorry about the wine," said the giant. "I only brought one bottle."

I waved a hand at him. "It's fine."

Valen wiped the wine as best as he could with the towel. "I'll have to let Jimmy know to send someone to clean the wine stain." He stood up and tossed the now burgundy-stained towel in the small sink.

My eyes moved to the large discoloration on the carpet. It reminded me of the bloodstains the hotel's cleanup crew had to clean when the hotel was plagued with demons.

I took another large gulp of wine. "There's still my murder charge. How do I prove I'm innocent without dragging Catelyn's name into this?" I would never let her take the fall for that. She was still human, in a way. She didn't belong in a paranormal jail.

"She could tell the truth," said the giant. He washed his hands in the sink and walked over to the table.

"And have her thrown in jail?" I shook my head. "She doesn't deserve that. Not after what she suffered."

Valen looked down at me. "That's just it. If she tells the truth, tells the Gray Council what happened, they can't lock her up."

"I wouldn't be so sure about that." I didn't trust the Gray Council. Not when one of its members was blackmailing me and was behind Adele's freak show.

Valen's eyes traveled over my face. "You've got Bellamy to testify to that. He knew she was human. He knows what they did to her. He's involved in this. If the council hears his version of events, Catelyn will never see the inside of a cell."

"I hope you're right." But I wasn't convinced. I didn't want to gamble with her life on "maybes." It was too damned dangerous unless I knew I could speak to someone who was trustworthy. "Hey. Didn't you tell me you knew someone on the Gray Council? Someone you can trust? Someone we could bring my case to?" The paperwork was nearly done. I just had some final comments to add. But I wasn't about to bring up a case against one of their members without knowing I could trust them.

"Yeah, I do," answered the giant. "Her name is Migda. Tough old werecat. If you want someone you can trust, she's it. I'd trust Migda with my life. She was there for me when I moved here. She knew my wife."

I tensed at the mention of his wife. I knew deep down this was a sensitive subject for Valen, as it should be. "Okay. Good. That's really good. It'll help."

Valen eyed me. "Then why don't you look pleased? That should be one less thing for you to worry about. You haven't smiled since you got here. What else happened?"

I took a deep breath and said, "Are you ready? It gets worse."

"What do you mean?"

"I did something. Something I can't take back. Something I wished I hadn't, now that I think about it."

Valen's body tightened with tension. "What? Tell me?"

I set my glass of wine on the table and rubbed my temples with my fingers. "When I got here, I was already stressed with not finding the jewel, and Shay not being able to conjure her magic. You know, so she can protect herself if I'm not there."

"Wait? What? Shay can't call her starlight magic?"

Oh, right, I hadn't told him yet. "No. We tried earlier tonight. But she couldn't. She could manipulate mine somehow, but when she tried to call on hers… it didn't work. She was really devastated." The same guilt struck me at leaving her again. But I had no choice. Now seeing that I hadn't found the jewel, it seemed it was all for nothing.

Valen let out a breath. "That's gotta be hard for the kid. But maybe all she needs is more training. It'll come. I'm sure it was the same for you. Right?"

But it wasn't. "I'm sure more training will help her. So, you see, when I crossed the lobby and headed for the elevator, I was tense. And when Errol threw the message card at my head—"

"Wait—what did he do?" Valen crossed his thick arms over his chest, a tiny vein throbbing on his temple.

"Pitched the message card at my head. I lost it. Literally lost my mind. And I hit him with my starlight. Hard. Not hard enough to kill him, but hard enough to hurt him. Burned his clothes right off. Burned his skin too. I'll never get my job back after that. And I'll probably need a new place to live. Basil will never let that go. I assaulted the freaking concierge. The *concierge.*"

"Errol deserved what he got," said the giant. "He's lucky I wasn't there because he would have gotten more than a little burn."

I let my head fall into my hands. "I just want this night to end. So I can start over tomorrow."

"Is that all?"

I looked up to see Valen's expression pulled into a smile, making my heart transform into liquid gold.

"What do you mean, is that all?" I stared at him, my mouth slightly open. "Uh. Haven't you heard what I just said? I burned the lizard." Yeah, that didn't come out right.

"I did." Valen grabbed my hands and pulled me to my feet.

"I almost killed Errol."

"But you didn't," said Valen. He let go of my hands and wrapped his arms around my back.

"No. But still."

"That's really what's been bothering you?" he asked, and I was very aware of his hands massaging my ass.

"That. And Shay. And the jewel. And Darius."

He pulled me closer until my breasts were pinned against his hard chest. His arms around me tightened for an instant and then relaxed. "One thing at a time, Leana. Before you give yourself a stroke."

He wasn't wrong about that.

His hands felt amazing around me, and his eyes held passion and desire. I felt myself move my arms up to slide around his waist. They felt nice there. Natural.

"You can forget about Errol. He's not worth stressing about. You can find other work. You did before the hotel hired you."

"I know. But the hotel was a stable job. Now with Shay, I

know it would be better for us both if I still had *that* job." She needed stability, and a steady paycheck every week would give us that.

Valen leaned in and planted a kiss on my neck, sending delicious thrills down my spine. "Shay's going to be fine. She's a tough kid. She's a lot like you in many ways."

That drew my eyebrows up. "Really?"

"Really." His hot lips dragged over my jaw.

I sighed, trying not to moan. Too late. "Are you going to kiss my worries away?"

"Yes."

"Everywhere?"

Valen's tongue darted out, making me shiver. "You bet."

Okay, maybe this night wouldn't be so bad after all.

His lips worshiped my neck. "I'm going to talk to Catelyn tomorrow. I know she'll be on board to help you. She's told me so. I'll reach out to Migda and see if she has time to see me tomorrow. We'll get your name cleared. I promise."

I tried to smile, but my facial muscles seemed to be stuck forever in a frown. "Okay."

He pulled his lips away from my neck; his eyes met mine, and I could tell there was something else he wanted to talk about.

"What?" I asked him.

Valen continued to rub his big, manly hands all over my behind. "I want you and Shay to move in with me," blurted the giant, like it was something he'd been thinking about, and he wanted to come out and say it already.

My heart did the tango, a ballerina spin, and a jumping jack for the finale.

My breath tripped in my throat. "Are you serious? You want me and my new kid sister to move in with you?" I sounded daft, but I had to say it again, just in case I'd heard wrong.

"You wouldn't be far from the hotel, so I'm certain you won't lose your job."

"I've already lost my job," I told him.

"You'd be close to your friends," he added. "I know you think of them like family. I want to be your family. Yours and Shay's."

My heart just about melted into a puddle at my feet. I searched his face. "You've been thinking about this. A lot. I can tell."

"I have. You wouldn't have to work or worry about money if you're worried about that," he said.

The fact that he said it meant the world to me. "Thanks, but I *have* to work." I could never imagine my life without work. Work had always been there for me when times were rough, like when I lost my mother and when things were bad with Martin. I could always fall back on my work.

Valen smiled. "I know. I know how your independence is important to you."

"It is. I love my work, actually. It's part of who I am." I cared about Valen. Hell, I was in love with him. But I wasn't about to let a man take care of me in that way. I could take care of myself, well, on most days.

"I get that." The giant leaned in and kissed me, sending my skin on fire. "But I wanted you to know anyway. It'll be good for Shay. To have the both of us here with her. To protect her. She needs consistency in her life right now. And we can take turns with her schooling."

My throat was tight when I said, "You *have* been thinking about this." My heart lodged in my throat, nearly choking me at the concern and the love the giant had for my little sister. He cared about her. He wanted to take care of her and protect her. Hell, he wanted us to move in with him!

"Let me think about it." It was already a yes on my part. I'd been thinking about waking up next to this hot specimen every morning. But I had Shay to consider here. "I have to talk to Shay. She gets a vote in this. I won't agree to anything before I speak to her. I won't force her, though your offer is tempting."

Valen shook his head. "You shouldn't. But I do hope she votes yes." He planted another kiss on me. This time it was deeper. "I know she likes me."

"How can she not," I purred. "You're one hot giant."

Valen's eyes widened as they traced my face, my mouth. His lips parted, and he breathed in my scent. He let out a growl as his hands tightened around me, pressing me against him. The hardness in his pants told me just how much he wanted me right now.

He leaned closer and nibbled one corner of my mouth and then the other side, pulling gently on my lips. My lower regions pounded in response.

Oh God, what is he doing? His kisses made me ache for more.

My skin tingled where his fingers touched my ass, my back. He dropped his mouth onto mine, slipping a tentative tongue between my lips. My breath came fast as he darted his tongue deep into me.

A stab of desire went straight to my core, sending a wave of heat through my body. I let out a little moan and wound my fingers around the nape of his neck, pulling him closer to feel him. This was insane at a time like this, but we both needed it—a reminder that we were here for each other.

Sensing my desire, his touch became aggressive, and hot ribbons of need spiraled through my body.

My nether regions pounded in time with my heart. I was about to spontaneously combust if we weren't doing the deed soon. Yup. It was on.

I pulled back. "Guess what?"

"What?" said Valen between kisses.

Clever as I was, I said, "I'm not wearing anything under this robe."

Valen froze. But it was cut short when a feral growl emitted from his throat. Damn. He was hot and wild and looked somewhat smugly victorious.

Then, in a blur, he tugged on my bathrobe's belt. The next thing I knew, cool air hit my naked skin as the bathrobe disappeared.

I laughed, not at all bothered that I stood there in my birthday suit or that my nipples were rock hard. "How did you do that?"

Valen gave a sly smile. "Can't give away all my secrets."

His hands slid over my back, shoulders, and waist, and the roughness of his callouses sent my skin tingling. Then he cupped my breasts with his hands, his fingers brushing my nipples and sending shivers into my core. Heat rushed through me, making me crazy and impatient.

I couldn't take this anymore.

I jumped on him, I really did, and wrapped my legs around his waist. He growled as he grabbed my ass and hoisted me higher on his hips.

"Thought I'd move things along," I said, loving how his big hands felt on my skin.

Valen grinned. "Smart witch."

He swung me from the dining area and into the bedroom. No, wait, there was no separate bedroom. It was just one room with small additions. Good choice.

The giant lowered me carefully onto the bed. Then, in a flash, he pulled off his shirt, pants, and underwear to stand there in his naked glory, his long, perfect manhood pointing in my genital direction.

Then he lowered his big, giant body on top of mine, sending tiny kisses along my jaw, neck, and collarbone. The man knew how to turn me on.

Delicious heat pounded through my belly, my fingertips, everywhere. He dragged his mouth from my lips, staring down at me as hunger flashed in his eyes.

I wrapped my legs around his waist and drew him closer, enjoying the feel of his weight over me.

Valen, my giant, wanted me and Shay to move in with him. My heart suddenly felt too big to fit inside my chest.

It was my last coherent thought before he thrust his hips and buried himself inside me.

CHAPTER 21

"You look well-*rested*." Elsa spied from the fridge as I attempted to sneak in without anyone noticing.

"Nice robe," laughed Jade. "You stealing hotel property?"

I straightened. No point in pretending I wasn't here anymore. "I'm going to give it back." I dumped my dirty clothes into the hamper in my room and came back out to join them.

I'd texted Elsa last night after my first round of orgasms to tell her I was spending the night with the giant in one of the hotel guest rooms. She'd assured me Shay would be okay and that Julian had offered to sleep on the couch. I couldn't ask for better friends. Better family.

I tightened the belt of my robe as I spotted Shay sitting on the couch, her head down as her fingers brushed her tablet.

"Hi, Shay." I waited, but she didn't look up, didn't as much as acknowledge my existence. Apparently, she hadn't forgiven me for ditching her last night.

It stung. I'd admit it. And seeing her now, I felt even worse about my night with Valen. Maybe I should have canceled with him and come straight here. It was just one floor up.

But I also needed some me time. And that included time with Valen. Staying with him, talking until all hours of the night really did me some good. Helped me to unwind somewhat and clear my head.

I thought about what he'd said last night about moving in with him. At first, I had the feeling Shay would have said yes. Now, looking at her, I wasn't so sure anymore.

I met Elsa's face. She gave me a *leave it alone* kind of expression.

Fine. "Is there coffee?" I woke up in a strange bed to a missing Valen, though he had left a cute note and had even attempted to draw a flower. Could have been a rose. Could have been a cat's face.

Went to check on Bellamy. Call you later.
—Valen.

I needed coffee, like I needed air, at the moment.

"Fresh pot." Elsa pointed to the coffee machine. Her red hair was piled on the top of her head and held by a bamboo stick that people used for their tomato plants. She wore a long corduroy navy skirt and matched it with a bright-red wool sweater.

I grabbed a mug and poured some steaming coffee into it. "Thank the goddess for fresh coffee."

"And orgasms, apparently," said Jade. Her blonde hair was in tight curls, like she'd given herself a perm. White leg warmers wrapped over pink-and-black zebra-patterned tights, which she paired with an overly large, off-the-shoulder sweaterdress, also pink. Jade really did rock the eighties' fashion.

I pointed a finger at her. "If I'm going to talk about my orgasms, you better start talking about yours."

Jade's face went bright red and began to spread down the sides of her neck. "Jimmy and I are still in the very early dating stages. Nothing like that… yet."

"So, it's been a dry week?" I teased. But the grin on Jade's face told me that soon she was going to get some orgasms of her own. Go, Jade!

"When did Julian leave?" I grabbed my coffee mug and sat at the table.

Elsa poured herself a cup of coffee. "You just missed him. He went home to shower. He's taking the twins out for lunch."

Right. I'm sure that included their hot mother too. Go, Julian!

"So?" Jade pulled out a chair and sat. She leaned forward, her blue eyes on mine. "What did you do to Errol? I want all the juicy details leading to his ass kicking."

Shit. "You heard about that?"

"The whole hotel heard about it. Well, his version. And there were a few witnesses too."

From the corner of my eye, I saw Shay look up our way. "What's *his* version?"

Jade blinked. "That you savagely attacked him when he was only trying to do his job."

"Says you nearly killed him," added Elsa. "Says you had a murderous glare in your eyes."

Jade leaned forward in her chair and placed her elbows on the table. "And if it wasn't for his quick thinking, he'd be dead by now."

I shook my head. "Yeah. Bet he said that." I let out a breath. "But he's not wrong about the almost killing him part."

"Leana?" Elsa's face was twisted in horror. "What happened?"

"When I came back to the hotel last night," I started, seeing their wide eyes, "I was angry. I didn't find the... what I was looking for," I said, not wanting to tell Shay about my search for the jewel and what not finding it implied. "And Errol, being the nice concierge he is, flicked a message card at my head."

"And you lost your temper." Elsa crossed her arms over her chest and leaned back. "It's not going to be easier to get your job back. Not after that."

"I know." I looked at my friends. "I'm really sorry."

Elsa blinked at me. "For what?"

"For ruining your hard work. All those spells and pixies mayhem to try and get rid of Oric. I messed it all up."

Jade tutted. "We're not done. Not even close."

"You'll be working for nothing," I said, taking a sip of my coffee.

Elsa looked at me, her expression torn between concern and something darker. "You let us worry about that. Okay. So, you burned the lizard. There are worse things in life."

"Is he okay?" Errol wasn't my favorite lizard, but I was "partly" sorry I had fired some starlight at him.

"He'll live," answered Elsa. "Polly took a look at him. Just needed some ointment for the burns. Won't leave a scar. If you ask me, I think he's being a little overdramatic about the whole thing."

Jade laughed. "But he's loving the attention."

"At least someone is." I couldn't have made things worse for myself if I had tried. *Nice going, Leana.*

"Basil's been looking for you." Jade pursed her lips thoughtfully. She didn't have to say it. I knew what she was going to say. That Basil wanted me out of his hotel. But with Valen's offer, I wasn't too stressed about that. At least Shay and I had a place to go. But I wasn't about to give up my apartment to Oric. Not yet.

I could feel Shay's eyes on me, but I didn't want to look at her for fear of the disappointment on her face. I didn't want her to worry about us being kicked out. I'd tell her about Valen's offer. Just not yet. It wasn't the right time.

"Morning, ladies." Jimmy came strolling into the apartment. "Hi, Shay," he said, and my kid sister gave a nod in greeting before going back to her tablet.

The assistant manager came up to Jade, leaned over, and kissed her on the lips. He pulled back, and Jade's eyes sparked with what I could only describe as some serious love.

"That will never get old," I told them, beaming. "You guys make such a nice couple."

Jimmy straightened. "I know." He looked at me and said, "So? Any luck? Jade told me you went out to look for the—ow." Jimmy rubbed his arm where Jade had smacked him. She cocked her head and rolled her eyes in Shay's direction. He mouthed "oh" and then lowered his voice and said, "With the second location last night?"

I shook my head. "Nothing." Movement caught my eye, and I saw Shay put on her headphones. She was probably tired of hearing us. I didn't blame her. I wouldn't have wanted to hear boring adult talk at her age either. I leaned forward and said in a low voice, "I went to both locations, and I didn't find it."

Elsa's face went hard. "You think that Darius character lied?"

"I don't know. I don't think so. This whole thing doesn't make sense. I mean, he did have me arrested and then blackmailed me to find this jewel. Did he make it up to have me run around the city? Just to get his kicks?"

"Maybe." Jade gave a shrug. "Maybe it's some sort of power trip. See how far you'll bend."

I let Jade's words sink in. "I'm sure you're right on some level. But he seemed genuinely ticked that I hadn't found it yet. And why give me a deadline?"

"Because he needs it by then," said Jimmy. "Whatever it does. He wants to have it in his possession by tomorrow."

I leaned back in my chair and took a drink of my coffee, rolling over what Jimmy had just said. It's something I had thought about too. That is why I didn't suspect Darius had sent me on a wild-goose chase. Well, not anymore. The more I thought about it, the more it rang true.

I set my mug down. "This jewel is probably some kind of weapon. Right? I mean, why else would someone like Darius want it so badly? Because it's a weapon. He means to use it."

"But what kind of weapon is it?" Elsa's face was tight with worry.

I shook my head, tapping my mug with my fingers. "No idea. My guess is it's magical. And very powerful. If I had found it, I might have had an idea what he was planning." And then it hit me: "Darius wants this thing by tomorrow. Right?"

"Right," answered Jimmy and Jade simultaneously, and then they smiled at each other. God, they were cute.

"Jimmy." I stared at the assistant manager. "Is something happening tomorrow? Like something big in our community?"

Jimmy thought about it. "Actually, there is."

My heart slammed in my chest. "What?"

Jimmy grabbed the backrest of the empty chair next to Jade, leaning over it a little. "I can't believe I didn't think about it until now. But there's a national assembly tomorrow at the Gray Council headquarters in New York City. It happens only every seven years. All the members of the Gray Councils in North America will attend. And all the heads of the paranormal races. It's one of the reasons Basil's going a little nuts. He was hoping to book the hotel with very *important* people, but because of the recent… disturbances, the hotel's not doing so well."

"So, everyone who holds power will be there." I felt my tension rising and mixing with my fear of the unknown and my anger at Darius.

Elsa leaned forward. "You think the jewel and the assembly are connected?"

I looked at the older witch. "Yes. That's why he needs this jewel. Because he's going to use it on everyone at this assembly. He's going to kill them all." And then he'd be free to do whatever he wanted. Like to continue the HTO project, and worse, much worse.

"Goddess, help us." Elsa gripped her locket, a terrible kind of fear and grief making her look much older.

I nodded as the realization dawned on me. "He's going to remove everyone of power so he alone will sit on the throne. He'll make all the decisions. So he can rule over us." It made sense. It was why he needed me to find this weapon for him.

"But he can't. Right?" Jade's eyes widened, and she shifted in her seat. "You didn't find it, so he can't kill anyone."

"True." Yup. Thank the goddess for that. "He still expects me to go looking for it. Because without it, he's going to either stuff me away to rot in a cell for the rest of my life or kill me. I'm pretty sure it's the latter." Yet I was pretty sure Darius wasn't the type to rely on only one strategy. If the jewel was the object to remove those in power, I was certain he had something else planned if I should fail. Which I had.

"If he's waited seven years for this," I said. "I think he's got other schemes going. Not just with me."

"But these are all extremely powerful and capable paranormals," said Jimmy. "I'm talking about the most powerful witches, vampires, and werewolves in the country. It won't be easy to kill them all—and all at once, if I'm following what you're saying."

"You're right," I told him. "Which is why he would need something of enormous power. Like a bomb. A magical bomb." I felt a shiver run across my skin at the thought. But it made sense.

"Then we must warn them," said Elsa, her voice rising. "I don't want this on my conscience. We have to tell them."

"You're right. But we need to tell someone we can trust. I have a feeling Darius isn't the only shady character on the Gray Council." I thought about Valen. "Valen knows someone on the Gray Council. He's supposed to be in touch with her today. I'll ask him if we could meet her. I'll bring Bellamy along with me and my case file I've put together on Darius and Adele."

"You'll have to tell her everything," said Jimmy. "About who really killed Adele, if you want to clear your name."

"I know." My heart gave a squeeze when I thought of Catelyn. "But Valen says Catelyn wants to come forward. He thinks nothing will happen to her because she's—was—human."

"He's right." Elsa was nodding. "You have Bellamy to back you up. You should be fine."

Should be fine wasn't what I wanted to hear. But I couldn't think of that right now. Right now, we needed to stop Darius.

And we had to do it fast before it was too late.

CHAPTER 22

Valen had managed to make an appointment with Migda for 3:00 p.m., which explained why Bellamy, Catelyn, and I were in his Range Rover Sport on our way to the Gray Council headquarters in New York.

I sat on my fingers, trying to hide their shaking. I didn't want Valen, but mostly Catelyn and Bellamy, to notice how nervous I was. I'd brought all the paperwork on my case and my laptop, or rather Eddie's. I knew the case through and through, but I couldn't help the trembling of my hands or the tightness in my chest.

Yes, I was anxious about meeting this Migda. I mean, the only other Gray Council member I'd ever met was Darius, and he was a real bastard. Who's to say she wasn't an icy bitch? But if Valen trusted her, I had to believe we could confide in her. But the cold feeling kept rolling up and down my spine at the thought of walking into the building again. The last time I'd been there, I was a prisoner. Locked up in some dingy basement cell. I knew now that my friends had tried to reach me while I was incarcerated, but it had still been a horrible and frightening time, if only three days. I couldn't imagine what it would be like to spend a week or a month, or even a year.

But we weren't going to the basement level. We were meeting Migda in her office, probably on one of the upper floors. Well, at least that's what I was hoping.

I was really surprised Catelyn had been so willing to come along. I mean, with Bellamy, we'd had to use some threats—mostly Valen showing his fists and making them clench and unclench. But the giantess had said yes right away, like it had been something on her mind.

"You sure you want to come?" I'd asked her in Elsa's apartment, which she shared now with the giantess. "I mean, it would mean you'd have to tell her about what really happened with Adele. You know, that crazy witch who did this to you." I could still clearly hear the sound of Adele's neck snapping.

"I know," answered Catelyn, her eyes going distant for a second, like she, too, was remembering that moment. "And it's still a yes. I'm coming. I'm going to tell them everything. Valen says that will remove the murder charge they have on you. So that's why I'm doing it. I killed her. Not you." There was a definite determination over her brow. She wanted to do this for me. Like I said before, Catelyn was my hero. Even now, after everything that had happened to her, she still wanted to help even though it would expose her and reveal she'd killed Adele—though Adele totally deserved it.

And once again, I'd left my poor little sister in the care of my friends.

"I want to come with you," Shay had said as I sat next to her on the couch with my bag and laptop ready to go.

"I have so much to tell you," I began. "But the Gray Council is no place for girls." It's no place for anyone, really, just contemptuous people who want you to obey them. I didn't want to go back there, but I had to.

Shay had narrowed her eyes at me. "You're leaving me. Again."

I felt like she was ripping out my heart with every word. "I don't want to. I *have* to. I have to do this." Shay didn't look impressed with me. I wasn't either. This was going worse than it had when I acted it out in my head. "Listen." I reached out to touch her hand, but she pulled it back. Okay. Ouch. "Valen's going to take us out to a movie right after the meeting. Then we're going to have a nice dinner at his restaurant." *Because there's something we need to discuss.*

But then Shay had gotten up and marched into her bedroom, slamming her door.

"Don't be nervous. It'll be fine," said Valen as he slowed down at a red light.

My face flamed. I was nervous, but I didn't need him to call me out.

"Why are *you* nervous?" Bellamy shifted in the back seat, and from the corner of my eye, I saw him lean forward as much as his seat belt would allow. "Is there something you're not telling us?" His voice rose in pitch. "If you're nervous, that means something's wrong. Turn back. We have to turn back. Turn back now!"

I let out a sigh. "Relax. It's fine. I'm just anxious because I want things to go smoothly. That's all. This is a big case. Nothing for you to worry about."

Bellamy made a sound of disapproval in his throat. "Of course I'm worried. You're throwing me to the wolves. And I don't even have a say in the matter. Might as well just kill me now and be done with it."

I rolled my eyes, my body pressing into my seat as the SUV started forward again. "We're not throwing you to the wolves." I caught a smirk on Valen's face. Good thing Bellamy couldn't see it.

"I beg to differ." The witch scientist leaned back, and when I turned my head, he'd crossed his arms over his chest. "What if she decides to throw me in prison? You promised to keep me out."

I did. But that wasn't up to me. "She won't. You're coming voluntarily to expose what Adele did and what Darius is doing.

This is a good thing. It's going to blow up the council, and not in a good way."

"Like what?" asked the witch scientist.

"Well, for starters, I'm hoping what we're doing will expose the other bad apples on the council. Because it can't just be Darius. He'd need others to cover for him and allow his plans to have gone on for so long."

Bellamy's face was screwed up. "Then I'll need twenty-four-hour protection." He blinked and then added, "For the rest of my life."

Yeah, he loved to be a drama queen. "You won't. Darius won't have anyone working for him after we're done. Those Dark witches won't come after you anymore. And after we expose Darius and his plans to use the jewel on the assembly tomorrow, it'll be rocky for a while, but I'm sure the council will be back and operating in no time." I had no idea, but I needed Bellamy calm. I didn't want him to ruin anything with Migda.

"What jewel?" Bellamy's voice held a faint ribbon of worry. "I knew it! There's something of great importance you're not telling me!"

My eyes swept over Catelyn, and I saw traces of suspicion across her face like she thought I was hiding something from them too.

Crap. My own stress was making me not focus. I'd never told Bellamy or Catelyn about the jewel. Bellamy because I thought he might use it for himself, like his "stay out of jail card" with Darius to keep them from trying to kill him. But Bellamy was smart. He knew things, and maybe he knew about the jewel.

I stared at him and asked, "What do you know about the Jewel of the Sun?"

"The Jewel of the Sun?" repeated Bellamy, like he was committing it to memory. He pursed his lips and said, "Never heard of it. Why? What is it? Is it valuable?" His eyes widened, and I could see *exactly* what kind of value he was referring to.

I shook my head. "Not in the way you're thinking. But it's

valuable to Darius. I don't know what it is. He never told me what it looked like, just that he wanted it. And that I would somehow find it with my starlight magic." He'd been wrong about that. "He had me look for it, his way of giving me leave from my jail cell."

"So, *that's* how you got out," the witch scientist said, as though he'd been thinking about it, and somehow it bothered him that I was out of that cell.

I clenched my jaw and suppressed my growing anger. The last thing I needed was to lose my temper and blow Bellamy out of the SUV with bouts of my magic.

"I never found it."

"Too bad," said the witch scientist. "If it was worth money, I could have bought myself a new life."

I narrowed my eyes as Catelyn shook her head. I knew the witch was self-centered, but this was pushing it. I was glad I hadn't told him sooner. He might have ditched me and gone after it himself. He totally would have.

"We think it's a weapon," said Valen suddenly. "Something he's going to use on the other Gray Council members tomorrow during the assembly. That's why it's imperative that we speak to Migda today. She needs to know. She has to warn the others."

"I'm surprised a high-ranking member of the council would kill his own associates." Bellamy began to run a hand over his seat belt. "Poor taste, I say. I'm very surprised."

"I'm not." Catelyn stared out the window. Of course, she wouldn't be. Her entire world had changed overnight due in part to Darius. Adele acted on his orders, though she might have gone a little rogue. The giantess was still adjusting. Valen told me he'd been practicing with Catelyn a few times a week to get her giant form or what I like to call her "big girl" alter ego under control. But if anyone hated Darius more than me, it was Catelyn.

I turned back around, my thoughts going back and forth on what I brought, hoping I didn't forget anything.

I looked over to Valen as the SUV slowed at a stop sign. "You think she'll believe us? We're basically telling her one of the guys she voted to take a seat on the council next to her is planning a mass murder. And that he was behind the HTO project."

Valen glanced at me, and then the Range Rover started forward again. "Migda's good people. You'll like her. And, yes, she'll believe you."

"She better," muttered Bellamy. "Or all of this"—he spread his hands—"will have been for nothing."

After that, silence dropped between us, all lost in our thoughts.

Valen turned left, and the SUV pulled into a large parking lot. He found an empty spot and killed the engine.

He turned to look at me. "Ready?" Worry pulled his features a little tighter than usual, but he was still handsome in that rugged, beast-man way.

I smiled. "Hell, yeah."

We all clambered out of the Range Rover and headed for the double glass doors at the entrance of the building. They weren't familiar to me, even though I'd been here before. None of the building's exterior frame was recognizable. I'd been so distraught, angry, and scared that I only cared about getting into that cab to take me away from the Gray Council building and back to the hotel. I never paid much attention to it.

It looked like a typical, mid-high-rise building with its gray exterior and many windows on all the levels. You wouldn't glance twice at it walking by. And the humans wouldn't even know it was headquarters to us paranormal folk. It didn't even need a glamour.

Valen held the door open for us, and I walked in.

I strolled into a large entryway the size of the Twilight Hotel lobby. It was a spacious, two-story-tall room with towering windows from floor to ceiling, letting in vast amounts of natural light. Large doorways hinted at equally spacious rooms down the hallway. Occasional artwork hung on the walls, but nothing drew my attention.

And like the Twilight Hotel, a long front desk sat at the end of the entrance across from us. It stood empty.

"It is normal that it's so empty?" I asked Valen as he walked beside me, Catelyn and Bellamy right behind us.

"Maybe they left early for the day." The giant didn't seem bothered at all that the Gray Council headquarters building was so empty, so quiet.

But I was.

All my warning flags were up and flapping in a burst of emotional wind.

"It's not as luxurious as I thought it would be," stated Bellamy. "Very plain. I always imagined it with more of a modern flare. But it looks like it was modern. Back in the nineties."

My eyes flicked to the black metal door next to the elevators, and my pulse hammered. That door I recognized. It led to the jail cells below the first floor, where I'd spent three days—a place I most definitely didn't want to see ever again.

The clomping of my boots sounded so loud on the dark, polished floors that I could barely hear Valen's heels scuffing next to me. That, and also because of the pounding in my ears.

The elevator doors opened, and we all followed Valen inside.

"She's on the top floor." Valen pressed the number twenty on the panel. "She's anxious to meet you. Says she's looking forward to meeting her first Starlight witch."

I tried to smile, tried to shrug off this nervous feeling that was now wrapped around my throat, but I couldn't.

I wanted to be more relaxed like Valen. I wanted to trust her. But I couldn't. What if she didn't believe me? What if she sent me back to that cell?

The elevator doors opened, and we marched down a short corridor. A single door stood across from us.

A metal plate with the inscription *Migda Madden, Gray Council Member* hung on the side of the door.

"This is her," said Valen. "It's the only office on this floor." He walked up to the door, knocked twice, and pushed in.

We stepped into an extravagant office, which looked about the size of an entire building floor. The ceiling was at least twenty feet high with floor-to-ceiling windows, giving us a view of Central Park. Not too shabby. Dark, polished hardwood floors greeted us as we made our way toward the center of the office. A seating area was just off to the left, with modern gray sofas sitting upon a lush, light-beige-and-blue Persian rug. A massive desk, made of some expensive polished wood, which made me wonder how it fit in the elevator, sat to the right of the office across from us. Tall bookcases lined the side of the wall without windows. Classical music floated in the air, giving the office a warmer, more inviting feel. The faint scent of candles found me, along with something else.

Blood.

Thick, almost choking. The sudden tension along Valen's shoulders told me he'd smelled it too.

"This is nice," said Bellamy, smiling as he took a deep breath, taking it all in. "Wonder how much she gets paid." Damn that witch scientist.

Catelyn was silent as she stood in the middle of the office. She looked as nervous as I was. And possibly a little green.

Nothing looked out of place. I couldn't see any signs of a struggle. But it still didn't explain the smell of blood. Or why it was empty.

"Where's Migda?" I asked Valen, my voice thick with tension and barely perceptible.

Valen shook his head, muscles around his neck and shoulders taut with tension. "I don't know. She said she'd be here."

"She's probably just running late," said Bellamy, admiring the office. He stared at the sofas, looking like he wanted to try them out.

"I don't think so," I said. This was too important a meeting to be late. Maybe Darius got to her. Maybe he scared her off.

Damn it.

I made for the desk and dropped my bag and laptop. Maybe I'd find something that would explain why she was late.

I did find something. But it wasn't what I thought it would be.

Lying on the floor behind the desk was a woman with dark brown skin, heavy wrinkles, and gray hair that matched her robe. She rested in a large puddle of blood, forming a sticky pool around her. Her dark eyes stared out, lifeless.

A deep red gash went across her throat. Dark blood sheeted down her neck.

Migda was dead.

CHAPTER 23

Dread squeezed my insides until I thought I might puke. "Is this her?" I asked Valen. Even though I had never met her, it was pretty obvious this was the council member we were supposed to be meeting.

And they'd killed her because of it. Because of me.

The giant stood next to me, staring down at the obviously dead woman, with a snarl on his face.

"Yeah. That's Migda." He knelt down next to her and dragged his hand over her eyes. When he pulled back, her lids were shut.

"That's disgusting," said Bellamy, who'd joined us. "So what now? If she can't help us, is there someone else? We came all this way. Maybe there's another council member we can speak to?"

I shared a look with Valen. His dark expression said it all. Migda had been the only person he trusted. And now she'd been killed. We had no one else on our side.

Catelyn's shoulder bumped into mine as she stood next to me. "Who would do such a thing?"

"I would," came an oily voice that I knew all too well.

The silver-haired Dark witch stepped into the room. A group of twelve men flanked either side of him, witches, too, by the strong warm and cold pulses of energies wafting through and the scent of sulfur. They were a mix of both White and Dark witches.

"Ah!" screamed Bellamy. "That's them! That's the ones that tried to kill me!" He pulled me around and crouched behind the desk, his shoes stepping into Migda's blood.

I cast my gaze over Darius. "How did you know?" Someone had told him about our meeting. It wasn't Migda. No. Someone she trusted, and she'd been played, just like us. And she'd lost her life for it.

Darius grinned. "I don't reveal my sources." His gray eyes traveled over me. "Looks like your little plan didn't work. What did you think? That you could somehow remove me from the council? Did you really think they'd believe you?"

I clenched my jaw. "I did." My eyes went to the tall windows. The sky was clear, and the sun was a brilliant yellow globe. No way could I reach my starlight, what little I could, not when the sun was cockblocking me like it was doing right now.

Shit. This was one of those times I wished my magic wasn't so goddamn limited.

Darius clasped his hands in front of him. "You disappoint me, Leana. I thought we had a deal. Imagine my surprise when I found out you were going to stab me in the back. After I kept you out of that cell."

"You mean after you manipulated the system to have me put in there in the first place?" My eyes traveled over the twelve witches. Their magic was different, but they were all wearing the same heavy linen robes. "What's up with those robes? Going to a *Star Wars* convention?"

"Your plan didn't go so well. Did it?" Darius's face spread into a false smile, and I wished I had my starlights with me so I could blast him through those windows. "Women. You're such deceitful creatures. Manipulative. Beautiful, yes, but still bitches that need to be broken."

At that, Darius's gang of witches all laughed and snarled at me, all of them together, casual and offensive. They didn't seem to care that they'd killed one of their own, a Gray Council member, no less, and that she was still sprawled on the floor.

My mouth parted. "Did you just call me a bitch?"

"Women need to be put in their place," continued the silver-haired witch. "No females should have even been on the board. Too emotional. Can't make the right decisions. Take Migda here. She was thinking with her heart, not her head, when she decided to hear your case. And look what happened to her?"

Guilt hit hard. I'd never met the woman. But she was dead because of me. I had no doubt about that.

"Face it, Leana," said Darius as he pulled on the sleeves of his dark navy suit. "Female witches are useless. Your power is limited. You can never be as powerful as your male counterparts. You don't have what it takes. You lack the strength, the intelligence. That's why it's better that you stay home, stirring your cauldrons."

I cocked a brow. "Stirring cauldrons sounds like fun to me." I saw Catelyn tense next to me. She wasn't stupid. She knew what was about to go down, and I had no magic to spare. I had nothing but my smart mouth and my wits, which wouldn't help at the moment.

Real fear gnawed in my stomach. Not for me, but for my friends. For Shay.

Darius cast a slow gaze over me and the others. "Any last words before you die?" he laughed. "Nothing?" His face pulled into a mock sadness. "Oh, well. You should have minded your own business. Now your friends are going to die because of you."

Yeah. I didn't need more of the guilt trip. I was pretty good at doing it on my own. Still, I really, really wanted to rush over there and pull on his stupid silver hair.

The air buzzed suddenly with raw energy, pulsing through the room.

"Oh, no. Oh, no," lamented Bellamy. "It's happening. We're all going to die. You told me you'd keep me safe. And now I'm going to die because of you!"

Yeah, part of me wanted to pull on his hair too.

My clothes and hair lifted around me as the witches continued to pull on their magic. The scent of earth, grass, and water mixed with rot and sulfur rose in the air. I felt the power of the elements interacting, moving, and flashing energy.

Chants filled the air. Their voices took on the edge of cruel satisfaction as some of the witches continued some incantation I didn't recognize. Dark, demonic syllables thundered from other male witches' lips.

A combination of White and Dark magic. This should be interesting. If I could conjure my Starlight magic, it would have been a magical party.

A flash came from my right. With a pull of his muscled arms, Valen ripped off his clothes. By the time they fell to the floor, instead of his normal six-foot-four frame stood his eighteen-foot one. A giant with hard muscles bulging along his arms and with hands that could crush a car, let alone a human head.

Taking his lead, Catelyn yanked off her clothes just as her face swelled, until her body was triple her normal size. A frown marked her prominent brow, and her protruding upper jaw was cast in a snarl. Her giant form stood at about fourteen feet. Not as large as Valen but close.

Seemed like she had reasonable control over her giant form. She could shift just as fast as Valen. Looked like he's been training her well. Hopefully, he taught her how to fight too.

Guess we were about to find out.

Another witch clapped his hands together, muttering some incantation. Red sparks flew about his hands, and then red fireballs hovered above them. The smile he gave me said it all; you can't starlight yourself out of this one.

He was right. And I hated that I would have to rely on Valen and Catelyn for protection. But what choice did I have?

Shit. "Stay down," I told Bellamy, but I needn't have. He was practically inside one of the drawers of the desk, the way he was pressed so tightly against it.

I noticed that Darius moved inside the room and pressed his back against the wall, hands over his chest, clearly not wanting to get them dirty. He caught my eye and flashed me a knowing smile, the kind that said I was about to die.

Frustration hit hard, but fear had settled deep in my core. No matter how hard I tried to push it down, it just kept growing until it tightened so hard, it made me nauseated. My shoulders tightened with tension. I felt trapped. Yes, I had two giants with me, but I didn't know how or if they were susceptible to magic or if they were impenetrable.

It was twelve against… two, really. And with odds like that, if it were nighttime, and I had my starlight magic, I wouldn't have given it a second thought. But I was magic-less, and with twelve experienced witches, things just got a lot more complicated.

I was so screwed. Why were these situations always happening to me? Maybe if I caused a distraction, we could all run out. Yeah, didn't think so. It was too late for that.

Cold seeped up my back. My gut clenched. We should have stayed home.

Darius's low, mocking laugh grew in depth but then faded with a bitter sound. "Don't worry," he purred. "It'll all be over soon."

"Fuck you," I snarled. My hatred for the Dark witch was making my body shake.

Darius's face rippled in anger. He lifted his hand and snapped his fingers.

A mix of energy blasts, red, blue, green, and black, all came spiraling our way.

Okay, time to panic.

I wasn't stupid. I wasn't about to get my ass fried. So I did what any smart Starlight witch would do in the middle of the afternoon. I ducked.

I heard a deafening crash, and splinters of wood and bits of paper showered over me.

"Stay here," said Valen in his giant form, his voice loud over

the ringing of my ears as he exploded into motion and rushed to meet the onslaught of witches.

Catelyn, the giantess, sprinted after him. Thank the goddess, the ceiling was high enough. 'Cause, that would have been awkward.

Seeing as I never do what I'm told, I crab-crawled to the other side of the desk, opposite where Bellamy was crouched and cowering, stepped over Migda, unfortunately, and peered out.

Energy rushed out of the witches. Fireballs and kinetic forces, all went for Valen and Catelyn.

A blast of blue energy exploded on Valen's chest into a roar of blue flame.

I froze, thinking he'd burn. But the giant swatted away the flames, like they burned or were uncomfortable but not enough to stop him. At first, I was relieved, thinking that giants were immune to magic. But with one look at his charred chest, I knew that wasn't so.

Catelyn screamed as she took a hit in the thigh by some green lightning. The scent of burnt hair filled the room.

Damn. I hated not being able to do anything. I felt like a fool—a useless witch fool.

Speaking of said fools, Bellamy let out a cry, his body shaking, as another blast of kinetic energy slammed into the desk. Shards exploded, showering us both in wood dust and wood splinters.

I coughed, wiping my eyes. When I looked around, the desk was gone. Well, it wasn't *gone* gone. It was just a pile of wood and dust.

Heart thumping, I shot to my feet. I wasn't about to die on my knees.

Valen threw a couch at one of the witches. It caught the witch in the chest, and he rocketed back, hitting the wall with a horrible crunch. He slid down and did not get up.

One down, eleven to go.

Catelyn, following Valen's example, tossed a bookcase at two of the witches. It hit one of the witches, burying him under it, but the other witch leaped out of the way. With his hands dripping in blue energy, he thrust out his wrist, and a string of blue electricity slammed into Catelyn.

She grunted and fell to her knees, the blue magic coiling over her body like sparks of electrical current. The witch kept hitting her and hitting her with the same magic.

Fear gripped my throat. I thought she was going to die. But the giantess lurched to her feet, grabbed the witch by the throat, and slammed his head against the wall, flattening it like a raspberry pancake. Okay, that was gross.

In a flash, Valen knocked out another witch with a powerful thrust of his hand. In a burst of muscles, the giant grabbed the same witch and lifted him as though he were just a doll, before tearing him in half.

Yeah. That was pretty gross too.

Two more witches fired their magic at the giant. Valen stumbled, and my breath caught. He roared, swatted the closest witch, like an annoying mosquito, and took the witch's head between his massive hands, crushing his skull. I heard a pop and the sound of bones crushing before the witch went limp in his hands.

He whirled and kicked out, his foot landing against the neck of another witch. With a snap, the witch's head hung at a ninety-degree angle.

Even if it looked like we were winning, several very capable witches were still pitted against two giants.

I looked over at Darius, who hadn't moved. His shoulders rocked up and down as he laughed. He looked at me, his gray eyes glistening with amusement.

He pushed off the wall as a strange, dark language spilled from his lips. The air in the room dropped a few degrees. Darkness dripped from his hands, a sort of black energy I'd only seen on demons.

"Time for this to end."

Darius thrust his hands out. Tendrils of black electricity hit Valen and Catelyn, enveloping them like black ropes. The energy tightened, snapping their arms against their sides. They couldn't move.

Valen cried out as he tried to break free from the magical bonds, but he couldn't. And neither could Catelyn. She fell to the floor on her side, the building shaking with her weight, unmoving and stiff, as though she were made of cement.

Okay. Well, that wasn't good.

Bellamy seemed to have picked up on that too. The next thing I knew, I caught a glimpse of the witch scientist's large rump as he ran, faster than I thought possible for legs that short, right out of the room, leaving behind a trail of bloody footprints.

"Bellamy! You coward!" I shouted. I really shouldn't have been surprised. This was Bellamy, the most untrustworthy bastard chicken witch who ever lived.

A fist came out of nowhere and hit me in the side of the head. It threw me hard to my left, and if I hadn't planted my legs at the last minute, it would have thrown me to the floor. I stumbled and whirled around, blinking black and white spots from my eyes.

"Stupid bitch," snarled the witch who had hit me. "You thought you could defeat us with your little pets?"

I guess my little pets were Valen and Catelyn. "I did." No point in lying.

Darius came forward, and the witch who had struck me stepped aside. "You should have done your job and kept your mouth shut. None of this would have happened. Now, your friends are going to die because of you, which is a shame. Giants are 'in' at the moment." He glanced at Valen, who was still struggling against the magical restraints. "But before I do, I will take what is needed from them both. Adele had the right idea, though her methods were a little sloppy. Giants will rise again. As will all the paranormal races."

I met Valen's eyes. His face was a mask of fear—for me, not for him. He was powerless to save me. Just as I was powerless to save my own ass. What a gigantic clusterfuck this was.

The thought of losing Valen woke up something in me. And a

slow burn of fury took root. "This again. You're still going to try and breed out the humans? It's not going to work. The community will stop you."

"The community will stop you," mocked Darius in what he thought sounded like my voice. "Leana, Leana, Leana. When will you ever learn? Can't you see? The humans are a cancer. They are ruining this world, taking away its natural resources, plaguing it with industrialization. In a few years, the world will face devastation. But I will save it. I will return the earth to who it was meant for."

"You?" I guessed.

The Dark witch flashed me a smile, his teeth too bright, and took a closer step. "That's right."

He was so close now, I could smell the sulfur and something like alcohol oozing from him. My next thought was probably not smart. No, it was really stupid. But desperation called for a little crazy.

So, I gave in to crazy.

I made a fist and attacked, putting everything I had into my speed since I could barely see. My fist met his jaw. Yay! I had no idea I had such remarkable combat skills.

Darius's head snapped back. He glared at me, both furious and surprised I had actually hit him. Me and him both. Woo-hoo!

He laughed, baring his teeth, and I could make out streaks of blood. At least I'd hit him and not the air next to his head.

A strangled cry came from Valen, and when I looked at him, I saw more than fear in his eyes and face. I saw a desperate panic. Yeah, he thought I shouldn't have hit the Dark witch. Too late for that now.

A hand grabbed a fistful of my hair, and a fist slammed into my chest, knocking out any air and sending me to my knees with buckets of pain. I looked up just as a shoe pummeled my face.

The blow knocked me back, and black stars blocked what vision I had left.

Ow.

I hit the ground, my face wet with tears and possibly blood.

I blinked. A shadow danced before my eyes. "You can kill me," I said, tasting blood in my mouth as my vision slowly came back. "But it's over. So whatever plans you had for tomorrow, they're over. Yeah, I know what you were about to do. And trust me, we told everyone." Not true, but he didn't know that. "So, you can kiss that goodbye."

Darius started to laugh and then started to clap. "You're a liar. Just like all women. But you're probably the worst liar I've ever seen. You need to work on that."

"Screw you."

"I know that's not true. I know you only told Migda. Do you want to know how? Because that's what she told me before I killed her."

I spat the blood from my mouth. "It's still over. Your plan won't work. I never did find that jewel you so desperately wanted me to find. I looked. I really did. But it's not here in this city. So, you're screwed."

A smile spread over Darius's mouth. "Oh, but you're wrong, Leana. You did find my jewel."

"Excuse me?"

A cruel smile spread over the Dark witch's lips as he stared at something behind me. "Imagine my surprise that you would bring it here with you."

I turned around and about just died.

Shay stood in the doorway.

CHAPTER 24

Shay, my eleven-year-old sister, who was supposed to be back at the Twilight Hotel with my thirteenth-floor gang, stood on the threshold of Migda's office. What the hell was she doing here?

Ignoring Darius, I ran over to her just as Shay rushed toward me. I caught her, and grabbed her in my arms, feeling for the first time how tiny she was. She was just skin and bones.

I pulled back and stared at her face. "Shay?" I shook my head, wondering if maybe I was having some sort of mental breakdown and she wasn't really here. "How did you know where I was?"

Shay blinked at me. "I heard you talking with Elsa and Jade. I knew you were coming here."

Guess her earphones were just for show. She'd been listening to our conversation the whole time. "But... how did you get here?" No. No. No. This was wrong. This wasn't happening!

Shay shrugged. "I took an Uber."

"With what money?" Unless our father had given her some, I never had.

"I stole fifty bucks from Elsa's purse."

I slapped my forehead. "Goddess, help us." I shook my head. "But how did you know where to find me?" The building was massive. No way she could have found us on her own.

"Bellamy told me. I saw him in the lobby downstairs."

I swear, that witch scientist was going to end up dead by my hands. He knew we were getting our asses kicked. What the hell was he thinking letting her come here?

I grabbed Shay and pushed her behind me, protecting her with my body as best as I could. Tears were streaming down my face. Darius saw them, and he chuckled. I didn't care. The words he used came flashing back. But they didn't make sense.

"I knew if I waited, if I was patient, you'd find her," said Darius, and I saw the remaining witches all gather next to him. "I knew you could do it."

"What the fuck are you talking about?" My rage was oozing out of me. I was mad with the overwhelming feeling of protecting my little sister with everything I had. She had to get away. She had to run.

Darius pointed to Shay behind me. "The Jewel of the Sun. Really, Leana. Your stupidity is starting to get annoying."

I turned my head and whispered to Shay, "When I say *run*, you run like hell."

She nodded, her eyes wide with fear.

My throat hurt as I pulled my eyes back to Darius. "I don't know what you're talking about."

The Dark witch let out a dramatic sigh. "See, you're a Starlight witch. So is your little sister. Yes, I know she's your sister. I know more about you than you know."

"Wonderful."

"The thing with Starlight witches," he began, "is that you don't know which stars will respond to you, which ones are linked to what witch. Like you, your power is somewhat limited to those three stars. But your sister… well… she's different."

My father's words came rushing back. Shay was powerful. I'd never seen it, but it didn't mean it wasn't true.

"She's just a kid," I said, my heart pounding through my chest. "Take me instead. Just let her go."

Darius stared at me like I'd lost my mind. "Let her go? Are

you mad? I've been waiting for this chance for years. And you brought her to me. Thank you for that."

"Go to hell. You can't have her." A dark panic took form in my gut. "Take me. Or are you afraid of me? Afraid of a woman? Is that it?" I could see by the frown on his face that I'd hit a nerve. So I kept going. "Oh, I get it. You *are* afraid of me."

"Don't be ridiculous." Darius had lost his smile, tension making his shoulders tight as his fingers twitched at his sides.

So, I smiled for both of us. "You are. Deep down, you know you want me. Want to thrust that little pecker inside me? Am I right? But you can't. You can't do it. Because you need me to be restrained. Right? It's the only way you can get it up." I flicked a finger for a better demonstration. "You can't make love to a woman because no woman would want you. No. You have to take them by force."

The male witches were staring at Darius like they weren't sure whether to believe me or not. Darius saw that.

Fury etched his face. "Shut up, you whore!" he hissed as he came closer.

"You know it's true," I continued. He was closer still. "You can't get it up unless we're tied up. Look. I made a rhyme."

Darius's hands dripped with that same darkness as he came at me. Whether to punch me or hit me with his magic, I didn't know.

But if my plan was going to work, it had to be now.

Adrenaline flooded me. "Run!" I screamed, pushing Shay back, just as I threw what little starlight magic I could muster. The tiny ripple of magic sailed out of my hands and hit the Dark witch. He stumbled. It wasn't much, but it was enough for the distraction I needed.

Darius waved his hand. A volley of dark electricity soared over my head. I spun around just as the dark magic grabbed hold of the door, like black, spindly fingers, and shut it.

Shay stumbled and slapped her palms on the door to stop her momentum. Then, grabbing the handle, she tried to pull it open, but it wouldn't budge.

She turned and met my eyes. "I'm sorry."

I shook my head. "This is not your f—"

I cried out. Searing pain flared up my back, striking deep. Doubling over, I crashed onto the floor, convulsing. I curled into a ball as whatever curse had hit me spread through my bloodstream, burning. My head felt like it was splitting in two, and my vision blurred as the pain swelled. The scent of burnt flesh filled my nose. My flesh. I was burning from the inside.

The curse seemed to shred me into thousands of pieces, held together only by my skin and my will. Scorching pain exploded in my head, and blackness flooded my eyes. I couldn't see, but I still held on.

My muscles quit seizing, and I sucked in a ragged breath. I took another breath and then another. My muscles relaxed, leaving only my pounding head and the taste of something metallic in my mouth.

"Bring me the girl," I heard Darius say through the pounding of my ears.

I threw my gaze around the room. Two male witches grabbed Shay by her arms and dragged her to Darius.

"No," I wheezed. "Let. Her. Go." I could barely breathe, let alone speak.

"Let her go?" Darius leaned over me. "Never. Now that I have her. I need what's inside of your sister. I need that power. And it will be mine."

Fear cascaded down Shay's face, and my heart shattered at what I saw there. I couldn't do anything. I couldn't save her.

"Don't. Hurt. Her."

Darius blinked at me, his expression carefully blank. "You've served your purpose. I don't need you anymore. But I will keep your sister. Until she has served her purpose. Until she gives me what I want."

My lips trembled. "She's just. A little. Girl."

"She's just. A little. Girl," mocked Darius again. His eyes were patronizing. And with a flick of his wrist, he sent another shot of

his dark magic at me, sending forth a gust of darkness from him, rippling like a wave of death.

Darkness slammed into me. It was the same kind of pain as before. Only more intense. And everything went dark.

I didn't know how long I was out, but I woke and blinked into a set of pale-gray eyes.

"You're not what I expected," said Darius. "You're much more irritating and simple than I thought."

A cry reached me, and I raised my head to see Shay fighting her captors. She kicked and tried to bite. Atta girl. But they were much stronger than her. She stopped and looked at me. Tears came spilling down my face. I wished I could have had more time with her. Wished I had gotten to know her better, and she me. Only then did I realize how lonely I had been all these years after my mother died. Family was important. I'd always pretended it wasn't so I wouldn't feel the hurt and emptiness.

And now that I had family, a sister, I was about to lose her.

And Catelyn. And Valen. My eyes traveled to where he was. He hadn't moved. He couldn't. He was still trapped in those magical ropes, not able to do anything but watch as they took Shay and then would kill me.

"I'm sorry, Shay," I wheezed, wishing I could tell her more, but my body felt broken. I wouldn't last much longer.

Darius knelt. He ran a hand over my face. "I'm going to kill you like I killed her bitch mother."

Holy shit. Darius had killed Shay's mother.

His eyes crackled with some evil delight at the thought. He was a creepy sonofabitch. But that's not what had me staring with my mouth slightly open.

Shay's face was flushed, and her eyes sparkled with some wild fury.

And then something extraordinary happened.

Shay's body started to glow. Small at first, and then the glowing intensified until it was hard to keep looking. But I did.

Even if it felt like my retinas were burning, I just couldn't look away from Shay.

She shone like a star, a brilliant star. But how could that be? Starlight witches couldn't draw their magic during the day. At least, not like that.

Rays of light emanated from her like heat waves. The two witches who were holding her cried out in pain, let her go, and scrambled away from her.

I could barely see her face in all the light, but what I could see was a mask of dark fury. Her eyes found Darius.

"No," he said, backing away from me. He spun around and ran toward the door.

And then, a beam of light shot out of Shay's middle and hit Darius.

He let out a strangled cry as his body exploded into ashes.

Holy shit on a stick.

Next, Shay spun around, and again, beams of her light fired from her and hit two, three more witches. With popping sounds, like the crackling of a fire, their bodies combusted into ash, just like Darius's.

The remaining witches didn't stand there and wait to get fried by my baby sister's apparently badass magic. I heard a loud bang and flicked my eyes in time to see the office door rebound off the wall as they ran out.

I glanced back at Shay, trying to see her face to determine if she knew what she'd just done. It wasn't every day that you took a life, and she'd just taken four. But I couldn't read her face, not with all the light. I wanted to tell her it was okay. That she didn't have a choice. I didn't want her to feel guilty. Strangely, I had a feeling she wouldn't.

"Leana!"

I blinked to see Valen's face, his human face, and then the next thing I knew, he was holding me in his arms. Guess Darius's magical restraints vanished with his death. Good.

"She looks bad." Catelyn appeared next to Valen. "We need to get her to Polly."

I knew they were right, but I needed to see Shay. "Shay?"

"Here." Shay stood next to Valen. She wasn't glowing anymore. She looked me over, and big fat tears leaked from her green eyes.

"That bad, huh?" I asked her with a smile. I probably looked like death.

"Worse." Shay glanced down at her body. "I don't understand what happened."

"I do." I raised my head, Valen's arms holding me tightly. "That was your starlight magic."

Shay's face wrinkled in confusion. "But it's daytime. I don't get it."

I smiled at my sister. "You're the jewel of the sun. Your star *is* the *sun*. The most powerful of all the stars." It's why my father wanted her protected. It's why Darius wanted her. Wanted to use her to kill the members of the council, and God knew what else.

Shay's face brightened, and a smile spread over her. "Cool."

I laughed but regretted it instantly, as everything hurt. "Cool."

And then the darkness took me.

CHAPTER 25

The thirteenth floor was bursting with life. Every tenant was out of their apartment, all clustered around the long tables, topped with food and every alcoholic beverage you could think of, enjoying the company, the happy conversations, and the celebrations.

Said celebrations were the festivities that Elsa, Jade, and Julian had decided to throw in my honor, or rather, the honor of all charges of murder being dropped.

It was a "the bastard's dead" kind of celebration, and everyone was invited.

I woke up four hours after my blackout, in my bed, surrounded by my friends, Valen, and Shay, who'd curled up beside me and was fast asleep. Didn't blame her. Using her starlight magic would drain her. She'd taken a lot. And being her first time, she needed to rest.

"You've been asleep for hours," Elsa had told me.

"Four hours," Jade had corrected.

I propped myself up on my elbows, seeing Valen in a chair next to my bed with a smile on his face. "What happened?"

"You blacked out." Polly came forward and thrust a mug at me. "Drink this. You took quite the magical beating. You're going to need lots of time to recuperate, and you'll need to be monitored."

"Monitored?" I took the mug. It was cold.

"To make sure you don't have a relapse," said Polly. "Just a precaution."

I took a sip and winced. "Yikes," I wheezed. "That's nasty."

"Oh, shush," Polly ordered. "Drink it up. I'll wait." The chef crossed her arms, giving me a look that meant business.

I did as I was instructed and gave her the empty mug. "Thanks." I already felt less dizzy, and my insides didn't seem like they were liquifying anymore. "So, I blacked out. Then what?" I looked beside me at a still-sleeping Shay and smiled. God, she was cute.

"She's been there since we put you to bed," said Valen, emotions raw in his voice, which had tears welling up in my eyes. "Hasn't left your side."

I blinked fast and cleared my throat. "She needs to sleep."

"I called the other members of the Gray Council after you passed out." Valen shifted in the chair. "Catelyn took you and Shay to Polly while I waited for them."

My eyes found Catelyn, who stood by the door. "Thank you, Catelyn." She'd fought bravely, fought for us, for her new community.

Valen leaned forward, his eyes on mine. "I also called the heads of all the paranormals in New York. I wanted them to see what Darius had done. What he did to Migda. I told them what happened. I gave them your notes and your computer with all the files on Darius. Hope you don't mind. It's evidence now."

"You owe me a new computer," I told him, smiling. "What about Darius's witches who ran away?" I remember a few bolting out the door when they saw what my little sister was capable of.

Valen's teeth showed in a smile. "They sent a team to look for the witches. Trust me, they'll be found." He raked his fingers through his hair. "Speaking of runaways. I went to find Bellamy."

I swallowed, my throat still raw. "And? Did you find him?" I felt a string of anger rise. The bastard had left us and then had sent my little sister where he knew she'd be in danger. I didn't think I should see him again—ever. I didn't think I could stop myself from strangling him.

Valen's smile grew. "Oh, I found him. He's with the Gray Council now. I left him about an hour ago." He searched my face, beaming. "Those trumped-up charges against you are gone."

"Really?" I looked at Catelyn.

"Catelyn came back and spoke to the Gray Council members after she dropped you and Shay off," said Valen. "She told them everything."

"I told them *I* killed Adele," said the giantess, her gaze on me. "They listened. They took samples of my blood to make sure I was who I said I was. Had to show them my ID, proof of my work, and my birth certificate. They believed me after that. They told me they were sorry for what happened to me and that no charges would be brought against me."

I smiled at her. "Glad to hear it."

"You're off the hook," said Jade, giving me a knowing smile. "They should give you a raise. You know, for saving their asses."

After that, I'd gotten out of bed, careful not to wake Shay, and opted for a nice hot shower. It felt amazing, but my body was still in pain. Emotionally, I was drained. I'd need a few days off.

Which was why I found myself hours later with a mug of Polly's cold healing brew, force-sipping because, one, it tasted like feet, and two, because I knew I needed it.

I was under Polly's strict instructions to avoid all alcohol for a week so my body could heal. That, and I had to ingest her special healing brew three times a day with a meal.

I spotted Julian next to the twins. Both were in black, Goth-like dresses. He was holding the hand and kissing the neck of a pretty brunette I recognized as the twins' mother, Cassandra.

"Well, well, well." I smiled, knowing how long he'd been in love with her. It was my theory that all those other women he'd been sleeping around with were his way of trying to forget

Cassandra because she wouldn't give him the time of day. And now look at them. I was happy for my friend.

Jade stood with a glass of wine in one hand while running her fingers through Jimmy's hair as the shifter looked positively enamored that his woman was taking such good care of him. They were so cute, I could barf.

It was a wonderful party. And it probably cost a small fortune, but I couldn't bring myself to talk about my lack of funds at the moment. I was out of a job. Once I was feeling better, I'd have to start looking.

Catelyn was conversing with one of the tenants, but I couldn't remember his name. He was a witch, nice looking, and he was leaning close to her, seemingly really engaged in whatever she was telling him.

I found Shay standing with Valen. Her face was bright red, laughing at something the giant had told her. She gave Valen a fist pump and then stuffed her mouth with what looked like chips.

"She's a different girl now," said Elsa as she joined me. "Just look at her. She's changed."

I nodded. "She has. And it's a good change. She's more confident now. But…" I sighed.

"What is it?" Elsa surveyed my face. "Are you feeling tired? You want to go lie down?"

"Later. But I was referring to Shay. I was just worried that she might have a small freak-out moment after killing those witches. She did burn them to tiny bits. And she's so young. That would mess with anyone's head. I don't want her to suffer through something like that. Even though she saved our lives. It's a lot to take in."

"It is." Elsa turned her gaze to Shay. "She looks fine, but I agree. Maybe in a few days, you should sit with her and talk. Just to be sure."

"Yeah. Good idea. I will."

"Leana."

I turned at the sound of my name to find Basil standing behind me. "Here about the apartment?" I figured he wanted me out because of what I did to Errol. I'd accepted it. "You can't fire me because of what I did to Errol. I'm not on the payroll."

Basil waved away my comment with his hand. "Forget Errol. He can be insufferable. I'm here on business."

Elsa and I shared a look. "What business?"

"I'd like to offer you your job back."

No shit. "What about Oric?" My gaze traveled over to Jade and Jimmy, who were both eyeing us and beaming.

"Gone." The manager let out a breath. "It might have been a bit premature to remove you from your post. And I…" He cleared his throat. "I apologize."

"That hurt. Didn't it?"

Basil narrowed his eyes. "Will you accept your job back at the hotel?"

"On one condition."

"What?" asked Basil.

"I want a ten percent raise."

Basil's eyes widened, but he clamped his mouth shut.

"I have a sister to look after now, so I'll need more money. What do you say?" I stuck out my hand and waited.

Finally, Basil took it, and we shook on it. "Deal." He spun around on his heel and disappeared into the crowd of paranormals.

"Even more cause to celebrate," said Elsa, raising her glass to my mug, and we clinked them together in a toast.

I felt the pricks of eyes on me. I followed the feeling. Matiel, aka my father, stood in the doorway of my apartment. He glanced at me and then disappeared inside.

"Excuse me for a second." I left Elsa and marched, more like waddled, over to my apartment. "Nice of you to show up," I told him as I joined him in the living room.

"Shay looks so happy," he said with such a sappy sadness in his eyes that all my anger evaporated.

I sighed. "She is. Why didn't you tell me her starlight magic came from the sun?"

Matiel shrugged, an action very similar to Shay's. "Because I wasn't sure. I felt her power. I knew it was extraordinary. But I couldn't tell if it was the sun or the moon or even just a large selection of stars."

I dragged myself to the couch and sat. "Well, Darius knew."

"You're injured. I'm sorry that happened."

I looked up at him. "The angels were never after Shay. It was Darius. A crazy, silver-haired member of the Gray Council. Did you know that?"

"I didn't know who was after her. I just knew someone was. Though the legion might still want to have a look at her."

"Not a chance," I growled. "No."

Matiel smiled at my anger. "I'm glad you love her. As you should."

"Yeah. She's my sister. I'd do anything for her." The words rang true as they flew out of my mouth.

"I knew it was a good idea to bring her to you," said the angel, proudly.

I raised my hand. "Easy, now. You're just lucky it all worked out. It might have gone the opposite way. Shay might have been taken. She might have been killed."

Distress wrinkled the angel's face. "I know. But she's fine. You're fine. And I'm very glad for it. Really I am."

I looked away from the emotions on his face. I didn't want to go there. "He killed her mother, you know," I told him. "Darius. He killed her. And then Shay killed him. She killed him with her… sun-starlight power." I didn't know what to call it. She'd obliterated him like he was nothing. If she wasn't my cute little starlight sister, I would have been scared shitless.

Matiel was silent a moment. "I didn't know. I knew she'd been killed, but I didn't know who did it. I found Shay two weeks later, living on the streets with some kids her age." He frowned at some recollection. Probably the state he found her in. Half-starved, dirty, and out of her mind with fear.

Damn. "She'll never be on the streets. Ever again." Something occurred to me. "Did you try to hide Shay in a convent? A church? A psychiatric ward?"

Matiel nodded. "Failed attempts. How did you know?"

I brushed it off. "It doesn't matter now." Because Darius was dead. Somehow he'd figured out where my father had tried to hide her. That's why he'd sent me to those locations, hoping I would discover my sister and lead her to him.

I shifted on the couch, trying to stand, but fell back, wincing. "Okay. I think I'll stay down here for a while."

Matiel stepped closer until he was right next to me. "I can heal you, if you want."

I thought about it. "No thanks. This is a reminder of how close I came to losing everything. I'm good."

"Dad!"

We both turned to the sound of shoes flapping the carpet as Shay came galloping through the apartment and crushed her body against her father.

"Hey, knucklehead," said Matiel as he kissed the top of his daughter's head.

"Guess what!" said Shay, her eyes big as she stared up at her dad. "I'm a Sun witch!"

I smiled. Guess that was a proper name for her abilities. She might be a Starlight witch like me, but somehow Sun witch sounded better. More badass. It was perfect.

My eyes stung as I finally hauled my ass off the couch and left father and daughter to have some time together. I wandered back to join the party, my body aching, but I could hardly feel it anymore.

I was too damn happy.

CHAPTER 26

I stood on the Twilight Hotel's roof, next to Shay, staring down at the cars and human pedestrians who walked the streets at night. The air was much cooler up here. I was beginning to get dizzy back on the thirteenth floor all crammed with paranormals, the smell of body sweat, cigarettes, and booze.

"You come here a lot?" asked Shay, leaning over the railing.

"Sometimes." Especially when spying on a naked giant. "I can feel my starlights better when I'm outside and up high."

"Cool."

I flicked my gaze over to Valen. He was standing a bit farther off to give us some time alone. In his giant frame, the moonlight reflected off his massive body, all eighteen feet of it.

I was glad Valen had taken my advice and had some makeshift shorts made for his giant self. You know, to cover up some flapping bits. Totally inappropriate around an eleven-year-old girl.

I stared at Shay. "I'm glad your dad came over tonight."

Shay turned her head to look at me. "He's your dad too."

"He is. But it's different. I didn't know him when I was your age. My mother didn't want him around."

"Because of the legion of angels?"

I raised my brows. She was a clever little thing. "Yes. She was scared. I'm not sure that was the right decision, but she thought it was. And I respect that."

Shay's face scrunched as she thought about it. "But you know him now."

"I do. And I like him."

That seemed to be the right answer, as her face lit up. "He's a cool dad. He's going to come visit us once a week. I made him promise."

I laughed. "I'm happy to hear that." Yes. That would be nice for Shay and for me to start knowing my birth father. But I was happier for her. She needed him. I was way beyond the need for a father figure.

"Shay, I wanted to ask you something. It's why I came out here." I waited until I had her full attention. "You see, Valen was wondering if you and I would move in with him. In his apartment above his restaurant. It's nice, big, and fancy. A lot more room than my apartment."

"Would I have my own room?" Shay watched me, her green eyes large, and she wasn't blinking.

Of course, that was important to her. Even more so as she got older. "Yes. A huge room. Twice the size of the one you have now. And it has its own bathroom."

Her green eyes sparkled. She shrugged and said, "Okay."

My mouth fell open, and I glanced at Valen, who looked just as surprised as I was. But then his features spread into a huge grin. As a giant, that look was both terrifying and exciting. You weren't sure if it meant he would eat you or kiss you.

My gaze flicked back to Shay. "Really? You sure?" I mean, I wanted to live with him, but I wouldn't if she wasn't comfortable with the idea.

Shay shrugged. "Yeah. Valen's cool. But what about your apartment?"

"I talked to Catelyn. She's going to take my apartment." I'd found Catelyn in Elsa's apartment right before the party and had brought it up. She was genuinely surprised and thrilled at the idea of having her own place. I still hadn't worked it out with Basil, but seeing how desperate he was to have me back as a hotel employee, I didn't think he would refuse anything I asked at the moment. And I was going to milk that. Besides, it was the least I could do for her after what she did for me: coming clean, to the Gray Council, about killing Adele and having those charges against me dropped.

"Okay. When do we move?" asked Shay.

I hadn't thought of that. "In a few days? How does that sound?"

Shay pursed her lips. "Okay. But don't forget to tell Dad."

I laughed. "I won't." I breathed in the cool night air. "Umm. There's another reason why I wanted you to come up here with me."

I tapped into my starlight, to that well of celestial magic, to the core of power from the stars high above me. The cool night air pulsated with energy just as a ball of blazing white light floated over my hand.

I blew on my palm, and the ball burst into thousands of tiny stars of brilliant light. The miniature stars fell over Shay, circling her and leaving trails of glimmering white dust. The starlights spun and danced around her, lifting her hair, some settling on her palms like pet fireflies.

Shay let out a laugh as my starlights welcomed her like a friend they'd been missing for years. Her happy face made my ribs crush my heart. That, and the new man in my life. Valen. It was hard not to think about all the sexy times we would have once we were living together. The strong, sexy man-beast was all mine. All mine.

"Are you ladies ready?" asked the giant, stepping toward us.

I looked at Shay. "You want to go for a ride?"

Shay's eyes darted from Valen to me. "Yeah."

"Okay, then. We're ready."

Valen came forward and carefully picked up a giggling Shay.

He placed her on his left shoulder and then picked me up and settled me on his right.

Shay let out a squeal. "Whoa! This is so cool! Where're we going?" Her voice was high with excitement.

I laughed and stared down below. "Wherever the night takes us."

Valen's chuckle was a rumble in his chest, and I felt it in his shoulders and along the base of his neck. I shifted my weight as I sat on the giant's shoulder, getting comfortable and feeling a mix of excitement and happiness. I had a new man in my life. A new sister. The perfect job. I had everything I'd ever wished for and then some.

It was time to start my new life as a Merlin for the Twilight Hotel and with Valen and Shay.

For the first time ever, I felt content and complete.

And then, with Shay and me on the giant's shoulders, he moved to the roof's edge and jumped.

Don't miss the next book in the Witches of New York series. Try it now!

BOOKS BY KIM RICHARDSON

THE WITCHES OF HOLLOW COVE

Shadow Witch

Midnight Spells

Charmed Nights

Magical Mojo

Practical Hexes

Wicked Ways

Witching Whispers

Mystic Madness

Rebel Magic

Cosmic Jinx

Brewing Crazy

WITCHES OF NEW YORK

The Starlight Witch

Game of Witches

Tales of a Witch

SHADOW AND LIGHT

Dark Hunt

Dark Bound

Dark Rise

Dark Gift

Dark Curse

Dark Angel

Dark Strike

ABOUT THE AUTHOR

Kim Richardson is a *USA Today* bestselling and award-winning author of urban fantasy, fantasy, and young adult books. She lives in the eastern part of Canada with her husband, two dogs, and a very old cat. Kim's books are available in print editions, and translations are available in over seven languages.

To learn more about the author, please visit:

www.kimrichardsonbooks.com